CW01507214

Chapt

Marian Chase had two perfectly good reasons to remember 5 February 1885. One was the weather. She awoke to find, not the bleak grey chill of winter but a near summer's day, unusually mild for the time of the year and brilliantly sunny. From the upstairs window of her bedroom in Adelaide Drive, the sea appeared a deep, almost sapphire blue. Close to the shore, white horses pranced courtesy of a brisk offshore wind which encouraged the waves to break early on the thickly pebbled beach running from Brighton to Hove.

The second and significantly more poignant item worthy of note in her diary was the news in the Morning Post of the fall of Khartoum. According to informed reporting, the city was sacked, the garrison massacred and the fate of General Gordon, though unconfirmed, believed to be grave.

Though the best efforts of British journalism attempted to paint an accurate picture of events in the Sudan, it was impossible for Marian to draw from those efforts a truly evocative flavour of the unfolding tragedy.

Consequently, in spite of the welcome sunshine and promise of spring like warmth beyond her tightly closed windows, she found herself in sombre mood and frustrated by an inability to picture with any accuracy the hideous tapestry of events taking place on a continent which was so completely beyond her experience.

Even years later that morning remained vivid in her mind. She could never quite eliminate from her thoughts the sense of guilt she felt for savouring as she had the sun warmed comfort of her settled, pampered existence, while in a far-off land men, women and children lay butchered on the streets of an Arab city, the same sun she so relished, rotting their flesh and bleaching their bones.

Ironically however, there should have been another, more potent inspiration for her diary entry on that particular February morning. Precisely one year earlier, aged twenty three and possessed of a maturity beyond her years, she met for the first time a certain young army captain by the name of William Radford.

The occasion itself was of no great note. Indeed, it merited barely a sentence in her daily journal; 'Dinner party at Princes Gate, Sir Charles and Lady Strachey, Colonel and Mrs Butterfield, the two Miss Hudsons, cousins George and Fred and Captain W. Radford (a friend of Fred's from Cambridge).'

There was no need for anything more, no cause to detail his dark good looks, deep brown eyes or impeccably tailored dinner suit. He was a friend of Fred's from university, something of a celebrated rower, and came only with the added reputation of being a young man destined for great things.

All else she learned of him was that he hailed from Sutton Coldfield where his father still laboured as a respected member of the clergy, being as he was a diocesan bishop. In addition, it appeared that the young Captain Radford recognised few ambitions beyond those promised him as a serving officer in Her Majesties armed forces.

Indeed, on that occasion, just another in a long line of dinner parties given at Princes Gate during the winter months, Marian was little moved by the presence of one more guest at the London home she shared with her parents, two younger sisters and a modest retinue of household staff. Dinner parties were a regular feature, 'at homes' almost a daily occurrence and balls a monthly ritual. William Radford, or Willy as he was soon to become known, made his debut into Marian's life as just another face in a roll call of visitors to the Chase family home, be it resident at the time in London or in the more clement environment afforded them on the south coast.

However, fate decreed 5 February 1884 to be the day for a seismic shift in the balance of Marian's uncluttered and hitherto comparatively untroubled life. There was no evidence of it at the time. The dinner party passed off much as most dinner parties did at 32 Princes Gate. The guests arrived punctually at seven and tailed away around eleven o'clock. In between there was food, wine and vibrant conversation and although Marian was sat within easy hailing distance of the said Captain Radford, she retired to bed with no particular recollection of anything exchanged between them worthy of record.

Yet, and it was a 'yet' with the open space and resonance of the Albert Hall itself, on the following morning, while gainfully employed at a vicarage working party along with her two sisters, Margaret and Katie, her thoughts wandered in his direction. Quite beyond any conscious intention on her part, occasional, even coincidental interest in him turned to a genuine and moderately urgent desire for the two of them to meet again.

A compulsive writer for many years and inspired by several visits to the Indian Sub-Continent, Miles Lamdin lives quietly with his wife and daughter in the heart of Suffolk. Historical fiction provides him with opportunity to explore the life and times of people and places easily forgotten, people who lived beyond the conventional wisdom of the day and places now so altered as to be unrecognisable.

To my mother.

M S Lamdin

FLIES TO WANTON BOYS

AUSTIN MACAULEY PUBLISHERS®

LONDON * CAMBRIDGE * NEW YORK * SHARJAH

A CIP catalogue record for this title is available from the British Library.

ISBN 9781035870721 (Paperback)
ISBN 9781035870738 (ePub e-book)

www.austinmacauley.com

First Published 2024
Austin Macauley Publishers Ltd®
1 Canada Square
Canary Wharf
London
E14 5AA

When he left on the previous evening, there was no suggestion of their being reunited unless by chance at some future social event. No invitation was offered for a renewal of their acquaintance and cousin Fred gave no hint that the gentleman in question was intent upon returning to stay with him in the near future.

Besides, Captain Radford had recently arrived home on leave from a tour of duty in India. He was soon to be on his way to the bosom of his family in the midlands. Marian had no idea how long he was to stay in London and, on the night in question, certainly gave no hint she cared whether he made a second appearance or not.

Over the following days, however, her private diary told a different tale. Like the slow advance of an incoming tide, his name crept ever more forward in her daily entries. On the night of the dinner, he was no more than a footnote. By the end of the week his name was writ bold in her opening lines. Queries, questions and observations about him reigned supreme over reports of her visits to the theatre or opera, rides in the 'Row' with her father or the fruits of her learning at bible class. Captain Willam Radford successfully dominated her thoughts and the ever-growing need she felt to meet him again became as essential as it was imagined to be pleasurable.

The first concrete hint that something was seriously amiss came a week later. Marian and her two sisters accompanied their parents to Brighton. More than a year in the building, their new out of town residence was finally ready for occupation. On previous occasions their extended breaks to the south coast were in rented homes. The house in Adelaide Drive, Hove, however, was the culmination of several years' planning and a considerable investment of funds. It was a time of huge excitement for the whole family. During the final weeks of construction and internal decoration both Marian's mother and father were frequent commuters, keen to oversee and orchestrate every last detail leading up to its completion. After each trip, they brought back with them explicit news of progress for their offspring to share.

Then finally the day was upon them. It was time for the whole family to see for themselves. During the train journey from Victoria station, the conversation was lively and the general impatience to see their new home for the first time infectious. Strange then that as Marian tried her best to join in, with every mile the train drew away from London, its hot breath tainting the cooler country air along their route, so her disappointment grew. She found herself staring out of the compartment window, her thoughts preoccupied by the reluctant realisation that the further south they travelled, the less likely she would be to encounter for a second time, the young man she had regarded so casually at their first meeting.

There was no good sense to her melancholy. Never before had she been aware of such irrational or inhibiting emotions. She was confused by and self-critical of her reduced enthusiasm for a day to which the whole family, herself included, had been so looking forward. And yet, she found herself powerless to alter her mood. Involuntarily she willed the train to falter, hoping against hope it would turn itself around and head back to the city.

Margaret, three years her junior and with each passing month more fervently dedicated to her theological studies and desire to join the scattered ranks of female missionaries across the globe, saw nothing of the anxiety in her sister's thoughts. Katie, younger still by a further four years and by contrast to Margaret, whimsically silly and, though equally devoted, uniquely focussed on an adult existence of Hedonism, noticed in Marian a rather annoying mood of introspection which had begun at the breakfast table. However, she was too enthused by the day ahead to express concern.

As usual, Marian's father was the only one to notice her plight and cast an anxious eye towards his eldest offspring. He and Marian were close, as close perhaps as any father and daughter might be. Much of him was in her. It was true she bore some traits exclusive to her mother. Like her mother she was neat, methodical and a deliberate organiser. Like her mother, she cared for people and for nature in equal proportion and very much like her mother, with a smile alone, she could disarm even the most unwilling of recipients. Her intelligence and intellect, however, came direct from him. An academic at heart, a man compelled by circumstances and family obligations into a life of commerce, his genes were the ones which had gifted Marian with the capacity for deep thought. It was he alone on that morning who recognised in her a distraction serious enough to warrant occasional monitoring.

He said nothing. That her silence was no petulant ill humour he knew for sure. However, as the rest of his family chirped and chattered around him and pestered him constantly for more or repeated details of what they should expect upon their arrival at Hove, he kept Marian in view out of the corner of his eye, assured that his intervention would only be needed if and when she asked for it.

Over the years, almost from the earliest age she was able to sit a horse, he and Marian had ridden out together. Mrs Chase was a well renowned pedestrian.

She was more than happy sitting in the blanketed comfort of an open landau or, when in town, quite relaxed about employing the services of a hansom. But she was no horse woman. Consequently, her husband rode 'The Row' alone in the mornings until Marian was old enough to join him. Thereafter the two of them went together, using such precious time to establish a bond of intimacy and compatibility he had found impossible to achieve with either of his two younger daughters.

In effect, their relationship was such as to make Marian in many respects the male heir he and his wife were not able to produce. In complete confidence, the two of them shared so much of what was reserved traditionally for a father and his son. In turn, Marian treasured her father not merely as the provider and head of the family but as her most trusted confidante. As surely as he knew something was troubling her, he also knew she would confess it when and if she were ready to do so. There was no need for interrogation, no need to hold out the hand of concern. Marian would keep a silent vigil with her thoughts until she chose otherwise. Then, probably, on horseback, somewhere aloft in the comparative remoteness of the South Downs, she might turn to him for assistance. Meanwhile, a glance in her direction and a meeting of their eyes across the railway carriage was enough to secure contact and give her he hoped any reassurance she needed.

The burden for Marian, however, was not the solitude of her vigil but the accompanying confusion. She could not fathom her frustration. Try as she might and indeed had been for more than a week, she could not account for the obsession she appeared to be developing for a man she had met but briefly and about whom she knew almost nothing. Short of the fact of their having sat for one evening at the same dinner table while he entertained the assembled party with varicose tales of his and Fred's exploits while at Cambridge or his time served in the Punjab, Marian could identify no adequate reason for his continued and predominant presence in her thoughts.

Only with their arrival at Brighton station was she granted a brief respite. Frenzied excitement within the terminus and during their twenty-minute carriage ride along the sea front to Hove, eliminated any prospect of silent introspection. There were fine buildings to be admired, out of town fashions to be commented upon and the vastness of the English Channel to be gasped over, the fast-running waves on that morning a sight for repeated mention. Moreover, when, finally, they drew up outside their new home at number 16 Adelaide Drive, even Marian could not remain aloof from the general clamour.

One year on from those first days in February 1884, the atmosphere within the now familiar house was conspicuously deprived of the near hysterical excitement so obvious and so loud on that first morning. Then there was no opportunity for Marian to sit quietly in the alcove of her sea view bedroom window, her heart saddened by newspaper reports of so great a military loss as had occurred at Khartoum, her head raised from time to time to take in the tranquil sea. Instead, it was rush and bustle and the clamour of many voices all raised at the same time in exaltation for a house which promised so many years ahead of happy times.

And to her credit, Marian had joined in. She was beset by a problem as perplexing as any she had yet encountered, but she was not selfish enough to let it spoil the day. Less ebullient perhaps in her expressions of excitement she still followed her two younger siblings from room to room, examining with them every detail and marvelling at the ultra-modernity of fixtures and fittings and each design ingenuity contrived by the builders. And indeed, their enthusiasm was hard to resist. Quite likely there was not a home on the south coast as cleverly appointed or with so satisfying a combination of elegant comfort and technological innovation. Not even their home in Princes Gate could boast as much.

By evening, and their first dinner together, the conversation still resounded to astonishment at so much that was new. There was also continued praise for the father whose inspiration and unwavering industry had brought it about. And, for a while at least, Marian was distracted.

Only when the whole family retired to bed did the face of William Radford return to taunt her. The following day her diary entry read simply 'rode with Papa,' a quite inadequate paraphrase of the two hours they were alone together on the Downs with more than enough time to broach if not resolve her dilemma. However, when they returned home to lunch, Marian felt only marginally relieved of her burden.

For much of the time they had talked of anything but Captain Radford. They agreed upon the kindness of the weather and Marian dutifully heaped praise once more upon her father for the triumph which was their new home. They mused over the prospect of making new friends and expanding their social life. They even discussed the quality of the various entertainments available in Brighton over the coming weeks, Marian herself noting with some pleasure the news of a forthcoming Richter concert at the Dome. However, it was not until well into their ride that, having exhausted every other avenue of discussion, her father ventured into the uncharted territory of his daughters troubled soul.

They were completely alone. Behind and below them stretched the ever-expanding coastal conurbation of Brighton and Hove. Ahead lay the soft but exaggerated undulations of the South Downs. Above them, almost invisible to the naked eye, skylarks followed their progress, their shrill but sweet chatter too soon for the time of year.

For as far as the eye could see, not a soul threatened their solitude. Their privacy was spoilt only by the ever active but uneducated ears of their two mounts, able to hear and conscious of their every word but incapable of understanding the least syllable. No more perfect an opportunity was likely to arise during the course of the day for father and daughter to exchange confidences.

'Would you like to tell me what's been troubling you for the past few days?' her father asked, his question releasing the pressure like a sloes gate let open to relieve backed up flood waters.

'I don't know, Papa,' Came the reply, not helpful, but in a tone which begged further probing on his part.

'Are you unwell? Do you need to see a doctor?'

'No Papa. It's nothing like that.'

'Then what is it? I can see something's the matter.'

'You're right Papa. But it's so hard to explain. I have no need of a doctor. In myself I feel quite well. And yet, I know there is something wrong. I have never felt this way before.'

And from that tentative first step, the words poured from her lips. The intimacy of comments and emotions previously expressed only to her diary were released for her father to mock or mourn as he saw fit, her faith in his compassion and discretion such that she held nothing back. The name William Radford was pronounced over and again during a confused and unrehearsed monologue which lasted until interrupted by the opening, closing and passing through of a gate to another open expanse of downland.

When she was finished, the words drying up like the last dregs draining from a barrel, there was a moment or two of silence between them prompted by her father's desire for reflection. In the company of either of his other daughters, his immediate inclination would have been to smile and patronise, but not with Marian. Her strife was sincere. Her emotions were neither fickle nor flimsy. That he was worldly enough to recognise infatuation for what it was, no more or less threatening than a summer cold, was no licence for him to belittle so frail and yet so intense a sensation. Clearly his daughter was struggling. Clearly, somewhat overwhelmed by the symptoms of an illness she was unable to identify, her disquiet was real. Here was an intelligent and deep-thinking young woman experiencing for the first time a disease of the heart, cause unknown, cure a mystery. Not in his wildest dreams was he inclined to whisk her discomfort away as he might a fly from the neck of his horse.

'Marian, my dear,' he began in a tone so like a warm blanket, 'I know this Captain Radford rather less well than even you. He and Fred have been close for some years, of that much the two of us are aware. However, suffice it to say that your heart has clearly found something in him far beyond anything I noticed during the evening we were all together. I have to confess; I don't suppose he and I exchanged more than half a dozen words. I'm afraid my time was rather taken up either with Sir Charles or fighting to get a word in edgeways with the two Miss Hudsons.'

Excuses aside, he then went on to suggest motive and means for her unsettled state. Confining his examination of her symptoms to the more tangible aspects of human development and leaving the metaphysical to someone better qualified, he attempted to convince her of the inevitability yet ultimately harmless nature of first love. He avoided the actual word 'love' of course. That word would have been too easily associated with the silliness of her two younger sisters for Marian to grasp willingly. Any notion that she was 'in love' with a man who was a virtual stranger would have been dismissed by her as quite absurd. 'Infatuation' too was unsuitable by way of a definition and, in the context in which she understood the word, would have been considered by Marian a slight to her intelligence. Margaret or Katie, each in their own ways, might well be susceptible to such shallow emotional whimsies, but not her.

To her father therefore lay the task of pitching his interpretation of this most delicate of ailments somewhere in the middle of the two. 'Love' was too dramatic a definition, but 'infatuation' was too mean. Consequently, the verbal solution to his dichotomy lingered longer than he would have chosen and was punctuated with somewhat prolonged pauses for consideration. Needless to say, each word was chosen with great care, each syllable pronounced with the cautious footfall of a man walking on eggshells.

In the end, their natural and long-standing empathy got him through. His explanation of and prescribed treatment for what ailed her settled slowly, like the rippled waters of a pond after a large stone has been cast into the middle. By the time they reached home, some two hours after they had set out upon their ride, Marian's condition, though by no means cured, was at least labelled. Understanding the symptoms and being given a name to her disease was half the battle towards a cure.

And, as they walked back in through the front door of their home in Adelaide Drive, that was the thing most forward in her mind; cure not compliance, elimination rather than incorporation. She wanted none of it, not the unsettling mystery of her emotions, not the irrationality, not the incapacity.

And yet, as each day passed, she could not rid herself of it. Initially, the lunch time hubbub of conversation after their ride eased somewhat the irritation of having to admit that her symptoms matched so accurately her father's prognosis. Much of the talk was of her sisters and their own morning ride, not on horseback, but on board the new tram running the length of the sea front all the way from the bottom of Adelaide Drive to the Aquarium on the esplanade in the centre of Brighton itself.

Mrs Chase also recounted at some length many of the smallest, if trivial, details she had already noticed concerning the occupants of the house opposite who, like themselves, were new residents to Hove. And in between sisters, mother and to a lesser extent father whose occasional contribution to the conversation was mostly confined to requests for rather less chatter while he was trying to digest his food, all of which were ignored, Marian was given little opportunity to dwell on matters of an amorous nature.

Moreover, later in the afternoon, she found herself press ganged into an 'at home' being given in Grand Avenue by the two Miss Macaulays. She, Margaret, Katie and their mother were all invited and thus, all were expected to attend. It was a welcoming gesture extended by two happily cohabiting spinster ladies destined as it happened to be among the closest of their friends over the coming years whenever they were resident on the south coast. And, not by coincidence, their attendance was encouraged wholeheartedly by Mr Chase who dreamed of an afternoon alone, during which he intended an hour or two of quiet solitude, a brief spell for self-satisfied appraisal of their new home.

Not until late into the evening therefore was Marian able to snatch an opportunity for recording in her diary the full and unwelcome truth of what she had been compelled to confront during her ride across the Downs, along with a clear determination to achieve full recovery at the earliest possible moment. She wanted nothing from William Radford and certainly not any form of emotional attachment. She liked her life just as it was. If and when it took her fancy, she was happy to flirt occasionally, even accept complementary attention from members of the opposite sex. But she simply refused to allow this or any other man to intrude upon her life in so debilitating a manner. Captain William Radford was not of the slightest interest to her and, as if to reinforce a conviction at present under threat from forces beyond her control, she exaggerated the importance of her resolution by underlining a denouncement of him several times.

Aware, however, from her frequent and instructive attendance to bible classes at Brompton Church, that the deed is invariably so much more difficult to effect than the word, and regardless of how earnestly she applied pen to paper with words of defiance, she continued to struggle in vain against feelings and impulses bearing a more resistant strain than anticipated. Fortunately, and by no means the most difficult of tasks, she was able to conceal the scale of her catastrophe from sisterly and maternal observation. However, though she was in the company of her father the least, she was unable to convince him of anything but her continued and fast-failing battle.

Although he knew full well it was a fight Marian was unlikely to win, he resisted reminding her of the fact. He was old and wise enough to understand the unstoppable forces of nature. Long ago, he had succumbed himself. His only contribution therefore was in offering to ride with her again just as soon as the weather permitted and as often as she chose. In addition, and to defy somewhat the pledge he made not to intervene, he took it upon himself to manipulate a rather risky and clandestine invitation.

While on a day trip to London, excuse business, true motive to get away from a seaside household completely overrun by the sound of women's voices, he engineered a brief detour to the home of his brother-in-law in Gloucester Place. There he cornered the unsuspecting Fred, his nephew, and insisted he should be their guest in Hove at the earliest opportunity on the express understanding that he be accompanied by Captain Radford.

The plan hatched, and after a solitary meal at his club in Pall Mall, Charles Chase returned by the late evening train to Hove and the bosom of his voluble family. He could only hope against hope that in time his eldest daughter would grow to forgive him for the plot she would surely suspect and almost certainly uncover moments after of her cousin's impromptu arrival.

Thus, within the week, Fred arrived at Adelaide Drive. A sense of duty and a small dose of metaphorical 'boot up the backside' from his father encouraged early compliance to the request of his uncle. He was reluctant to leave the heady social whirl of London for what he envisaged as the parochial blandness of life on the south coast. But he went nevertheless. Furthermore, fulfilling his instructions to the letter, he persuaded William Radford to accompany him, a task which proved rather easier than he had anticipated. Indeed, if anything, William resisted the idea rather less than he did himself, admitting even, something of a joyful enthusiasm at the prospect of visiting Brighton, a concept which Fred found highly suspicious.

Of course, blissfully ignorant of the true purpose behind his uncle's summons, Fred suspected nothing. He was unaware of the ailment afflicting his cousin. Likewise, not for a second, did it cross his mind that William's acceptance of the invitation was anything other than a desire to share his company. After all, their friendship was set in stone. Strong bonds tied them. Mutual interests at university, some academic but mostly of a less instructive nature were the foundation of that friendship. Continued affinities afterwards served to strengthen it, even though their individual and very different career choices kept them apart for long periods.

Indeed, there were times when Fred felt closer to William than his own brother. What could be more natural therefore than he and William spending a weekend together away from town. Brighton was not London, Hove even less so. However, the air was clear, the wind often bracing, the scenery beautiful and the company of a close family with a reputation for generous hospitality no undue hardship.

In many respects, Fred's aunt was a mirror image of his own mother. She was kind, generous, occasionally over protective and, though not conspicuously so, as often as not the anchor of the family. Margaret was a friendly enough girl. However, theirs had always been a relationship built on ambivalence. To his mind, she was too intense for her own good. An overzealous devotion to her faith contributed to a somewhat dull personality, particularly when it came to a consideration and pursuit of more earthly pleasures. By contrast, Katie, barely sixteen, was still too young to be considered in a serious light. She was flighty, had the empty headedness typical of a girl her age and was by far and away too pretty for her own good. More dangerously, she showed regular evidence of a wayward streak which Fred believed would one day come to furrow the brows of both her parents. This of course, was an observation he kept to himself. Had he but known it however, it was one not only shared but much to the fore on the mind of her father.

Marian was a different matter altogether. She was a young woman whose company Fred always enjoyed. To within a month, they were both the same age, he being just the older. As children their respective families were together much of the time, whether in London where they lived only a short distance apart or during shared summer holidays on the Isle of Wight. He knew Marian as confident, witty and ever ready to join in with boyish pursuits. She was neither fearful, shy nor easily intimidated by danger. Indeed, he could recall how readily at an early age she learned to defy the supposed inadequacies of her sex.

Of all his cousins, both male and female, including the four who lived at Durley in Hampshire and two more from Sutton in Surrey, Marian was his favourite. As children they had bickered and squabbled for supremacy in almost everything but always ended their feuds as friends. Now, as young adults, when in the same room together or sat at the same dinner table, their debates were more verbal than physical but no less hotly contested and they were no less evenly matched, she inevitably stretching him to the limit. Frequent were the times the two of them monopolised the conversation, drowning out others as they clashed over some moral, political or social difference of opinion. Equally frequent were the number of times, when as a truce was called, no clear victor emerged, Marian simply refusing to bow to the Victorian concept of male supremacy.

Fred was puzzled by the rather sudden nature of his uncle's invitation, and the latter's insistence that it be complied with so promptly. However, he offered no opposition, particularly when the invitation also extended to William. On the train down from London, they invented for themselves an itinerary of things to do and places to visit. William gave not the slightest hint that behind his own ready acceptance of their foray to the south coast lay a secret desire to meet again a young woman whose eloquence, wit and good looks had neither escaped his notice at their original encounter nor left his mind for a day since.

Unusually, he had confided nothing of this to Fred. During all their conversation, most of it relating to the normal hedonistic pursuits sought by two young men in their twenties, Marian's name was mentioned no more than in passing. No counsel about her was asked of Fred and none given.

And yet, William was indeed impatient to make Marian's acquaintance again. He spent much of the journey preparing himself for just that event. Little did he expect her to have been running a similar emotional gauntlet since news of his and Fred's imminent arrival was announced at the breakfast table the same morning.

Though she concealed it beneath a wafer-thin veneer of disinterest, much as she might news of a change in the weather, in truth Marian was quite caught off-balance. She spent most of the morning in her room, the view over the coast no distraction from the sheer terror she felt inside. For the first time and for as far back as she could remember, she found herself wanting. Her courage and self-confidence evaporated. The absent William Radford was already causing her enough consternation. How she would react when placed in the same room with him or faced with the prospect of shaking hands in a 'how d'you do' was almost too great a torture to bear.

She prayed for a delay, a benign catastrophe. A train derailment would have been a convenient blessing, assuming of course it was without casualty. Failing that, a severe bout of the mumps on her part would have been equally as welcome. Anything to keep her from a reintroduction until many hours of rehearsal could guarantee the same polite but bland behaviour expected of her when entertaining the local vicar or some distant great aunt.

Had she known the catalyst to her consternation was no less unsettled, she might have been more willing to face him. However, she had not the slightest idea he recalled her name, let alone concealed a secret and urgent desire to meet her again. Apparently, fate had decreed that each should be woefully ignorant of the others affliction, an affliction all the more exacerbated by their being thrust together under the same roof for the second time within a fortnight.

In typical style, when they arrived at the front door, Fred was all smiles. Those greeting him were his family. They were familiar, generous in their affection and genuinely delighted he had taken the time to come and stay. Mrs Chase hugged him in a manner reserved by aunts for nephews. Margaret behaved more coyly than was necessary, while Katie, dear Katie, swung her arms around his neck and kissed him on both cheeks, announcing as she did that this was the

French custom and one she intended to adopt in future for all those deserving of her embrace.

Marian kept to the background, retreating from the greeting ceremony rather than taking the initiative. As delighted as she was to welcome the nearest person she could claim as brother, she hesitated lest she be thrust too close to or, worse still, directly into the path of Captain Radford. To be face to face with him would have been too awkward by far. Rather than fuss around Fred and in so doing risk some accidental brush with his companion or perhaps even the need for an exchange of words, she faltered in the drawing room doorway, making certain her passage for retreat was assured.

As it happened, she need not have worried. William was equally desperate to avoid contact of any kind. With careful deliberation and some sleight of hand, he kept both Mrs Chase and her two younger daughters in front of him and engaged each of them in turn in trivial conversation well beyond what would normally have been expected of him. Save for a brief 'how d'you do,' at all costs he avoided speaking to or looking at Marian, preferring the monosyllabic shyness of Margaret and the somewhat irritating exuberance of Katie to any notion of meaningful dialogue with the one lady present in the house who really interested him.

Just how long either he or Marian would be able to sustain the charade was of interest to Marian's father alone. Since he was the only member of the household privy to her true feelings, he watched with mischievous fascination as his daughter squirmed her way out of any situation likely to produce even a moment of direct communication between herself and the man most the subject of her interest. That William Radford was equally and reciprocally infatuated was not known to him. Had it been so his delight in watching events unfold would have been heightened still further.

However, his entertainment was in no way spoilt by the lack of this additional information. This was the first occasion any of his daughters had displayed the cumbersome symptoms of being upset by the proximity of a young man. It was an added bonus that the exquisite discomfort he was able to observe unchallenged, as if he were present at some penny arcade peep show, was manifesting itself in Marian, his eldest daughter. Under normal circumstances, she was the cool one. She kept her head when all around, his wife, Margaret and Katie, were likely to lose theirs. Regardless of the crisis, it was Marian who could always be relied upon to rise above the situation. To see her so flustered therefore, so stumbling in her manner was an amusement for him almost too much to bear without an incriminating smile.

Fortunately, he resisted. To have succumbed would have been a mistake, a betrayal of the trust his daughter placed in him when confiding so personal and revealing an admission. Consequently, as soon as the initial greetings were done, he invented an excuse to be in another part of the house, quitting the scene as an absolute necessity lest he surrender to his impulse for creating further mischief.

By the time they all went in to lunch the atmosphere was measurably less charged. With a certain dexterity both William and Marian had managed to avoid any direct physical contact and, as far as they could, had maintained a whole family of chattering voices between them. However, the initial awkwardness was passed. Gradually both took the first tentative steps, testing the water with polite if rather abbreviated conversation and the meal came to an end without incident.

For the afternoon it was decided they should all visit the Hove School of Art there to witness Katie's 'work in progress' and to consider her development as an artist. A young man by the name of Mr Kenneth was the tutor and it was felt high time, particularly by Mrs Chase, that some attempt should be made to decide whether her youngest daughter's frequent morning visits to the school were prompted by a desire to emulate the old masters or something more earthly.

Nothing had been seen of her work to date, not from the previous winters efforts when she had first asked to attend the school or from the few days she had been attending since their recent arrival from London.

Marian was most concerned. As a keen devotee of the fine arts herself, she wanted to see if Katie had been gifted with any of the talent for execution, she so sadly lacked herself. She was equally enthusiastic to clarify the depth of any relationship between the often talked about Mr Kenneth and a sister who, by unanimous agreement, was still too young to bear thoughts of anything beyond the strictest of tutor student relationships.

Worryingly, Mr Kenneth's comparative youth, he was believed to be twenty-two or twenty-three years of age, and his well-publicised good looks, were cause for concern. Katie was a girl whose head was both easy and ready to turn. Thus, a family outing, 'én masse' as it were, to the school, with the additional accompaniment of two male members, was a perfect opportunity to assess the situation and perhaps pre-empt the future development of anything which might cause embarrassment to the Chase household or to Mr Kenneth.

Should that mission go according to plan, the evening's entertainment would be an ensemble visit to Hove Town Assembly Hall to witness a duo of theatrical comedies entitled respectively 'A Scrap of Paper' and 'Perfection.' Amateur productions both, they were bound to be less than the Chase family was used to at 'The Haymarket' or 'Drury Lane.' However, Mrs Chase and Marian were practiced theatre-goers. In London rarely a week passed that they did not attend an Opera at Covent Garden or sit through at least one or more of the current popular plays. Add to that equally frequent visits to musical concerts at the Albert Hall which was virtually on their door step and their evenings were rarely free from some cultural entertainment or other.

Temporarily resident in Brighton, they might be deprived of the scope and undoubted professionalism of London's West End, but Hove Town Assembly Hall was just one of several venues offering perfectly adequate alternatives. Brighton, after all, was no south coast backwater. It had lost little of the prestige or popularity it enjoyed from the heady days when playing host to the court of the Prince Regent. The 'Dome' itself, one of the largest and most luxuriously decorated concert halls in the provinces, was more than able to attract the best of European talent.

That said, the venue of their afternoon outing, namely the 'Hove School of Art' made no claims to be a Sussex answer to the Royal Academy. Indeed, the title 'academy' was not in truth an apt description of it.

Furthermore, Katie herself exhibited no enthusiasm for having the whole family descend on the place. However, she was sensible enough to present no obvious objection to the idea either and since it was within easy walking distance of Adelaide Drive on what proved to be a more clement afternoon than forecast, there was little excuse for the whole family to delay the visit.

Mr Chase was the only absentee. He asserted his seniority and declined on the grounds of preceding duties. This was unlikely, but went unchallenged. Mrs Chase knew better than to press her husband on such matters. If he said no, he usually meant it and was not a man to court debate. For the rest, there was no such easy option to decline. Even Fred and William were persuaded to tag along, not the most arduous of chores but one which gave Fred pause for thought when William accepted so readily.

Shortly after two o'clock therefore, Mrs Chase, her three daughters and their two male house guests arrived at the 'Hove School of Art,' breaking in upon the unsuspecting and clearly surprised Mr Kenneth who, along with some fifteen or so pupils of similar age to Katie were in the midst of reproducing in watercolours every subtle detail of a large vase of flowers placed on a velvet covered table in the centre of the studio.

The room itself, more a small hall than a room, was on the upper floor of a red brick building in Palmeira Road. Light and airy courtesy of large windows set into the south facing slope of the roof, it was otherwise quite plain. It was also far from warm and, due to the fact that nothing was laid down to cover the bare floor boards, every sound of shuffling feet, the movement of furniture, or the spoken word, were magnified to an annoying pitch. Nevertheless, there was obvious artistic endeavour in progress for each member of the raiding party to witness and occasional evidence of some talent among the majority of rather less promising work on display. Furthermore, Mr Kenneth presented himself as a quiet and dedicated young man bent entirely upon the furtherance of good artistic endeavour.

Consequently, when after about ten minutes of interruption, Mrs Chase turned to leave, she and Katie's other two most sceptical critics, namely her elder sisters, Marian and Margaret, appeared confident that her skills as an artist might be honed to the better, albeit in such a stark environment. They also appeared unanimous in their opinion that Mr Kenneth, though polite, affable enough and certainly handsome, if a little on the Bohemian side, was unlikely to pose a threat to Katie's morals, placed as he was among an assemblage of young maidenhood, several of whom possessed more obvious attractions than Katie to a bachelor of his demeanour.

The walk home, therefore, took place in congenial mood. Katie appeared content enough with her mother's reaction to the school and its tutor. Where criticisms lay, they were directed at the fabric of the school rather than at the gentleman conducting it. He was, Mrs Chase declared, a 'pleasant enough fellow' although it was obvious to anyone he was in 'dire need of both a barber and a tailor.' That aside, the school was deemed to offer some benefits to a girl of Katie's age and temperament. Accordingly, she was granted full parental permission to continue her twice weekly sessions as long as the family remained in Brighton.

So preoccupied was the small troop with the summing up given by Mrs Chase, no one noticed, least of all the two people concerned, that Marian and Captain Radford found themselves walking along the comparatively narrow pavement side by side and at some distance detached from the rest of the party.

That they should complete their walk in silence was unlikely. However, it did take some minutes before either plucked up the courage to speak. When they did, William made a throw away remark about the general quality of painting he had seen on display during their brief visit to the school. Nervously, but losing none of her innate talent to amuse, Marian declared a certain relief that their unannounced arrival had taken place when the topic for study was a neatly arranged vase of flowers rather than a life class.

Ice suitably broken, they embarked upon a steady stream of conversation which continued with only short pauses and interruptions, through to the end of their walk and beyond. During tea, rather than continue the previous tactic of careful separation, they sat next to each other, their conversation unstoppable. Later, at dinner, though seated opposite, there was no change. Indeed, had not the duo of short plays at the Hove Town Assembly Hall proved more entertaining and better performed than expected, they might well have continued throughout those as well.

It was as if the tide knew no high-water mark. Fred valued William as man possessed of natural confidence. He was well travelled, well informed and more than able to hold centre stage at any social gathering. Similarly, his cousin Marian, had gained a reputation as the saviour of many a dull dinner party, her outspoken but eloquently expressed opinions regularly provoking even the most reticent of guests to lively debate. But this was something quite new from both of them. Unaware of being closely observed by all interested parties which meant the whole family with the possible exception of Katie who rarely concerned herself with the affairs of others, the two of them were mutually absorbed. Sleep it seemed would be the only distraction to halt their interrogation.

For a time, William talked of his years at university, of his home in Sutton Coldfield, his tour of duty in India and of his future ambitions. Then it was Marian's turn. She confided her life in London, her love of art, music and literature and gave hints as to the sort of future she envisaged by the turn of the century. Then came exchanges of attitudes towards religion, politics and world events, their record of accord in all such matters astounding those who from time to time paused to listen in on progress.

Almost every subject they touched upon achieved a degree or other of consensus. William did not agree with Marian over her doubts as to the need for Britain to sustain such a sprawling empire. In turn, and naturally enough for a young woman of such independent opinions, Marian took issue with him over his rather pessimistic anticipation of the meek contribution he imagined women making towards society over the coming century. However, as her father was pleased to observe in a purely self-congratulatory manner, their differences were as naught to the astounding clarity of their common accord.

Quite clearly, though hesitant at the outset, this was the coming together of two matched souls. Not once before had Marian shown the slightest glimmer of serious interest in a member of the opposite sex. Young men came and went. All were greeted warmly and entertained with an open mind but without any one of them creating the least ripple on the surface of a pool her father believed to be deeper than in any woman he had encountered. Convinced of her exceptional qualities and setting to one side as best he could any natural paternal bias, he was never disappointed.

Though his wife longed to see her eldest daughter well matched and off her hands, fast breeding a clutch of healthy grandchildren for her to fawn over, Mr Chase was less keen to be rid of Marian. He was relieved she did not succumb to the first young man with good looks and promising career prospects. Of course, she needed a partner in life, but it was essential she chose one to challenge her. Without intellectual stimulation how else would she grow into the woman he truly believed she was destined to become.

For Marian, marriage and motherhood would not be enough. 'At home,' dinner parties and teas at the vicarage would not serve long term to fulfil her. She needed and was capable of so much more.

As sure as he could be, Mr Chase knew William Radford was the man for his daughter. He had no hard facts to bolster such conviction. He held little information about the lad beyond what was general knowledge. However, after his initial visit to 32 Princes Gate, Mr Chase was satisfied enough. Should his daughter be introduced to a hundred similarly reared young men, not one of them would be as suitable to her needs as the one now so determinedly preoccupied with her.

During the following three days, Marian and William were rarely out of each other's sight. Mrs Chase, Margaret, Katie and even poor Fred became an irrelevance. Only on the evening Canon and Mrs and Miss Butler came to dinner were they compelled to put on hold their mutual approbation. Then, for an hour or two, courtesy demanded they reunite with the rest of the family to engage three guests who though not close family friends were nevertheless deserving of undivided attention throughout their visit.

As it happened, Marian found the Canon a fascinating man. After dinner, in the drawing room, liberated from the overzealous interruptions of his wife throughout the meal as she expressed concern over what he hate, how much he ate and whether or not he should eat at all, bearing in mind the frail condition of his stomach and the perilously fragile state of his heart, he inspired Marian with his radical views as to the obligations of the clergy in modern society. Convinced though he was as to the efficacy of missionary work abroad, a topic so close to Margaret's heart, he believed vehemently that the glamour and romanticism of such endeavours and the attractions such a career held for newly ordained priests should be treated with caution. It was vital such things were not permitted to divert attention from the very real and ever-increasing problems of moral and physical deprivation within the great cities of Britain.

He conceded readily that the recent industrial expansion had brought with it great wealth for the few and a rise in the standard of living for many. However, he urged Marian as he did his congregations and priests alike to recognise that huge and rapid population growths had also created a new under class, a whole raft of society, poor in the extreme and morally bereft, whose resulting severe poverty was in danger of being entirely overlooked unless the church and parliament adopted a novel stance. Inward spiritual investment was essential lest for every heathen brought to Christianity on the other side of the world, ten souls were lost beyond redemption in the heart of the empire.

This was not a view given much credence by Margaret whose sole ambition in life was to give herself to the self-same missionary work the Canon spoke of with such reticence, but it was a message Marian found hard to resist. Committed as she was to the ambitions of her sister, she could not but offer in equal measure every encouragement to the Canon. Clearly, he was a man of acute social conscience, alert to what he saw as an impending crisis and not embarrassed to acknowledge a very real danger that the institution of which he was a leader showed signs of letting the nettle slip from its grasp.

By the time Mrs Butler came for her husband and, in the same deft movement, extricated her daughter from the attentions of Fred, Marian was deeply committed to the Canons' cause and in full agreement with his philosophy. His ecclesiastical doubts seemed to mirror at least in part her own scepticism with regard to present Imperial priorities. She was intrigued by his radicalism, captivated by his depth of knowledge and much impressed by his preference for humanitarianism over religious zeal.

By the time her head hit the pillow that evening, however, subject to the fore was no longer inner-city decay but pleasurable anticipation of another day spent in the company of Captain William Radford.

Chapter Two

For Marian, the day of William Radford's departure brought with it the termination of her pleasure at being in Brighton. Yet she, her mother and two sisters were not due to return to London for a further week.

In between there were dinner parties both to host and attend. There were theatre visits planned and the much looked forward to Richter concert at the Dome. Added to that was a trip to the newly restocked Aquarium with promise of a dolphin to see and various members of the shark species imported from oceans across the world. In all, she was faced with the prospect of an uninterrupted schedule of social activity, something normally embraced with willing participation and a degree of intellectual curiosity not expected of the agonisingly shy Margaret or the frustratingly exuberant Katie.

But everything had changed. Marian wanted little to do with family and friends. In their place and in the absence of any sign of an early return to London, she craved solitude in her room, solitary walks along the beach or occasional rides with her father, the only relative she owned with whom she was comfortable sharing her deepest felt emotions.

In short, Marian was ill at ease, incapable of participating in or gleaning any reasonable satisfaction from the many simple pleasures of normal family life. Her sickness precluded entertainment, stifled any desire to travel unless towards the source of her ague and specifically excluded any notion of enjoying the company of others. Quite without precedent, she found herself incapacitated, giddy and morose in ways she neither recognised in herself nor admired.

If the name and memory of William Radford was the inspiration for such an overwhelming sense of ill humour and melancholy, she wanted to loathe him for it. Instead, the more she cursed his name, the more eager she became to see him again. And, the deeper she descended into a slough of her own making. Her diary, no longer a picture book commentary of places visited, people well met and things done, became a dower soliloquy concerning loss and the pain of affection.

Love was given no quarter. She did not, could not, love Captain Radford. Nor, and every bit as much to the point, was she 'in love' with him. That was a ridiculous notion. The act of being 'in love' required dedication. Love was not a whim, an impulse. Love was as broad as an ocean, as enduring as tempered steel. How could she possibly claim to be in love when her time thus far spent in the company of Captain Radford and her knowledge of him were both so limited.

In the end, and in spite of her reluctance to admit it, she concluded that the term 'infatuation' best summed up her state. Yet, even that was almost more than she could bear. She despised the very word. It implied something fickle, weak and she scolded herself for the possibility of owning so feeble an emotion.

From Katie, she expected it and more. Katie was the sort of easy come easy go girl enamoured with a different man at the drop of a hat. She was butterfly like in temperament and already possessed of a flirtatious personality destined to envelope trouble like spider's silk about careless flies.

Perfectly conceivable as well was the spectre of Margaret, shy and unworldly, readily exposing herself to such sudden a flight of fancy. Indeed, if evidence were needed to prove the point, there was not a soul in the family who did not fully expect her present zeal for missionary work to thaw as quickly as a spring frost in favour of more moderate goals.

In both Margaret and Katie, the condition of 'infatuation' could be eminently possible and not the least surprising. For Marian, however, such a definition of her feelings bordered on intolerable. She was faced therefore with a two-edged sword of shame. If the secret sentences contained within her diary were the pronouncements of a woman caught in a sudden infatuation, she wanted rid of it as soon as possible. There was no place in her life for such trivia. If, on the other hand, she owned up to love, she sensed a deep and irrevocable lessening of the emotion as she recognised it, imagining as she always had that love grew and developed not like a flower, quickly blooming and then easily spent, but like a great oak tree, the germ of a seed striving for generations to produce its mighty, unmoveable trunk, resistant to all storms, enduring beyond every other living thing.

Night after night, she strove to find the words to write, words which would both define and purge. She wrestled with every grain of knowledge in her head to explain her torment. Kind words from her father eased the pain but suggested no satisfactory remedy.

One year on, confined to the same room in Adelaide Drive, with the same view of the sea and no less a conflict in her heart, she mourned the tragedy unfolding in the Sudan. She found herself no less frustrated than the newspaper columnists themselves at the British governments apparent tardiness in sending forces to aid the heroic General Gordon. However, in one thing at least, her emotions were clear. No more was she compelled to torment herself in applying labels to her feelings. Love and infatuation were merely two ends of a many-coloured rainbow. They were the two poles, north and south. In between were vast expanses of varied terrain and in twelve months she had walked most of them. She recognised every pothole and bend in the road.

For a period of one year she had been on a journey, visiting én route the highest of peaks and the lowest of valleys. She had entertained the most exquisite and the ugliest sides of that branch of the human psyche named 'amour.'

By the February of 1885, it was over. During the same month in 1884, however, it was just beginning. The day after Fred and Captain Radford returned to London, the former to the pursuit of his career as an itinerant barrister, the latter stopping off only briefly before continuing on to the home of his parents in Sutton Coldfield, Marian was faced with a return to the normal round of social activity as prescribed for her and her sisters by their mother. The first was an 'at home,' given, rather than received. For a whole afternoon their new house was filled with a host of neighbours, come to pay their respects, proffer their kindest regards, take tea and inspect an interior which had been the subject of local speculation since the laying of the foundations.

As the eldest daughter, Marian was compelled to play hostess with enthusiasm to match that of her mother. With studied charm and a carefully manufactured smile, she welcomed the likes of Miss Butler, Miss Munday, Mr Anstead, Mrs and Miss Grimlow, Mrs Kemble, Mrs Johnstone and Mr and Mrs Hill. Only when they were gone and the house finally silent again could she return briefly to her private thoughts. Then, all too quickly, she was expected on parade for another outing to the Hove Town Assembly Hall, this time to watch a humorous review staged by various amateur thespian elements of the 4th Dragoon guards.

It was a harmless enough hour or so of fun, a show of meagre artistic merit. However, since its' precise 'raison d'etre' was to raise funds for charity, it was an extremely well attended evening. The Assembly Hall was filled to capacity. Both laughter and applause were offered in equal abundance. Mrs Chase was even bold enough to pronounce it the best entertainment of the year, a declaration sweetly agreed to by both Margaret and Katie but greeted with a wry smile from Marian who doubted the guards themselves would have claimed such merit for their efforts. Fortunately, the long-awaited and first visit of the great Richter to the Dome on the following evening was enough to dampen her mother's generously offered bias.

The Dome itself was no Albert Hall. Smaller, plainer and less resounding than the acoustic grandeur of its London counterpart, there could be no doubt it was a lesser venue for a performance by the great man. Nevertheless, in his presence, even Marian temporarily forgot herself. Mesmerised by every note of the music he orchestrated, she disappeared into a world free from the artistic judgements of her mother, the giggling intrusion of her two less appreciative sisters and, for a short time at least, the ever-present image of the man who had become such an obsession.

This relief, however, did not last long. Two hours and the music was over. Two hours and waiting ahead of her was another night of tossing and turning, another darkened room plagued by Cupid's demons.

Not a moment too soon therefore did their stay in Brighton come to an end. No more was she compelled to tolerate the spectacular view from her window or the daily search for yet another pleasurable activity to divert the family.

Once back in London she was no nearer a resolution to her problems. Encamped as he was in Sutton Coldfield, Captain Radford was no more accessible than had they all remained on the south coast. But that mattered not a jot. In town, at home in Princes Gate, there were many serious diversions to distract Marian. Regular trips to bible class and afternoons spent at vicarage working parties would serve to ensure fewer and less arduous periods of painful introspection. Once settled back into her daily routine, with problems to solve and a mountain of weighty reading to be done, she would surely restore her sanity. She would look forward to seeing William again; of course she would. His company would be hard to better and his conversation difficult to replace. Just as certain, she was unlikely to meet a man whose features appealed more, whose interests matched her own or whose presence pleased her quite as much.

However, as the rolling South Downs were left behind in favour of urban sprawl, Marian anticipated the days ahead being far less rigorous a penance than her last week in Brighton.

On their first evening home, they went 'en famille' to the Opera at Covent Garden, that is Marian, her mother, two sisters, Uncle George Mountfield (her mother's brother, father of Fred and therefore a third joint conspirator in the plot to place William Radford in her path) and, for a rare change since he professed no love of shrill sopranos or portly tenors, her father.

When questioned as to his sudden change of heart, his initial refusal to attend being no less vociferous than was his wont, Mr Chase insisted his motive was merely the desire to share an evening with his wife and children. In truth, since he had not spoken to Marian for three days, that being the length of time he had been in London prior to their return, having come away earlier to fulfil certain professional commitments, he was anxious to observe her condition. The opera was no place for the two of them to talk privately. That could wait until they were alone in the 'Row,' but what originally began in Hove as scrutiny based upon mild amusement had turned to genuine concern. To witness his daughter so unusually flustered simply by being introduced to a young male house guest was one thing. However, to see her unnerved by a fast-developing relationship over which she appeared to have little or no control, was quite another.

Pressed to do so he would have denied vehemently any favouritism among his three daughters, loving them and caring for them as he did in equal measure. However, he could not deny, nor had it gone unnoticed that an affinity existed between himself and Marian, a combination of empathy and sympathy if you will, which he failed to achieve in his relationships with either Margaret or Katie.

The opera was something of a passion for Marian. As a little girl when she was first taken, her father noticed at once a light in her eyes which was repeated each time she went. Consequently, he could think of no better place to assess her mood than from the dress circle of the finest opera house in England. If he saw no light then his best or worst fears would be confirmed dependent entirely upon the intentions of her young suitor.

Marian of course was ignorant of his scheme. She was delighted her father had decided to join them. She was also open in her appreciation of a return to a standard of musical theatre capable of leaving her breathless. Nevertheless, by way of confirming his fears, the light in her eyes shone less brightly than Mr Chase recalled. The evening was a success. Katie was somewhat restless. She made mischief by over using her glasses and commenting upon anyone in the boxes of amusement to her. Finally, her father was forced to remove and pocket the offending articles. For a while, but only during the final act, Mrs Chase fell asleep and snored roundly until a gravely embarrassed Margaret nudged her urgently and the poor lady woke with a start, almost leaping to her feet.

But it was Marian whom Mr Chase observed the most. What he witnessed was enough to convince him that through her acquaintance with William Radford she had brought to the surface a range of emotions which had hitherto lain dormant. This was precisely as he had suspected when first she mentioned his name while on their early morning ride across the Downs.

The following morning Marian breakfasted early with Margaret. As soon as they were finished, they set off for Victoria Hospital in Chelsea to visit the children's wards, returning barely in time for lunch. When they did so they found their father had left home bound for Sutton Coldfield.

Naturally enough, Marian quizzed her mother as to the purpose of his trip and found herself envying his ability to come and go as he pleased upon a whim, particularly in a northerly direction. Quite sensibly, however, Mr Chase said little to his wife beyond the fact that he would be away overnight. That being the case, he would be unable to attend the dinner party to which they were both invited at the home of Colonel and Mrs Webster who lived in a delightful house just off Russell Square. The only guarantee he offered was to be home the following day in time to spend the better part of his birthday in the company of his family.

Wise to the result of his previous clandestine trip, Marian was in little doubt that his intentions were connected with her. He had no business in Sutton Coldfield that she knew and unless by coincidence some relative or other had moved to the region while they were away in Brighton, his plausible motives were few.

An appointment with Captain Radford seemed the only logical explanation for his sudden departure and, though logical, it was the answer she least wanted to accept without having first had the chance to approve the idea. Too late, however. Her long morning of charitable concern for the sick was the perfect opportunity for her father to slip away uncontested which was his planned intention. Knowing Marian as he did, he wanted to avoid her obvious opposition to his mission. Pride and an oft times infuriating stubborn streak were two traits of her personality he knew well, since they were both attributes inherited from him. Had she been aware of his proposed journey to the midlands it might have ended before it was begun.

Pride would have led her to deny her emotional discomfort and that same stubborn streak would have encouraged her to resist any attempt at a remedy.

'I think Papa's really mean to have gone off like he has,' was Katie's contribution to the unanimous criticism of his absence on the eve of his birthday.

'Quite so,' Margaret agreed pithily.

'Even if he sets off for home immediately after breakfast tomorrow morning, he still won't be home in time for lunch,' Katie concluded, having clearly gone to some lengths in working out train times.

'Never mind,' said their mother, always quick to offer a defence. 'He promised he would be here and I know your father won't let us down.'

'But why did he have to go away today of all days?' Katie moaned, the early morning birthday surprise to her father facing ruin.

'Katie dear,' came the response from her mother, 'Don't make a fuss. Your father went away because he had to and that's all you need to know. Now be a good girl. He'll be home tomorrow in plenty of time.'

'But Mamma…'

'No more buts, Katie. For once just accept things the way they are and make the most of them.'

Peace reigned after that short exchange. Katie did keep quiet for the rest of the day. It was hard for her. Her mildly rebellious streak, never far beneath the surface, urged her on to more complaint but she held back. Recognising the rarely used tone of authority in her mother's voice she knew better than to provoke further.

Marian said nothing either. She was not so much disappointed by the absence of her father as she was anxious. If he was off on some sort of errand on her behalf, she wished he was not. She realised at all times he had her best interests at heart but in this instance when she was in a total quandary as to any satisfactory solution for her delicate state of mind, she would have preferred less direct action from him and more of a shoulder to lean on.

In an effort to dampen her anxiety, she and her mother took themselves off to an exhibition of Ecclesiastical Embroidery at the British Museum. An exquisite and sober display of religious artefacts assembled from churches and cathedrals the length and breadth of the country, it served to occupy them for most of the afternoon. Later, she, Margaret and Katie, the latter most reluctantly, attended a confirmation service at Brompton Church and listened with varying degrees of attention to a long sermon given by the Bishop of London, a man whose words were wont to be as profoundly delivered as they were intended. For nearly an hour he regaled the assembled innovates to the church, emphasising the seriousness of their calling to Christianity and warning them against any dalliance from the path of righteousness.

The bishop was a renowned orator. It was unlikely anyone would have been inclined to engage him as an after-dinner speaker, but mounted in a high pulpit, he was formidable. Martin Luther himself could not have bettered his pristine Puritan idealism. He offered no compromise and gave no quarter. Christianity was a serious ship to board. The cruel seas of heathenism might easily swamp even the mightiest vessel if the crew slackened. The way for a true Christian was therefore hard and fraught with pitfalls, but the rewards were great.

It was a message couched in grand metaphor and delivered with a theatrical dexterity rarely achieved on the best of London stages. It was also a message Marian had heard from him before. Stock in trade were his allusions to ships and the savagery of the open seas. High on his agenda was the predominance of sin in modern society and powerful were his words of condemnation for those who having committed themselves to the church then strayed from the path. None of it was new. Like well-rehearsed propaganda, it poured forth from his lips with studied synchronisation, every emphasis exactly on time, every pause profoundly manufactured for best effect.

Quite whether they were the most comforting words to heap upon a host of new converts, Marian had her doubts. Fire and brimstone, suffering and retribution seemed the least desirable offerings from a church keen to attract a new generation to its congregations. To her mind and certainly to her instincts, words such as compassion and understanding appealed the more. Threats of eternal damnation were all very well and she was quite prepared to accept that modern society was, morally at least, on a downward spiral.

However, she was not prepared to see sin in everyone and everything. Many people she knew and certainly all those she loved were predominantly good. London was indeed an overcrowded, dirty and often sinful metropolis. That there was ample evil abroad could not be denied. But equally, not a day passed she did not witness acts of good, deeds of kindness and thoughts of generosity.

The Right Reverend Bishop of London was a man to be respected, the spiritual leader of a vast population, as diverse as any across the world but having borne the brunt of several similar sermons previously, Marian held to the opinion that he saw little hope for humanity and that this lack of hope for, or faith in, his own congregation would come back to haunt the very institution which he held in such awe. Parents who find no joy in their children rarely reap the rewards they profess to covet.

By contrast, Margaret remained supremely impressed by him. The very stature of his title, his majestic robes and the bellowing force of his words were the stuff of her inspiration to become a missionary. While Marian willed him to end his sermon wishing only to rebuke him for his ferocity and to challenge the core of his ideals, Margaret sat like a startled rabbit. Spellbound, she committed every syllable to memory, ready to reproduce it all again somewhere on the other side of the world. And Katie, poor Katie, squirmed with impatience and indifference, too wilful to mind his words but still too ignorant to invent for herself a moral or spiritual creed.

The overall result was that three sisters arrived home all very much in a similar frame of mind but each for different reasons. Marian felt depressed, brought down by the sheer wanton negativity of a church she wanted so much to admire. Margaret was frustrated that her desire to join the front line of Christian soldiers was still beyond her reach and Katie bemoaned the waste of an afternoon when she might have been more gainfully employed finishing the dress she intended wearing to commemorate her father's birthday on the following day.

Needless to say, without her husband to parry the disgruntled mood of her three daughters, Mrs Chase was left to face them alone, something not at all uncommon but no less unwelcome. Marian went to her room. There she filled two pages of her diary with contradictory evidence illustrating as many as she could the positive sides of human endeavour. She also took the Bishop of London to task. Finally, she noted that she could not recall a time she had waited for the coming day with such apprehension. She forgot to make any critique with regard to the exhibition of ecclesiastical embroidery and she overlooked completely any reference to the fact that although it was the beginning of March their journey home from church was made rather more remarkable than it might have been by the onset of a flurry of snow. When finally, she fell asleep it was no deep repose. She was restless all night, the day ahead an ever-present irritant to a good night's rest.

The following morning, as soon as breakfast was over, she press ganged her two sisters into a stroll to and back from the Albert Memorial. She could not ride with her father so a walk was the most she could hope for, a walk which actually proved more interesting than any of them anticipated.

Once in the park, they came across a parade of horse drawn coaches assembled for all to see. It was a crisp day. There was a thin layer of snow on the ground left over from the previous day. The branches of the bare trees were coated with a frosting which sparkled in the bright sun. The hot, muggy breath of the carriage horses threw up a fog around their heads. That aside, it was a fine morning, a morning made for celebrating a birthday, a morning when to see three sisters walking together, arm in arm through the park belied much of the cynicism expressed the previous afternoon beneath the grand vaults of Brompton Church.

Strangely, Marian felt herself at ease, not at all what she anticipated after so broken a night's sleep and a sensation somewhat remote during the last few weeks. She chatted casually with Margaret and Katie, sharing with them nothing more weighty than observations of the fashions being shown off by the ladies in the 'row' or the likely faces they might see at the 'at home' they were due to attend in the afternoon courtesy of Mrs and Misses Kekewich. In fact, to her surprise when she considered it, she quite forgot William Radford. He was gone from her thoughts, replaced by a certain light hearted nothingness incapable of stimulating emotional highs or lows. As fresh and as crisp as the air itself, it was as if for a short while a window had been thrown open. The heavy, burdensome constitution of her thoughts was gone. In its stead a light, zephyr breeze cleared her mind, bringing with it a transparency much needed but so regretfully absent all the while she had been in Brighton.

Reminiscent of days past when they were three girls together, she, Margaret and Katie laughed, teased and joked with each other right up to and beyond the front door of their home in Princes Gate, bringing back with them a frivolity their mother had missed and would have welcomed on the previous afternoon. For a brief moment they were children again and the house echoed to the sounds only children make as they share and entertain with the innocence and charm of youth.

'You enjoyed your walk then?' came the rhetorical question from Mrs Chase.

'Oh Mamma, it was so lovely,' Katie replied with boundless enthusiasm. 'The horses were all got up, the coaches gleamed in the sun and some of the uniforms were really splendid.'

Since their mother was unaware of the event, Marian elaborated, explaining how they had stumbled upon the historic coaching club, all decked out in their traditional finery with even the passengers in period costume.

'Well,' their mother sighed, 'that will teach me for being a "stay-at-home", won't it? I should very much like to have seen that. It must have been quite a sight.'

'Oh, it was Mamma, it was,' Katie bragged.

'And what about you Margaret?' her mother inquired, 'did you enjoy your walk in the fresh air.'

'Yes, thank you, Mamma,' came the reply. 'It was very edifying.'

'Edifying. Was it indeed? Well, it must have been good then. And did you find it edifying as well Marian?'

'It was lovely Mamma thank you,' Marian replied, not keen to prolong any further mocking of her sister.

'That's good, because your father will be home soon and today is his birthday. So, if you all feel suitably "edified" by your walk, I shall expect a lot of happy, smiling faces to greet him.'

'Yes Mamma,' came the chorus of response, Marian particularly aware that her mother's pointed remark was perhaps levelled at her rather than the other two. Katie, after all, was tirelessly exuberant and therefore not likely to be in need of a reminder and Margaret, though laconic by nature, a rather too serious young lady for her own good, a girl whose natural 'joie de vivre' was curtailed by her devotion to the Lord, was accepted for the way she was.

In the end, Mr Chase arrived home just before dark, having caught a later train than expected due to an earlier derailment just outside Oxford. However, when he did walk through the door, his wife and all three of his daughters welcomed him with no less enthusiasm than if he had been around the world; a hero's welcome.

Though tired, he could not avoid the flattering attention of his family. With somewhat weary resignation he allowed himself to be dragged into the drawing room where a roaring fire was set in the hearth. Tea arrived within minutes and, at the side of his favourite wing chair, a small stack of neatly wrapped presents lay waiting for his attention. A fine new pig skin portmanteau was the largest package from his wife, the complete works of Shakespeare in lush half calf bindings was Marian's offering, while Margaret had bought him a pair of soft leather gloves and Katie a finely engraved silver calling card case.

It was a haul received with much sincere gratitude. For many minutes while his tea went cold in its cup, he pawed over each gift, admiring, relishing and assuring all four donors of the guaranteed use he would put to each object over the coming months. Afterwards, he announced that he too had a gift, not for himself alone, but for the whole family.

With a teasing flourish he produced from the inside pocket of his jacket an envelope.

'I've had this a few days,' he said, 'but I wanted to keep it until now before giving you all the news.'

'What is it Papa?' Katie asked on behalf of them all, the impatience in her voice magnified to accommodate the interest of her mother and two sisters.

'Well,' he replied, delaying a second or two in order to build the suspense, 'It's an invitation.'

'Yes?' Katie begged, her impatience by now too much to bear.

'Do tell us Charles,' Mrs Chase added, 'You know how hard Katie finds it to be patient.'

He smiled, pleased to have achieved such an air of expectancy.

'This card,' and he held it aloft, 'is an invitation for me and as many members of my family as I so choose to attend the opening of the International Health Exhibition.'

There followed general howls of approval, sporadic applause and an affectionate kiss on the cheek from his wife. Prior to this announcement pressure from all quarters had been placed on him to obtain just such an invitation. The International Health Exhibition was the most talked about event to be staged in London since the Great Exhibition of 1851 and since it was to be erected almost within sight of their home, everyone resident at 32 Princes Gate had been looking forward to it for months. Invitations for the opening ceremony were extremely hard to come by, but it was always hoped that through their close friendship with Sir John and Lady Strachey, he a long serving parliamentarian and sometime equerry to His Royal Highness the Duke of York, something might be done.

'Thank you, Papa,' Marian said quietly after the initial clamour had died down.

'That's quite all right my dear,' he replied and smiled, and Marian knew that as pleased as he was with their individual gifts, no greater birthday present could come his way than to witness universal happiness on the faces of his family.

Charles Chase was a man who made few demands upon life. Successful in his field as a civil engineer but at heart, very much the academic, fond of literature, the arts and music, though not opera, he harboured few complaints with his lot. An inherited income guaranteed him relative financial security.

However, his career, his interests and, most particularly, his family were the real substance to his modest fortune. Money permitted him an elegant London home with a retinue of staff. Money also provided a comfortable retreat in Hove, the freedom to travel and the enjoyment of knowing that his family would never go hungry. However, without his family, money meant little to him. For himself he was not extravagant. Material things he considered to be of negligible worth unless shared and when all was said and done, his wife and three daughters were his only significant source of pleasure.

Smiles on their faces were worth many thousands in the bank. Their happiness was his, their sorrow a burden almost too great to bear. Invitations to the International Health Exhibition were trinkets, in themselves of no significance at all. However, as a ticket to contentment within the walls of his home, they were the most precious thing available and to produce one at that moment gilded what had been a long day.

Only one problem remained unresolved. Marian was as pleased as her mother and two sisters with his surprise. In fact, it was she more than anyone who stood to gain most benefit from the forthcoming event. Her insatiable desire for knowledge would be fuelled by so diverse a display of modern technological achievement and so imaginative a reconstruction of societies and cultures from across the world. While his two other daughters would be impressed by the prestige of attending the opening and thereafter gain hours of amusement from the many things on show, for Marian it would prove a deep well, filled with the most refreshing and reviving water.

Yet, his overnight absence bore no relevance to such comparative trivia. His mission was a matter more urgent than any hard-won invitation, its outcome more poignant than a hundred such exhibitions.

'Marian, my dear,' he said as he sat on the edge of her bed later that evening, when the birthday festivities were at an end and the remainder of the family had retired for the night, 'I'm sorry you've had to wait so long to hear my news.'

'That's all right, Papa. I understand.'

'I knew you would. But I'm still sorry we've not been able to find a quiet moment together until now.'

For a second or two he paused, his hesitation partly to allow time for the process of thought but equally to absorb the sight of her. In her night dress, her hair loose, her womanly face paint washed away, he recalled for a moment the times when, as a small girl, he would go to her room each evening to bid her goodnight; times unparalleled for joy.

'I want to tell you something,' he began again, betraying not the least hint of what had just passed through his mind. 'Years ago, before you were born, when I was young and brash and completely unaware of what life held in store for me, I was introduced to a young woman. It was at a dinner party. Nothing out of the ordinary. Just one of those dinner parties, similar to those we have; family, friends and friends of friends. She was eighteen, I twenty-three. Your age exactly. In those days I was happy, single and, in spite of your grandfather's constant urging to the contrary, not in the least interested in settling down. However, that night, something extraordinary happened.'

'Across the dinner table from me sat quite the most beautiful and vibrant creature I had ever seen. Instantly, and I do promise you, it was in an instant, in the blinking of an eye, my life was altered forever. I fell deeply in love. I was not infatuated; I was in love. I barely knew this girl, hardly spoke a word to her all evening, but I was quite hopelessly and positively in love. It was your mother, of course and not for a second was there slightest doubt in my mind that this was the woman I was destined to marry. Furthermore, since that night I bless every day we have been together.'

He stopped speaking to wait for a reaction but none came. Marian was rather overwhelmed by this sudden stream of confession.

'You may be wondering why I should choose such a time to tell you this,' he continued, taking his daughters nod of the head as his cue to proceed. 'Well, I can confess it now. I very nearly missed my chance with your mother. I didn't know it at the time but her parents, grandfather Arthur and grandmother Elise, already had plans for the man she was to marry. He was a smart, young cavalry officer, quite the catch. He and your mother had known each other from childhood and it was taken for granted they would be married when she came of age. Consequently, my case was hopeless. Besides which, on the night we first met and for several months after that, it never crossed my mind to see her again. I could not forget her though. She was in my thoughts, night and day. I was in agony, but I did nothing. And in doing nothing, I came close to losing her. You see I hadn't the least idea whether or not she felt the same way towards me. I simply assumed she did not. After all, why should she. We'd only met once. Anyway, to cut a very long story short, we did meet again and, thank God, we did marry.'

'I'm glad, Papa.'

'So am I if only because had I not married your mother, I would not now have three of the most beautiful daughters in the world.'

'But no son,' Marian interjected, changing the subject somewhat.

'No son could better you,' he insisted. 'You must never think I would have preferred a son to you. I am a fortunate man. I have my health, a fine home and loving family. Son or no, I could not ask for more. Anyway, that's not the point of my being here at this hour. I came to talk about you and your future and the reason for my going to Sutton Coldfield.'

'Yes Papa.'

'As you may well have guessed, I went to speak with young Captain Radford. You may think I had no right to do so and I'm quite prepared for you to be cross with me for interfering. However, because I love you and because I want so much for you to be happy, I couldn't help myself. Over the past weeks I've seen it in your eyes. You may not want to admit it. You may not even recognise it. But you are in love with Captain Radford.'

Marian was about to object but he raised his hand for her to remain silent.

'Let me finish my dear, then you can scold me all you want.'

Marian obeyed and settled back into her pillows.

'More to the point and the chief reason for my train journey to the midlands is that when he was staying with us, I saw in young William's eyes exactly the same emotions I felt for your mother a quarter of a century ago. I was absolutely convinced his feelings for you exactly match yours for him. I was also equally convinced that should you spend the rest of your lives looking, neither of you will find a mate better suited. Consequently, I went to find out Captain Radford's intentions. In short, I've been match making. Now I know this role is usually reserved for the mother and it is not a very complimentary pastime but in my opinion, it had to be done.'

'Captain Radford is off to India again shortly. A year down the line, with you still on his mind but with resignation in his heart, he will meet another respectable and available young woman. They will marry, raise a family and be perfectly content. But I promise you he will always regret not having seized the moment with you. His life will be full, yet incomplete, satisfactory yet lacking. Simply put, I couldn't sit back to see that happen, not for his sake or yours. You my dear, will never get this chance for true happiness again.'

Marian made no reply. She was speechless. Of course, she suspected her father's motive for going way. Indeed, she anticipated what he would say when he returned. But she had not expected his determination to have her so quickly and permanently linked to Captain Radford.

'I can tell you now,' he continued before she had time to collect her thoughts. 'Lest you were concerned, William Radford is a fine young man. His parents too are most pleasant and respectable people. More to the point, however, his feelings for you are exactly as I thought. He is deeply in love with you. Consequently, I made it clear to both him and his parents that should he ask for your hand in marriage, I would not stand in his way.'

'Marriage Papa!' Marian exclaimed, the word like a gust of cold wind rushing past her face.

'Yes, marriage,' he replied, saying the word again to soften the blow.

'But Papa, I've never thought about getting married.'

'Of course not, and you don't have to now. You can turn away from it, tell me and yourself that this man means nothing to you. But I know you, Marian. You are my daughter. You have my blood in you. In you, now I see myself twenty-five years ago. It's like looking in the mirror, the only difference being that then, as a man, I had control over my own destiny. I won the hand of your mother because society permitted me the privilege of choice. As unjust as it is, you do not have that choice. You cannot take the initiative. You can only wait and hope and if fortune smiles on you thank heaven for it. I could not let that happen. William Radford is the man you were destined to spend your life with, to raise a family with. Since you cannot speak up for yourself in these matters, I felt I had to do it for you. You can still turn him down. You can send him packing, deny your feelings and I will say nothing, but I could not bear for the chance to pass you by just because William lacked the confidence to pursue you.'

Marian was truly stunned. In an assessment of her father, unorthodox was not a word one would most normally associate with him. Such extreme behaviour, therefore was completely out of character, or so she thought. She was caught in a whirlpool of possible responses to what he had done and his reasons for doing it.

She could not deny her feelings for William Radford. That would have been futile. Her father knew her too well. But the word 'marriage' writ bold by his public pronouncement of it when till that moment it had remained but a vague, subconscious thought in the back of her mind, was a severe shock to the system. As for the rest, she was bemused. She had no idea what to think or how to react.

When he left her room, she lay in the darkness for what seemed like hours, trying to come to terms with the implications of what her father had said and done. She wanted to be angry. That would have been the simple solution. To be cross with her father for interfering was the obvious response, particularly if partnered with denial. But it was not that simple. She could not disclaim her feeling for William Radford. She was even willing to accept that no man she had met before, or who might come after, was likely to stir her soul the way he did. Secretly, she was even relieved that in recognising her impotence to act for herself, her father had taken it upon himself to become a broker. But 'marriage'; that was the huge stumbling block. That was the storm in her tea cup, the single most persistent obstacle to sleep.

When she arrived at the breakfast table the following morning, some time after her mother, father and Margaret, beating only Katie who was habitually late and forever being scolded for it, she felt exhausted before the day had begun. She spoke only occasionally and avoided direct eye contact with the man directly responsible for her insomnia.

Afterwards she returned to her room until Margaret arrived to remind her that this was the morning for their visit to the dentist, a diary date so uninviting Marian laboured hard for an excuse to compel her absence. None came, however, and in any case, it was unlikely Margaret would have accepted one. The dentist was a hateful ogre, a man accustomed to inflicting pain and notoriously unapologetic for doing so. The only consolation was that contemplation of an appointment with him was enough to focus the attention, even distract a troubled mind from the prospect of marriage.

Chapter Three

11 April was Marian's birthday, the day she would have liked to announce formally her engagement to Captain William Radford. Unfortunately, it was also Good Friday, a day in the calendar not normally associated with celebration. Therefore, in the name of good taste, she agreed to delay the glad tidings for a week, the following Saturday being the date of the spring ball at Princes Gate, a little earlier than previous years, but suitably convenient for her purposes.

As was commonplace, her father had been right. Try as she had to deny his analysis of her feelings for William she could not. The evening he had sat on the edge of her bed after returning from Sutton Coldfield and for days afterwards, she strove to avoid what to her father was as transparent as crystal water. In the end, however, she was forced to concede. Rightly or wrongly, for better or worse, she was in love with the young captain. He was in her thoughts day and night, the subject of her every longing, his absence the source of perpetual misery. There was no escaping the truth. Only his prompt return would offer her relief.

And, fortunately, appear he did. Within a week of her father's trip to the midlands, his courage fortified and new best suit to the fore, William arrived back in London with the express purpose of asking for Marian's hand in marriage. Of course, there were preliminaries. He did not leap out of the 'hansom' from his club in Pall Mall where he had taken rooms, rush to the front door of 32 Princes Gate and propose there and then.

Rather, in advance, he made the family aware of his arrival in town and waited for the invitation he so urgently desired. Then, on a fine Thursday afternoon, he arrived. For an agonising half hour, he exchanged pleasantries with Mrs Chase and her three daughters in the drawing room, chit chatting about nothing in particular while aching to be alone with Marian. Finally, and not a moment too soon, he was given leave to escort her to the Grosvenor Gallery spring exhibition where on display for several weeks was a retrospective collection of portraits by the grand old master himself, Sir Joshua Reynolds.

William himself held little interest in art. Good music he enjoyed enough and literature was something of a passion, but halls lined with eighteenth century portraits were not his first choice venue for what he had in mind. Marian, on the other hand, though not entirely swayed by the palette or style of Reynolds, was a regular visitor to such places. She and her mother were keen critics of both the ancient and modern in the art. The Grosvenor Gallery itself and Royal Academy were favourite venues. On rainy afternoons with nothing else to occupy them, a tour round one or other was more than adequate distraction from miserable weather.

In this instance, however, Marian was also less than best pleased with the location. Nevertheless, beggars could not be choosers. If compelled to share their brief time of privacy overlooked by lifeless images of the great and good from a previous century, then so be it.

For an hour or more they entertained the muse, admiring, commenting upon and, of course, criticising. Their conversation was generally academic, but their emotions were highly charged. Finally, came the drive back to Princes Gate and just as their closed carriage rounded Hyde Park corner, William began the opening paragraph of a well-prepared speech, its' conclusion destined to include the much-anticipated proposal. His hesitancy in leaving the matter so long was not apprehension, nor was it to be blamed on any element of doubt in his mind. On the contrary, he was as confident of this decision as of any he had made. To marry Marian seemed the most logical and natural thing in the world. His delay was simply the inadequacy of their surroundings.

Hyde Park, on the other hand, was not without its appeal. The weather was dull but dry and warm enough for the two of them to go at least part of the way on foot. William began the delicate process while they were still seated in the carriage. However, Marian caused him to pause while she ordered it stopped and they got down, leaving their coachman to follow at a discreet distance. If 'Marian my dear there's something of great importance I want to ask you…' was the prelude to a proposal, she wanted it to be between them alone, not something to be shared with a servant, albeit it a man who had driven her since she was a babe in arms.

In the end, it was over all too quickly. William was used to brevity. He was a military man, not a politician. He professed his deepest respect and love for her. Then he asked the question to which the answer was an unequivocal 'yes,' taking neither of them by surprise. For Marian was past the stage of self-denial.

She had given up denouncing her emotions as alien or unwelcome. True they defied the norm, but equally, they had become inescapable. Her reply to William therefore was immediate and given without the least concern that she might not be doing the right thing.

Thus, by the time the carriage returned them home, their future together was sealed. They were holding hands, had kissed and were greeted by a family resigned to the outcome of their afternoon together. Applause, smiles and hugs assured the happy couple that their news was entirely to be celebrated, a mood shared unanimously by all present at the Saturday ball after a carefully orchestrated proclamation by her father.

'Thank you, Papa' were the only three words entered into Marian's diary that night. Any more and a book would have been needed to accommodate everything she wanted to say. In the space of scarcely two months, she had met and was betrothed. Not in her wildest dreams had she anticipated such good fortune, imagined herself capable of such impetuous behaviour or believed herself deserving of such rare happiness. At times she was tempted to pinch herself, just in case the whole thing was an elaborate hoax, but it was not.

William was real. Every day he called at the house, flaunting his own considerable self-satisfaction by showering gifts upon her and insisting on as much time alone with her as convention permitted. Together he and Marian stood cheering on the banks of the Thames near Chiswick bridge, watching Cambridge beat Oxford in the boat race. Touring the summer show at the Royal Academy they selected with considerable care those pictures of mutual appeal. At the opera they sat side by side. On 5 May, Katie's birthday and the day when the whole family were finally able to make use of the tickets her father had secured for the opening of the International Health Exhibition, they walked arm in arm, willing every person in the vast throng to acknowledge the bounty of their alliance.

Not until the end of the month did a single negative thought enter Marian's head to spoil such perfection. On 23 May however, William went away. He took the train to Sutton Coldfield. For four months he had been on leave. Now he was to rejoin his regiment, but he could not do so without first bidding adieu to his parents. India was a long way off; too far for any mother. There were tearful farewells to be said in London, but none more wrenching than between Mrs Radford and her only son. The sole surviving child of four children she had borne, there was no measure to the love she felt for him or the agony of knowing he was leaving to be so far from her reach in such a hostile part of the world. And William was sensitive enough to realise it.

He and his father were men. At times of separation, they did as all men do. They shook hands and wished each other God speed. Few words were said or necessary. William's father respected his son's decision to join the army. He admired and even, to a certain extent, envied him a career with the promise of travel and excitement. For his mother, however, it was a different story. Given the right to choose, she would have pressed her son to follow his father into the church or take up a profession, anything to keep him on home shores and close to the bosom of his family.

Instead, each time it came for him to leave, she felt as if her heart were being torn from her chest by a giant claw. Try as she might she could not hide the pain. Tears rolled down her face like a waterfall and though William was ignorant of it, for days after she mourned him no less than if he had died.

That he was returning to India only served to compound her anguish. So many mothers had lost so many sons to that sorry continent, she could not escape the prospect of hers being another one. Assurances from her husband offered no relief and nothing William could say made a lot of difference to the absolute conviction she held that India would take him from her.

Not without a heavy heart therefore did William finally take his leave and head back to London. There had been times he considered resigning his commission specifically to save his mother the torture of his going. But at any hint of such a thing his father would forbid the idea, assuring William that a mother's pride in his achievements far outweighed the torment of his absence. Though prone to extremes of emotion, much exaggerated by the agony of losing three children in infancy, Mrs Radford had taught herself the art of self-counsel. She denied herself demonstrative displays of grief or sorrow and in so doing had acquired an inner strength sufficient to master whatever the fates held in store.

By the time William's train arrived at Paddington station therefore, any weakening of his resolve was as dust in the wind. He was resigned to leaving his mother. Now he faced a new ordeal, one beyond any previous experience. To say farewell and to be parted from the most recent focus of his affections, namely Marian, was pioneering stuff, a challenge with no precedent. He had as little idea of the outcome as Marian herself.

As spring turned to summer, storm clouds gathered on the blue horizon of her recent joy. During May, the of date June 2nd had seemed a long way off. Her diary entry for 29 May read 'Sunday. Flower service at Brompton Church.' The following evening, she wrote simply: 'Rode with Papa. Went to lawn tennis party at Mr and Mrs Owens.'

Each day she recorded less and less, deliberately avoiding any mention of William as if in so doing it might delay his departure. However, the sands of time ticked by irrevocably, bringing their separation closer until one morning it was upon her.

'William has gone,' she wrote to herself afterwards. 'How will I bear so great a burden?'

The moment of their parting was deliberately brief. He arrived at 32 Princes Gate shortly before ten in the morning, but almost immediately, the two of them quit the house, walking to the Albert Memorial by way of a favourite route through Kensington Gardens. Arm in arm, their conversation was patchy. Words were not sufficient to communicate their mutual distress. Silence spoke more than a thousand words. Emotions poured back and forth between them as if by some telepathic power and with the touching of hands a link of steel was forged.

When they returned an hour later, William was quick to take his leave. His farewells to Mr and Mrs Chase were filled with gratitude for their kindness towards him. Then he assured them over and again of his permanent affection for their daughter. For Margaret and Katie, his future sisters, there was an appropriate kiss on the cheek. Then he was gone, not once looking back from the 'hansom' lest his strength fail.

The next day, he was on the open seas. The weather was kind, the winds set fair but his heart ached, a symptom felt with equal pain and vigour by Marian herself. Too proud to pine or pout, she did her best to assume a normal regime, arriving for breakfast promptly. Afterwards she attended bible class with Margaret and Katie. In the afternoon she went with her mother to a 'Moody and Sankey' meeting held in a hall near the temple. Together they sang hymns and listened to the strong American twang of a rather stout Mr Moody as he preached his discourses to a crammed audience. Later in the day, after dinner, the whole family strolled in Hyde Park, admiring the illuminations and stopping to appreciate the stirring music of a German military band.

It was a day as any other. Nothing was out of the ordinary. Nothing was said or done to suggest any deviation from Marian's usual untroubled existence. And yet through it all, deep in the pit of her stomach lay a feeling of nausea no tonic could ease and beneath her breast there was the stabbing pain of a thousand daggers. She felt miserable, alone and abandoned; frightened and convinced her parting from William would never be relieved.

***

How cruel is hindsight, how casual an abuser of the mind. 5 February 1885 was remarkable for the weather. It was also remarkable as the day a whole nation awoke to read the fate of General Gordon and his brave garrison of soldiers at Khartoum. Yet, in spite of everything, in spite of her pain and ever-present guilt, it did not remind Marian of her first meeting with William Radford exactly a year earlier. On the other hand, 2 June 1884 and every 2 June thereafter, were as clear as crystal, as stark as any of the choices set before Gordon in the face of his greatest and final adversity. Not one day went by that she did not blame herself for letting William go.

She should have known. She should have halted him, prevented his departure. Every fibre of her body rebelled at his going. Every instinct screamed the finality of their last embrace, their last touch of the hand, their last contact of the eyes. But she did nothing. His carriage pulled away from Princes Gate and she let it go, her emotions willing her to call him back, her every muscle desperate to race after him. And when he was gone her days were empty, her nights desolate. So absolute were her feelings of loss and so irrevocable the conviction of his parting being final, she should have acted. But she did not.

At five minutes past ten on the morning of the 12 August 1884, the letter arrived. It was addressed directly to her. The contents were short and to the point. Mr and Mrs Arthur Radford informed their future daughter-in-law with the deepest regret that their only son William had been taken from them by cholera on the night of 18 July.

They gave no details. A letter was not the place to tell the full story; how on a four-day sea voyage from Bombay to Karachi over two hundred passengers and crew succumbed to the vile contagion. The scale of their loss, possibly greater than Marian's herself, cared naught for detail. That William was dead was enough. There was no time to paint the scene, to concern themselves with the sequence of events, was he the first or last, was it a Monday or a Friday, was the sea rough or calm. Their son was dead, a fact so appalling it required no embellishment to relieve the devastation.

Marian was in the drawing room at the time. With ever thinning patience, she was trying to convince Katie that on such a beautiful sunny day a walk along the banks of the river to Walton would do her the world of good. It was only a mile or so from their temporary residence at St Georges Hill, a house their father had decided to take for a few weeks to give them an airing from the acrid summer pollution in London. However, since their arrival nearly two weeks prior, Katie had shown a concerted reluctance to involve herself in anything remotely connected with the outdoors. She was suspiciously inert, something her mother assumed to be the result of a random physical malady.

When Dodds came into the room carrying the small silver salver, Marian reached for the letter on it with notional interest, the debate with her sister still in full flow. Indeed, had it not been for the thin black band of trimming to the envelope she would probably have laid it to one side for later reading.

Instead, she broke off from her somewhat matronly lecture on the efficacious nature of brisk exercise to reach for a fine ivory and mother of pearl paper knife which lay neatly atop a writing table in the bay of the window. A second or two later, with the unfolded letter falling from her fingers, she reached for the edge of the table to find a purchase, something to support the weight of her body as her legs began to crumple beneath her. It was no good, however. One hand found momentary support. The other brushed the back of a chair, but neither were sufficient to prevent her fall. With no strength to her legs and consciousness receding rapidly, she fell. Like a rag doll, she lay motionless, a trickle of blood seeping from the side of her head where it had taken a glancing blow against the skirting board.

Dodds and Katie reached her together, the former having cast aside the salver like a worthless piece of scrap. Fear and panic reduced Katie to tears, rendering her incapable of any practical assistance. Dodds on the other hand, as if well-rehearsed for just such a crisis, manoeuvred Marian into a more comfortable position, loosened the fastenings of her chemise at the neck and, as if by magic, produced a velvet cushion to lay beneath her head. Finally, he rearranged her skirts.

'Miss Katie,' he instructed. 'Ring the bell if you please.' Then he turned his attention back to Marian who was beginning to stir.

Within seconds Mrs Chase was in the room; also Margaret and two maids. Rather too closely, they flustered around Marian who by this time had been transferred to a 'chaise lounge' only a foot or two from where she had fallen. She was pale, confused and blood still flowed from the wound on her head, although until something more appropriate could be brought, it was covered with a clean white handkerchief borrowed from Dodds inside pocket.

'I'll send for the doctor immediately,' he informed Mrs Chase without waiting for the instruction. 'In the meantime, I will arrange for a cup of warm tea to be brought in. Warm, sweet tea will help.'

Mrs Chase said nothing. As Dodds left the room she attended Marian, mystified by her daughter's sudden collapse, until Margaret retrieved the letter from where it had fallen to the floor.

By the following morning, Marian was recovered enough to get up from her bed. The doctor had been and gone. The flow of blood on her head was stemmed, leaving rather obvious evidence of a tear in the flesh and bruising which was bound to become more dramatic in appearance over the coming days. Otherwise, she moved about the house as before. She took breakfast with the family and, in spite of vigorous opposition from her mother, rode with her father by Addlestone, Ottershaw and Byfleet, calling on Mr George Money, the new Rector of Byfleet as they were passing.

The day after was her mother's birthday. A trip to London was planned and although Marian was invited to remain behind, she insisted on carrying on as if nothing had happened. First, they went on a shopping spree, buying fabrics for new curtains at Princes Gate, dress material for Katie whose enthusiasm for making her own clothes was being given every encouragement to succeed, and a potpourri of trinkets to please the whims of Mrs Chase. After lunch they called in at the International Health Exhibition, staying only a short time before deciding they could no longer cope with the steamy, perspiring masses of humanity. They returned to St Georges Hill in good time to attend the evening Harvest Thanksgiving service at Byfleet church.

The third day was no different, nor the fourth. Though the letter from Mr and Mrs Radford was laid out in full view on her dressing table, a prominent and dreadful reminder of the terrible news which a few days before had caused her legs to buckle and for her to lose consciousness, Marian walked by it as if it were not there. She neither looked at it nor picked it up. In public she said nothing about its contents and refused even the slightest gesture of sympathy. For all the world her life was unchanged, her apparent disregard for the fact of William's death leaving her mother and sisters quite mystified and, in light of her extraordinary reaction, or lack of it, unable to proffer any positive consolation.

They wanted to offer solidarity. They willed Marian to break down so they could add their tears to hers, mourn in unison as was their place and the custom. But as long as she played the part of the stoic, they were helpless.

It was an eerie, foreboding atmosphere in which to behave normally. However, there was no alternative. Marian held the baton. With no cue from her, the one person most sorely wounded by the terrible news, Mrs Chase was compelled to marshal her troops as usual, conduct herself and instruct her two other daughters to behave as if nothing were amiss.

Little could they have guessed the scale of the storm just beyond the horizon. The calm was macabre; such normality and yet such universal need to express and share grief. Somewhere, not far off, were crashing waves and a treacherous, jagged shore line. Slowly but inexorably the Chase family ship was drifting towards it. At the helm, Mr Chase knew the rocks were there. However, through the dense fog of Marian's denial, he had no idea how soon they would be thrown upon them.

For a week the shroud lay about them. Their brief stay in St Georges Hill was at an end and they moved back to Princes Gate where they were destined to remain until after Christmas. And all the while Marian, though more pensive and less talkative than usual, remained in control. Only her diary told a different tale. Since the news of William's death, she had not made a single entry. The pages lay blank, a silence of words as gaping as a chasm, empty spaces more eloquent than a thousand adjectives to describe her state. Shock had struck her dumb. There was nothing to say. For what indeed could she say to report an event which she found so impossible to believe.

There had to be a breaking point, a moment for the fog to lift, leaving the rocks ahead raw and terrifying, but somehow Marian kept about her the eerie blanket of cover where all sound is muffled and vision is limited to a but few feet. Day after day she continued on as if nothing had happened, unchanged and yet altered for all time. Her physical appearance was as neat and tailored as ever and her conversation, more concentrated on the trivial than was her normal preference, denied the essence of her every waking thought.

What was needed was a trigger, something to breach the barrier. Ahead lay rocks and shipwreck. For a while at least the pain would be terrible, her loss almost too great to endure. However, unless she risked all, there was no hope of her ever reaching again the soft shore beyond.

In other circumstances, a funeral would have served as the spur. The sombre drama and a congregation of mourners would have made it impossible to continue on in an emotional vacuum. But for Marian there was to be no such convenience. Cholera is a cruel servant to death. In the four days of a short sea voyage it came aboard ship, claimed at random the lives of two hundred men, women and children, striking them down in a matter of hours, wrenching the life from them with no mercy and leaving those behind in a state of terror. In the face of such a death, there is no time for lavish ceremony, no time for loved ones to gather. Scarcely can creed, sex or nationality be determined in the race to conceal corpses beneath the earth, to be rid of a contamination so threatening to those fortunate few who escape the first onslaught.

In the small military stronghold at Landi Kotel, high and dry at the farthest reaches of the Khyber Pass, a brief service of remembrance was offered for Captain William Radford, two other officers and fourteen enlisted men whose journey from Bombay to Karachi proved so tragically fatal. A brief eulogy was offered by the Officer in Command in praise of a small body of soldiers who had succumbed too soon to arrive at their new posting or for him to salute.

Later, a letter was sent to William's parents by his regimental commanding officer, extending to them his deepest personal sympathy.

But there was no body, no grave, no quiet corner of an English churchyard. William was gone, wrenched from the world by a vile ogre, consumed by a repellent disease and in the process became as infected and invidious as the disease itself, his corpse not to be revered but disposed of as quickly as possible.

In Sutton Coldfield there was a memorial service, a small family affair to which Marian was invited, but declined to go. During the early hours of one night, she wrote a letter to William's parents, thanking them for their concern and generosity. It was short but constructed of the right words and phrases; enough to excuse her presence and in so doing cause no offence, but saying nothing of her true feelings.

Her father offered to go with her. Indeed, he pressed hard to make the journey, believing such an occasion would do much to relieve her dangerous state of denial. But she was adamant. To attend such a service would be to close the book on William's life. She wanted it left open, page one, chapter one. How could she end a book which was only just begun, so few pages written, so many to come. Barely had she accepted William into her life than she was being called upon to discard him. Scarcely had the flame between them been ignited than it was extinguished.

She could not and would not condone such finality. The fact of his death was not in dispute, but as long as she was spared any direct confrontation with the facts, she could continue to imagine him alive, in a far-off place perhaps, but alive. It was a delusion more corrosive than she was able to see for herself, but in the short term it served a purpose, at least for Marian.

Her father continued to worry, however. During their regular morning rides in the 'Row' he tried vainly to stimulate in her the beginnings at least of acceptance and grief. He wanted to act as her guide but for the first time she refused to confide in him, side stepping his every effort to console her.

On the morning of 4 September, a wet and windy day the length of the country, as hymns were being sung and prayers said in a grey stone church on the outskirts of Sutton Coldfield and all thoughts were concentrated upon the memory of William Radford, Marian did not stay quietly at home, keeping to her room, her thoughts turned towards a young man with whom she had uncovered so brief a spell of joy. Instead, as was her wont, she attended morning bible class. Later she accompanied her mother to the South Kensington Museum for a tour of the newly opened plaster casts room and to view the Raphael cartoons. Later that evening, she did not excuse herself from attending a dinner party given by Mr and Mrs Gerard Fox, presenting herself at their home with not the least suggestion that life was other than it should have been, their host and hostess oblivious to her dreadful secret.

It is not without some irony therefore that it falls to the narrator of this tale to report the most unlikely of catalysts which released the maelstrom of emotions brooding within Marian. The fickle and often spiteful master that fate is, one sadness within a family may necessarily not be enough to satisfy an appetite fuelled by tragedy and heartbreak.

Generally speaking, Mr and Mrs Chase led a charmed life. Moderately well off, generally healthy and blessed with three children, all of whom had thrived, as a family, their cup was full. Marian's paralysing sorrow, though well cloaked, was a pressing hardship, casting, for the first time, a dark shadow over the household. There was more, however; worse to come. Sorrow compounded is sorrow doubly felt. Pain heaped upon pain is exaggerated anguish.

It was the first week of October. Katie asked for permission to spend a few days with her aunt and uncle on the Isle of Wight. Originally the invitation had been extended earlier in the summer. All three girls were invited. However, circumstances as they were and with the weeks passing quickly, the trip went begging, a disappointment voiced only by Katie whose previous memories of times spent in Sandown, included sunny days, golden sands and elaborate picnics in the countryside.

Neither Mr or Mrs Chase therefore were the least suspicious that by autumn there was no let-up in their youngest daughter's pleas to be allowed to make the journey alone, chaperoned only by the ever vigilant Miss Branfoot, stalwart nanny and governess to the family for almost twenty years.

With more luggage than was absolutely necessary, they left Princes Gate together on a Monday morning, by carriage to the station and then by train to Portsmouth. The following morning a telegram arrived to announce their safe arrival. Two days after that a further telegram was brought in to Mrs Chase as she was in the process of preparing herself for an 'at home' a few doors along at number 26 Princes Gate. It was from Miss Branfoot. It was necessarily brief but clearly a cry for help. Katie had disappeared. A note left on the dressing table in her bedroom indicated she had eloped with a certain Mr Kenneth. They were in love and intended to marry. There was no mention of where they were going, simply a bland assurance that they would be fine and that she, Katie, the future Mrs Kenneth, would be in touch as soon as they were settled.

Had Mr Chase been at home when the news arrived there is no guessing whether or not the house would have been able to contain such a combined accumulation of rage. Fortunately, he was not. He was across London on business and was not due back until the evening. Nevertheless, Mrs Chases anger alone was quite enough to shake the rafters. Add to that Margaret's moral outrage and Marian's sudden, explosive outpouring of emotion and the mix was highly charged. Blame was cast like confetti. Miss Branfoot was at fault for failing to keep an eye on Katie at all times and Mr Kenneth was culpable of the most appalling deception. Not only had he very obviously planned and executed the scheme but he had grossly misled them all during their visit to his art school in Hove. More than that, he had given no hint of his having the least interest in Katie. Indeed, he had persuaded Mrs Chase with little effort that should he be so inclined his attentions would certainly be drawn to other, more mature women in the classroom. His deceit was immaculate and thus, by implication, his crime the worse for it.

Mrs Chase also laid a degree of blame at the door of her sister and brother-in-law for their lack of supervision. Lastly, she blamed herself for not having noticed any deviation in Katie's behaviour over the previous months. And, in doing so, though without voicing any such notion, she also blamed Marian for having distracted her attention from adequate scrutiny of her two other children.

A festival of blame therefore echoed through the corridors of 32 Princes Gate as Mrs Chase fumbled to construct a suitable response to Katie's actions. By luncheon, however, she brooded rather than raved, preferring to cast accusing looks at Margaret in case she might have plans to spring a similar surprise on the family. There were also glances of recrimination at Marian to indicate her own significant contribution to this latest catastrophe.

Unfortunately, throughout it all, not a single constructive pledge was made to search out the deviant pair. Nothing was done to invent a scheme for Katie's safe return. By the time Mr Chase arrived home, unaware of and unprepared for the scene of devastation poised to greet him, Mrs Chase and her two faithful daughters had withdrawn to three separate areas. She went to the drawing room, the largest room in the house and therefore ideal for aggravated pacing up and down. Margaret skulked off to her bedroom and there immersed herself in suitably supportive passages from the New Testament. And Marian retreated to the conservatory where she attempted some sort of resolution to the new torment of jealously which the contents of Miss Branfoot's telegram had caused to erupt deep within her.

His wife and second daughter were the vanguard for Mr Chase's own emotions. Disbelief, disappointment and extreme anger filled the remainder of his day. Less vocal perhaps than his wife and less of a threat to the pile in the carpet, he sat to consider their dilemma rather than join in with the pacing. Neither did he retreat for comfort to the bible. He wanted to do something. Inactivity suggested apathy. However, he forced himself to think the problem through rather than charge off in a futile gesture which would serve no purpose. He did consider setting out for the Isle of Wight, but rejected the idea.

Katie had worked on him at length to go there. Quite obviously, in hindsight, she and her lover had been planning their elopement for some time. Secretly they had plotted their escape. Sandown was merely a convenient springboard from which to launch their future life together. Their destination was any one's guess. Where and when they would surface was an equal mystery, but for certain, nothing would be gained by journeying through the night to the scene of the crime.

As beside himself as he was with his youngest daughter's recklessness and as frustrated as he felt at being unable to respond more positively, Mr Chase finally concluded that remaining in London and waiting for news was his best, though perhaps least attractive, option. Mrs Chase stopped her pacing long enough to hear his conclusions and though agreeing to them took no comfort from the idea of doing nothing. Margaret stayed in her room to continue reading and praying for her sister's safe return. In addition, she beseeched the Lord on Katie's behalf for salvation from what was evidently a serious case of moral decay.

Meanwhile, Marian, usually the lone female voice of reason in times of crisis, kept to herself, her feelings bearing little comparison with those of her father. She was not worried for Katie. She was not fearful for her sister's safety either physical or moral. She was distraught. In that much at least, she matched her father blow for blow. But her distraction was built from different timbers.

An unaccountable and strangely tearful envy raged within her. With the impetuous irresponsibility so much her trademark, Katie had snatched happiness for herself. Without the least concern for her family, she had run off with her lover. For months, she had deceived them all. No one had the slightest inkling of her relationship with Mr Kenneth. On the few occasions his name cropped up during round table conversations, usually in a rather mocking manner, poking harmless fun at his ill-equipped art school, his rather contrived scruffiness and the thought of him coping in such a female dominated environment, Katie smiled her accord. Not once did she leap to his defence or appear wounded by what she must have perceived as hurtful remarks.

Her powers of deception were so efficient, mature beyond her years. And now she was reaping the rewards. She was with the man she loved. She had him to herself. They were free, alive and with their whole lives ahead of them. Marian had nothing. Too strict with herself, too mindful of what others expected of her, too foolish to respect the whimsical nature of the Gods, she had let happiness slip through her fingers.

She never considered eloping. She entertained no conspiracy to keep William Radford by her side. Instead, she waved him off into the distance and turned her back on him with smug confidence of his prompt return. How crass was her stupidity, how woeful her crime. Katie had what she most desired. She, Marian, did not and she wanted to hate her sister for it.

Chapter Four

With the return to London of the lone Miss Branfoot came a revival of general agitation at 32 Princes Gate. There were no publicly voiced recriminations. Although she was abject with apology and roundly determined to accept full responsibility for her negligence, no one laid the blame at her door. Parents and sisters alike knew all too well that, at the best of times, Katie was a wilful, headstrong girl. With a plan so clearly conceived over a considerable period of time and executed with such accomplished deceit, Miss Branfoot was to be officially exonerated. But she carried guilt as if it were a trophy. Knowing Katie from infancy, she should have suspected something, or at the very least been on her guard against just such an eventuality.

However, the family would have none of it. Katie had deceived them all. Not once during their stays in Brighton had she hinted at the least sign of an affection for Mr Kenneth. That she visited his painting classes on a regular basis was deemed quite natural. Perhaps she did not possess the talent to become a great artist, or much of an artist at all. Nevertheless, Miss Branfoot and Mrs Chase alike had been combined in their delight at seeing Katie apply herself with enthusiasm to a single task for more than five minutes. Just as she professed no ulterior motive for attending the school, Mr Kenneth gave the impression that he was interested in Katie less even as an individual than as an artist.

Sole blame therefore was levelled full square at Katie and her lover. The short note she left in her room before fleeing, outlining the true affection she held for Mr Kenneth, the integrity of his intentions towards her and guarantees of their well-being together, served in no way to lessen the general dismay at her behaviour. As much as Miss Branfoot was offered immunity from any culpability or complicity in what was indeed a shameful affair, Katie was vilified for her thoughtlessness, selfishness and hitherto unrealised talent for deception.

Overall, for the first few days, anger continued as the overriding emotion within the walls of 32 Princes Gate and the majority of that anger was directed squarely at the absent pair. For one person, however, namely Marian, although there was anger, it was of an entirely different nature. With an almost biblical wailing and gnashing of teeth she turned on herself. Alone in her room, a place she frequented more than was good for her and not unnoticed by her father, she raged against herself. Envy at her sister's courage and good fortune heightened her own sense of loss. Mourning of a sort had begun. While the majority of her family were united in their condemnation of Katie, Marian accused herself of dire carelessness in letting a life time of happiness slip through her fingers, cursing William Radford for deserting her so soon after having employed such determination in capturing her affection.

An exacerbation to, rather than relief from, the general anger came with the contents of Katie's first letter arriving as it did almost a week into her elopement. It was sent from Cannes. To be precise, it was written on stationary bearing the mark of the Hotel Elite in Cannes. Quite why the two of them decided upon the south of France was left unspecified. Emphasised, however, was their good health and happiness. Living on a small inheritance Mr Kenneth received after the death of his maternal grandmother, they were not immediately in need of money. Shortly they would be leaving for Italy, Sienna their ultimate destination. Once there Mr Kenneth wanted to pick up his own artistic career within the cradle of Renaissance art, surrounding himself in and taking inspiration from the old masters.

Not a single word of apology or contrition appeared in the letter. No excuses were given, no explanations for their deceit and there was absolutely no suggestion that Katie acknowledged the pain or shame she was inflicting upon her family. It was a letter as if written on holiday; bright, newsy and full of expectation. That she had run off with a man some years older than herself and forsaken her family was apparently of little significance.

Mrs Chase read it. Then she filled the room with yet more words of incredulity and recrimination. Predictably, Margaret was equally vocal, but preferred a continued dialogue ruing the moral morass into which her sister was fast sliding. Mr Chase on the other hand made little comment. His anger had abated. He saw no constructive purpose in it. Anger was an emotion best reserved for irritants in his life, aggravating obstacles or people for whom he felt little respect and no love at all. Katie was the last born of his children. Compelled to grow up more quickly than she should in the company of two older siblings, she had skated through so much of her childhood. Now, at only sixteen, she had struck out for womanhood prematurely and was alone.

Mr Kenneth was clearly a man of poor breeding and low character, else he would never have sanctioned, let alone encouraged, such a venture. For him, Mr Chase reserved only contempt. That he should have been attracted to Katie was unfortunate but excusable. That he should have permitted himself the luxury of falling in love with her was a clear sign of his own immaturity and deep irresponsibility. To have forged or even complied with a plan for elopement however, was unpardonable, ignoring as it clearly did Katie's youth and easy impressionability.

But Katie was a different matter. Imagining herself in love with Mr Kenneth was not relevant. Her precipitous actions and the tone of her letter spelled imminent disaster. She was blindly delighted with what she had accomplished and naively optimistic about the future. Her horizons were filled with the kind of blues skies and sunny days only the blinkered eyes of infatuation perceive.

Mr Chase could not bring himself to rant in similar fashion to his wife and second daughter. Instead, he adopted a more pragmatic approach. He did not condone any of it, but set his sights on accepting the situation for what it was. From the start he realised that his chief concern should be Katie's continued welfare over the weeks and months to come after the expiration of what was, no doubt, a modest inheritance belonging to Mr Kenneth. He was also determined to keep open a way for her to return should the worst happen and she find herself abandoned on the other side of Europe. This was a scenario he truly hoped would not occur. However, he very much feared just such a final outcome to so foolhardy an enterprise.

Quite sensibly, he turned to Marian for support, believing, wrongly as it turned out, that her similar public appearance of calm in the midst of general family uproar, was motivated by concerns similar to his own.

It was not. On the surface, she was calm. But that was her way. It was not in her nature to leap up and down or remonstrate in the manner usually associated with her mother and two sisters. As a rule, she was a thinker rather than a speaker, a firm hand on the rudder rather than a rocker of the boat. In times of trouble, if her father were not present, she it was who could be relied upon to steer a course through troubled waters and between the rocks.

However, her calmness now was a veneer, her apparent readiness to be a steadying influence confusingly deceptive. Her father looked to her for a rational approach and found her wanting. Not only was she reluctant to condemn Katie, but in a manner which left him more at a loss than ever, she wished her sister God speed, proclaiming that however hard the road ahead might become for the two miscreants, a few months, weeks or even days of happiness in each other's arms were surely worth the heartache to follow.

That her mother and Margaret were destined to endure considerable social embarrassment was of little importance. That Katie was risking her virtue and good name seemed a small price to pay. Even the prospect that if the worse came to the worse, Katie's lover might prove himself a thorough scoundrel, abandoning her hundreds of miles from home, held no horrors for Marian. All she could say to her father was that in Katie's shoes she would surely have been tempted to do the same thing. Love, delicate bloom though it was, should be grasped tightly in both hands, not squandered as she had done. To her eternal regret, she could not turn the clock back. Had it been within her power to do so, she would never have allowed William Radford to take his leave. Her complacency cost her everything. Should Katie's happiness last a week only, no price could be too dear. A full cup of sorrow and regret was the price Marian was paying and would pay for the rest of her days for having so readily let slip the chance of happiness. As much as she praised Katie for her courage and good fortune, she surprised and confounded her father.

Consequently, with little or no constructive support from the other two women in his household and such an unexpected twist to Marian's frame of mind, Mr Chase found it hard to be positive. After considerable pondering, the brief telegram he dispatched to the Hotel Elite in Cannes neither passed censure nor promised hope. It merely acknowledged receipt of his daughter's letter and assured her of his continued affection. There was to be no attempt at a rescue. No agent would be sent to track the two of them down. Scoundrel though he might be in absconding with his youngest daughter, Mr Kenneth was to be let off the hook. There appeared to be little option but to accept that Katie, no more than a girl and with little experience of the world, had set her heart on roaming Europe as mistress to a man with limited means and the rather eccentric ambition of walking among the ghosts of the Italian Renaissance.

For a while, the usual harmony of life at 32 Princes Gate acquired a strange note of discord. Public gossip as to Katie's absence all too soon became rife and the cause of considerable inconvenience. In her efforts to avoid unwanted interrogation and minimise the humiliation, Mrs Chase cancelled or postponed much of her social calendar. Meantime, Margaret turned for consolation to God, spending inordinate amounts of time rifling through the pages of her bible and making numerous visits to bible class, dedicated towards purging herself of shame. It was a burden of considerable proportions to own a sister so completely devoid of morals.

Marian continued along the arduous road of self-condemnation. The mourning process, for so long postponed, now became a daily torture. Grief held her on the rack and turned the handle without remorse. Every day Katie stayed away, gorging herself on the happiness she had the good sense to snatch, Marian squirmed beneath the yoke of regret.

And poor Mr Chase, seemingly a lone voice of common sense among all the madness; what of him. How was he to soothe his pain? His youngest daughter was gone, so recently a babe in arms, so far from womanhood. What opportunities were there for him in all this? Few but to carry on as usual.

A fortnight or so later, as soon as Katie was settled in Sienna, he wired regular consignments of money, pressing her with each dispatch to believe that his thoughts and his heart were with her always. Beyond that, he carried on as usual, deviating little from his role as head of what had become, within a few short months, a rather troubled household.

Christmas passed off much as always. There were the same friends to see, relatives to greet. On Christmas morning the whole family, minus the much missed Katie, went to morning service at Brompton Church. In the afternoon Marian and Margaret visited the University College Hospital to join in with a Christmas fete being held in the women's wards. There were wreaths, mistletoe and bright lights and, where possible, the children were brought from their beds to join in with the festivities.

Later in the evening the Chase household swelled. Long since cleared of any blame in respect of Katie's shady departure with Mr Kenneth, Mrs Chase had invited her older sister and brother-in-law from the Isle of Wight. Their daughter, Nora, and her husband accompanied them with their own two sons and babe in arms, a little girl. In addition, though not strictly family, Mrs Kekewich, Marian's godmother, came with her two daughters Alice and Florence. Widowed at the age of only thirty-four, her husband having been killed by a runaway carriage as he was crossing Oxford Street on a foggy January morning, Mrs Kekewich and her children were regular guests to 32 Princes Gate and as near to family as made no difference.

As usual it was a happy occasion. There was good food, the smiles and laughter of children and a generous exchange of presents. To the unfamiliar eye all appeared normal. However, Katie was absent. Though mention of her name was studiously avoided, she was sorely missed. Concern for her welfare cast a permanent shadow. Neither the Christmas season nor a room filled with people could fully disguise her absence.

Margaret said prayers for her on a daily basis, doubling her efforts over the Christmas period. Mrs Chase voiced sorrow at the opportunities her daughter was missing, parties, the theatre, changing fashions and the very real chance that in London she might meet a young man more eligible to cater for her needs than a hapless nomad like Mr Kenneth. For the rather superficial roll call of deprivations Katie was experiencing by being absent from her family, Mrs Chase laid herself open to the charge of being somewhat silly and shallow. Tongues of strangers might well have chattered about her doubtful priorities. However, it was a ruse, a mask to hide her true sense of loss, a truth she was in no mind to share with the outside world.

In fact, Emilia Chase was as desperate and as wounded by the whole affair as her husband, the two of them blaming themselves in equal measure for what had happened, neither living a waking moment without the real fear they might never see their youngest daughter again.

Mr Chase immersed himself in work and his duties as head of the family, the only obvious sign of his anguish the regular vision of him at home with his head buried in a book. Sitting and reading, or both combined, were occupations for which he was well known, particularly in times of family crisis. Less clear an indication of his preoccupation perhaps was the extended length of his morning rides. A ritual which normally used up no more than an hour of his day was doubled to two or more.

In consequence, the family moved out of London earlier than planned. The New Year round of dinner parties and 'at homes' was scarcely at and end. Nevertheless, Hove seemed a more private place to be at a time of such universal consternation.

Bearing in mind the season, as expected, January began cold and bleak. The sea, a torrid brown, tossed then turned and crashed down against the shore as if angered. Few people, if any, strolled the promenades. Many houses in Hove were closed up. Adelaide Drive itself felt deserted, an impression supported by the paltry number of lights burning in the windows at night.

Only towards the end of January did the temperature improve a little and the cold winds ease. Marian and her father were able to take short rides together. In the newspapers there were reports from Sudan. General Gordon wrote in dispatches to Lord Wollesley 'Khartoum all right—could hold it for years,' a much needed morale booster after previous reports of the wounding of General Stewart during 'sharp fighting' with the Berbers. And on the first day of February, a day of splendid sunshine, Mr Chase's brother Tom arrived from Shenfield to stay for a week.

No wonder therefore that the news of General Gordon's defeat and supposed death only a few days later, so much the reverse of what he himself predicted, came as such a blow to the nation and to Marian in particular. The mood of reflection she found herself in on the morning of 5 February 1885, belied the real progress she and the whole family had made since their arrival in Hove. She stayed in her room not because the weather encouraged it and not because of any attributable illness. Her uncle, a man whom she liked enormously and of whom she saw all too little, was waiting downstairs.

He was to escort the ladies to an entertainment being given at a recreation room in the heart of Brighton to support shop girls, pupil teachers and milliners' apprentices. For here was a whole raft of young women much in need of financial assistance from those of their peers who were not compelled by circumstances to work as a means of feeding their families. A weekly event in most major cities it served as both entertainment and education to the women it was designed to assist. There were recitations, musical performances, readings, lectures etc and through the generous patronage of those more fortunate, such events provided money which was later distributed among them.

Under normal circumstances, Marian would have been first into the carriage. She relished the company of her uncle and, earlier in the day, had voiced approval of the cause. But when the time came to leave, she kept herself upstairs longer than was perhaps polite. She stared blankly out of the window, watching as waves broke and broke again along the shore line. Eventually, however, she did go down. With her mother, Margaret and uncle, she attended the benefit. On the way, much was made of the better weather, her uncle remarking upon it as a particular bonus to his stay. At the small hall in the centre of Brighton they sat and watched as forty or more young girls danced with each other; lancers, polkas, quadrilles and cabals.

Their laughter and delight was infectious. Forgetting that most of the girls present were the same age as or younger than her absent daughter, Mrs Chase wore a broad smile, tapping her feet to the music. Mildly envious that she could not join in, Margaret brooded somewhat. Tediously pious as a rule when it came to more hedonistic pursuits, the one pleasure she did permit herself was that of dancing. She found it mildly frustrating therefore, merely to sit and watch.

For his part, Uncle Tom, the younger of the two brothers by three years and by far the more outgoing, focussed his attention on Marian. Unused to her silent abstraction, he pestered her into conversation, addressing all his observations directly to her, trying to solicit a response. He knew she was in mourning. Though he was a confirmed and happy bachelor, he recognised the tragedy of loss. His sympathy for the whole family in a time of dual crisis was sincerely felt. However, like his brother, he was struck by the very real possibility of unhealthy consequences for Marian if such a prolonged and deeply grained period of sorrow were allowed to persist.

Five months had passed since the news of Captain Radford's death, time enough, he believed, for Marian to permit herself a partial reprieve from the painful guise of stoic. It hurt him to see a young woman of her extraordinary personality and intellect wasting away as she was.

He was present at 32 Princes Gate on the day she was born. Besides her mother, father and the midwife, he was the first person to hold her in his arms. She was his favourite niece. His pride in her achievements was paternal and his belief in a sparkling future for her, both as a woman and mother, unblemished. In this instance, however, he was at something of a loss to know how to approach her. Personal tragedy had been spared from him. He had never loved and therefore by implication not lost. Sympathy rather than empathy was the flavour of his condolence. Yet, he was wise and well-travelled and in so far as he was able to comprehend her condition, he believed his niece deserving of less heart break than she was affording herself.

As the young girls danced, their laughter rising above the music, he targeted Marian with conversation, trying as best he could to draw her out. And to a point he was successful. She was genuinely pleased to see him. For a while, something resembling a smile returned to her face. But it was short-lived. Once back at Adelaide Drive, while her mother and sister set about irritating Mr Charles Chase with an explicit and prolonged narrative of an outing he had so carefully avoided, Marian returned to the window seat in her room.

Beyond the glass the daylight was fast fading. A bank of clouds had begun to drift in from the distant horizon, a promise perhaps of returning bad weather. In her diary she wrote; 'News of General Gordon seems grim. Khartoum has fallen to the Arabs and Sir C. Wilson has been driven back. God save brave soldiers from the whims of politicians! Went with Mamma, Margaret and Uncle Tom into Brighton today. Fine weather all day. Like spring. Came back on the new electric railway which runs from the Aquarium to the end of Madeira Road. Uncle Tom did his best to cheer me up but I can see no cause for good cheer.'

There was no mention of William. She did not record the anniversary of their meeting, nor was there any suggestion he played a role in her life. And yet, when the day ended it was with a sense of relief she retired to bed. Missing him was a daily ritual, as constant and inevitable as breathing. However, in truth, 5 February was a day of special agony, a commemoration to be endured.

Uncle Tom was generous. His patience and understanding were more than Marian expected or deserved. February 6th was bound to be a day much as any other. William would still feature strongly. On the hour, every hour a memory of him would be there to taunt her. But it would be easier, a day of no particular note, a day not written in stone, a day not marked down in history either for the slaying of a great warrior or the contrived introduction of two souls later so cruelly separated by fate.

As ordained, a week after his arrival, Uncle Tom took his leave and returned by train to Essex. On the same morning, the newspapers confirmed the death of General Gordon and the sun returned after several more days of rain and miserable skies.

Marian woke shortly after seven. Curiously she had slept well, stirring only once from a fitful dream. For months her nights had been as tormented as her days. Real sleep was a rare luxury, a pleasure she could recall but not replicate. Instead, it had become her habit that while the rest of the household slept, she wrestled with the unbelievable truth of William's death. Each night, he appeared in her dreams to haunt her. Each night he died a new death and each night her loss seemed magnified. Such had become the custom. She dreaded the emptiness of every day, but feared the night more, trying every discipline she could think of to achieve sleep but forever failing. The simple fact was, William would not release her. Clearly for her part in his going she was to be afforded a lifetime of insomnia.

However, this morning something was different. She rose early. Beyond the closed curtains of her bedroom, it was still murky. The winter sun was struggling somewhere below the horizon, a reddish glow heralding its appearance. Brighton and Hove were yet to receive benefit of either light or warmth. Had she gone to the window there would have been little to observe. Soft waves patted the beach and there was an unseasonal stillness to the surface of the sea, reflecting rather than resenting the great iron skeletal piers as they thrust outwards from the promenades like stiff tentacles. Delivery vehicles of all kinds were beginning to fill the streets and below, within the house, Marian could just hear the grates being cleared.

Nothing was out of place. The weather was again more spring like than winter pall, but otherwise everything was or, at least, should have been the same as when she retired for bed the previous evening. The moment she awoke, however, she sensed a change. Once dressed she drew the curtains, settled into the stiffly buttoned chair which she kept permanently by the window and watched the last of the dawn come up. When it was light enough outside, she picked up her copy of 'Memorials of Westminster Abbey' by Dean Stanley and read for an hour, finding herself absorbed by the oyster shell ceiling in the chapel of Henry VII and the legends of the Scone stone. When finally, the low bright sun reached round to shine directly into her face, she closed the book and made her way downstairs to join the family for breakfast, carrying with her an appetite she had found wanting over recent months.

'Papa. Shall we go for a ride this morning?' she asked without any prompting. 'It looks like it's going to be a lovely day and we haven't been out together for ages.'

'Of course,' he replied, showing not the least hint of his surprise at the sudden change in her mood. 'I was thinking precisely the same thing myself.'

Mrs Chase carried on with her eating, noticing but like her husband, choosing not to remark upon the apparent revival of her daughter's spirits. Margaret on the other hand could not resist.

'You're bright and cheerful this morning,' she suggested with a rather tactless degree of accusation.

'Am I?' Marian replied, at once feeling guilty, as if to be bright or cheerful, or worse still, both was in some way a crime against grief, as if over her black widows weaves she proposed the wearing of fine, sparkling jewels.

Mrs Chase cast a scolding eye at Margaret while her father was quick to pre-empt any change of heart by instructing Dodds to have the horses made ready for ten o'clock.

For a moment or two, Marian paused to consider the veracity of Margaret's observation and whether or not she should revoke her decision to go riding. Had she committed a sin in finding the early morning view from her bedroom window pleasing to the eye? Was reading a pastime she should deny herself? Should the idea of riding out with her father give her cause to feel she was in some way committing a betrayal?

Since William's death she had ridden out with her father often. In London an hour on horseback was virtually part of her daily regime. It was a ritual interrupted for a while by the death of her fiancé but when resumed, undertaken out of habit rather than any conscious desire for gratuitous pleasure. Should she now feel remorse at being the one to propose the idea?

Perhaps, but she did not. In spite of her sister's tone, she felt no guilt. Instead, involuntarily, she embraced a sensation of light headedness, as if she were in some way in the process of setting down a burden she had been carrying too long.

Quite what it meant, if anything at all, was too early to say. It was a fine morning. The skies were clear and she could not resist the desire for activity. Though they said not a word on the subject between them, both mother and father recognised the signs. Their relief was mute but mutual. So small a change in their daughter was what they had been waiting for. They could only finish their breakfast in the hope that Margaret's unfortunate intervention did nothing to halt or reverse the progress.

Fortunately, it did not. The ride was an unqualified success. With the sun on their backs Marian and her father made their way up on to the Downs. From the top they could see the whole of Brighton and Hove stretched out below them and beyond, the vast emptiness of the English Channel, an occasional sail the only interruption to an otherwise desert like panorama. Further out, of course, were the busy shipping lanes, broad maritime trunk roads, avenues to commerce, but those they could not see.

Above their heads seagulls whirled and wailed, battling into headwinds or running with them, passing over their heads at high speed, steering clear of the busy, bare branched rookeries in the woods away to the north.

In spite of the clement weather, they were sensible to remember that it was still winter. The sun walked low across the sky, the trees and hedgerows were bare, and a cool dew lay heavy on the deep turf beneath the hooves of their horses. That said, Marian sensed spring.

'Isn't this wonderful, Papa?' she crowed as they paused to take in the view.

'Yes, my dear. It is,' he replied, aware that the view was the lesser aspect of what Marian found so wonderful about the day. For months she had been lost in the deep, dark tunnels of some awful labyrinth. There were times he feared she might be lost for good. But at last, she was finding her way out and this 'wonderful' February morning was clear evidence of it.

'Yes, my dear. It certainly is,' he repeated and they exchanged smiles before continuing on their ride. Nothing more was said. Nothing more needed saying. This was no sudden transformation. The Marian of old would not return entire. It would take time for the healing process to take full effect and even then, there would be scars, but at least the process was begun. Quite by chance, Marian had stumbled out of the darkness and back into the light. Their ride could continue and end without another word being spoken.

Chapter Five

The fine soft morning Marian spent with her father riding over the Downs was not repeated. The following day the rains returned and when finally, the sun appeared again, it was accompanied by a bitter east wind. Along the promenades a few people braved the elements wrapped up in warm long coats. From behind the protective glass of her bedroom windows it was easy for Marian to imagine the pleasure to be gained from such constitutionals. However, those hardy enough to venture out, and she was not one of them, were afforded no pleasure. There were thick frosts and anywhere water lay it was iced over.

On 16 February, Mrs Bowderie and her sister, Mrs Thomas heeded an invitation for lunch and later Mrs and Miss Donovan called in for tea, two pairs of guests among many to drop in during a time of the year when the weather lent itself to little else but house calls. 'At homes' were a simple alternative to idle inactivity. Either Mrs Chase and her two daughters raised smiles and hellos to greet small bands of guests as they arrived on their doorstep in Adelaide Drive, or they bundled themselves into a carriage for short rides to the likes of Dr and Mrs O'Brian who lived in Palmeira Road.

There were no large dinner parties or balls. Those would come later once they were back in London. Lunches, teas, 'at homes,' the occasional concert at the Dome or Hove Town Assembly Hall and regular visits to St Andrews Parish Church were sufficient to pass the time. It was a social life of small events. Conversation was mostly gossip and rarely stimulating. Nevertheless, for the fortnight during which the weather worsened rather than improved, depositing towns all along the south coast with a liberal coating of snow and ice, it was sufficient as a bare canvas for Marian to begin the painstaking enterprise of recreating her life.

After six months of emotional coma, she returned slowly to consciousness. Anew, she felt, sensed and breathed life in around her. She was ready to begin again. The clock could not be turned back. William's death left a gaping void. But there was hope for the future.

10 March was the date set for their return to London. And so it was. Shortly after breakfast they decamped. The skies were still clear. There was a crisp layer of frost over everything, but the wind was turning slowly from north east to south west implying warmer, wetter days ahead, days when the black fogs would return to choke the city. However, it was with unanimous pleasure the Chase family took their leave of the south coast.

Their home in Hove was modern and luxurious, making their various and frequent pilgrimages there so much improved from the days of rented properties. Brighton itself was a vibrant resort and the general climate usually healthier than in town. And yet, by implication, it lacked the sophistication and excitement of London. Socially and culturally, it could not compete. It tried. The Dome was a fine concert hall, visited by many of the top performers of the day. The 'Pavilion' and terraced esplanades afforded elegant architectural vistas and huge efforts were made by the temporary winter society to entertain themselves as best they could.

Nevertheless, London had so much more to offer; parks, theatres, exhibitions and a social calendar bar none. As much as Marian looked forward to their extended stays on the Sussex coast and as grateful as she, her mother and sisters were that Mr Chase had thought to build for them a permanent residence in Adelaide Drive, by the middle of March, they were more than ready for their exodus.

As if to emphasise what they had been missing, on the evening of their arrival at 32 Princes Gate, they went as a family to the Savoy theatre. On show was the 'Mikado,' the latest operatic offering from the highly talented pairing of Messrs Gilbert and Sullivan. In tune with the current and seemingly insatiable fashion for everything Japanese, it was the sort of treat Brighton simply could not stage. No matter their seats were not the best. That Mr Chase obtained tickets at all to a show which had advanced bookings until June was quite sufficient to remind them of the contrast between the two different parts of the country in which they owned homes.

The 'Mikado' was exciting, amusing and performed to the highest standard, the shimmering costumes and elaborate scenery clearly inspired by everything on display over the previous year in the replica Japanese village at Knightsbridge and at stores across London. Indeed, as much as Marian enjoyed the show, the music and songs filling her head like a draft of fresh air through fog filled halls, she could not but leave the theatre reminded of how poignantly tragic was the accident half of London witnessed, prior to their leaving for Brighton. The Japanese village caught fire and was entirely engulfed by the flames. At the time, she was too caught up in her own sense of personal tragedy to feel the anguish of so causally begun yet so devastatingly ended a conflagration. A single spilled cooking pot, a few hot embers on a wooden floor and panic ensued, the newspapers reporting five dead with the exhibition completely destroyed.

The morning after their visit to the theatre, she and her father rode together in the Row. When they left Brighton, the air was cold and the ground crisp. In London it was warmer, damper and frost free. The park, however, was not full. There were few people on foot and more than enough space free from pedestrians for a canter. They stayed out for more than an hour, reaching Marble Arch before turning homeward. And all the while they talked, not of tragedy or drama, not of dead lovers or missing daughters, but of spring, the coming season and just a little politics, their dialogue only interrupted by the approaching carriage of the Queen and Princess Beatrice.

Chaperoned by two equerries on horseback, two gillies in the rumbles, several policemen and out riders drawn from the household cavalry, the stately carriage moved slowly, both the Queen and Princess taking time to acknowledge the bowed heads of those fortunate enough to come within glimpsing distance, a pointed reminder, if one were needed, to both Marian and her father that they were back in the capital city.

When they arrived home at Princes Gate, any plans Marian had for the rest of the morning were sidelined by preparations already under way for Margaret's forthcoming trip to Paris with cousin George. Great excitement accompanied the choosing of dresses and hats, the packing of cases and a review of the itinerary. Had Marian been going, there would have been talk of the Paris Opera house, the Louvre and Versailles. Margaret's fervour however centred on Sacre Coeur, Mont Matre and a convent she was to visit on the outskirts of the city where novice nuns were specifically trained for missionary work in many of the more desolate centres of poverty and spiritual deprivation around the world.

Quite what poor George would find by way of recreation during their weeklong stay on the continent was something of a mystery. Though he was considered responsible enough to make the trip with Margaret and keep her from any harm, a lieutenant to Mr Chase who could not spare the time to go, he was not in any way likeminded when it came to matters of the church. In sympathy with Marian's more sceptical view of the clerical community, no one expected George to return with the light of Saul burning brightly in his eyes.

In many respects, it was an odd pairing. Cousins they were, but in everything else there was little compatibility between the two. Margaret was a rather thin young woman, awkwardly shy in public, rabbit like in her fear of the unknown and devout in a manner quite unhealthy for someone her age. Her single-minded dedication to the church and what those nearest and dearest to her saw as an unhealthy determination to take up a career as a missionary, rendered her a rather dower companion. George, on the other hand, first cousin via Mrs Chase, was quite the opposite. Well-fed and tall, he towered over his travelling partner. A successful sportsman at school and university, rugby football, cricket and rowing being just three aspects of his many facetted athletic repertoire, he was not the obvious choice as chaperone. He did, however, speak French, proof positive if it were needed that his academic education had not been entirely wasted.

Furthermore, over the years, Mr and Mrs Chase had clearly observed in him a warmth for Margaret which, though unexplained, assured them he would not ignore or abandon her should they run into any difficulties. He might also save her from any precipitous leap into the arms of a clerical order which would have her confined for life behind the walls of some inaccessible convent on the other side of the Channel. George was an affable young man, easy to like and though gifted with the reputation of being somewhat aimless, gentleman enough to place the welfare of his temporary ward before his own.

They left from Kings Cross station mid-morning barely three days after the family's return from Brighton. Mrs Chase and Marian went with them in the carriage and there were tears all round when the moment came for Margaret to board the train. But it was a brief farewell. The platforms were awash with people and the noise made normal conversation virtually impossible. Blowing whistles, the violent hissing of escaping steam and a thousand voices all raised to speak at once resembled all the sounds of Bedlam, but personified. A stench of sulphur filled the air and a thin film of coal dust covered every stationary surface. It was not an environment conducive to fond goodbyes. However, with one daughter already lost to her, Margaret's mother was determined to part from her second leaving no doubt as to the affection in which she was held or the degree to which she would be missed. To this end, she proved the point by waving furiously until the final second the train disappeared from view and she was staring at vacant steel tracks.

Back at 32 Princes Gate, the atmosphere was deflated. After a quiet lunch, a lunch starkly deprived of Margaret's sanctimony as well as Katie's twittering, Marian and her mother took themselves off to the Grosvenor Gallery, leaving Mr Chase to himself, the latter too restless to enjoy this rare spell of solitude.

In the evening, the three of them walked up to Hyde Park. For an hour or so they strolled, lingering longest at the covered band stand to applaud the band of the Coldstream guards which was playing military marches with great gusto. But all in all, it was a lack lustre outing. Neither parent was at their ease and Marian struggled to raise any enthusiasm.

When they returned home, they said their good nights and retired to separate rooms, Mr Chase preferring a period of time alone in his study, helping himself to a glass of port and settling into his favourite wing chair, the upholstery on the arms just beginning to show the effects of many years wear. Then, with unique irony of which he was completely ignorant, he brooded over the prospect of a house entirely devoid of his children.

Meanwhile, Marian was upstairs in her room. That much at least gave him comfort, though he was all too aware of just how markedly William's death had provoked such frequent bouts of withdrawal. Furthermore, he recognised how unyielding were the doors behind which she had chosen to closet herself. However, with Katie absconded and Margaret temporarily absent, he took it as a warning of how empty his future existence might become should all three of them desert him.

Of course, on the rare occasions he was prepared to be honest with himself on such matters, he always anticipated as much. He had even rehearsed for the day when all three of his daughters would make lives for themselves beyond 32 Princes Gate. But the taste was bitter. It soured his port to the extent that he left it unfinished on the table. In a few weeks it would be his birthday again, a day usually set aside for thoughts of an optimistic nature. However, two of his daughters would not be there, an omen of all birthdays to come and he took no comfort from the thought. Finally, he quit his chair to go upstairs, yearning to turn the clock back and recalling with each footfall on the staircase the days when his home was alive to the giggles and shrieks of small children, when the elegantly balustraded staircase was an adventure playground rather than a simple thoroughfare from one level of the house to another.

At breakfast the following morning, on the surface at least, his mood was improved. Neither his wife, nor sole remaining daughter were conscious of his melancholy from the previous evening. He was, as usual, himself, the mask of ambivalence back in place. Marian as well appeared better equipped than might have been expected of her to take on a new day.

'Shall we go for a ride again this morning, Papa?' she asked in a tone which prompted a positive response.

'Of course,' came the reply.

'Perhaps the Queen will be out again. Mama? Did Papa tell you we saw the Queen and Princess Beatrice yesterday?'

'Yes dear. He did. And so did you, I seem to recall.'

'Oh yes. How silly of me. Of course I did. I remember telling you about Princess Beatrice's heavy old dress. Ghastly thing it was too. Even more ghastly beside the Queen's permanent black. Her hat was nice though.'

'Yes dear. You mentioned.'

'Sorry, Mama.'

'That's all right dear. Perhaps the next time you see her the weather will be warmer and she'll be in something nice.'

'I doubt if we will see them,' Mr Chase intervened. 'I'm sure I read in the court announcements that the royal household is off to Sandringham for a week or so. I believe they are leaving town today or tomorrow. No doubt there will be bigger crowds at the station to see them off than there were yesterday. That should mean the park will be quieter. They must be going up for Easter.'

'Oh yes,' said Marian. 'Easter's early this year, isn't it?'

And so, it continued until father and daughter were alone in the park. Then their conversation took on a more sober tone.

There was a heavy dew. Stretched across the high wrought iron entrance gates, saturated cobwebs straddled the empty spaces like intricate lace curtains, the weak sun causing them to glisten as if they were constructed of a thousand tiny jewels. Yellow pools of daffodils were coming into bloom beneath the mighty beech and chestnut trees either side of their route and, in spite of there being little likelihood of spying the royal carriage, more people rather than fewer seemed to have turned out to enjoy the morning, as many on horseback as on foot. On the distant band stand there was already music being played and every so often Marian's horse made as if to shy from occasional squirrels as they fled the ground for safer territory in the branches above their heads, as often as not carrying with them nuts, newly unearthed from beneath the turf where they had been secreted since the previous autumn.

Marian, it was in this cool but pleasant environment therefore, who felt the timing appropriate to broach the subject of India. More precisely, she wanted to sound her father out on the plan she had hatched to go there. Unfortunately, she was ignorant to her father's period of lonely introspection during the previous evening, his mind taken up with images of a childless home.

Of course, she was sensible enough not to have introduced the subject as part of breakfast conversation. She realised all too well that inclusion of such a venture was hardly in keeping with an agenda of daily activities such as visits to the theatre, lunch with the Kendals or the need to purchase a new dress. However, she misjudged entirely the more relaxed forum of their ride in the park. Rotten Row was the perfect setting. The scenery was kind on the eyes and the unique intimacy she shared with her father was historically at its best when they were together on horseback. Notwithstanding, on this occasion, the ingredients alone were insufficient to dampen the initial shock to her companion of such a bold scheme.

'I beg your pardon?' he said, hoping against hope he had misheard her.

'I want to go to India, Papa,' she said again, this time more confidently.

'India?' he repeated, the note of surprise almost tangible.

'Yes Papa,' she confirmed, hoping in vain that the needed repetition was merely the fault of a temporary impediment to his hearing.

'Out of the question,' came the blunt reply.

'But Papa, you haven't...'

'No, I haven't and I don't want to. You may not go to India, Marian and that's all there is to it. And, if you don't mind, I would ask you not to bring the matter up again.'

Dutifully, Marian said no more. The tone in her father's voice, something she rarely heard levelled at her, had an air of finality about it. She was not happy, but she obeyed. She respected her father too much to quarrel.

However, as far as she was concerned, the matter was by no means closed and, regardless of her father's immediate and emphatic response, she determined to raise the subject again when he was in a more receptive frame of mind. After all, this was no whim, no spur of the moment fancy. It was a scheme which had been brewing for weeks. Much depended upon her making the journey, more indeed than he might realise. Many hours of solitary confinement and soul searching had culminated in the absolute conviction that this journey above all others was vital to her future well-being. She could not afford to have the matter dismissed in a sentence. Nor would she permit it. When the time came to try again, and timing would be everything, she was confident of being afforded a fairer hearing. Clearly on this occasion, she had chosen both the wrong time and place, misjudging his mood entirely.

After all, it was rare for Mr Chase to refuse Marian anything, least of all so perfunctorily. It was his habit to say no to both Margaret and Katie as an immediate response to almost any request. This was based upon years of experience and thousands of ridiculous propositions from each of them. Margaret's regular pleas to commit herself to missionary work were dismissed without debate. She was too frail in body and mind for any such career and no amount of religious zeal could compensate for these two debilitating flaws.

Consequently, every time she brought the subject up, a patronising 'yes dear' from Mr Chase was enough to postpone her departure for any of the darker continents in search of souls to save. Indeed, dispatching her to Paris was a roundabout way of exposing her to a somewhat more secular environment, convinced as both mother and father were that their second daughters desire for a life of self-sacrifice could be turned as readily as the pages of a book.

In much the same vein, but on opposite sides of the coin, as a rule Katie was so recklessly fickle, scarcely had she uttered her desires than they were changed, as often as not making the need to refuse her redundant. As surely and as frequently as night turned into day, so what was in one moment declared a desperate need became a forgotten cause the next. The most essential blue hat on a Monday was by Wednesday the poor relation to a red one which in turn might be superseded for a white one by Friday. During his many hours of self-recrimination, Mr Chase took some comfort in the certainty that, however sincere her affection, Katie would soon tire of living with a penniless artist and that, in turn, Mr Kenneth would become less and less attracted to a girl whose convictions blew like the wind.

In his treatment of Marian however, as a rule things were very different. Her needs and wants were not so readily dismissed. Over the years she had earned for herself the reputation of taking a more measured approach to whatever problem or project lay ahead of her. As determinedly negative as his initial response was, Marian believed that, in time, her father could be relied upon to oblige her with at least an open debate on the subject of India. Although she was disappointed by his unusually forthright interruption to her request, she was optimistic of a more open-minded response to her case. In time, she expected him to come round. As long as she presented herself intelligently and with a degree of logic alien to either of her sisters, she was confident of a reversal in her favour.

Her mistake, however, was to assume that sense and logic were the only criteria by which her father assessed an argument. So consumed had she been over the previous few months with her own emotions, she failed to consider that for once her needs might take second place to his. She underestimated completely the anguish her absence would bring. The consequences of Katie's elopement were embarrassment and worry for the whole family. Margaret's holiday in France carried with it the outside chance of her becoming more rather than less committed to her 'calling.' Both girls were a constant cause for concern. Nevertheless, in spite of their equal failings of silliness on the one hand and self-righteousness on the other, they were missed.

To have Marian away as well for what would undoubtedly be a prolonged period of time, was simply a punishment too hard for Mr Chase to bear. In Marian he could confide. With her he could interact on an even intellectual plane. No matter how many scrapes Katie got herself into and no matter Margaret's zeal, with Marian close by he felt secure. She was daily evidence of the satisfaction to be gained from and the justification in creating a family. Without her the house would be empty in a way he cared not to contemplate.

Thus, if Marian hoped to win her father over at a second attempt any more readily than at the first, she was mistaken. Leaving a gap of only two days was another poor decision. Rather than giving him time to warm to the idea, the scant delay only served to harden his resolve. As if drawing up battle lines he prepared himself for the second onslaught, committing to memory a menu of objections to confound any efforts on her part to sway him or to promote such an enterprise as in any way essential.

First mention of India as they rode together in the park produced from Mr Chase an instant, if flimsily considered, rebuttal. That refusal remained intact after their second skirmish, albeit that he granted his daughter more in the way of debate. Marian put her case and her father made as if to weigh it in the balance. However, he was resolute. His motives were selfish, of that he was well aware, even though he was not prepared to admit as much to Marian. In the normal run of things, he would have tempered such selfishness in favour of her needs, but not this time.

They parted company at odds. There was no ill feeling. Marian adored her father too much to permit anger. Nevertheless, she was once again thwarted. Her request was not proffered lightly. She insisted again that it was a deeply felt need, not a whim. For months, she had mourned William. So complete was her conviction of their mutual destiny, his death ripped through her like a tornado, reaping havoc. That surge of destruction was now abated. It was time to rebuild her life. This much she recognised. This much she was resigned to. It had been a hard struggle. In the beginning she wanted to die alongside Richard. When that need passed, she ached to yell and scream in rage at the cruelty and injustice of his being taken from her. Then she determined to mourn him for a lifetime.

All that was now behind her. Sanity had returned and with it an acceptance, albeit reluctant, that life must go on. However, to move forward was impossible unless she could detach herself from the past. Somewhere on a far continent his body lay, a few feet below the surface of the hard, baked soil and above him there would be a stone bearing his name, proof if proof were needed that he was no more. And Marian needed to see it. Deep within her was the compulsion to stand over his grave and read the words inscribed on his headstone.

On the day it took place, she had not been able to face the memorial service held in his honour. She refused all urging to go to Sutton Coldfield, a mistake she now freely admitted and regretted. Now, India was the only solution. Oceans away and as intimidating as it might be, she was resolved to make the pilgrimage. Unless and until she did, there would be no peace of mind. She could not properly begin her life again. Without that last sight of him there would be no way to fill the awful vacuum.

All this she explained calmly and dispassionately to her father. There were no tears or tantrums and no brittle tremors in her voice. She included in her speech only the good common-sense aspects of her argument. Yet, still he refused. He paraded before her a well-rehearsed mandate, some of it, though not all, giving Marian cause for reflection. However, the single most crucial reason for his denial was left unsaid. That he could not bear to be parted from her for so long, he was reluctant to admit to himself let alone to his daughter.

Consequently, Marian made a second retreat from the field, but more determined than ever to win the day. She could not go, nor would she without his blessing. If he continued to deny her, she would stay. She would not defy him. The task ahead therefore was to strengthen her argument. Somehow, she must conjure another, better approach, invent a manoeuvre to out flank him.

Beaten but not bowed, she let the matter drop for a week or so. In public she presented her father with the face of resignation. In private however, she set herself to regrouping, preparing herself for a final decisive assault. Only, the next time, the moment and the presentation would be everything. If she failed to sway him at her third attempt, she doubted a fourth or fifth would be anything other than flying directly in the face of the wind.

Chapter Six

In the end Marian did get what she wanted. Her father's surrender, when it came, was not easily achieved nor his accord lightly given. Her persistence, however, was not to be ignored. From the start his refusals were motivated from an entirely and uncharacteristically selfish perspective. Regardless of some perfectly valid but surmountable objections to the enterprise, the simple truth of the matter was that he did not want to be parted from her. With a dexterity acquired from years of saying no to literally thousands of trivial requests from his wife and daughters, he hid the truth of his resistance behind a thick smoke screen, siting dangers to Marian's health from the sea, disease and even the native population. He accused her of desertion, of insensitivity to the needs of her mother and, as a last resort, of being entirely self-centred in pursuing this particular desire with such stubborn resolve. Eventually though, his guilty conscience prevailed. It was his rather than her selfishness more in the need of curbing.

Once resigned, his task became clear. The battle over, it fell to him to facilitate her departure as best he could. Through the spring and into the summer he laboured to plan an intercontinental journey with every eventuality covered. On the day of Marian's birthday, 11 April, had presented her with a leather-bound atlas of the world and a finely engineered pocket compass housed in pigskin jacket, lest presumably she find herself abandoned somewhere in a featureless desert or impenetrable jungle.

These gifts were received by Marian with record levels of gratitude, the compass, a permanent guide home in the face of adversity, guarded as if it were a rare piece of jewellery. However, though not given on the morning of her birthday, the best gift of all and the one for which she owed and offered most gratitude, was his final acceptance of her need to go.

She knew he did not understand. Of course he was sympathetic to her loss. From the moment news of William's death arrived; her father could not have been more supportive. Even with the added crisis of Katie's elopement to distract, he continued to give as much or as little of himself as Marian demanded, not once belittling the nature or stature of her personal tragedy.

Nevertheless, the impulse to go to India remained something of a mystery to him. He agreed to it, but only in response to her insistence. He did not pretend an understanding. To his mind, the voyage was unnecessarily long, the risks to her health and personal safety too many and for what; just so that she could stand at the side of a dirt covered military grave to say a final farewell.

However, the deed was done and it could not be undone. The date for departure was set and delayed only to avoid the worst of the monsoon season on the other side of the world. By the end of April preparations were in full swing and dinner table conversation was of little else than India. Poor Margaret had returned from France with tales to tell but little in the way of an audience. Those around her appeared more interested in the future than her recent past.

Much to his credit, George had done an admirable job as chaperone. How he endured the task was considered something of a miracle by both Chase parents and Marian. But he had fulfilled his responsibilities and brought Margaret back home unscathed from her encounter with the Gallic race, their food, their levels of hygiene and their reputation, in Paris at least, for a somewhat decadent approach to the values of Christian morality.

Margaret herself appeared unchanged. For the first few days she was more eloquent than usual, filled as she was with accounts of her adventures. She entreated the whole family to reserve a place in their lives for a sight of Notre Dame, giving as detailed a description of its majesty as her vocabulary would allow. Then she listed the various convents she had visited. She remarked upon the ever-present odour of garlic on the breath of those she engaged in conversation, the number of whom was somewhat limited by her ignorance of the language. Finally, and fortunately for him, she confirmed what a perfect travelling companion her cousin had been throughout the trip.

In light of such opinion, no doubt she would have liked him to accompany her on future journeys as a missionary. However, she was at least savvy enough not to mention her thoughts of further trips, nor George's useful contribution to or part in them. She was also sensible not to re-open the India debate by adding her three-penny worth of objections to the idea. Possibly she preferred to support the plan on the assumption that to do so would stand her in good stead later. If Marian's pilgrimage were to be concluded satisfactorily, then perhaps when she set her sights on a venture as bold, the way would already have been paved for her.

It was a gamble of course. Should Marian meet difficulties or fall foul of any of the perils previously outlined by her father, Margaret might very well find herself confined to the house for a lifetime, a walk in the park being her only and furthest excursion. Whatever her reasoning, she appeared unusually quick to lend support, voicing her approval and offering practical help at every turn, something Marian did not expect but greeted with some satisfaction.

If pleased to do so, Margaret could sulk unmercifully. Given the necessary incentive she was well able to brood for days. When she did so, and it was not infrequently, she inflicted upon all those in her company the most vile and insidious of silent moods. Fortunately for all concerned and with gratitude displayed by her father in the form of a small gift, a pocket book of common prayer, mounted on its cover with an embossed silver plaque in the form of three angels, she embraced her sister's scheme with magnanimous approval. This was so completely out of character; alarm bells should have started ringing. Instead smiles of relief were exchanged and preparations went ahead undisturbed.

The only absentee of course was Katie. By now she was in Sienna. That much the family knew for certain. The rest was patchy to say the least. She wrote, not in the form of letters, but dispatches, brief and to the point. She said nothing of her relationship with Mr Kenneth. She gave no hint as to the success or failure of his ambition and apparently, she saw no point in referring to the climate, the native Italians or their social habits. All she boasted was their continued health and happiness, a scanty and irregular style of communication which did nothing to ease the ever-present sensation of dread lingering in the pit of her mother's stomach and encouraging her father to continue with responses in the form of monthly money orders.

Katie was sorely missed. Her absence did leave a gaping hole in the life of her family and reminded her father every day just what an additional wrench he faced with the loss of Marian as well. Nevertheless, preparations carried on apace and, having acquiesced, not once did he resurrect his objections. Rather than risk alienation, he set aside his personal disappointment in favour of whole hearted compliance, measuring carefully every eventuality.

Campaigns involving whole armies were scarcely better planned. Logistically, Charles Chase examined every detail, nothing being left to chance. Every day for weeks he proposed a new addition or alteration to Marian's schedule, presenting her with a never-ending list of items to add to her luggage; one day a piece of essential clothing, the next a pill or potion to ward off a catalogue of diseases.

So predictable were these addenda changes, mother and daughter made a game of them, second guessing what his next little package might be. In all other things, Marian carried on as usual. That she was going to India lifted her spirits immeasurably. The delay was frustrating but the reasons for it sound and therefore she gave no hint of impatience. Instead, she settled into a normal life, looking forward to the adventure as something she absolutely had to do in order to be rid of the ghosts haunting her.

The day Mr Chase accepted her scheme was a watershed. Without his consent she could not and would not have gone. On the other hand, with it she felt she had gained not just his approval but an understanding of the need to go. For months, she had felt entirely alone with her grief, believing herself embarked upon a solo voyage into a dark world of despair from which there were few avenues of escape. While all those nearest to her offered sympathy, their lives carried on as before. Only hers was in tatters. Only she could envisage for herself a bleak, hopeless future. That her father believed in her enough to permit such a journey was the spur she sought. He professed at least to understand and that was all she asked.

With the arrival of summer, she was ready. India beckoned. More than anything she yearned to be on her way. The delay, as common sense as it was, made the chore of each passing day a burden of patience she found hard to endure. Rides in the park relieved the strain but most else was little more than mundane ritual. She found it impossible to focus on bible classes or the meaningless chit chat of 'at home' gatherings when her heart was bound for distant shores.

Just occasionally there was some relief. On 4 May, the whole family went to the grand opening of the International Invention Exhibition in Kensington. Guest of honour was His Royal Highness the Prince of Wales. In addition, and contributing to a respectable turn out of the royal family were the three Princesses of Wales, the Duke and Duchess of Edinburgh, Princess Christian, the Duke of Cambridge and in their party an unknown face who was reported in the papers as the Turkish Ambassador.

Watching from the balcony of her bedroom, Marian had an uninterrupted view of the royal carriages as they processed along Exhibition Road, the crowds lining either side of the thoroughfare waving and applauding, happy to glimpse each open carriage in turn and feeling rewarded by the courteous hand of royal acknowledgement.

As soon as the caravan was passed, she left her vantage point and joined the others. Together they walked up to the opening ceremony, fortunate once again to have obtained tickets to such an event when so many were compelled to remain outside, their only reward the chance of a second sight of the royal carriages as they departed.

For several hours they toured the various galleries, marvelling at the scale and variety of exhibits. There were shining railway locomotives and carriages, tram cars and massive manufacturing engines, examples of the finest in British engineering, a tour de force of, Imperial might, each example firm proof of the irrevocable superiority of Her Majesty's reign.

It was with some sense of irony therefore that the item which caught Marian's eye the most was both American by invention and rather smaller in size than the impressive steam driven locomotives around which were gathered most of the first day visitors. In her diary, she recorded impressions of having witnessed the firing of a new 'Maxim Gun.' It was capable of releasing several hundred rounds of ammunition a minute in a Halestorm of destruction and with only the simple turning of a handle. She could not but be moved by the awesome potential of so lethal a weapon. Never before had she witnessed the firing of any gun.

Wars and death were statistics she read about on the pages of newspapers and discussed with her father. They were staged on the other side of the world. Consequently, so violent a piece of machinery left a deep impression. With this ingenious but comparatively simple addition to his armoury, one soldier alone held the power of life and death over hundreds. In a matter of seconds, tens of lives could be taken, snuffed out at random. It was a black omen for the future, a thought so terrible to comprehend, she felt compelled to mark its invention with dire words of warning in the private pages of her journal.

What impressed Margaret the most, or for that matter her mother and father, Marian had no idea. General 'oohs' and 'aahs' accompanied so much of their extended visit to the exhibition. It was impossible therefore to note any particular favourites. But for Marian at least, the Maxim Gun, was the most memorable, if shocking, item on display. Clearly it was a weapon of mass destruction quite able, as its brochure stated, to change the face of modern warfare. This was a boast to send a shiver down the spine, so much so that when, a few days later, she and her mother made one of their regular visits to the Royal Academy, Marian found herself still haunted by the shrill rat-a-tat of rapid gunfire and a vision of the carnage in its wake. Somehow paintings of pretty Venetian ladies by Luke Fildes and romantic landscapes by Vicat Cole or Benjamin Leader lost their relevance in a world where other creative minds worked with equal vigour to invent tools so casually lethal.

Privately she struggled to understand a society which on the one hand could value so highly the aesthetic achievements of men wielding no more than brushes and raw pigment while on the other, and almost in the same breath, display with such pride the obverse side of a coin so readily tarnished with the blood of easy slaughter. It was a problem which troubled her for days. To her father she declared the finest painting at the Royal Academy to be 'A Reading from Homer' by the self-acclaimed Don Juan of contemporary art himself, Lawrence Alma Tadema. Decoratively it had no equal at the exhibition. In quality of execution, she admired no other painting more and its allusion to classic literature appealed to her on an intellectual level that no rustic view could achieve. She was quite adamant in her selection and could find no praise sufficient.

Yet, her diary spoke of war, not art. For two days, she wrote exclusively of 'the gun.' As if to impress future generations as to the magnitude of what she had witnessed, she wrote down every last detail she could recall, its size, shape and operating mechanism, devoting to it several pages, obliterating almost to a footnote any reference to the Royal Academy.

On Whit Sunday, 24 May, she and Margaret went to the flower service at Brompton Church and finally her thoughts were released from the depressing darkness of warfare. For a while, surrounded as she was by the sight and smell of nature at its finest, she sensed again the joy and reward of being alive. At the same time, the weather changed for the better. The beginning of the month had been dreary. The days were lengthening, but the skies remained grey and overcast.

Finally, however, the sun was out. The air was warm and summer felt just around the corner. As May turned to June, the Strauss band from Vienna played for the first time at the 'Inventories,' the nickname she gave in her diary to the International Inventions Exhibition. Strauss himself was there to conduct, proving hugely popular, drawing large and universally appreciative crowds at every concert. So inspiring was his music it was common place to see people in the audience dance in time to the music, mindless of the time or place.

On 6 June, all but Mr Chase attended the Trooping of the Colour in celebration of the Queen's official birthday. A few days later Marian and Margaret went for the day to Kew Gardens, returning in the evening to witness the Indian Museum ablaze. For several hours from a vantage point on the upper floor, they watched as an army of firemen and appliances fought in vain to bring the inferno under control, desperately entering and re-entering the building to rescue treasures from within. The Prince of Wales himself appeared on the scene to assess the fate of presents he had brought back with him from his tour of the Indian continent. In the midst of it all, Marian paused to consider whether or not, so close to home, this was some significant portent of which she should be aware.

By the following morning, only the smouldering ruins remained of a once fine building, blackened streams of water flowing from it in all directions along gutters the length of Princes Gate. Palls of smoke delayed any warmth there was to be gained from the early morning sun as exhausted fire fighters drifted about, resignation their scant reward for a sleepless night.

It was also the morning the Chase family set off for Shenfield. They arrived at the old rectory shortly before luncheon to find Uncle Tom and assembled friends in the middle of a highly animated lawn tennis party. At the same time and much to the consternation of the ladies present, the gardener was employed in the removal of a rogue swarm of bees which had settled itself somewhat inconveniently into a nearby oak tree.

Setting about the task in the old-fashioned way, the elderly Mr Smithers wrapped his head and shoulders in a coarse veil, donned a thick pair of woollen gloves and set off up the tree after his prey. He was armed only with a makeshift straw hive into which he swept as many of the bees as he could, hoping in the process to capture the queen among them. Any which refused to be budged, he squirted with a water filled garden sprayer until he was satisfied that those either watching or playing tennis were no longer in any danger.

Marian kept an eye on the procedure with some fascination, finding the sight of Mr Smithers perched precariously on the top step of a rather rickety old ladder clutching a swarm of bees in one hand and a gleaming brass sprayer in the other far more interesting than the tennis below which had been brought temporarily to a halt by his antics.

When the task was completed to every one's satisfaction, she wandered the gardens alone. Being June there was more a promise of the feast to come than the feast itself. Some braver shrubs were showing off their colours in the borders. The rose garden was beginning and, some distance from the house, the rhododendron walk needed only a few days more of sunshine before turning to a river of pinks and mauves. Nevertheless, it was an afternoon to savour. In London their garden was a formal affair. Regiments of annuals were planted, flowered and removed at each point in the season, in beds bordering carefully manicured lawns. It was a neat, disciplined setting, maintained to perfection, providing a suitable place to stroll, sit or entertain. Sadly, however, it was no place to dream. There were no private corners, no secluded avenues, no secret arbours.

The gardens at Shenfield, however, unending, rambling and husbanded to let nature choose the way, were magical. As children, Marian, Margaret and Katie had been used to running wild in them for hours. They played hide and seek, stalked poor Mr Smithers who, for reasons they could not fathom, never noticed their presence until they were upon him despite their lack of stealth or unstoppable giggling. They also explored the darker reaches as if they were big game hunters, expecting at any minute some wild animal to pounce out upon them. That the occasional rabbit and squirrel or their uncle's old ginger cat were the most ferocious beasts they encountered mattered not a jot.

As she walked alone, Marian recalled vividly the many afternoons she and her sisters had spent at Shenfield and it was with some reluctance she heeded the call to go in for lunch.

By the time they arrived back at 32 Princes Gate it was late into the evening and almost dark. There was little to be made out of the still smouldering remains that was once the Indian Museum, but the smell of charred timbers lingered in the air.

Margaret and her mother spent the following morning shopping and visited Westminster Abbey in the afternoon. They left shortly after breakfast and did not return until about four o'clock. As a result, Marian had the house to herself, her father having also got up early to catch the train to Birmingham where he was due to attend a conference.

For an hour or two she enjoyed the sunshine in the garden. Seated on an ornate wrought iron chair hard up against the sunny most wall some distance from the house, she made as if to read. 'Gordon's Letters' was a birthday present which had lain unopened, waiting its turn until she finished Stephanik's 'Russia under the Tzars.' Sadly, progress had been slow. Under normal circumstances Marian could bury herself in a book for hours, reading one a week and sometimes two in tandem. However, planning the trip to India had consumed most of her spare time. Her mind was filled with lists, things still to do, things to get, things to expect en route and, most to the fore, things ready and able to prevent her from going. There was little time left for reading. A Jane Austen novel would have been all right. That she could have picked up and put down at will, consuming only a few pages at a time as was Margaret's habit. But it was not Marian's way. She preferred books of a more substantial genre. She liked history and historical biographies.

It was a discipline she acquired when still quite young. Innately inquisitive and with a thirst for knowledge well beyond her expectancy for employment of it, the weightier the tome, the more intricate the topic, the more determined she became to digest the contents of its pages. Such was her appetite she set her sights on a never-ending flow of predominantly factual literature and such was her reputation for reading, family and friends were united in their generous donations to the cause, providing for her the makings of a small library which she guarded jealously.

Of late, however, she had neglected the written word. Left alone in the house and with the garden to herself it was a perfect opportunity to catch up. With the loss of General Gordon still so poignantly poised on the breath of the nation and the political ramifications of the massacre at Khartoum unresolved, the opportunity to commence a study of his letters was perfect, particularly with the warm sun to illuminate the pages.

An hour passed and such was her concentration, she paid no heed to a fledgling blackbird hopping around in the flower bed a few feet from where she was sitting or the mother anxiously calling out from her lookout position on the garden wall. Then came a passage dedicated to an opinion of General Sir Charles Napier. With the open candour reserved for private correspondence, General Gordon, laid bare his interpretation of the successes and failures of his predecessor's campaigns in India. In an instant, Marian was transported there herself, her mind distracted from the pages of the book to every footfall of her own imminent campaign on the same continent.

How she longed to be on her way and how frustrated she was by the delay. Much about her trip filled her with apprehension. Undoubtedly there were physical dangers to be considered and uncharted emotional waters she could only test once she arrived. Yet, regardless of the tranquil scene all around her, she was restless depart.

She returned to the pages of her book, but her mood had changed. Leaving it closed behind her on the bench she prowled up and down the closely cut grass paths between the flower beds, pretending to admire the early blooms while she rehearsed again exactly what she would do and say the minute she made landfall on the Indian continent after a month at sea.

Eventually she did return to the words of General Gordon but not in order to continue her reading. Instead, she gathered the book into her arms and walked back inside to endure a solitary lunch and an afternoon of fidgety seclusion in her bedroom. There she sorted dresses to take with her, as well as hats, shoes and gloves yet to pack and what, if any, further shopping was required before her cases could be satisfactorily declared ready.

Fortunately, over the following days the season provided many reliable distractions to prevent her from going out of her mind. General Gordon's letters were picked up and put down more often than was good for the binding. The Oxford versus Cambridge cricket at Lords came and went, leaving Cambridge the victors, much to the delight of her father and Uncle Tom, both of whom were graduates.

Then came the annual outing to Henley for the Regatta on 2 July. Without Katie, their party was four; Fred, George, Margaret and herself. On a fine summer's morning they started together from Paddington station at about 10.30, reaching Henley at noon and going straight to the Isthmian Club where Fred had several friends. They lunched and listened to a military band play selections from among others Carmen and the still highly popular Mikado. When the rowing began, they watched from the river bank, she and Margaret cheering loudly as Eton won the Ladies Challenge Cup against strong opposition from Oriel College, Oxford.

So hot was the sun, regular supplies of cold lemonade were required to keep them cool and where in past years Marian was in the habit of taking herself off and strolling along the water's edge down towards the start, this time she stayed with Margaret and the others, her parasol permanently open to shield her from the worst of the heat.

Even when they set out for home shortly after six o'clock, the sun was still unrelenting. Their railway carriage was stuffy and uncomfortable. However, it had been a most enjoyable afternoon. Fred and George were the perfect companions and Margaret declared it to be the best Regatta she had attended, an opinion possibly swayed by the hovering presence of a young man who appeared rather taken with her.

On nodding terms only with Fred and George, neither of whom could quite recall where they had met him before or, at first, what his name was, he lingered all day on the fringes of their party, his eyes rarely leaving Margaret, her every need catered for almost before she had invented it. He was pleasant, well spoken, from his disappointment at the rowing results clearly an Oxford man and, at the very least, a good six inches taller than anyone else about him. Wiry and irregular like the branches of an ancient olive tree, he was all arms and legs over which was draped, rather than fitted, a pair of white flannels which looked as if they had been screwed up in a ball since the previous summer. He also sported a many-striped blazer with more alternating colours than a rainbow.

His name was Giles Fairfax. He was both polite and softly spoken. More to the point according to some rather revealing and whispered gossip to reach their ears during the course of the afternoon, he was the only son of Sir Gerald and Lady Fairfax. Their chief claim to fame was apparently that they 'owned half of Hampshire.' They were also said to be regular visitors to Osborne House when the Queen was in residence and though clearly their son was in dire need of a good tailor, his general behaviour did have something of the aristocrat about it.

Whatever truth there was to the rumours, The Honourable Giles Fairfax was clearly extremely taken with Margaret. Too shy for her own good, she did nothing to encourage his attentions but they came nevertheless. By midafternoon he had inveigled himself into becoming the fifth member of their party and when they made to leave, he presented Margaret with an elegant calling card and an earnest request that, with her approval, he be permitted to call on her the next time he was in town. Quite when that would be he could not indicate. All he assured her was that although his trips to London were generally rare, he would make it a priority to see her when next the occasion arose.

The consequence of all this attention was a quiet Margaret for the rest of the day. During the large dinner party which they all returned to in the evening and at which there were at least a dozen guests over and above immediate family, she scarcely spoke a word. This was not unusual in itself, though rarely was she reduced to absolute silence for the duration of a meal. However, when the conversation turned to challenging the actions of certain more notorious missionaries on the African continent whose fanaticism was deemed by many to have overwhelmed their common humanity, she barely responded. This was a lack of reaction which caused her mother some consternation, the immediate assumption being that her daughter was ailing in some way.

The idea of Margaret being unsettled by the attentions of a man did not cross her mind. In that they were capable of being impressed by men and sometimes attracted to them, Katie and Marian were quite normal. Margaret, on the other hand was not known to have shown even once, however briefly, the slightest interest in matters pertaining to the opposite sex. The simple word 'hello' spoken to her by a stranger with a voice other than soprano or contralto was wont to bring on an instant cowering response, like a threatened snail retreating suddenly into its shell. Generally, around men of her own age, she was awkward, painfully shy and determinedly unwilling to become involved. Consequently, her more than usual reticence at the dinner table was labelled as ague rather than any form of budding amour.

Nothing was done or said and certainly Margaret was in no mood to mention the elongated Giles Fairfax during her brief summary of events at Henley. On being pressed, she described the rowing in some detail. She and Marian agreed that as fine a day as it had been, the sun was just too hot. They were also as one in their praise of Fred and George as companions. However, there was no reference made to the fact that Margaret had caught the eye of a would-be suitor. She studiously avoided the subject and an anxious glance in Marian's direction was sufficient to discourage any such rumour reaching the ears of either parent.

But a seed had been sewn. Of that Marian was sure. Had Giles Fairfax raised a substantial banner aloft over his head with Margaret's named emblazoned on it; he could not have made his instant attraction to her more obvious. That he would indeed call on her when he was next in town, was not to be doubted. Marian was as confident of it as she was that day turns to night. Where lay the deceit was in the implication that he would surface only as and when he next drifted in her direction. Quite clearly, before the words had left Giles Fairfax's mouth, his thoughts were directed towards ways in which he could adjust his diary so as to have him in London at the earliest possible moment. Had he succeeded in negotiating for himself an invitation to that evening's dinner party it would not have come as any surprise. Nevertheless, Marian expected to see him shortly, an expectation she believed was matched by her sister for whom, in fact, expectation was undoubtedly more an earnest hope.

After dinner, the party divided into two. The older and less athletic retired to the drawing room for liquors, more comfortable chairs and a continuation of what had been already an evening of lively and varied conversation. For the remaining quests, a walk in the park was the order of the day. Brilliantly lit and with cooling waters playing in the fountains it was a welcome relief from the pressing midday sun of Henley. Strauss waltzes were being performed by bands from the Pomeranian Hussars and Grenadier guards and for a fleeting moment Marian was compelled to imagine there was nowhere else on earth she would rather be. The air was cool. The smell of fresh grass and summer flowers pervaded her senses and around her was assembled a small group of people who represented the core of those she most admired and loved.

Just for a second, William Radford left her thoughts and, had she been broached on the subject, she might have declared India a far-off land she had no mind to see and was even less likely to visit. In reality William lived in her mind as vividly as if he were standing at her side, tapping his feet on the ground to the rhythm of the music, his hand clasped in hers. Now that Henley was over for another year, India was the next pressing appointment in her diary.

'I liked Giles Fairfax very much,' she whispered to her sister as they walked back to the house arm in arm and in a tone she trusted would be taken as encouragement.

'Thank you,' Margaret replied, nothing further needing to be said, the fraudulent glow of anticipation guarding her from any chill in the night air.

Chapter Seven

On Saturday morning the 14 July, as was usual, Marian rode with her father. It was a perfect summer's day, not a cloud in the sky, the sun shining with a brilliance and warmth that belied the generally erratic British climate.

It was expected to be their last ride together for many months. Consequently, their conversation was occasional and brief. There were no more plans to be discussed, no more debating necessary. The following morning Marian intended rising early for church. Then, on Monday, she was due to depart for India.

As if she had never ridden in the park before, she absorbed every detail along their route, committing to memory every inch as a precious keepsake. The trees were in full leaf, casting great lakes of shadow on the lush grass below. Birdsong filled the air and the park was busy with the traffic of father's and daughters, husbands and wives, gentlemen and mistresses all dedicated to making the most of so fine a day.

It was no day for melancholy and she felt none. She was apprehensive lest in the final moments the parting tears of her mother or the sadness in her father's eyes gave her cause to falter. But so certain was she of her crusade and so impatient was she to be done with the weeks of waiting, no chink of doubt remained to spoil her ride. Rather, she savoured the moment, lapping up every nuance of colour, smell and sound, watching her father as if from a distance, admiring him and wanting to thank him again and again for his tolerance.

In giving her leave to go, he had done what few fathers would have had the courage to do. One daughter was lost to him already. With unbelievable irresponsibility, Katie had run off with a man of little character and few prospects. She had brought shame to herself and her family. Yet, through it all, she was missed and loved without compromise. Now it was time for Marian to leave, bent on a mission fraught with a catalogue of possible perils too numerous to record and a motive so intangible as to confound every contemplation of it.

As they walked their horses the length of the Row, she recorded the deepest possible affection for her father. Without his unswerving help and guidance, she could not have considered such a journey. Now it was upon her and though she knew his heart was tearing itself in two at the prospect of her going, he gave not a hint of any such thing, his smile, his voice, his manner immaculate to the last.

Two days later, as scheduled, she was gone. Lieutenant Colonel Sir Archibald and Lady Caroline Farrer were to be her escort as far as Bombay. Their final destination was Delhi where the Colonel was to take up a position as military secretary to the Governor. The Farrers and Chases were not acquainted but shared a mutual friend in Sir James Strachey who lived at number 38 Princes Gate. He was a gentleman in his early eighties, a man of wit and wisdom, knighted for his services to overseas development. As a senior administrator within the East India Company, he had spent many years in India where he was chiefly responsible for the initial planning and later construction of a railway network destined one day to reach into every corner of the continent.

Much respected by Marian's father, he was a regular addition to dinner parties at 32 Princes Gate and, in turn, the whole Chase family were frequent guests at his lavish home a few doors away. His recommendation of and introduction to Colonel Farrer was the single most fortunate circumstance in Marian's search for the means to secure a passage to India. Without an escort, the simple fact of the matter was that she could not have gone.

A young woman travelling alone was unthinkable. This was something even Marian accepted from the outset. She knew her father would never agree to her going unless she found a suitable or, as luck would have it, two suitable travelling companions. Sir Archibald and Lady Caroline came highly recommended. He was an experienced soldier, a man who had served in many foreign campaigns. She, Lady Caroline, in possession of an immense inherited fortune, was the only daughter of a certain Hector Covington who, though deceased for some years as was his wife, still commanded respect as the founder of a business empire which included shipping, canal construction and heavy engineering.

Rumour had it that he was one of only a handful of English investors to appreciate the extraordinary potential in the building of a canal through Suez to link Europe with the east. During its planning stage, directors of established companies like Peninsular and Orient shipping line procrastinated, exhibiting only muted enthusiasm and failed initially to invest in larger, modern ships capable of making the voyage from London to Bombay. Even the Royal Mail service stuck doggedly to the old overland route. Hector Covington though, got his hands on as many shares in the Suez Canal Company as he could, his faith undaunted by an engineering project the like of which the world had never seen. Firmly convinced that a passage via Suez would transform travel into the twentieth century, his foresight secured his fortune and that of his family for generations to come.

As luck would have it, Marian's father could not have hoped for better chaperones. Into the hands of Colonel and Lady Farrer he was content to release the precious cargo that was his daughter. With them to protect her he had no fear that the journey as far as Bombay would be anything other than a safe one. Arrangements for the onward leg by sea from Bombay to Karachi, overland to Lahore and beyond into the barren and troubled north west territories were quite another matter. Every inch of the way was prepared, however. The names and ranks of each individual Marian was to encounter were established in advance of her leaving London. Of course, names and ranks were one thing. They were an assurance that at no time would she be abandoned to her own devices. But without a face put to the name there was still cause for concern, a concern her father expressed repeatedly and which Marian at times feared might be the stumbling block to her plans.

In the end it was Colonel Farrer who stepped in to assure him that every officer serving in India could be relied upon to treat Marian with respect. As long as she remained under the umbrella of the British army, she would be quite safe. She was, after all, a British memsahib. As such therefore, she was beyond the reach of any native intrusion, a guarantee extended not only by Colonel Farrer to Mr Chase more than once prior to their sailing, but repeated in private by Lady Caroline to Marian on their first night aboard the P & O ship SS Egypt as it left from Victoria docks.

Whether or not this information set her father's mind entirely at rest is doubtful, but on the surface at least, he accepted the word of Colonel Farrer and promoted it with vigour to Mrs Chase when she too showed signs of weakening. Bearing in mind Marian's motive for going to India and the fate of the man on whose behalf she was prepared to travel such a vast distance, the Colonels words of encouragement were essentially flawed, but they were a comfort nevertheless, a life belt to which both parents clung for relief.

The long sea voyage itself was not upper most in their thoughts. It was not without its' dangers, but generally speaking such voyages were seen as nothing by comparison to the very real perils Marian would confront the moment she set foot on Indian soil.

Consequently, the letters arriving at 32 Princes Gate during the first weeks of her absence, commencing with one posted in Marseilles, were opened with pleasurable anticipation. When inclined to be, Marian was a good letter writer. She could transpose with ease the flowing and often humorous style of her diary writing to that of correspondence, although the latter was inclined to exclude the more intimate or emotional revelations inscribed on the leaves of her private ledger.

However, unlike the paltry efforts of her two sisters, the missives from Katie in particular being short and sadly lacking in any detail of her new life in Italy beyond affirmations of continued good health and blissful happiness, Marian was able to fill several pages and more whenever she sat down to write.

In the first epistle, she spoke at length of her two companions. As if to reassure, she made much of her quick affection for both Sir Archibald and Lady Farrer, relating more details of the Colonels illustrious career, something his wife was pleased to pass on whenever she and Marian were alone. Marian also stressed the fast-growing friendship she and Lady Caroline were developing.

The latter very soon became a constant companion. Rarely did she leave Marian's side and in the company of others showered her with attention. Indeed, had Marian been her own daughter she could not have been more cosseted, so much so that within a few days of sailing, she actually came to treasure somewhat the increasingly rare occasions of being left to her own devices.

In effect, Lady Caroline became her shadow. No sooner did Marian find for herself a secluded spot than her privacy was invaded. In her letters she wrote nothing but kind words. From the outset she realised that her news was of secondary interest. What her parents really hoped for each time they opened an envelope was confirmation of her being in safe hands. Lady Caroline's permanent attachment and their mutual regard one for the other was just exactly the balm Mr and Mrs Chase needed for their wounds.

As previously mentioned, Lady Caroline was a woman of considerable wealth. She was born into a privileged lifestyle few shared and even fewer could imagine. Consequently, her opinions on almost every aspect of life were necessarily slanted. Sadly, however, she was unaware it. In spite of certain modest intellectual short comings, no doubt encouraged by her often-quoted declaration that literature was the root of so much unrest in the world and therefore to be avoided, particularly by those whose class or status denied them most of what literature exposed, she was rarely short of an opinion. She was wont to take advantage of any gathering of two or more people to flaunt her views on every topic from social deprivation, of which she was boundlessly ignorant, to political and economic progress about which Marian was of the opinion she knew even less.

Nevertheless, she was extremely well meaning. She showed Marian nothing but kindness, favouring her with compliments and gifts at every turn. And at no time could she be considered wanting in the application of her duties as guardian. When Marian wrote to her parents declaring Colonel and Lady Farrer to be beyond reproach, it was the absolute truth. As long as she remained in their company no ill could befall her. That said, there were times, and they became more and more frequent as the voyage progressed, she craved solitude.

For Lady Caroline was very much a larger-than-life character. When she appeared on deck or arrived in the dining room, there was a conspicuous lull in the general conversation, a hush as if a member of the royal family had just crossed the threshold. Taller than most women, standing shoulder to shoulder with her husband who was by no means himself a short man, with an abundance of flame red hair the envy of any Rossetti model and always attired in the most extravagant of outfits, she cut an imposing figure. Furthermore, she exploited in equal part her celebrity and the rather obsequious respect in which she was held.

By contrast and almost by way of a balance to the overt and thoroughly relished attention Lady Caroline encouraged toward herself at all times, Lieutenant Colonel Sir Archibald Farrer, was a quiet, self-effacing man. He was naturally courteous and kind, asking little of Marian beyond an occasional assurance she was being looked after adequately. At the side of his wife, he rarely found either the need or the opportunity to speak. Yet, strangely, he did not appear diminished in any way by her presence. In spite of a slight limp, he carried as the result of a wound sustained during a campaign twenty years earlier, he remained both elegant and charismatic.

This charisma was not encouraged by any effort on his part to be noticed but hidden within the depths of his intense hazel blue eyes. Never before had Marian met a man who spoke so little yet appeared to say so much. While his wife bloomed like an open flower, he remained silent, giving her centre stage. Yet, invariably, all eyes were drawn to him. He had a presence and magnetism quite beyond the reach of fine jewels, rich fabrics or outspoken opinion. Reticent, but not shy, he made no effort to outshine his wife and yet did so without trying, a fact no less fascinating to Marian as it must have been devastating to the somewhat frail ego of Lady Caroline herself.

All in all, however, Marian's favourable reviews in her letters home were sincerely felt. Both Sir Archibald and Lady Caroline, though quite opposite as personalities, shared a generosity of spirit which shone like a warm sun. Furthermore, they showed themselves to be a genuinely well-matched couple. Even though, they were no longer star-crossed lovers, their deep mutual affection, so freely expressed, was clear and, rather surprisingly, as far as Marian could tell, it was Lady Caroline, the younger of the two by some considerable margin who courted more the attention of her partner.

In spite of her rather forthright manner and his undemonstrative style, it was she who worked the harder to earn his approbation. In public she hung on his arm at every opportunity and when the coast was clear they exchanged barely noticeable but intimate glances and gestures, activities as amusing to Marian for their mischievous quality as they were pleasing. It all served to remind her of home and in so doing saved her from feeling more homesick than she might had the atmosphere between her two guardians been cold.

Much to Marian's surprise therefore, as their days at sea passed, the three of them began to mould well together. Disparate to the casual observer perhaps, they soon became ideal companions. Though they were three different personalities with very different means of expressing themselves, when thrown together in the same mixing bowl, namely the confines on board ship, they united to produce a well-balanced trio. Invariably debate between them was lively but cordial. Disagreements were settled by returning to their respective corners with no victor being declared. A few weeks into the voyage and Marian felt as if she had known them for a lifetime, warming to them equally but perhaps favouring Sir Archibald fractionally the more.

Lady Caroline was bold and brazen, the legacy perhaps of an upbringing free from personal sacrifice or the least suggestion of going without. Her opinions were outspoken, often harsh for their apparent lack of sympathy and rarely altered by sound argument. She was also an unashamed hedonist, a quality no doubt which the errant Katie would have much admired. She revelled in life, exploiting every opportunity to increase her pleasure of it, often exceeding accepted social graces in order to transform a dower assembly or event into something amusing and memorable. Quite appropriately, she was also unstoppably open hearted, spoiling Marian at every turn, sometimes to the point of embarrassment.

In all, Lady Caroline was quite unlike any woman Marian had previously encountered. She was a lot to take in and, at first, small doses were as much as Marian could bear, assuming as she did that beneath the glossy veneer lay yet more veneer. Only later did she become aware of an intellect and empathic quality in Lady Caroline, quite different from her own perhaps, but there nevertheless and it was this which both intrigued her and strengthened their friendship.

With Sir Archibald things were very different. A camouflage of shyness once recognised for what it was, shielded a man who reminded Marian closely of her own father. Consequently, it was a short step from stranger to confidante. His appearance was different. He was tall but thin, almost gaunt. His hair was faded to grey. However, his uniform, from which he was never parted, was at all times immaculate and tailored to perfection, rendering him an imposing figure, more so than her own father and every bit the equal of a wife whose annual wardrobe expenditure must have been heart stopping. No less than six porters were employed in the formidable task of carrying her ladyship's numerous valises from shore to ship prior to their departing British soil, the contents of which were merely for use while at sea.

More trunks were stowed in the hold to be opened upon their arrival in Delhi. Though trivial, this was a statistic remarkable to Marian and therefore necessary to relate to her father if only by way of admonishment for all the occasions he had criticised his own wife for her clothing excesses. Of more interest was the vivid picture Marian drew of their passing through the Suez Canal. Quite simply, she wrote to her mother and father, it was the most spectacular construction she had ever seen, dwarfing anything and everything at the International Inventions Exhibition.

She was too young at the time to recall the political infighting as to which if any political party would have the courage or imagination to foot the bill for its construction. Equally, she was ignorant of the sums involved and the acrimonious recriminations which followed its dramatic opening only a few years after she was born. All she could do was salute the French for their own imagination, the engineers for their genius and the thousands of sweating labourers for their endurance and sacrifice in the face of a task so gigantic and undertaken in a climate so hostile to their endeavour.

At the Mediterranean end, Port Said guarded the entrance to the canal. There they paused for a day and a half before continuing on, moored alongside a flotilla of ships waiting their turn to pass through, while fresh provisions were taken on board for the last leg of their voyage to Bombay. There was time enough for Colonel Farrer to escort the ladies ashore. There were bazaars to visit and a thousand sights and sounds completely alien to the streets of London. As their rather moth-eaten carriage passed through the narrow, dusty and dirty streets, drawn by a single horse which was no more than an emaciated carcass of skin and bone, they were plagued by a throng of similarly emaciated beggar children, all jostling for position with roadside vendors raucously pressing them to buy everything from roughly beaten brassware to embroidered shawls and traditional head gear.

There was little in the way of architecture to admire save the occasional public building with varying degrees of French influence. The heat was oppressive and made all the more unbearable by an acrid pungency in the air resulting from a total lack of even the most basic sanitation. When they returned to the ship, it was with no desire to prolong or repeat the outing.

Marian, indeed, found herself quite shocked. The poverty and squalor were like nothing she had witnessed before. Even on deck she was besieged by a hundred shrill voices from the quayside beseeching her to buy some trinket or other and she was in no way relieved by the knowledge from Sir Archibald that she could expect the same and more when they docked in Bombay.

To his eyes, none of it was new. He had seen it all before; the dirt, decay and massed humanity scratching an existence in a hostile climate, where filth and disease rubbed shoulders. For him the shocking impact had dulled to an irritable loathing for so conspicuous a display of degradation. Over the years he had disciplined himself to ignore or ride rough shod over those things which were beyond his power to alter.

Marian, however, was less immune. Her conscience was sensitive to the plight of every child, to the pain of every physical handicap and to the cruel hardship embroidered on almost every face. She reeled from the stench and struggled to contain her disgust for so much of what confronted her, faltering slightly in her enthusiasm to reach India.

If what she witnessed in Port Said was no more than an aperitif, she questioned her resolve to go on. She was overwhelmed, much disturbed and in need of reviving encouragement from the Colonel who consoled her with the truth that she was not the first nor last Peninsula and Orient passenger to be affected in similar manner. He conceded that it was impossible not to be shocked. He was quick to own up to similar emotions the first time he was posted far from the comfort of English soil.

Fortunately, the canal itself provided a satisfactory distraction. Quite simply, a wonder of the modern world, it carved through the desert like the shining steel blade of a sword dropped by Allah himself. Giant like was its construction. A feat of engineering too extraordinary to contemplate, a labour so arduous, it was impossible for Marian to consider the sheer numbers involved or the volume of dry earth displaced.

For a hundred miles it stretched before them, a watery thoroughfare, slicing the desert in half, broad enough only to allow one great ship at a time, though long enough to accommodate a fleet. After their departure from Port Said, she stayed up on deck for more than an hour. The sun was blistering but the view too spectacular to ignore. With what appeared to be only a few feet of water on either side of the ship and riding as they were high above the rim of the canal, the impression was one of the ship itself scything through the desert, a desert stretching without interruption to infinite.

The only evidence of human encroachment was the old railway line running parallel on one bank of the canal for its entire length and the occasional sight of nomadic settlements. Otherwise, the view was as barren as the surface of the moon, nothing to be seen and yet spectacular. It was a wasteland of sand which possessed a beauty quite unlike anything she might have imagined. Accustomed as she was to green fields, rolling hills and broad oaks, she was spellbound by the majesty of so vast an open space and man's ingenuity to traverse it.

Eventually, however, she was forced inside. Heat radiated from every surface and the suns bleaching rays bore down on her like flames from a fire. By comparison, the saloons and cabin were cool. Sir Archibald, familiar with the scene, and Lady Caroline, rather less able to tolerate the extreme heat on deck, were playing bridge with a couple from Pirbright in Surrey. Their conversation was punctuated by brittle laughter and since they were mostly absorbed in with their cards, Marian lingered only long enough for introductions. Then she retreated to her cabin, there to continue her scouring of the horizon through the constricted aperture of a porthole.

It was the middle of the night before they made the ocean once more, the Red Sea opening up to them like a broad funnel, the land on either side slipping from view by stages until finally there was nothing port or starboard save watery emptiness. The Western Ghats was the next land they would see, rising up from the ocean like a vast bank with Bombay in its shadow.

In one sense, it would be the end of a journey for Marian, in another the beginning. Before that, there were days of open ocean, days with little to view from the promenade deck or to stimulate the mind. For all the passengers, letter writing was a popular pastime. Every sheet of headed note paper on board was used up. Tales of Port Said and the Canal filled pages, some more eloquent and evocative than others. There were detailed accounts of parties, games and the occasional amorous affairs begun by an accidental meeting over deck coyts and pursued with as much discretion as could be maintained within so small and confined a community. Gossip, of course was rife and inevitably, with gossip, came misunderstandings and resentments. By no means was the atmosphere at all times convivial.

Marian was invited to take charge of the entertainment committee, a role she accepted merely to relieve the creeping boredom she struggled in vain to resist. Sir Archibald and Lady Caroline were attentive and their company stimulating enough. However, there were occasions when the latter displayed an exasperating ignorance of the world about her, inviting as often as not a softly spoken but vitriolic response. There were other passengers as well whose company Marian enjoyed or whose conversation she courted. Nevertheless, for much of the last leg of the voyage, she spent more and more time alone in her cabin, writing in her diary, reporting not just impressions of places seen or the people she had come to know, but questioning her possible reaction to a country which promised to be so uniquely different.

Privy to many of the Colonels previous experiences, courtesy of long after-dinner conversations and, in Port Said, having sampled a morsel of the social deprivation she could expect to confront on the Indian continent, Marian was considerably more circumspect about her mission than she had been within the walls of 32 Princes Gate.

There were times indeed she felt inclined to turn back. She experienced bouts of apprehension. The gravity of what she had set out to do weighed heavily on her shoulders. In Bombay she would say farewell to Colonel and Lady Farrer. As they boarded a train for Delhi, secure in the knowledge of their destination and what would be there to greet them, Marian was due to board another ship to

Karachi. From there, she would travel overland to a corner of the world as remote and forbidding as any she could have chosen.

The North West Frontier was a hostile environment. That much she had been told countless times. A barren and essentially lawless part of the world it was populated by warlike tribes who as much as they fought among themselves were united in their violent resentment of the British.

Second thoughts therefore dogged her. In London she wrestled with her father long and hard to be on her way. In spite of all the many objections he proposed, she remained steadfast to her cause, making light of his words of caution. Then, her mind was firmly made up. Nothing could or would prevent her from going.

Yet, as Bombay drew ever closer, she was riddled with doubt. Should she go ashore or stay on board for the return voyage back to England. Certainly, Colonel Farrer was in no doubt. In his opinion, an opinion he was not afraid to express and did so to Marian on more than one occasion, India was no place for the white man, let alone the white woman. Statistically the odds were not in their favour. The climate, disease and violence all conspired to make their presence on Indian soil perilous.

'Flies to wanton boys,' he declared philosophically, 'That's what we are in India you know.'

There were those who considered India the jewel in the crown of British empire and in many respects they were correct. However, the price paid to keep that jewel was a dear one, paid with the lives of countless English men and women. The Colonel was a loyal soldier, a man of duty and, as such, returning to India for the third time. However, he was under no allusions as to the risks posed to himself and his wife. To a certain extent, in Delhi, he would be cocooned, spared the worst rigours. Gathered together in one area, the British contingent was segregated. With conscientious dedication and residing together in an environment as Anglo-Saxon as they could contrive, the English kept themselves to themselves. Integration was studiously avoided. Social or physical contact with the native population was all but outlawed, effecting, it was earnestly hoped, a degree of immunity from the many guises by which death might be visited upon them.

It was not full proof. Even in Delhi, in the heart of such clinical isolation, death was a frequent visitor, multi-facetted, indiscriminate and sometimes calling with a ferociously unforgiving appetite. Nevertheless, at least the odds were lengthened. Where Marian was headed it was entirely a different story. Harsh was the least forbidding adjective used to describe so bleak a corner of the world. It was not without some dedication on his part that Colonel Farrer tried to encourage an alteration to her plans. If she wanted to see India, she was more than welcome to continue on to Delhi with himself and Lady Farrer. Once there, she could stay with them as their house guest for as long as she wished. But he urged her not to proceed north to Karachi and beyond.

He had said as much before they left London, but his words fell on deaf ears. Repeating the same between Port Said and Bombay was more likely to provoke a favourable reaction. Marian listened and paused for thought, her resolve less resolute, her determination less determined.

Whether or not she proceeded was by no means set in stone. Bombay was to be her Rubicon. Should she cross it or not was a question which haunted her during the remaining long and often sleepless nights at sea. In the airless, throbbing confinement of her cabin she tossed and turned, one minute sure of her purpose, the next confronting a fast-failing willpower.

Lady Caroline, of course, knew exactly what she should do. Delhi was the only sensible option. There, as her guest, Marian would be safe, well cared for and able to mix in a society better suited to a woman of her age and class.

'If,' as she put it, 'one has to come to such a God forsaken country, the least possible contact one has with the natives, the better.'

It was advice given with her usual uncompromising bigotry, but in this instance not without some good sense, if somewhat brutal. That the whole native Indian population should be avoided was an extreme view and helped her husband not a jot, particularly if it was expressed with any conviction on her part. The task of governing India, of which he was an active part, required the good will of the indigenous peoples, an accord not easily achieved in the face of such forthright opinions should they be trumpeted as the general consensus.

But it was a stark fact. Marian was heading into a world brim full of hazards. Just how many of them she was equipped to face remained to be seen. In reality, the two options were poles apart. The one was to reside in comparative comfort within a closed circle of her own kind. The other was to stray into uncharted and unfriendly territory where her safety could not be guaranteed and her welfare protected only as best as conditions permitted.

In the end, she decided to compromise. Assuring both Sir Archibald and Lady Caroline that her journey to the north west would be conducted with all possible haste and only for as long as was absolutely necessary to achieve the purpose of her mission, she agreed to return by way of Delhi. She would not leave India without first being their guest for a week or two, a promise given not under duress but with some sensible anticipation of the pleasure she would gain from the detour.

In spite of Lady Caroline's strongly held, loudly pronounced and often absurdly arrogant opinions on every subject from the ungodly habits of a whole nation, to the sorry dress sense of a certain Miss Elisa Threw who was bound for India to bag herself a husband, she was a surprisingly likeable and generous woman. Had she been mean spirited in any way, Marian would have found her company loathsome. However, she was not. Much of what came from Lady Caroline's lips was said for effect. There was little real sincerity in her radicalism. Strangely, all the money in the world was not enough to compensate for the mysterious lack of self-confidence she kept hidden behind a barrage of bluster.

On the surface, and certainly at first meeting, Caroline Farrer was not an easy woman to like. Marian remembered writing unfavourable lines in her diary the evening they sailed from England. It was a few days before she reviewed her opinion. Then the change of heart was only achieved because circumstances on board dictated their constant companionship. By the time they reached Port Said, Marian entertained a genuine liking for and admiration of her chaperone. In many respects, they were much alike. In that Lady Caroline was prone to speak before thinking, they were as chalk and cheese. However, in some of their other personality traits they were twinned. That they became firm friends was no coincidence. Time and dedication were required to forgive each other their failings, but by embracing their similarities, in the end, they formed a strong bond.

Marian's promise to pass through Delhi before returning to England was given with ready enthusiasm. Quite how she would fulfil said promise remained to be seen. Before then she was committed to an adventure as open-ended in its duration as it was in content. Nothing was certain, least of all the common sense of what she was setting out to do.

As the Indian coastline drew ever nearer, at first a dark, distant cloud like shape then becoming a solid, sustainable contour, she wished she had heeded the scepticism of her father.

Chapter Eight

Marian tried to imagine the weather in London at the end of August. Warm, dry and sunny she hoped, but not as blisteringly hot as in Bombay. Neither would it have the draining humidity brought on by regular torrential monsoon downpours.

It was nearing ten o'clock in the morning when they began to disembark from the SS Egypt. The temperature was already in the eighties. Below them was terra firma in the form of Ballard Pier. On it was gathered a mass of humanity seemingly as dense as the grains of sand on a beach. A thousand individual voices, all talking and yelling at once combined to produce a brutal cacophony.

Not with any great glee did she quit the comparative quiet and security of the promenade deck for the swaying gangway which had been lowered into place within minutes of the ship docking. There was an almost threatening look about the mob on the quayside. Consequently, Marian kept close to her companions, leaving what had been her temporary home for the best part of five weeks only when compelled to do so.

In Port Said they had been greeted by similar scenes; beggars and street vendors swarming to the side of the ship like bees to honey, small children with dirty faces and staring eyes clinging to the coach work of their carriage, clambering for attention, each determined to be singled out for some tangible display of benevolence. There were cripples with withered limbs, pox scarred faces and the putrid odour of poverty. But it was escapable. Their stay in Port Said was for a few hours only, their trip ashore brief.

Bombay, on the other hand, was where their voyage ended. Marian was leaving the ship for good. In a few hours it would be gone, its berth lying empty aside syrup waters. The pier would be deserted until the next packet ship arrived. In the meantime, she and all those who had travelled out from England on the same vessel were at the mercy of every alien face, every glaring example of humanities worst social deprivations.

Beneath too many starched layers of clothing, she was already hot and perspiring. However, the fast-growing feelings of nausea in the pit of her stomach were the consequence of mild panic as much as suffocation. Sir Archibald and Lady Caroline were at her side. Their vigilance was constant. Not for a moment did they lose sight of her or permit her to stray more than a few inches from them. Yet, Marian was afraid lest she find herself alone in the midst of a hostile crowd.

There were tugs at her skirts from insistent tentacle like arms. There were leering, tooth decayed and foul breathed faces only inches from her own and in the midst of this strangulating sea of humanity she was helpless.

Under different circumstances she would have cried out, turned and run back to the safety of the ship. However, undaunted, she carried on, deeper and deeper into the melee until all at once relief arrived as the sea of bodies around her opened.

A clearing had been formed by a small troop of armed soldiers. Standing to attention in the form of a semi-circle, encompassing a lone, immaculately spit and polished young captain, they gave no quarter to the mob, claiming space for the Colonels party with cold efficiency.

With a much exaggerated raise of the knee, stamp of the foot and synchronised salute, the officer in charge introduced himself.

'Captain Raymond Spencer, Sir,' he announced himself to the Colonel, clipped and half shouted.

'At ease, Captain,' came the reply from a man who by the superiority of his rank was permitted a more leisurely and, dare one say without wishing to offend the military psyche, more natural tone to his voice.

There followed brief introductions, several words of instruction from the captain to a corporal regarding the transportation of luggage and then they there led to the comparative privacy of an open landau. From there and with only the briefest words of instruction from the captain, they left the waterfront.

For the next couple of days, they would be staying at the Taj Mahal Hotel. This news was greeted with much relief by Lady Caroline and Marian alike. Both women shared the distinct and unsettling sensation of continuing to feel the roll of the ship in spite of their feet being firmly planted on dry land.

Privately, Lady Caroline hoped their stopover in Bombay would give her a final opportunity to persuade Marian of the common sense in continuing on to Delhi rather than heading off alone into the unknown. Albeit that she had come to know Marian well enough during their voyage to appreciate the poor likelihood of success, she liked her well enough to try. Less driven by passion than Marian and therefore perhaps the more objective of the two, she was filled with concern for her younger companion. As much as anything, she was inspired by the firsthand experience of her husband. He was frequent in his advice to her, just as he had been to Marian, that the North West Frontier was 'no place for a woman.' A couple of nights in Bombay might tip the balance or not, but they could do no harm.

The drive was short. As escort, both ahead and to the rear of their carriage, were three mounted guards. Riding with them on a handsome chestnut whaler, the captain kept in close contact, ever mindful to the needs of his party.

Turning into Mint Road, they swept past the Gothic splendour of St Thomas' Cathedral, its eighteenth-century granite structure copying to perfection both the style and grace of a medieval cathedral, acacias rather than oaks in the surrounding gardens sole evidence of it not standing on English soil.

At the bottom of Apollo Road, they crossed an open convergence of five streets, dominated by an elevated equestrian statue of the Prince of Wales. Then they ran along Colaba Causeway for a distance before turning left down a short avenue to the hotel. They might have gone by way of Apollo Bunder and the Royal Bombay Yacht Cub, but the captain was keen for the Colonel and ladies to gain the most favourable first impression of the hotel. It was, after all, the most newly erected of grand buildings, a further extravagant addition, setting Bombay apart as one of India's most modern and sophisticated cities.

There existed no larger or more luxurious hotel anywhere on the continent, its massive red brick bulk set off by a huge Italianate dome rising skyward from its centre, towering over everything in the vicinity with the exception only of the university clock tower.

And, it would be fair to say, those in the carriage were impressed. Not for a moment had Marian anticipated such an imposing sight. And that was not all. No hotel in Bombay boasted greater luxury. As elegant as was the facade, the huge reception area, public rooms and the fourth-floor suite to which she was shown, were no less than majestic, combining subtle influences of the east with the most modern of imported refinements.

Over the course of the next two days, and in certain respects with the assistance of Captain Spencer who appointed himself their guide as much as their guardian, Marian discovered a city which reflected not only the dominance of the British in India but the scale of their enterprise. As resplendent as the Taj Mahal Hotel was, it turned out to be but one building among many of similar grandcur.

A drive along Rampart Road and into the broad avenue of Esplanade Road, the route of royal processions, took them past the university, high court buildings, Great Western Hotel and Bombay Club to the business quarter, an extraordinary convergence of two extreme cultures. On the one hand Marian witnessed in its buildings the absolute arrogance of Imperialism. Architecturally and administratively Bombay was a British city. There was an unmistakable sense of London and Brighton about it. And yet, on the other hand, in the midst of it all as they returned by way of Hornby Road, they were forced to detour around two cows which had decided to sleep in the middle of the busy thoroughfare.

To their backs was the mighty Victoria Terminus, in places still under construction. It was as magnificent and intricately decorated as a great mogul palace, and yet, in the same breath, it was uncompromisingly Anglo-Gothic in its overall architectural flavour. Meanwhile, immediately in their path stood, or rather lay, that most unique and immovable symbol of Hindu faith, the recumbent sacred cow. The contrast between old and new, of belonging and alien, could not have been more dramatic. As their carriage rounded the animals, Marian smiled at the irony. Two such potent but disparate symbols; the one massive and intimidating, a temple to the age of British might and empire, the other placid, yet patiently confident. The cows and the faith they personified were as potent and powerful an influence as any bricks and mortar over four hundred million souls, nominally constrained beneath the yoke of British Imperial rule.

Of course, her appreciation of Indian politics and culture were necessarily limited. English newspapers rarely attempted to poison the milk of Imperialism. Little was reported concerning exploitation and the ever-growing resentment towards British occupation. Marian knew therefore only snatches of the tensions beneath the surface, tensions which had been brewing for years. As far as she recollected, the mutiny of '57 was reported as an isolated incident of unrest, quickly suppressed and certainly not a symptom of any underlying cancer. Through no fault of her own, she was profoundly ignorant of the ferocity with which the rebellion was put down and, like most of her generation, lived with no conscious anxiety as to the future of British rule in India.

The necessary circumnavigating of two cows was laughed off as nothing more than the accommodation of a quaint local tradition. Nevertheless, the poignancy of the moment was not entirely lost on her and although she was unaware of it at the time, recognising the irony of the situation would come to stand her in good stead.

When they returned to the station the following afternoon, the cows were gone, having moved themselves on at their own pace and in their own time, no doubt to become a temporary traffic island in some other quarter of the city. However, a seed of doubt had been sewn, a seed which, with almost equal irony, tipped the balance in Marian's final decision as to whether she should continue forward or adopt the safer option urged by Sir Archibald and Lady Caroline.

Travelling with them in first class she could have been in Delhi in no time at all. Relatively safe from disease and danger she would have been transported from one great colonial city to another. As their house guest, her stay in India would have lacked for nothing. Sir Archibald was a man of some influence, his wife wealthy beyond the majority of her peers. As a couple, they would quickly establish themselves within the resident British community, second only in status perhaps to the Governor himself.

And indeed, until the incident with the cows, Marian was very much of a mind to take the easier option. Temporarily unnerved by the heat and somewhat intimidated by the malaise of their disembarkation at Ballard Pier, she was not much relishing the idea of another sea voyage or the uncertainty of the unknown. But the cows intrigued her. Their refusal to budge was not the puzzle, nor their rather unorthodox choice of place for a snooze. Logic would dictate that there were more suitable locations other than a major thoroughfare brimming with horses, carriages, rickshaws and a multitude of pedestrian traffic.

However, more than a little intriguing to the inexperienced eye, was contemplation of the fact that in the middle of a city where British Imperialism paid no heed to the wishes or culture of the indigenous population, that same Imperialism was compelled to negotiate its way around two indolent four-legged beasts.

Her final decision therefore not to accompany her friends to Delhi was greeted with dismay. Nevertheless, their generosity remained to the last. All said and done, Sir Archibald and Lady Caroline permitted Marian the liberty to choose for herself, their efforts to dissuade her an expression of how sorry they would be to lose a companion of whom they had become so fond.

Sir Archibald repeated his various lists of 'dos' and 'don'ts.' Lady Caroline shed tears. She also handed Marian a small package which, when unwrapped, was found to contain a finely set gold and pearl brooch taken and given from her personal jewellery collection.

Then they were gone. As the train pulled out of the station, its plume of billowing smoke engulfing the hundreds of sorry passengers whose limited resources required them to ride on the roof of the carriages, Marian remained on the platform, Captain Spencer at her side, the latter rigidly to attention until the last possible moment that the Colonel might have had sight of him.

It was then Marian realised the enormity of what she had set her mind to do. For the first time since leaving England, she was on her own. Captain Spencer's brief was to look after her for a long as she needed him. But he was a stranger. Suddenly India seemed a very big country indeed.

'Miss Chase, if you're ready I think we should return to your hotel,' the captain suggested with a hint of authority in his voice.

'Yes,' she replied, following him like a child being led by a parent.

As soon as they were out in the bright sunlight, hordes of wretched children set upon them, pleading for a few rupees. With well-practiced dexterity and as if he were scattering seed for birds, the captain dispersed them by hurling a small fist full of coins to the ground. With nervous fascination Marian's attention was drawn for a moment as she watched the urchins scratching and scrabbling in the dry earth for a share of the bounty.

Once in their carriage they were safe. However, it was another reminder of what she faced ahead. Where she was going there would be no more Taj Mahal Hotels and no longer would Sir Archibald or Lady Caroline be there to clear a path for her. As onward escort a certain Lieutenant Jerry Hugo had been assigned to her. They were scheduled to meet that evening over dinner at which time, Captain Spencer would be relieved of his 'baby-sitting' obligations and return, with some relief Marian felt sure, to the bosom of his regiment. And, no doubt, his replacement would be highly competent, selected specifically as he had been.

His appointment was just one of the many arrangements pre-planned in London. Lieutenant Jerry Hugo RA was a name writ bold on Marian's travel itinerary. She had formed a clear idea in her mind of how he would look, his age and his manner. Somewhere in one of her diary entries, written while still at sea, she speculated and committed to paper a brief summary of him, subconsciously inventing for herself the sort of man she expected.

Not one like Captain Spencer, she hoped. He was pleasant enough. He was efficient and polite. But he was no conversationalist and gave the impression of being less than inspired by the temporary assignment he had been set. He fulfilled his duties to the letter. Sir Archibald and Lady Farrer were dispatched safely and on time. Their stay in Bombay was comfortable, trouble free and taken up with an appropriate amount of sightseeing. But he smiled only rarely, if at all, and tended to speak only when spoken to. At first, Marian supposed him to be intimidated by rank. After all, Colonel Farrer was an officer of considerable reputation. He was known for his achievements as a soldier but also for his candour. And this was not to mention the strident temperament of Lady Caroline.

After a few hours in his company however, Marian believed Captain Spencer's mood was determined by boredom rather than temerity. This was the root cause of his coldness, a condition she had no choice but to endure, determining it to be acceptable for a day or so only because she was with two people whose company she enjoyed.

Lieutenant Jerry Hugo would need to be more resourceful. He and Marian were going to be together for the better part of a week before reaching Lahore. Silence inspired by apathy on his part would inflict upon her a journey too solemn to tolerate. Above all else, she prayed he was capable of good conversation. A sense of humour would be an added bonus but she was content to settle for the former as a bare necessity.

At seven o'clock precisely that evening, speculation on the subject came to an end. Lieutenant Hugo arrived for duty. Of course, he was not in any way the Lieutenant Hugo she prescribed for herself. He was a little short while the one she had imagined was tall. He was fair rather than dark, with an abundance of freckles and a youthful appearance which made it hard for her to imagine him as a capable bodyguard. And, in marked contrast, he was a chatter box.

From the moment Captain Spencer took his leave, quitting his responsibilities to Marian with politeness but an acceleration akin to hounds being set loose after the hare, Jerry Hugo rarely paused for breath. He exuded enthusiasm on every topic from the splendour of Bombay to the extraordinary beauty of the Indian countryside. As far as possible, he was self-evidently in love with India, considering himself among the most fortunate of men in having chosen a career which kept him there. Furthermore, he appeared impatient, beyond measure, for Marian to share in his good fortune.

Their meal together was like nothing Marian could recall. Many dinner parties at 32 Princes Gate were exuberant affairs. Busy chatter, laughter and lively debate were familiar to her as an aid to good appetite. But Lieutenant Jerry Hugo was quite unexpected. He monopolised the conversation, clearly assuming Marian was content to listen. With hyperbole heaped on hyperbole he extolled the myriad virtues of India, leaving her in no doubt as to the exciting adventure ahead.

Had the hotel manager thrown open the windows of the dining room to let in great gusts of fresh air from the ocean, Marian could not have felt more invigorated. Rather than being the source of annoyance she would normally have expected, her new companions' unbridled enthusiasm was surprisingly infectious. Before long, the fact that she spent the greater part of their initial dinner listening rather than talking, mattered not at all and went unnoticed.

Captain Spencer had proved himself reliable and efficient, but he was a dower man. He clearly considered himself worthy of better assignments than that of nanny to an elderly Colonel, his larger-than-life wife and some naïve young thing probably come to India like so many of her kind in a last-ditch attempt to land herself a husband.

Jerry Hugo, on the other hand, was delighted with his mission and, it must be said, though Marian was unaware of it, instantly smitten with the lady whose future safety rested in his hands.

By the time they parted company later that same evening, they were firm friends. Marian retired to her room, while Lieutenant Hugo departed for the more modest but still perfectly respectable accommodation on offer at the Bombay Club, membership of which for him was assured on the grounds that his father was steward there and had been for some fifteen years. In fact, a fact he was keen to point out to Marian more than once over their dinner together, he, the son, had been born in India. As far as Jerry was concerned India was his home. Twice only had he been to England. Once to attend the Royal Artillery Academy in Woolwich and the other on leave when he had stayed in a small village outside Royal Tunbridge Wells where his uncle farmed hops.

Such revelations encouraged Marian to feel better about her immediate prospects. Her new appointee appeared to have been selected with some thought. Were she expected to put up with Captain Spencer, the absence of Sir Archibald and Lady Caroline would have been sorely felt. As it was, she was inspired with immediate confidence by his replacement. With Jerry Hugo she was ready to embark upon the next more arduous leg of her rather tenuous pilgrimage.

Within twenty-four hours, she was back at sea again. Shortly before midday the following morning, she and Lieutenant Hugo took a carriage to Ballard Pier and boarded the MV Indus bound for Karachi. A rather lesser vessel than the great P & O steam ship which delivered her safely from London to Bombay, Marian was impressed, or to be more precise, unimpressed, by the vessels general state of decay. This was no flagship. In front of her was an old work horse, used and abused over countless years, plying the same route week in week out, year in year out with little regard to her condition or general appearance.

All about them on the quayside was chaos. Cargo of every shape and size was being carried aboard by an army of coolies and, in an area designated for passengers, there was a scene similar to that which had greeted her upon arrival from England.

And immediately, Marian felt panic returning. The crush, the noise and the heat set internal alarm bells ringing. In unison, she felt over heated, mildly nauseous and in danger possibly of feinting. Too many people, too much noise and a too, too cloying confusion of stale odours were a slice of India she found hard to bear with any equanimity.

Fortunately, Jerry did not leave her side. Whether he noticed her distress was unlikely. However, he quickly intervened to clear a path ahead. Like Moses parting the waters, but cursing profusely in Hindi and gesticulating wildly, he steered them through the mass of bodies and straight up the gang plank on to the deck of the sad old ship.

'She's not as bad as she looks,' he said, realising at once Marian's reluctance to board a vessel which seemed likely to take her and all of those on board straight to the bottom of the ocean.

'She's a bit of a chugger, the old girl, but she'll get us there, don't you worry. And I've made sure we get a couple of half way decent cabins. Most of these poor creatures,' he said waving his hand in the general direction of the mass of human flotsam through which they had just come, 'will be sleeping on deck for four nights. I don't know about you, but I wouldn't fancy that a bit.'

'No,' Marian replied her tongue too tied to add more.

Eventually, with the aid of a young boy sporting what was once a white steward's jacket, three sizes too large and three years at least past its last scheduled wash, they found their adjoining cabins. Not long after by some miracle of planning which Marian suspected was in fact pure chance, their cases also arrived.

Somehow and with a steely determination not to let them out of her sight again, Marian found space in and around her cabin for the six large cases and one small valise she had brought with her from England. Meanwhile her ship mate made do with a single, albeit bulging, suit case, clear evidence Marian guessed that he was not expecting their journey to be punctuated by too many formal engagements.

When finally, the ship departed, some two hours after boarding, she summoned up enough courage to leave the seclusion of her ice cooled cabin for the heat and crush of what was rather laughingly referred to as the promenade deck. With Jerry Hugo firmly at her side to ward off any uninvited attention, she watched nervously as the ship slipped its moorings, the fine panorama of modern Bombay receding ever further into the distance, the university clock tower rising tall and proud like a lighthouse, its Gothic structure so poignant and distinct a symbol of British rule.

Unfortunately, the comparatively tranquil, even romantic image of their departure was soon shattered. Once out at sea, the old ship set to rolling and pitching like a cork. The weather was fine, a light breeze all there was to disturb the water. Yet the MV Indus behaved as if she were navigating her way through a force ten in the English Channel. Before long the bulwarks were lined with people unable to control the contents of their stomachs and before too long, Marian craved the luxury and stillness of the hotel she had so recently quit.

By contrast and somewhat to her annoyance, Jerry seemed to revel in the whole affair. For him, a sea voyage aboard the MV Indus epitomised so much of what he loved about India. The chaos, the general shabbiness and the sound of several hundred seasick natives loudly committing their souls to a variety of Gods, was precisely the sort of thing which persuaded him to refuse 'home leave.'

He never met Captain William Radford. He could neither share Marian's grief at his passing nor fully understand her motives for wanting so badly to trace his footsteps. He was, however, refreshingly open in his admiration of her having set out upon such a journey of discovery. Quite sensibly, he preached caution in certain matters and encouraged her to stay close by him at all times. For the rest, he promised her spectacular scenery and a country rich in culture. It simply did not cross his mind to join the ranks of doubters who believed Marian would have been best served by remaining in London. Inwardly he admired her courage. Outwardly he promised her the journey of a life time, 'just as soon as we get off this old tub' as he put it, making what Marian felt was perhaps a rather rash assumption that they would.

And there were numerous times during their four-day voyage she had her doubts. Clear of Bombay harbour and with Elephanta Island at their stern, the ship ventured into open waters, traversing the Gulf of Cambay. For the remainder of the time, they hugged the coast as best they could. But throughout, there was no let-up in their unpleasant and often violent forward momentum. Sleep was virtually impossible and the mere thought of food had Marian filled with the undeniable urge to join the ranks of fellow passengers already hard up against the bulwarks, their necks craned seawards.

As luck would have it, in spite of every adverse condition of both ship and weather, she managed to maintain her dignity. Keeping to her cabin served as the best option. Cooler and quieter than elsewhere on board, she outwitted the best, or worst, efforts of the ship to render her incapable. Jerry made regular visits to check on her and their increasingly shabby cabin boy pressed her to take occasional sustenance. The former irritated her with his cheery enjoyment of the whole unruly voyage, insisting as he was wont to do, on relating to her some of the sights she was missing by staying below. The latter, less annoying but no less persistent, she received with the detached superiority expected of her. However, she would have parted with any number of precious jewels to find herself for an hour or two on flat, dry land.

Karachi could not and did not come soon enough. Land never seemed so dear to her as the moment she stepped ashore again. If the previous four days and nights were a sample of what was to come, she regretted having spurned Lady Caroline's urgent pleas to travel with them to Delhi. For the majority of the time as she lay in her bunk, all she could focus on was her family and 32 Princes Gate.

She imagined her father riding alone in Hyde Park. She saw her mother, forever busy, forever in the process of organising the next social function or clearing the aftermath of the previous one. She envied Margaret the tranquillity of weekly bible classes and tried to draw for herself a mental picture of what life was like for Katie among the ancient streets of Sienna. As a last resort, she imagined herself not on the high seas aboard a ship the creaks and groans of which spoke of terminal decay, but in her bedroom at Adelaide Drive, the ocean noises those of waves falling benignly on the Brighton shore, not of breakers crashing against the side of the hull.

Her diary entry to cover the leg of her journey from Bombay to Karachi was brief and written several days after the event, the mere thought of putting pen to paper while at sea too much for her. In it, she spoke only of a helpless physical condition worsening with each day and the pledge not to repeat the exercise. When the time came to make the return trip to Bombay it would certainly not be courtesy of the MV Indus or any of her sister ships. Her dear William contracted cholera on board just such a ship, while completing precisely the same voyage.

As she went ashore with Jerry warding off the worst of unwanted attentions, she felt weak, sick and quite overawed by the poignant sadness of the moment. William's life ended in Karachi. His sickness, deeper and more desperate than anything she experienced over the previous four days and nights, overcame him. There was no way she could or would want to replicate the suffering he experienced.

As Jerry carved a swathe through a new crowd, his preoccupation granted Marian enough privacy for a few tears, overcome as she was by the emotion of the moment. Shielded from the curious gaze of onlookers behind the protective veil covering her face, she could not deny a public display of the grief she had kept hidden so effectively for months. Nor did she wish to, struck as deeply as she was by the pitiful nature of her fiancé's death.

Had William died a warrior, gone out in a blaze of glory while in defence of empire some small grain of good might have come from it. Left with memories of pride in his achievements and personal sacrifice, Marian might just have found some solace. But the demeaning and useless nature of his passing bequeathed her nothing.

Karachi was no Bombay, no splendid emblem to the majesty of empire. It was a dreary and dirty place. The northern most port to the west of the Indian continent, it bragged no great hotels or public buildings and hosted no royal visits. As the last resting place for her beloved William, it seemed a grey and heartless city. Like Sodom or Gomora, it gave the appearance of being beyond redemption. Or at least so it appeared to Marian's biased eyes, doomed as it was to eternal damnation for the part it played in depriving her of the happiness she was due as a wife.

One night only would she tolerate the army bungalow made ready for them a short carriage ride from All Saints Church. She would agree to no longer. Jerry pressed her to stay for three or four days. He felt she needed to build up enough strength for the onward journey. But she was adamant. Karachi was a hateful, ugly place. Of that she was certain. No amount of evidence to the contrary would sway her from that conviction.

Away from the port, attempts had been made and were continuing to construct a more modern, Anglo-Saxon style to the city. There were a variety of pseudo-Gothic churches, a cluster of administrative buildings mimicking in a lesser way the grandeur of British presence, but for all that it was a place readily forgotten.

Inside All Saints Church, Marian was taken to see a newly erected brass plaque. On it were recorded the date and circumstances of the deaths of officers and enlisted men as the result of a cholera epidemic contracted aboard the MV Cambay in the summer of 1884. There for the gaze of any passing eyes, in order of rank first and then alphabetically were the names of all those who had succumbed, including that of Captain William Stephen Radford.

Outside in the bleaching sun stood a substantial marble statue of Queen Victoria, high on a carved granite plinth. With pride and majesty, she surveyed the city with the self-satisfaction of any conqueror over the conquered. But there was no pride or majesty in what Marian saw. A modest brass plaque boasting a pathetic list of names etched deep into its surface, the only epitaph to a body of men whose deaths did precious little to secure either the empire or their places within it.

At home in England, she had fervently battled to be permitted the trip to India. Precisely to be in Karachi and to see for herself that plaque was why she had travelled all those thousands of nautical miles. Few women of her age ventured abroad. Fewer still went alone and of those few, only a handful were intrepid or perhaps rash enough to set their sights as high as she had done. The Indian subcontinent was a long way from home. As she stared at the plaque fixed to the inner wall of the church, the distance she had covered opened up like a yawning chasm.

She wanted to reach out for her father's hand or cry on her mother's shoulder as she had done when she was a child, but there was no one there. Jerry stood quietly, a pace or two from her. However, he did not intervene. His only brief was to act as custodian. That Marian was on a personal and tragic pilgrimage was only just becoming clear to him. That his future career with the regiment

121

and the British army depended upon a successful outcome to his assignment had already been made clear.

Marian was not at all what he expected. Prettier by far and clearly a young woman of considerable determination, as she stood in the gloom of the church, vulnerable and sadder than any person he had witnessed before in his short life, he doubted her ability or resolve to continue.

At sea, her feminine physical frailty was obvious. She was unused to the harshness of life in India. As well as from the heat, she reeled from the people, the sights and the smells. But he anticipated no less. While staying at the Taj Mahal Hotel she was fine. Protected and confined, with 'India real' at arm's length, she coped well. However, away from conventional comforts he was all too aware of just how difficult their proposed journey ahead would be. Privately, he rather hoped that her lonely vigil in Karachi would put an end to any idea of going further.

Therefore, from a discreet distance he looked on. He found himself torn between the desire to know her better and an equally determined belief that the best service he could perform was to return with her to Bombay. There they could wait together until the first passage home to England became available. At that moment, she was a pitiful sight. Weakened by four days at sea and reduced to tears by the sight of her 'would be' husband's name on an insignificant brass plaque, Jerry was in little doubt they should retreat rather than advance and, eventually, he felt compelled to say so.

As their carriage drove them back across the more pleasant quarter of Karachi to the modest army bungalow at their disposal, he ventured to suggest returning the way they had come. Not knowing Marian well, indeed barely at all, and not privy to the private pledge she had made to herself upon making landfall, he was unaware of the wasted breath involved in voicing his thoughts in such a way.

Marian was a woman and therefore, by definition, of the weaker sex. She was physically less able. She suffered from sea sickness and as a consequence was temporarily incapacitated. However, on an intellectual level, she had been educated to believe herself the equal of any man. Frail though her body was, her mind shone like the brightest of lights and her determination to succeed in what she had set her heart and mind to, or indeed at whatever task she set herself, was that of an ox. In this case, the load she carried was a heavy one, the road ahead rugged and filled with obstacles, but no amount of sympathetic persuasion was going to alter her itinerary.

Fortunately, she quite liked Jerry. What she had seen and heard of him during the short period of their acquaintance impressed her. There were times she would have preferred a little less conversation, particularly during those periods when his enthusiasm denied her a two-way dialogue. However, he was amicable, attentive and clearly demonstrated a sincere desire to place her safety and comfort ahead of his own.

But in one matter he needed to be enlightened. By assumption rather than hard fact, she guessed his experience of women was limited and probably to a single type. From the outset, it was important for him to learn just how severe a mistake it would be to judge her by those few examples of the opposite sex he already knew.

On returning to the bungalow, they retired to separate rooms, she to rest, he to ponder the forthright notification he received that there would be no turning back. His orders were clear and would remain unaltered. Any doubts he harboured as to Marian's fitness to continue were set straight. She had not come half way across the world to turn for home at the first sign of difficulty. Her sea sickness was a temporary condition, rendered unimportant the moment they set foot again on dry land. Any feelings of anxiety she had were hers to overcome and overcome them she would.

It was a brief lecture, no more than a few sentences and spoken calmly as they sat next to each other in the rather antiquated open carriage available to them as transport. It was enough, however, and Jerry was left in no doubt as to how he should proceed. He was also left curiously impressed. English women generally were scarce in the remoter corners of India. He had forgotten much of what their company offered a man of his age. And yet, search his memory as much as he did, he could not recall having come across a woman quite like Marian.

In every respect, she was a member of the female sex. She dressed, walked and talked like any other of her gender. That she was perhaps prettier than most of those with whom he had come into contact was to place her at the head of a comparatively short list. There was no London season in colonial India. In his life, he had attended only a few social gatherings playing host to more than a dozen women and of those the majority were either married or matronly. But some instinct told him Marian Chase was the exception to the rule. The tone in her voice possessed a certain tenacity quite unlike anything he recognised. Her vocabulary exceeded his own and that she was well read seeped out by bits and drabs whenever they spoke. Where he knew India at first hand, understanding it, the people, customs and country, she knew some of its history.

Self-evidently, she had taken time to make a study of it prior to leaving England. She could relate details of the '57 mutiny and the Sind campaigns of General Charles Napier. More impressive still was her desire to learn and understand the politics at work within so vast and complex a human gig saw. Of course, she professed considerable ignorance of such matters, but Jerry was not deceived.

When they left Karachi the following morning, his confidence in their mission was renewed. He would make no further attempt to change her mind. Their destination was Landi Kotal. Positioned as it was, hard up against the border with Afghanistan, there was no more desolate or remote a military outpost in India, far from anything one might reasonably think of as civilisation. Captain William Radford was to have reported there for duty but never made it. Clearly, Marian was set on reporting for duty on his behalf, a strange and inexplicable obligation only she fully understood. Jerry certainly failed to solicit from her a suitable explanation. However, he vowed his allegiance to her cause, satisfying himself that the task she had set was no whim.

Some one hundred miles to the north east of Karachi lay the city of Hyderabad, a journey by train lasting approximately four hours. For much of the way, running parallel to the mighty river Indus, the scenery was impressive, the air temperature relatively cool and the wooden first-class carriage in which they were placed a fraction less uncomfortable than those further back. Second and third class were little more than glorified cattle trucks and, in some cases, not as much as that. Beneath Marian's seat however, there was a freshly filled ice box to counteract the worst of the heat and with several stops for the engine to replenish its water supplies, she had the opportunity to stretch her legs. Had she continued to shows signs of distress she and Jerry could have thought again. However, she did not and as the train proceeded, so her health and countenance slowly improved.

Beyond Hyderabad was a further six hundred miles by rail to Lahore. The more northerly their direction, the more inhospitable and thus potentially dangerous the journey became. There were fewer opportunities to leave the train, less comfort and the temperature soared to levels Jerry guessed Marian had not experienced before.

Years later, while flipping through the pages of her diaries, Marian came across the entry which recorded her state of mind the evening before leaving Karachi. It was a water shed moment. On the flip of a coin her decision to proceed or go back could have gone either way. By no means fully recovered from her days and nights aboard the MV Indus and full of doubts, her head told her to go no further while her heart urged her forward.

It was all written down. Every emotion was analysed, every physical ailment catalogued. Against the cause were all the same common-sense arguments begun in London by her father and echoed by Sir Archibald and Lady Caroline Farrer. For the motion, was the absolute yet inexplicable conviction that this was something she must do. If she turned back, she would regret it for the rest of her life. She had no idea why. She could not explain it, even to herself. The journey promised to test her physically and emotionally, perhaps up to and beyond endurance. Anxiety and panic attached themselves to her like limpets, vile and draining, her energy seeping like water from a dripping tap.

In the end a single and simple notion tipped the balance. No grand and honourable gesture made her go on. No vain attempt to impress Jerry Hugo or to convince him of her metal persuaded her to choose north over south. In the final sentence of several pages the 'fors' outweighed the 'againsts' on the simple basis that given a choice between train or ship as her next means of getting from one place to another, be it further away from or closer to home, she opted for the former.

In the light of documentary evidence, that night in Karachi was a defining moment. Her decision to proceed catapulted her into a life she never envisaged during her growing up at 32 Princes Gate. That it came down to a preference of transport between train or ship would one day give her cause to smile, though on the morning she and her companion boarded the train, she remembered well that smiling was the last thing on her mind.

They arrived in Lahore five days later. From Hyderabad, on an ever Northward track they passed through Sukkur, Bahawalpur, Multan and Sahiwal as well as a hundred smaller towns and villages. From the windows of the carriage, India opened up to Marian a world as exciting as it was different. With Jerry and his infectious enthusiasm, she sat for hours in wide-eyed amazement, the beauty and scale of it quite overwhelming.

From Karachi to Hyderabad, the heat affected her badly. She felt weak and lethargic, too leaden to move, too burdened to bother with the view. She was still suffering from the effects of her sea voyage and the high collars and thick layers of skirts engulfed her like shrouds, restricting her every movement, preventing her from breathing.

In Hyderabad, however, she effected a transformation, shedding all but essential layers and releasing many of the buttons and stays instrumental to her discomfort. At first, she was vaguely suspicious of the young lieutenant for proposing such an idea. Although appearing no more or less covered than at the outset of the garment shedding exercise, she experienced a certain embarrassment for the first hour or so, conscious of his every glance in her direction.

But the relief she gained soon overcame her maidenly modesty. Though she was unaware of any such thing at the time, this act was the first tentative step along a path of integration destined to have her one day labelled by some as Bohemian and unfit for 'polite' society.

A few miles beyond Hyderabad, however, she was aware only of how much more comfortable she felt and how much more willing she was to embrace the journey ahead. That the discarding of a few underskirts made her any less inhibited than she was or should have been, escaped her consideration. She felt released as if from a straitjacket, a sensation more wonderful than she was at liberty to express to Jerry Hugo and, thankfully, less of an encouragement to his male ego than she might have imagined. Indeed, he appeared unmoved by occasional glimpses of her ankles or the ivory hue of her neck.

Sitting as they did at times opposite and at others side by side, he ventured to explain every twist in the track, every variety of tree, every crop in a field, every action of native workers as they toiled within sight of the train as it trudged past, its arrival and departure apparently an event of singular disinterest. With the knowledge of a man who knew the country well and a deep affection exposed only rarely to strangers, he read every changing panorama to her as if from the pages of a book.

Occasionally they passed within sight of the river. At Bahawalpur, they crossed over a great iron bridge. For the most part, however, the land either side of them was flat. For eyes more accustomed to the lush greenery and rolling downs of southern England, it appeared at first dry and unforgiving, the heat making toil in the fields a futile labour. Gradually, however, as Marian's eyes adjusted to the novelty of the view and Jerry filled her with his own encyclopaedic wisdom, she saw not one featureless landscape but a rich tapestry, not a monotone canvas but a kaleidoscope of shapes and colours.

So transformed was she, she longed to admit her growing joy in having made the decision to head north. The train rattled incessantly, the seats were hard, the facilities for personal hygiene basic to say the least. Quinine taken five times a day irritated the nauseous sensations she hoped she had left behind when disembarking from the MV Indus and sleep came more in the form of involuntary naps than deep slumber. But by the time they arrived in Lahore, she felt herself changed and enriched by the experience.

In Jerry Hugo she had discovered more than a competent guardian. Officer and gentleman he was, but beyond that she sensed friendship. He was attentive but not cloying. He approached his responsibilities towards her seriously, but he was possessed of a sense of humour and zest for life which made their time together in such close confinement a pleasure rather than a burden. He was also intelligent enough and gifted with enough wit to act as a worthy adversary to the pleasure she took in verbal sparring. And he was boyishly good looking, with a physique not unlike many of the rowers she recalled at Henley.

Strangely, however, she did not find him attractive in the same way she did sometimes when in the company of other men and had certainly done when she was close to William. And for that, she was grateful. She liked him enormously and welcomed the further development of their friendship with every mile they travelled in a northerly direction. But she wanted nothing else from him and sincerely hoped he would not expect more from her.

In short, she could not have asked for a more compatible male companion. Lady Caroline was generous and open hearted, but she was a woman and could be exceedingly irritating if she so wished. Her arrogant assumptions, her half knowledge on almost every topic and her absolute lack of sympathy for those worse off than herself, drove Marian at times to the point of distraction, persuading her to seek out private corners of the ship where she could fume in peace.

With Jerry she felt no such needs. Even confined together as they were in such a small space, she sought no escape from him. His attentions were welcome and tailored to her needs. His conversation was invigorating and his concern for her welfare weighted perfectly. He did not fuss over her but by the same token he was at her side to fulfil her every need. Had their arrival in Lahore implied an imminent separation, she would have been sorely disappointed. As it was his orders were to accompany her all the way to Landi Kotal, a further journey of some three hundred and fifty miles, a journey more arduous and more dangerous than anything yet undertaken. Most of those involved in arranging her itinerary doubted she would attempt it. The exception was Jerry Hugo who, by the time they arrived in Lahore was no longer in any doubt as to her extraordinary resolve.

Chapter Nine

Unlike Karachi, the city at the end of their five-day train journey was no dreary commercial shipping port. Lahore boasted a proud, if sometimes violent, history.

When Marian arrived during the second week of September 1885, it was the seat of British government for the Punjab. Before that and throughout the seventeenth and eighteenth centuries, it had been the favoured city of residence for successive powerful Moghuls. As a result, it had broad avenues and a predominance of fine Moslem architecture, including the magnificent 'Golden' Mosque and uniquely beautiful Shalimar gardens, laid out some two centuries earlier by the great Shah Jahan himself. A later addition but standing proud over the city was the fort, its soaring, red sandstone walls shining flame red with each sunset.

And under the Victorians, new buildings had been added year on year, each challenging for its rightful place in an ever-growing list of architectural superlatives. Among others, the university lecture hall stood as an emblem to the civilising influence of benign British occupation. All in their own ways served to reflect the expanding strategic importance of this particular city and the might of empire.

Sadly, Marian's first impression of it was marred by fatigue. After five long days and nights of being jostled and buffeted about on the train from Karachi, with little rest, she and Jerry were exhausted; not spent physically and emotionally as she had been when disembarking after the four-day sea voyage from Bombay, but exhausted nevertheless.

This time it was simple fatigue, the sort that as they left the station in a covered carriage, their luggage following behind on an ox cart, had Marian longing for a soft bed and warm bath. A modestly appointed army bungalow was what she expected and a modestly appointed army bungalow was what they got. But on this occasion, there was something else. She and Jerry also received an invitation for dinner.

General Leonard. M. Leighton, Commander of British Forces in the Punjab, sometime writer of military history and infamous womaniser, was more than a little curious to meet Miss Marian Chase. For months, letters had crossed his desk regarding this lone female traveller. For reasons which both amused and irritated, much of his busy schedule had been interrupted in the planning of a smooth passage for her to Lahore and beyond. Time, men and resources had been commandeered for the explicit purpose of satisfying some rather obscure and, to his mind, pointless meander through a particularly dangerous part of India.

He neither approved of the venture nor set about the task of securing a satisfactory conclusion to it with any enthusiasm. To his way of thinking, Miss Marian Chase was likely as not the same as all the others of her ilk; bent on a fool's errand. The army in general, but more significantly, he in particular, had better things to do than pander to the whims of a spoilt middle-class girl from London.

However, in this instance, his curiosity was aroused. Irritant though she was to his routine, he was mildly intrigued, interested to meet a young woman whose mission appeared, on the surface at least, untypical of the majority. She was certainly quite the opposite of his own wife. Mrs Leighton loathed India, the army and, to a lesser extent her husband. Consequently, she was passionate in her frequently expressed desire to be back in Bournemouth.

Bigotry to the fore, the General imagined Marian as a plain, young woman of little character, another candidate from the 'fishing fleet,' out from England trawling for a husband and, as likely as not, bound inevitably for the return trip as one of the 'empties.' So persistent was her father, however, that no expense be spared to ensure a successful outcome to his daughters stay on the Indian subcontinent, the General could not help but conclude Marian to be either the ugliest of young women and therefore in need of extra effort, or the most inconsequential; perhaps even, both. That she was travelling alone aside from a single male escort was a novelty and it was this fact which encouraged him to extend an invitation for dinner.

He had also received a telegraphed communication from Lieutenant Colonel Sir Archibald Farrer, newly arrived in Delhi, indicating that he would look upon it as something of a personal favour if the General were to offer Miss Chase whatever assistance he could while she was travelling within his jurisdiction. In itself, this was not unusual. Many such messages batted the length and breadth of India, from one ranking officer to another, requesting a favour in respect of some relative or friend. India, after all, was a vast country. Distances were great and conditions could be harsh. Favours were a bankable form of currency. Furthermore, the General was well aware of the Farrers' distinguished military lineage stretching back as it did for three generations.

After all, was this Lieutenant Colonel Farrer not one and the same as a young Captain Farrer known to have marched with the forces of Sir Colin Campbell when he relieved the beleaguered inhabitants of Lucknow in the autumn of 1857. And was this not the same Captain Farrer who was recommended for the Victoria Cross during that campaign.

More to the point, perhaps, the General was acquainted well enough with the popular press to have read many times of the fortune Colonel Farrer came into the day he married the beautiful and celebrated Caroline Covington. Thus, on this occasion, however inconvenient, a favour towards the newly arrived Miss Marian Chase was as nothing to the rewards it might reap at a later date.

For her part, Marian could have done without the irksome duty of dinner with a General she had not met. However, good manners obliged her to comply. Duly attired, therefore, with Jerry at her side, she reported for dinner that evening. And it has to be said, though weary from the long train journey and just a little put out at being summoned quite so soon after her arrival, she acquitted herself well.

Jerry was even less prepared to attend so formal an occasion. At short notice, he managed to borrow a full mess kit. The regimental insignia was not his own but at least, it fitted reasonably well. However, his modest efforts paled beside the sight of Marian upon announcing she was 'as ready as she was ever going to be.'

In an evening gown she was quite simply the most dazzling woman he had ever seen and he absolutely could not resist telling her so. She thanked him of course with necessary modesty, but was somewhat embarrassed by his candour. Inside, she felt no such thing. Her hair was a travesty and the dress she had selected weighed heavy on her shoulders. Furthermore, she was in no frame of mind for polite conversation, particularly with people she did not know.

Jerry however, was undeterred. His first compliment, accepted with good grace, was followed by a procession of others. For his endeavours, he received courteous 'thank you's' but no more. If his words were the prologue toward the laying of foundations as suitor, they were in vain.

Marian was flattered but unimpressed. In the best of lights and with several hours of preparation she knew herself to be reasonably pleasing. In a crowded ballroom of moths, she was never the butterfly. At best, she accepted that to some men she might be thought attractive. But since she was not at her best, only through a pair of heavily rose tinted spectacles could she be mistaken for a beauty.

Throughout their short carriage ride, however, on a night when the evening air was filled with the lazy scent of hibiscus and honeysuckle grew wild on either side of the broad avenue, she was conscious of Jerry's eyes fixed upon her in admiration. Accordingly, she felt considerable discomfort. A small part of her enjoyed the attention. In other, very different circumstances, she might even have felt tempted to tease him a little, encourage praise from his lips. Instead, on this night, she found his over blown remonstrations rather trying. He was a thoroughly pleasant travelling companion. Indeed, in the week or so they had been together, she had grown to like him enormously. His conversation was entertaining, his sense of humour a blessing during their long journey and his love for India infectious. But she had no desire whatsoever to encourage or invite his or anyone else's amorous advances.

In spite of possible assumptions to the contrary, she was not in India to secure for herself a husband. Her purpose was altogether more sober. Besides which, though she had not the heart to tell him, were she indeed on such a quest, he would not foot the bill. Jerry had proven himself kind and attentive and, quite readily, Marian felt a generous friendship developing between them. In time she could even imagine herself looking upon him with sisterly affection; but never passion. Only once during the course of her short adult life had she met a man whose close proximity caused her heart to race. Only once was there a man who stirred in her desires which years of bible class studies decreed morally unhealthy. Now that man was dead. As if by way of dreadful punishment for crimes committed or yet to come, he had been snatched from her. She doubted there would ever be another man capable of igniting such fires within her. Stronger than doubt however, was the conviction that Jerry Hugo could not be the one.

In his favour, however, was that he bore no resemblance at all to General Leonard Leighton. Before Marian knew where she was the carriage pulled up outside the home of their host. A whitewashed Palladian style mansion set in the midst of a tropical paradise, with covered loggias and formal walk ways, for many years it had been the official residence of successive Governors. Outgrown by the demands of bureaucracy it found its way into the hands of the Indian army and subsequently was allocated for use as home to the Regional Commander in Chief. Sadly, such grandeur only served to inflate the General's already over-inflated ego.

From the moment of their introduction, Marian found him a remarkably unpleasant individual, her opinion of him worsening by degrees as the evening progressed. By contrast, the hapless and ineffectual Mrs Leighton was a well-meaning woman. She extended a warm welcome toward her guests and, on the rare occasions she was permitted to speak, engaged both of them in amicable conversation.

By Marian's estimation, in her late fifties or possibly early sixties, Mrs Leighton showed all the signs of once having been a woman of considerable beauty. She was also clearly well-educated and gifted with a politeness of manner utterly absent in her husband.

He was a bull of a man, apparently imagining himself lord over all he surveyed. He spoke to his wife in the same tone as he addressed the servants and patronised Jerry in a quite unforgivable manner, throughout the evening emphasising both the gulf in their rank and his clear contempt for any officer below that of Major.

Quietly, Marian fumed. Oft times she was desperate to speak out in Jerry's defence. She wanted to educate the General as to his gallantry in performing for her the services he had, his competence, his wit and his uncompromising friendship. However, she was thwarted at every turn. Any such attempts were dismissed out of hand almost before they were begun. Instead, and as astounding as it seemed, throughout the evening she was compelled to parry the General's unwanted advances.

Barely were she and Jerry through the front door of his home than they began. Unhindered by anything as trivial as the presence of his wife and oblivious to the growing agitation of a mere lieutenant, he waded in with the subtlety of a runaway train.

Marian was fresh meat, a young woman recently out from England, still with the smell of dew on her skin, untainted and untanned by the cruel Asian sun. Apparently, she was ripe as a new target for conquest, a trophy as yet untarnished by the handling of prior contestants.

That he should 'go after her' in the manner he did was inexcusable. Moreover, that he should consider himself free to proceed in so direct and overt a manner with his wife in the same room so shocked Marian as to render her speechless. Several times in past years she had found cause to divert unwanted advances. Usually, they were from young men of her own age. To one, they were merely clumsy examples of adolescent infatuation, easily snuffed out by a few well-chosen words. Once, an acquaintance of her father became a little out of hand during a summer garden party. However, his behaviour, partly drink induced, was readily brought to nothing with a few stern glances from his wife.

This though was a novel and altogether more alarming experience. It was one which had Marian torn between outrage and fear. Self-evidently, poor Mrs Leighton was quite past the days of having any control over her husband at all. She was afraid of him. Remaining silent throughout save for the odd muted effort to distract her husband from his intent, she permitted his insulting behaviour to proceed not because she was impervious to it, but because she was years late in being able to prevent it. Marian could only wonder at the scale of misery inflicted which could result in a woman of Mrs Leighton's intellect becoming so utterly bereft of self-respect. The fear in Mrs Leighton's eyes was crystal, the capitulation in her voice when she addressed her husband as resonant as a bell.

Not once in any true sense of the word did she attempt to intervene to prevent her husband's lewd behaviour. Instead, she left the luckless Marian to fend for herself, hoping against hope that perhaps Jerry might summon up the courage to affect some sort of a rescue. That he did not, however, was to be anticipated and excusable. Short of openly challenging the General's unforgivable display of lechery, there was little he could do. Out ranked, any rebuke from his lips would have been futile and reaped its own dire consequences. In truth, he was powerless to act. Inside he seethed. Resentment and anger willed him to emit some heroic outburst. But he was struck dumb in the certain knowledge that should he intervene, the evening would end in disaster.

And the General behaved as he did because he was aware of the weak battalions assembled against him. Mrs Leighton possessed no armoury. She had been relieved of her weaponry years before. Since that time, she had remained helpless in the face of his abuse. Jerry was proud and gutsy but surrounded on all sides by superior forces. Any manoeuvre from him would have been no more than a short-lived distraction.

Tired and unskilled as she was in the rules of engagement, Marian was easy prey. The 'dinner' therefore was an ugly farce. Little of the food was eaten by anyone other than the General who clearly fought better on a full stomach. While his wife, Marian and Jerry toyed with the contents of their plates, their individual attentions drawn to quite separate solutions for the unfolding crisis, he gorged himself, stocking up his bulk as if for a long siege.

That the evening did not end in the disaster Jerry felt rapidly coming upon them was by coincidence rather than design. There were moments when Marian feared the General would claim his prize, ravaging her there and then in front of her helpless allies like some marauding Viking. So overtly expressed were his attentions, she was in no doubt at all of his desires. She was stunned with disbelief at the thought of it. However, she had no choice but to resist as best she could for as long as she was able. In spite of his wife, Jerry Hugo or the implied responsibilities of his rank, he meant to have her. He illustrated his lust shamefully and made it abundantly clear he intended having that lust satisfied. It was an incredible situation made no less frightening by Marian's oft-repeated but silent mantra that such things simply did not happen in polite society.

When rescue came, it was in the form of an urgent communication delivered to the house by a rather out of breath young captain who, from the general state of his clothing, had been galloping at speed for some time. By chance, his arrival coincided with the appearance of a large decanter of port which Marian assumed the General intended consuming by way of further fortifying his brazen behaviour.

However, somewhere in the northern quarter of the city, two Sikhs had been set upon and beaten to death by an enraged mob of Moslems. The ensuing chaos of retaliation and counter retaliation threatened to become a full-scale riot. Worse still, the small contingent of troops sent to quell the situation were fast becoming overwhelmed. They were coming under attack from both sides in an ever more vicious confrontation. The situation was ugly and growing uglier by the moment. Consequently, the Major in command was looking for the intervention of a more senior officer and a subsequently increased force. Fortunately for Marian, just in time, he had dispatched his captain to distract the General from the increasingly aggressive campaign he was embarked upon within the walls of his own home.

With no alternative but with loudly voiced annoyance, he stormed from the soiree, unsympathetic to the captain's graphic tales of natives bent on slaughter in the streets a few miles off.

'Wretched bloody natives,' was the only decipherable phrase uttered as he strode from the room, further expletives no more than a muffled blur.

For a few minutes those remaining in the dining room were silent. Marian made eye contact with Jerry, while Mrs Leighton fidgeted and focussed her attention at random about the room, clearly struggling for the right words to compensate for the extraordinary behaviour of her husband.

Eventually she ventured an 'I am most terribly sorry my dear,' followed by what was clearly a well-rehearsed and over used catalogue of excuses. That she was mortified by the whole affair went without saying. As it happened, Marian was more relieved by the General's departure than distraught at what had taken place immediately prior to it. While she shuddered to think just how far beyond the pale his actions might have taken him had he not been diverted, concern for Mrs Leighton preoccupied her thoughts.

'Please,' she said in a tone softened by compassion, 'there is no need to apologise. I'm sure your husband meant no harm.'

Of course he had 'meant harm.' That was precisely what he had meant and both women knew it. His designs on her were as blatant as they were inexcusable, designs not of a gentleman but of a cowardly, crude man. He insulted his wife and guests in a manner for which there could be no satisfactory recompense and it was with considerable relief that their carriage was ordered to the front door barely ten minutes after the General himself quit the dining room.

Once returned to her temporary home, Marian began to feel the full effects of the experience. Shock in the form of uncontrollable shaking and fierce anger stayed with her until the advent of fitful sleep. Not in her worst nightmares had she anticipated such a threat to her person and most certainly not from such a source. Every so often throughout the night, she was woken from sleep by nightmares of marauding natives bent on doing her ill, of being abducted and being carried off. But in all such encounters, she was rescued by men in uniform, men of gallantry and 'daring do.' Never were the roles reversed. But for the presence of witnesses, the looks on their faces evidence of their part in the macabre event, she might have believed herself to have imagined the whole sorry thing.

The following morning however, she awoke to no lasting after effects. She was angry and incredulous but otherwise unscathed. Then, shortly after ten o'clock, she received a letter from Mrs Leighton. It arrived by courier, was personally written and contained within a securely sealed envelope.

'My dear Miss Chase' it began.

As you can imagine, it is with considerable difficulty I write this letter. In the affairs of last night, I am guilty of compliance to a degree for which I bear a heavy burden of shame and responsibility. I cannot apologise adequately for the behaviour of my husband because anything I say would be scant compensation for treatment of so foul a nature. I can only hope you will find it in your heart to understand and, in time, forgive my inaction. That I should have prevented such embarrassment and injury to yourself goes without saying. I have no excuse save the weakness of my sex and the weariness of years spent with a man so morally bereft.

If there is any way at all I can redeem myself in your eyes I would welcome the opportunity. I have lived in India for more than a quarter of a century. During that time, I have met and befriended a significant number of influential people. Should you require at any time an introduction or assistance I would deem it a privilege and indication of your forgiveness if you would call upon me.

I remain your humble 'would be' friend.

Clara Leighton (Mrs)

It was a brief note, but Marian read it several times. Then she folded it carefully, placed it back in the envelope and secreted it away deep inside the 'portmanteau' she carried with her at all times. There might come a day, she thought, when she would have cause to bring it out again, a day or a time when she would be able to hold the writer to her word. The behaviour of General Leighton could be forgiven but would never be forgotten. He was a disgrace to his uniform, a man for whom the word 'gentleman' obviously stood for naught. No actual physical harm had been done but Marian felt tainted by the experience of that evening. Newly arrived in India, she should have been welcomed. Instead, she was openly insulted.

Her first instinct was to write to Sir Archibald Farrer. So enraged was she and, initially at least, so bent on retribution, she wanted to send a stinging account of events to the man who had in part at least initiated the introduction. However, after some consideration, she determined it would serve no purpose other than to embarrass Sir Archibald and his wife for having erred so greatly in their recommendation. And she had no wish to do that. Quite obviously they knew nothing of the General's disgraceful character. Had they done so, they would surely not have steered her into his path.

After some thought therefore, Marian decided to keep the sorry events of that evening to herself, insisting Jerry do the same in spite of his calls for public exposure of the General's actions. Public humiliation was, he declared, the least the General deserved and although Marian was inclined to agree, she remained firm to her call for silence on the matter. After all, as cruel an injustice as it was, when all was said and done, Jerry was a lowly lieutenant and she a mere woman, newly arrived from England with few allies. Should the matter be made public, it would be their word against that of a man whose reputation and rank were well established. The General was a respected figure within the resident British contingent of Lahore. Marian might be taken for a young woman perhaps come to India precisely to create mischief.

She concluded therefore that a public outcry would very probably see her cast as the villain of the piece and condemn Jerry to a life time in the ranks. She was not prepared to chance either. Her mission in India had yet to be completed. She was half way to her goal and still fit. Her pride was dented. She had been insulted in a manner and by the stature of man she would not have expected. Nevertheless, at the end of the day, she had escaped intact. Her revenge if she needed it, would come in time. With Mrs Leighton's letter tucked away securely; she possessed the perfect ammunition. One day she would use it in earnest. But for the present, she held Jerry to a vow of secrecy.

At first, he was reluctant, his appetite for direct confrontation with the General spurred by an impetuous nature and transparent admiration for Marian. In the end, however, he was persuaded, impressed not as much by the quiet logic of her argument as by his desire to fulfil her every wish.

Cutting short their stay in Lahore, within twenty-four hours they were aboard another train, the next leg of the journey under way, Rawalpindi their destination nearly two hundred miles to the north west. Their intended visit to the Shalimar gardens would have to wait.

And during the course of those two hundred miles, there were distractions enough to soften the stinging irritation of circumstances which had placed Marian as the victim and a certain General as the unpunished perpetrator. Events played on her mind, an ugly distraction, but not for long. And Jerry proved his loyalty by not reminding her of a topic she declared best put behind them.

Then came Rawalpindi, the most significant military stronghold in the region. A fast-growing, sprawling conurbation dominated by substantial army presence, but not blessed with the sophisticated architectural setting afforded the likes of Bombay or Delhi, it was enhanced instead by a distant but spectacular backdrop of the mighty Himalayas. It was also marginally cooler.

And it was here that Jerry originally expected their journey together to end. Though Marian mentioned more than once her plans to proceed all the way to Landi Kotal, his presumption was that Rawalpindi would be far enough for a young 'memsahib' travelling alone from England. However, circumstances and his feelings for Marian had changed. The further north they advanced, the less willing he was to be separated from her and thus the more he hoped she would want to go on.

His impressions were that Marian Chase was quite unlike any woman he had previously met. Indeed, he suspected she might well remain unique among any yet to come. Her fortitude and dedication impressed him. However, the manner in which she staved off the advances of General Campbell and her remarkable ability to shrug off the whole sordid episode, encouraged him to admire her more than ever and certainly than he anticipated when first they met at the Taj Mahal Hotel in Bombay.

It was with a heavy heart therefore he prepared himself for the parting of their ways. In Rawalpindi, he supposed her spirits would flag, her resolve to carry on melt away. No real preparations had been made for her to proceed any further because, by committee vote, and in spite of all her previous protestations to the contrary, it was assumed she would be all too willing to end her journey in what was effectively the last outpost of recognisable civilisation.

However, they, the committee, a triumvirate of officers none of whom had previously met Marian, and, latterly, Jerry himself, were mistaken. Apparently, it had not crossed their minds that far from having grown weary of the heat and dust of India, day by day the country was growing in her affections. With encouragement from Jerry who devoted so much of his time accentuating the positive and making light of the negative, Marian had come to greet each day with renewed vigour. What was begun as a 'tour de force' of the heart, a trial imposed by herself on herself to test her devotion, had altered.

As to be expected, much of the time she found the heat oppressive. It sapped her strength, leaving her by the end of each day quite exhausted. Since her departure from the comparative comfort of Bombay, each mode of transport seemed progressively worse and her diet had changed so drastically as to assure her of one malady or another.

Nevertheless, her spirits were undaunted. She was filled with raw fascination at everything that came into view. From the fertile plains of the Indus delta surrounding Karachi, she had travelled for over a thousand miles, a slow, uncomfortable passage but one filled with a constant variety of terrain. Much of what she had seen from the window of a train compartment was barren wasteland, harsh, inhospitable landscape with no obvious beauty or charm. To Jerry, however, a man as unfamiliar with the picturesque qualities of the English countryside as his companion was with the path of the Indus, there was a scale and grandeur to be found in the Indian panorama quite beyond bland superlatives. His affection for India was awe inspiring.

Against all odds the British had colonised the continent from top to bottom, searching out the remotest corners. In spite of the dangers, heat, disease and death, they had made India their home, conceding nothing to climate or landscape and going to quite extraordinary lengths to avoid compromise. In the cities the architecture echoed that found in the heart of London. The hill stations were as Anglo-Saxon as any small town in Sussex. In matters of dress, habit and lifestyle not the slightest concession was made towards integration or accommodation of Indian customs or climate regardless of the inconvenience or hardships endured in the process.

The rigours of Imperialism demanded that 'Englishness' be implanted wherever English feet trod the soil. Native cultures, customs and history, regardless of their merits were shunned. Be the climate as aggressive as it liked, the starch remained. To the conqueror fell the burden of imposing superior customs, cultures and clothing habits upon the conquered regardless of the practicalities.

Jerry, however, was the clear exception to the rule. His philosophy included close assimilation, or as close assimilation as his rank permitted. Contrary to the majority of his peers, his eyes were open to the vast and varying beauty of the Indian countryside and his mind was intrigued by the unique history of a people whose architectural and social heritage could be traced back over a thousand years. Rather than greeting the climate, terrain and native population as something to be endured, he embraced all three, adapting to them rather than struggling to overcome.

Marian was rapidly becoming of like mind and with equal stubbornness. She had no intention of turning back. She was as excited by their advance as she was enthralled. To the original motive for travelling to India was added a new element. With her underskirts discarded, her neck collar unbuttoned and her hair left to fend for itself most of the time she assumed the mantle of petty pioneer.

General Campbell believed her weak. His insulting behaviour was based upon the rash presumption that all women were defenceless creatures quite unable or unwilling to fend for themselves. He was accustomed to thinking of them not merely as the 'weaker sex' in name but the 'weak sex' in deed and in that custom, he was by no means alone among his peers.

As one and then another uniformed but uninformed 'gentleman' counselled an early end to her journey, so Marian became steadfast to the cause, insisting that with or without their approval she still intended reaching Landi Kotel.

Originally, even Jerry was among the ranks of doubters. However, he was now a convert. He also had the benefit that having travelled part of the way with her, he had already sampled the inherent Marian Chase resilience. Consequently, although he was inclined to question the wisdom of carrying on, he found himself defending her right to do so.

Not surprisingly therefore his duties were rearranged to accommodate such outspoken confidence. Since he boasted Marian's fortitude over and again and promoted the seriousness of her mission with equal eloquence, Major Bruce Morgan-Mann, officer commanding in Rawalpindi, or 'Triple M' to the troops under him, soon gave up the struggle of persuasion.

'So be it,' he declared after a lengthy debate during which he found himself outnumbered two to one.

'I've done my best,' he said, a note of resignation in his voice.

He was sitting behind a large desk, the burgundy leather top a shadow of its former glory. Above his head two swathes of heavily pleated but faded cotton swayed back and forth courtesy of a punka wallah who was seated on the dirt outside pulling on a cord which passed from worn hands up into the eaves and along the ceiling. Sadly, the rhythmic motion barely stirred the thick, hot air, and thus offered little relief from the stifling heat.

All four walls were white whitewash no more. They were cream from age and peeling, a none too proud backdrop to the single framed portrait of Queen Victoria, whose severe almost scolding eyes seemed to mimic the sentiments of the gallant but portly Major.

'I'd like to emphasise however, Miss Chase, that I consider it completely foolhardy on your part to venture any further. I'm not at all happy, Lieutenant, either that you seem so ready to encourage the idea. But I suspect I'm wasting my breath. As I'm certain Miss Chase, it has already been pointed out to you, probably even by the lieutenant here if he has any sense at all, the North West

Frontier is a particularly perilous part of the empire and no place for an English woman. What am I saying? It's no place for any of us. But we're soldiers. Like it or not, we have a job to do. This is a troubled part of the world, not the promenade at Brighton and…'

'Oh, you know Brighton then?' Marian interjected flippantly, hoping to end his rather patronising lecture before it descended into the realms of insult.

'Whether or not I know Brighton is beside the point Miss Chase,' he replied more sternly this time, unused to being interrupted in mid-flow.

'I think sir,' Jerry intervened, trying to defuse what he predicted was in imminent danger of becoming an unnecessarily heated exchange 'what Miss Chase means is that she is aware of the risks. Reaching Landi Kotel is of great importance to her sir. She has not undertaken this journey lightly and from my experience sir I'm sure she is more than up to it.'

'I don't doubt her determination, Lieutenant. Neither do I doubt the motives behind your rallying to her cause,' the Major responded, embarking upon a conversation with Jerry concerning Marian while seeming to ignore her presence in the room.

'Gentlemen,' she interrupted with some irritation. 'While I realise, I'm entirely dependent upon your good will for my safety in India, I would be grateful if you would refrain from discussing this matter as if I were not here. I may only be a woman and therefore in your eyes Major a rather poor, pathetic creature, but actually, I am quite able to think and act for myself. With or without your help I'm afraid, it is my intention to proceed to Landi Kotel. Naturally I would prefer it was with your help. I would feel much safer.

However, please be assured, whether you help me or not I will go on, unless of course you intend preventing me by force and physically ejecting me from the country.'

'That will not be necessary,' the Major insisted, feeling himself backed into a corner while Jerry looked on with equal shares of surprise and admiration. 'I cannot, nor will I, prevent you from doing anything you want Miss Chase or, for that matter, from going anywhere you wish. However, you must understand. I am responsible for the welfare of all British personnel in this region. The vast majority of them are soldiers who, fortunately, are obliged to observe my wishes without question. As is plainly clear, you are not and therefore, within certain limits, free to come and go as you please. My advice to you stands however. This part of the world is…'

'No place for a woman. I know,' Marian interrupted again trying to adopt an equally patronising tone but in danger of sabotaging any good intention the Major might have. 'So, I've been reminded on numerous occasions since leaving England. But Major, have you considered that perhaps, just perhaps, the reason why there are so few women in this part of the world is simply because men don't want them here. They might threaten your...'

'Have it your own way Miss Chase,' he replied with angry irritation. 'Go to Landi Kotel if you must. Keep on going all the way across the border into Afghanistan for all I care. I'll provide you with whatever you need. But if and when things go wrong, and as sure as I sit here, they will, please remember the lieutenant is my witness to the fact that I tried to persuade you otherwise.'

And that was how Marian finally not only gained Jerry as a permanent fixture. It was also a contributory factor in nudging Major Morgan-Mann a good way along the road towards despairing of women altogether.

If that was not enough, he was further discouraged by her choice of transport. He would have been more than happy to provide either a bullock cart or, perhaps more appropriately if not quite as robust, a carriage. Instead, Marian opted for a horse, assuring both men, with some bravado, that she was a match for any horse they might provide and the equal of most men on horseback.

This was doubtful. Both Lieutenant and Major alike were accomplished horsemen, men who by dint of their chosen profession were inclined to spend as much of their time in the saddle as on two legs. Furthermore, when stationed in Meerut as a more lowly ranked Captain and with rather less weight around his mid-drift, the Major established something of a reputation for himself as a polo player. Twice he had competed in the Inter Regimental Cup, winning it outright in 1879, against, it was reported, some of the stiffest competition since the Seapoy uprisings.

As a gentleman he made no mention of this matter, preferring to let Marian have her way than prolong their meeting with further exchanges on which of them could better the other in the saddle. His mood was such that if Miss Chase wanted to continue her hazardous journey on horseback, then that was precisely what Miss Chase would do. One provision, however, he did insist upon. As well as Lieutenant Hugo, reassigned to continue as her escort, a further four mounted troops would be added to provide some sort of protection should anything untoward occur.

The road to Peshawar was not without its hazards. And beyond lay the Khyber Pass, a lawless landscape of scraggy mountains and deep ravines. The track up to Landi Kotel was no more than just that. It was narrow, steep and winding. Land slips were regular and the hills all around were populated by heavily armed bandits whose resentment of the British manifested itself in violent skirmishes on an almost daily basis.

These men were fierce and ruthless fighters, afraid of no one and impervious to the rule of law from whichever quarter it came. Many atrocities were recorded and they thought nothing of taking on forces far superior in number to their own.

Whether they would molest a white woman travelling alone with only a handful of men to protect her remained to be seen. However, as the Major considered such a notion, he was minded to think Miss Marian Chase more than able to give some bearded, armed to the teeth ruffian a good run for his money.

Much about her annoyed him. 'No,' he thought. Most about her annoyed him. He was used to commanding men who obeyed orders with a brisk salute and no questions asked. His somewhat limited experience of women led him to believe he might equally expect similar acquiescence from them. Marian therefore came as something of a shock to his system, her independent ways and attitudes catching him off guard in a manner his did not like at all.

When the time came for her to leave, he was relieved to be rid of her, not having the slightest inclination to swap places with a young lieutenant who had already endured her all the way from Bombay. At the same time, and with the deepest reluctance to admit any such thing even to himself, for a few minutes after the conclusion of their initial meeting, he could not help but smile with favour at her outspoken manner, secretly wishing the bandits of the Khyber Pass God speed should they cross her path.

For her part, Marian was experiencing something of a metamorphose in her frame of mind. What had begun in London as a pilgrimage was fast becoming an adventure. Walking through the stalls at the remount station, she took her time in selecting just the horse she wanted to ride, impressing Jerry with her discretion, opting as she did not for the first placid mare to be suggested but selecting instead a sturdy charger with legs and feet well used to difficult terrain.

In front of them lay a hundred miles and more of hard riding. It would take them a day to reach Campbellpore. There they would rest and change mounts before carrying on and, as was becoming his custom, it was there Jerry hoped she would have more second thoughts. As usual, he voiced his reservations and repeated the risks, risks which increased in direct correlation to their height above sea level. The higher they climbed into the hills, the more danger they courted.

Major Morgan-Mann lent additional 'double barrelled' support with his own small speech of foreboding immediately prior to their departure, but it was all for nought. As their small party set off, Jerry to the fore with Marian riding beside him, four armed guards in their wake and a bullock cart bringing up the rear, laden with equipment and provisions, there was apprehension in all but Marian herself.

She was filled with memories of being with her father, high up on the South Downs, the two of them alone with their horses, lingering over long views of the countryside, feeling the fresh breeze in their hair and the warmth of the sun on their backs.

As they left the outskirts of Rawalpindi the sun was not yet fully up. The heat would become oppressive by noon and, save for the far distant hint of snowcapped peaks, their route would be dry and featureless. Nevertheless, she could recall no time since the news of William's death when she had felt more alive.

Jerry was alert to every shift in the wind, every rustle in the sparse undergrowth. By contrast, Marian relaxed into a tranquil state as pleasurable as it was unexpected.

At Campbellpore, for the last time until they reached their destination, they slept on beds enclosed within the walls of an army bungalow. Thereafter the contents of the bullock cart came into play. For each of the three nights before reaching Peshawar a tented camp was erected. For Jerry, this was a worrying affair of sleep taken in shifts. For Marian it was an opportunity to relish the chill of the air and a night sky blacker than the blackest velvet and bejewelled with more diamond stars than she ever thought present in the firmament.

To Jerry, the hours of darkness were a time for anxious expectation. Of a hundred and one possible disasters, he thought of them all. Raids by bandits, attacks by stealthy predators, flash floods, he imagined the lot. His fears were ungrounded. History recorded few such incidents on the route from Rawalpindi to Peshawar save that of flooding to the west of Attock during the monsoon season when the river Indus regularly enveloped vast expanses of the landscape.

However, since the early autumn weather was as dry and hot as it had been for some years, there was little likelihood of their being swept away by a tidal wave of mud and debris.

In the event, Jerry would have done well to reserve his worrying until after Peshawar. From there on, the Khyber Pass did indeed pose threats to their small party. Prior to that he might just as well have shared at least a little of Marian's optimism.

She was as far from Victorian London as it was possible to get. Yet, she felt utterly liberated. From her clothing which had become positively peasant like, to the very regime of her daily life, there was no comparison to that for which she was brought up and educated. More significantly, the Marian of London and Hove was fast disappearing to be replaced by a new woman.

As she lay in her tent, unwilling to sleep, a thin canvas wall the only thing separating her from the blackness above, seemingly so close she could have reached up and touched it, she wondered at the sudden and dramatic transformation in her life. Twenty feet away a hot red fire burned, the embers stoked through the night by one of the three wallahs to come with the contents of the bullock cart. Somewhere in the darkness two armed guards stayed awake to protect her, the whites of their eyes and glint of moonlight on brass buckles scant witness to their presence. Little disturbed her save the swooshing of giant bats intrigued by the flickering light of the flames and occasional wild dogs calling to each other in the far distance.

Her transformation was greater than that of being merely four thousand miles from Piccadilly. She believed herself transported to another planet and in another time. She was the same Marian and yet utterly different. She saw through the same eyes, thought with the same mind and spoke with the same voice, but she was fast becoming an entirely different person to the one who had boarded the SS Egypt at Victoria docks a month or two earlier.

Fate was notoriously fickle. That much she knew. Consequently, she made no attempt to predict the future. She had an idea what to expect in the days ahead. That the Khyber Pass was 'no place for a woman' was not in any doubt. Sir Archibald Farrer was the first of several to bring this fact to her attention even before they landed in Bombay. For the rest, however, she preferred not to know. In London or Hove her weeks were planned in advance. Parties, 'at homes,' visits to museums and even bible classes were contrived to take place as part of a convenient and well-ordered time table. Her life was full but routine, stimulating but rarely if ever exhilarating or spontaneous.

India however was changing that. In India, nothing was predictable. Everything was new and, precisely because her journey was taking her to places that were 'no place for a woman,' she wanted to go all the more. Rising to the surface was a spirit of daring and adventure, a spirit which she had no idea existed but which she relished at every moment.

She was impressed by Jerry's vigilance. His determination to see her safely through to the end was as commendable as it was gallant. There were moments indeed she felt tempted to reward his ardour with some small hint of reciprocal feelings.

However, most prominent among a raft of emotions swirling around inside was that of exhilaration. With each new dawn it increased. As Jerry's reluctance to proceed made itself more evident, so her impatience to go on grew, her careless disregard for the perils ahead in stark contrast to his anxious and constant appraisal of them. Were he less afflicted by the subtle yet pervasive wound of Cupid's arrow, his words of caution might have initiated in her a more sensible comprehension of the very real dangers their party faced. Instead, he voiced the words but shied away from the instigation of them, permitting her ignorant enthusiasm to win the day.

Peshawar came and went almost unnoticed. Another sprawling, chaotic, rather 'back of beyond' setting, it served briefly as a place to rest and replenish their supplies. Fresh horses and oxen replaced the ones they were loaned in Rawalpindi and Marian noticed a large box of ammunition being stowed aboard the cart along with their rations of food and water. Other than that, she found little to note in her diary, preferring to leave the pages free for a highly coloured record of the final forty miles or so up into the hills.

Chapter Ten

'28 September. Entered Khyber Pass early this morning, just after dawn. Jerry's nervous. Sees demons at every turn. I think he worries too much. We've had no hint of trouble since leaving Rawalpindi. But progress has been slow. The ox cart is struggling up the steep gradients. It's very cold now at night. Once the sun goes down the temperature can drop to below zero. It's important to keep the fire high. Night's wonderful though; blackest sky I've ever seen and so many stars it's impossible to count them. Tomorrow if all goes well, we should reach Landi Kotel at last. If we do Jerry will be relieved, I know. I'll be sad. I suspect it will seem rather an anticlimax after all the trouble we've had getting here and all the miles we've travelled.'

So read the diary entry Marian made as she wrote by the light of the camp fire. That she remarked on Jerry being anxious was precisely because he was. Though he did not bring the matter up, he was, like Marian, a stranger to the pass. Indeed, since leaving Rawalpindi it was as much a journey of discovery for him as it was for her.

By reputation, however, he knew the last leg of their journey would be the most dangerous. Invited to do so, he would have turned back, but he was a soldier. His orders were to escort Marian as far as Landi Kotal and, come hell or high water, that was his intent.

During the day, Marian gazed in awe upon the landscape from the saddle of her horse. She was shielded only slightly from the burning heat of the sun in the shade afforded by a rather flimsy parasol, more suitable for Henley or Ascot than the Indian subcontinent. Meanwhile, Jerry scoured the surrounding hills for signs of life. He imagined bandits lurking behind every large rock or jagged outcrop, their guns trained upon them, ready to cut them down for the contents of the ox cart. He had no time to look back down the road, to realise the extent of their climb or to appreciate the raw beauty of the landscape. All he could think of were hostile forces set against them, out numbering them ten to one, their ruthlessness cruelty the stuff of legend.

As best he could he tried to conceal his feelings, but it was not easy. Every so often during the course of the day their eyes met. Each time they did he knew Marian recognised his apprehension. Around the fire, though their conversation was as light hearted as he could engineer, there was a brittle tone to his voice which betrayed the fragile state of his nerves.

Perhaps, he considered, she was the braver of the two. Perhaps her relaxed mood reflected a stronger character. Perhaps he was essentially a coward, a man fearful of his own shadow, a man not fit to wear the uniform of an officer.

Such thoughts gnawed at him. They compounded the realisation that Marian might never come to admire him in the same way he did her. Long after she retired to the privacy of her tent, he stayed by the fire, peering into the flames, searching for some grain of hope to dispel his mood of pessimism and self-doubt.

A few feet away two riflemen kept lookout, peering into the darkness for any sign of movement, their ears pricked, wary too lest they be caught off guard. Near the fire, the other two slept until the time came for their turn on watch. In the shadows the horses and oxen shuffled restlessly, pawing at the ground from time to time, toying with the fodder at their feet. Elsewhere an eerie silence filled the darkness. In this treeless, rock-strewn landscape there were few visible signs of life; the odd scurrying of tiny rodent feet, an occasional movement of falling shingle or the eerie swoosh of bats attracted to the light of the fire. Otherwise, all was silence.

During the day, kites soared over head, their wings rarely moving as they swept across the hills, sharp eyes in search of anything dead or dying which might serve as a meal. Once or twice, though almost invisible against the mottled greyness of their background, Jerry caught sight of mountain goats and had they paused to look, no doubt they would have found beneath every boulder some small reptile or insect. For what appeared at first glance to be a hot, desolate wasteland was, like almost everywhere else on the continent, teaming with life. However, it was neither the time or place. The longer Jerry's eyes settled on an empty horizon the better he liked it.

When the new sun rose, bringing with it a warmth, welcomed before becoming a burden, he hoped the fast-ageing oxen would have stamina enough to take them through to their destination before another sunset.

In the event, his interest in the physical condition of such lowly creatures was tinged with irony. Barely an hour after striking camp, with the low early morning sun in their eyes and progress reduced to a snail's pace as the climb became ever steeper, their run of good fortune came to an abrupt and violent halt.

Rounding a sharp bend in the road as it traced the tortuous contour of the hillside, Jerry's attention was drawn to a noise which at first, he took to be that of distant thunder. Before he had time to register the likelihood of imminent disaster however, it was upon them. The thunder was not the rumblings of troubled skies but the closer and more devastating roar of a rock slide a hundred or so feet above their heads.

Barely had he and Marian time to turn in their saddles to look for the source of the commotion than thousands of tons of rocks and boulders came crashing down, crushing anything in their path. There was no time for action, not even time for Jerry to call out. As he and Marian looked on, helpless, the ox cart, still with oxen in their yokes, three wallahs and all the supplies were swept from the track and into the deep ravine below.

Ahead and behind the cart their mounted escorts escaped the worst of it, having to contend only with occasional stray but potentially lethal smaller rocks which detached themselves from the main fall. One rider was knocked clean off his horse, sustaining a serious blow to the side of his head and breaking an arm as he landed awkwardly on the hard ground. Similarly, another was unseated. However, as luck would have it, his horse caught the worst of it. A massive boulder struck its hind quarters and pinned the wretched beast hard up against the cliff face.

The fall itself was over in a matter of seconds, though to Jerry and Marian who could do nothing but watch aghast from their vantage point in the elbow of the bend, time seemed to stand still, the rocks coming in slow motion, the noise carrying on and on like a violent symphonic finale and the dust taking forever to settle.

When the last trickle of pebbles came to an end, the devastation was clear to see. Within seconds, the injured soldier was being cared for by his comrade who escaped with no more than a grazed brow. Equally, on the far side of the slide and consequently cut off from the rest of the party, the latter two were gathering their wits and counting injuries, the dreadful cries of pain coming from the stricken horse of secondary importance to their own welfare.

And in the ravine below, Jerry strained his eyes to see signs of life among the appalling chaos of rocks. But there were none. Bits of cart were scattered like matchwood. He identified part of a wheel first. Then smaller details; splinters of planking, a folded tent, pots and the butt of a rifle. However, there was no sign of either the oxen or their three accompanying natives. They were buried under tons of rubble, their broken limbs and wretchedly maimed bodies entombed.

Suddenly there was a loud report. In the crook of the hill, the sound of a rifle being discharged was magnified many times. Its echo travelled back and forth among the surrounding peaks and troughs for what seemed like an age. However, it brought to an end the pitiful wailing of the stricken horse, its hind quarters shattered beyond repair.

Just at that moment, time stood still. Silence descended on them like a smothering blanket. For a second or two, Jerry and Marian were frozen to the spot, their shock and dismay at the sudden desperate turn of events rendering them helpless.

Everything had been going too well. Save for the discomforts of travelling in the manner they were and setting aside Marian's encounter with the lecherous General Campbell, thus far India had provided nothing more or less intimidating than she might have expected in London or Brighton.

In the spring of 1884, she, Margaret and Katie had spent several hours on the beach at Hove their attention riveted by the rescue of crew members from a stricken trawler which had run aground on sand banks close to shore. It was a frantic battle against time to save the men before their stranded vessel was torn apart by heavy seas.

In London, consecutive fires at the Japanese Exhibition and the Indian Museum had been the subject of deep concern for days. And once Marian's uncle, Mr Ridout, who lived on the Isle of Wight, broke a leg when his favourite carriage horse shied and crushed him against a stone gate pillar.

However, this catastrophe was something quite different. Unexpected and despite its brevity, utterly devastating, the rock slide brought death and injury into sharp focus. Overcome with shock, Marian had no time to register just how close she had come to death. That flash of reality would come later. In the interim, she fought to cope with sight of bloody injury and the foul odour of death, not yet real, but filling the air around her nevertheless.

Jerry leapt from his horse and went first to look after the injured rider whose head clearly needed some form of bandaging and his arm required a sling. A belt served for the latter while, with Marian's help, the hem of her skirt served to bind the head. Both were makeshift, the belt supporting the broken arm but doing nothing to hide the splintered bone protruding through the poor man's flesh. His pain was excruciating. However, with all their supplies, including medical kit, buried at the bottom of the ravine, there was nothing to be done by way of relief.

A further problem lay in their being cut off from the two men and remaining horse on the other side of the rock fall. They could not negotiate a way around, nor could Jerry make his way to them. Thus, the only option for them was to limp back to Peshawar. They had no food or water and nothing for shelter. In the day time heat, their one horse would carry the two of them only a short distance. However, they both had rifles for protection and Jerry was confident that failing any further misadventure, they should make it back in one piece.

For himself, Marian and the two remaining guards, one of whom needed urgent medical attention, the only course open to them was to ride for Landi Kotal as speedily as they could. Without supplies and with only two able-bodied men among the party, they would be vulnerable. The single rifle shot fired in order to put the poor horse out of its misery would have been noted by any bandits for miles around.

How fast they could proceed, however, and therefore how soon they would reach the safety of the fort at Landi Kotal, depended entirely on the best speed bearable from the wounded. Clearly suffering from concussion and consequently, though mounted, unsteady in his saddle, the courageous fellow feigned ambivalence to his injuries. Nevertheless, in spite of his best efforts to resist, he cried out pitifully with each falter in the step of his horse and threatened to topple to the ground at any minute as he struggled to remain conscious.

For three dreadful hours, they laboured up the trail. Their pace barely greater than that of a walk, progress was impossibly slow, confronting Jerry with the daunting prospect of their being caught out in the open when darkness fell. With no supplies, no shelter and one of their party badly injured, he did not care to contemplate the consequences of such a further ordeal.

Needing to find an alternative, it was not long before he reached a decision. Although it would deplete their numbers still further and leave then hopelessly vulnerable to assault, he ordered his lone able-bodied horseman to ride on ahead just as quickly as he could and bring back assistance. On his own and driving his horse on, he should be able to cover twice or even three times the ground. Then he could return with more men to protect them, a medical orderly and everything for another night in the open should it become necessary. The alternative offered few if any positive prospects. That they could survive a night out in the open with no food and no protection from the cold was a matter for conjecture. Very possibly they would, but it was an exercise in endurance Jerry was determined to avoid. He certainly doubted if the injured member of their party would survive for that long without treatment to his wounds.

Marian trusted Jerry enough to go along with whatever he judged best. At the forefront of her mind was the awful realisation of what she had witnessed; men and animals swept aside by the force of nature, crushed like match sticks beneath tons of rock. In one fickle moment, a moment either side of which she herself might as easily have become a victim, all the thrill and excitement of her journey was dashed to pieces. She felt sick at the thought of what had happened and, as if in some way to punish her, she was reminded of it with each moan and grimace of pain to issue from the barely conscious soldier a few feet from her.

She imagined crippled bodies lying in the ravine, possibly still alive, their cries for help going unheard, their agony unnoticed by Jerry when he peered over the edge to look for signs of life. Echoes of rifle fire continued inside her head long after they died down among the hills, reminding her over and over of the final death-defying spasms of the cruelly pinioned horse as she witnessed its struggle to stand in spite the agony of so doing.

She could not think ahead. The immediate past demanded her full attention, rendering her useless to make or aid in any decisions with regards to their future safety. Jerry taking charge was a blessed release. As she watched the last of their able-bodied guard ride on ahead she made no move to question the wisdom of this plan.

She was not prepared for death. Nothing in recent history had given her cause to contemplate the fragility of her own life. With no hint of impending disaster or her dangerous proximity to it the shock of so close an encounter with death rendered her numb. Any practical use she might have served vanished. She was as helpless as a child, unable to contribute, relying entirely upon the capabilities and courage of a young man several years her junior who, until that moment, she had looked upon with a degree of benign amusement, smiling at his boyish infatuation and making light of his authority.

Fortunately, Jerry did not disappoint. Though severely unnerved by the crisis, he did not falter. Death by violence was as new to him as it was to Marian and as shocking to witness. That said, though he carried in his head dreadful images of the event, as cruel as any Marian fought to ignore, somehow, he managed to be the master of them long enough to remain alert. Vital decisions had to be made, decisions necessary to keep them from further danger.

As they laboured on, the sun beating down, the wounded man now kept on his horse only by means of being sandwiched between them, occasional drips of blood from his inadequately bandaged head wound falling on to Marian's clothing, all hope for their salvation rested on the efforts of the rider who had gone on ahead. Should he meet with misadventure or his mount succumb to the gradient, their fate was ominous.

In the event, the rescue party arrived half an hour or so before sunset. Just as Jerry was preparing himself for the worst, namely a chill night out in the open, prey to any number of nocturnal predators, about twenty men on horseback met them on the road, the sound of their approach music to the ears of both Jerry and Marian alike. Within two hours they were passing through the high gates of the fort in Landi Kotal and their wounded colleague was being attended to at the infirmary.

Marian was shown to quarters previously made ready for her arrival. There she was brought something to eat and drink and was advised to rest. For Jerry, however, there was no such easy release from duty. He was summoned to the office of the officer commanding, a Major Jonathan Cole. Before reporting, he was given water for his thirst and approximately five minutes of preparation. Then he was expected to deliver a detailed account of circumstances which had resulted in him losing most of the small contingent with whom he started out from Peshawar less than two days earlier. There was no time to change, no time to regain his composure. Explanations were required immediately so that a clean-up operation could be set in motion as speedily as possible.

As a matter of urgency, the road would have to be cleared where the fall had taken place. The fort was a substantial structure. Those contained within its walls were comparatively safe from attack. There were sufficient supplies, arms and ammunition to sustain a prolonged siege. Nevertheless, there was only one road to and from Peshawar. Though deeply rutted, prone to rock falls and vulnerable to bandits, it was a vital and busy life line and it was essential to keep it open at all times.

And since rock slides were a frequent hazard of the region, the necessary men and equipment were always on hand to clear them. However, such events rarely claimed lives. That Jerry and his party were caught so suddenly and lethally was extremely unfortunate. It was important therefore to discover whether or not it was triggered by a freak coincidence of nature or by something more sinister, by sabotage for instance and with just the intent which resulted. In addition, if at all possible, it was the Major's responsibility to recover the bodies of those who perished ahead of the vultures commencing their gruesome feast.

Jerry was not expected to participate but with death and injury involved, a record of events as he recalled them and his subsequent actions was a priority. His personal comfort would come later. Consequently, while Marian was permitted solitude and a moderately comfortable bed to lie on, Jerry faced an interrogation, still dressed in his blood-stained uniform, the smell of sweat heavy upon him, the pangs of hunger unheeded.

It was not until the following morning, over breakfast in the officers' mess that Marian and he renewed their acquaintance. She was rested and her face was clean, but in appearance she looked much as she had done on the previous evening. With no fresh clothes to change into, all her belongings having been swept into the abyss along with the ox cart and three men, there was little she could do to improve herself. It was with a degree of self-consciousness therefore that she was introduced to Major Cole and other officers in the mess.

Unfortunately, there were no women other than 'natives' resident at the fort and not for a moment would it have been considered fitting for her to exchange even soiled and blood spattered European clothing for a 'sari.'

The Major, however, was no dolt. He noticed Marian's discomfort immediately and made a silent commitment to resolve her problem at the earliest opportunity. New clothes could be brought from Peshawar, but not for some days and not before the road was re-opened. In the meantime, he took steps to address the problem rather more pragmatically. He could not pretend he was particularly happy to have Marian at the fort and he was less than pleased at the problems thrown up in his path as a result of events which had occurred while she was 'en route.'

Having said that, he did not, nor indeed could he, blame Marian in any way, even though the temptation was there. In reality, the likelihood was that no one was to blame. It was no one person's fault that tons of hillside came crashing down upon them just at the moment their small caravan passed beneath. Nevertheless, he could have done without further problems being added to his already fraught daily routine.

In the midst of an unusually troubled period, with bands of heavily armed tribesmen entering the town, brandishing their weapons in an open and provocative manner, the fort was in a state of heightened expectancy. Two suspected cases of cholera added to raw nerves, casting doubt and fear into the minds of every internee at the fort be they in uniform or native rags.

The Major was loathe to spare the time or manpower for what was bound to be an arduous and risky recovery operation. Furthermore, the last thing he wanted was to lose more lives in a secondary fall set off by the shifting of debris already blocking the road. Retrieving the bodies of the three men who had been killed would be difficult enough. He had no wish to compound the situation.

Of course, he made no mention of this to Marian. If she noticed the many armed tribesmen within the vicinity of the fort, their chests crisscrossed with bandannas of bullets, she said nothing and she was ignorant of any cholera threat. And it would have been ungallant of Major Cole to make mention of problems which were of her making, however indirectly.

Besides, unlike the rather dour Major Bruce Morgan-Mann in Rawalpindi, who within a day of bidding adieu to Marian had forgotten her existence completely, his recollection of their brief spat barely discernible above the relative chaos of his daily schedule, Major Jonathan Cole, unashamedly alert to the advantages one could gain from the company of an intelligent and attractive woman, could not bring himself to apportion any blame in her direction.

The moment of their first meeting was not memorable, not at least in its setting or context. The officers mess in the fort at Landi Kotal could best be described as adequate. Lacking the extravagance of regimental silverware or portraits of previous commanding officers, it was no more or less than Marian expected from so remote an outpost of British empire, a bare room set with table and chairs but little else. It was functional for the purpose at hand. Other than that, there was not a lot more to be said for it.

Major Cole greeted her politely enough but was clearly distracted. And as for Marian herself? Her hair was a shambles, her dress blood-stained and dirty and her mood sombre. Aside from the remorse of knowing full well that had she stayed in Rawalpindi, as was so sensibly suggested, three lives would not have been lost, her arrival in Landi Kotal was a stark reminder of the original sad motive for her journey.

In fact, she had achieved her goal. She had completed her pilgrimage to the place where, had he lived, William would have served as second in command to the very man upon whom she had descended in so dramatic a fashion. But there was no joy to be had in her accomplishment, no sense of victory over adversity, no triumph at having reached the end of her marathon.

And Jerry was equally subdued. An irrational but evident sense of guilt also weighed heavily on his shoulders. He too was blameless for what had happened. He could have done nothing to prevent a large slice of the hillside crashing down upon them. Equally, there was nothing he could have done to prevent the loss of life. Those who perished were pawns to fate. Indeed, but for Jerry's good common sense in sending his last able-bodied man on ahead, the death toll might have been higher. As it was, their injured companion was making good progress. His arm was set, his head wound cleaned and bandaged. The concussion would take a few days to pass, but the medical officer was quick to assure Jerry and the invalid himself that he anticipated a full recovery.

All in all, however, a rather melancholy mood settled over the breakfast table.

'I hope you will quickly put the events of yesterday behind you Miss Chase,' the Major offered Marian as a consoling gesture. 'I fully appreciate just how frightening the whole experience must have been for you. The only positive thing to come out of it is that you arrived here yourself in one piece and I'm very pleased for that.'

'Thank you,' Marian replied.

'You've had a long journey all the way from Bombay. As you are aware now if you weren't before, it was an enterprise not without its dangers and I must say I respect your courage in undertaking it. For fairly obvious reasons, we get all too few visitors up here. I know your motives for coming were not in the pursuit of pleasure. Nevertheless, I hope you will attempt to enjoy your stay with us. Comparatively we're a small contingent here and this outpost comes with its own unique difficulties, but I for one will try to make your time here as relaxed as possible.'

It had the cut of a prepared speech; the sort Marian might have expected to hear delivered from a dais. However, she was grateful for the generosity of content. She was also relieved to find herself in the company of a man, other than Jerry, able to resist the immediate temptation of reminding her of just how inappropriate a part of the world it was for a woman.

'I couldn't have made it this far without Lieutenant Hugo,' she responded. 'Without his close guidance and companionship, it would have been impossible.

Thank you, Jerry,' she said, turning to look at him, a smile of gratitude his for the taking.

'Indeed,' the Major agreed. 'Up to and including the events of yesterday, Lieutenant, I must commend you. That the final day of your journey should have ended as it did was in the lap of the Gods. You should know, in the presence of Miss Chase that I believe you acted with commendable good sense. Without your quick thinking, Private Chowdri might well have gone the way of those three poor wretches who were overcome by the slide.'

Thus exonerated, Jerry relaxed somewhat. However, his first experience of death in the raw had inflicted a deeper wound than he anticipated. With time it would heal, but the scar would remain, a witness to the fragility of life and a constant reminder, if he needed one, that a second or two either way is all the margin required to alter irrevocably the course of one's own life.

He and Marian had cheated death by a hair's breadth. That was the rub. His culpability or the lack of it was relevant, but not the defining ingredient to what would become over time his and her lasting impression of the incident. That they had escaped death so narrowly was ignition for the shock which so thoroughly dampened their appetite. It also curbed any sense of achievement either of them might have savoured in the expediency of their post avalanche actions.

After breakfast, Marian was invited by the Major to attend the quartermasters' stores, there to select at will any articles of clothing she deemed suitable, temporary replacements for those she had arrived in. The latter were taken away by the dhobi wallah for washing, leaving Marian attired in khaki shirt, the smallest pair of male riding breeches available and an assortment of undergarments best left to the imagination.

A short while later, in a mood of frustrated defiance, she also obtained a sharp pair of scissors to perform drastic surgery on her hair. By the time she re-emerged from her modest quarters no trace of polite London society remained. She looked boyish, a combination of strident feminist and Bohemian artisan.

Jerry, of course, mourned the loss of her flowing, deep brown locks. On the other hand, Major Cole, already quietly impressed by Marian's fortitude, found her unique if somewhat startling appearance rather fascinating. He tried to imagine her as hostess to an elegant dinner party in Kensington, or on a summer's day strolling the promenade in Brighton, but he could not. Instead, somewhat to his consternation, and in spite of all efforts to the contrary, from the moment of their initial introduction, he found himself oddly attracted to her.

Equally noticeable, at least to the Major, was the fondness afforded Marian by Jerry. His constant attention and immediate readiness to perform for her even the most modest of tasks were as obvious as they were relentless, rendering the imminent termination of their relationship a thorny subject for the Major to initiate.

New orders had Lieutenant Hugo back in Rawalpindi before being sent on to a new posting in Zhob, a similarly remote army stronghold in the heart of Waziristan. With it came what the Major imagined would be welcomed news, namely Jerry's promotion to Captain. However, there was also the strong likelihood that some real soldiering would be expected of him. Waziristan was a part of the empire every bit, if not more, as lawless as Landi Kotel.

Sensitive to Jerry's highly charged emotions, however, he chose to procrastinate for a day or two, justifying his decision, if justification were needed, with the simple fact that the road to Peshawar and therefore Rawalpindi, remained impassable.

When it came, however, the time to say their goodbyes, was poignant. Marian's gratitude to Jerry for all he had done, set against to his obvious affection for her, made for a tearful farewell.

At the moment of departure, in an unbridled display of positively Arthurian gallantry, he raised Marian's hand to his lips, affected a smart salute and stared into the middle distance, refusing point blank to make eye contact. His heart was bursting, yet he showed no sign of it and no hint of the emotional torment due him over the next weeks and months.

Marian knew something of his feelings for her. She could not mistake his dedication or the reasons for it. Her deepest regret was that she could not reciprocate, deeper even than watching as he passed through the gates of the fort, any notion of when or if they would meet again in the hands the Gods and an anonymous directorate of military movements.

'You were fortunate to have Lieutenant Hugo assigned to you,' Major Cole remarked once the gates were closed. 'He performed his duties impeccably.'

'Yes, he did,' Marian agreed, all too aware that in Jerry she had gained a friend whose sense of duty was more than equalled by the generosity of his spirit.

'During the course of the next week or so,' the Major added, 'I've to submit a report. I thought you might like to know I intend putting his name up for a commendation.'

'That's good of you.'

'Well, credit where credit's due, Miss Chase. And Lieutenant Hugo is a credit to his uniform. I can't say I share entirely his unique affection for the Indian continent, but in the present climate of unrest, we could do with more soldiers of his ilk. Whether we like it or not, eventually, I believe, all of us will do well to acquire something of his empathy and willingness to integrate. From my experiences thus far, I've gained the distinct impression that if we don't learn to share this country with the natives, the natives might well take it back for themselves. If we continue trying to subdue it and them, we will rue the day. Sadly, I'm inclined to believe we've learned little from the dreadful events at Lucknow and Cawnpore back in '57.'

Marian knew too little of India or its indigenous peoples to quarrel with his views one way or the other, particularly just at that moment. However, instinct told her the Major was probably right. Thinking back to her evening spent in the company of General Campbell, she doubted the long-term benefits of such men being permitted to orchestrate the future of so many diverse peoples and cultures.

She remembered Jerry once remarking, during their train journey from Karachi to Lahore, that as long as men with empty bellies were willing to sanctify their cattle, they would never be subjugated. This was a philosophy perhaps more relevant to the thinly stretched forces in on the North West Frontier. Somehow Marian doubted it would gain the same attention along the broad, Imperial avenues of Bombay or Calcutta where finely painted colonial carriages and their white occupants remained blind to the significance of a need to circumvent sleeping cows in the road.

Chapter Eleven

Major Jonathan Cole was thirty four years old, some ten years Marians senior. He was of medium height, medium build with mouse brown hair. He had no particular distinguishing features, boasted no remarkable wit and, prior to his meeting with Marian, hoarded few souvenirs of past romantic encounters. His father was a Methodist preacher in Braintree, his mother a modest home maker. He had two elder sisters, one a talented but unexhibited artist while the other was a stoical sufferer of relentless ill health.

Since leaving school in Colchester, his career in the army had been text book and relatively dull. He had fought in no campaigns worthy of history and his posting to India was a simple matter of routine, his promotion to Major similarly orthodox.

Consequently that he decided to ask for Marians hand in marriage barely a week after their introduction, was as much against the rub for him as it was for Marian. More of a surprise still, and one bound to dismay poor Jerry Hugo as much as it was to shock both the Major and Marians' respective parents, was the latter's immediate acceptance of the proposal.

In her diary Marian wrote; 'This morning, October 6th, Major Cole asked me to marry him. I accepted.'

No mention was made of William. There was no explanation, no attempt whatsoever to chronicle the logic of so extraordinary a decision and no account of the days prior to it.

Had Marian agreed to wed Jerry there would have been at least some small semblance of the rational. For several weeks the two of them had been thrown together. Each had ample opportunity to observe the other. They had laughed together, exposed, each to the other, many of their most intimate thoughts and shared a fatal tragedy. Furthermore, Jerrys affection for Marian was transparent. Equally, since Marian was familiar with his character and personality, there was no denying a certain reciprocal fondness. In such a pairing there was at least partial sanity.

Marian Chase and Major Jonathan Cole, however, was a very different matter, a completely unknown and unexplored quantity. During the first seven days and nights of her residency in the fort at Landi Kotal, she saw little of the man to whom she was to become betrothed and, by the same token, he little of her. Their hours in each other's company were countable on the fingers of one hand.

All Marian knew of him was what she saw in front of her. Equally, all he knew of her was the figure of a somewhat boyish looking woman, clothed in breeches rather than skirts and whose primary purpose in coming from London to the far reaches of Empire was to purge herself of a uniquely personal process of mourning.

That Marian looked upon Landi Kotal as a watershed was well documented in the pages of her diary. The determination to reach there against all odds had never been in doubt. In ways too convoluted to explain, even to her father, she was seeking a conclusion to her relationship with William. His death left a vacuum, a vast empty space in her heart, open to the skies. Landi Kotal filled that space. Although she could not define the exact nature of the therapy, in completing the journey William had started out on, she concluded a love affair cut short by his death.

Her engagement to Jonathan Cole, however, was a radical departure from the plot. Her original intention was to reach Landi Kotal, perform a silent ritual of cleansing and then return to London, possibly by way of Delhi for the express purpose of renewing her acquaintance with Sir Archibald and Lady Caroline Farrer. Nowhere had she sight of a script bearing a proposal of marriage. Even further from the text of any master plan she envisaged for herself was the possibility of accepting such a proposal from whatever quarter it came.

But she did. She agreed to marry a man of whom she knew almost nothing. In one week she saw enough of Jonathan to verify only that he was neither too objectionable in his manners nor too repulsive in his looks.

One hour in the company of General Leighton had been enough to satisfy her of his credentials. Without a shadow of doubt, he was one of the most odious of men. Similarly, less than an hour in the same office as Major Bruce Morgan-Mann, was ample time to satisfy herself that he was polite but had about him a patronising tone which rendered him immediately ineligible. And so the list went on. Marian could readily identify a roll call of men on two continents to whom the answer would always have been an emphatic 'no' had they chosen to ask for her hand in marriage.

Even poor Jerry Hugo would have fared no better, albeit that there was little about him to fault. He was kind, generous, gentlemanly and completely blind to any of her own misgivings. His devotion to her was self-evident and he had laboured ceaselessly to earn her respect and affection.

So why Jonathan Cole. When everything Jerry had been and done was not enough, why was 'yes' the only response possible to a question which, in truth, Major Cole had no business asking in the first place. Marian was a virtual stranger to him and he to her. So little time had passed since their introduction, neither could claim with certainty any virtue in the other.

For days, with pen in hand, Marian tried to answer 'would be' critics by writing down her thoughts in the pages of her diary. What was there about Major Jonathan Cole so different from all the others. What mystery ingredient did he possess to have her so beguiled; and beguiled she had to be. Or else why would she have contemplated such a dramatic leap into the dark. How was it possible for him to run her customary gauntlet of cross examination and yet escape unscathed. More significantly, why were there so few answers.

Each time Marian sat down to write, the words faltered on one and the most critical topic. She analysed the weather patterns in some detail, remarking how abrupt was the chill each evening as the sun dropped from the sky. She described her temporary home, its rather Spartan facilities, the exaggerated fortifications and the magnificent, if somewhat intimidating, views from the modest battlements. Brief mention was also made of threats from beyond the walls. She went on to construct an epitaph of gratitude for all Jerry had done, the name 'Jerry Hugo' writ large, immortalised over and over. Several pages alone were dedicated to the events as she recalled them during and after the rock slide.

Major Jonathan Cole, however, remained as much an enigma on the written page as he was in real life. The words 'Major Cole asked me to marry him and I accepted' stood as the only substantive evidence of his existence.

One thing alone of significance was deserving of comment. Before Christmas he was due to surrender his commission. His days of soldiering were drawing to a close. Landi Kotal was to be his last posting, the rank of Major was as far up the military ladder as he had elected to climb. His future lay not on the

North West Frontier but on the other side of the continent in Assam, as a planter and harvester of tea.

It represented a distinct change in his circumstances, a complete reversal of all the plans he and his parents made one winters evening around the family supper table in Braintree almost fifteen years earlier. But this was no sudden change of heart. For some time, even before his posting to Landi Kotal, when he enjoyed more relaxed conditions at the 1st Mule depot in Sialkot, his mind was on other things. He no longer wanted a career in the army. As a young man with few concrete ambitions and even less sense of direction, it was the easy option. Respectable, reliable and, provided he managed to avoid stray bullets, with the guarantee of a satisfactory pension, it promised excitement, stability and opportunities for travel, two things his father's modest income could not otherwise have funded.

Progress for Jonathan Cole, however, had been slow. He was an officer, but not essentially of the officer class. Colchester College was no match for Eton or Harrow and 'Supply and Transport' was a long way from the glamour of the Cavalry or Artillery. The likes of Major Bruce Morgan-Mann, with whom he had come into contact on several occasions, General Leighton and, for that matter, Lieutenant Jerry Hugo whose father called in many favours to have his son accepted into the 4th Hussars; all these and more were members of an exclusive club into which he would never be fully admitted.

True enough, in 'Supply and Transport' he could climb the promotional ladder. If he persevered, over time, he might make Lieutenant-Colonel. However, as far as he was concerned it would be a 'Pyric' rise to the higher orders. The army needed horses, tens of thousands of them. It needed mules, camels and elephants as well. Without a constant supply of four legged beasts it could not move at all. Transport was a vital ingredient to the effectiveness of a successful fighting force. But, it was not what Jonathan wanted and his posting to Landi Kotal offered little opportunity for advancement, albeit that a garrison command was one step removed from his previous equestrian duties.

High in the hills, the border with Afghanistan was a desolate part of the world; a small company of men, for the most part cooped up behind the walls of a cramped sandstone fortress playing policemen to a local community of brigands and cut throats. There were cross border skirmishes and the potential for danger was all too real. However, it was also a place to brood, a place where more than enough time was available for negative introspection.

Over weeks and months, Jonathan had examined the course of his life and career. He had viewed it from every angle and reached the undeniable conclusion that he was destined for something else. He wanted broader horizons, greater challenges and a wife to share them. Marian Chase was indeed a stranger. More than that and rather ominously, she was the first English woman whose company he had shared for some considerable time. Consequently his proposal of marriage might have been viewed as no more than an impetuous, even desperate impulse. With little to go on short of a few brief and far from intimate conversations, there were those who were bound to proclaim his behaviour as profoundly foolish. Moreover, that Marian, was prepared to embrace his request for her hand, displayed a similar lack of maturity.

At no time had Jonathan the opportunity to examine Marian, the woman. Her hair hacked to an untidy stubble, her clothes forever army khaki and her rather contemplative state, none of these bore evidence of a worthwhile personality. Thus he could only hazard a guess at best in respect of their prospects as husband and wife. And, the same scant information was all Marian had to feed upon. So why, she could hear her parents pleading, the readiness to throw herself so readily off a cliff with no sight of the bottom and no idea how long the drop.

With the 'yes' of her reply to Jonathan still ringing in her ears she could hear the weeping of her mother and sanctimonious mockery from Margaret. Comparisons would be made to the selfish irresponsibility of Katie. Her elopement with Mr Kenneth had heaped shame enough upon the family. Any such similar and untypical behaviour from Marian would only serve to compound the corporate heart ache at 32 Princes Gate.

Marians only hope was her father. Denied any of the written mitigation included in the pages of her diary, he might struggle at first for an understanding. But knowledge of, and trust in, his eldest daughter would encourage him toward a deeper search for the truth. In the end, the bond he nurtured with her, like none he held with Margaret, Katie or indeed his own wife, would fuel his blessing of the union.

For the time being, however, Marian was alone. She and Jonathan confirmed their betrothal but told no one, for there was no one to tell. There were no celebrations, no 'God speeds' and no wishes of good fortune. The moment came and went and the days followed with nothing to mark the event. Alone as a noteworthy occurrence was the arrival from Peshawar, some two weeks into her

Khaki wearing regime, of a sizeable trunk, packed tight with garments thought befitting to a young woman of her breeding and station in life.

The sizes were mixed, the garments clearly having been donated from a variety of different sources. The styles were rather less than contemporary, some being positively of a past generation, and the broad colour range eliminated at least half of them as being of any potential use. Moreover, as grateful as Marian was for the effort everyone had clearly gone to on her behalf and their generosity, she was strangely reluctant to make use of her newly acquired wardrobe.

The under garments were welcome, but for the rest, fine evening gowns and dresses more suited to a stroll in Regents park on a warm summers day, she avoided even trying them on. She was not the same woman any more. Day by day, India was changing her. She had become infected, not with some dire, life threatening disease but with an energy and a vision of the world quite beyond the limits of her experience in England, quite opposed to the trivia of urban society.

Jerry was the carrier of that infection. By way of a legacy, his excitement in and affection for everything Indian had passed to her. She revelled in each sunrise, sunset and every hour between, gasping at the scale of it all, ever hungry for more. Fine dresses were no match for the majesty of landscape. In Landi Kotal, fashion was an irrelevance. It was a symbol of something she found herself needing to leave behind, a past not forgotten or entirely abandoned but exchanged for a new and different future.

In accepting Jonathan's proposal of marriage she was indeed taking an extravagant leap into the unknown. At home, in London, such action would have been preposterous. She would have dismissed the possibility of it and her 'would be' suitor, out of hand, pouring scorn on the impertinence of being asked to sign her life over to a man she barely knew, let alone held in any high regard. Had she paused for a moment to examine herself in the mirror running full length of the door on the wardrobe in her bedroom at 32 Princes Gate, attired as she was, her hair cropped, she would have cried out in anguish and confined herself to the house in shame. But she was a world away from home. William was not forgotten. The pain of his death was no less acute and her sense of loss in no way diminished. He owned her heart. In death as in life she had given it to him and she cherished the privilege of experiencing and having experienced a raft of emotions not afforded those never to have succumbed to the arrow from Cupids bow.

How better therefore to secure her single minded devotion than in marrying a man such as Jonathan Cole. In 'accepting' him as a husband, her immediate future in India was secured. In addition, she would gain a companion, she hoped, of equal wit and integrity while her heart remained the property of another. Jonathan had known her too short a time to be in love or demand affection from her. The limited attentions he paid her, the tone of his voice, the look in his eyes betrayed none of the classic signs. Whatever his motives, and Marian was of no mind to dissect them closely, they did not emanate from the heart. Exactly to what extent or in which direction was not certain, but, without doubt, their dual motivation for such a union was platonic rather than driven by passion.

Marian needed no feminine guile to lure him. His proposal came before the arrival of the trunk of new clothing from Peshawar. Their betrothal was sealed not in some heady moment but in as mundane a fashion as could be imagined. In a matter-of-fact way, the same way he might have planned and executed any matter of daily routine, he placed the proposition before her, adding to it a brief precis of the benefits, but making no apologies for the absence of traditional courtship rituals or emotional baggage.

At the time, they were seated in his office, a small, featureless room set against the outer, North, and thus fractionally cooler, wall of the fort. There was a stark wooden desk strewn with papers, two wood seat chairs and a tiny slither of a window looking out towards an horizon obscured by a lunar like escarpment. Without the door propped wide open it was dingy and cupboard like, no place at all for so vital a topic of conversation.

As far as Marian was concerned however, it was the perfect setting, emphasising as it did the strict limits to their relationship, giving neither of them cause to stray from the purpose of their treaty or misinterpret the rules. Theirs was to be a union of minds and ambitions, of practical needs and a certain mutual regard, but no more. Their hearts were their own, excluded utterly from the transaction. With no wooing or winning to be done, the trunk of seduction from Peshawar could stay tightly shut. Marian was free to continue her embrace with Bohemia. Whether her dark hair cascaded waterfall like to her shoulders or framed her face to inspire a Rossetti masterpiece was of no mind or matter.

Betrothed, they could proceed. Assam was as distant as the moon itself. The getting there would entail a journey of equal measure to the one Marian had recently completed with Jerry. And, once there, on the other side of the continent, assuming their safe arrival, a new life had to be forged from nothing. With no previous experience, the life of a tea planter would not come easily to either of them.

Above all else and before leaving the fort for the last time, Marian was obliged to write home. During the pause in their voyage at Port Said, she posted a short note assuring her family she was well and looking forward to their arrival in India. Later, in Bombay, while resident at the Taj Mahal Hotel she committed herself to a more detailed epistle, recounting much of the sea voyage and the welcome development of a friendship with Sir Archibald and Lady Caroline Farrer. More importantly, she took pleasure in being able to assure her family that there were no regrets in venturing from English shores.

However, leaving aside the novelty of her impending marriage, she still had so much to tell of her travels across India with Jerry Hugo. She knew her father, especially, would be impatient for word of her progress, although, in the writing, she was quick to censor either the implications of her evening with General and Mrs Leighton or the severity of the accident in the mountain pass below Landi Kotal. As far off as was her family and therefore in no position to assist or alter events, she saw no purpose in worrying them with tales of difficulty or disaster.

Early one morning she began to write. The sun was barely up. The chill of winter in the mountains was fast approaching and most of what she could see through the narrow window in her quarters was in soft silhouette. Candle light was all she used to illuminate the paper and she had a blanket from the bed wrapped around her shoulders to stave off the chill.

For an hour or more as the sun assumed its gradual ascent, she sketched a picture of her weeks in India. As best she could she added colour, trying to approach each episode with the same enthusiasm and affection as Jerry might have done, not comparing or contrasting with what was familiar to her at home but, exploring with an entirely fresh eye. As she described the brightness of the sun and the intensity of the heat she was reminded of all those 'Avant Garde' artists from France whose paintings she had seen in exhibitions at the Grosvenor Gallery, their bright, unspoiled colours and canvases full of light, so akin to her 'Impressions' of India.

Barely half way through her correspondence, she was interrupted. By the most extraordinary if trivial of coincidences, on the very morning she sat down to write home, a letter arrived for her bearing a variety of post marks one of which showed its origin to be London. Immediately she recognised her father's handwriting on the rather weather beaten envelope. But, as impatient as she was to open it, she tucked it away in one of the pockets of her army regulation blouse until she found both time and space alone to read it.

It was dated July 30th, only two weeks after her departure from England. Clearly it had followed in her wake. By the manner of its writing, however, it was intended to arrive in Landi Kotal before her, overtaking her perhaps while she paused in Bombay or Lahore, the postal service itself, even in India, requiring no such relief regardless of how far flung the destination.

By mid-morning she was alone. Jonathan had gone out on patrol with a small troop of men, leaving her with little to do and the privacy of his tiny office should she want it. With a cup of tea and a 'punka wallah' at his post outside, she settled down to read.

'My Dearest Daughter' it began, the 'Est' on the end of 'dear' something her father reserved for her alone. When addressing Margaret or Katie in letter form it was always 'My Dear Daughter,' not an indication that in any way he denied either of them the fatherly affection which was their due, but that, as his first born, Marian held an undeniably special place in his heart. Her conception was entirely the consequence of a love and passion between himself and his young wife of only a few days and it was never surpassed. Margaret and Katie were planned children, the product of two desires, one the wish to expand their family, the other, unfulfilled, to produce a son.

When Marian was conceived, however, neither Mr or Mrs Chase were concerned as to whether their baby was to be a boy or girl. Tangible and irrevocable evidence of their deep love was enough, a child whose features would include something of them both and much that was a union of the two, a child whose eyes would reflect the sincerity and conviction of their marriage vows.

Margaret and Katie should have been boys. Indeed, had Margaret turned out to be so, it is unlikely Katie would have been conceived at all. Unfashionably neither of Marians parents were of a mind to reproduce in numbers. When three successful pregnancies failed to produce a boy they were resigned. Neither Margaret nor Katie were a disappointment, even though Katies most recent escapades were a severe test of parental patience.

Nevertheless, Marian remained special. The fact was never mentioned. Every effort was taken to ensure public equanimity with all three children. On no occasion was Marian ever singled out or held up to her sisters as in any way superior or more loved. However, 'My Dearest Daughter' was a small token of her father's bias and one Marian guarded jealously.

'Barely two weeks have passed since your departure' the letter began, *'and already your mother and I miss you terribly. We worry about you constantly and wish you were still here at home with us. The house seems so empty without you. My morning rides are a bore and our dinner parties lack the sparkle you inspire with your provocative conversation. In pursuit of my own selfishness I wish you would turn around and come home.'*

However, you must not consider doing anything of the sort. In spite of the weather being unseasonably poor and almost daily reports in the papers of gloom and doom for the future prosperity of us all, both your mother and I wish you God speed in your venture.

We know that in the company of Sir Archibald and Lady Farrer your safety is assured. Short of a natural catastrophe which is in God's hands, and there your mother beseeches him directly with each new day (twice on Sundays) to spare you, we are ready to believe that the gentlemen of the Peninsular and Orient Steamship Company will get you to Bombay in one piece.

By the time you read this letter of course all our fears will have been for nought and all your mothers prayers answered. You will be near to or at 'Landi Kotal,' a strange sounding place which I find hard to imagine with any clarity. Therefore when you reply and we wait with impatient and open hearts for you to do so, I trust you will be highly detailed with your descriptions. Neither your mother nor I have travelled beyond Europe. Consequently we find it impossible to picture for ourselves what you will experience. Details, details and yet more details are what we would like to read. Above all else, however, we long to hear you are well and that you will return to us with your mission resolved.

Dare I say this my dear girl. Captain Radford was a fine young man. His loss was deeply felt by us all. Your future together was filled with promise and it was a great sorrow he was taken away from you so cruelly. You will not and must not forget him. However, I hope the journey you have undertaken will bring you home in the knowledge that life goes on and you must go on with yours.

You are, Marian my dear, a quite exceptional young woman. I say this not because you are my daughter but in spite of it. You have too much to offer to discard it all because of one tragedy. Undoubtedly, as you will discover, your life will contain many tragedies along the way. They come to us all in one form or another. Although it may not seem like it at the moment, how you rise above these tragedies will not only be a measure of your stature as a woman but a reflection of the richness to be gained from living.

Wherever you go, my dear, whatever you do, our hearts are with you. Our deepest wish is that you keep well and happy. How you achieve the two is in your hands and I, for one, am confident you will never let yourself down in the pursuit of either. What you must remind yourself however, is that the pursuit is all. One life, one 'mortal coil,' is all each of us has. The search for happiness therefore should be relentless. Only the method or methods of achieving it should give you pause for thought.

Katie, may God bless her, has little use for, or understanding of, either the words 'pause' or 'thought.' She rushes in where angels fear to tread. Consequently there will be many occasions to regret her actions as I suspect she will herself in the not too distant future. You, my dear Marian, however, are blessed with the capacity for deep thought and the intelligence to apply it, both virtues, incidentally, which I flatter myself you have inherited from me rather than your mother. Use them well, my dear. Test them both to their limits and you will find the happiness your deserve. Then come home to us with your treasure chest of good fortune.

In the mean time we long to hear news of you. We have had no word yet but wait for the post each day in anticipation. 'Your loving father.'

P.S. Your sister, Margaret that is, speaks of little else these days save becoming a missionary. Please do your mother and I a favour. While you are in India look out a position for her, preferably somewhere remote and, more to the point, where the missionary work needed will keep her occupied for some years. With you and Katie both out of the house her obsession knows no bounds. Mine and your mothers patience however has its limits.

P.P.S It was reported in the newspaper the other day that the fire at the Indian Exhibition was probably started by of all things sunlight shining through a window on to some jewel encrusted artefact which in turn sent a concentrated beam of light on to a piece of fabric. Bearing in mind your destination I thought you might be interested to know this small item of trivia.

Marian read the letter twice over before folding it and then placing it back into its envelope. Precious as it was she then stowed it away carefully within the leather bound writing wallet which was among her most treasured travelling possessions. For some time, she remained in Jonathan's office, but her mind was far away. She was at home.

As if to reassure herself, she imagined strolling from room to room, unseen and unheard, but observing every detail. She watched as Margaret took up her usual seat in the window of the drawing room, bible in hand, her thoughts on distant corners of the world where the word of God had yet to be heard. She followed her mother about the house as she busied herself in the role of home maker. Then she lingered in the doorway of her father's study as he sat with his back to her, bent over his heavy desk, writing the very letter she had just secreted away. She knew every inch of the house, the noises from the kitchen, the activity in the street outside.

For a moment or two she was not in India at all. She was transported, the walls of the room in which she was sitting no longer there, Landi Kotal itself as distant as it had seemed before setting sail from England.

The word 'Memsahib' brought her back. Repeated twice to attract her attention, it was alien to 32 Princes Gate. It was familiar but misplaced, an interruption to her day dream.

'Yes' she replied, the dream at once shattered, the walls of the office again closing in around her.

'Many pardons Memsahib.' The voice came again.

'Yes.' She said, turning to see a young native boy framed in the doorway, his urchin clothes, dark complexion and jet black hair so much the hall mark of his race.

'Is the Memsahib wanting something to eat?' he asked in broken English.

'No thank you Rashid.' She replied. 'The Memsahib does not want anything to eat for the moment. Perhaps later. But thank you for coming to ask.'

The boy smiled, broad and, one might have imagined, fondly. Not yet was he old enough to resent the likes of Marian and all other British Sahibs and Memsahibs. However, his interruption was enough to bring her thoughts back from England to the task in hand.

She had a letter of her own to finish, a paragraph at least should be dedicated to expressions of her fondness for home and family. If the truth were known, since leaving England there was not a single occasion she had in fact felt homesick. Sometimes, on quieter days, during the long sea voyage when there was nothing to see from the deck of the ship but an open expanse of water or when the conversation was at an ebb, she thought of London or Hove. She recalled people and places familiar to her, warming to them as one would to the glow of a winters fire. But she felt no sense of deprivation, no desperate need to be back among her family and friends. There was a purpose to her leaving and with each day some novelty of experience or fresh encounter saved her from brooding on what she had left behind.

This was made more so once she arrived on Indian soil. Every sight and sound, every mile travelled, promised and delivered something new. There was no time to feel sorry for herself, no place or occasion when the reality of where she was, or with whom, became so overwhelming she longed to be spirited back; not perhaps until that fleeting moment immediately prior to the arrival of Rashid.

Seeing her father's handwriting, reading his words, feeling his affection close around her like a soft blanket, a deep longing to be near him surged through her, introducing tears to her eyes and a sudden realisation of just how far she was from home. There were no second thoughts however. She did not regret leaving England, nor did she feel the urge to leap up and ready herself for immediate departure. She was confident in where she was, why she had gone there and, surprisingly, bearing in mind the reckless nature of her most recent decision, certain of her future.

Yet, the flavour of home lingered for a moment on her lips and she could not deny the urge to taste it again. She imagined herself riding the length of Rotten Row with her father, the early morning Autumn frost still heavy on the grass, squirrels scampering between trees, the mist of horse breath like steam from a hundred small engines.

Returning to the task in hand, she picked up her pen and continued to write the letter from where she had left off, acknowledging the one she had just finished reading and returning assurances of her affection before embarking on the announcement of her betrothal. As she wrote, and it was a feat of Herculean proportions, she struggled for a rational explanation of her intentions, something, anything, to convince her father she was still sane and not affected by sun stroke or some such debilitating illness which was fast sending her mad. Above all else, if not his blessing, she wanted his understanding. His good opinion of her was everything. Without it she was handicapped, like a man with only one arm or a dog with three legs.

She had no thought of changing her mind. She intended marrying Major Jonathan Cole and going with him to Assam. Starved of her father's approval, however, the future would be but a half-life. For an hour or more she teased the words on to the blank surface of her writing paper, each syllable as if hewn with great physical effort from stone, each sentence an exhausting exercise. No more daunting a task had confronted her. By the time she was done the afternoon sun was beginning its impatient downward spiral.

***

Chapter Twelve

As Marian had already discovered, almost to her cost, no journey on the Indian continent was to be undertaken lightly. Aside from the crushing heat and general discomfort, whatever the mode of transport, there were many physical obstacles and dangers to be negotiated at every turn. Added to that was the unenviable catalogue of killer diseases. Malaria, cholera and typhoid were all as easy to attract as the common cold and invariably by the time symptoms became evident treatment was futile. The catching of any one nearly always brought with it a sentence of death.

She had already travelled over a thousand miles, experiencing, on the way from Karachi to Landi Kotal, a broad sweep of terrain and various modes of transport. No wonder therefore she should join with Jonathan's apprehension at the prospect of setting out again to cross from one side of the Indian subcontinent to the other.

Assam with its mighty Brahmaputra River and tropical climate was as far to the east of central India as Landi Kotal was to the west. Had they been birds with the ability of soaring to great heights, their straight-line journey would have taken them high into the Himalayas, passing through Nepal and the tiny kingdom of Bhutan before setting them down on the riverside mooring ghats in Dibrugarh barely a day or two from the border with China.

As terrestrial beings, however, their route, a deep circuitous bow taking them first to Delhi and then in an arc across the continent until Calcutta, was dictated by the roads and railway systems already in place.

In all, even if they chose not to break their journey at any point, it would take several weeks and the odds against the two of them reaching their destination unscathed were no more than fifty-fifty. Consequently, careful preparations were required, preparations which in themselves took weeks rather than days to organise.

Jonathan was not the kind of man to embark upon any venture lightly. He was methodical; a military man with a military mind. Planning and logistics were meat and drink to him. Had he travelled alone he would have been no less clinical in his preparations. However, with the acquisition of Marian as both his companion and future wife, attention to the smallest of details was doubled. Many letters were sent ahead inviting temporary assistance or calling in favours, establishing for the two of them helpful points of contact at each stopping off point along their way.

At Rawalpindi and Lahore, they would pause only long enough to rest and catch their breath. On reaching Delhi, however, the intention was to linger for a while, guests it was hoped of Sir Archibald and Lady Caroline Farrer who were the first after her father to be notified of Marian's intriguing if somewhat erratic change of heart and plans.

Jonathan also had friends in Delhi, not perhaps as well placed as those Marian could boast, but true and of long-standing acquaintances who would offer them hospitality and assistance. They too would be similarly perplexed, no doubt, to find their friend in the company of a future wife. For so many years and with such insistence Jonathan had professed the ardent desire to embrace the bachelor life on a permanent basis.

Time at the fort passed quickly. Second thoughts, if there were any, came and went in a moment. As curious as Marian found it, she was fast becoming more rather than less dedicated to the task and prospect of becoming Mrs Jonathan Cole.

With each new day, she studied her fiancé more closely, not looking for faults or searching for excuses to withdraw from their contract but uncovering in him virtues and attributes to impress. She watched with the deepest scrutiny his movements, his treatment of those subordinate to him and the methods by which he conducted his daily routines. And, as one day passed to another, she found herself becoming more rather than less confident they were doing the right thing.

Upon some strange instinct she had agreed to marry him. There was no love between them. Their knowledge of each other was scant. Yet, when he proposed she accepted without hesitation, in the full knowledge that he and their journey together were both unknowns fraught with possible pitfalls.

Whether her family and friends would understand such rashness remained to be seen. For herself, however, Marian entertained no feelings of irresponsibility or portents of disaster. At certain points during the course of each day, she did think of home. Foremost in her mind was the reality that, destined for Assam with Jonathan, there was little chance of returning to England in the foreseeable future and she could not pretend she received this wisdom with any great comfort. She was too fond of family, home and England not to pine for all three.

But there was not a single germ of doubt in her mind. Whether or not she would come to love and admire the man to whom she was betrothed, remained in question. Still devoted to the memory of William and filled with images of what their marriage might have been, she neither needed nor anticipated any such relationship with Jonathan. She had fallen in love once. That was enough for one lifetime. Simply because William had been snatched from her was no reason to abandon him.

What she expected of Jonathan and, as one day followed another, what she believed he would offer, was a combination of worthy companionship and dedicated dependency. She hoped for his friendship, loyalty and fidelity although, should she remain true to William, she was quite prepared to relinquish her expectancy for the last of the three. Jonathan was, after all, a man. Married or single he had a man's needs and if, as his wife, she failed him in that quarter, she would not find any blame in his seeking satisfaction elsewhere.

None of this was discussed in advance. With each passing day, their time together and the words which flowed between them improved. Emotions and conjugal rights, however, were rarely on the agenda. When they did come up, both she and Jonathan did little but skim the surface, preferring instead to discuss the availability of certain essential supplies or the prospects of affecting a seamless transition from his military life to that of plantation manager.

Competence was not the issue. Jonathan was confident of his own abilities as commanding officer in Landi Kotal. He knew also his years of experience in 'Supply and Transport' would stand him in good stead. What worried him more and, in turn, became Marian's most urgent cause for concern, would be his ability to adapt to a civilian way of life. Thus far he had spent his entire adult life in uniform. It fitted him well. He wore it with the look of a man at ease. Little wonder therefore, courting rituals and endeavours to propagate the seeds of love were overlooked.

Keeping her courage up was the most time-consuming task in her daily agenda and it was not easy. In the middle of the night, she would wake. Lying on her back, the darkness was absolute, the silence broken like the roar of thunder by every slightest sound, rafts of anxiety and fear drifting into view. Marrying

Jonathan and trekking off across a continent with him glared at her as the most ludicrous of ideas. Placed before her were visions of a cruel, heartless individual, a man bent on using and abusing her, a man who would break her, body and soul, and then abandon her when his brutal scheme had run its course. Ahead of her on their long route lay almost unimaginable dangers; diseases which inflicted unbearable pain and disfigurement prior to death, marauders and bandits of the most sadistic kind, disasters of incalculable scale. Against her will and quite beyond her prevention such nocturnal horrors acquired an intensity demanding every ounce of her courage to contain.

With the coming of day, they all but evaporated, leaving only a shadowy legacy to haunt her thoughts. With so much to do, so many plans to set in motion, she was distracted. However, some nights such was the intensity of doubt and apprehension against which she battled, the easier path seemed simply to turn tail and head for home.

Many were the mornings Marian woke from a fitful sleep convinced that her charted course should be south to Bombay, to Ballard Pier and the first steamship headed for England. One nudge, one offer of a helping hand would have been enough to divert her, but none came. As each day's sun rose and warmed, so the mood of her heart altered with it, the nights tortured visions dissolving to dust.

She said nothing of course. Had Jonathan been aware of her fears he might have, indeed probably would have, cancelled everything. He would have remained in the army, escorted her to the first train on a south-bound track and allowed himself to be posted to another remote military encampment, his career carrying on as before with none of the twists or turns the resigning of his commission suggested.

He was not a selfish man. He could not deny that Marian was the final catalyst to his decision for change. She was the spur, pricking him into motion. Something about her inspired him. Something he could not identify with any certainty, persuaded him of the need for change and, more to the point, persuaded him that the changes he had in mind would only bear fruit if she were at his side. Without her his project was doomed to failure before it was begun. However, he would have abandoned it in an instant had he thought her needs were best served in doing so.

None of her fears were mentioned however. In his presence, she was positive and practical. No hint of hesitation or reservation were visible to the naked eye. That he forged on regardless therefore was no evidence of a character flaw or blind self-interest. Both his pace and determination to proceed were dictated by her continued encouragement. Together, they bolstered the courage one of the other, the day for final transition approaching not with any backward glances or second thoughts, but with mutual enthusiasm and bravado.

On the morning of Monday, 8 December, a chill morning with grey skies and mists drifting ominously between the hills and threatening snow, Jonathan sat down to breakfast with Marian for the last time as Major Cole. Later, as the morning proceeded, he accepted salutes as usual. He was addressed as Major or as 'Major sahib' and he was still in uniform. However, his temporary replacement as officer commanding was already up from Rawalpindi. He was a rather striking young man who, in possession of his first sole command, showed distinct signs of leaping into Jonathan's shoes with the haste of impetuous ambition emblazoned on his forehead.

His name was Simon Pettit. Like Jonathan he had reached the rank of Major, but he was two years the younger and bore in his eyes the expectancy of an excited ferret.

In a climate of ever-increasing unrest right across the North West Frontier, only time would tell if he would prove to be more effective in the post. However, his impatience to embrace the task ahead was unmistakable, giving Jonathan some reassurance at least that the place and men he was leaving behind would not want for leadership. Quite what perils that leadership might take them into was a matter for conjecture. However, Major Pettit was clearly more in favour of action over diplomacy, a fact he expressed variously during the brief spell he and Jonathan were acquainted.

Far from entertaining the possibility that one day India might be ruled by Indians, it was the formers firm conviction that the 'natives' were little more than children. Their ignorance and idleness, blind faith and paltry ability to grasp even the simplest of tasks rendered them incapable of self-rule. Without the British as their guardians, they would undoubtedly embark upon a backward slide into barbarism and he was not alone in that view.

However, such an assessment of the tribesmen of the North West Frontier ignored their resilience, courage and ability toward savagery quite beyond anything taught on the square at Sandhurst.

Such opinions, expressed so openly and with such conviction, were not shared by Marian or Jonathan, but they were by no means unique. Marian herself preferred another view. She believed whole heartedly that, wherever possible, all peoples, and in her case as a firm supporter of the suffragette movement, women, should be entitled to self-determination, just as she had been in deciding to leave England for India. Anything else was tantamount to compulsory subjugation and consequently to be abhorred.

Not entirely at odds with this view and taken from the considerable first hand experienced he had gained while serving on the Indian continent, Jonathan adopted the approach that, with history as his guide, all past Empires had proved themselves beasts of an ephemeral nature. Inevitably, whatever the political bias of the day or the preferred philosophy, the time would come when a hundred thousand plus British soldiers and an equal number of civil servants would find it impossible to hold in check a population of four hundred million. Better therefore to negotiate a tenable position in advance than be forcibly ejected. The mutiny of '57 failed. After initial successes on behalf of the mutineers and some appalling human tragedies, it was crushed mercilessly. Reprisals for the impudence of rebellion and loss of European lives were swift and with little discretion.

However, unlike his replacement, Jonathan's opinion of the uprisings themselves and the brutality meted out to quell them was that every British man and woman on Indian soil should heed such events as an omen of possible things to come. Unless active steps were taken towards reconciliation for past deeds and conciliation for those yet undetermined, there would be more Cawnpore massacres and more Lucknow sieges. To his mind, growing unrest in the region was enough to cement his belief.

Major Simon Pettit, a 'young gun' preferred to embrace not the future but reflect the past. Thus, in many ways, he was indicative of the broadly held views which had helped to persuade Jonathan his future lay in another career.

At morning parade, he took the salute as he had done every morning for the best part of a year. Later there were a few personal farewells to fellow officers and enlisted men and several last-minute bits and pieces of administrative red tape to go over with his successor. There was little sadness, however, and nothing to regret. The countryside around Landi Kotal had a raw splendour but the town itself, no more really than a rather dishevelled border trading post with a somewhat mongrel and ceaselessly changing population, was a dreary backwater. It was a petty cauldron of unrest where violence lay just beneath the surface, a place where no man walked the streets unarmed, where no white man ventured alone and, with such beauty as there was, only to be enjoyed from behind high walls, the one guaranteed place of safety being within the compound of the fort.

Jonathan was under no illusion as to the difficulty of the journey ahead or the additional responsibility he had taken on by asking Marian to go with him. He was also deeply aware of the gamble involved in relinquishing his commission. Yet, his impatience to be gone and his self-belief were strong. The prospect that within army ranks prevailing attitudes were still linked inextricably to past glories, reinforced his vision of the downfall of British rule. Be their journey to Assam three weeks, three months or three years, be it fraught with danger, be they reduced to poverty, both he and Marian would serve each other and ultimately their country better by absenting themselves from a regime so clearly held together with paper and string.

'Good bye, Major and good luck,' were his final words of farewell to Simon Pettit. Such was his colleague's apparent control of the situation, he felt no particular urge to short list any hints he might have had as to his own methods of command. He neglected even to explain the simple kick technique he employed when opening the bottom right-hand drawer of his desk which was prone to stick fast when closed with any gusto.

Marian and he rode out through the gates of the fort with barely a backward glance. As she had been on her way up from Peshawar, they were accompanied by four armed guards and a heavily laden ox cart, the latter supporting not only provisions and Marian's newly acquired hand-me-down wardrobe, but all Jonathan's worldly goods. There were no second thoughts, no pulling of heart strings. As if on cue, though it was still very cold, the sun pierced the overhanging clouds shining bright and strong and the way ahead looked clear. Marian cast an encouraging smile in Jonathan's direction. In turn, he reached out to take her hand. Their great adventure had begun. God willing, or perhaps Shiva, for it was he who reigned supreme in these rugged mountain ranges, the icy, snowcapped peaks his palaces, the hills and valleys his domain, they would reach Delhi safe and sound.

Passing the spot where she had brushed with disaster on the way up, Marian paused. There was no sign of the rock fall on the road itself, nothing to mark the tragedy. Teams of men had cleared away every last obstruction, sweeping tons of debris into the ravine below, further burying those poor unfortunates who succumbed to the initial slide and whose bodies were never retrieved in spite of all efforts to do so. She felt for them and for their families, sharing their grief and committing them to her memory. But for the fickleness of fate, she might have been entombed herself beneath tons of coarse granite, too deeply buried for retrieval, too far from home to hear the mourning of those by whom she was loved.

On this occasion, however, they met with no calamity. The passage down was considerably quicker than the long upward haul. Consequently, by dusk on the same day, they were safely in Peshawar. The following evening, they made Attock, then the sprawling Supply and Transport depot at Campbellpore before finally abandoning their horses in Rawalpindi. From there, the train took them back across the great iron bridge over the River Jhelum to Lahore where they stayed only two days and nights, barely pausing for breath before carrying on to Delhi.

Jonathan had various formalities to complete with regard to the termination of his commission. Military bureaucracy demanded of him a certain volume of form filling and a final report on his command, including an outline of relevant conditions in Landi Kotal and present circumstances at the time of handing over to Major Pettit. Protocol also demanded he attend a personal interview with his overall commanding officer, namely General Leighton.

With wings of eagles, gossip travelled fast in India. Very little occurred which was not public knowledge within days if not hours. It was not surprising therefore that the announcement of Jonathan's engagement as partial mitigation for his decision to leave the military was already known to the General. What did catch Jonathan off guard, however, was the General's boast of a previous encounter with his fiancé. Furthermore, he was shocked by the less than complimentary remarks the General saw fit to make on the subject of a woman whom he readily accused of harbouring dangerously low moral standards.

Not slow in coming forward with open condemnation of her, the General was adamant as to Marian's considerable faults as a person and as a woman. She was clearly out from England in search of a husband, clearly prepared to latch on to the first officer foolish enough to come under her spell and, as was now quite apparent, clearly careless of the havoc she left in her wake.

No explanation was given for the General's outspoken opinion of Marian, but he spared nothing in his vitriolic attack upon her character and motives, leaving Jonathan unduly perplexed. Marian was not the sole reason for his quitting the army. In fairness, his decision was reached long before her arrival in

Landi Kotal. Plans for his future in Assam were well forward before mention of her name or sight of her.

Lying for some time in the drawer of his desk among other files and letters was an invitation to join the newly established Lepetkatta Tea Company in Dibrugarh. Bearing the address of their head office in London and emphasising the open-ended nature of an employment contract, it had already been answered. Marian took no part in his decision to accept the offer. The only part she played was in the timing of their departure from Landi Kotal and, even then, to a certain extent, that was dependent upon the arrival of his replacement.

Had she not come to Landi Kotal, he might have stayed on through the winter to assist Major Pettit, helping to wean him into a command probably very different from any he had previously experienced. Instead, her arrival and his subsequent proposal of marriage to her persuaded him that the fates were guiding his hand. Something about Marian, something inexplicable but compelling, urged boldness and haste. She was not the temptress but the catalyst. Far from doing anything to cast the shadow of doubt in his mind, she arrived in the nick of time to shore up the weakening supports of his resolve.

Had she not reached Landi Kotal, had she and Jerry Hugo rather than three unfortunate coolies been swept off the road into the abyss, then the letter from the Lepetkatta Tea Company might have lain in the drawer undisturbed for some time. Indeed, the open-ended agreement might have stretched to months, the offer of employment shelved day after day and week after week, until just the right, convenient moment.

Refusing to accept the General's outspokenly low opinion of Marian and his assertions as to her failing moral standards, Jonathan preferred to trust his own judgement.

Fortunately, therefore he dismissed them out of hand. Nevertheless, seeds of doubt were sewn. With spite in his heart, the General outflanked his subordinate, catching him off guard and, unprepared, inflicted on Jonathan a wound which though not fatal to a relationship only just begun, did open a sore, tarnishing for a time the prospect of his ambition and marriage.

Of course, he said nothing of it. A closely guarded secret, he kept it hidden from Marian, none of the General's words being repeated, none of his accusations pursued. He and Marian quit Lahore together on the train as they had arrived, no hint of a cloud on the horizon. However, a zephyr's chill passed between them, barely noticeable but there nevertheless, his wide-eyed optimism for their future smarting from a sting so deftly inflicted by his commanding officer. Only time would tell if he had the strength of character to rise above the influence of slurs proffered out of malice.

Marian was made privy to none of the content of Jonathan's meeting with General Leighton. However, she was more astute than he gave her credit. From the subtle change in his mood, she was wise enough not only to suspect the worst of the General but to keep her silence. It was a first test in their trust of one towards the other. Only time would tell.

Finally, however, on the morning of 17 December, they arrived in Delhi. They were tired and hungry. Jonathan was still in uniform and though no longer in shirt and breeches, Marian was dressed in a simple cotton blouse fastened at the neck and a plain beige skirt to the ankles. Her boots were scuffed and her hair was little altered from the boyish cut she had inflicted upon herself while in Landi Kotal.

It was no wonder therefore, that she noticed Sir Archibald and Lady Caroline before they recognised her. As usual, he was the epitome of elegance. In full whites, his regimental pith helmet festooned with intricate regimental regalia and topped off by the whitest and proudest of plumes, he seemed to tower over all those around him. At his side, Lady Caroline was no less distinguished, her elaborate outfit newly imported from Paris, her boots, gloves, hat with jewelled veil and even parasol, a match for any woman in India. Had the Governor himself turned out to greet them they could not have been more feted.

Of course, they had no idea there was to be a welcoming party at the station. Marian had telegraphed Lady Caroline indicating her intentions and giving vague details of their travel itinerary. As warmly as possible, she also expressed a desire to renew their acquaintance, hoping to rekindle old ties and share time together before she and Jonathan continued on to Assam.

However, she did not expect to be greeted with such ceremony. Nor did she anticipate that they would be invited to become house guests in Delhi for as long as they chose. A brief skirmish ensued while Marian protested against such generosity, insisting that she and Jonathan should take rooms for themselves at an hotel in the city. But resistance was futile. Lady Caroline had already made up her mind and there was to be no negotiation.

It lasted no longer than a few sentences before capitulation. Outside the main entrance of the terminus in Queen's Road an open landau was waiting. Like returning prodigals, Marian and Jonathan were bundled aboard, the pleasure in their safe arrival clearly evident on the faces of their hosts. Not a word was uttered to indicate concern for the strangeness of their appearance or the rather hasty development in their relationship.

A journey of two miles took them west and then to the north. Beyond the walls of the old city among the broad avenues and open spaces of the fast-expanding civil station, Sir Archibald and Lady Carloine kept what the latter described as a 'modest villa,' a term clearly relative to her wealth and stature. 'Petit palace' was more the thought which passed through Marian's mind as the stately landau swept up the gentling curving drive to a pedimented porch supported by a pair of whiter than white columns.

Once inside, their meagre luggage was whisked away to adjoining rooms by immaculately uniformed boys, their little dark faces and legs the starkest of contrasts to the whiteness of their tunics and shorts. Then Marian and Jonathan were introduced to a lifestyle far beyond anything the surroundings of Landi Kotal could afford.

As a rule, each morning, after a hearty breakfast which he was quite used to taking alone, Sir Archibald left home to fulfil his duties as a soldier. If permitted to do so, Lady Caroline preferred to remain in her 'chambre' until midday. However, she had already determined to bathe Marian in every conceivable luxury. And she began by apologising incessantly and quite unnecessarily for the Spartan conditions in which she and her husband were still being compelled to live.

'It's absolutely scandalous just how many of life's basic needs are still not available in this part of the world.' she moaned. Meanwhile Marian and Jonathan, their eyes wide to the honey pot of extravagance into which they had fallen, marvelled not only that such opulence was indeed available so far from the centre of London.

The 'bungalow,' 'palace,' call it what you will, secure within high walled gardens was newly built. It was a bungalow only in as much as all its many rooms were contained on a single storey. It was cool, airy and sprawling. It included more bedrooms than Marian was able to discover, a dining room fit for a regal banquet and, of all things, a ballroom. Shortfalls there may have been but at first glance, Marian was unable to find any. Throughout the house servants scurried to and fro, their voices never above a whisper, the sound of their movements muffled by silken slippers on marbled floors.

In the space of only a few days she and Jonathan had been transported from the primitive simplicity of a military outpost at the farthest reaches of empire, to the epicentre of Imperial splendour. In Landi Kotal, Marian felt entirely at ease with her hair cut short and khaki breeches covering her legs. In the palatial surroundings of the Farrer household, the reflection she saw in gilded mirrors was that of street urchin.

'My poor dear,' Lady Caroline consoled her, misunderstanding completely the processes of her altered state, assuming hardship and tragedy to be the cause of such obvious deprivation, 'we'll soon have you sorted out. A day or two here with Archie and me and you won't know yourself. I can see for myself most of your needs. But you mustn't hesitate to tell either of us if there's anything you want, anything at all. I've instructed Shelal here to look after you. He's my best house boy. He works hard as long as you keep him busy. Otherwise, he has a mischievous streak in him a mile wide. All you have to do is ask and he will see to it.'

Shelal was about twelve years old. He was thin and somehow dwarfed by the starched white folds of a uniform which was his to wear yet seemingly completely alien to him. However, his smile was broad and he possessed the darkest of brown eyes, eyes which latched on to Marian and followed her everywhere she went.

'Thank you, Caroline,' Marian responded avoiding the futility of explaining her voluntary slide into rusticity. To do so in terms her host would understand was a task she decided to avoid. Trying to convince someone of Lady Caroline's spoilt and pampered existence would have been a waste of breath. Her concept of deprivation was worlds apart from that of Marian.

Giving in to her hosts generous, if misguided benevolence therefore, within hours of their arrival, Marian found herself bathed, perfumed and dressed once again in Parisian couture. As much was done to salvage her short hair as possible and she reappeared just in time to hear the deep tone of a large brass gong announcing the coming of dinner.

Shelal escorted her through the house to a modest dining loggia with views looking out over gardens still hard pressed to fulfil the expectations Sir Archibald and Lady Caroline had of them. In India, nature was a reluctant servant. Constant husbandry would prevail. In time Lady Caroline expected her lawns and flowerbeds to echo the contrived majesty of Versailles. For the present however, the view from where Marian sat was one of sparsely populated beds, young saplings straining against thirst to gain height and raw edged pathways crying out for the softening effects of irregular planting.

For Jonathan also, the scene which confronted him was one of complete contrast. Like a desert after a sudden and unexpected downpour, Marian had blossomed into a vision quite beyond anything for which he was prepared. Dressing for dinner himself, he had washed and changed into his mess kit. A glance at himself in a mirror revealed nothing new, nothing out of the ordinary. But for his crimson jacket, he was the same Major Cole as arrived in Delhi a few hours earlier, if a little cleaner. The Marian seated opposite him however, was absolutely not the same woman with whom he had travelled from Landi Kotal, not the same woman whose hand he had requested in marriage.

In Lahore an unfortunate meeting with his commanding officer had left him bewildered, momentarily wrong footed. However, his resolution to quit the military remained intact and General Leighton offered only token resistance to the resignation of his commission. However, such was the concerted effort to dissuade him from any and all involvement with Marian, such were the accusations levelled at her by a man whom Jonathan held in some esteem, the onward journey to Delhi had been teased with misgivings and suspicions. Had he acted rashly in asking Marian to be his wife? Was he making a fatal mistake in proceeding?

'Yes' and 'probably' were the two answers which occupied his thoughts, so much so that by the time they arrived in Delhi and were met by their new hosts, he did consider momentarily exploiting their goodwill as a means to extract himself from his obligations. Perhaps if he conducted himself with dexterity and a certain sleight of hand, taking advantage of their influence over Marian, he might eventually continue on to Assam alone.

The moment she walked into the dining room, however, all such doubts and devious schemes evaporated. In an instant, nothing the General Leighton had said of Marian mattered a jot. The veracity or not of his accusations was irrelevant. In spite of the shortness of her hair and indeed almost uniquely as much attributable to it, she was quite the most striking of women. His heart knew not what direction their relationship was headed. Perhaps he and she were destined to fall in love, perhaps not. Only time would tell. Meanwhile, his determination to marry her held firm.

With some pride and an almost uncontrollable desire to embrace her, he showed her to a seat, the soft perfume of her a heady mixture of spring flowers and sensuality.

'Call me Caroline. Please,' Lady Caroline announced as Jonathan rounded the head of the table to take his place, almost as if they were half way through a conversation. 'If you and Marian are to be married, Lady Farrer will just not do. I insist you call me Caroline. Since Archie and I are the nearest thing Marian has to family in India, you must both treat us as such. I'll not hear of anything else.'

'Very well. Thank you,' he replied. 'However, Sir,' he continued turning towards Sir Archibald who was still waiting for the ladies to sit before claiming his own chair. 'If you will permit me, I would prefer to address you as Sir Archibald. I would feel uncomfortable with anything less formal.'

'Whatever you like, my boy,' his host agreed. 'I can assure you, it's neither here nor there to me. I'm addressed in many ways by all sorts of different people, some of them unmentionable I'm sure in present company. But I answer to most of them and that's all that's important don't you think?'

'Yes sir.'

'Very well then. We're agreed. Now we can eat.'

As both Marian and Jonathan expected, all five courses of the meal were accompanied by an intricate interrogation of their past, present and future activities, the last of the three coming under the most intense scrutiny. Lady Caroline led the charge of course. As was his wont, her husband preferred a more stealthy approach than the open fronted assault adopted customarily by his wife.

Jonathan was asked to account for every detail of his life, parentage, education, career and prospects, so that a judgement could be made with regard to his suitability as a husband. And, he complied, fully aware of the reasons behind so bold an invasion of his privacy. Not once did he evade a question or show resentment. Indeed, upon occasion he elaborated a tale previously told, his intention as much to pass information to Marian as to either of his hosts.

For the first time since their introduction, he felt the distinct urge and need to impress. In Landi Kotal he went about his daily business unaffected in any way by Marian's presence. Her arrival with Jerry Hugo was of little moment. All he recalled, with a degree of satisfaction, was the genuine concern she had exhibited for the families of the three men who perished in the rock slide. Out of the corner of his eye, as it were, with each passing day, small details about her had caught his attention, insignificant building blocks which, when brought together, finally persuaded him she could be the companion he needed for his life ahead in Assam.

However, nothing about her had shaken him to the core. Nothing she said or did distracted him from the priorities of his command. Their betrothal was a contract entered into with mutual ignorance one of the other. All they shared was a unity of purpose, a partnership based upon a certain respect and regard. Jonathan knew as little about Marian as she did of him, that knowledge growing with each mile they travelled together but by no means essential to their cause.

At a stroke, however, all that changed. Each time he looked across the dining table his eyes fell on her. With accelerated urgency, he found himself devoted to the notion of her finding him the most interesting man in the room, a task made relatively easy by the simple fact of their being only one other gentleman present at the table. He was an elderly and rather retiring Colonel whose sole expressed desire was to act as a competent host.

For her part, Marian was similarly affected. Perhaps it was a return to the more conventional realms of civilised society. Perhaps it was that, for the first time in weeks, she was aware of her own femininity, conscious of the contrast in their sexes. Whatever it was, it made for a heady mixture. Eager for every syllable of information coming from Jonathan's lips and ready with every new detail to be impressed by the wisdom of agreeing to take him as her husband, she consumed the sound of his voice and gestures with an appetite not easily sated.

Noticeable to her alone was an increase in heart rate and the urgent need to hold his attention. Lady Caroline pursued her interrogation of Jonathan throughout the evening, believing herself the arbiter of a union hitherto bound together with only the most fragile of knots. What, in fact, she achieved was the unleashing of desires both Jonathan and Marian alike believed dormant.

Prior to leaving Landi Kotal, Jonathan wanted and expected nothing of Marian other than she be to him a loyal and intelligent companion.

As for Marian, the words written in ink on the pages of her diary, made no mention of her motives for agreeing to marry him. All she hoped for in return for their contract was that he provide for her, give her shelter and offer her a life more challenging than any she could have expected within the portals of 32 Princes Gate, London or 16 Adelaide Drive, Hove.

After dinner, Sir Archibald took his young male guest away. They withdrew to the privacy of a panelled library, not unlike but smaller than at his club in Pall Mall. Without the volume or verbosity of Lady Caroline, they settled into the comfort of well-padded leather chairs and the quieter exploration of life as a tea planter. Brandy and cigars were brought to fuel or punctuate the conversation, while the ladies, far from the chill of mountain air, braved the cool evening breeze out on a veranda which ran the whole south side of the house.

Shawls were brought for their shoulders and, as if not to be outdone, their spirits were reinforced with generous glasses of Madeira, an elixir to which Lady Caroline herself was much devoted and had imported with her from England by the case.

Marian felt flushed and each whisper of breeze was a welcome fan. Something had occurred over dinner for which she was quite unprepared. Something within her had stirred. She had no idea what it was or why. Nothing she had done invited so confusing an emotional whirlwind. What she needed was not the warming embrace of sweet wine but an ice-cold blast from the highest Himalayas.

Lady Caroline sipped, her red hair the colour of flame in the light of a dozen flickering torches, the angle of her chin and confident ease of her posture irrefutable evidence of her breeding. She was matriarch of all she surveyed, infinitely wise, proudly aloof and as rooted to the traditions and dogmas of her age as the sturdiest of great oaks. Her dynasty would last forever. Her kind would live out the century and enter a new one quite unshaken by the forces of change revolving all about her.

As she looked out across the India she endured for the sake of her husband, she felt no inkling of things stirring. She wondered only how best to continue her contribution towards the building of the new Jerusalem. She sensed none of Marian's unease. To her, passion of any kind was an Achilles heel, an affliction to be avoided as surely as the plague itself. Debilitating and quite unnecessary, she believed it a silliness, an ague for those whose societal responsibilities were clearly less formidable than her own.

Hedonism was a distraction she could afford. She had the wealth and freedom to flaunt excess. But emotions such as her companion was feeling beneath the same stars and with the same moonlight on her face, were as unfamiliar to Lady Farrer as the people and landscape of India itself.

Marian was alone on an unsettled sea, her unease a solitary burden and sleep a haven on a distant horizon.

'In the morning, we shall take the carriage into Delhi,' Lady Caroline announced without noticing the discomfort of her companion. 'There are many fine old buildings and something in particular I should like you to see before you set out on your travels.'

Chapter Thirteen

'This clock tower is quite new,' Lady Caroline said as their carriage paused at the western end of Chandi Chauk.

'Apparently, it's over two hundred feet tall. But I suspect it's rather less than that. At the other end of this street there's the red fort of Shah Jehan. And over there,' she added motioning with her gloved hand 'You can see the dome of the great mosque. Both are remnants of an empire long gone now. On the other hand, it seems to me, this Gothic monstrosity is supposed to be a bold statement of what Delhi has yet to become.'

'According to those in the know, we, the British, are going construct a great new city here. There is talk of "New" Delhi becoming the most important city in all India. But I suspect if this is to be the case, it will be built by the next generation not ours. Archie and I are too old now. We're just holding the fort for you young folk. Like it or not, this country belongs to you my dear and your children. It's hot and dirty and personally I pine for the green fields of England. But there is a future here for you. So go. Marry your young officer. Plant tea if that's what he wants to do. And if you want my blessing? You have it. Here and now is where you should make up your mind. At the foot of this hideous tower, begin your new life.'

'Don't worry about what anybody else thinks. Think for yourself. Feel for yourself. No matter if you're not in love with the man you've agreed to marry. There will be plenty of time for love. All that matters is that he's the right man for you. That's how I came to marry dear Archie. He was the right man for me. That was the most important thing. Love came later. I confess quite openly he's never made my pulse race, but he was then and still is the right man.'

She paused for dramatic effect, enjoying the element of surprise which rendered Marian speechless in the seat beside her.

'You see, dear girl, Madeira may dull my brain a little,' she continued in triumph, 'But not my senses. Poor, dear old Archie may not have had it in him to make my heart skip a beat, but I am still a woman and I have eyes to see. You can wait for word from your father if you like, but I say do it now. Marry this Major Cole. Somewhere there may be a better catch, another man more worthy of you. Indeed, I know you believe there has already been one. But as sure as the sun comes up each morning, the past is past. You can't undo it. So move on. Take the best life offers you. I did and not once in nearly thirty years have I regretted it. Of course, I have enough money to surround myself with compensations aplenty should I need them, but that's not the point.'

The sun was warm. Their stationary carriage had attracted the attention of several urchin beggars. All around them there was noise and clamour; ox carts bearing great loads, people, camels, men on horseback. And above it all the chimes of the clock rang out the hour.

'Tempus Fugit. My dear. Tempus Fugit,' Lady Caroline said with humorous irony.

'I'm not sure I quite understand what you…'

'Yes, you do my dear. I saw you last night. I saw the way the Major looked at you and you at him. You understand very well. The only thing you don't understand fully yet about life is the need for haste. Life is short. Take a hold of it while you can. Of course, there are still those who say we women have a long way to go before we're the equal of men. In most things we just have to tag along making the most of what they serve up to us. But in this, you have the power. Do it now. Make the decision before the clock strikes again. Let this great edifice of bricks and mortar be your symbol for a new beginning, just as it's a symbol of the New Delhi to come.'

Marian continued to feign bewilderment. Throughout the rest of their tour around the city, she puzzled in silence the implications of her companions impassioned monologue. When they returned to the residence she recalled being impressed most, not by the majesty of Moslem architecture, but rather the urgency of Lady Caroline's tone.

Five days after Christmas she stood beneath the modest cupola of St James' Church, just a stone's throw from the ancient Kashmir Gate at the northern end of the city. There she exchanged marriage vows with Jonathan. Sir Archibald and Lady Caroline acted for her, while Colonel and Mrs Reginald Smythe offered their support to the groom. With granite portico as back drop, photographs were taken before and after, to record the event. There were no bridesmaids and no guard of honour. As ceremonies go, it was an under stated, rather muted affair, a long way removed from the image Marian had of herself as William's bride. And it appeared as an entry in her diary with the same economy of words she provided to record her engagement.

'This morning at eleven o'clock, Jonathan and I were married. I am now Mrs Jonathan Cole. How strange and rare a thing is life.'

Preparations were hasty. The reading of the bands was overlooked and at such short notice a reception of any kind was a lot to ask for. Lady Caroline did her best, however, bringing into use for the first time since her arrival in Delhi the ballroom of her new home and filling it with as many of her recent acquaintances as she could muster. And through it all, Marian thought of two things; how like Katie she was behaving and how disappointed her father would be.

There was something else as well, something far more compelling. Every now and then she imagined she could hear the striking of the clock tower in Chandi Chauk. Each time she did the words of her friend rang in her ears. 'Marry Jonathan and be done with it,' was what she had said. And so it was. For better or worse, for richer or poorer, in sickness and in health.

'This will be something to tell your grandchildren,' Mrs Smythe whispered in her ear as she and Marian found themselves alone together for a moment or two on the veranda.

'Yes, I suppose it will,' Marian replied, grandchildren the very last thing on her mind.

Mrs Reginald Smythe was a small Welsh woman. Her Swansea accent though shackled was still clearly evident. She was short and rather unflatteringly stout, appearing as if she were trussed up, somewhat like a chicken, so tight were her corsets.

'You wouldn't believe it to look at me now,' she continued, undeterred by Marian's rather limp response, 'but when dear Colonel Smythe and I were your age, of course he wasn't a Colonel then just a young, dashing lieutenant, more than anything in the world, we wanted to elope. Oh, the thrill of it. The sheer joy. But it wasn't to be. We were engaged for three long years before our marriage. By the time he walked me down the aisle he was a captain and all the excitement was gone. How I envy you, my dear. Such a thrilling adventure for you both and such a handsome young man.'

There was a hint of girlish glee in her voice. Her face was lit up with a mischievous smile, at once endearing yet, at the same time, resting rather uneasily on a woman of her rotund frame and flushed complexion.

Marian had no cause to doubt her word, but it was hard to enthuse. She was alone among strangers, feeling herself more a curiosity than blushing bride. Somewhere in another part of the house, her husband of a few hours was surrounded by his peers, the vows so recently spoken lost in a confusion of male conversation whiskey.

Below her bare shoulders, Marian wore what began life as an evening gown. It was sumptuous in every detail, once the possession of Lady Caroline and hastily concocted to fit, but it was not a wedding dress. It was cold silver rather than pure white. There was no train and no veil. It was more than she deserved but less than she dreamed of. Though it was she who goaded Jonathan into getting married before their onward journey to Assam rather than, as he had planned, after their arrival and once they were settled, she felt a distinct sense of anticlimax.

Not that she was plagued in any way by doubt. Lady Caroline was a woman whose mind, once made up, was rarely changed and she had studied the two of them well. Jonathan, she determined, was a good man and his credentials appeared more than adequate. Added to that and in spite of all efforts to the contrary, Marian could not deny or hide the growing attraction she was beginning to feel for him.

It went without saying that she wanted to remain loyal to William. From the outset, her purpose for going to India was to honour him and cement the love they shared. And, as best she could, she remained committed to that mission. She thwarted Jerry Hugos every effort to win her affection, saved her virtue from the aggressive attentions of General Leighton and, in the end, agreed to marry Jonathan solely as one half of a contract between two people with converging aspirations. With the recent changes in their circumstances however, she was failing miserably and failing fast. Guilty though she felt, the rush in to marriage made a lie of any platonic idealism.

In the comparatively short while they had been in Delhi Jonathan had become captivated by her and, to a lesser extent perhaps, she by him. That Mrs Smythe should have noticed it so readily was no cause for celebration. For her to draw inspiration from the newlyweds and be reminded of her own youthful infatuation some thirty-five years before, only served to illuminate what Marian took to be

195

her own fickleness. She was not ashamed by the seemingly easy transference of her affections from William to Jonathan, even if, at times, she felt she should be, but she was disappointed.

'If you are worried about tonight,' Mrs Smythe added, noticing her discomfort but fully one hundred and eighty degrees away from the source of Marian's consternation 'don't be. Very probably, like my dear Colonel Smythe, your husband will prove to be a kind lover. The first time is never pleasant, but if your Major Cole is the man I've always believed him to be you will learn to find pleasure in such moments of intimacy. I had nine children by Colonel Smythe. Two passed away while they were still babies which was a great source of sorrow to us both, but seven survived, thank God and each one was created with love in our hearts.'

No doubt, Mrs Smythe was a good woman. All she asked of life was to receive in equal measure the kindness and generosity of spirit she so readily gifted to others. She and Marian were complete strangers and normally she moved within social circles far removed from and below the likes of Sir Archibald and Lady Caroline. Nevertheless, the intimacy of her conversation rested entirely upon the most altruistic of motives. She wanted simply to make a new friend. She had no desire to embarrass Marian or to invade the sanctity of her deepest emotions. Sad to say, unfortunately, she achieved both, securing for herself in the process, not the foundations of a firm friendship, but a rather abrupt rebuttal with Marian excusing herself to go in search of a more secure place of sanctuary.

She did not intend to be rude, but she was. Mrs Smythe moved away to lick her wounds by the side of her husband, while Marian pursued the course of her inappropriately timed introspection. In the weeks that followed, after their departure from Delhi, she often invented ways by which she might one day prove her contrition to Mrs Smythe.

Sadly, however, it was not to be. The next time she heard of her, the unfortunate lady was in her coffin, cut down in early old age not by some fatal disease, the like of which was a daily hazard in every Indian city, but as the result of falling down a flight of steps and not a long flight at that.

Reports suggested Colonel Reggie Smythe was a broken man after the accident, so devoted was he to his small Welsh wife. What the self-same reports omitted to mention was the pang of guilt Marian carried with her like an unwelcome keepsake, the penalty for a moments lack of common courtesy towards a woman who was the model of kindness herself.

And, as if to punctuate the hurt she had caused with such casual disregard, in the throes of her bridal bed Marian did find Jonathan to be every bit the fond lover Mrs Smythe hinted at. With or without the preoccupation of Willam, the consummation of her marriage vows took place as ordained by convention. Why or how her husband knew so much of the art of love making when Marian knew nothing at all was rendered unimportant set against the relief she felt that with his help the pain of entering womanhood was less than she expected and no more than she could bear. More disturbing was that in spite of her wish to avoid it, she was aware of a conscious desire to repeat and repeat again the luxurious invasion of her body. Far from enduring the attentions of her husband, each time they shared the same bed her passion matched his own, her need equalled his and her satisfaction cried out to be heard.

Had Lady Caroline been the sole conspirator of Marian's immediate future, she and Jonathan would never have left Delhi. Their spoilt existence might have continued on into old age. No day was less comfortable than the one before, no evening less extravagant.

Only the combined discipline of them both resulted in the firm determination to depart. Ahead lay a journey by rail to Calcutta of some nine hundred and fifty-six miles, their intention on the way to exploit this their best opportunity for tourism.

South of Delhi lay the sacred city of Agra and the glorious tomb of Arjmand Banu, the Taj Mahal, reported to be the crowning glory of Emperor Shah Jehan's extraordinary architectural legacy. It was also promoted by Lady Caroline as the perfect site to visit for two people in love embarking on a new life together.

Beyond Agra and of particular interest to Jonathan were Cawnpore and Lucknow. The former lay on the banks of the Ganges and, as an important junction for an ever-expanding railway network was clearly destined for growth. Jonathan's interest, however, was historical. He wanted to see for himself the memorial well, to stand on the Suttee Chowra Ghats by the river, the same steps up which and upon which over two hundred English men, women and children were slaughtered during the worst days of the mutiny. In Lucknow he intended walking among the ruins of the Residency. Something in him longed to hear echoes of the past, to see bullet scarred walls and experience a little perhaps of the heroism and drama of a siege so courageously resisted.

For, as far as he could see, thirty years on, few lessons had been learned. In the immediate aftermath of such terrible events, the bloodshed and massacres were heralded as evidence of extraordinary sacrifice by ordinary English men and women, all of whom had shown with unimpeachable courage that they were prepared to defend the empire no matter the cost. Their bravery quickly became the stuff of legend, more crimson red patches of cloth on an already rich quilt of Imperial tradition. For their sake, to glorify rather than sully the brutal deaths of these men and women, the empire was duty bound to endure. It must go on in perpetuity. India must carry on as the jewel in the British crown lest the horror of what took place at Cawnpore or the unique courage of those who held out for so long and against such overwhelming odds in Lucknow should be belittled.

In their own way, both had become shrines, the blood stains as indelible as dye, the atmosphere at both sites no less charged than for the thousands of Sikhs whom each year made their pilgrimage to the Golden Temple of Amritsar.

No one spoke of the unholy reprisals which followed the events of 1857, no one that is of an Anglo-Saxon complexion. For each English life lost, hundreds, if not thousands of Indian lives were taken in retaliation. Rivers of blood flowed to transfuse broken English hearts. Corpses by the thousand were claimed to balance the scales of justice. Retribution of medieval dimensions was required to exact revenge and confirm the title of Queen Empress in the minds of every native of India.

For some time, however, and with increasing intensity, Jonathan was becoming cynical. He doubted the renewed confidence of British rule in India. Something told him that at Cawnpore and Lucknow, at Meerut and Lahore, fissures had been opened which would prove themselves too deep and too wide for repair. Something for which he had little in way of evidence save his own gut feeling, persuaded him that 1857 was the beginning of something, not the end, that the trough of Imperial rule was half empty, not half full.

Plans for the Golden Jubilee Celebrations to Queen Empress were well advanced. From London to Landi Kotal the Imperial flag would be flown in triumph and glasses raised to salute the first fifty years of Victorias reign. For some months Jonathan had received various communications outlining precisely how, what, where and when numerous displays of affection and respect should be observed by his small garrison, no heed being given to the remoteness of their position on the Imperial map or the impression any of it might have on the indigenous tribal communities.

And all the while, he had grown more disillusioned, convinced that, safe behind the walls of his fort though he might be, the British presence in India was as a small fish swimming in a very large ocean. His was an existence of looking out rather than looking in. Every instinct told him that those on the outside, the armed warriors and worshippers of Shiva were merely biding their time. They were tolerating rather than capitulating to those such as himself, representatives of a monarch and ruler in a distant land on the other side of the world who was becoming less relevant and, more significantly, less intimidating with each passing day.

In Landi Kotal he had felt vulnerable, not empowered. Each night he had slept, firm in the belief that at any moment and at any time his fortress and every other like it in India would prove no more protection for the empire than had they been built of cards.

He longed to see Cawnpore and Lucknow to purge such fears. He wanted to feel his confidence in empire renewed and gain inspiration by affinity. More than anything and, now married to Marian, more than ever, he wanted to feel secure. He longed to share in her optimism for the future. Perhaps on the banks of mother Ganges he too might be cleansed, his faith revived, like the pilgrims of the Kumbh Mela who gathered at Allahabad every twelve years to bathe in sacred waters and be reborn.

Their quitting of Delhi, however, was the first and most delicate of tasks. Caroline Farrer was a persuasive hostess. She guarded her guests jealously, enticing them with seductive favours and a calendar of social functions which threatened to become a season.

In order to extricate herself and her husband without causing offence, Marian needed every ounce of tact and diplomacy at her disposal, something she had failed so miserably to display in the company of Mrs Smythe. In the end she turned to Sir Archibald for support, shifting the burden of insistence on to his shoulders, making it his responsibility to sue for their early release. Like rescued, wounded creatures which she had nursed back to health, Lady Caroline was reluctant to let them go. She knew they would want their freedom. She knew she could not keep them forever. But when the time came, it brought pain and a degree of sacrifice to inspire guilt into the hardest of hearts.

Farewells on the platform of Victoria station were wretched. Tears flowed like rivers between Marian and Lady Caroline. Decorum vanished. The latter of the women was genuinely distraught, choking on her words and abandoning all thoughts of public image. Her sole concern was the imminent prospect of once more being hurled into an oblivion of solitary confinement. Delhi was abundant with sahibs and memsahibs. Substantial wealth and the reputation of her husband guaranteed an invitation to every social function in the city. She was feted like no other recent arrival, perhaps even more so than the Governor himself. Yet, among all her new acquaintances, not once had she encountered a soul whose company she enjoyed better or friendship she desired more than that of Marian.

Lady Caroline was older now and therefore too old probably to grasp an opportunity for adventure the like of which Marian had secured for herself in agreeing to marry Jonathan. Nevertheless, her affection for Marian was genuine and without parallel. Furthermore, the pleasure she gained from Marian's company was unequalled by that of any of her new acquaintances. She felt she was losing not a friend but a sister.

And as for Marian; she was truly touched by so open and sincere a display of affection, so much so indeed that had Jonathan not been there to encourage her on to the train and Sir Archibald not at the side of his wife to console, the whole parting procedure might have been delayed by several years.

The train was nearing Agra before Marian could do anything other than shrink from the pain and guilt she felt at being parted from her friend. Lucky therefore that her silence was accepted by Jonathan with patient stoicism, particularly since he too had left behind friends in Delhi of whom he was equally fond. As many as possible of these were at the wedding, although they constituted only a small proportion of the guests. Chief among these were Colonel and Mrs Smythe who stood in for his own parents, Jonathan having been acquainted with them on and off from his earliest childhood.

Indeed, they were his God parents. They had known him all his life and in spite of their infrequent meetings, treated him as if he were one of their own. That they were in India was a considerable source of comfort to Jonathan's mother and father in Braintree who shared in equal measure the daily anxiety of having their only son abroad in a country from which so many did not return. Not a day passed without his father offering a prayer for his safe return.

Fortunately, the sadness and disappointment of Marian and Jonathan's leaving Delhi did not last. Before long they were standing together in the shade beneath the gate entrance of the Taj Mahal, humbled by the beauty and majesty of the tomb in front of them. It seemed there could be no greater evidence anywhere in the world or at any time of the love one man might hold for a woman. Their spirits soared. The simple symmetry and beauty of the white marble mausoleum held them in awe and wiped clean away all former disappointment at leaving the protection and hospitality of Sir Archibald and Lady Caroline.

It was in Agra therefore that their great adventure truly began, the holding of hands a symbol of their union. And, for the first time as they stood side by side, their dual reflection a motionless portrait in the long pool leading to the entrance of the tomb, they felt the poignancy of their wedding ceremony. Not without some surprise but with almost tangible delight did Marian find herself more rather than less convinced that what she had done was for the good.

Dear Willam was not forgotten. That would never happen. The memory of him was etched on her soul, the promise of what their life together might have been, ever vivid in her imagination. But she was grateful, in ways she had no idea how to express, for the good fortune of having stumbled across the man to whom she was now married.

Their becoming lovers was unintended and unexpected. She could not regret it, nor did she want to. However, it was not what she anticipated when first he proposed marriage. Physical union was not a consideration. No more so was there any suggestion of that deep affection which bears the name 'love.' From the outset, any such notion was eliminated from her thinking. She was clear what she wanted from Jonathan and what she was prepared to give him in return. Neither of them had been under any illusions. Theirs was no more or less than a mutually beneficial contract.

Delhi altered all that. The time, the place and to a greater or lesser extent depending upon who was invited to express an opinion on the matter, Lady Caroline; all were to blame for the metamorphoses. If Marian suspected a conspiracy, however, she was wrong. Like it or not, neither the time, place nor encouragement from Lady Caroline were singly or wholly to blame. Nature was the compelling force. Try as she might to stop the tide from coming in, hope as much as she liked for the sun not to rise or fall, Marian had no more control over the forces of nature than she did over her own emotions or the intricacies of physical attraction. She was not disloyal to her cause or to the memory of William. Her fault, if she stood accused of one, was in resisting what in her heart of hearts she knew to be true from the first days she and Jonathan were thrown together.

'This is a wonderful place,' she said, standing so close to her husband she could feel the weight of his body against her shoulder.

'Yes, it is,' he replied, neither of them shifting their gaze from the white marble mausoleum, its tranquil majesty provoking a mutual sense of their own great good fortune.

'If this is what heaven is like,' Marian continued. 'Then one day I should very much like to go there.'

Chapter Fourteen

In as much as neither Cawnpore nor Lucknow changed in any way his personal predictions for the future of British rule in India, both locations were a disappointment to Jonathan.

In their own way, the memorial well and crumbling steps down to the river at Cawnpore, were as evocative as the Taj Mahal itself. Both stirred his emotions.

The original, unremarkable well head of course was gone. Over it had been built a substantial earth mound laid to lawn. Atop that was a fine marble angel, specially commissioned by the then Governor General, Lord Canning. Surrounding it had been erected a high octagonal Portland stone screen in the Gothic manner with mullion openings and delicate tracery work. A single stepped entrance offered sole access. And the whole was contained within a garden of some fifty acres into which no Hindu or Moslem might pass.

There were inscriptions, the simplest and yet to Jonathan's mind the most poignant of all; 'Sacred to the perpetual memory of a great company of Christian people, chiefly women and children who, near to this spot, were cruelly massacred by the followers of the rebel Nana Dhundu of Bithur and cast, the dying with the dead, into the well below on the 15 July 1857.'

There were also two small cemeteries nearby with a variety of personal monuments and the fine red brick All Souls Church which had been completed only ten years prior to Jonathan and Marian's visit.

The former was deeply moved by his careful inspection of the site. Later, he stood on the banks of the Ganges, the early spring sun low in the sky, ancient blood on the steps beneath his feet dried to dust, and he mourned for those who had perished. There were no faces he could recall, no names to recite in his silent eulogy but he could not resist.

He was acquainted with none of those who were slaughtered as they tried to escape in their frail but exposed barges and yet he felt he did know them. He had met the women and children of British India. The names on the memorials were unfamiliar to him but the faces he knew all too well.

And in Lucknow, the experience was much the same. Scarred walls retained echoes of pain and suffering. The roof of the residency was gone. Dereliction was all around. Trees and creepers had begun the slow process of smothering all that remained, but it made no difference. The voices lived on, demanding attention, deserving to be remembered. Ruin though it was, Jonathan had little difficulty in imagining the residency as it had been or sharing the desperation of those who clung to life so valiantly in the hope that eventual relief would come.

His only regret was that in spite of it all, he came away with his mind no less made up. Omens of the future still troubled him. Heroes, he believed, were not born but created by circumstances. Cawnpore and Lucknow enticed many quite ordinary people into acts of extraordinary heroism. But still they had died and with their deaths, though another page in British folklore was written, their names bold and proud, he saw no evidence of lessons having been learned or resolutions taken to proceed with more caution.

Within the ranks of British armed forces and equally so in the seats of government back in Westminster, the majority opinion still held that a firm, and if need be, brutal hand on the tiller was the only way to preserve the status quo. Those in command remained convinced that there should not, nor would there be any compromise with the hundreds of millions of indigenous Moslems and Hindus, the greater proportion of whom were plainly thought of as ignorant and indolent, not much more indeed than savages. British rule was the best, indeed the only option for India whether India realised it or not, whether India wanted it or not.

No matter how many or how often the Cawnpores and Lucknows, Jonathan could see no circumstances which might bring about a change in that resolve. During his time in India, he had seen nothing to suggest a shift in philosophy. The foundation of and royal seal of approval for the Indian National Congress was nothing more than an act of expediency, window dressing from the government in Westminster, a toy to pacify the sulking of spoilt children.

The conviction of his vision for the future took no account of Jonathan's personal prospects. As pessimistic as was his mood, during their onward train journey towards Benares, he retained at least a degree of optimism. He took comfort that in having resigned his commission and having acquired for himself a wife whose desire for adventure was a match for his own, he could at least make the most of the untroubled years remaining.

When or how the British would be forced out of India he could only guess. That they would be, he was in no doubt. One day Indians, be they Hindu or Moslem, would take control of their own destiny. Until then, however, he was determined to exploit fully the time he and his new bride had at their disposal.

In Assam, with Marian at his side, there was the promise of an exciting and prosperous future. In tea there were fortunes to be made. The growing, harvesting and manufacturing of it were not easy. Both climate and conditions were not for the faint hearted. Many went to Assam only to be disappointed, returning home empty handed, unable to endure the hardship.

But it did not matter. By the time they reached Benares, both Jonathan and Marian were impatient to be in Calcutta and subsequently to embark upon the final leg of their journey into the jungle and beyond. Apart from what they were able to see from the window of the train, there was no more sightseeing they wanted to do.

At Benares however, they were compelled to pause for a night. Most sacred of cities to the Hindus, a place for pilgrims from across the continent to bathe and unite in worship, it was also the coming together of railway tracks.

At first sight it was a city like any other; ancient, labyrinthine but falling away steeply to the water's edge, where temples and shrines to a thousand lesser Gods jostled for position in their haste to be closer to the one true God, Mother Ganga herself. Its resident population was comparatively small. No more than a hundred thousand souls claimed Benares as their home. Its narrow streets, however, and, more particularly, water front ghats were forever swollen with a sea of pilgrims come to offer single sentences of gratitude and to bathe in the holy waters.

In her diary, a book whose daily entries were fast becoming a tome, Marian recorded as best she could the sights and smells which greeted her, particularly during the brief tour she and Jonathan took as close to the river as was considered acceptable for non-believers.

For as far as she could see in either direction along the banks, on high platforms or at the base of steep steps leading into the water, funeral pyres burned. Some were newly lit, their tightly shrouded corpses still aloof from the flames and smoke. Others were reduced to smouldering ash piles, pitiful remnants of lives soon to be swept into the water to become at one with Ganga.

To the buildings, there was no single pattern or design; no planning. It was a shambles of architectural shapes and sizes, the only unity being the pinkish hew of the sandstone from which every structure was built. As well, and so much a feature of India, there was no order to any of it. Hundreds of impromptu funeral services were taking place at once. Everywhere men and women were wading chest deep into the river, washing themselves and drinking, as small craft came and went, adding to the congestion. At the same time, earthly remains floated past, sodden garlands starkly colourful against the rich brown water.

Strangest of all were the many sadhus, their individual rituals of personal physical humiliation as bizarre as any sight Marian was likely to witness, devotion carried to extremes quite incomprehensible to the Christian mind. Acutely embarrassed by their frequent nakedness and open mouthed at the excruciation of their various tortuous inventions, she could not but look on in amazement, made aware in an instant of the centuries separating herself from so demanding a faith and so zealous a race of believers.

Upon arriving in India, she had heard of such things. From time to time Jerry spoke of men who covered themselves with ash and went naked through life, men who pierced their bodies with cruel shafts of steel or slept on beds of nails, but Marian did not imagine for a moment she would witness at first hand such extremes.

Benares was like no other city she had visited. It offered no compromise to the Raj. Victoria was not honoured there. There were no examples of English architecture. There was no infringement upon Hindu culture or Hindu traditions. As a white woman Marian was exposed, her voyeurism ripe for rebuke, her presence an intrusion upon a scene unaltered for hundreds if not thousands of years.

Thus, when the time came to leave, she found herself disappointed at the brevity of their stay in a place of such intrigue and extravagant disregard for the onward march of modernity. Yet, at the same time, she was relieved, the constant feeling of intimidation producing in her an anxiety she had no wish to prolong. Calcutta remained a distant goal. Another sun would set before they reached India's capital.

'Remarkable country?' Jonathan said as the temples of a very different faith to his own became the last they could see of Benares.

'Yes,' Marian replied, her thoughts still on the ghoulish Sadhu figures, eyes staring and penetrating, glaring out from their ashen, disfigured and emaciated bodies like cold black jewels, accusing yet all knowing.

'I've not been to Calcutta,' Jonathan continued, completely changing his focus 'but I'm told it's quite something, the London of the East, with parks and gardens and buildings as grand as anything back home. We'll have plenty of time to see it all. There's a lot to organise before we head to Assam. You know,' he added, noticing in his wife of only a few days, a somewhat distracted mood.

'You shouldn't let the things you saw in Benares concern you too much. I know India's holy men appear rather frightening at first but they can't do you any harm. I believe they look the way they do to intimidate, but only ignorant people. They're a little like clowns, really. Of course, there are those who believe they have mystical powers or some such stuff. But I'm not convinced. I think, more likely, they're just mad men, poor sad souls gone out of their minds. After a while, you won't notice them; like the beggars. They're everywhere but they needn't affect what we do or how we go about our daily business. They say, in Assam, there are fierce looking tribesmen. Nagas they're called. To this day they're still untouched by civilisation. They roam the hills and jungles, completely naked for the most part, performing rituals the like of which we can't possibly imagine in this day and age.'

His concern was appreciated, but not necessary. Marian was certainly moved by the sadhus. Indeed, sight of them in Benares left her with precisely the feeling of intimidation Jonathan mentioned. She also came away with the strongest sense that she had intruded upon something quite beyond the comprehension of her kind. At the same time, however, there was a degree of exhilaration at having witnessed, however briefly, something so extraordinary.

Quite often during their time together, Jerry Hugo had steered her away from sights and sounds which he thought might be the cause of discomfort. Unaware of Marian's resilience he was over protective, as often as not offering simplistic or mollifying explanations to the mysteries of things Marian would have preferred left to her own interpretation. His and now Jonathan's apparent need to show her and yet save her from the real India, to temper the arcane and shocking, was done, she knew, with the best of intentions, but it was quite unnecessary.

From the moment she stepped ashore on Indian soil in the company of Sir Archibald and Lady Caroline Farrer, and in spite of her initial anxiety, it was precisely the novelty and charged atmosphere of everything which encouraged Marian's onward progress. In London and Hove, she found life rather dull and unchallenging.

Her childhood was happy and uncomplicated. She was nurtured and educated with the utmost care so as to ready her for an adult life in middle-class society. She lived in a home, or rather two homes, almost totally cushioned from any of the harsh realities of those less fortunate than herself. There was money enough to clothe and feed her. She never went without and the fundamental purpose of her education was to prepare her for continuity into married life.

The only controversy, or controversies, were those encouraged by her father in the form of open debate. He wanted, for each of his daughters, the same stability he had always known. He expected them to wed men of similar class and income to his own and, in time, to raise their own families, families which themselves would carry on again in similar vein. Where he varied his approach with Marian in a manner he did not with his other two daughters, was to recognise in her and encourage to blossom a capacity for intellectual stimulation beyond that normally anticipated in a young woman of her background.

Given the choice, he would never have permitted Margaret or Katie to leave home. Margaret insisted she had it in her to become a missionary. She spoke of a calling. She boasted the courage for travel to the most distant and inhospitable corners of the world. She claimed she had the sense of purpose and dedication to endure any number of hardships. But she had none of those things. She lived with her head in the clouds. She had neither the intelligence nor stamina for such work. Beyond the comfort blanket of 32 Princes Gate, she would falter at the first hurdle and, by ignoring rather than fanning her ambitions, everyone in the family hoped and expected them to fade away.

Devotion to her Christian beliefs was laudable and much applauded, but beyond that Charles Chase quite expected her to take a husband of equal blandness to herself and settle down somewhere within easy reach of home.

Katie, on the other hand, had already thwarted any designs to keep her from the possibility of doing something stupid or discrediting. Her elopement was forgiven on the grounds that such recklessness was committed by an impetuous and easily led child and not in any conscious way as a rejection of her family. Neither, Charles Chase believed, was it her deliberate intention to disgrace them. That she had achieved both and caused untold grief to her mother was a matter of untimely coincidence rather than some master plan.

In Marian's case, however, he had deliberately opened her mind. Therefore, he risked the blossoming of desires and needs beyond those which could reasonably be satisfied within the cloistered environment of a middle-class marriage. He had given Marian her wings so to speak. The inevitable consequence was that one day she would want to fly. And fly she had, with his blessing but tinged with regret. She had taken advantage of the gifts he bestowed upon her. But the price was high. He had misjudged her, not in the least anticipating the distances she would cover or just how far behind she would leave the nest.

Accidentally, he had triggered in Marian appetites she had no idea she possessed. Once stimulated, the further she travelled from home the further she wanted to go. The more extreme her experiences or contrasting the sights and sounds she witnessed, the more she searched the horizon for novelty.

Jonathan's concerns were expressed with the best of intentions but were unfounded. Marian was ready to embrace any land he led her to and she was willing to engage any culture along the way. Having seen into their eyes, she was convinced the sadhus were anything but insane jesters. Beneath the ashes, dyes and layers of matted hair, set apart from the obvious humiliation and self-mutilation of their personal ordeals, she glimpsed something of great depth, a spiritual insight too complex for her well-nourished soul to fathom.

In Cawnpore, as Jonathan stood, his feet on the exact spot where British blood once flowed into the Ganges like a waterfall, staining crimson the murky currents, he had been visibly moved. He felt the pain of those who perished. He suffered alongside them. In their sacrifice, he tried in vain to see hope for the future.

In just the same way, Benares left its mark upon Marian. Rather than alert her to the realities of how far from civilisation she had strayed, the sadhus, burning funeral pyres, temples and petty ceremonies going on all around them, inspired in her a thirst to see and learn more.

A few days in Calcutta would be a welcome relief from the rigours of train travel. However, a return to the superficiality of Anglo-Indian society in Delhi, was to be endured rather than entered into with any great relish.

Without question, Lady Caroline Farrer had proved herself a good and loyal friend. Beyond the arrogance and self-indulgence which came courtesy of her wealth, she was joyously irreverent and earnestly exuberant. She was not at all like so many of the social climbing acquaintances Marian encountered in London or Hove and whom she endured by way of regular and often tedious dinner parties. Lady Farrer had nowhere to climb. She sat atop the social ladder, 'cow towing' to no one.

Nevertheless, she was in so many ways a typical example of the British in India. Making no concessions at all to climate, terrain or the physical difficulties of being thousands of miles from her place of birth, she, and the vast majority like her of Europeans compelled by circumstances to live in India, ignored and were ignorant of the indigenous population, reacting to them only in as much as they made useful servants or beasts of burden. With careful contrivance Lady Caroline erected about herself a little England. The faiths, customs and habits of those into whose country she had alighted were absolutely of no moment at all; barbarians and heathens occupying dark skins. Their needs, wants and above all rights, were inconsequential. They were dismissed out of hand as an irrelevance or, more seriously, and very much the theme of Jonathan's quietly observed anxieties, ignored as if they did not exist at all. To his mind, this was significantly more dangerous.

Marian could not pretend she was anything but grateful for the hospitality she and Jonathan were afforded in Delhi. Their wedding, on the spur of the moment and not without its critics, was planned and executed selflessly. No expense was spared and no inconvenience too much to ensure a memorable day. And, a memorable day it had been.

But something was not right. The closer her train got to Calcutta, the more Marian shied away from a repeat of the social whirl manipulated for herself and Jonathan by Sir Archibald and Lady Caroline. As if in some way hypnotised by the piercing stare of the sadhus in Benares, she found herself wanting to detour around Calcutta altogether. She agreed to a short reprieve before the last leg of their journey into Assam, but in her heart, she would have preferred to pass it by lest she be deprived of the passion and thirst coursing through her every vein.

Regretfully, there was no choice. They could not avoid Calcutta. However, while humouring her husband, Marian made a silent vow not to be distracted from her quest for answers to the thousands of questions India posed each time she opened her eyes in the morning.

They arrived at the Hooghly River just after dawn, the terminus at Howrah, gaunt in the grey early morning light. On the opposite bank, a short carriage ride across the old pontoon bridge, lay the great city itself. Fine eighteenth century architecture, broad avenues, spacious green parks and the largest gathering of humanity in one confined space on the Indian continent, Calcutta was home to some five million or more people, the trading heart of the British empire and the seat of British government.

From the Palace of Belvedere, the Governor General reigned supreme. Upon his whim was the power of life and death over an entire continent, the population of which was larger than all others within the jurisdiction of the British empire. In Calcutta rested not only the fate of a single nation but the well-being and prosperity of an empire. India was the jewel in the crown, Calcutta its brightest facet. Right and proper therefore that one should enter with some humility.

In the width of a river, the blinking of an eye, Marian was transported to another world. There was the heat, there was the inevitable tide of humanity and there was the all-encompassing clamour and chaos. But Calcutta was not India. Here was a modern European city, a city of straight-lined avenues, order, elegance and definition. Central to it all, a short distance to the south of the bridge, was Dalhousie square, a tree lined lake surrounded on all sides by a quadrangle of fine public buildings. It reminded her not of the country she had just crossed, but of Paris or London.

So extreme was the contrast she found it hard to take in. Barely a few hours earlier she had stood on the banks of the Ganges looking at naked warrior monks and sorry funeral pyres, her senses heady. Now, all around her were bleached white buildings and horse drawn carriages. In Benares she was the outsider, an alien presence, encroaching upon rituals and customs far removed from any to which she could readily assimilate. In Calcutta, the setting was reversed, like the negative image on an enormous photo plate. Everywhere she looked there were Asian faces, but it was they, not she or Jonathan who looked out of place. Their turbans and loosely wound clothing, even the colour of their skin was an anachronism amid so much that was British.

Eventually the carriage arrived at the esplanade, an open maidan spotted with trees and crisscrossed with neat walk ways. Ahead of them was Chowringhee Road and the Great Eastern Hotel but as they looked to their right, they could only marvel at the residence of the Viceroy himself.

Standing central in its own vast compound of formal gardens it rivalled even Buckingham Palace for splendour, a symbol in every way not just of the might, majesty and permanency of Imperial rule, a flagrant reminder to the whole Indian nation of continuing British supremacy, but also an affirmation to every European living on Indian soil of their personal legitimacy and infallibility.

Once, India had been ruled by the Moghuls. In every city the great Moghul Emperor built mosques and palaces the scale and beauty of which no Hindu had ever seen. For hundreds of years, these buildings were the symbols of their power and dominance over a people they had subjugated in battle. But the Moghuls were gone, their place taken by yet another nation with Imperial designs. Calcutta belonged now to the British, an elegant modern city quite able to compete with any in Europe.

Yet, something was not right. There was a fragility about it neither Marian nor Jonathan could satisfactorily explain. He looked at Government House still with the images of Cawnpore and Lucknow on his mind and could not help but speculate on the eventual fate of so pretty and vain a structure. If pride indeed comes before the fall, then this building of all others, the very epitome of British rule in India, was an alter to pride on a scale at least equal to the wondrous constructions of the magnificent but ultimately mortal Shah Jehan himself. How long would it be, Jonathan wondered, before this temple to pride was reduced to a crumbling ruin, its occupants brought low by a people whose numbers alone would one day make them an unstoppable tide.

Marian was still held by the spell of what she had witnessed in Benares. She was altered in a way she could neither describe nor understand. All she could identify was an uncomfortable feeling, a notion that she and Jonathan, far from belonging, were actually out of place among such architectural superlatives, that their stay in Calcutta should be as brief as they could make it. There was no real cause for her to feel unsettled. Government House and the streets and parks around it were familiar to her. She was a Londoner, born and brought up in a fine city. There should have been nothing strange or intimidating about the Georgian facades, straight paved roads or manicured gardens. Benares was an anathema to her, a place of mystery and disturbing visions. Landi Kotal was a settlement more remote than any she could have imagined from the drawing room of 32 Princes Gate or the upper window of her bedroom in Adelaide Drive.

However, her mind was turned upside down, her thoughts on their head. Something had happened the day she stepped ashore in Bombay. She was infected by and with India. At first, she tried to reject it. Her intention was to remain on the outside looking in. She expected to endure India long enough to complete her mission and then return to England unscathed, the same woman as before, her opinions, philosophies and prophecies for the future unaltered by her travels.

Arriving in Calcutta should have been akin to a home coming. Every aspect of the city was familiar to her. As she and Jonathan walked into the foyer of the Great Eastern Hotel it was not too far removed from taking tea at the Savoy. There were concessions made to the different climate and there were decorative variations consumed within the term colonial, but to all intents and purposes the Savoy and Great Eastern were one and the same. The only difference, the only unfathomable change was her own unease, the distinct feeling she sensed of no longer belonging.

In Delhi, there was a hint of it. Hospitality on the scale for which Lady Caroline Farrer was legend could be unnerving even to the most conventional and well-practiced of social animals. There, however, she attributed her unease to tiredness and, more particularly to the rather unusual circumstances of her marriage. Perhaps in Calcutta she was still experiencing more of the same. Perhaps her whirlwind and headlong plunge into matrimony, when it had been the very last thing on her mind, was taking its toll. Perhaps she was weary of trains. Perhaps the sights, sounds and smells of India were altogether too potent.

She had no idea. She could explain none of it, nor rationalise it with any good common-sense excuse. All she was aware of was a certain and overpowering discomfort, like the sensing of a coming storm in spite of being bathed in sunshine. Fight it though she might have wanted to, and she was not at all sure she wanted to, she was no longer the Marian of 32 Princes Gate, no longer the Miss Chase whose looks and ready wit encouraged a woman such as Lady Caroline Farrer to call her 'friend.'

For a split second, at the moment the door of their suite closed behind them and Jonathan hesitated before walking across the room to inspect the facilities, Marian wished she could have had Jerry Hugo at her side; not because she preferred his company to that of the man who was now her husband but simply to show him what she had become in his absence and thank him for his considerable contribution. She knew and understood little enough about the changes going on inside her. However, she suspected his influence, albeit sometimes overzealous and at others irritating, was the root cause of her welcome discomfort.

For the remainder of that day and night she and Jonathan did not leave the confines of the hotel. Their time together was spent quietly. In deep rattan chairs on spacious verandas and saloons with marbled floors, they sipped ice cooled drinks. They talked, but neither spoke of their disquiet. Jonathan's predictions for the future of British rule in India were clear in his mind but for a time, he hoped, further off than would affect either himself or his new bride. He was committed to the premise of Imperial frailty, that in time the walls would come crashing down, but he was comforted by the conviction that he was of a generation still immune from such impending disaster.

Since Lucknow, since the crushing of the mutiny, since the vicious punishments inflicted upon all those who were directly involved and many thousands who were not but who found themselves caught up in the aftermath, those behind the walls of Government House were able to eat and sleep peacefully in their beds. They rested, secure in the knowledge that the hole in the dyke had been plugged. India would not have been India and Imperial rule no challenge were there not occasional skirmishes or public expressions of resentment. Here and there small pockets of resistance were inevitable, like single, infrequent clouds on a blue-sky day. But storm clouds, the heavy, thundering, lightning filled storm clouds which Jonathan believed were headed in the direction of the Indian continent, storm clouds which would ultimately engulf every province, north to south, east to west, were beyond his immediate horizon. He feared they were there, but for the time being, they were far enough off and he could continue his enjoyment of the unbroken sunshine.

From time to time, such as in the decision he took to alter the path of his career and the poignant moments he spent standing at the entrance to the Cawnpore Well Memorial, his visions came all too near, the blackness in the clouds sending a shiver down his spine. However, with Marian at his side and a prosperous life in Assam ahead of them, the white splendour of Government House and the formal elegance of Calcutta were a tonic to his pessimism.

That night he went to Marian's bed. Passion and affection were not emotions Marian expected to feel for the man she had married in the place of William. Yet there were both. They emerged from the experience into the morning sunlight united, their onward journey and plans set firm. Before leaving the Great Eastern Hotel, Marian sat down to write home. With every word, she tried to confirm the confidence of her unfamiliarly impetuous plunge into marriage and urged all members of her family to rejoice in her new found happiness.

Meanwhile, Jonathan went to fulfil his various appointments at Fort William, entering the sunken complex with its heavy fortifications and deep dry moats, impressed by the ingenuity of a place so carefully contrived to cater for calamity. Should the worst happen. Should the icing on the white palace begin to flake, should Calcutta fall, Fort William was prepared. There would be no Lucknow in Calcutta.

Almost completely hidden from view to the outside observer, there existed a fortressed town. And within it was a maze of buildings which included barracks, accommodation for every European in Calcutta and even a parish church. Deep below ground level, secreted away on the edge of the capital, its construction a credit to nineteenth century engineering skills, this secret city was the antithesis of everything boasted of in the extravagant peacock display that was the residence of the Viceroy.

It was also headquarters of the army, the place where, finally, Jonathan was expected to resign his commission formally, where he would receive the final shilling for service to Her Majesty and empire. It was an obligation he needed to fulfil on his own. No sense of great pride or relief accompanied his resignation. His years with the army had been good ones, his service loyal. Though now his ambitions lay elsewhere, his heart was heavy in the formal declaration of his intentions.

When he returned to the hotel, he did so as a civilian, accompanied by a certain sense of nakedness which he found difficult to translate into words. Marian was sensitive enough to offer sympathy but it was nigh impossible to communicate her empathy to such an exclusively masculine sense of loss.

What they needed to do, and with some haste, was find their way to the Brahmaputra. Both felt ill at ease in Calcutta. Their reasons were different and, though their intimacy was complete, they stumbled when it came to sharing their innermost thoughts. There existed only between them a telepathy of accord. The Great Eastern Hotel was not home. It was a strange environment in which neither felt at ease, the acceleration of their leaving therefore something to which they addressed themselves in unison.

The railway terminus at Howrah, on the opposite bank of the Hooghly River, beckoned and they were quick to answer the call. Within forty-eight hours of their arrival in Calcutta they were once more entrained.

Chapter Fifteen

Given their impatience to leave, there was much in Calcutta Marian and Jonathan did not see. There were people they might have visited. Sir Archibald had written letters of introduction on their behalf before they left Delhi, providing names of former colleagues whose positions of influence might be of assistance to them. Jonathan himself knew of various previous acquaintances presently serving at Fort William.

Had Lady Caroline been in Calcutta, no doubt she would have enrolled them rapidly into the sumptuous social life of the city. Invitations, even to Government House, would have been a simple matter of a few well-chosen words in the right ears. She was not personally acquainted with the Governor General, but working her way into his inner circle would have presented only a minor challenge.

Had they chosen to do so Marian and Jonathan could have stayed on almost indefinitely, secure in the knowledge that the hospitality would have continued as long as they chose to take advantage of it.

However, they were of one mind, leaving at the first possible opportunity, not looking back and with no second thoughts. Their only decision was to select a route. From Howrah terminus there were two possibilities. One train of the Assam and Bengal Railway Company would take them due north to within sight of the Himalayas. Then it would swing Eastwards following the line of the Brahmaputra until reaching Gauhati. From there, it was a steamer journey of two nights to Dibrugarh.

Alternatively, and the route they chose, there was a shorter train journey, initially along the same track but then veering off sharply to reach the river almost at its southern most end in Goalundo. Here it merged as a tributary of the Ganges Delta. And from there, the steamer would carry them for nearly four hundred miles upstream before their final destination. Marian needed no prompting. She had seen quite enough of trains to last her some time.

Within a few months, the monsoons would be upon them, widening the river to miles. Clearly marked channels would disappear making navigation a dangerous adventure. But for now, the comparative luxury of a first-class cabin aboard the SS Pagan appealed more than another prolonged ride in a cramped railway carriage.

Sadly, two nights into the voyage, their sleep was interrupted by the loud and prolonged tolling of the ships bell. It was not done specifically to awaken the passengers but as a warning to other vessels on the river lest they too ride up on the same sand bank as had impaled the SS Pagan on its lumbering progress upstream. Helpless in thick fog but reluctant to pause, the boat had floundered, like a beached whale, all efforts to free itself under its own steam, useless.

Naturally, the best was made of a bad situation. Jonathan and Marian were not the only British passengers on board. For the most part, the majority of those employing the services of either the steam ship company or the Assam railway were headed south. They were going to, rather than from Calcutta. However, Major Robert Hutchison of the Assam Valley Light Horse Volunteers and Norman Bayden who they later learned was 'en route' to Assam to supervise the construction of a further rail link from Jorhat to Dibrugarh, were but two of a modest European contingent.

Others comprised a new doctor for the region, himself an Irishman by the rather predictable name of Patrick Murphy, Mr and Mrs Laws who were tea planters and later to become close friends, Herbert Forbes, chairman of the Indian Tea Association and two young men who were, by their own admission, as new to Assam as Marian and Jonathan themselves.

It was a small clique but adequate enough to ensure spirits remained high in spite of the obvious hazards of being stranded in mid-channel with no immediate expectation of rescue. In a small corner of the ship's saloon, prayers were said while the bell continued to toll irritatingly, the doctor for some reason being chosen as the most appropriate among them to officiate. Quite why this decision was taken presented something of a mystery. Stranded they were, stuck fast, but no member of the crew, nor the captain himself suggested that their lives were in any real danger.

Rather inexplicably also, a flask of brandy was produced from which the men sipped while toasting the health of Her Majesty. Little other ritual was observed save a private thought from Marian for her family at home in London. She had no difficulty in picturing all those she loved at 32 Princes Gate and far from finding such fond recollections an exacerbation to the discomfort of her predicament, she took advantage of them to bolster her hope for a safe and speedy deliverance from the firm grip of the Brahmaputra.

Eventually their salvation came in the form of the SS Sherani, sister ship to the Pagan, the one on a downstream course while the other should have been making her way up. Sounds of distress from the Pagan in the form of her bell, were instantly recognisable to those aboard the Sherani who were familiar with such incidents.

That said, in the thick fog and the pitch darkness of night, attaching hawsers from one stern to the other was no easy task. During the process of manoeuvring back and forth and the casting of lines several of which failed to reach their target, much hysterical shouting from the two crews ensured a lively entertainment. Poor Major Hutchison mustered all his powers of verbal restraint, so impatient was he to set the 'wogs' right in what he considered to be the simplest of tasks. Accustomed to issuing orders and having the men under his command get the job done, it was as much as he could do to refrain from usurping command of the vessel. Only with assurances from Mr and Mrs Law, with whom he was clearly acquainted prior to their embarkation, was he persuaded to let the pantomime reach its own conclusion, but not without first making the rather disturbing, over loud and self-illuminating exclamation, that 'these bloody natives are only so far removed from animals in that they can speak.'

Apparently, this belief was his chief motive for wanting to interrupt the performance of their rescue. It was also abundantly obvious that this was a general rule he applied through his daily life and a comment typical it seemed of the attitude which Jonathan encountered all too often among military ranks, and one which served as a spur to maintaining a discreet distance between himself and the Major.

However, finally, and it was a 'finally' accompanied by much self-congratulation and applause from all those directly involved in the salvage operation, not to mention much audible sighing with relief from all the paying passengers on the SS Pagan, the rickety craft was re-floated. Steam was got up, propellers turned and she was under way again, her master it was greatly hoped showing more diligence than he had done prior to their impromptu running aground.

As a prelude to their future life as tea planters, the incident was not particularly auspicious. Their only consolation was in assurances from the likes of Jack Laws and the cabin steward who not only spoke perfect English but boasted of having once been in service to an aristocrat in Hertfordshire, that running aground was not uncommon, nor was the unceremonious manner of their retrieval. Either way, it was an incident Marian would remember.

'I came out here back in the forties, not long after this whole tea malarkey began,' Jack Laws said to Marian on the following morning as the fog began to lift. They were both on deck looking out over the guard rail towards the south bank of the river. 'Met my wife here, you know. Had our children out here too for that matter. In fact, now I think about it, I've only been home to England once in the last twenty years. It's a bit rough and ready out here. None of your Calcutta smart life if you know what I mean. But if you give it a go I can promise, you'll never want to leave.'

He appeared concerned that events of the previous evening might have been the source of some discouragement to Marian. Fortunately, his worries, if indeed that is what they were, had no foundation. She was neither frightened by their mid-stream mishap, nor put off by it. At one moment during the furore, she did turn to Jonathan to see if he was at all anxious but he was not and his calm was enough.

Every day, Marian was presented with something new. India was a constant source of novelty to her; unique and unpredictable. And that was precisely the attraction. In England life was comfortable, orderly, without extremes and, more particularly, predictable. Were she to take to the water at Henley, there was absolutely no chance at all of finding herself stranded or in need of rescue. Every day was the same; different names perhaps and different places, but the same.

By contrast, in India she awoke each morning without the slightest idea what to expect before going to bed the following evening or, as often as not, where she would find to lay her head. Running aground in dense fog on a mud bank thrown up by the currents of the Brahmaputra, was no deterrent to her growing fondness. It enhanced her excitement and stimulated her desire to continue on, albeit in the full knowledge that without Jonathan at her side, very possibly she would not have had the courage to proceed.

She leaned against the well-worn, wooden guard rail, not out of weary dejection, but in reflection of what further adventures lay in wait.

'It's such a beautiful part of the world,' she said as if she were referring to some quaint corner of Sussex, but in an effort to quell any fears Jack Laws might be harbouring as to her fortitude.

For half an hour or so they chatted. At any moment she expected him to ask for news of home. She anticipated fond reminiscences on his part of a country he had not visited for so long, but none came. Almost from the start of their conversation she realised that Assam was Jack Laws' home. Clearly, he loved every inch of it. If he did pine for English soil, he hid it well. He spoke instead of rivers and jungles, of tea and jute and red earth and he did it with a passion Marian had not heard since the days of her long train journey in the company of Jerry Hugo.

By the time Jonathan appeared on deck, his previous mission a brief consultation with the captain in broken Hindi concerning the likelihood of any further delays, Marian and her companion were firm friends. They shared it appeared a mutual affection for horses as something other than a convenient means of transport. More than that, however, by a rare coincidence when taking into account the number of years since he had been in England, they also shared the dual acquaintance of a certain Mr James Keith. He lived in London and had been a close business colleague of her father since Marian was a small girl.

If it was the same Mr Keith, and it seemed likely that it was, then Mr Jack Laws recalled him with fondness as the young boy with whom he shared a dormitory during his first and second years at Harrow. It was a matter of no consequence and formed the basis only of a slender strand between them, but it was a beginning and in a corner of the world where friendships were an essential aspect of everyday life, Marian believed she had made a good start.

Of course, she had the advantage of being blessed with a naturally gregarious nature. She found it easy to make friends. Though their sojourn on the sandbank was an event guaranteed to bring people together, for Marian the ability to strike up a conversation with comparative strangers had been learned during many years in the less stressed atmosphere of dinner parties and 'at homes.'

Charles Chase was always determined his children should acquire self-confidence at an early age. To that end therefore, rather than confine them upstairs when there were guests in the house, even when quite young, his three daughters were invited to be present during social functions and encouraged to contribute. It was a form of liberalism, or perhaps modernism, which did not necessarily sit well with all his friends. However, in his own home, Marian's father stuck to it regardless, devoted to the notion that as they matured to adulthood his children would have no trouble assimilating into any society or situation.

In Marian's case, his philosophy brought with it obvious dividends. She and Jack Laws were already well settled into each other's company by the time Jonathan joined them on deck. Almost certainly, Margaret would not have coped so well. Her innate shyness, inherited it seemed from more distant members of the Chase family, since it was a handicap from which neither Mr nor Mrs Chase suffered, would always be a stumbling block to her social advancement. It was relieved only somewhat by her readiness to explode into a diatribe of missionary zeal at the least opportunity.

As for Katie, her past precipitous actions spoke for themselves. The youngest of the three Chase girls and therefore perhaps feeling the need to compete for attention, she had already taken her father's ideals to and beyond their limits. A flirtatious child from the day she was old enough to recognise her own reflection in a mirror and blessed or cursed, dependent upon one's viewpoint, with an exuberance of spirit not matched by an equal measure of common sense, her silly and, ultimately shameful actions, were the unenviable consequences of a policy defended so rigorously by Mr Chase whenever he was challenged on it.

Had he been at Marian's side, he would have applauded her easy manner and the inconspicuous effort of her conversation with a fellow passenger. Whether he would have cheered so readily the manner and circumstances of her being cast adrift in the middle of the Brahmaputra on a day when she would and should normally have been at home with her family was a different question, the answer to which Marian could only guess. The exchange of letters between herself and her father was a precarious thing. She had no way of knowing if hers had reached him or if his, assuming there were any, would catch up to her eventually when she ceased constantly shifting position from one side of the continent to the other.

Either way, Jonathan was impressed by the intimacy she had already established with Jack Laws. He too had no trouble engaging strangers. However, it was a pleasant surprise to find the ice broken and confidences already being exchanged before he had been formally introduced.

By the time SS Pagan reached Gauhati, without further incident and for the most part in fine sunshine, Marian and Jonathan were conversationally 'well met' with every European on board. Dr Murphy was not new to India but he was new to Assam. Young, unmarried and a keen polo player he was immediately welcomed into the fold. Moreover, his professional qualifications added further to his eligibility in a part of the world where all his attributes were in short supply, save one, that of his bachelor status.

Assam had its full complement of young unmarried men. It was a harsh place. The work was difficult, conditions regularly medieval and the tropical climate set firm against human habitation, particularly human habitation by those used to the more benign European climate. Add to that a paucity of young women and morale was always under threat.

The arrival of yet another single male therefore would only serve to exacerbate what was already a significant imbalance in the sexes. However, the doctor's added skills as a polo player were bound to be viewed as adequate compensation for the handicap of his being without a wife, more perhaps even than his ability to cure all or many of the sicknesses capable of rendering his peers in the region incapacitated or dead.

By contrast, Norman Bayden was newly returned from England where he had been for the express purpose of acquiring for himself a wife. He was alone on the SS Pagan. However, his new bride was due to 'come up river' within months, giving him breathing space only to prepare a home suitable for a young woman previously more accustomed to the sleepy, cushioned environment of Wimbledon, its rough common land the nearest to jungle she had been in her comparatively short life. It was also time enough, he hoped, for the new Mrs Agnes Victoria Bayden to prepare herself physically and emotionally for transportation to a region which might just as well have been on another planet for all the knowledge she had of it.

Mr and Mrs Jack Laws were more fortunate. They were both from among the old tea planting families. Assam was their home. To the both of them, England was the more alien country of the two. Mrs Laws, nee Braithwaite, had only been to England once during the course of her fifty-three years on the Indian subcontinent and then not at all to the county to which her name alludes. She was born in India. Her father was a soldier. In fact, he was one of the many casualties during the worst of the '57 uprisings. Fatally wounded as he was in a relatively minor but violent skirmish which history did not see fit to record, he died, leaving a wife who subsequently returned to England. His daughter, the said Marjorie Braithwaite, stayed on however and took a young tea planter named Jack as her husband. She knew the climate, understood the harshness of the life and endured the Spartan ways. She had also long since come to terms with the ephemeral nature of human existence in a remote corner of empire where jungle and insects were united to resist human intervention.

That Norman Bayden saw the need to travel to England to find himself a wife was not at all unusual. Indeed, for the young men of northern Assam it was something of a ritual, almost an essential rite of passage into manhood. The drawback was that so desperate were the tales of jungle living which filtered back to England, gaining in momentum with each sea mile covered between the two, even in England the finding and capturing of a wife was no easy matter. Not many rosy cheeked English girls with prospects were prepared to risk such a notoriously unpredictable and uncomfortable enterprise as marriage to a tea planter.

As often as not, those few who were gullible enough to let some young buck talk them into it, were as desperate for a husband as their future mates were for a wife. Invariably therefore and regretfully, the rule rather than she exception tended to be that Assam wives were either plain and uninteresting, financially indisposed or, worse still, both. The most important skills required of them were to keep a good house for their husbands and spawn a plural number of healthy children, neither task easy under such conditions, but the latter of the two more difficult. Child mortality was tragically high, any alleviation of which was an added blessing with the arrival of another doctor to the region.

Of all those on board whom Marian encountered, Major Hutchison was the only one to arouse some suspicion that all might not bode well. Although it was obvious he and the Laws were acquainted, it was equally apparent that there was no love lost between them. Courteous good mornings and other innocuous exchanges passed one way and the other but there was no camaraderie. Marian gained the definite impression that Major Hutchison was deliberately kept at arm's length, particularly by Jack Laws.

The major himself was an exceptionally tall man, well over six feet, broad shouldered and with a heavy, purposeful stride which, on the teak decking of the ship, announced his arrival from some distance. During their stranding on the sand bar, he spent the majority of his time in the midst of the action, issuing instructions to the ships master in spite of himself and cursing in Hindi at the two crews engaged in the passing of hawsers from one ship to the other. Evidently, he was a man who liked to take charge. Moreover, he had most definitely little or no respect for non-whites.

First impressions indicated he was more than a little self-satisfied, rather too quick to assume the infallibility of his commands and possibly, Marian considered, a man apt to cross swords rather than sue for peace. First impressions of course can be misleading. She made it a habit where possible not to judge people on such narrow parameters, preferring to reserve judgement until suitable hard evidence of character presented itself. However, Jonathan's instant disquiet about the Major and resentment of the manner in which he appeared so ready to assume control at the least provocation, was a spur to her instinctive feeling that Major Hutchison would be a hard man to befriend and, very probably, might prove himself a man best avoided.

At Gauhati, several more European passengers were taken on board. One or two had come up from Calcutta by train, just as Marian and Jonathan themselves might have done, taking to the water only when the tracks ran out. Others were in Gauhati on business, ordering provisions or buying machine parts. All of them appeared to be on speaking terms at least with the Laws and some of them knew Norman Bayden, leaving Marian to assume they also were 'planters,' an assumption confirmed during the remainder of their voyage as one by one she and Jonathan were introduced.

When it was made public that they were headed for Dibrugarh and, more precisely, to the recently established Shahjan Tea Company and that Jonathan was to be the new estate manager, a vacancy the filling of which had been the topic of general speculation for some time, one gentleman in particular was quick to engage them in conversation. His name was Philip Dunn. It was his elder brother, John who had taken the unusual decision to fill the position at Shahjan with someone new to the region and industry.

Under normal circumstances 'tea men' were apt to fill vacancies where they arose with other 'tea men.' A close-knit community, knowledge of the product, familiarity with the growing and manufacturing processes and previous experience of living in a tropical climate were usually viewed as the only reliable qualifications.

However, the commercial production of tea in Assam by the British was barely half a century old and the general population of plantation owners and managers was not exactly in the first flush of youth. Most planters in Assam were either, like the Laws, 'in at the start of it' as he was proud to boast, or brought in from other parts of the world with a similar tradition. Some, like Philip Dunn and his two brothers, were second or, in their case, third generation. Precisely for those reasons, John Dunn, the eldest of the Dunn boys and consequently heir to the largest tea enterprise in Upper Assam, was bent on attracting new blood.

He wanted to introduce into the industry and into his new, independent enterprise, both the energy of youth and the broad canvas of fresh ideas a man such as Jonathan might bring. That he had no direct experience was not necessarily a handicap. If he was intelligent and quick-witted, he would soon learn the skills. And there was no shortage of men to teach him.

It was a philosophy the cause of considerable debate around the meal table at Kurmi where his father resided in some splendour, king of all he surveyed. Much heated argument came and went before John got his way, advertising the position not through the local community or by way of the Indian Tea Association, but more broadly, hoping to attract a man of a different stamp.

Among his sceptics was his brother Philip. Consequently, it was with some reticence he welcomed the former Major, now plain Mr, and Mrs Cole to Assam over dinner on board the SS Pagan the evening they departed Gauhati on the final leg of their journey up river. Although his attitude and tone were that of welcome and he was generous in his offers of assistance or advice should they feel inclined to ask, his approach verged on the inquisitorial. Nevertheless, neither Johnathan or Marian were naïve. They were well aware of the scrutiny their arrival was bound to generate. For a while at least, they expected to find themselves under a microscope. It was only right and proper they should be. Running into the brother of Jonathan's future employer before they had even arrived in Dibrugarh was somewhat unsettling, but with Marian as his ally, beguiling all would be critics with her every word, Jonathan was ready to face his examiners.

In the most polite manner and hidden beneath a veneer of otherwise trivial conversation, Philip Dunn probed Jonathan for details of his and Marian's backgrounds and, in the formers case, career to date. As much as anything he wanted to understand for himself what had persuaded his brother to offer the position of manager to a man who was not only a stranger to Assam, but whose nearest encounter to a tea plant was at the bottom of a cup.

Fortunately, it was all taken in the spirit intended. None of the gentle interrogation spoilt the pleasure of the trip. In fact, so much did Marian enjoy the company of Mr Jack Laws and his somewhat retiring but genial wife, she was a little disappointed at the prospect of their separation upon arrival at Dibrugarh. For at that time, she did not know the eventual closeness of their relationship.

Jonathan fared no worse himself. Intrinsically he and Philip Dunn had little in common. The latter's only experience of military life was his occasional brushes with the likes of Major Hutchison, for whom he held few compliments.

However, it was under the same Major's command that he delivered himself during his duties as a serving member of the Assam Valley Light Horse Volunteers and as such it was beholden upon him to express his opinions with restraint.

Even less was Philips broader knowledge of the Indian continent. This was due to the fact that during the course of his thirty-one years, he had never been further afield than Calcutta. Of course, like his two brothers, he had received an education in England, cared for while there by his mother's sister. However, he would never have counted himself well-travelled or worldly. Indeed, he found it difficult sometimes to think of himself as an Englishman.

Second only to being a planter, Philip was an almost fanatical polo player, wasting no time in mentioning to Jonathan his position in the Dibrugarh 1st Team. He also bragged somewhat of his ambition to be selected to play for Assam, ahead of his elder brother, or at the same time if needs be.

By the same token, Jonathan was equally handicapped. He was ignorant of the difference between Orange Pekoe, Broken Pekoe and Pekoe Souchong, a knowledge he would quickly need to acquire if his employment was to continue beyond the first six-month trial period negotiated with John Dunn. Furthermore, his rather take it or leave it attitude towards polo, was no help to the building blocks of mutual respect between the two men. Jonathan did hold one ace card though, one which he would come to guard jealously. Like Jack Laws, but possibly with completely different motives, Philip Dunn quickly showed that he too was captivated by Marian.

Her open conversation, good humour and under stated attractiveness were a breath of fresh air, particularly to a young man who, like Norman Bayden, held the best hope of finding a suitable wife for himself in a long sea voyage back to the main reservoir of English maidenhood. So starved indeed was he of passable feminine company, had Jonathan been a man easily brought to jealousy or quickly offended by harmless indiscretion, Philip might have given offence with his over generous attentions towards Mrs Cole. Instead, Jonathan was flattered to be considered so fortunate. He realised immediately the degree to which the fates had smiled upon him soon after Marian's arrival at his fortress in the mountains.

All in all, their five days and nights on the Brahmaputra were a pleasant and well-chosen alternative to travelling by train. In spite of the slight mishap in the fog, an incident which was in truth considerably less perilous than the risible and increasingly frantic attempts at re-flotation seemed to imply, all hands and passengers were re-floated without injury and with only the least of inconvenience. Damage done to the ship, if any, remained a closely guarded secret between the SS Pagan and her captain. Their next pause was at Silghat before the final haul to Dibrugarh.

In between meals and the inevitable cross examinations, Marian and Jonathan spent the majority of their time together on deck. Although the forward progress of the boat stirred a cooling breeze, with the sun overhead for most of the day, the weather was unusually humid. It reminded Marian of mornings that she and her father took themselves off on horseback for several hours at a time across the South Downs, their view of Brighton, Hove and the sea beyond unhindered by haze or cloud.

In this case, the scenery to port or starboard of the boat was equally captivating, although very different to the English south coast. Beyond the deep brown waters of the river, the red soil at its banks was dotted with sleeping crocodiles. Beyond that still lay dense, impenetrable jungle, while on the port side only, in the far distance, the white snowcapped peaks of the Himalayas, shimmered like a spangle of jewels. It was a romantic setting for two newlyweds. Not only were Marian and Jonathan on the brink of an adventure, the highs and lows of which they had no way to predict, but they were blessed with the growing awareness that their decision to marry was being rewarded by a depth of mutual regard and affection neither originally anticipated.

Somewhat reminiscent of the morning P & O delivered Marian and her travelling companions safely to Ballard Pier in Bombay, the arrival of the SS Pagan and her passengers to Dibrugarh was greeted with modest jubilance by the miniature throng gathered at the moorings ghats. The scale of the occasion was less, the tired river ship a poor, rather dishevelled thing set against the impressive dimensions of an ocean-going steamer.

Nevertheless, the enthusiasm of those waiting was no poorer for it. This was in part due to the fact that the SS Pagan brought not just passengers, welcome though they were, but supplies, vital equipment, foodstuffs and medicines all of which were sorely needed for the continuance of an acceptable existence in a part of the world as yet inaccessible by any other means. To native and European alike, the Brahmaputra was a life line, the ships plying up and down indispensable. No wonder therefore every time the SS Pagan docked she was met with cheers and whoops of delight and no less a ceremony being afforded her two sister ships.

Not knowing what John Dunn looked like, Jonathan and Marian stuck close to Philip in the hope of affecting a smooth introduction to his brother. This they did while negotiating the rather unsteady and worryingly narrow gang plank which bridged the gap between ship and shore. As it happened however, John Dunn was not there to greet them. In his stead, the youngest of the three Dunn brothers, Terence, was commissioned to the task, John being otherwise detained by the annual visit of the dentist, himself up from Calcutta a few days prior. At the very moment of Jonathan and Marian stepping ashore, their future employer was having the nerve removed from a rather offensive upper molar.

'How was the cricket?' Terence asked his brother as they negotiated their way through to various waiting carriages, a brief handshake sufficient apparently as a sign of filial affection.

'Not bad,' Philip replied, a note of ambivalence in his voice.

'Did you win?' came the impatient demand.

'Of course we won. Beat them hollow.'

As the rather abbreviated conversation ran its course, Philip divulging information piece meal to his sibling as if by painful extraction, it transpired that, while in Gauhati on various commissions to do with tea and the forward march of an ever-expanding Dunn family plantation empire, he had also found time to represent Dibrugarh in the recently instated annual winter cricket match between the two towns. 1886 was the year of sweet revenge. Twelve months previous, Gauhati's European community had conspired a narrow victory, chiefly through the efforts of their own resident doctor. Before venturing to Assam, the said doctor had played cricket regularly for Middlesex, his bowling subsequently the scourge of every Dibrugarh batsman. Sadly, for his fellow cricketers in Gauhati, severe gout provoked his early retirement from the game and from Assam itself to a small cottage on the outskirts of Worthing. This opened the door for the recent result which Philip Dunn acknowledged with less exaltation than his brother expected.

And so they proceeded, Jonathan listening politely while Marian found herself otherwise distracted by the rutted and uneven surface of the road as they began their nine-mile carriage ride to the Shahjan estate. The climb up to and the descent from Landi Kotal had not been without its discomforts. However, neither compared with those inflicted by the crashing and lurching of their lumbering carriage as it appeared to attract every pot hole and deep ruts along the route.

Terence was seated immediately opposite Marian, quite unruffled it seemed by the roller coaster ride, although she noticed he did maintain a vice like grip on a sturdy piece of the coach work. Possibly accounted for by his youth, for he was certainly no more than twenty-two or three, he seemed much slighter in build than his brother, the sort of frame which encouraged Marian to imagine the benefit he might gain from a hearty meal. Lean was the best single word she could think of to describe him when she made mention of him as part of that day's diary entry, an entry not made in fact until several days after their arrival.

His hair was dark, his eyes a rather insipid cross between hazel and pale brown. Indeed, sitting as he was in the carriage by the side of his brother, there was not a single obvious feature they shared which would have identified Terence immediately as having hailed from the same loins, an observation made all the more acute when later she saw Philip and John together. They were most definitely peas from the same pod; both fair, both robust, both polo players.

Of course, this knowledge was still a laboured carriage ride away. To distract herself from the awful state of the road and the aching in her kidneys, Marian chose instead to scrutinise the countryside, leaving her male companions to talk of batting scores and, as it happened, the February cold weather race week in Dibrugarh.

Green pigeon accompanied them along the way. They seemed to be everywhere, as prolific as house sparrows, flying from tree to tree on the edge of the jungle, disturbed by the noisy approach of the carriage but not frightened. Every so often the dense undergrowth gave way to a clearing of long, coarse grass until, eventually, the virgin landscape subsided to reveal a panorama of gently sloping cultivation.

They had arrived. As far as the eye could see, on either side of the carriage, the land had been cleared for the planting of tea. At first sight, there appeared to be little activity in the fields.

'Not much to look at I'm afraid,' Philip Moran remarked as if guessing her thoughts.

'There's not a lot to do during the winter months. In February, we start pruning; five to ten acres a day. But the leaf doesn't start coming till the middle of March. Most of what we do during the winter is repair work; fixing machines, rebuilding and clearing new land for cultivation. We also manage to squeeze a few games of polo in and the odd cricket match. Once things hot up on the picking side, it's all hands to the pumps as it were.'

'The weather's lovely,' Marian offered, taking note of what Philip said, keen to gain any snippet of information which would help her adapt to an industry and part of the world she knew absolutely nothing about.

'Yes. We call this the cold season. At night it gets really quite cool. Most of us have fires. The days are usually pleasant though. Not too much rain. But you'll find out all this for yourself soon enough. The two worst things about living up here are the heat and the rain. Not really the sort of place us English are bred for at all. Usually, it's raining so hard you think it'll never stop. Then, just when you've given up all hope of seeing the sun again out it comes ready to fry you to a crisp. Still if it wasn't for the climate there would be no tea and all of us would be out of a job. That reminds me, if you're not in the habit of doing so already, you should both start taking your quinine as soon as possible. The mosquitoes up here are vicious devils. They're not too bad this time of the year but they'll give you the fever at the drop of a hat and you don't want that. Once you get it there's no getting rid of it. It'll make your lives a misery. It can kill you if you get it badly enough or often enough.'

His 'matter-of-factness' was a little alarming. Clearly Philip Dunn was the sort of man not used to gilding the lily. However, Marian was happy with his frankness. Better that than for lack of taking the necessary precautions, she or Jonathan should fall foul of some dreadful illness. Jonathan had served in many different parts of India. He was used to the threat of disease and the taking of steps to prevent calamity. By comparison, Marian was a newcomer. Willams death was enough to make her aware of the dangers on the Indian subcontinent, but her recent good health might well have led her into complacency were it not for the warnings of Philip Dunn. He had lived since childhood with the constant threat of diseases for which there were no easy cures and whose effects were both rapid and debilitating.

'Please don't worry yourself too much though,' he added by way of consolation, assuming in Marian an exaggerated concern stimulated by her sex. 'My family has lived up here for more than half a century. John, Terence and I were all born at Kurmi and we're all going strong. My mother is hale and hearty and my father is still one of the fittest men in Assam; Still does a full day's work and still plays polo once or twice a week.'

One of the things which drew Marian to Jonathan when first she made his acquaintance in Landi Kotal was his quiet reticence. He was not by any means a shy or excessively introverted man. Somewhat like her own father, he was, however, economical with his use of words, well used to handing down commands in short, exact sentences and listening to excuses or explanations along the same lines. He spoke only when he had something to say and then denied himself the pleasure of hyperbole or the over use of adjectives.

Quite clearly, Philip Dunn was not the same. He was verbose, but in a manner Marian found refreshing. In time she would come to find both his speech and manner endearing, but as they passed through the tiny village of Barbaruah, just two miles from Shahjan, its small bazaar in noisy full swing and its only significant building the post office, she knew him only well enough to smile at his harmlessly verbose if occasionally patronising manner.

Chapter Sixteen

No more than a few yards short of the two miles Philip Dunn claimed as the distance from Barbaruah to Shahjan, their carriage turned off the main government road which, had they continued on, would have taken them to Dawan.

As they passed the small marker indicating their arrival at the Shahjan Tea Company, Marian's relief was palpable. The nine-mile journey from Dibrugarh had been nothing short of an endurance test, so much so that, at times, she would have preferred the option of getting down from the carriage to walk. The highway along which they had come, government maintained or not, was no highway at all. A centuries old Suffolk farm track would have afforded them a more comfortable ride. With some reluctance, this was an observation she kept to herself, conscious as she was that neither of the Dunn men seemed in the least bit perturbed or discomforted by the ordeal. Obviously, and in spite of their schooling in England, they were ignorant of the significant progress made in modern road surfacing.

'Garden road,' the half mile or so of similar but narrower track leading up to the bungalows and plantation buildings was no better than the main highway, but by the same token, it was no worse.

'Here we are,' Terence said, three of the possible dozen words he had spoken since their initial introduction, preferring it seemed for his older brother to dominate the conversation.

The first buildings they came to, a scattering of four or five large sheds with sturdy wooden sides and thick palm thatched roofs, were positioned either side of the lane and the carriage passed neatly between them. From the outside, there was no activity to be seen, but Marian assumed they were in some way pertinent to the manufacturing side of the enterprise.

'As I say, it's quiet at the moment,' said Philip, 'but when the machines are fired up in March the noise is horrendous. All tea houses are the same and hot too, like the devil himself sometimes.'

Marian was interested in what he had to say, but her attention was drawn to a neat and reasonably large bungalow directly ahead of them. Raised several feet above the ground on stilts it too was built of timber and thatch but there was a covered veranda skirting the entire building. Standing to one side of what she took to be the front door was a man, John Dunn, she presumed.

Like his brother, he was tall, broad shouldered and fair, with an overlong and untidy shock of hair. He was dressed in a white open neck cotton shirt, riding breeches and a pair of heavily laced highly polished riding boots. In one hand, he was holding a crop and his legs were apart, his stance a provocative exclamation mark to the overall suggestion of his being a rather intimidating character.

As the carriage came to a halt in front of the bungalow, he walked down the few steps from the veranda to greet them, ignoring his two brothers in preference to making the acquaintance of the only lady in the party.

Taking Marian's hand, he affected a rather unpractised bow and kiss before straightening himself up to look her full in the eyes in a manner so penetrating she felt quite caught off guard. To Jonathan he then offered a firm handshake.

'Welcome to Shahjan,' he said, his voice the echo of his brother Philip, but with more of the baritone. 'Your home,' he added, pointing with a sweeping gesture of his arm to the building behind him. 'I'll leave you both to settle in. Tomorrow I'll come by at seven o'clock for breakfast. Then we can talk. Meanwhile, Terence will take care of anything you need and show you the ropes.'

With that, he walked over to where a dark brown colt was loosely tethered to a corner post of the veranda. He unhitched the reins, mounted and rode off without a backward glance, disappearing out of sight at a slow canter.

'You must forgive my brother,' Philip said. 'He's not one for social graces. All he thinks about is Shahjan. It's his baby. Apart from polo, this estate is his pride and joy. He eats, sleeps and breathes the place. I can assure you; he treats everyone just the same. You mustn't take offence at his manner. It's just his way.'

'That's quite alright,' Jonathan replied. 'Mr Dunn must be extremely busy, otherwise what need would he have of me?'

'Quite right. Good point,' Philip agreed, relieved by Jonathan's tactful response. 'It might not look like it from the little you've seen so far, but this time of the year is, in its own way, just as hectic as any other, particularly at a new garden like this. There's the pruning to be done, jungle to be cleared for next seasons planting and at the present time I know my brother has a large contract to fulfil supplying sleepers to the railway company. They're working like blazes at the moment to bring the line all the way from Gauhati to Dibrugarh. It should be open in the next couple of years or so. They're as far as Nazira already. So, it doesn't leave them too much more to do, always assuming John can cut enough sleepers for them. That gentleman you were introduced to on the Pagan, Norman Bayden. He he's come up here to take charge of the project. So with luck, we'll soon be able to take the train all the way from Dibrugarh to Calcutta.'

This was not an aspect of life in Assam which Jonathan had considered at any length. However, one of the most pressing problems in Landi Kotal, as with so many similarly remote military outposts on the North West Frontier, was the lack of a connecting railway. Year on year there were promises of a rail link from Rawalpindi to the border with Afghanistan. As the crow flies, it was barely forty-five miles from Peshawar to Landi Kotal, but with no train it was a long and tortuous journey, as Marian would be the first to testify. Without the railway, not a day had passed for Major Cole and the troops under his command when they did not feel isolated and vulnerable, a truth all personal in such under-manned military positions wisely kept to themselves lest hint of it invited attack from beyond the walls of their forts.

Sleeper cutting conjured up less of the romantic image Jonathan envisaged of plantation life. It had the ring of hot, hard labour about it, but he needed no impressing as to the importance of a comprehensive rail network. Under these circumstances therefore, he was more than ready to forgive the abrupt departure of his new employer.

Some few minutes after their arrival, the bullock cart carrying their luggage and other cargo brought up from Gauhati lumbered up to the front of the bungalow. With his customary frankness, Philip expressed surprise at how few trunks Marian possessed. Some vague acknowledgement of contemporary etiquette led him to stay silent on the subject of her unconventional hair style and the rather masculine styling of her attire.

However, he could not resist a small remark as to the number of suitcases to her name. Between Jonathan and herself, he pointed out with some personal amusement, their total luggage was not half the amount normally expected of any young lady travelling out alone from England. Had Marian perhaps misplaced some of it along the way he asked. That, or perhaps she had deposited some of it safely with friends in Delhi or Calcutta for later transportation.

Neither, was the answer, as Marian was happy to admit. Apologies therefore followed quickly but were as quickly declined as quite unnecessary.

Terence, who was fast confirming Marian's opinion of him as being a young man of few words, did not involve himself in the exchange. It seemed he preferred instead to oversee the removal of said luggage, whatever its quantity, from the cart and into the bungalow while Philip began a brief guided tour of their new home.

That night, their first night at Shahjan, should have passed quickly. Together, Marian and Jonathan had crossed a continent. They had been on trains, boats and unspeakable cart tracks not worthy of the name road. Fatigue should have granted them both deep slumber.

However, Marian lay in her bed for what seemed like hours, eyes wide open, head spinning, her ears on constant alert for every new and unusual sound. The noise of rats scurrying through the roof rafters gave cause to wrap the bed clothes tight to her chin, but their rampaging was as nothing to the exotic chorus of sounds emanating from the jungle a few hundred yards through the darkness.

What had she done, she wondered. Perhaps she was dreaming. Perhaps Assam, the journey across India, her marriage to Jonathan, India itself, was all a grand hallucination. Perhaps, any minute she would wake to find herself in her bedroom at 32 Princes Gate, the glow of a warm fire in the hearth, heavy curtains drawn across the windows, the only sound outside that of carriage wheels on paved roads or of rain falling on tiled roofs.

But it was no dream. The mosquito net shrouding her bed was real. She could reach out and touch it. The night time calls of tigers and elephants, leopards and monkeys, wild boars and buffaloes were not the product of her imagination. They were the cause of her insomnia.

In the next room, separated from her by the flimsiest of partition walls Jonathan lay, sleeping. She could hear his relaxed breathing, sense the nearness of his body. And outside, on the veranda, there was the occasional shuffling of the chowkidar as he shifted position, the heady perfume of his hookah potent evidence of his presence through the long night.

Where was the Marian Chase she once knew? What had happened to the safe, conventional young women who rode out with her father along the Row, attended bible classes with her sisters and entertained at dinner parties. Was she lost, gone for all time? Had her place been taken by this strange, Bohemian impostor whose appetite for adventure far outstretched any former flights of fancy, the product so often of unemployed time in London or Brighton?

If she were to meet herself in Knightsbridge or Regents Park would there be a spark of recognition or would the new Mrs Jonathan Cole pass by the old Miss Marian Chase without the least hint of having once known her?

In the dark, question after question popped into her head. Sleep came, but eventually, her wide-eyed alertness defying fatigue, steering her into a maze of questions, none with ready answers.

With the dawn she was up long before her husband, dressed and out of the bungalow, impatient to explore her new surroundings. On the veranda, the chowkidar had finally dosed off on a crude charpoy, his hookah still smoking beside him, his duties as night watchman vanished in a narcotic haze, his mind presumably lost in a dense fog similar to the one which greeted Marian as she stepped into the early morning air.

Save for the absence of urban congestion it was like a damp January morning in London, cold enough for her to feel the need for an overcoat and the dense mist enough for buildings no more than twenty yards away to appear like ghostly ships. It was becoming light, but the sun was a long way behind, most unlike the early mornings in Landi Kotal.

During the season, the manufacturing of tea began early. Drowned out by the brutish noise of heavy machinery, there was little in the way of a dawn chorus to please or impress. But in winter, the tea houses were silent. As Marian descended the short flight of steps from the veranda and positioned herself on the track exactly at the point where it formed a junction leading off in three directions, she paused to select a heading for her dawn stroll.

'This isn't the safest time of day to be out on your own,' came the warning voice of a man from behind her who appeared out of the mist on horseback as silently as if he had materialised from the ether. 'But then, I imagine you already know that,' he added, taking care not to patronise.

It was John Dunn, looking for all the world like a character from the Buffalo Bill's Wild West Show which her father had taken the whole family to see in London just a couple of years before she set out for India. John was wearing a broad brimmed hat, long hide overcoat and the same riding breeches and boots of the previous afternoon. His oversized frame seemed to dwarf somewhat the rather small pony he rode.

'Why's that?' Marian asked, resisting the impulse to express alarm at his sudden appearance.

'We're quite close to the jungle here,' he explained, his tone friendly, no sign of impatience at her ignorance. 'From time to time the odd tiger or leopard pass through here about now. Normally they're fairly secretive creatures. You can hear them, but you rarely see them, unless of course you're out after them with elephants. But sometimes, if they're short of food, they'll come prowling around in search of a goat or anything else to fill their bellies. Close to town you won't see them at all. You could live in Dibrugarh twenty years and not see one. But we're a bit off the beaten track here and the jungle's only a stone's throw.'

As he finished, he dismounted and removed his hat.

'Here,' he said handing her the reins of his horse as if he were offering her the use of his umbrella, 'I've got an hour's work to do in the store over there, the one next to that long leaf house; stock taking would you believe. I have to get an order for supplies off to Gauhati as soon as possible otherwise nothing will arrive before the season begins. If I leave it any longer, it'll be difficult to get the stuff through before the monsoons start. Anyway, if you follow that path over there, the one to the right of your bungalow, it'll take you as far as our coolie lines. Turn left there and keep turning left then eventually you'll get back round to the garden road where you came in yesterday. You'll see more on my pony and its safer. He knows his way. Just follow his lead.'

Marian hesitated.

'You can ride?' he asked, the tone of his voice hinting that should she reply in the negative he would be surprised and disappointed.

'Of course.'

'Well then take him. His name's "Snowden". He'll see you home all right. But keep to the road. Plenty of time for wandering off when you get to know the place a bit better.'

With that, and not giving the least thought to its positioning, he placed his hat back on his head, cupped his hands and, bending down slightly, offered them to Marian as a foothold in order for her to mount up.

'In these parts,' he added by way of a parting remark, since it was said as he turned and began to walk way, 'we do almost everything on horseback. And I'm afraid to say, these days few women in these parts ride side saddle. We are a long way from London here.'

When Marian returned about an hour later, the fog had lifted. The ground was still wet with dew and there was little to be said for the soft warmth of the sun. Of the four hundred and fifty acres owned by the Shahjan Tea Company, she had covered barely one fifth in the course of her short circuit, the circuit prescribed her and one from which she did not deviate.

However, what she saw was enough to make her forget the chill in the air and the slight nervousness she felt during the first few minutes of her solitary ride. Along the route she passed row upon row of neatly pruned tea bushes, their lines the very soul of military precision, disappearing into the distance, apparently never-ending. Some way off from the bungalow, there was an equally regimented group of rough huts, the 'coolie lines,' a makeshift village of temporary homes for imported labour to work the harvest.

And at one point the road passed within a few feet of the jungle, a dark, impenetrable morass of lush foliage within which lurked, unseen, the shapes and forms of those creatures whose nocturnal wailings had kept her awake for so much of the night.

But it was enough. A brief glimpse was all she needed for a flavour of the landscape, enough at least to convince her of its raw and unique beauty. Jonathan was up and sitting on the veranda, but rose to his feet to help her dismount, a simple act which, although he was completely unaware of it at the time, was to become something of a habit.

Very quickly he and Marian learned that in the running of a tea plantation as with most occupations, life becomes a matter of routine. On this particular morning, she was up before him, having risen shortly before dawn, leaving him to sleep on. Within days, however, he was usually gone from the bungalow before her, his working day beginning shortly after six. But each morning, at about eight o'clock, when he came back to the bungalow for 'chota haziri' it was timed to coincide with Marian's return from a morning ride. And, on each occasion, he was there to perform this modest act of gallantry.

On that first morning, 'Snowden' was a reliable companion. He brought her back just as John Dunn predicted, negotiating every petty crater in the road with faultless agility, convincing Marian that where and when possible, she would choose for herself the back of a horse for transport rather than the bone jarring discomfort of a carriage. This early conclusion she expressed as she handed him back to his rightful owner. The result was that although she was deprived of 'Snowden' on future rides, before the day was out a new pony was delivered for her exclusive use.

The 'Dun pony' had no name. She was referred to simply as 'The Dun pony.' Less the athlete than 'Snowden' whose primary duties were to champion John Dunn to victory in the Dibrugarh 1st polo team, she was also older and, of course, dun in colour.

She died of colic less than a year after being donated to Marian, a cruel incident which underlined the harsh and fickle reality of life in Assam for humans and animals alike and focussed an acknowledgement of just how fond Marian had become of her. However, in the meantime, the mare fulfilled her duties with unstinting generosity of spirit, always sure-footed, always head up and ears pricked.

Thus, the morning ritual began. Sometimes Marian performed the same circuit several days in a row, knowing exactly what time she would return, using it as part of her routine. On others, she and the 'Dun pony' would stray, exploring different tracks or, venturing further afield, visiting neighbouring plantations such as Medla or Bollai, both of which were part, but operated independently of, Shahjan itself.

Jonathan was also allocated his own horse, a large sturdy black waler, on occasion prone to bursts of accelerated and uninvited activity. Theirs was something of a love hate relationship. Without a horse, Jonathan would not have been able to perform his duties as overall manager of the three plantations. But he and 'The Geisha' were never the best of friends. The name itself was as completely idiosyncratic as the man from whom John Dunn inherited the horse. The story went that the gentleman in question abandoned tea planting in favour of a new life logging in Tasmania. Apparently and much to every one's astonishment, he announced his intentions at the club one night, directly he said as the result of a recently acquired conviction that the fashion for tea in Europe was about to expire.

The morning after her arrival in Shahjan, however, 'Snowden' brought Marian back to the bungalow not only in one piece but with a brightness in her eyes and glow to her face which Jonathan interpreted quite correctly as delight at their new surroundings. His initial concerns for her well-being evaporated. Booloo, their bearer, took the horse from her and tethered him to the same veranda support as used by John Dunn. Then he disappeared inside the bungalow to return a few minutes later with a breakfast laden tray. Not long after, John himself joined them to share their meal and retrieve his horse.

In this rather informal manner, Jonathan's employment at Shahjan began. In the years to come, Marian's life was destined for twists and turns beyond any she could imagine on that veranda in the February of 1886.

She, Jonathan and John Dunn were to become inseparable. Over time, it was easier for Marian to think of the two men as brothers, so close was their relationship. And though she would never have believed herself capable of it, so much in love with both men did she become, eventually she found it impossible to part the two in her affections.

In 1901, barely twelve months after the turn of a new century, Queen Victoria died. With her death came a new era of unprecedented social change. The 'Victorian' way of life withered. Conventions, manners, class structures, all were invaded by the shock of the new. In northern Assam, however, the new morality was sparked not by the death of an Empress but by subtle events fifteen years prior, with the first breakfast shared between two men and a woman, each blissfully ignorant of what fate had in store for them in the coming years.

'When our father's dies,' John announced with a candour which surprised Jonathan and Marian, 'my two brothers and I will inherit the largest tea company in Assam, producing and shipping more tea than any other. But Shahjan is mine. Everything you see around you was virgin jungle just two seasons ago. I've done just so much, come just so far. Now I need you Jonathan, or someone like you, to help me make the Shahjan Tea Company what it has the potential to become. The hours will be long, the work hard but the rewards, I can assure you, will be great. This is the challenge of a lifetime if you're ready for it. I ask only one thing, that Shahjan become as important to you as it is to me. If it does, we can't fail. If not, then now would be the best time to say so. That way we needn't waste each other's time.'

As he finished, he looked first to Jonathan and then Marian, the steel in his eyes adding emphasis to the words from his lips.

'As far as I'm concerned…' Jonathan began but was interrupted.

'There's no need to say anything. Just show me,' said John. 'You know nothing about being a planter now. But you'll soon learn. I'll make a planter of you. All you have to do is show me how much this place means to you.'

Jonathan was satisfied. He understood completely.

'In time, I promise you,' John continued, addressing Marian directly, 'you'll grow to love this country. What you've seen this morning is but a glimpse. Of course, there will be times you may think you want to be anywhere else but here. But when it comes down to it, there's no better place on earth. This country gets under your skin and when it does, you'll never want to leave.'

He seemed so sure of himself. His passion was so raw. Marian was reminded of spiritual evangelism and her heart beat a little faster in the presence of a man who was so completely focussed.

Three months later, by the end of April, the weather had turned hot and humid. Picking had begun and the questions of that first morning were answered. In Jonathan, John Moran discovered a man with few short comings. He was dedicated to the task, quick to learn and uniquely placed to introduce a fresh perspective on many of the day-to-day administrative demands of a comparatively new plantation. Morning breakfast meetings became the rule rather than the exception as the two men established a working bond united in a common cause.

And Jonathan; he was like a man reborn. Shedding his army skin left him not vulnerable, but invigorated. Enthusiasm for his work and life generally, soared to levels he thought lost, the challenges presented with each dawn stretching him in ways he had not been for years. Landi Kotal was forgotten. Far from feeling himself awkward out of uniform, the informality of his clothing ignited in him an appetite for life and a freedom of movement he had not felt for as long as he could recall. And plenty of manual hard work kept him fit. Each day such experience and skills as he was able to bring to the job were put to the test by a man with whom he found it a constant race to keep up.

Picking, laying the leaf out to wither, rolling, firing and drying; all these soon became a matter of course, a daily pattern of work from dawn to dusk throughout the long season, interrupted only by the most extreme of weather. But at the same time, there were plans for the future, visions in the mind of one man to create, in shorter time than his father could believe, a tea company to rival any in Assam. John Dunn's ambition was singular unrelenting. It was all as clear to him as daylight and, by way of the extraordinary bond which developed rapidly between the two men, a vision to which Jonathan could relate precisely, quickly setting his own mind on a similar heading.

Marian revelled in the sight of her husband so absorbed, so content with his lot. As the weather warmed, so the rains increased and with the rains came mosquitoes, leeches and the spawning of a cocktail of ills ready to strike either of them down at moment's notice. In places the roof of their bungalow leaked. Unpaved roads became quagmires. Even on horseback the shortest journey was a chore, as often as not best left undone.

And Marian herself was isolated, regularly too weary to enjoy her husband's company and, so far were they from the sophistication and glamour of the Caroline Farrer circle, she all but forgot the means to impress her femininity on the male environment she inhabited.

And yet, she too was happier than ever before. Married to a man who, as each day passed, endeared himself to her the more, her morning rides on the 'Dun pony' were an opportunity to reflect upon the extraordinary good fortune she had stumbled into. Within two months of arriving at Shahjan, she knew well every track and pathway on the estate. Trees and shrubs she had no idea existed before arriving in Assam, were as familiar to her as gnarled oaks or English roses. Sounds which had disrupted her first night, sending shivers down her spine, came to herald a new dawn or announce the evening finale. Each day she was captivated by the untrammelled beauty of the countryside and, at times, exhausted by the sheer pleasure she gained from it all.

In her diary she wrote of novelty and delight, detailing the smallest experience, observing the briefest of moments with the palette of an artist and the poetic ingenuity of a Bryon or Shelley. And, in her letters home, written and sent every fortnight, she implored her father to forgive any hurt she may have caused by her marriage and exile. Instead, she invited him to share in her good fortune and new found contentment. She beseeched him for his understanding, promising in return that one day he would see for himself the rare happiness in her eyes.

That Katie made similar claims in less eloquent speeches from her hideaway in Italy was conveniently put to one side, although the irony was not lost. Occasionally Marian recalled with horror the scathing criticism she heaped upon her younger sister at the time of her elopement with the luckless Mr Kenneth. Now, in her diary, conscience alone decreed that she admit openly the guilt of so glib a judgement of poor Katie. In doing so, she hoped that eventually, though undeserved, she would be granted absolution and recognition that her hypocrisy was unintended.

In all else, she was happy. And that was all her father truly needed to know, happier than she believed possible, happier than she deserved, the ghost of

William and thus the suffering his name demanded, fading like the January mists beneath the warmth of the sun.

Weeks earlier, on 26 February to be precise, as recorded by Marian in considerable detail over several pages of a letter home she, Jonathan and John travelled together into Dibrugarh for the cold weather race meet and polo tournament. John encamped on the polo ground itself to be near his ponies, while Mr and Mrs Cole, hitherto only known through gossip to the majority of people, were given accommodation overnight at the club.

For forty-eight hours, sleeper cutting was halted, repair work, pruning, hoeing and the clearing of new land set to one side. By custom, everything stopped for an annual entertainment guaranteed to assemble the European community from far and wide.

By the time they arrived, the club was bursting at the seams. Innocently unaware of their novelty value, Marian imagined she and Jonathan would be able to blend in unnoticed. Deciding on what to wear for the occasion she chose simplicity. She set aside any one of the half dozen glamorous outfits bequeathed her by Caroline Farrer. For the sake of her husband, she wanted to remind him she was still a woman, but to avoid any suggestion of dressing to be noticed she was careful to select the least provocative colours and styles at her disposal.

In that she tried, she was to be applauded. In that, she failed dismally was no less than John Moran foretold. Like it or not, she and Jonathan were on show. Their name, their appearance and, in particular, the stylish manner in which Marian had won over Jack Laws at their first encounter aboard the SS Pagan, were already the subject of universal speculation.

As a newcomer himself, Dr Patrick Murphy had come under similar scrutiny. However, the peripatetic nature of his employment had already brought him into contact with a broad cross section of Dibrugarh society. Those who had not yet found cause to summon him professionally were curious to make his acquaintance. They needed to size up his skills, skills which as often as not were likely to mean the difference between life and death and therefore as vital as climatic extremes or news of tea market values in London. On the other hand, motives for a sound knowledge of Mr and Mrs Cole were primarily based upon themselves as individuals and their future social contribution to the community.

From the moment they entered the club on the morning of the race meet, all eyes seemed turned towards them. More people than Marian found comfortable wanted to make her acquaintance, peering and probing with their every glance and gesture. It was then she felt a certain empathy with the primates on display in Regents Park Zoological Gardens, an attraction she had visited many times with Margaret and Katie.

The Dunn clan had much to occupy them. They were gathered for the occasion as a force to be reckoned with on the field of conflict, Trevelyan Dunn, the father, being the only one not expected to appear in the actual heat of battle.

Fortunately, before long, and possibly noticing their discomfort, Mr and Mrs Laws removed Marian and Jonathan from the general fray, claiming a discreet corner away from centre stage.

'Bit of a bun fight what?' Jack Laws said by way of re-introducing himself. 'Annual shin dig like this brings them into town from far and wide. New people like yourselves bound to be a bit of a draw. Shallow old lives we lead in these parts, I'm afraid. Not what you're used to I expect.'

'Quite the contrary,' Jonathan replied 'This is all quite suburban by comparison to my last posting on the North West Frontier.'

'So, so,' came the acknowledgement.

'Still,' Marjorie Laws said to Marian as an aside and in something of a whisper, 'you mustn't be alarmed by all the attention. It'll soon pass. They just want to take a look at you. It's the same with all new arrivals. It didn't happen to dear Jack and I because when we came up here, we were among the first. We were all new then. Times have changed now though. The old guard, which includes us I suppose, we like to cast an eye over new comers. Get a look at them to make sure they're the right stuff. In your case of course, the other ladies just want to get a glimpse of what you're wearing. See if there's anything new in fashion they should know about.'

'Well,' Marian replied with a wry smile, 'I'll be a disappointment then. Even at home in London, fashion and I were never the best of friends and since I've been in India I'm afraid I've lost interest altogether. This dress is as old as the hills and all my others are hand-me-downs.'

'Never mind that, dear. No one will notice. To the rest of us you look quite the thing, particularly your hair. If you are not careful, you'll have every lady in Assam running around just the same.'

Though she had no intention of altering it now, Marian was still conscious of her hair, so much so she had contemplated letting it grow again to a more conventional length. No for a moment did she expect her boyish cut to be mistaken for a new trend, a fashion import in danger of being taken to heart by those whose scrutiny she was compelled to endure like a fish in a bowl.

Declaring herself the very last person to set trends or lead fashion, she emphasised to Marjorie the farcical nature of such a notion. Together they shared a secret laugh, the envy of the other ladies in the club room, all of whom were keen to make her acquaintance but had not yet done so.

Meanwhile Jonathan was introduced to a cross section of the Dibrugarh business community. Norman Bayden, he remembered from the SS Pagan. So too Dr Murphy and, fortunately at a distance across the room, Major Hutchison. He caught Jonathan's attention only because he was busy regaling an unfortunate bar steward over something or other, his arrogant outburst pitched at exactly the desired level to claim the attention of a small audience clear across the other side of the room as well as those in his immediate vicinity.

Of the others, there was mention of many names and equally as many tea companies, most of which Jonathan forgot immediately, so unrelenting were the number of introductions to be got through. One man, however, he was duty bound to commit to memory.

Trevelyan Dunn waited until the initial enthusiasm drew to a close. Then he made his way across the room, shaking hands with Jack Laws first before turning his attention to Dibrugarh's newest interns.

'I hope you've got what it takes,' he said to Jonathan without the bother of the usual pleasantries. 'One or two good meals were ruined in my household on your account. True to form, my son, refused to heed my advice. I told him he should take on an experienced man to work Shahjan. Instead, he insisted on bringing in an outsider. I hope you were worth it. Not often I give in to one of my sons. I'm more used to them doing what they're told. But John likes to have things his own way. Like his mother in that.'

'I think I have,' Jonathan responded, confident he and John had already established a good working relationship and also that, during the course of his military career, he had encountered more formidable characters than the man standing in front of him.

Trevelyan Dunn was something of a legend in the region. He was a buccaneer, a larger-than-life figure who thrived on his reputation and glorified in the idea of himself as the founder of a dynasty. Where others met to socialise, he held court. He was big and brash and oblivious to criticism of any kind or from any quarter, save that on occasion from his wife.

Within the boundaries of Kurmi, and they stretched far and wide, his word was law. On his estates he ruled like a petty dictator, benign to those sensible of his power but ruthless to anyone foolish enough to challenge the smallest of his whims.

Verity Dunn, his wife of thirty years and mother to his three sons, reigned at his side. Compassionate, intellectually her husband's superior by a country mile and in her youth a woman of unrivalled beauty, she had learned well over the years the art of subduing the man whom most people feared by reputation alone. She curtailed many of his excesses and contained his piratical instincts. Within weeks of their marriage, it was she who had channelled his energies into the business his own father had begun.

Later it was she who kept counsel with him, applying her natural skills for planning and organisation to help him achieve for herself and for her children what the Dunn Tea Company had now become. Without her influence and without the rigours of life in Assam, his self-ruin would have been a foregone conclusion, at least in the opinion of his father. This was a philosophy which subsequently he chose to propose for his own sons.

Assam was the perfect environment for Trevelyan Dunn and tea the perfect industry; hard, cruel, a Gorgon for him to pit his brutish strength against. Verity Dunn supplied him with his every other need.

Now the wheel had come full circle. In many respects, his own eldest son was the mirror image of himself. Also larger than life, fearless and unstoppably independent. Since his earliest steps towards manhood, John and his father were destined to cross swords. By great good fortune, however, John had inherited from his mother a degree of wit and intelligence denied his father. Above all, he also possessed a certain sensitivity which encouraged him to gain the respect of his employees by consent rather than outright tyranny.

By the same token and to his credit, Jonathan was not a man easily intimidated. He was warned in advance of the legendary status surrounding Trevelyan Dunn. It hung in the air like a halo of steel. In his dealings with both Philip and Terence, Jonathan was well aware of the awe in which the old war horse was held. Unlike their elder brother, they had not inherited the courage or killer instinct to move out from beneath the shadow of their father. Terence positively quaked at the mention of his name.

But for Jonathan, it was a different story. He was on home ground. For the best part of his adult life, he had thrived in a regime of command and counter command, of orders given and orders received. It was a way of life where General's administered power as if by the waving of a wand, the lives of thousands were held in the palms of their hands to do with as they saw fit, their motives unquestioned, their eligibility as often as not an accident of birth.

Consequently, the mystique of Trevelyan Dunn cast no such spell over Jonathan. Had the world slowed to half speed for a second or two, there were those in the club room that morning who might have witnessed a rare hint of frailty in the old man as Jonathan stood his ground.

'Glad to hear it,' he replied. 'My eldest boy claims to know his own mind. Be that as it may, the pair of you would do well to heed the dalliance path you tread lest it led you to disaster,' and with that he turned away, pausing only for a few words to his sons. 'Be sure you win tomorrow, boys,' he said for all to hear. 'I'm counting on you. Remember, second place is no place at all.'

'We'll do our best sir,' came the threefold response.

'Not good enough. Do better,' came the caustic final command.

It was a brief exchange. Clearly in addressing all those deserving of his attention, he permitted only a few moments of engagement with each fortunate participant be they family or not.

During the exchange between Jonathan and Trevelyan Dunn, Marian was absorbed in conversation with his wife. However, she also held an ear to their exchange of words, noting most of what transpired while, at the same time, appearing intent upon fashion and the opinions of other ladies present. She was therefore pre-warned of the abrupt manner likely when the moment arrived for her own introduction to the great man.

Leaving his sons to contemplate the seriousness of his demands upon them, Trevelyan Dunn did indeed turn his attention to Marian. When the time came, she braced herself. She summoned the courage to return his opening salvo with ammunition of a similar calibre to that which Jonathan had used from his arsenal. In the event, she had no need. Over the course of many years, Verity Dunn had moulded her husband well. He was at liberty to behave in the company of men just as he pleased. If he chose to bully or intimidate that was his prerogative. In the company of a lady, however, he had been taught that his manner and tone needed to be tempered.

Besides which, he was in possession of an altogether unfettered ego, an ego more than adequate to convince himself that he had been and still was irresistible to the opposite sex. Thus, he was able to transform, chameleon like, when in the company of a woman he wished to impress.

'Mrs Cole, you defy the best I've heard of you,' he said to Marian as he cupped her hand in his. 'My sons told me you were a beauty but as usual they failed to give an adequate account.'

Such was the direct manner of his approach, for an instant Marian had the feeling he might as readily have adopted the same to describe a newly acquired breeding mare. She realised of course, that in his own distinct if unconventional manner, he was trying to be charming. It would have been churlish to take offence. However, she stole herself to resist the temptation of replying with a similar submission as to his own impressive proportions or the gnarled ruggedness of his features.

Unfortunately, retaliation would have been in vain. For, in vain, or rather in respect of his vanity, her irony would have been lost. Trevelyan Dunn was a man in no doubt as to his own worth, both materially and physically. He was so used to praise, so accustomed to his own superiority over others that the full force of any sarcasm targeted in his direction would have washed over him like the finest, thin spring water off a duck's back.

Instead, Marian responded to his courtesy with a feigned smile, lending a lie to the success of his flattery and giving relief to Jonathan who knew only too well her outspoken dislike of being patronised or being cast in the role of the little woman.

'Thank you,' she replied, leaving unsaid the addition of 'and you are everything I expected as well' which was poised on her lips like a perfectly round glass marble on the edge of a polished table top.

Chapter Seventeen

Not once, for as far back as anyone could remember had the winter race meet in Dibrugarh been completely spoilt by rain. However, this was a declaration made public by a chorus of voices when, by the middle of the first afternoon, both the polo ground and the race track surrounding it were deemed unplayable. The weather in February was usually more reliable. True it had been milder than the norm, but such a deluge after what had been a reasonably long, dry spell was quite contrary to expectations.

This, at least, was the general consensus, becoming fact the moment the likes of Trevelyan Dunn stated it to be so. For Marian and Jonathan, it was their first race meet, their first February in Assam. Consequently, they had no way of knowing the legitimacy of such universal disappointment.

The Dunn brothers appeared particularly upset at having their weekend ruined by rain. No polo meant no chance of another trophy. More to the point, it denied them an opportunity for showing off their skills to the selectors of the Assam team. Although Marian was unaware of it, this was no mere irritation to John or Philip. Their dedication to the sport was not to be taken lightly. John, in particular, had his sights set high on the polo field and approached the sport with almost as much passion as he reserved for his plantation.

The racing was frivolous entertainment, a chance for everyone, men and women alike to join in with an afternoon of harmless fun. To all intents and purposes, it was a spectacle, an excuse for people to gather together who otherwise might not have seen each other from one picking season to the next. For the gentlemen, it was also a day for a wager or two, while their respective wives engaged in the timeless hobby of tittle tattle or the subtle art of upstaging each other with the flourish of a newly imported hat or a surprising insight into the latest Paris fashions.

On the other hand, polo was taken seriously by competitors and spectators alike. Much local pride was at stake. Every chukka was watched with keen scrutiny, every strike of the ball admired or criticised from a broad depth of knowledge. Heroes were made on the polo field in Dibrugarh. Reputations were won and lost, a certain kind of fame sometimes spreading to Calcutta and beyond.

John Dunn was a man of ambition. Even in the short time Marian had been at Shahjan, that much about him was evident. There were many aspects of him she found enigmatic and, to her regret, intriguing. However, his dedication to the success of Shahjan was never a matter for doubt. Furthermore, on meeting his father, she understood in an instant the motivation behind this ceaseless endeavour. Nothing was more important to John than he prove himself as good as, if not better than, his father.

It was an all too familiar scenario, one typical of the age whether in Assam or London; young men, overshadowed by a domineering father, desperate to prove themselves worthy.

As a woman, Marian faced no such debilitating obstacles. She was the eldest of three children. The most her father expected of her was to act responsibly and retain the generosity of spirit he and his wife had worked so hard to instil in each of their daughters from birth. Therefore, she had enjoyed the luxury of a freedom denied John Dunn. As the eldest child himself, his responsibilities were onerous enough. However, in devoting himself not just to equalling but exceeding the awesome achievements of his father, he was setting out along a path which demanded of him more than most ordinary men would be able to give.

Until the rain arrived to spoil the occasion, Marian had no idea of this dual obsession. Only once before had she seen polo played. It was on a not very memorable occasion in Windsor great park. The speed and agility of the ponies was fascinating, quite unlike anything she was used to in the course of her own riding experience. But with no knowledge of the rules or etiquette of the game, it was little more than a confused blur of equine activity interspersed with long breaks while ponies were changed, wounds licked and a close examination of every twist and turn pawed over by the assembled spectators.

Consequently, she was deceived into imagining that the opening of the heavens was neither unusual nor a sign of anything other than a minor irritant to life in the community. In the event, John's bitter disappointment was mirrored on the faces of almost everyone present. Some returned to their homes, finery mothballed until the next occasion for a substantial public gathering. Others, like the Dunn boys, stayed on, morosely searching the skies in vain for a break in the clouds, refusing to give up on the chance of a stray chukka or two.

Unfortunately, their long and forlorn wait meant that Jonathan and Marian were compelled to stay behind at the club as well. It also resulted in a drying up of conversation. This in turn led to boredom, frustration and, in certain cases, excessive drinking. Trevelyan Dunn became boorish and was prevented from exceeding the bounds of good taste only by the intervention of his wife. At the last moment, she stepped in to interrupt what might have become an ugly exchange between himself and a stately dowager by the name of Lady Pendrith who appeared to take relish in reviving some long-term disagreement between them.

Such as she could gather, Marian overheard the gist to be that of an ongoing squabble concerning a tract of land which the honourable lady claimed, probably with some justification, that her immediate neighbour, namely Trevelyan Dunn, had snatched from her by stealth during the period when she was distracted and in mourning over the death of her husband. Later Marian learned this particular incident had taken place some ten years previous. Nevertheless, passions were still enflamed between the two protagonists, wounds still raw. This was enhanced on the part of the male participant by whiskey, only to be encouraged by Lady Pendrith herself who gave an excellent impression of a dog refusing to give up on a juicy bone.

To all but the two most directly involved, there was considerable amusement to be gained from the spectacle. Apparently, the locking of horns between Lady Pendrith and Trevelyan Dunn had developed into something of an annual ritual. Verity Dunn was well used to performing a deft intervention whenever their paths crossed, but not until a degree of entertainment had been gained by all those present during such spats.

Small, tight knit communities are inclined to elongate such rivalries. No doubt a resolution was impossible. Their dispute would go on until one or either of them expired, and certainly beyond a time anyone would be able to recall exactly what started it in the first place. The sparring match between the unmoveable Trevelyan Dunn and the unforgiving Lady Pendrith was as much a feature of public gatherings as the reason for the gathering itself.

On this occasion however, exacerbated possibly by the cancellation of the polo, their spat was in danger of becoming an embarrassment to one or other of them. In spite of considerable goading from those on the fringes, eventually the referee, namely the dextrous Mrs Dunn, was obliged to put an end to the confrontation.

At the same time as this land dispute was raging, John Dunn retired to a corner of the club to brood. His two younger brothers were more stoical about the appalling weather. They became part of a noisy pride of bachelors gathered together for bawdy relaxation. John, however, behaved as if her were in mourning. His expression was desolate, his mood sombre. In effect he sulked, an aspect of his personality, when she saw it, which took Marian quite by surprise and not one she found particularly endearing.

Like his father, John was tall and broad. Around Shahjan he strode with the assurance of a man who knew exactly what he wanted from life and how he was going to achieve it. He was frank to the point of bluntness, fair in the treatment of his employees and seemingly quite unimpressed by the common perception of a woman's frailty or inferiority. He behaved towards Marian with respect but with the same even handedness he showed to her husband or any other person with whom he came into contact. As a result, she thought well of him in far quicker time than she planned, looking forward almost to their brief times alone together.

Seeing him in the corner of the club room, however, alone and with a face akin to that of a spoilt child, she was disappointed, reducing somewhat her otherwise unblemished impression of him. Eventually he resolved his mood alone, casting off his disappointment like a snake shedding a skin. After an hour or so he reverted, taking time on his way back to their party for a short but smiling rebuke of his father for further ruffling the inimitable Lady Pendrith's feathers. His melancholy lifted as quickly as it had descended upon him, but Marian remained puzzled as to its origins and its depth.

Eventually, with the rain still showing no signs of letting up, they all returned to Shahjan. Deep troughs in the road became miniature rivers and potholes ponds, the horses struggling against the elements to maintain their forward progress. It was weather the like of which neither Marian nor Jonathan had experienced since their arrival in Assam, but as naught to the extremes scheduled for the months ahead.

That weekend in February therefore served primarily as useful education. They mad the acquaintance of Trevelyan Dunn and learned at first hand the substance of his reputation. He was indeed larger than life, embracing as he did much that was to be admired, namely in the scale of his business achievements over the years. At the same time, he proved there was an equal if not greater portion of his character which did him no credit at all. That he was a petty tyrant was plain for all to see. That his tyranny was based upon intimidation and fear, even within the more sensitive members of his own family, gave Marian instant cause to distrust, even dislike him. Unusually, she determined to go with her first impressions of him, finding him guilty of the crimes she attached to him until such a time as he might prove his innocence.

She and Jonathan alike were also enlightened to the fact that above all, in Assam, the life of a planter was ruled by the elements. Work or play the daily routine, leisure activities, their very existence, 'like flies to wanton boys,' was in the laps of the Gods, a truism she recalled as part of a brief conversation she once had aboard the SS Egypt with Sir Archibald Farrer long before her arrival in India. At any time, a weekend of racing and polo might be dissolved by rain. A whole year's harvest could disappear in a night upon a climatic whim. Even their homes were not safe.

In this instance, with the exception of John Dunn, the loss of a weekends sport was endured with smiling resignation, gifting all the recent new arrivals, of whom Jonathan and Marian were but two, an example worth emulating. Elsewhere on the Indian subcontinent, indeed in most other parts of the empire, it was the habit of the British to ride rough shod over the inconveniences of weather, terrain or indigenous peoples. Cities like Bombay and Calcutta bowed to an ever more obvious English architectural palette. Hill stations such as Darjeeling or Simla were parodies of Sussex villages, rising as they did from the steep hillsides in the Himalayas regardless of the cost, difficulty or eventual absurdity of their appearance.

In Assam, however, the jungle was not so easily tamed. Land cleared for cultivation returned to its original state in short time unless husbanded daily. Roads, railways and buildings, the basic infrastructure of existence, were as fragile as butterflies' wings. Nothing was secure, no living readily acquired. And, in realising as much, perhaps it was unsurprising that men of the stamp of Trevelyan Dunn continued to thrive. Their stubborn, unforgiving natures were precisely what was required if, in the end, tea was to find its way to the tables of middle-class society in London and the home counties.

Unfortunately, the postponement of race day became a cancellation of the entire race week. Between the end of February and the commencement of picking in March, there were no suitable opportunities to revive the occasion.

Polo was played. Two afternoons a week John set aside the tools of his trade for a polo mallet, leaving Jonathan to manage the estate while he was gone. But there was no replacement tournament, no reorganised assembly of the local European community.

June would be the next occasion for general festivity. The Dibrugarh Cup Shield was the enticement for another coming together of polo clubs the length of the Assam valley. By then the weather would be unbearably hot and sticky with rain once again equally if not more than likely to spoil the event.

In between times, Marian was presented with a choice. She could do her best to join in at Shahjan, living the life of the men, working alongside them in any capacity deemed to be within the scope of her sex or she could labour with the chore of paying visits to neighbours or having them call on her.

Generally, she preferred the idea of work. For most women, the latter of the two options was the more usual. Tea production was not light labour in any aspect. From picking to packing the processes were an endurance test, the bulk of the manual labour being done by 'coolies.' And though many of these were women, none of them had white skins and most of them were born into the life.

However, Marian could not sit idly on one side. Above all people, she needed stimulation. Paying house calls on neighbours was pleasant enough, but not 'enough,' not any more. She had spent years doing that in London and Hove.

There was one exception. She did particularly look forward to her weekly visits to and from Jack and Marjorie Laws. Their stories of a lifetime spent in Assam and their careful education of her in the ways and habits of planters, rapidly became as much a part of her routine as her morning ride.

Many hours were spent with them on the veranda of their bungalow at Mancotta. Cool lemonade and slow conversation was as pleasant a way as Marian could imagine to pass an afternoon. Theirs was a 'tea garden' worthy of the name. A few hundred acres only, a mere minnow by comparison to the thousands controlled with the Dunn corporation. Yet, it was a truly magical place. Tea surrounded the house on four sides, but like a picturesque patchwork quilt, the countryside at Doom Dooma some three miles to the north west of Shahjan being more hilly. Terracing was required to sustain successful exploitation of the land on the Mancotta estate, transforming the view to a scale and collaboration of shapes more appealing to the eye than the bland sameness of cultivation on the larger plantations.

Quietly and for more years than they cared to recall, the Laws had worked their modest tea garden, tending it with the care and affection one might usually expect to be reserved for gentle acres of roses. There was no escaping their love of the land. When she was there, Marian found little incentive to leave. If there was paradise to be found in Assam, the Laws were living in it. She envied them not merely the beauty and tranquillity of Mancotta, but the calm satisfaction they enjoyed every time they looked out upon it. Her only disappointment was the revelation of their impending retirement.

'Mancotta' was to be sold. In his own words, Jack was getting a 'bit long in the tooth.' Running a tea estate, even one as modest as his, was work for a younger man. Both he and Marjorie would miss 'the old place.' It had been their home and the source of their livelihood for as long as they had been married. During the many hours Marian sat with them on their veranda, it was a mystery to her how they could bring themselves to leave.

They had a son who might have carried on the estate, but he was in England. Educated at Winchester and then Cambridge, rather than returning to Assam after his studies, to continue what his father had begun, he declared his intention of a career in medicine. In many respects, it must have been something of a blow to both his mother and father.

However, wanting nothing but the best for him, they had no option but to give him their blessing. As for their two daughters. The elder had married a trapper of exotic animals for transportation dead or alive to collections across Europe and was never to be found on the same spot of the Indian continent for more than a few weeks at a time. Meanwhile the other had taken up the position of governess to three young English aristocrats whose time was divided equally between Calcutta in the winter months and Darjeeling during the long, unbearably hot summers.

Their son was sorely missed. There was no telling when they might see him again. There were nights Marjorie cried herself to sleep so greatly did she pine for him. But medicine was a noble calling, a profession which, in the circumstances of life in Assam, she knew to be of the utmost importance. She lamented his absence, but at the same time, shared equal pride with her husband at what he had set his sights to.

Marian regretted the prospect of losing two people who were fast becoming her closest friends. Within the first few months of their arrival at Shahjan, she and Jonathan made the acquaintance of a host of perfectly pleasant people. Mr and Mrs Russell Wood ran a medium sized estate at Diglie Baree. Arthur Donelly, a tall, lean bachelor with a stutter was the general manager of the sprawling plantations belonging to the British India Tea Company. He lived with his equally awkward sister Jane who might have remained an isolated spinster were it not for the fact that their widowed father was a High Court judge in Calcutta. His power and influence were a considerable attraction. Consequently, she was rarely seen in public without an escort bent on seduction, a somewhat incongruous concept but appreciated by all onlookers for its potential.

James Barrett was also unmarried. He owned and operated Balijan, an estate similar in size to Mancotta. However, it was not long before he went home to England in search of a wife, returning with a fresh-faced bride by the name of Marie Studholme. She was a sultry young lady, supremely confident of the power she wielded over men. Much later she was to become notorious for the cuckolding of her husband with a string of lovers, one of whom was a native government land agent and another, it was often reported beyond his hearing, Trevelyan Dunn.

Then there were the partners, Reginald Evans and Gerald Dickson, not 'planters' in the true sense of the word, but shopkeepers and successful businessmen. They owned and operated two highly lucrative 'Planters Stores,' one at Kobo and the other in Dibrugarh. Evans himself was a qualified pharmacist, Dickson an astute man with figures. Not surprisingly, the latter was also Adjutant to the Assam Valley Light Horse, a coincidence which maintained for their business a customer base destined to carry them on to greater things. In both towns, the 'Planters Store' was an indispensable focal point. To the surrounding estates they supplied everything, from quinine to a crated and cased Davidsons 'Sirocco' drying machine imported via Calcutta directly from the manufacturers in England.

Neither men were married, nor did they appear to be concerned to become so. This gave rise to a degree of whispered speculation. However, such was their importance to the community in general, it remained no more than that. Questions which might have been asked of them never were and the legitimacy of their presence in church was never tested.

Perhaps most conspicuous of all, though rarely seen as far north as Dibrugarh, was AHW Bentinck. He became commissioner of the region by virtue of his predecessor, Donald McKenzie having been drowned in a tragic boating accident on the Brahmaputra during the previous rainy season. The consequence of this freak incident, which involved the sinking of a small craft, with thirteen men aboard including the poor commissioner himself and three horses which were the only survivors, was a new man in the post. For understandable reasons and bearing in mind the circumstances of his rise to prominence, he refused point blank to travel anywhere in Assam other than by train or carriage; hence the fact of his being rarely seen as far north as Dibrugarh.

With the railway network far from complete and susceptible to collapses or mud slides throughout the year, his progresses through the region were painfully slow. However, he did manage a brief sojourn in Dibrugarh towards the end of March and it was then that Marian made his acquaintance.

That she was instantly reminded of her encounter with General Leighton in Lahore spoke volumes for the sort of man he appeared to be. Their introduction was short and his memory of her fleeting. But an image of him lingered in Marian's mind for days afterwards.

He arrived with all the pomp and circumstance of a petty Viceroy, accompanied by an entourage of aids, servants and hangers on, making his tour of the countryside like a medieval warlord. Quite why he was feted in the way he was or why so many people broke off from their labours to present themselves to him at the club, Marian was initially at a loss to understand. Presumably, she surmised, within his gift were favours and privileges unobtainable without certain public displays of subservience.

Both she and Jonathan were quickly persuaded of his importance and of the need to make his acquaintance. Dutifully, they joined in, waiting their turn for an audience, observing as they did a general atmosphere of jealous impatience among those whose turn to do so appeared a long way behind the rest. Notable exceptions were Mr and Mrs Trevelyan Dunn, their obvious complacency either a sign of a fall from grace or, and what Marian guessed more likely, an act of defiance to prove their independence and, in Trevelyan Dunn's case at least, inherent superiority; Trevelyan Dunn bowed to no man, not even a commissioner.

Otherwise, the majority of Europeans and natives alike turned out to glimpse or, if white, to shake the hand of Mr Bentinck whenever he deigned to acknowledge them. Marian could only guess what sort of reception was required when and if the Viceroy himself were to put in an appearance.

AHW Bentinck reminded her a little of General Leighton not because in his build or physiognomy he was at all alike. He was smaller, balding and in many respects terrier like. However, when he shook her hand and looked into her eyes, there was somehow that same sense in her of being invaded, that were she to be left alone in his company, under different circumstances and in a different place, she would have been wise to fear for her safety.

'Loathsome little man really,' Marjorie Laws whispered to her as they endured the sermon—like speech which was his habit to deliver at whichever small town his caravan halted. 'Why we suffer all this nonsense each time he or his like come up here is beyond me. Still, it's the way of things. It's part of 'doing business' I suppose.'

'Is he very powerful then?' Marian asked, echoing rather her companion's low opinion of the man.

'Oh dear me, no. Not really. There are bigger fish in the sea than our Mr Bentinck. But he does have a certain influence, particularly when it comes to matters concerning the railway. That's why Jack and the others pay him so much mind. The more he can be encouraged to pass this way, the quicker the rail link will be finished and, in the end, only when the track reaches Dibrugarh and beyond will we be able to compete with the estates further down the valley. At least, that's what Jack and the other planters say.'

It was a simple equation which made good sense. Persuade the water phobic commissioner to look upon Dibrugarh with special favour and the future prosperity of all those who worked in the immediate vicinity would be guaranteed. Give him the least incentive to think of Upper Assam as no more than a troublesome backwater and vital government resources might be channelled elsewhere. A degree of fawning, public adulation and perish, she thought, behind the scenes favours, were a small price to pay for the part Mr Bentinck might play in securing so important a link to the outside world.

Whatever the politics, Marian was able to summon up no great spirit of welcome for him and offered no words of regret at his departure. Twenty-four hours after his grand entrance he turned himself around and went back the way he had come, leaving what was left of the month of March to draw to a close with no further incident. The only tangible evidence of his visit seemed to be an extended contract for the supply of sleepers, the cutting of which both John and Jonathan devoted a large part of their working week to before the picking season commenced in earnest.

Felling trees for their lumber was a curious introduction to the life of a tea planter, but once persuaded of the importance of such hard manual labour,

Jonathan expressed no objection. He devoted himself to the task with the accustomed discipline of a military background and the goodwill of a man in possession of new found contentment.

By the end of March, Marian thought of Shahjan a home. If Jonathan had any regrets or misgivings about his sudden metamorphosis from soldier to civilian, or from bachelor to husband, he showed no outward signs. Though dissimilar in so many respects he and John took to each other from the word go, united in their pleasure of work and a common vision of what the estate might one day become. Together they plotted the future. Jonathan, pragmatic and well used to the preciseness of military routine, scored high on the detail of management and tactics, while John, inflicted with an unrelenting passion, an almost obsessive determination to exceed the achievements of his father, kept in his head a clear picture of what he expected from every one of the several hundred acres of land he owned. There was nothing random about his plans for Shahjan, Medla or Bollai and Jonathan was fast turning out to be exactly the man to help him complete his dream.

To see her husband as he was, pleased Marian. As the months passed his affection towards her grew steadily. She sensed in him a certain satisfaction in having her as his wife and in turn she could not help but reciprocate. To admit she loved him or was in love with him was not an easy matter. Her relationship with Jonathan was in no way similar to that which she experienced with William.

For the short time it lasted, theirs had been a glorious kaleidoscope of amour, a rich, exotic passion which thrived alone on the promise of what it might one day become. They had held hands together, stood so close to each other that the warmth from their bodies fused and whispered words of love more tender than the average heart could bear. And yet, in truth, it was all of no more substance than a zephyr's breath, no more real than the searing pain of cupid's arrow. To admit she loved William, had once reduced her to a helpless wreck and, when it came, the news of his death raised her emotions to the ground. She was desolate, helpless and resolved to an eternity of grief.

But that was more than a year in the past. By the spring of 1886, she was in a different land, living a completely altered life. She was the wife of a man who though rushed into marriage, applied himself to the task with diligence and apparent satisfaction. If he believed himself following in another man's shadow he gave no hint of it. And, for her part, quite genuinely, Marian let slip the memory of her beloved William like a silk ribbon passing slowly between her fingers. He became, like the glow of a setting sun, little more or less than the fondest of memories.

Jonathan offered sincere affection and she returned it. He respected her independence of spirit. And, in doing so, he permitted her the freedom to roam and express herself as freely as she was accustomed to do. He was kind, generous and proud to have her at his side. In return, Marian approached the title of Mrs Jonathan Cole with a readiness even she had not expected, finding it a small endeavour to satisfy both the emotional and physical needs of her husband.

Regularly, he came to her bed at night. However, far from finding his attentions an onerous chore, a distasteful obligation, with each coupling, she learned to desire him more. Intercourse was no ugly event, no sordid indignity to be endured. Whether with the act came the art of truly making love, she had yet to determine. So confused was she by the definition of her emotions, it was impossible for her to label the sexual labyrinth into which she and Jonathan had stumbled. All she could be certain of was that somehow and in some way, in penetrating her body he awakened extravagant desires which had previously lain dormant.

Far from avoiding his attention or regretting his presence, there were nights she craved his body next to hers, waiting in the dark impatiently for the first suggestion he might come to her. And when he did there was true exhilaration, carnal lust, instinctive and unavoidable. Parts of her, the parts which attended bible class at home in London, the parts which still clung to the purity and perfection of her love for William, they pricked her conscience. But they were overruled. If there was love in sexual passion, then for Jonathan she felt love and, want it or not, that love could not be denied. Nor was she of a mind to have it so.

Jonathan took her and used her, satisfying desires he felt no need to disguise. But he was also tender and caring. He caressed and touched her in ways and in places which cried out for more. He stimulated desires of equal measure to his own, so much so that on occasions they were together for hours on end. When it was over they lay contented, coiled in each other's arms, light sleep a companion to their tenderness.

Later, when he returned to his own room, Marian would be left with the warm memory of him till morning. During the following day, the shadow of their lust was reflected in the holding of hands, a caress, a shared smile, or a look of longing as full of intent as the act of love making itself.

Eventually, Marian confessed to her diary that she and Jonathan were lovers. It was no easy admission. Somehow by committing it to paper, she registered a sense of guilt, a sense that she was betraying or had betrayed the exclusivity of her vows to William. She hesitated to define her new emotions as those of being in love. Of that and about that she remained deeply sceptical. As far as she understood it, to be in love was a singular occurrence. Though they were not lovers, she most certainly had been in love with William in its truest possible guise. Lust and passion were an irrelevance to such a relationship.

She was compelled to believe that what she felt for William and he for her was pure love. If not that, then why had his death hurt so brutally. Why, like Portia, in her grief had she yearned to consume live coals. Why had her heart been split in two and why had it been so imperative for her to embark upon a pilgrimage which obliged her travel to the other side of the world.

General Gordon's slaughter in February 1885 and the massacre of all those who fought so gallantly at his side; that was a tragedy of greater proportion to the death of one young soldier from cholera. General Gordon was a great man, a hero, a man who shaped and changed the course of history. His death and the fall of Khartoum offended a nation. William Radford's demise caused pain and sorrow to no more than a small handful of those who knew and loved him well. Yet it was the news from India, not from the Sudan which had stabbed Marian like a thousand knives and caused her to weep selfish tears.

In her diary, she declared a growing respect for the man she had married in such haste. Moreover, she admitted to an affection she believed ripening with each new day. And in sentences filled with the hesitancy of one not used to graphic confessions of the physical, she described the most intimate details of what she was experiencing for the first time in her life.

And, she went further. She documented the day-to-day activities of both herself and her husband. She outlined the tea manufacturing processes. She drew a picture of Shahjan and the surrounding countryside with the precision of a miniaturist, sometimes devoting several pages to the sights and sounds of a single morning ride and recording, she hoped, an indelible picture of life in Assam.

Much of it was later paraphrased into letter form for dispatch to 32 Princes Gate, leaving out the intricacies of her internal emotional struggles or any allusion to the fact or frequency of the nights she shared a bed with her husband.

It was a simple matter of inevitability therefore that in the first week of May, when her letter home was devoted to the number of 'maunds' of tea being manufactured and the level of rain in inches to have fallen during one twenty-four hour period, she chose not to inform her mother or father of the growing discomfort she was experiencing in the early weeks of pregnancy.

Chapter Eighteen

At first, it occurred to Marian that she might be in for a bout of 'the fever.' It was also possible her persistent nausea was due to the extra doses of quinine advised by John Dunn to combat the higher than usual number of mosquitoes as the rainy season approached. His warnings of the sickness brought about by, and inherent dangers of, something as small as the bite from a mosquito were submitted with his usual lack of embellishment. As unpalatable as it was, quinine was the only and best defence. It was also better by far than submitting to the disease itself.

Therefore, the warnings were heeded. Neither Jonathan nor Marian needed reminding of the speed of transmission or fatal potential of illnesses contracted on the Indian subcontinent. However, disease was not the cause of Marian's ague. The reason for her slump into listlessness and the frequent desire she felt to remain within the privacy of her bedroom, avoiding sun, heat, rain or the attentions of two men who, for different reasons, expressed growing concern over her welfare lay elsewhere.

16 May was the date she first diarised the truth of her condition. Since she had not called for confirmation from Dr Murphy, there was a degree of speculation. However, she knew enough of the condition and the routines of her own body to be convinced without need of a medical examination. Not until 23 May, a week later however, after the smiling face of Patrick Murphy confirmed the news, did she confess to her husband what she already knew.

It was early evening. All day it had rained. Picking continued but it was almost impossible to get a wither on the leaf and production was slow. Jonathan was frustrated, tired and dirty by the time he returned to the bungalow, his high leather boots no defence against the water, his clothes wet through. Some three miles along the road to Dibrugarh, John gave up on his plans for an afternoon's polo and returned to Shahjan equally disgruntled, making a point of cursing loudly against weather which had been the ruin of too many matches already.

Whether or not it was an appropriate moment to break the news remained to be seen. But Marian felt she had little choice in the matter. Jonathan had been too busy in the leaf houses to notice the coming and going of the quietly mannered doctor. However, John met him on the road as he was leaving and with only a moment or two of interrogation extracted the pithy news.

'I'm perfectly well thank you,' Marian replied to the initial enquiry as to her good health.

'I'm glad to hear it,' John remarked having joined Mr and Mrs Cole on the veranda to take a cool drink out of the rain. His attention was drawn to a fast clearing sky which promised by evening to reveal the pleasant glow of a sinking sun.

'So why the need for Patrick Murphy?' Jonathan asked, surprised that the doctor had called without his being made aware of it. 'I'm sure he's far too busy to pay social calls.'

'If you must know,' Marian replied disappointed that on this one occasion she was not alone with her husband, 'Some days ago, I asked Booloo to send for him. I wanted him to confirm whether or not I am going to have a baby.'

There was a brief silence as both men exchanged looks of equal incredulity, though in John's case, the cat was already out of the bag and his own expression of disbelief was therefore contrived.

'I beg your pardon?' Jonathan spluttered.

'I'm pregnant,' Marian repeated.

After that the conversation moved quickly, a chaotic bombardment of questions, corresponding answers and general all-round congratulations. If Marian was nervous of the reception the news was likely to engender, she need not have been. Jonathan was delighted and John's praise flowed in abundance.

'This will be our first baby at Shahjan,' he declared with pride. 'I should say that's a good omen for the future,' then he took his leave, sensitive enough to realise his place at such a time was elsewhere. Collecting up his mud strewn coat and unhitching 'Snowden' from his usual post on the corner of the veranda, he rode off through the semi-darkness to his own bungalow some three hundred yards across what had become in the course of only one day of rain a muddy lagoon.

As for Jonathan, his obvious delight at the news came as something of a relief. He and Marian had not discussed children. She had no idea whether he would be horrified or overjoyed by her revelation. She anticipated the latter, or rather, she prayed for it. But when it came it was the acknowledgement she needed, the blessing which would enable her to enjoy the prospect of motherhood.

By the beginning of June, the monsoon season was well upon them. During ten consecutive days the heavens yielded no less than twenty-two inches of rain. The Brahmaputra rose by an astonishing fifteen feet. In places downstream, where in winter there was a channel barely half a mile wide it had become ten, inundating vast tracts of land on either side and ruining untold acres of cultivated land.

A disaster of spectacular proportions one might have imagined. But to old hands, it was greeted with stoical resignation, the engulfing waters down river shrugged off by John as an annual inconvenience, becoming important only if they threatened to disrupt the Dibrugarh Shield polo tournament.

A revelation of considerably more interest across the region was news of Marian's pregnancy. Notified to Marjorie Laws as a piece of privileged information, she was solicited to serve as midwife. However, it quickly became common knowledge, spreading like wild fire, a morsel of gossip to be bartered even among ladies yet to make Marian's acquaintance.

As best she could, she carried on as usual, taking appropriate measures where necessary to conceal any physical manifestation of her condition. Unfortunately, Jonathan had other plans. He was quick to curb her morning rides and, as far as Marian was concerned, devoted far too much of his time to her welfare, fussing over her more than she welcomed. That his pleasure at the nearness of becoming a father was writ large on his face and in his every action, was of considerable comfort. However, in her customary independent manner she tried and failed to hide the irritation of being so restricted. She was reluctant to be confined to barracks.

Fortunately, Marjorie offered her services as 'aide de camp' and devoted confidante. At times she also found herself acting as referee, frequently taking Jonathan aside to remind him that women had been giving birth with remarkable success since the dawn of time, even in Assam. And, as if to justify her credentials she produced photographs of the two daughters to whom she had given birth during the years she and her husband struggled virtually unaided to wrestle their estate from the relentless grip of the jungle. In addition, she promised to remain at the side of his wife up to and until the first cries of his son or daughter.

Quite why Marjorie took to Marian and Jonathan with such a generous heart was never fully explained. Perhaps having her only son in England and her two daughters far off with families of their own to consider, she was encouraged in her surrogate impulses. But she was not alone. Jack was equally loyal. From a chance meeting aboard the SS Pagan his liking for Marian had developed to such an extent, he vowed to delay the sale of 'Mancotta' and his subsequent retirement to the alpine beauty of Kashmir until the christening of a child over whom he pledged his vigilance should he be enlisted as Godfather.

In the event, by the end of June, the deal was struck willingly on both sides. During a lively dinner party held at Kurmi to celebrate. not the impending birth, but a home team victory in the Dibrugarh Shield, Marjorie and Jack Laws were formerly appointed to the task they requested.

For on a day when the rain had relented, the name of Dunn appeared once more on the sizeable silver trophy.

Save for their shared seniority among the local European community, on the surface at least, the Laws and the Dunn's had little in common. Jack Laws was David to Trevelyan Dunn's Goliath. He was an essentially quiet, gentle, man, a devoted Christian, tireless worker and conscientious master to his work force. Over the years he had sacrificed personal aggrandisement and wealth to the principals of fair play and honesty. He treated all men as equal and earnestly believed in the sharing of any bounty gleaned from the soil, particularly soil upon which he was the alien presence.

By contrast, Trevelyan Dunn was the antithesis of everything Jack Laws believed in and practised. He was ruthless, heartless and utterly devoted to the power and wealth he wielded with such feudal forethought. For the most part he held his workforce in contempt and exploited their labour as best he could to enrich a very small circle of family members.

And yet, it was not at all unusual for both he and Jack, with their respective wives to be gathered at the same table, displaying one towards the other a most unexpected and somewhat incongruous respect, even affection.

Clearly there was a history between them. Only this could explain such apparent inconsistency, things of which newcomers to the region like Marian and Jonathan knew nothing. Evidence of their closeness, however, offered an opportunity to imagine a side to Trevelyan Dunn which he appeared reluctant to reveal and hid with considerable success.

They might have been mistaken. There might have existed between the two 'older statesmen' a deep loathing, restrained only as a courtesy to their wives who were transparently the closest of friends, relishing each other's company as might two sisters, laughing and teasing together in a relaxed manner only credible after many years of intimate contact. But somehow Marian doubted it. She complimented herself on understanding human nature sufficiently to recognise that between Jack Laws and Trevelyan Dunn there lay buried something deeper than the acting out of a part simply to please others.

As it happened, had she but known it, this was an observation deserving of applause for its accuracy. For twenty years earlier, Jack Laws had saved the life of Trevelyan Dunn. With a singular but typical display of selflessness on his part, and later a matter of public record, he had thrown himself into the swirling, muddy currents of a swollen river and pulled the stricken Trevelyan Dunn to the safety of shore. Had he not done so, the man would have been swept to a watery grave. It was an act of courage and physical fortitude Trevelyan Dunn could never repay in kind and for which he was forever indebted. Though he was a man who trifled with conventional codes of fair play and justice, within his own somewhat distorted morality, Jack Laws was a man he had come to respect almost beyond all others.

Understandably, Marian was preoccupied with matters of a more pressing nature. Having secured prospective Godparents for her child, there was still the small matter of sending word to England. Verity Dunn suggested that rather than the dispatch of a letter, Marian should go home for the duration of her pregnancy. Sooner rather than later she should pack her things and leave. In England she would be more comfortable, and in a climate more conducive. Moreover, when it came to the birth itself, she would be in safer hands.

This was probably true. Many wives did make the voyage home for precisely that purpose. However, Marian had already made up her mind. She wanted to stay close by her husband. That is not to say there were times she longed for home. Not a day passed without at least a thought for her family. Being absent from her father was a particular agony. But she had new responsibilities, a new life and one to which she was committed wholeheartedly. When the time came Patrick Murphy would be on hand. With his help and the support of those around her, she was confident of having her baby at Shahjan.

This decision was applauded by Marjorie and even received the royal seal of approval from Trevelyan Dunn, taking as he did a moment off from his enlivened discussions concerning the polo tournament to admire her pluck, blurting out the rather extraordinary and clearly chauvinist observation that only a woman who gave birth to her children in Assam could truly consider herself a planter's wife. Fortunately, but more by luck than judgement, this remark caused no offence to the other women at his supper table since those of them who were mother's, namely Marjorie and his own wife had themselves complied with this standard.

However, it was typical of his somewhat medieval principles. Of course, there was always the possibility he made such remarks in order to call attention to himself, a habit Marian began to suspect was at the root of much of his intolerable behaviour in public. Having said that, without doubt, he was a man so spoilt and so used to obsequious obedience to his every whim from all those he had subjugated, it was not beyond him to believe his own propaganda.

She could well imagine he saw little difference between the male contribution of siring children and the pregnancy which followed. In those circumstances, since he had no problem staying in Assam to fulfil his part in the birthing process of several offspring by his own wife and, it was rumoured, two or three by a string of mistresses, he saw no particular reason for the general exodus of women to 'finish off' their half of the enterprise.

The subject of Marian's pregnancy aside, the evening at Chunkier went well. Around a huge dining table, cut from the blackest Nahore trunks and polished to a mirror shine, were collected the most unlikely group of people. As far as Marian could tell, the only common denominator was tea.

Trevelyan Dunn sat at the head of the table with his wife at the far end. On his immediate right he had Marjorie Laws, while on his left there was poor Patrick Murphy. With the diplomatic skills so essential to his profession, he absorbed all suggestions as to the inadequacies of help on hand for women forced to endure labour in Assam. Instead, he took confidence in Marian's determination to remain at Shahjan throughout, assuring her, as she sat next to him, of his intention to be within easy reach whenever she needed him.

Jonathan sat next to Marjorie which made for easy conversation while to his right he had a young lady by the name of Rosemary. She was companion to Terence and, like him, she remained mute through most of the evening, responding if spoken to directly with soft, monosyllabic affirmations or negatives, none of which were audible to anyone other than the two gentlemen in her immediate vicinity.

Even Jack Laws, sitting immediately opposite her and trying his level best to engage her in conversation, gave up, convinced he must be hard of hearing, so limp were her responses to his questions. In her defence, however, it has to be said that she and Terence appeared comfortable together. Much of their evening was spent in mutual, if silent, admiration. They were like two dozing lovebirds on a perch, side by side, at one but silent and motionless.

John and Philip also had guests, sisters, the misses Julia and Emily Fenton, the former a worldly, flirtatious creature of twenty-two years, the latter a delicate rose of barely twenty. Had it not been for the fact that their father, ex-Major Horatio Fenton, was the local chief of police, convention would have decreed them too young to be abroad without a more mature female escort, particularly in the company of two men yet to prove the extent to which they were likely to mature into 'chips off the old block.'

However, the 'Major' and John shared a mutual affection for horse flesh. The former was an adequate polo player, if not of first team potential. Consequently, the virtue of his daughters was less of an issue than it might have been had their presence been requested at a similar event in the company of two other young men.

Sadly, neither girl contributed much more than to the making up of numbers. Julia was ebullient and, though not beautiful in any classical way, had engineered for herself an undeniable attractiveness which entitled her to regular attention from both married and unmarried men alike. Whether her rather too obvious and often tactile flirting with John was an indication of serious intent, Marian could not judge with any certainty since it was her first encounter with the two young sirens. She found herself hoping not. Julia possessed many attributes. She was vivacious, rather too much so, and with even the older men in the room glancing in her direction rather more often than they should, it was quite apparent she appealed to the eye.

However, sadly, she gave no indication of having even a modicum of serious intelligence. She held and expressed opinions with gay abandon, but displayed a desperate lack of knowledge and although Marian owned few enough women friends since her arrival at Shahjan, she doubted Julia Fenton was destined to become one of them.

By contrast, and attached to Philip for the evening, rather like a limpet, Emily Fenton reminded Marian to a greater or lesser extent of her own sister Margaret. She lacked the religious fervour. No indication on her part was given of missionary inclinations which, to Marian's mind was a blessed relief. Indeed, rather like Rosemary, so shy and quiet was she, raising her voice barely above a whisper if and when she spoke, any indications at all as to her heart's desires were kept securely to herself. For a while, as hostess to the soiree, Verity Dunn tried to engage the two more timid girls in conversation, but like Jack Laws, she soon abandoned the task as hopeless. Furthermore, though verbose, in a marked exhibition which proved her somewhat lacking in the social graces, Julia showed little interest in responding to the sound of a female voice.

One other guest was present at the dinner table. His name was Thomas Gulliland. He was a man possibly in his late fifties or early sixties. Though he was slight in build and not particularly tall there was something rather imposing about him. Marian found herself noticing him from time to time during the meal. He too was softly spoken and although he contributed freely to the conversation, it was at all times with a marked economy of words, responding to rather than inventing questions. Nevertheless, he was clearly at ease in the company of all those present which was something of a curiosity.

For he was unique in one unmistakable respect. He was Anglo-Indian. Indeed, but for his Christian name and a lack of any obvious native accent, his colour and complexion were that of an Asian. His hair was jet-black, his skin the colour of seasoned timber. To all present save Marian and Jonathan he was well known, as open in the warmth of his smile to Marjorie Laws as to Trevelyan Dunn and, in turn, received from everyone at the table equal courtesy. Even the Misses Fenton appeared to be on familiar terms.

Unfortunately, he had no companion. He sat on the left on Verity Dunn, leaving an empty space opposite. Whether this was intended from the outset, when the evening was planned, or a simple inconvenience caused by a last minute cancellation, compelling him to come on his own, Marian knew not. No one spoke of a Mrs Gulliland either black or white. That much about him, as with so much else, remained a mystery up to and beyond the end of the meal.

All Marian gathered from occasional snippets of conversation overheard as her attention shifted around the table was that he enjoyed the general 'bon ami' of all those present. She gathered also that he had recently returned from England where he had been to care for and then bury his recently deceased mother. This indicated but by no means confirmed the notion of his having a white mother and black father.

Marian was intrigued. She had been in India long enough to know how, particularly in former years, it was common practice for young British officers to form liaisons with native girls. Back in the forties and fifties, the East India Company actively discouraged officers or enlisted men from taking wives to India. They were an unnecessary distraction from the onerous and precarious task of maintaining a business empire the like, size and complexity of which had not been seen before. With disease rife and the day-to-day life of a soldier peripatetic to say the least, wives were considered more of a hindrance than a help. No one was deceived. India was a wild and dangerous corner of the globe, no place at all for the pale complexions and frail physiques of white memsahibs. This was a belief vindicated, if vindication were needed by the appalling loss of civilian life during the darkest days of the mutiny.

Deprived of winsome Anglo-Saxon maidens therefore, sexual relief for the average soldier, officer class or no, was sought elsewhere. Diminutive Hindu girls were readily available. They were exotic, plentiful and educated to a culture of sexual liberalism far beyond anything previously experienced by their pale skinned soldier suitors.

Sadly, this somewhat misguided policy of such frequent inter racial co-habitations resulted in a propensity towards the full range of venereal diseases and a burgeoning population of children with mixed parentage. Though these offspring were eliminated from the inner circle of the British community, it was common place by the 1880s for Anglo-Indian children to be more conspicuous in certain Imperial strongholds than those of pure Anglo-Saxon origins.

What was entirely more unusual, however, and when encountered invariably met with the full weight of Victorian moral indignation, was the reverse union of an Asian man to a white woman. Such irredeemable scandals occurred rarely, but when they did were kept a closely guarded secret. For a woman to become pregnant as the direct result of so iniquitous a union was quite beyond the bounds of acceptable standards. Few British women in India were unmarried or without at least some form of betrothal contract. Consequently, for a white woman to become pregnant by a black man and to produce his child represented a degree of public shame and humiliation from which there was little chance of recovery.

As Marian was to discover later, shortly after Thomas Gulliland was born, he was removed from his mother. She was sent home to England in disgrace. There she remained for the rest of her life, ostracised from respectable society. She was nurtured by the church only in as much as she could be held up as an example to others of the appalling consequences of straying so blatantly from the true path of righteousness.

He, Thomas that is, was brought up in Calcutta, in the home of his father, loved and cherished by aunts and cousins but denied either the unique succour of a mother or the right to a national identity. The one advantage he had was that his grandfather was one of the wealthiest silk merchants in Bengal. He had amassed a substantial fortune. From this he furnished his grandson with an education in England, an education intended to exaggerate rather than deny the Anglo-Saxon blood in his veins. In turn, Thomas' father impressed upon his son the importance of gaining respect for himself within the white community.

The unintended result of course was confusion and a certain bitterness. Thomas grew up in suits and stiff collars yet ignorant of and disconnected from his mother. At the same time many of his formative years were spent far from the protection of his father. Much of the time he was lonely, unhappy and completely unsure of his identity. He spoke with an English accent, read Shakespeare, and worshipped in a Christian church. Yet, when he looked in a mirror he was as dark as any Hindu native. He saw in his reflection, not the son of a sahib, but the servant of a white master.

Eventually he returned to Calcutta, a young white man in a black man's body, a misfit wherever he went and although welcomed back into the household of his father with all the love and affection due him, his days passed as if he were a fish out of water. At the age of twenty-two he set out on his own, finally fetching up in Dibrugarh. There his race, colour and disgraced parentage were of lesser importance. He immersed himself in a community which was struggling to steal a harvest from an unforgiving jungle. With hard work, he provoked little censure in a part of the world where graft and contribution, not race or creed were what earned one man the respect of another.

During her long accounts of him to Marian in the days after that dinner party, Marjorie Laws told the tale of Thomas' unconventional life; of how he had risen above the tragic consequences of his parents' extreme indiscretion and of how he had earned the friendship and respect of black and white alike, eventually able to mix in both worlds with ease.

Destiny suggested that one day he would return to Calcutta, there to claim his inheritance. As the first-born son of his father, he held title to a business enterprise stretching from Shanghai to London, from Cairo to Paris.

In the meantime however, Dibrugarh was his home as it had been for many years. The people who lived there were his friends. Trevelyan Dunn and others like him, respected Thomas Gulliland and invited him to their homes for the man he was, not for the one that Victorian social dogma would have him painted.

Almost single handed and without the need or inclination to take a wife, Thomas Gulliland managed for himself a meagre plantation sandwiched between Kurmi and the River Dibong, one of many small tributaries feeding into the Brahmaputra. His land was not the best. It flooded regularly and produced a poorer quality of leaf than most. Yet he flourished. A man of gentlemanly resignation and modest goals he had come to terms early on with the hand dealt him by fate. In a manner later embraced by Marian herself as an example during times of the worst self-pity, he had risen above his own handicaps. He set them to one side, preferring instead an acceptance of life for what it was rather than for what he had been denied by it.

That evening at Kurmi, she knew little of Thomas save for what was immediately obvious. When she and Jonathan returned to Shahjan, the cool night air and sounds of the surrounding jungle a heady cocktail to minds made light by wine, she invented intriguing and mysterious images to satisfy her curiosity. None of them were fact, something she was educated to over the coming weeks, but she could not resist. Though Thomas Gulliland was an eloquent man in the company of that evening, he preferred to let others take centre stage, thus making him a delightful subject for exotic invention.

In the end, the true story of his life was barely less extraordinary than any Marian invented for herself. Brought up a Hindu, but educated to the standards of a white sahib, he was caught between two worlds, walking a tight rope between two cultures and two opposing sets of prejudices. On the one hand, he was the first-born son a wealthy Indian merchant family. On the other, he remained loyal to the mother who bore him, requiring no encouragement to be at her graveside and erect a stone in her memory. He bore both a Christian and Hindu name, an advertisement to his genetic impurity. However, he refused to shrink from the stigma inflicted upon him by the union of a mother and father who themselves did not escape the retribution of having committed so heinous a crime.

Initially Marian was puzzled by his presence at Kurmi. She was confused that a man of Trevelyan Dunn's uncompromising imperialistic views should welcome into his home the likes of Thomas Gulliland. But then, Trevelyan Dunn was a man of many contradictions and fully accustomed to setting his own rules. Imperial he was, or perhaps, to be more exact tyrannical; but his empire was of his own making. Kurmi and its surrounding lands were an independent fiefdom of his own construction and constitution, with him as its head of state and sole law maker, all of which were subject to change upon a whim.

In truth, the more Thomas Gulliland faced rejection from the great Queen Empress and the society over which she held sway, the more Trevelyan Dunn was likely to welcome him in.

Proof of this, if proof were needed, came in observing first the evident discomfort of both Miss Julia and Miss Emily Fenton. They appeared somewhat unsettled at having to share their end of the dining table with a man whose complexion and race contrasted so clearly with their own. On the other hand, there was palpable delight in Trevelyan Dunn's eyes each time he observed their discomfort.

All in all, and contrary to expectations, Marian returned home to Shahjan having enjoyed the evening. By comparison to the standards of any other bungalow she had visited since being in Assam, Kurmi was palatial. There were no classical columns, no refined Georgian architectural allusions. Indeed, bricks and mortar were few and far between. Yet there was opulence. No elite social gathering in London could have boasted better fare or more sumptuous surroundings.

Of the evening itself, Verity Dunn was clearly the conductor of the orchestra. She it was who ran the household, prepared the menu and directed events. However, the general tone was set by her husband. In the grand entrance hall, his many hunting trophies festooned the walls; several tigers heads, that of a buffalo and a variety of smaller animals Marian could not identify, a gallery of lifeless creatures, all with clear bright eyes and vanquished looks. In the dining room the furniture was heavy, ornately carved and overtly masculine, the masters preferred chair at the head of the table a veritable throne. There was a snooker room for the gentlemen, the Burroughs table having been imported directly from England, perhaps the most unique item yet handled by Messrs Evans and Dickson of the 'Planters Stores.' Even the drawing room favoured the Trevelyan Dunn hallmark rather than that of his wife. It was a house fit for a king and it was hard for Marian to see herself as anything other than one of his subjects.

Therefore, though sated and at ease with the company of the evening, there was also some relief to accompany their arrival back at Shahjan. The following morning life resumed as normal; the strange, almost surreal setting of the previous night no more relevant than had it been a dream. The Misses Fenton, so prim and pristine and so obviously inappropriate to the needs of either John or Philip, were perhaps a bizarre figment of her imagination, their invention a curious caricature. More strange still, was it possible that no man existed, black or white with the unlikely name of Thomas Gulliland?

As she was to learn all too soon, it had been real. John came over to the bungalow to apologise for both the marked resentment shown toward her by Julia Fenton and the silliness of her younger sister. The two young women, he assured her, had been invited simply to repay a small debt to their father. In his capacity as chief of constabulary, he had recently performed a modest favour for the Kurmi estate. He was unable to attend the dinner for himself. However, sending his daughters was considered by both parties fair repayment. Overt evidence of their being unready for such company, in Julia's case because she flaunted herself so visibly and in Emilys because she appeared so inept at any social interaction, was a matter which caused John considerable embarrassment.

After begging the pardon of Marian and Jonathan in turn, he made his excuses for the morning on the grounds that he needed to visit Thomas Gulliland to affect a similar and perhaps more urgent apology. Although previously acquainted with him, the two young ladies were disdainful and rude in their refusal to attempt anything but the bare minimum of conversation with Thomas. This was something for which John would not forgive them readily and which his father was bound to make known to their father, the ex-Major Fenton.

Marian of course, dismissed John's apology in an instant as being entirely unnecessary. She insisted that no fault lay at his door for any ill manners of others who should have known better. However, she was strangely relieved that Julia Fenton's rather too inflated opinion of herself was not deemed attractive by John. Clearly, he was of a mind that her vanity overshadowed the more obvious physical attributes she employed so frequently to ensnare members of the opposite sex.

When he left his intention was to be away for the rest morning. Jonathan was fully occupied in the tea houses. Consequently, Marian decided to take advantage of a dry day. Banned from riding because of her condition, shortly after ten, she set off on foot to walk the trolley lines to Medla.

Bearing in mind her condition, it was an ambitious venture. Four months and more into her pregnancy was not the most appropriate time to embark upon such strenuous exercise. In Hyde Park, on even ground and in more temperate weather, a short stroll might have been efficacious. However, there was no easy walking in or around Shahjan. The ground at every step was uneven and the humidity such that even before reaching the coolie lines, the effort was beginning to tell. Quite clearly Medla was too far. Reluctantly, she turned for home, the yards become more arduous by the minute, until she found herself pausing for breath more frequently than she anticipated.

By the time she returned to the bungalow, she was weak with exhaustion. Booloo came to her rescue, bringing her cold drinks on the veranda where she intended waiting in the shade until Jonathan came home for something to eat.

When he did, he was hot and fatigued. His open necked shirt was wet through and his hands were covered in black grease, acquired in the all too familiar practice of wrestling with a belligerent drying machine. It was not surprising therefore that he failed to notice his wife's distressed condition, particularly since she went out of her way to disguise it beneath the pretence of expected symptoms.

After a light lunch which he devoured, but which she picked at, he kissed Marian on the forehead and returned to work the way he had come, the drying machine having proved a more stubborn adversary than originally expected.

When John appeared, just as the afternoon sun was beginning to cool, he rode straight past the noisy industry of the leaf houses to Marian and Jonathan's bungalow, on his mind a long cool drink sitting in the shade on something rather more comfortable than a saddle.

Booloo appeared exactly on cue to relieve him of his horse as he dismounted. He came from the vegetable patch behind the bungalow rather than from the interior. A few minutes later, both men were surprised therefore to hear Marian's faint cries of distress coming from within, barely audible above the din of machinery no more than fifty yards away and self-evidently inaudible to anyone further than a few feet from the open front door.

John was the first to enter. In the gloom, it took him a few seconds to adjust his eyes to the light. However, when he did, he was appalled by what confronted him. Marian was lying on the floor half in and half out of her bedroom. She was clothed in little more than a white shift. There were no shoes on her feet and her short hair was unbrushed. Most obvious though were the deep crimson stains against what was effectively only a thin undergarment. There was blood on her hands and blood on the floor.

'Help me please,' she cried out as she saw John. 'My baby! My baby!'

And help her he did, as best he could. But there was little to be done. Booloo ran to the leaf sheds to fetch Jonathan. During the minutes which elapsed before his arrival, John lifted Marian from the floor and replaced her on the bed, her deadly pale face filled with the ghastly truth of what was happening to her. This was no figment of her imagination, this no nightmare from which she might wake at any minute. This was as real and as ugly as it could be. No more were her thoughts of Thomas Gulliland or Misses Julia and Emily Fenton. No more was the biggest disappointment of her day the need to cut short her walk to Medla. This was real and frightening. Deep within her, she could feel the life of her child slipping away.

Chapter Nineteen

It was a fortnight before Marian ventured beyond the confines of the bungalow. The monsoons were upon them as never before. Barely a day passed without a deluge. Nevertheless, where possible picking continued and the leaf houses continued to fill. If they could achieve a satisfactory wither on the leaf, there was promise of record yields. The estate was producing anything from fifteen to twenty maunds of tea each day (a maund being approximately eighty pounds in weight). With the market in London holding up well, expectations were high that by the end of the year, Shahjan would turn a profit for the first time since work began clearing the land. Together, Jonathan and John worked twelve-to-fourteen-hour days. In John's case, he only rarely spared himself the time off for polo in Dibrugarh.

Late one afternoon, he and Jonathan took guns and went into the jungle with the intention of shooting a tiger. The local 'babu' had been to Shahjan. He pleaded with Sahib Dunn to save his village from the ravages of a beast which had already killed two of their cattle. How long would it be, he implored in frantic tones, before this ferocious animal gained a taste for human flesh.

Accordingly, a platform was erected for the two men in the crook of a tree some yards from the partially consumed carcass of its last kill. For hours the two men waited in anticipation of the tigers return to claim the remains of a feast already half eaten. Under normal circumstances it might have been the perfect opportunity for John and Jonathan to talk man to man, but they did not. Instead, they perched uncomfortably and silent, their guns at the ready while darkness descended and the jungle closed in around them. Eventually, with neither sight nor sound of their prey, they abandoned the task, coming in a poor second to the stealth of the tiger.

Since the loss of Marian's baby, a heavy air of despondency had lain over Shahjan. There was still the noise of machinery, the jabbering of coolie workers, the snorts, grunts and whinnying of assorted animals, but the language of communication between herself, Jonathan and John had all but vanished.

Through the first few days, Marian was too ill and too weak to talk. Marjorie Laws and Patrick Murphy were her most frequent visitors. The former as often as not stayed through the night, sleeping in a cot next to Marian's bed, secretly fearing the worst but in a burst of renewed devotion, praying on bended knee for the Lord God almighty to save her young friend.

Whether through faith or medicine, or perhaps a combination of both, Marian did pull through. Marjorie saw times when her young friend wavered. She knew herself, only too well, the absolute desolation of losing a child. Her own second-born survived barely three months in the world before he was snatched from her by fever.

In Marian's eyes, Marjorie witnessed the same pain and sense of hopelessness she herself had felt. In the long silence of the night, she heard, or thought she could hear, echoes of her own thoughts, remembering vividly the times she had pleaded to be left alone to die alongside her tiny infant.

But it was not to be. Marian was not allowed so final a solution. Patrick Murphy visited each day, administering in equal doses both advice and the limited drugs at his disposal to bring down her fever and prevent infection. Meanwhile Marjorie kept watch, willing Marian to regain her strength. For hours at a time, she read to her. That, or she recounted episodes from her own life, fact and metaphor mixed seamlessly to create a detailed patchwork. And when Marian slipped into sleep, she held her hand or bathed her brow with a cool damp cloth.

Through it all, Jonathan stayed away. By day he worked, harder than he had ever done. At night he shut himself in his room, taking his meals alone. If he spoke to Marjorie or to Patrick Murphy it was only to receive assurances as to his wife's improving condition. However, he could not bring himself to see her.

He knew he should. The look of anguish on Marjorie's face each time their paths crossed was a reminder to him only too well of the duty he owed his wife. But it was no use. Guilt and anger were at work. He felt guilt that as Marian had writhed on the floor of their home, the lifeblood of their child draining from her, he was ignorant of her suffering. But then there was also anger. Anger, all consuming, that in so vain and selfish a fashion, she had deprived him of the son he so hoped for.

Alone in his room, like a slave thrown to the gladiators, he waged war against blame. But it was a battle he could not win. More than anything in the world, he wanted to go to the side of his wife. He longed to hold her in his arms, console her and will her back to health, but he could not. Blame shaped his every mood. It forbade compassion, pity, even love.

Marjorie's words of sympathy and encouragement stood for nothing. Her pleading for him to visit his wife went unheeded. He had but two avenues of consolation; hard physical labour until he was too dirty and too tired to think; and John Dunn, silent friend and witness to the horrors torturing him.

Thus, the morning Jonathan returned from the leaf houses to find his wife up from her bed, dressed and sitting on the veranda, was like the meeting of two strangers. Marjorie was there, a frail, sinewy rope bridge stretching across the deep chasm, but neither Marian nor Jonathan were brave enough to take the first step. Though she made no move to do so, Marian longed to rush headlong toward her husband, careless of the flimsy structure or the terrible drop below. But she was held fast on her side of the precipice, tangled in a web of confusion. And for his part, Jonathan stood on his side, frozen to the spot, Marian's isolation no spur to his courage.

He smiled and bid her good morning, asking after her and advising her not stay outside too long. However, his smile was as brittle as the ice formed by frost on the surface of an autumn puddle. His voice was that of a stranger. He neither touched her nor stayed long enough for Marjorie to begin the process of reconciliation.

Sadder still, their estrangement lingered through the next day and the day after that, until the days ran into weeks, with little apparent hope of healing the rift which their dual tragedy had created.

With each new day, however, Marian's health improved. By the end of July, she was well enough for Marjorie to shorten the time and frequency of her visits. Twice a week only she called by, leaving Patrick Murphy to drop in when passing and then only by way of a social visit. Soon Marian was confident enough in her strength to take to riding again, spending sometimes a whole morning or afternoon on the 'Dun pony,' venturing further and further afield, Shahjan, Bollai and Medla no longer the limit of her range.

But between herself and Jonathan the distance remained. The few months of happiness they once shared were gone and there seemed little chance of their return. For the second time, Marian felt herself a widow. William had been taken from her by cholera, his death a cruel punishment, endured but not forgotten. Losing Jonathan, however, was beyond endurance. Fate had brought them together. Fate had them meet and fate had them marry. And their child was to have been an expression of a love born from mutual trust in that fate. In a single afternoon, however, with no more than a blink of an eye, fate made mockery of that affection, callously denying all evidence of the happiness to which Marian believed she was entitled.

Jonathan continued to share their home but not her bedroom. He embraced the letter of their marriage but not the law. He was caring, kind and laboured long hours. He displayed polite affection, but the passion was gone. If he still loved Marian, he made no show of it. If he still desired her, he kept it to himself.

To all intents and purposes, Marian was alone. She walked a lonely path, the shroud of self-recrimination becoming heavier by the day. And, there was no consolation, no relief. Shahjan became a hateful place; not a home but a prison; no bars and the freedom to roam, but a prison nevertheless.

More than ever, she sought salvation in tiny souvenirs of 32 Princes Gate. And one Saturday morning, a letter arrived from England. It was from her father:

My dear Marian, it began.

So many months and so many miles separate us, I can only imagine how far your life may have moved on since I last had news of you. No doubt you will be settled in Assam by now which is why I have addressed this letter to you there. Your last correspondence bore the crest of the Great Eastern Hotel, Calcutta at its head, but by the time you read this I expect your stay there will be but a distant memory.

You will be pleased to hear I have invested in a new atlas. That way I can follow your progress across India. The distances you have travelled are greater than I imagined and I expect were not without their difficulties or dangers. This leads me to be concerned for your safety. I therefore wait impatiently for your next epistle so that you can assure us all that you are well. Your mother, of course worries more than I. She has not the benefit of appreciating your intelligence or resilience. Passing each day as she does with Margaret as her only companion, she has no measure by which to adjust her fears. She imagines Margaret in similar circumstances and promptly thinks the worst. This is not surprising, but heightens her anxiety in direct proportion to my exasperation.

For myself, I am certain you are safe and in good health. From your description of the man you have taken to your heart, you are certainly well protected. Nevertheless, I would be no father at all if I did not worry a little. Not a day passes I do not wish you here with your family. Our home is a poorer place for your absence. I miss your companionship, your humour and your affection. I wish you well, of course. I also wish you happiness and good fortune. And I am confident that wherever you are and whatever you do, nothing you embark upon will be done rashly or without the due process of thought.

Here in London, sadly, those same due processes rarely break cover. Your mother carries on as ever. Loving, caring and forever with a smile on her face, she surpasses anything I deserve. I know she cries for you, but I have never been witness to it and were she able to do so at this very moment, I know she would also encourage you to follow your heart. Margaret, on the other hand, continues to be a far greater source of concern to me than either of my other two daughters. She remains painfully shy, absolutely refuses to blossom into anything other than the plainest of young women and persists with irksome monotony in the extraordinary notion of one day becoming a missionary.

For two half pence, I would put her aboard the first package to Calcutta. From what you have told me, Assam and many other parts of India appear to present opportunities beyond Margaret's wildest dreams for conversions on a biblical scale. Sadly, I doubt if you, or Assam would be able to cope. She really does not have an ounce of sense in her head, so filled is it with nonsense and girlish imaginings.

Last, of course, but by no means least, Katie. All I can say in defence of dear little Katie is that her letters are more frequent than yours. If only, however, your mother and I did not receive them with such trepidation. She claims to be happy. She speaks in glowing terms of Mr Kenneth, never failing to predict a bright future for him. Yet it is I who continues to subsidise his search for artistic recognition and your mother and I who live each day in a permanent state of fear for Katie's moral welfare. They have now moved to Rome. Apparently, Rome is the place for young artists to be these days; there or Paris. Personally, I think his time would be better spent in England. Here he could find himself a respectable teaching position and provide for Katie as he should instead of expecting me to settle all their debts.

In the last letter we had from Italy, Katie announced their intention to be married shortly. Your mother of course was delighted. She is disappointed that

Katie will not be coming home for the ceremony but is pleased to hear the sound of wedding bells at long last, even at so great a distance and to a husband of such unpromising potential. What I have not told your mother yet, though in all probability, by the time you read this, I will have, is that the cause of Katie's headlong rush into marriage after so many months of living in sin with her Renaissance lover, is the imminent arrival of her first child. Wisely I believe, rather than permit your mother to read Katie's letters unexpurgated, I intercept them for sensible editing prior to her consumption of the salient passages. In this way I can ration or dilute the bad news. This is a good thing since always, without fail, there is some portion of bad news to relate.

Of course, Katie does not see it that way. To her, everything in life is 'que sera, sera.' She fumbles her way along, oblivious to the tears or worry she leaves in her wake. Your mother, however, is easily brought low by bad news. A little judicial editing or paraphrasing goes a long way towards keeping her nerves at a pitch she can control and I can bear.

Fortunately, my dear, although your welfare is a constant source of anxiety to us, you are never a disappointment. As a matter of course, we worry about you at all times. We wonder where you are, whether you are well and happy. But joyfully, you have a head on your shoulders. You think before you act. Katie, dear girl, never thinks. She acts entirely upon impulse and devil take the hind most. She is the most impetuous creature God ever put on this earth. We miss you terribly dearest Marian. But if you are happy then so are we. God protect you wherever you are. May he keep you well and from harm. That is our daily prayer.

Your loving father.

P.S. I see in the newspapers that the Indians are to get their own National Congress now. Perhaps self-rule is not so very farfetched an idea after all.

Ignorant of the recent catastrophe in Marian's life, there were no words of regret or consolation from her father. Clearly, he was writing in response to a note she had cobbled together during their short stay in Calcutta. Although he knew of her marriage to Jonathan and she had drawn him a brief sketch of their journey across India from Delhi, letters detailing their trip up river had yet to reach him. He knew nothing of Shahjan and nothing of the latest leaden anguish weighing her down. Those letters were to come and one, at least, the one recounting her most recent cause for sorrow, had yet to be written. For his part, her father wrote as he always did, minimising his own true feelings, supportive yet at odds with his other two daughters. Little could he have known the wound he opened with news concerning Katie's impending motherhood. Had he an inkling of the wretchedness his eldest daughter's life had become, his tone no doubt would have been very different and he would have kept such poignant news to himself.

Nevertheless, Marian took from his letter what comfort she could. Though merely words on a page, she did her best to imagine the sound of her father's voice, to see his face and feel the warmth of his arms embracing her. For a while, after she finished reading, she sat with the letter on the table in front of her, staring at the pages, willing herself into the drawing room at 32 Princes Gate.

Over by the window seat, Margaret would be sitting, staring out into the garden and dreaming of a selfless career she would never attain. Her mother, never idle, would be at the writing table preparing a guest list and her father would be in his favourite wing chair reading. It was a scene repeated a thousand times, one which changed little whether they were in town or on the coast. It was home and although it was far removed from the view presented to her as she looked across Shahjan towards the jungle, its familiarity was like the resting of her head on a soft cushion where formerly there was one of stone.

How she yearned to be transported. There was no beauty left in Shahjan, no comfort to be gained there, only stark reminders of her terrible loss and the cancer of her own dreadful irresponsibility. What she deserved from her father were harsh, scolding words of rebuke. Had she not been so complacent of her good fortune, had she not squandered the advantages she possessed in abundance, had she not stubbornly embarked upon so strenuous a walk on that fateful afternoon, her baby would still be alive, waiting to be born into a world of bountiful mystery, to a mother and father more in love than either had believed possible.

As it was, the granite greyness of her days was more than a match for her father's prose. The comfort was temporary. Facing her now was the prospect of a marriage sunken into a loveless state and the excruciating agony of admitting her part in its downfall to the one man whose affection she valued more than ever. How she should reply to her father was a torment which lasted days. There were no gentle words to salvage so calamitous a passage of events. In her previous letter, not yet received in London, she had used the brightest colours on her palette to paint a picture of Assam. With pride, she boasted of her good fortune in finding a man like Jonathan. She blessed the day nature granted them the bounty of a child. But like the inevitable waxing and waning of the moon, the wheel had come full circle, bringing with it nothing but heart break. Shangrila had withered to dust. Now her nights were dark and lonely, her days sunless, the way ahead no way at all.

For days, her father's letter never left her side. She carried it with her as a comforter in the same way a child might carry a rag doll. As her riding out from Shahjan became longer and further, she racked her brain for the words to begin a reply.

'Would you like some company?' John asked one morning as she prepared to ride away in the direction of Dawan. 'I've got a couple of hours with nothing to do. Perhaps you would like me to show you a path through the jungle which leads to the river.'

His request was so unexpected that she hesitated.

'Yes,' came the reply and it was a 'yes' the consequences of which she could not begin to estimate. Born out of loneliness and desperation, it was a 'yes' which though Marian had no way of knowing it at the moment she spoke it, served as the key to a Pandoras box.

Jonathan was at Medla. The boiler on a drying machine was leaking. Tea production was at a standstill and there was nothing for it but to strip the whole system down to affect a repair. In the meantime, at Bollai and Shahjan work continued apace.

John had much to occupy him. Instead, he on 'Snowden' and Marian on 'The Dun pony' rode off towards the jungle along a path she had previously avoided exploring lest she were to encounter along the way creatures with an appetite for human or horse flesh.

For a while the track was narrow. The jungle closed in around them like a wall, forcing them close together, the flanks of their horses touching occasionally. Then the landscape opened out into an oasis of tall grass, pale green, dense and swaying like the sea. Somewhere within it there were buffalo and perhaps even tiger, but if there were, they remained silent and hidden, their closeness suspected but not proven, evidenced only perhaps by the aggravated twitching of their horse's ears as they scanned the dense vegetation for sources of danger.

John, however, was relaxed, confident. More than ever like Marian's images of North American cowboys, he sat astride 'Snowden' as if the two were moulded into one, back straight, head erect, his broad thighs pressed tight against the leather of the saddle.

As they rode, they talked. All the way they talked; he of Assam, his home at Kurmi, Shahjan and his plans for the future; she of home, of her father, mother and sisters. It was a conversation which lasted through the long grass, back into dense jungle and finally to the banks of the river Dibong where, swollen with monsoon rains, the waters rushed past them in a panic to reach mother Brahmaputra.

There they dismounted. The horses were left to pick at the green grass beneath their feet, empty saddles, jangling stirrups and the bits in their mouths no hindrance to concentrated grazing.

At no point were Jonathan or the events of recent weeks mentioned. Together John and Marian stood close to the water's edge, themselves close enough to touch, close enough that the narrowest shaft of daylight was all to pass between them. Marian stared at the swirling, headlong, muddy torrent. Wild, corkscrew currents caused disarray to the surface and temporary eddies, caught against resistant outcrops on the bank created strangely calm pools. Everywhere there was detail, not one mass of fast-flowing river but an intriguing patchwork of different shapes and forces, pulling one against the other in an inscrutable confusion. In vain, she tried to focus on the water alone, but all the while, even without looking, she could feel John next to her, so near that had she moved at all some part of their bodies would have made contact.

And how she tried not to move. How hard she fought to become, like Lots wife, rigid and lifeless. How urgently she struggled to thwart the astonishing surges coursing through her body. How determinedly she willed herself to comprehend her emotions and regain control.

But she could not. John also stood motionless. He too kept his eyes firmly on the water, falling silent, words no use against the mute roar of the river. One minute passed, then two. There was a violent, thunderous storm brewing. Both of them knew it, but neither could turn away. Something between them, on that spot and in that long moment had changed forever. Their relationship would never be the same. Whether at that precise moment Marian realised it or not she was a woman again and it was the man at her side, not her husband who had rekindled the flame.

Later, much later, in fact several months after she rode to the river with John, Marian discovered she was pregnant again. It should have been a moment of great joy. However, it was not. Instead, the creeping guilt she felt at losing her first child was rekindled. There was also the very real sense of her own moral decay.

Furthermore, she could invent no way to conceal the awful truth of her crime. Jonathan could not be misled. Not once since the loss of her first baby had they renewed the physical obligations of their marriage. Though she craved his affection, lying await night after night hoping he would come to her bed, he had stayed away. In battle, his courage was proven. As her husband he remained faithful. However, a high barrier with thicker walls than the most impenetrable fortress, kept him from her.

He wanted to explain. Many evenings they were alone. She prayed he would say something to her. He struggled in vain to find the words. And so, the silence remained. He lacked the courage or method to breach the imagined defences set against him. Instead, a sterility set in. He and Marian continued on as husband and wife in name alone. Though the tragedy of estrangement was obvious to them both, it was dread inertia that finally sealed their fate.

Jonathan was not and could not be the father of Marian's second child. There was no concealing the truth, no convenient ambiguity available for her to confuse the course of events. John was the father. She knew it, he knew it and Jonathan would have no doubt as to the truth of her adultery.

Given as much, what possible happiness was there for either of them to be gained in the knowledge of her physical state. That early August day on the river, that acceleration of her heart rate as she stood close to John, their compulsive slide into the oblivion of lust which followed over the coming weeks, that eviction of all moral decency, of every Christian principal Marian held dear, was the beginning of her downfall. Eventually, as hard as she fought to resist it, she and John made love wherever and whenever they could; on the banks of the river, hidden within the curtain folds of the long grass, or, sometimes even, and with every chance of discovery, in his bungalow.

There was no affection. There were no tender words. There was no expectation on either side of anything more. He, like a bull, she like Europa, they went at each other, their sin barren of excuses, animal lust their sole inspiration. For two months and then three it went on, unnoticed, a black secret made blacker by their easy observance of it.

And all the while, Jonathan knew nothing. He was deceived by a man he had come to respect, by a man he called friend and by the wife he loved more than his own life. In return, neither Marian nor John could have invented a language, written or spoken, eloquent enough to excuse the gravity of their crime.

When the truth could no longer be hidden, when the new baby inside her showed itself beyond any attempts at concealment, a tragedy of mythical dimensions waited in the wings Marian knew what lay ahead. She would become an outcast, a pariah. Society would spurn her, must spurn her for the disgrace she had brought not only upon her husband but upon all those beguiled into calling her 'friend.'

In the dark, alone, with sleep a luxury beyond reach, she came to curse the day she left England. Before then, life was simple. It was comfortable, convenient, controllable. She knew and understood London. Inside 32 Princes Gate she was secure. She was seen as witty, intelligent, the star in a small firmament. Young men courted her, old men admired her for her intellect and women of all ages envied the ease with which she negotiated the rigmarole of London society.

India had transformed her. With consummate ease she had become vain and selfish, happy to ignore every mantra of her upbringing. She had abandoned the very stuff of her previous life, exchanged honour and decency for a moral vacuum. Bohemia beckoned. Her hair was cut short. She wore men's clothing and rode in breeches; but obviously, all that was not enough. With missionary zeal, she plunged into the mire of adultery, mindless of her own shame or the hurt she was bound to inflict upon those she professed to love.

As punishment, she deserved eternal damnation. To the ounce, she knew the weight of her crimes. They rested heavily on her shoulders, a burden to subdue Atlas himself and through the long nights she winced at the thought of what lay in wait.

But fate was not finished with her. Too easy and straight was the pathway to damnation, too convenient the route to repentance. Jonathan was severely wounded by news no woman can hide. He knew at once the truth, guessed immediately the identity of the man who would make him a cuckold.

He reacted, however, as if to confound the stars themselves. There was no moral outrage. He remained as calm as was his wont; a military mind, designing strategy. While Marian's thoughts were in turmoil, his were focussed. And while John drew up his defences against onslaught, Jonathan stood his guard down, not raising his standard for battle but setting his table for peace. With a display of the most extraordinary and inexplicable self-discipline he carried on as if nothing had happened, tenderly embracing Marian's condition with the same compassion he might were the child inside her his own.

For several days, both wife and lover were perplexed. Marian had wounded her husband in the worst possible way. She knew that beyond a doubt. She was conscious of it during her every waking hour. His apparent acceptance of it served only to make rawer still the sense of shame.

And John was no less caught off-balance. He went about his business as usual, as much as possible on errands away from Shahjan. He visited Bollai or Medla and sought excuses to be in Dibrugarh, anything to avoid direct contact with Jonathan.

Exactly like the calm before a storm, the atmosphere grew stifling. Jonathan, eerily silent, yet strangely composed, behaved not at all as Marian anticipated. In the end, she, rather than he, broke the silence.

It was late in the evening. A full moon bathed Shahjan in a pale light. All day it had rained. Everywhere and everything was soddened but the air was still fresh.

For the time being, however, she and Jonathan were still able to sit out on the veranda, unmolested by mosquitoes, she with a shawl about her shoulders and he with a jacket, a scene as ordinary as on any estate in Assam. No doubt Jack and Marjorie Laws were similarly employed, perhaps planning together the retirement they spoke of in public so often but which somehow seemed destined for permanent postponement.

Trevelyan Dunn owned a veranda the length and breadth of a polo field. He never sat though. His habit instead was to pace up and down, drink in hand, decrees at the ready. Meanwhile, his patient wife did sit, poised, apparently attentive to his every word but in reality, day dreaming of her eventual return to England. Secretly, Verity Dunn longed for a life in the cool highlands of Scotland, a part of the world made vivid by the ceaseless pleasure she found in the novels of Sir Walter Scott.

It was a night indeed which invited occupation of every veranda in Assam. Patrick Murphy used his to ponder medical conditions beyond the scope of his training. Captain Hutchison, a solitary man with few friends to call his own, laid out on paper, troop movements for the next manoeuvres involving the Dibrugarh section of his beloved Assam Volunteer Light Horse, a matter he considered of significantly greater importance than any civilian occupation. When and if his strategies were played out in earnest, against violent uprisings by the Naga natives or invasion by the Chinese, he was determined to be ready, poised to become, not the man whose unfortunate manner denied him friends, but the hero and savour of every plantation owner within his jurisdiction.

Marian, however, was aware of only one estate, of one bungalow, one veranda and one burden. To delay further was to perpetuate an intolerable atmosphere of silence. She needed to know her fate. If she was to be banished, then so be it. If she was to be cast out for the adulterous wife she had become, she wanted to know it. The state of limbo into which she had been placed by Jonathan's silence was beyond endurance.

How best to relate the twists and turns of that evening is a problem of the utmost difficulty. Best to describe it as a debate, at times calm, at others fraught with passion. Marian began the best way she could, with apologies. In words both contrite and sincere, she begged her husband's forgiveness for the sins she had committed against him, sins she had compounded by their frequent and willing repetition over many months. She excused her actions on grounds of temporary insanity. Hurt by the loss of her child and wounded by his rejection of her, she was left floundering.

With no direction and far from the safety of shore, she reached out for the first secure hand hold she could find. She professed no love for John. She urged Jonathan to believe not that his affection warmed her like a blanket but that his desire for her was a balm to the tortured state of her soul. Shouldering the full burden of blame, she pleaded the case for her feminine frailty, begging him to accept that her love for him was in no way diminished.

It was a plea for mercy flavoured to achieve not an end but a new beginning. She was open hearted, open handed and uncompromising in her capitulation, effectively throwing herself at his mercy. She left out nothing, save perhaps the single most crucial element to her condition. While she employed the past tense, implying therefore the ending of something prior to a new beginning, she neglected to include the one undeniable truth that her desire for John still lingered, a smouldering fire, in need only of a breath of oxygen for re-ignition.

He was not, nor could he be half the man Jonathan was. He was too much the son of his father, too tainted, too much of the same mould. To a certain extent, the son was more sensitive and more caring towards others than the father. John's ego, ambition and ruthless cynicism were tempered by a softness inherited from his mother. Nevertheless, he was transparently a Dunn. His sultry introspection was born not from a mind preoccupied with thought, but of a brooding nature. He was selfish rather than self-possessed, obsessed rather than passionate. Much, indeed most, of what he set his sights to or achieved was to prove himself the better of his father. He had little time for people, conversation or the trivia of life, because his time was spent on a relentless quest to succeed on his own. Shahjan was not a love affair, filled with tender feelings and pride, but a means to an end. Polo was not a sport but a contest.

Every chukka was a trial of strength, every victory not a rare sweat meat, savoured for its taste but a spur, marking him out as a man. That he was courageous, dedicated, even generous to those he respected was not in doubt. Equally, however, Marian had no illusions as to the limits of his regard for her.

John was attracted to her. She was the antithesis of every other woman in Assam. She was precociously intelligent, outspoken and, a concept to which she was blind, the property of another man. He liked her enormously. He had also proved conclusively the pleasure he gained in possessing at least a part of her. And, as with so many things in his life, although Marian was a challenge he had overcome, she was not one he wished to keep.

She had cheated on her husband. Of that fact there was no doubt. She had deceived him and was found out. Remaining to Marian was the task of proving her contrition and then of persuading Jonathan of her continued affection towards him.

During their long discourse, had he at any point swept her up in his arms, she would have recanted her very faith itself, sworn to and complied with his every whim, so desperate was her need for his forgiveness.

Sadly, she was denied. If to be dispassionate was a flaw, then Jonathan had much to regret. John Dunn was a man who, met by fire, had no way to respond other than with fire itself. Jonathan however, knew pragmatism well. He was a peace maker, not a war monger. For many years he had worn the uniform of a warrior but had the mind of a diplomat. Ego was of little importance to him. Ideas, principles and devotion to both were his 'raison d'etre.' His choice of wife was no whim born out of physical desire. He selected Marian as his mate because he anticipated in their marriage a union of souls, a relationship whose longevity would outlive carnal desire.

After listening patiently, he responded with his own list of apologies. It was his fault, not hers, that she was tempted into infidelity. He had abandoned her, not she him. He had failed to comfort her when she was most in need it. He left cold the marital bed when it most required warmth and, so caught up was he in self-pity, he failed utterly to notice her unhappiness. The promise of a child, then the sudden loss of it was too much for him to bear. He admitted a long period of blaming her. Wrong though it was and quite without foundation, it was impossible to shrug aside.

He ached with repentance. As much as he struggled to turn the clock back, to feel and act differently he could not. All he had to offer was a scheme for the future, a way to absolve his part in the betrayal of their marriage vows.

After two hours, during which they vied one with the other for the greater portion of blame, a proposal hung in the night air. There was to be no exile. Nor was there to be any public parading of their joint failings. What was done was done. It could not be undone. Marian's crime was but one in a long list to be shared equally. In spite of her protestations to the contrary, Jonathan was not willing to have her the scapegoat.

He professed a love for her no less than it had been. Further, he pronounced a satisfaction with their life in Assam and, much to her surprise, his continued affection for John. He did not condone, but he would not condemn. Public disgrace for Marian would spell equal humiliation for himself and in the end serve no useful purpose. Furthermore, it would bring to a close a chapter in his life during which he had discovered for the first time true contentment. For years, he had been a soldier. As best he could, he had honoured both the uniform and the wishes of his father. No longer pursuing the course selected for him, but having chosen one of his own, one he cared for with a passion never realised while in the service of Her Majesty, he was determined not to see it thrown away.

Society would have him spurn his wife and reject his friend. Society would have him 'do the honourable thing.' However, he, not society, would have to live with the consequences. That being the case and with Marian's approval, he proposed the status quo. He sought no retribution. If blame was to be shared, and he expressed the earnest desire that it should, there was none to be taken. He wanted Marian to remain his wife, to stay with him and have the child.

More than anything he wanted her to have the child. She had been denied once. He was unwilling to believe mother nature would be so cruel again. Furthermore, if she agreed to remain as his wife, he would not intervene in whatever relationship she pursued with John. Clearly, he had failed in his responsibilities as her husband. His refusal to satisfy the normal conjugal demands expected of him had levied a dear penalty.

In a manner quite confounding to everything Marian anticipated, he accepted that penalty and was prepared, if necessary, to accept more. John was to remain his friend in spite of, and even if, he and Marian continued with their affair. Pride, his pride, was the only obstacle to the continued happiness of three people, three people interwoven by fate. He believed, and though it was hard for Marian to appreciate the extraordinary sincerity of that belief, he should do nothing to threaten the sanctity of what circumstance alone had wrought.

His pride was of little importance. Giving in to pride implied disgrace for them all, the destruction of all they had achieved together and, more to the point in his eyes, promised absolutely no benefit at all. To cut off one's nose to spite one's face, he believed, was as morally decadent as the many sins they all shared. To act was to heap disaster upon them all. To deny the truth was to show expediency.

They would know. He, Marian and John would have their consciences to punish any punishable offences. Their consciences would dictate the future far better than the appeasement of a spurious moral conscience imposed on them from outside. Who was to say whether adultery deserved a greater penalty than greed. Who among those ready and willing to condemn their failings was free from envy, malice of thought or selfishness. How many of those standing so ready in the wings to pass judgement on them from the floor of the 'Club' would prove themselves under examination to be more righteous.

Assam was a long way from the pulpits of Wrens churches, far removed from the moral regimes of Victorian England. The jungle was no place for self-righteous indignation, the life of a planter too precarious for keen inquisition. The burning of witches and exorcising of ghosts had little purpose in a part of the world where painted and naked natives practised sexual rites beyond the comprehension of their European overlords or where a tiny biting insect was the chief protagonist in a battle against death played out on a daily basis.

At any moment on any day, cholera might visit Shahjan, unseen and unexpected. Within hours any one of them or all three might be wiped from the face of the earth by an invisible enemy from which there was little defence. How significant the reign of pride then?

Chapter Twenty

Marian ended her second pregnancy, successfully, eight and a half months after conception. Emma Jane Albertine Cole was born at Perpetuate on 22 June 1887. The labour was short. Both mother and child came through the ordeal well. Patrick Murphy was on hand throughout, while Marjorie Laws took on the role of midwife.

It was as normal a scene of family life as could be engineered under the circumstances. Jonathan played the part of loving husband and proud father without falter. Marjorie kept secret the secret confided to her by Marian, observing with interest and a certain apprehension the behaviour throughout of both male protagonists, but giving no hint of her privileged wisdom. And John saw it through as if unaware of his true role in the drama.

The torrid relationship between himself and Marian was ended almost before it was begun. He was restored to the less demanding role of friend, once again silent and brooding, devoting his time to Shahjan and polo. He desired Marian no less and, though she gave no hint of it, her craving for the passion that was formerly theirs, lingered on.

However, a pact had been made. There was nothing in writing, no formal agreement. Jonathan made no demands of Marian. His generous acceptance of events which could not be undone was without condition. And so, the charade gained momentum. But it could not be ignored.

Marian was an intelligent woman. She realised how close she had brought herself to the edge of an abyss. For whatever reasons, uncontrollable desires had temporarily disoriented emotions and events she did not properly comprehend. But without doubt, they had brought her to within a hair's breadth of ruin. A lesser man than her husband might have exacted his revenge. But Jonathan was not such a man. He forgave her. And, in the process, he determined to shoulder the greater portion of blame.

In return, Marian undertook a solemn pledge. There was nothing written in stone. There were no documents signed or oaths sworn in front of witnesses. Jonathan received no verbal confirmation of her return to fidelity save an acknowledgement that she valued their life together in Assam as much as he did. She too was full of regret. More than that she expressed the deepest sorrow for having abused his love and trust in so blatant a manner. And in so doing, their truce became real. Not a sham declaration, animosity and bitterness hidden just beneath the surface, it was entered into with commitment and mutual sincerity.

Marian saw out the term of her pregnancy, fully restored to the position as Mrs Jonathan Cole. Marjorie was told because someone had to be. Such diabolical truths cannot be carried alone. They must be shared as if in the sharing, the burden is halved. For most of her life Marian had been accustomed to confiding in her father. He understood her, read her thoughts and kept precious every word or emotion to which he was entrusted. Were he available, there would have been no need of Marjorie. However, he was too far distant. Correspondence was no means to translate events so riddled with the seeds of disaster. On the other hand, Marjorie was close by and a willing vessel into which Marian could pour the contents of her heart without risk that the vessel would be spilled. She also knew Assam. She understood, better than anyone, the nature and impulses of a life so far removed from London.

Quite how Marian would have coped without the willing involvement of so devoted a friend, she did not care to consider. Nevertheless, she was ever mindful of her good fortune. There were occasions, late at night, or riding out on her own, sometimes even in a room filled with people, when she felt the anguish of loneliness. But they were few. Since leaving England and the cushioned environment of 32 Princes Gate, fortune had smiled on her.

Lady Caroline Farrer had asked nothing in return for her selfless if sometimes over enthusiastic generosity. She took to Marian as if they were sisters, reunited after a long absence. She had little to gain from such a protégé save her company. Self-evidently, she and Marian were dissimilar in most respects. Moreover, Lady Caroline's wealth and extravagance combined in themselves to attract a plethora of camp followers, thus making the acquisition and maintenance of a friend such as Marian a needless addition to her life. She and Marian shared few interests and held, for the most part, opposing views on almost every topic. Quite often during their discourses, either alone or in public, Marian made her disapproval known, hesitating to indulge in open conflict but displaying clearly the disparate nature of their philosophies.

It was all in vain, however. The more Marian had challenged the spoilt, often outrageous actions of her one-time sea-going companion, the more readily the open hand of friendship was extended. It was almost as if, in some obtuse way, Lady Caroline courted criticism, as if so, surrounded by sycophants was she, her conscience demanded a counter balance.

Regardless of their intrinsic differences, destiny determined to have them as friends and destiny was not to be denied. There were no women like Caroline Farrer in or near Dibrugarh. Oft were the times she missed the over indulgence and impropriety of her friend and many were the times she longed for the irrational, opinionated outbursts so demanding of a response.

Trevelyan Dunn was a bigot. He was also outspoken, egotistical and uninterested in any opinion lest it came from his own mouth. However, he was predictable and boorish. More to the point, Marian disliked him, finding it an irrelevance to mount any sort of challenge to his all too often repeated and endlessly simplistic views on life.

On the other hand, in many ways, Marjorie Laws as friend and confidante was more than Marian deserved. In the most unlikely manner, she filled the shoes left vacant by Caroline Farrer with room to spare. That is not to say she and Lady Caroline were at all alike. They were as chalk and cheese.

Marjorie was more akin to Marian's own mother. Flamboyant or extravert as adjectives to describe her were completely inappropriate. There was nothing remotely flamboyant about Marjorie. Nor was she in any sense of the word an extravert. She was quiet, content to stay aback of her husband, taking a lead from him, following the path he laid out for them but supporting him whenever he looked for it. In contrast, however, she did possess an alert mind.

As Marian discovered and very much to her advantage, Marjorie was capable of deep reflection. Over many years of often severe or tragic circumstances during her time in Assam, she had gained an understanding of life and a wisdom far beyond the repertoire of Marian's own kindly, but uncomplicated, mother.

Furthermore, Marjorie's vital contribution to the birth of Emma Jane Albertine Cole secured a place of special intimacy in Marian's heart. If Caroline Farrer was elder sister by proxy, then Marjorie became in 'loco parentis' the mother denied her by several oceans. It was only natural therefore that she and Jack be enlisted as God parents, a responsibility they accepted with the readiness of two people perhaps searching for yet another excuse to postpone their retirement.

On the face of it, everything was just as it should have been. After the appalling loss of their first child, Mr and Mrs Jonathan Cole were blessed with a healthy daughter. Within the local community this was cause for general celebration. At the 'Club' many a glass was raised to Jonathan in his absence. Good wishes arrived at Shahjan from across the region, even from people Marian knew only by name.

Such a commotion over one child was unexpected. However, as Marjorie was quick to remind Marian, the arrival of Miss Emma Cole implied far more than it might have done in central London. In the remoteness of Assam where the white population was both heavily outnumbered and struggled to procreate in conditions quite opposed to their natural environment, every birth was taken as a minor triumph against adversity. Every new child carried a promise for the future. Home rule, 'India for the Indians,' was the preoccupation of the native population. How better to combat such ominous intentions than with the successful enlargement of the race without which India would certainly slip into chaos and a new age of medievalism.

Emma was welcomed not simply because she was healthy, bright eyed and the 'spitting image of her father,' a truism flawed by the awful truth shared among four people alone, but because she was a rare addition to a new generation, a generation which would carry British rule far into the twentieth century.

One drop of bile alone tainted the milk of happiness. As if bound by an implied sense of duty, John remained loyal to his vow of silence. Without instigating the smallest interruption, he permitted the sham to proceed. Trapped into a public expression of his feelings, he perplexed no one by his sombre reticence. That was his way. He was by nature a man of few words, a man whose emotions were his own, a man well known for his antipathy towards conventional family life, his own having been so visibly dysfunctional and lacking in genuine affection.

His mother alone noted an added element of aggression to his polo. Then, during her infrequent visits to Shahjan, she also noted a certain novelty in having to track her son down in the heat and sweat of the leaf houses rather than on horseback patrolling the coolie lines. But the symptoms of any distress he suffered were too vague to signal illness, even to a mother.

Verity Dunn therefore did not suspect the truth. Instead, she contrived expressions of delight and approval in the 'happy event' quite masking the minor disappointment that none of her sons had yet provided her with daughters in law, let alone grandchildren.

Needless to say, for Marian, joy was dulled by heart ache. Emma was a miracle beyond description. There were no words broad or bright enough to include the many layers of pleasure or satisfaction she felt when holding the fragile infant to her breast. Yet Emma was a child born of lust not love, a child burdened from the moment of her birth with a dread secret which must never be revealed, a child who would not, and indeed must never know, her true identity.

There was no doubt Jonathan would love her as his own. She was not his. His genes would not endure through her. However, she was part of Marian. That was enough. During the long months after losing their child he had been unable to rekindle his desire. He deserted his wife's bed, ignoring the demands of her body. But he never lost faith in their love. In spite of his initial impulse to blame Marian entirely for their loss, over time he came to blame himself equally. The further he got from events on that day, the more guilt he took upon his shoulders.

Similarly, he blamed himself entirely for Marian's adultery. She was not wanton. She was not bereft of virtue, a deceitful woman who had fallen into the arms of another man to satisfy an animal need, tearing to shreds the delicate strands of her wedding vows. She did not go willingly to John. She was driven. And it was he, Jonathan, who had driven her, he who had rejected his wife and pushed her away.

His penance was to deprive himself of regret or recrimination. Hers, and it was a penance made harder with every day, was to keep faith with their secret. And as for John, arguably the least culpable of all when bearing in mind the nature of the beast, to him fell the worst punishment; never would he be able to call Emma his own. He might hold her in his arms, play with her in the fields, teach her to ride a horse, shower her with gifts and affection, but he would never hold title to her. Rare was the man to suffer without flinching the blade of so sharp a knife. Brave was the heart to endure so deep a wound without breaking.

But it was done. Life at Shahjan was restored. John and Jonathan repaired their friendship, working together as before, their vigour and ambition undaunted. Yields improved month on month. More land was claimed for planting. New machinery arrived from England to replace the old and worn. As Jonathan committed himself to the responsibilities of fatherhood, so John returned to the demands of being supposed one of the most eligible bachelors in the region. When not at work he was to be seen on the polo field or in the 'club,' surrounding himself as he had not before with companions of both sexes, encouraging gossip and prediction as to his intentions with regard to one blushing flower or another.

As a diversion, something to shade himself from the searing heat of a truth so artfully concealed, Jonathan turned to matters military. Abandoning any attempts to acquire a reputation as a polo player, he enlisted into the Assam Valley Light Horse Volunteers, assuming immediately the same rank he had held prior to the resigning of his commission. This meant that Major Hutchison was his immediate superior. However, overall Commander in Chief for all volunteer forces in Assam was elderly and none too agile General by the name of Sir James Wilcocks.

For Jonathan, commanding men in the field once more, albeit a comparatively rag bag of part time soldiers whose uniforms were as unimpressive and varied as their abilities to parade or perform manoeuvres, was a welcome relief. Though he and Marian displayed the facade of a perfectly contented couple, their daughter a banner to their success, it was a facade of eggshell fragility.

Shahjan thrived, but it too did so at some cost. The triumvirate of Marian, Jonathan and John continued on, but that continuance was no easy feat. As before, the estate flourished through hard endeavour. Every day, weather and nature contrived to claw back what had been won. Daily struggle was required to reap a harvest in the manufacture of tea and sustain an untarnished surface visible to public scrutiny.

Graft alone, however, was not enough. Jonathan loved his wife. In spite of everything, he admired and respected her. And it was with little effort he held his adopted daughter in his arms, caressing her as if she truly were his own. Marian too, continued in her affection for the man whose magnanimity was most responsible for her reprieve. The tender glances she shared with him, the pride she felt in his every minor achievement, the easy manner with which she encouraged his attention; none of these things were false. There was no confusion in her bank of emotions. She did love Jonathan and deny it as she might, that was the truth of it. Though she had betrayed him, there was no point at which she had ceased to love him. The chain was unbroken and as the days and weeks passed, the links became strengthened.

But there was a flaw to this picturesque perfection. John was as impeccable in his deceit as either Marian or Jonathan. His mother had detected in him a restlessness beyond what she was used to. He was her first-born. In him, she noticed nuances of mood which might have passed her by in the observation of either Phillip or Terence. Something was troubling John, but try as she might, she could not discover what it was. As was his way, he kept his silence, sharing his thoughts with no one.

Jonathan's good opinion of him continued to be important. Contrary to every omen, their friendship appeared strengthened rather than weakened by the sharing of a truth closeted from the scrutiny of the outside world. Yet, some indefinable wisdom, a knowledge shared equally between the three, but never voiced, warned of a fatal fracture buried deep within the structure of their seemingly buoyant craft. And for this reason, because of this microscopic threat to their continued good fortune, each selected an avenue of distraction.

Jonathan returned to recreational warfare in order to release a little of the pressure. Time spent away from Shahjan became an essential ingredient in his battle for sanity. In embracing his wife and her child as his own, in pretending the wounds inflicted upon him could be repaired cosmetically, he was flying in the face of his own deeply held beliefs. In fact, unknown to all those around him, he was bleeding internally. Every instinct, every moral fibre in his body cried out to be heard. In carrying on as he intended, in making the pact with his wife and John, he was denying his very self. It was done willingly. It was what he chose to do, but it was a trial of strength many times greater than his combined stamina and courage.

Days spent in the company of men like Major Hutchison were his best invention to ease the strain. The army he joined was amateur. It lacked the skills and disciplines he took for granted in the troops formerly under his command. Moreover, in Major Hutchison, he was also compelled to engage with a man whose manner and temperament were quite opposed to his own. For Major Hutchison inspired little confidence and his pompous tirades would have been the cause of deep consternation had their war games been played out for real rather than as an extended form of physical recreation.

The Naga tribesmen and women were plentiful. They lived in the hills, little more than savages to European eyes. They went naked through the countryside and carried on rituals believed by stout Christians to be beyond morality. However, in reality, they posed no threat to the British empire. They were an imagined foe. There was not the least chance they would rise up, come down from the hills and ravage the white community.

By contrast, and the main reason for maintaining a volunteer force so far north of Calcutta, the Chinese were a formidable race. Many an English widow owed her destitution to the hand of a Chinaman. Invasion from the north was a real possibility though perhaps not so obvious a probability.

Assam was a gateway to the continent of India and with little more than volunteer forces to defend it, an invitation to anyone with serious intent. Major Hutchison prided himself on being ready for any invasion, a boast he could be heard to express frequently. Apparently and without much effort, he and his troops would bloody the nose of the Chinese or any other 'nig no' foolish enough to challenge the might of empire.

In reality of course, this was pure vanity. Assam, and more particularly the Brahmaputra, was an open door, a fast-flowing highway to the heart of India, a fact on the mind of every European living and working with the tropical sun on their backs. However, it was set aside as something of minor significance by contrast to the more pressing day-to-day problems of surviving and prospering in the jungle.

It was with mixed feelings therefore, that one cool morning in the autumn of 1888, a full eighteen months after the birth of Emma, John welcomed Major Hutchison on to the Shahjan estate for a cross table discussion with Jonathan. On the one hand, the proposal as described by the Major made it necessary for Jonathan to be relieved from his obligations to the gardens for a period of possibly two months. On the other, such was the continued pressure on the relationship between John and Jonathan, exacerbated each day as Emma grew steadily from swathed infant to laughing toddler, a short-term sabbatical appealed to both men.

In short, Major Hutchison was looking for a volunteer. He and Jonathan were not friends. Indeed, the latter was compelled to smother his near contempt for the Major time and again during routine drills and training manoeuvres of the Assam Valley Light Horse. Save for the obvious pleasure Major Hutchison derived from the authority implicit in his rank and his love of a uniform which he was rarely seen without, he displayed a deplorable lack of aptitude for soldiering. He blustered and bullied, conducted parades as if his life depended on them and apparently proved his valour in the field again and again when his campaigns were mock and the ammunition harmless blanks.

However, he had no experience at all of actual combat. His understanding of the men under his command was pitiful and his arrogance in all things bordered on the offensive, at least to a man such as Jonathan who had served most of his adult life as a soldier and been witness to the very real brutality of conflict.

Jonathan had seen men die. He knew the sight and smell of blood. He had learned to respect his enemy, of whatever creed or colour, in a manner Major Hutchison did not. Such blind belief in one's own innate superiority was a failing, the proof of which was writ large in the annals of British history. It was also one from which the Major had clearly failed to learn.

For that reason alone; Jonathan usually kept his distance. On occasion they stood together, saluting the same flag and honouring Her Majesty as their sole supreme commander. However, there the camaraderie ended. When all was said and done, Jonathan did not much like the Major. He had not liked him from the first time they encountered each other aboard the SS Pagan and his opinion of him had not altered over the course of time.

Marian therefore was the first to question why her husband would entertain a plan the crux of which was to have himself and the Major thrown together for weeks on end. Of course, in her heart, she knew already the answer and although she was quick to speak out against it, there was no denying the sense of relief his absence would secure for herself and John.

If it were possible, she disliked the Major rather more than Jonathan did himself. Often, in words almost too audible and in places too public, she expressed her disapproval of him. He was a man whose company she preferred to avoid and whose good opinion she could well live without. What she was pleased to acknowledge was the unanimous agreement she received each time she mentioned as much, albeit alongside reminders as to her lack of diplomacy in making her views felt with quite such ferocity and almost within his earshot.

Needless to say, the Major's visit to Shahjan was brief and to the point. He was not invited to stay for dinner. Nor was it suggested he take time to admire the latest addition to the family Cole. His business was conducted on the veranda. Cold drinks accompanied talks lasting no more than half an hour. Then he departed on horseback the way he had come, his task completed, Jonathan's participation in his venture secured.

Their mission was to be two-fold. It involved them travelling alone together far up country, to the border with China and beyond if so required. Officially they were to be explorers. Their task was to trace and chart for the first time the course of the Brahmaputra to its source. Myth and legend were the extent of knowledge on the subject. Geographers were in dispute as to the origins of the great river, some believing it to stretch back right into Tibet, others preferring the theory of it trickling down from the Mishmi hills well inside the frontier. Academia was restless for a solution. What more harmless a motive could there be for such an expedition, particularly by way of a smoke screen to disguise any more serious intent.

The British government acknowledged a passing interest in the source of the Brahmaputra. However, to their mind and of far greater significance, was the need for factual reconnaissance information in regard to mapping the border territories with China and, more particularly, of assessing the possible success of an invasion should the Chinese choose to launch one.

It was to be a clandestine mission. Major's Hutchison and Cole were to adopt the civilian guise of geologists while, at the same time, actively spying for their country. They were to pretend an interest in rivers while mapping and recording the potential threat of invasion. They were to be financed and provided for from the national exchequer while being sponsored by the pale blue of Cambridge University. And such was the sensitive nature of their true mission it was made clear to both men that in the event of their being challenged or taken captive, all knowledge of their activities beyond those of waterways would be strenuously denied, both in Calcutta and London.

As was to be expected, Major Hutchison made mockery of any suggestion there might be danger. Beyond Sadiya, the most northerly place in Assam to boast a British military presence, the country was rugged and only thinly populated. Little was known of the people or terrain, but the Major stood firm to his belief that two British soldiers, in or out of uniform, were more than a match for man, beast or the forces of nature. His approach was without caution and, more dangerously, did not allow for the slightest inkling that anything could go awry. He appeared to believe that he was protected by the invisible shield of Imperialism, an impregnable superiority which would ensure their safe passage, to hell itself and back if necessary. He embraced the scheme as a child might the coming of Christmas, blind to any cautionary words delivered by his newly appointed companion.

By contrast, Jonathan had visited Cawnpore. He knew the price paid for arrogance. He had stood on blood-stained steps and heard the ghosts of those whose faith in natural superiority was shattered so cruelly. He understood the implications and responsibilities of being a stranger in a foreign land. He had lived for months on end inside the walls of a fortress at Landi Kotal in full knowledge of how delicately balanced was his life and the lives of all those under his command. Furthermore, and to his great credit, he was a soldier who recognised fear not as a weakness but as a sensible precaution for survival.

Every fibre in his body warned him against an alliance with Major Hutchison. He disliked the man, held no respect for him and seriously doubted his professional qualifications. Under normal circumstances he would have urged cancellation of so foolhardy a venture, encouraging those in Calcutta to think again and if not to reselect men more suitable to the task.

However, there was little in life at Shahjan which could justifiably be deemed normal. On the surface his marriage was to be envied. Emma was proof, if proof were needed, of both his and Marian's happily achieved aspirations. He and John were close friends, their compatibility evident for all to see, not only in their easy inter action but in the rapid success of their business enterprise.

But Jonathan knew it for the sham it was. Nights were long and lonely. Affections were strained, loyalties stretched. He did not hesitate in agreeing to the Major's proposal. Opposition from Marian and John alike was token.

He left Shahjan just after dawn on the fourteenth of November 1888. Marian recorded the event in her diary, writing how much she would miss her husband. It was the first time they had been parted in three years. Their marriage carried with it extraordinary challenges. The situation into which events had taken them was uniquely uncomfortable. But her love for him had never waned.

The fact of his going she expressed in one sentence. The emotions stirred by his parting, however, required several paragraphs to resolve, with emphasis being placed on the role Emma would play in consoling her aching heart.

On the day appointed, the two men left together from the mooring ghats in Dibrugarh. For a day, they travelled upstream as far as Sadiya. There they collected a heavily laden ox cart from the garrison; food, tents for camping out, cold weather clothing and a comprehensive range of photographic equipment, something which neither men had any experience of using. In addition, they were provided with several rifles, side arms and four bearers to look after their needs. It was a small caravan, their desire being to attract as little attention as possible. They were not the first white men to venture further north than Sadiya, but they were perhaps the first whose mission would have them away for so long and with so secretive a purpose.

Marian was assured there would be no danger. Jonathan insisted he would not have agreed to go had he felt there was likely to be any serious risk. Major Hutchison of course and in a manner so typical of him, dismissed out of hand any notion of peril or hardship.

The winter months were ahead of them. Therefore, they could expect it to be cold. The terrain would be steep and rugged, making the going slow. Otherwise, it would be an adventure the envy of every able-bodied man in Assam.

Not strictly true, of course, as these were assurances uttered by a man whose bravado was born out of ignorance and therefore, by implication, not to be trusted. But they were delivered with such confidence that Marian's anxiety was deceived just long enough to make the parting with Jonathan bearable.

Not until the boat was in mid-channel and well upstream did she and John return to the carriage. Their journey back to Shahjan was a quiet, lonely affair. There were no words of comfort offered and none anticipated. For the first time in over a year Marian was alone with the father of her child.

Jonathan was no explorer. All three of them knew the true motive for his absence. But it was no cue for the lowering of barriers. In the carriage, Marian and John were close enough to touch. Indeed, on several occasions unfriendly troughs in the road jolted the carriage and had them do just that. However, there was no embrace, no inclination on either part to resurrect the intimacy which once they had shared with such recklessness.

John kept his thoughts to himself. Many months had passed since the making of their pact and, like Marian and Jonathan, he lived each day with the consequences of his crimes. He put up with and survived the punishment allocated to him. Deprived of both Marian and the daughter he so yearned to hold as his own, yet forced to confront them during his every waking hour, he had taught himself to martial his defences. Jonathan's departure changed nothing. No spark to a flame, his own part in the triangle remained.

For two weeks, then three, life at Shahjan carried on as before. With the cold weather upon them and tea production stopped until the spring, John was still rarely idle. Repairs, renovations and renewals kept him occupied. When he was not otherwise employed, polo distracted his attention from the temptation of a lone mother and child.

Fate, however, is no friend to an ordered world. John knew how to behave, knew what was expected of him as a gentleman and as friend to Marian and Jonathan alike. Before Jonathan stepped aboard the SS Gunerwali, John, the instigator of so much torment between three good people, committed himself to a certain pattern of behaviour. There would be no attempts to beguile Marian into a revival of their passion. Nor would he infiltrate the carefully contrived stability of the Cole household.

His daughter was his daughter. Nothing would change the fact of her true parentage. But he had forfeited the right to proclaim himself as father. He intended Emma Cole to grow to womanhood with no hint that her birth contributed to so much pain over so many years.

Or so he proposed; until one afternoon in the 'club.' It was a Wednesday afternoon, the second week in January. He finished polo early. It was cold and the rain had decided to come down in sheets. The only pleasure left came from the contents of a whiskey bottle. It was a maudlin gathering of two Dunn's and three other men, all of whom sported mud strewn riding breeches and sodden jackets. They were disturbed from their dreary conversation concerning the preparations for the coming season by the arrival of a highly agitated and considerably out of breath messenger.

Details were sketchy, but the facts, apparently, substantiated. Some four weeks or so into their expedition, Major's Hutchison and Cole were ambushed by Abor tribesmen. Though they defended themselves courageously to the end, both officers were killed along with three of their bearers, the fourth, and sole survivor, escaping to return to Dibrugarh with the news.

At first, quite naturally, there was stunned silence throughout the club. There was no confusion as to the words the messenger spoke, simply the content. Such a thing beggared belief. Death in itself was not unusual, nor the news of it. More than likely every man present that afternoon in the 'Club' had lost someone dear or well known to him. The European community in Assam was small and close-knit. Premature death was visited upon it, all too frequently. Many were taken by disease, some by accident. However, whatever the circumstances, a good helping of stoicism was required to make life bearable for those left behind to carry on.

In this instance, the circumstances surrounding the killing of two British officers were quite beyond precedent. Elsewhere in India there were trouble spots, dangerous regions where skirmishes were expected and where the murder of British subjects by bandits was not uncommon. Moreover, there was still a generation who could recall with sadness the worst and most terrible days of the '57 mutiny.

As a general rule, however, Assam was a peaceful corner of the continent. Not once in living memory had the Assam Valley Light Horse Volunteers been called upon to bear arms in anger. Nor had any of their number been killed or wounded during a hostile encounter. Tent pegging competitions were about the most lethal activity to which the majority of them were accustomed. Their presence nevertheless was deemed necessary; at best as a precaution against any likely threat and a deterrent, be it in a modest way. If the Chinese ever chose to come down in their hoards from the hills in the north, little would in fact halt their progress and certainly not the combined but thinly spread forces of the Assam Valley Volunteers. Politics and diplomacy in London were the first and most efficient line of defence against such a scenario.

Elsewhere, the Nagas posed few problems, either real or imagined. True they were somewhat shocking in appearance. As often as not, their presence was an embarrassment to the modesty of European women. Nevertheless, for the most part, they lived quietly, their huddled villages of grass huts and camp fires well away from the urban population, their habits only visible to the most intrusive onlookers. Essentially, they were shy, suffering the invasion of their lands by the great Imperial Power with resignation rather than active resentment.

And, to the north, little was known of the Abors. They were believed to exist in large numbers. They were also promoted as warlike. Furthermore, reports had them more closely allied to the Chinese than to India under the British. Other than that, few Europeans were known to have encountered them.

Sadiya itself, the settlement from which Major's Cole and Hutchison had set off, stood on the north bank of the Brahmaputra at the union of three major tributaries, their ice cool contents pouring down from the mountains. The River Dihgang traced back like a squirming snake through China, Westwards into Tibet and beyond. Indeed, many thought it to be precisely the source of the Brahmaputra which Major's Hutchison and Cole were dispatched to investigate. But beyond Sadiya, few strangers ventured. However, debate as to the ferocity of those who had chosen to live in the forbidding mountain ranges to the north became academic on that cold, wet afternoon in early January.

For the Abors to ambush and slaughter two British officers was a stern declaration. Their action implied open defiance of British rule and Her Majesty the Queen Empress. It suggested a callous disregard for human life and obviously a belief however misguided, that they were large enough in number and well enough equipped to defend themselves against retaliation.

Incredulity followed by outrage was the general mood in the 'Club' upon hearing the morbid news. Calls for revenge were unanimous and soon echoed by every British citizen the length of the Valley even unto Calcutta where, it was expected, the Viceroy himself would act with ruthless efficiency to avenge so foul a deed.

Closer to home and of more immediate importance lay the pressing task of breaking such tragic news to Marian. Major Hutchison was a bachelor. His immediate family were in England. Those dearest to him would be appalled no doubt, but in Assam there were few if any to mourn his passing. He deserved and would receive of course a soldier's funeral. His heroism was taken as read in the fact of his being a British officer. No doubt he had fought bravely until the end against unequal odds, dying with gun in hand, cut down by merciless hoards. Ultimately his name would become a part of local folklore. He would be remembered as one more in a long roll call of British heroes.

However, the tragedy of his death would be felt only in England behind the closed doors of a modest terraced house in Hastings where his widowed mother and spinster sister resided. On the other hand, Major Jonathan Cole had family in more immediate need of attention. How would the news be broken to his wife? Who would do the telling?

Chapter Twenty-One

For better or worse, Marjorie Laws was elected to the task of telling Marian that her husband had been killed. Better because she was a woman. The best choice because she was known for her compassionate nature. And best because her close friendship with Marian was a matter of public record. On the other hand, this was news the like of which no one person would sensibly volunteer to pass on to another.

At first it was the general consensus that, since the Laws were not in the 'Club' when the messenger arrived, of everyone present John should be the one to perform the deed. However, for reasons he could and would not reveal to those present, he was adamant as to his being the most inappropriate of Marian's immediate friends to pass on so awful a revelation. It was a responsibility too far and one he shirked with an openness which was generally thought to be unlike him.

It was then that John's father came to the rescue and proposed Marjorie Laws for the task. Naturally enough, after that and albeit in her absence, the resolution was adopted without hesitation by the majority of those gathered. This left John feeling not only a sense of relief but a degree of gratitude towards his father which was quite out of the ordinary.

In agreeing so readily to volunteer Marjorie's help rather than relaying the news himself, John chose the easy way out and though it might have appeared so at the time, it was not entirely an act of cowardice on his part. He was not good with words. Nor was he any more accomplished in the handling of emotions. Physical desire and passion he expressed with ease. The physical was something he understood well. As Marian's past lover, he was all consuming. However, not once had he ever spoken of his feelings towards her. For that matter, if she were being honest, Marian had no idea if indeed he harboured any feelings for her. Such things lay, restless perhaps, but buried deep within him, possibly struggling to reach the surface but always failing to find a path.

To go to her at a time when more than anything else she would need eloquent words of comfort was to expect an empathy and the ability to express it which was simply beyond him. John's heart was broken for Marian. More than anyone gathered in the 'club' that afternoon, he recognised the true anguish soon to be heaped upon her shoulders. He understood, or believed he understood, the complex package of emotions which would have Marian on her knees with despair. And in that, he was shamed by his own weakness. But to masquerade as Mercury when he was Mars would not have been to serve her well.

Marjorie arrived at Shahjan as if by chance. Jack was with her but he did not go as far as the bungalow. He got down from the carriage as they passed between the leaf houses, inventing as an excuse the need to inspect the new drying machine which had been recently installed. It was not working but it was deserving of his appraisal.

His wife's main concern was to conceal the truth of the mission from her face until she had time to frame it in words. All the way from Dibrugarh, she worked on a scheme; what she would say, where and how she would say it. In the event, of course, rehearsals stood for nought.

There is no recipe for so foul a duty. There are no well tried or practiced words. There is no one more appropriate setting than another.

As she anticipated, Marian was with Emma. The two were playing together on the veranda, the one smiling and cooing in her crib, the other laughing with delight. There was no sense of foreboding, no hint that Jonathan's departing soul had been carried to her already on the wind and that Marjorie's news was too late. Mother and daughter were at ease, the former frustrated only that the rain had postponed her original plans of going for an afternoon perambulation to Bollai. The arrival of her friend, however, unannounced and towards the end of the day, was cause for a temporary revival of Marian's spirits.

However, it was short-lived. There was no time for evasion. Marjorie's deep sympathy for her young friend could not stay hidden for long. There was no opportunity for a diversion, no excuse for procrastination. When they came, the words fell from her lips in random order, all her well-rehearsed lines good for nothing. Instead, what she had to say and the manner in which she said it were entirely improvised. It was spontaneous but came from the heart, the truth but softened as best she could, ever mindful that Marian was no stranger to grief.

The message was as devastating as she suspected it would be. In her capacity as the harbinger of dire news, Marjorie had prepared herself as best she could.

As Marian's knees buckled beneath her, she was there to guide her limp body into a chair, quick to call out to Booloo for assistance and mindful that Emma would need for a while some distraction other than the encouraging words of her mother.

For several minutes there was absolute silence, as if the paralysis in Marian's legs had been transferred to her powers of speech. She sat with Marjorie holding one of her hands. Her tearless eyes staring straight out across Shahjan in wide amazement as if she were seeing the landscape for the first time. And she trembled, not the noticeable trembling induced as if by a biting wind, but like a butterfly on the petal of a flower fanned by a flickering summer breeze. Marjorie sensed it through the contact of hand on hand, but it was invisible to the naked eye.

'Thank you, for coming,' Marian said after what seemed a long time. 'Thank you, for being the one to tell me.'

'That's quite all right my dear. I wouldn't have wanted anyone else to.'

'I know. And I'm truly grateful.'

There was more to tell, of course. As Jack Laws fast exhausted his interest in the new items of machinery installed in the leaf house, lingering only long enough to allow for the privacy he knew his wife and Marian needed, Marjorie retold the details of Jonathan's death as they had been passed on to her.

The next days and weeks would bring more. How, outnumbered ten to one, the small party was set upon while negotiating a dried up river bed. How no mercy was offered, no quarter given. How the two dead white men's bodies were mutilated, their heads severed from their shoulders and carried aloft in triumph on spears until finally being discarded like used toys.

Eventually the full tale would emerge for public consumption and universal condemnation. For the time being, however, the fact of Jonathan's death, confirmed beyond a doubt, was all Marjorie had to tell and all Marian needed to know. The manner or his death was irrelevant. Accidental or by malice made little difference. Hero or villain of the piece, the result was the same. Grief, pain and widows weaves was the price Marian had to pay for events beyond her control hundreds of miles from their home at Shahjan.

It was unlikely Marjorie noticed the rage beating in Marian's heart before she took her leave. The silence was not unexpected. There might have been tears or the wailing of utter devastation. She was prepared to be moved by desperate pleas for another version of the truth and she was certainly ready to provide pity and sympathy in equal measures as they were demanded. But anger was the last emotion she imagined Marian concealing behind what she took to be a blank expression of disbelief.

From her own past experiences, she knew to restrict her time with Marian; long enough to cushion the fall but not so long as to deny that solitude which is the necessary overture to grief. All the sympathy in the world cannot ignite the mourning process. Lonely introspection is required from those left to confront the awful spectre of death.

Marjorie had made that journey herself more times than she would have wished. Anger and resentment, however, were never a feature of her descent into the emotional abyss of grief.

Jack relieved her about an hour after their arrival. Assurances were exchanged on both sides as to Marian's ability to face alone the darkness of the coming night. Then they were gone, the wheels of their carriage making little noise along the soft, muddy 'garden road.' Ringing in Marian's ears were not the words of comfort offered to her by Marjorie, like layers of warm blankets, but the harsh sounds of her own frustration, the screams and yells which had she uttered them would have echoed through the hills up to and far beyond the cold, rocky place where Jonathan had lost his life.

That night and for several nights afterwards, she was not ready to mourn. Emma played around her, impervious to anything other than her own selfish needs. She laughed in her mother's face or cried for attention, quite ignorant of death. Like a ghoulish jester she mocked harsh reality. She taunted her mother with her baby chirps and sniggers, sympathy and understanding a world beyond her imagination.

But Marian was unshaken. She remained focussed. How dare Jonathan leave her. Had he not pricked her enough. Was it not he who demanded she love him. Was it not his rejection she endured when she most needed his affection. Was it not he who drove her into infidelity. Had he not asked enough of her.

How was she to endure his death. What emotions did he expect from her. He asked no approval for his expedition to Abor land. Her permission was neither sought nor given. He needed time to be alone, somewhere beyond the confines of Shahjan to breath, think and re-align a reservoir of values sufficient for him to raise the daughter of another man. He it was who proposed compromise. However, in doing so, in agreeing to love his wife, befriend her lover and nurture their child, had he paused long enough to consider the strength of will required to accomplish so delicate and demanding a task; apparently not.

For when it was offered to him, Jonathan snatched at the opportunity of time in the company of Major Hutchison. And, he was a man for whom Jonathan had, on more than one occasion, openly expressed his dislike.

Perhaps he supposed that a period of hardship and solitude in a novel landscape would strengthen his resolve to sustain the façade that he and Marian had created. His absence, however, was not debated. His decision to join the expedition was a matter of self, of his needs and wants. Marian was considered only in as far as he expressed concern for her welfare while he was away, a concern which was catered for by the secondment of Terence Moran to act as temporary superintendent to the acres of planted tea, the hundreds of coolie pickers and the machinery used in manufacturing.

However, although born the son of a tea planter, Terence was no planter. Had he been or were he permitted to choose a career for himself, tea planting would have been the last profession he sought and Assam the last country in which he would have wanted to make his home.

Like his mother Terence held a deep longing for England. He dreamed of a life in academia, a life of history books, of intellectual scrutiny and rigorous mental exertion. Tea, jungles and a tropical climate were not what he aspired to.

But he was too young and, more significantly, too weak for rebellion. The spirit was willing but so dominated was he by the tyranny of his father and so easily seduced by the comfortable prosperity ladled out to him, the body had no strength to resist. He came and went as he was told, participating in a multitude of trivial enterprises without devoting himself to any one of them. Over all, he had come to be, by default, a rather vacuous young man. Consequently, in truth, he was certainly not a complimentary replacement for Jonathan.

The day of Jonathan's departure there were no tears. Husband and wife embraced, but there was no distress. Though she said nothing at the time, Marian resented his selfish intentions. Now, with the news from Marjorie that he would never return, that self-same resentment was fortified.

Grief could not compete for the space already occupied by anger. Sorrow, pity and remorse for having let him slip away so readily were resisted in favour of silent fury.

Over the following days, Marjorie called again and again at Shahjan. Renewing the role she had adopted in the dark hours after the death of Marian's unborn child, she administered the basic sympathy anticipated by convention, but she was at a loss to understand the situation at all. Whenever she arrived, no matter the hour, Marian was calm, seemingly unmoved by the ever more desperate details emerging of her husband's demise.

There was no funeral. Without a body, no burial was possible. In its place, there was a memorial service to which the whole of Dibrugarh turned out. Full military honours were accorded in recognition of the courage of two officers killed in action. Messages of condolence arrived from all over. The Viceroy himself sent word of his deepest regret and General Sir James Wilcocks was in attendance as a mark of the highest respect.

It altered nothing. Throughout the service, Marian stood erect, Jack Laws on one side of her, Marjorie on the other, both prepared to lend immediate support should she weaken. But she did not. She was made strong by her anger. There was no outward expression of it. She remained composed. But it was there, just beneath the surface like a simmering cauldron. When General Wilcocks offered her his hand, she took it. When, one after the other, generous expressions of sympathy were laid at her feet, she did not reject the kindness in their words. She did not turn her back on those who so desired to comfort her. Instead, she gathered up their good wishes and stored them away but, in a manner almost as if she had not heard them.

'You have my deepest sympathy,' the General offered. 'I'm well acquainted with what a fine officer your husband was. He will be sorely missed. I feel certain his most recent endeavours will not pass unnoticed by Her Majesty and you can rest assured, his death will not go unpunished.'

Marian, of course, cared little what Her Majesty thought of her husband. Nor was she particularly impatient for revenge. Her concerns were for herself and her daughter, their future, their welfare, their survival in a part of the world where to be a widow alone was unsustainable.

In the page of her diary bearing the date Monday, 19 January 1889; she wrote; 'Jonathan's service was this morning. The church was full. Standing room only. People came from miles around. Marjorie was very kind. I don't know what I would do without her. Many people spoke well of Jonathan. Emma Jane stayed in the bungalow with "ayah". I'm told much is to be done. A force is being raised to send into Aborland to find the men who killed Jonathan and Major Hutchison. There is much brave talk of fighting. For myself, I can see no sense in more men losing their lives. If they cannot bring Jonathan back to me, they shouldn't go.

But they must go I suppose. Everybody says so. Whatever happens, British pride must be avenged. I have no idea what will become of me. I can only wait and hope that fate will lend a hand. Emma and I are alone now. What sort of a future we can expect, I don't know.'

In the event, Marjorie and Jack Laws solved the immediate question as to how she should proceed. Jack came in his carriage to collect mother and daughter and insisted they stay at Mancotta for as long as she cared to.

It was not what Marian intended. Nor was is what she would have chosen had the choice been hers to make. However, neither Jack nor Marjorie would hear of her remaining alone at Shahjan. Ignorant of events, Emma clearly relished a week during which for much of the time, she was the centre of attention. Marjorie and Jack had grandchildren of their own, but they were scattered. Consequently, their home was made more complete with the sound of a child's voice.

For Marian it was no more than a short reprieve. Inevitably, there were serious decisions for her to make regarding the future. She was a mother with a child alone in a foreign land. She was far from her roots and the way ahead looked bleak. Worse still, she had absolutely no idea what to do or what would become of her. Shahjan could not support a widow. Eventually, John would have no option but to find a replacement for Jonathan.

The new picking season would be upon him soon enough and he would need all the help he could get. He could not do it alone and however much he wanted to show respect for Jonathan, especially with Marian a constant reminder of the past, the practical problems of running the estate required practical solutions. Terence was adequate as a temporary stop gap, but no more. A new estate manager would have to be found and quickly.

With an irony more painful than Marian cared to dwell upon, the most obvious solution to her problem was the least possible to achieve. As the father of her daughter, John could have taken her in.

They had been lovers once. What better than they rckindle the passion which brought them together. What could be more appropriate than John declare himself the father of her child. What simpler solution could there be than they become husband and wife, living together at Shahjan as a family.

What better indeed, save a list of negatives to render such a scheme impossible. Throughout January and into the beginning of February Mancotta served Marian as a quiet retreat. However, at Fort William in Calcutta, plans were afoot to raise an army, its purpose to enter Abor country and repay a debt. The expeditionary force was to include men from the 1st, 2nd and 8th Ghurkas, the 32nd Sikh Pioneers and a detachment of Lakhimpur military police along with two Maxim guns, the very same pieces of artillery which had so impressed Marian at the International Inventions Exhibition in London. General Charles 'Bonny' Bower would command with Colonel Giles MacKintyre as his second in command. With all haste they were to proceed north, seek out and capture those directly responsible for the murder of Major's Cole and Hutchison and come away again having persuaded the Abor peoples that to take up arms against subjects of Her Majesty Queen Victoria was as futile as it was abhorrent.

The Abors were to pay a substantial toll. In London it was decided that the rod was to be wielded with unrepentant vigour. And in General Bower, a man whose reputation for ruthless efficiency was legend among those who had served under him, the Governor General selected exactly the soldier to wield that rod.

In his hands, there would be severe retribution meted out to those responsible for so heinous a crime. The Mishmi hills would run red with the blood of those who had dared to confront the empire. Their punishment would be a dire warning, an advertisement to others in possession of a similarly misguided impression. British control of India in every way and in every corner was absolute and would remain thus in perpetuity.

Such was the scale of the enterprise raised in Calcutta and the acknowledged heroism of the two Major's on whose behalf the campaign was to be launched, Marian herself quickly became of little significance.

In an atmosphere of heightened xenophobia which radiated far and wide across tea estates the length and breadth of the Assam valley, with Dibrugarh at its heart, when all those selected to go thanked heaven for the opportunity and those not, bemoaned their misfortune, the needs and wants of one woman quickly became a matter of secondary importance.

Four weeks to the day following the memorial service, Marian moved back to Shahjan. Alone with her daughter once more and being kept at a discreet distance by the one man who would have been able to relieve her anguish if only he dared try; she was not altogether surprised to receive a letter bearing the announcement that the names of Major's Jonathan Cole and Robert Hutchison had been put forward as suitable recipients for the Victoria Cross. Such a recognition of valour was bestowed upon few men. It recognised in these two officers that they had performed their duties with courage and service above and beyond the call of duty. Such an honour also gifted their immediate families with a degree of public respect, the benefits of which would endure through the generations. Emma Janes children and grandchildren would reap the rewards of so great a tribute.

Consequently, to a widow, in mourning, it should have been an oasis of comfort, confirmation that although she had lost her husband, in so doing, she had gained the gratitude of a nation.

And Marian could not deny the pride she felt. However, her sense of loss was in no way diminished. Nor did such formal acknowledgement dispel her conviction, a conviction which, like a cancer, grew larger with each day, that Jonathan's death had been entirely futile. Posthumously, he was to be rewarded for outstanding bravery, but not for any success from his mission. Major's Cole and Hutchison were killed for nothing. A mountain of medals could not hide that fact nor would they bring them back. They had been dispatched on a fool's errand. Jonathan went for all the wrong reasons and both men failed to return.

Marian committed to memory the contents of the letter from Calcutta. However, the military campaign proceeding apace and the honours being bestowed, served only to constrain her in ways she could not have predicted, nor would have invited.

As the widow Cole, she inherited certain obligations, obligations which gathered momentum by the day; a substantial period of mourning, many weeks of solitude, little involvement in daily life and, when in public, a presentation of herself as befitting one racked by grief. Under normal circumstances it was a stern test. Victorian society demanded no less from a woman than she play her part in the theatre of death and no less was expected of her in Assam than had Jonathan died in the heart of London. As the wife of a publicly acclaimed hero, however, more was asked of her than she was able or willing to give.

What she wanted was to be relieved of her obligations. Also, she wanted relief from the bitter taste of bile on her lips and in her heart. Marjorie continued to called on her regularly. She consoled and fussed but gave no sign she fully understood the agony. And, of course, she suggested over and again |that Marian return with her to Mancotta.

All Marian wanted was the expedition stopped. She cared nothing for revenge. She despised the unanimous impatience for blood. She wanted no part of awards to honour a man who, for his own selfish reasons, had deserted his family. What she wanted were the arms of a strong man about her. Instead, the one man who could have helped, stayed away, mindful it seemed only of his duty to public perception.

Marian had a roof over her head, but little else and even that was only temporary. Unless John stepped into the breach, her options for the future would deteriorate with each new day. But he could not. He too was constrained, held in the straight jacket of convention. Any hint of a relationship with the wife of another man would cast a stain upon a dead hero. The repercussions would reverberate beyond anything he or Marian could imagine.

A wieldy machine was in motion, a huge, trundling juggernaut. An army was being mobilised, its size and strength exaggerated beyond any sensible response to the incident it was set to redress. But it was a symbol. Abor tribesmen needed re-education. They must bend low in the presence of British Imperialism. Theirs was to be a peculiarly public humiliation, a spectacle for the whole world to see and from which to learn.

Jonathan Coles death was not a personal tragedy, the property of one family to mourn in private, but the property of every man, woman and child born British. His name and that of Major Hutchison, their brutal deaths, their courage and the speedy retaliation for crimes levelled against them, were to be proclaimed across the world. In whatever corner of the empire there were British citizens, they were to be reminded of their safety while those who would dare take up arms against them assured of extreme penalties for doing so.

The day the expeditionary force departed from the mooring ghats; General Bower took the salute. Nothing quite like it had been seen before in Dibrugarh; so many troops assembled together waiting to board, while the General contrived a speech to suit the occasion; eloquent and of the moment, something to rally those called to arms and encourage the civilian population.

However, more poignant, more so than any grand soliloquy extolling the majesty of empire was the brief oration given by the Subadar Major of the 1st Ghurka regiment. Standing six foot two and 'a handsome fellow' according to the memory of Marjorie Laws who was one of fifty or more European men and women gathered to hear him speak, he began his address:

'I have eaten the sahib's salt since I was a small boy,' he began, his expression proud, his stance rigid. 'All I have, I owe to the sahibs and now you want something from me in return for all the salt I have eaten. I will go and fight to discharge my debt. If God wills, I shall come back. If not, I hope you will remember that Lakh Ram and his men went to fight our enemy.' Once finished, his broken English no hindrance to the meaning of his words, he called for three cheers for Her Majesty and for the empire. This was returned with three cheers from all those who heard his words.

Afterwards as many as could stepped forward to shake him by the hand.

'Quite the most extraordinary thing,' Marjorie declared in her recounting of the day. 'To shake hands with a native, quite the most extraordinary thing, but somehow it seemed the thing to do.'

And through it all, Marian became no ordinary widow. She was instead a pawn in a grand game, a game with only one winner. To sully the reputation of her husband in any way, to suggest even the slightest hint of impropriety or scandal would have been to collapse a pack of cards. Her role was clear. Deviation from it would have been to bring disaster down upon her own head. Any involvement with John, however innocent would see her ostracised from society. Her continuance in Assam would become impossible, her disgrace uncompromising.

Like it or not, Marjorie was her best hope of salvation. Their friendship was to be encouraged. Marian needed support and Marjorie was just the woman to give it. Her standing in the community was high and her sure-footed guidance would ensure her protégé presented the correct image of bereaved but much honoured wife.

And so, it was. Within two months of her husband's death, though living in lonely isolation, unable to approach the father of her child for affection or support, Marian was feted. Her name in conjunction with that of her husband became public property. If she left the estate at all, she was accosted with words both of consolation and congratulation. She was to be consoled for her loss, but with equal determination she was to be congratulated for the privilege bestowed upon her in recognition of a husband who in death had become one of the nation's more recent heroes.

By the time she determined to write the worst of all letters to her father, relating as much as she dared tell of what had happened to her, the birth of her daughter and the death of Jonathan, the latter was almost certainly old news at 32 Princes Gate. The Calcutta Times devoted its front page to the Abor affair from the beginning. Over many column inches it debated the whole issue of an Abor expedition; the costs, the lives bound to be lost, if only from accident or disease, and the benefits to be gained. After much deliberation, it yielded to public opinion, supporting the enterprise with the sort of glib rhetoric only to be found on the pages of a broad sheet.

The part played by Major's Cole and Hutchison was blown into a saga designed to capture the imagination of a nation. Before long, Fleet Street adopted the story as their own and the hitherto obscure name Abor, as obscure as the names of the two British officers whose lives were taken in so needless a fashion, was known throughout the empire.

Assam itself benefited. Children in schools the length and breadth of the British Isles learned for the first time of its location, pin pointing it on atlases and maps. They were educated to the knowledge that the noble men and women who thrived there in spite of terrible conditions and the constant threat of murder by savages, were at least in part responsible for every cup of tea served in British homes.

Indeed, and in a twist of fate well appreciated by the likes of Trevelyan Dunn, sales of tea on the London market, particularly those cases impressed with the mark of an Assamese estate, soared to new highs.

While British soldiers pursued their prey through the desolate mountain ranges bordering China, reaping a dreadful revenge on any Abors they encountered, further south, in the tropical jungles along the banks of the Brahmaputra, tea men looked forward to a new season in the sure and certain knowledge that market demand for their product was greater than ever before.

Sadly, all this was of little satisfaction to Marian. Events had overtaken her and she was being left behind. Every line she wrote to her father was old news. She wanted him to learn of her happiness and sadness in the order they occurred. She hoped that in giving him the more sober truth of all she had been through, he would be less disappointed than by the embellished facts, so often exaggerated in the retelling on the front page of his daily newspaper.

But it was too late. Her letter, indeed letters, trailed in the wake of international media like a tortoise following the progress of a hare. Any crumb of comfort she might have gained from the sympathy of her father was lost, his opinions and emotions distorted by news and events fed him by journalism.

Eventually, he would reply. When he did, she was in no doubt that his words would add comfort to those she had already received from so many well-wishers, but like theirs she guessed the essence of his sympathy would be coloured to imply some degree of congratulation.

In the minds of so many, Marian was not to be pitied for her loss so much as envied for her good fortune. So many women lost their husbands prematurely. So few, however, found themselves bathing in the bright lights of their heroism.

Indeed, as often as not, those who came to offer sympathy tailored their words of compassion with a curious note of jealousy, as if to suggest that the sorrow and grief Marian felt should take second place to pride at the accomplishments of her dead partner.

It was a strange phenomenon. It compounded Marian's sense of loneliness. Unable to relish exclusive and unsullied words of healing from her own family, always so eloquent when from the lips or pen of her father, she relied more and more upon the attentions of Marjorie.

She alone appeared unimpressed by anything other than the single, tragic fact of Jonathan's death. Although much of the time, she struggled to understand Marian's mood, Marjorie was the only one who came close to it. She recognised the loneliness of Marian's bereavement and the helplessness of her situation.

In time, when enough blood had been let, the Abor expedition would come to an end. Indeed, within two months it was all over. The perpetrators were found, convicted and executed in a manner as appropriate and as public as suited the general taste. Along the way, numerous other lives were lost in petty skirmishes. Many innocent victims fell afoul of British retribution, their sole crime that of association by race.

British soldiers also died, leaving yet more widows. Some succumbed to disease. Quite a few met with unfortunate accidents, devoid of glamour, as troops and heavy equipment struggled across difficult, uncharted terrain in harsh weather conditions. As many, and perhaps more, lost their lives in enemy fire. However, their names, were not mentioned in dispatches, their heroism, if any, went unnoticed. Even the gallant Subador Major, Lakh Ram, himself victim to a treacherous ambush, passed from life on earth to heavenly Nirvana anonymously, his name forgotten by those so proud to send him on his way from the mooring ghats at Dibrugarh.

One young lieutenant did become well known to the community. In the first of many exchanges with the enemy, he was pierced through the thigh with a poisoned arrow. Gravely ill and with his leg swollen to elephantine proportions, he was sent for treatment from the front to Calcutta. In the end, he made it only as far as the modest medical facilities in Dibrugarh itself.

So poorly was he, the onward journey proved too much for his sick body to bear. In spite of all efforts to the contrary, he died within the weak, his suffering reaching the hearts of everyone whose best attempts at a cure were in vain. His death, however, did serve in some small way to remind those so intoxicated with the idea of 'beating the Abors into shape,' that there was a price to pay.

Needless to say, the loss of one young officer, even the loss of many, was, in the eyes of a man like General Bower, no more or less than was to be expected in the course of such an enterprise. Without apology his philosophy was in this instance as it had always been in past campaigns under his command; the end was in itself ample justification for the means. Principals were at stake. British pride was at stake. The rule of law, British law, had been challenged. No matter the cost such a challenge neither should, nor would go unanswered. Lieutenant Robert Smythe, 2nd Ghurka regiment, only son of Mr and Mrs Manfred Smythe of Birch Grove House, Sandown Way, Esher in the county of Surrey and aged a tender twenty-two, yelled and screamed in agony as his gangrenous leg ushered him on his way to the grave. In his wake, some thirty-eight soldiers in Her Majesty's forces lost their lives to repay the travesty inflicted upon Major's Cole and Hutchison.

More significantly, several hundred Abors perished. Those directly responsible for the original crime were among them. They received summary, 'in the field' court marshals and were duly executed. Others were killed in battle. The remainder, some women and children among them were unfortunate enough to become the victims of an exuberant lust for killing which the brave General did little to curtail.

His message to the people in the north, one which he intended to have echoed across continents, was as ruthlessly expressed as he knew how. For his efforts, he was applauded by a grateful government in Westminster, many of whom were still smarting from the memory of the death of General Gordon, slaughtered along with his men by a rebellious hoard of barbarians who understood nothing of gentlemanly conduct or the rules of warfare.

Moreover, the name and actions of General Bower received warm praise from the whole British nation who, for some inexplicable reason, associated the humbling of an uncivilised tribe on the other side of the world, with their ability to sleep peacefully in their own beds at night.

Through it all, however, through the propaganda, the news of casualties and the highly charged reports of Lieutenant Smythe's excruciating journey to paradise, one person remained as the only constant.

Marjorie was not swayed by news from the front. She did not involve herself with the partisan hullabaloo going on all around. Far from being envious of Marian's lot, she appreciated the growing hopelessness of her condition. She watched also the manner in which John kept his distance, too deliberately, not intending to wound but adding pain to a heart already bursting.

His desertion of Marian was honourable. It was the only and best thing he could do. Anything else would have been to stir a hornet's nest. Nevertheless, Marjorie was moved to tears each time she witnessed the appalling denial of a man so uniquely placed to rescue Marian from the cold grip of grief and release an innocent child, his child, from the promise of vagrancy.

Her own charity was boundless. Each time she visited Shahjan, she brought with her the hope of a better future. She also proffered whatever practical help either she or her husband could provide. There were constant assurances that neither Marian nor Emma need go hungry or homeless. As soon as she was ready, and if she so chose, Mancotta could become her permanent home.

It was difficult to see how Marian could stay on at Shahjan. Soon enough Jonathan's replacement would arrive. Then her occupancy of the bungalow would no longer be tenable.

If she wanted to, Marian could return with her daughter to England. In many respects it was the most logical answer, but Marjorie was determined that should her friend choose that option it was to be taken as a preference, not as a last resort.

In spite of all that had happened, regardless of the sorrows and anguish she had experienced, Marian had demonstrated a love for Assam and the life she led there which could not be dismissed. There were clear practical advantages in returning to the country of her birth and the bosom of her family. Equally, however, Marjorie was convinced that however hard the death of her husband was, Marian's soul was as coupled to the jungles around Dibrugarh and the fast-flowing waters of the Brahmaputra as her own.

She could not deny there was a small part of herself which wanted to hold on to Marian, a small part desperate to sustain a friendship begun with such ease and maintained with such easy constancy.

General Bower 'went at' the Abors with the clear conviction so implicit in the military mind. Marian's options were less clear. There were opaque and muddled riddles for her to solve before she could achieve any clarity of purpose.

As best she could, Marjorie tried to be a catalyst, not an active ingredient. It was a delicate path to tread. On a daily basis, she wanted her own selfish desires to intervene. But she held back, disciplining herself to constructive advice and whatever assistance lay at her disposal, including the offer of her own home as a sanctuary.

With such a friend at her side, Marian should have suffered less, but she did not. Long after the Abor expedition was ended, she had reached no conclusion. John remained aloof. Her days were spent in continued and painful confinement with her daughter. Ahead of her lay stark choices, a new Rubcion, as wide as the Brahmaputra itself. Cross it she must, but where and how.

Chapter Twenty-Two

Among the many letters of sympathy Marian received after the memorial service one was from Verity Dunn. She wrote with a sensitivity not usually associated with the family name she had acquired through marriage.

However, no letter touched her more than the one from Lady Caroline Farrer. It arrived later than the others, the time taken for news of Jonathan's death to travel to Delhi and a response to come back being legitimate excuse for the delay. From a woman Marian knew well for her hedonistic approach to life and forthright, even tactless, manner, it expressed empathy beyond expectation. It appeared that beneath the tinsel of her so privileged upbringing, lay emotions in Lady Farrer as tender as any Marian could have hoped for.

Of course, there were demands for her to return to Delhi with all speed. Once there, assurances were given that her immediate practical problems would be over. Save for the process of grieving which she could take as much time over as she required, all other burdens of life would be lifted from her shoulders. The mourning of her husband could be her sole concern.

Of course, Marian could not go to Delhi. She had already made her mind up that either she was to stay on in Assam, continue the life she and Jonathan had begun together, or she was duty bound to return to England. Anything else would have been to deny the harsh reality of her situation. Delhi was a haven; rather too obvious and in so many ways too attractive. It was a temporary place of escape, not a permanent solution.

As a guest in the Farrer household there would be many advantages. Foremost among these undoubtedly was that Caroline Farrer would make it part of her daily ritual to promote postponement of any decision Marian herself was reluctant to make. Procrastination bore the tempting scent of a sweet-smelling flower on a summer's afternoon, but it was a luxury Marian could not afford and must deny herself, regardless of any encouragement.

A few days before the commencement of a new picking season, the Abor expeditionaries were mid-way into their campaign. The stick of retribution was being wielded harshly and with little obvious discrimination. Marian was sitting on the veranda at Shahjan with Marjorie and Jack Laws. It was a fine afternoon. The sun was becoming hot. The jungle was alive to the sounds of new life. Green pigeon swooped in chaotic formation, chasing each other over the roofs of the leaf houses and through the jungle canopy with frantic determination to be somewhere in a hurry.

Jack was talking about retirement again. He had already put off the day for the better part of three years. But his weary limbs were telling him to proceed with some haste. His plan was to build a home for himself and his wife in the cooler climes of Kashmir.

'Can't beat it,' he insisted. 'Clear crisp air. Cool as marble. Mountains like Switzerland. Lakes, valleys and views as far as the eye can see. Paradise.'

It was a eulogy spoken many times before. On this occasion, however, it was said with a ring of urgency about it. This time Marian could not ignore the serious intent behind his words. Nor was she left in any doubt that both he and Marjorie were expecting her to consider seriously an invitation to accompany them.

It was no empty gesture, not offered in the hope of it being rejected. With absolute sincerity they wanted Marian to consider going with them. That she could not require no more consideration and as little explanation as her response to a similar request from Caroline Farrer for her to return to Delhi. In their hearts, Jack and Marjorie knew she could not and would not go with them. Equally, in their hearts, was the real desire that she should.

Of course, they had a family of their own; a son, two daughters and grandchildren. But they were thousands of miles away and none of them were remotely interested in the life of a tea planter. So too, none envisaged for themselves living in Kashmir. Only their eldest daughter expressed any concern as to the manner or location of their twilight years. Rightly or wrongly, in the short time they had known Marian, both Jack and Marjorie had come to look upon her as a daughter and Emma as the grand child who brought smiles to their tired faces, rekindling for them memories of days when their own children were the same age.

Marian could not deny the attraction of Kashmir. Had she conceded, however, she would have been no better served than in fleeing to Delhi. The mountain ranges of the Himalayas were beautiful and mysterious, of that she was in no doubt. But she had mountains of her own to climb, great ranges of emotional hurdles to clear. With an irony she was at a loss to comprehend, the more often invitations were laid before her to leave Assam, the more she was drawn to the conclusion that she had to stay.

She endured Marjorie and Jack's cajoling with good humour. She was flattered by their affection for her and, as she was at pains to assure them, sorely tempted to follow in their footsteps. Jack's glowing words in praise of the Kashmiri hills were not new. They were a favourite and regular topic in his conversation. They were presented like sweet meats on a silver dish and just as difficult to resist. But resist Marian had to and did. She refused them with as little hurt as she could manage, seeing the disappointment clear on their faces yet hoping for divine intervention to excuse her from being the cause of any suffering.

She was surprised, but mildly grateful therefore, to have her attention diverted from the task of refusal by the sight of a covered buggy coming towards the bungalow along the 'garden road.' Since she was not expecting another visitor, the assumption had to be that the occupant, or occupants, were on their way to meet John. That being the case, she should have turned away. But she did not. Something persuaded her to stop talking mid-sentence. Ignoring temporarily her two guests and their pleas for her to quit life in the humid jungles around Dibrugarh for Shangri-La in the hills, she followed the steady progress of the buggy as it passed between the leaf houses. Finally, it came to a halt on the same spot where once she and Jonathan had alighted after their long journey from Landi Kotal.

For a second or two it appeared to falter, as if the driver were uncertain. Then, apparently spying the small party on the veranda, he carried on until coming to a halt immediately in front of the bungalow. There was a brief delay. Then the lone figure of Jerry Hugo jumped down.

He was gaunt, much more so than Marian remembered and his unshaven appearance was that of a man whose recent travels had denied him certain of the basic creature comforts. But without doubt, it was the same Jerry Hugo. Marian had not laid eyes on him since the backward glance he gave her on the afternoon he left Landi Kotal more than three years previously.

Fate had served up so many shocks over recent months, her reaction was perhaps not as startled as it might have been. However, in reality, Jerry was the last person she expected to see. In fact, so caught up with life and events centred on Shahjan, she had barely given him a thought for months, the memory of him having slipped into the background so far as to be almost out of sight. To see him once again standing in front of her and to have him there without a word of warning was motive enough for astonishment—and astonished she was, in spite of being unable to express it.

'What a journey,' he exclaimed to the three adults and single infant in front of him.

Good manners dictated that Marian perform the necessary pleasantries. In introducing him as Lieutenant Jerry Hugo, she was quickly corrected in so far as he had gained promotion to the lofty rank of Captain since their last encounter. The full extent of their relationship was abbreviated to suit the occasion. How or why Jerry was in Assam and without a word of warning, was his responsibility to explain, something he would have been happy to do at length but which he also cut short as a courtesy to Marjorie and Jack Laws.

Tea was brought and the foursome sat together for a polite duration. However, all further discussion of Kashmir ceased. When finally Marian's guests took their leave, she could barely contain her impatience for their departure. As fond as she was of them and as much as she looked forward to their visits, this was one occasion when she wished them gone. Jerry was the last person she expected to see at Shahjan or indeed anywhere in Assam. His arrival was a shock which could be alleviated only when and if he produced a satisfactory explanation as to why he had come.

'Why not?' was his initial response to the question. However, when pressed and conscious of the inappropriate timing for his flippancy, he attempted to expand upon his mere two words.

He began with his health. While on manoeuvres in Waziristan and after two years almost without incident, he had contracted a severe case of sand fever. This was followed by dysentery. In just a few weeks he lost over two stone in weight and, at times, felt himself preciously close to the pearly gates. As a consequence, it was decided he should take three months home leave.

Under normal circumstances this would have meant a voyage to England with all the benefits of fresh sea air and a return to the bosom of his family, there to feast himself on roast beef and care. Unfortunately, he had few relations in England. Those he knew of were virtual strangers and since he had never before set foot in the 'New Jerusalem' he could think of no motive for leaving India. Bombay was the obvious place for his recuperation. His father would have taken care of him. And indeed, that was exactly where he intended going until a three day old headline in a discarded newspaper drew his attention to the death and heroic exploits of one Major Jonathan Cole, recently slain in action while on active service in Abor land.

After that, the whereabouts of Mrs Marian Cole, nee Chase, required only nominal research. It was a process the fruit of which turned out to be surprisingly simple to pick from the tree. This then led him to embark for foreign parts not on board a ship but in and on almost every other means of transport available. His ultimate destination was the estate at Shahjan, the said journey being achieved in less than three weeks, something of which in the retelling he appeared inordinately proud.

His motives for coming were not as clear. They were voiced in a manner considerably less verbose than the convoluted tale of his travels from Lahore to the steamer ghats in Dibrugarh. The contrivance of his 'devil may care' attitude and his attempts to convince Marian he had given his trip across a continent as little consideration as he might have done a brisk walk the width of an open 'maidan,' failed to impress.

It was obvious to even the casual observer that he had been severely ill. His features were evidence enough of that. Marian herself was almost as shocked by his appearance as she was by his reappearance. However, his somewhat irritating enthusiasm and his refusal to treat her questions with the reverence she would have liked, were an indication that he was attempting to conceal the true motive for such an impassioned and ill-advised venture.

He would not admit that the whole enterprise had been in any way too much for him. He was reluctant even to admit to his evident exhaustion. Just how much damage it had done to the forward march of his convalescence Marian could only guess at. One thing was certain. No such journey would be undertaken merely as a 'jolly good weasel,' even by a well man. She suspected something else lay at the core; that heart rather than head had persuaded him to abandon common sense and the advice of his doctors.

The day they said their good byes in Landi Kotal, even then she recognised the look in his eyes. She needed no words or brightly coloured banners displaying the intensity of his affection. Indeed, though at the time he tried to hide it beneath a veneer of jocularity, Marian recognised all too well the symptoms of his 'amour' as far back as the morning they disembarked from the gallant old ship which had transported them from Bombay to Karachi.

329

That said, his arrival at Shahjan was still completely out of the blue. He was the last person she expected to see. That he knew of her marriage to Jonathan was something she took for granted. However, that he might be aware of subsequent events was something she had not considered. If pressed, she would have to admit she had not given him a second thought for longer than she cared to recall.

Nevertheless, faced with the fact of his turning up on her doorstep, she was prepared to entertain the idea that there was a certain inevitability about their reunion. Many people from her past might have stepped from that same buggy. In most cases she would not have believed her eyes, crediting their appearance to a dream or mirage.

But with Jerry, her astonishment was soon gone. With everything she knew and remembered of him, his behaviour was quite in keeping with the character she recalled. Moreover, the constancy of his affection, affection which she had done nothing to encourage or prolong, came as no surprise.

During their travels together from Bombay to Landi Kotal, Marian was unable to return his charged emotions, but she never for a moment doubted their sincerity. It was one of Jerry's most appealing attributes and formed the basis she believed of his optimism for life, India and the future. As infectious as it was endearing, during the term of their companionship, it was not then the stuff to capture the heart of a woman so recently and so deeply wounded by the death of her fiancé.

However, Jonathan's demands of her at the time, were less complicated. They were not likely to result in any additional heartbreak. By comparison to that of Jerry, his attraction to her and subsequent request for her hand in marriage, was as dispassionate as it was pragmatic. In agreeing to become his wife, Marian was fulfilling a need rather than a want. In Jerry's emotions, although never fully revealed, she anticipated demands upon her which at the time were greater than she was either willing or able to give.

'You shouldn't have come all this way,' was the rebuke Jerry received. But it was not the one his heart hoped for. Like a knight in shining armour, he had galloped across a continent to rescue the maiden in distress. She was widowed, alone and, to his mind, desperately in need of a saviour; all of which was true.

Yet his arrival, unannounced and uninvited, was too much for Marian to respond to in a manner more suitable. In truth, she really had no idea what to say to him.

For a while, there was silence between them as she tried to regain her equilibrium. Meanwhile, Jerry did his best and failed to conceal the disappointment of her immediate ingratitude.

'You must forgive me,' she said as her composure returned and she realised the paucity of her welcome. 'I had no idea you were coming. Your arrival like this, has taken me rather by surprise.'

'Oh believe me, I understand,' he conceded. 'I shouldn't have just upped sticks and come. But I couldn't resist. What else was I going to do. I had three months home leave and nowhere to go. When I read in the newspaper about your husband's death, it seemed the most logical thing to do. Send me away again if you want. I'll go without a murmur. Have me stay or go as you please. That will be punishment enough for my foolishness.'

Foolish he had been; impetuous as was his wont. But it was no more or less than Marian would have anticipated of him. Quite the contrary to Jonathan, Jerry was a man who wore his heart on his sleeve. He was a man for whom the notion of acting on impulse was as common place and as natural as breathing. By contrast, Jonathan was a thinker and planner. He neither did nor said anything without careful deliberation. At all times he had been methodical, neat and composed.

Much of Jerry's problem, if it was to be adjudged as a problem, was his youth. Marian had always supposed that over the course of time a degree of dilution, even cynicism, would serve to dampen the worst excesses of such an impetuous nature. There was always the possibility however that he was merely blessed or cursed with a personality given to extravagant gestures. This even went so far as to travel many hundreds of miles on a whim while under the illusion of it being the most logical and ordinary thing to do.

When it came to it, therefore, her scolding of him needed to be lukewarm. He had a Spaniel look in his eyes and a childlike innocence to his smile which forbade harsh words. Not that he was in any danger of being rejected or sent back the way he had come. The invitation for him to remain was given willingly. He was criticised for the method of his arrival, not the arrival itself.

Once Marian had gathered herself, she expressed genuine pleasure in making his acquaintance again. And indeed, his presence in the bungalow, even on that first night, enabled her to sleep less restlessly than she had done since Jonathan's departure with Major Hutchison.

She still woke several times, her head filled with awful imaginings of deserted mountains and violent struggles, but she returned to her dreams more quickly than had recently been her habit.

With the following morning came the time for introductions; Emma as her daughter and most precious possession and Booloo as faithful bearer. Then there was John, estate owner, former employer of her husband, benefactor and friend, with whom she took deliberate steps to eliminate any suspicion in Jerry's mind that their relationship might at one time have been more.

And true to the charade, John was polite and welcoming, more so than Marian expected. He too was surprised by the suddenness of Jerry's arrival. Nevertheless, and although they were two men separated by a catalogue of different character traits, they did appear to establish an opening rapport which promised hope.

Marian had no idea of Jerry's plans. She assumed however, that his cross-continental travels were not undertaken with any notion of a speedy return whence he had come. It was heartening therefore to witness a welcome from John and an open handedness from Jerry, which suggested an immediate future free from controversy.

Indeed, on a positive and surprising note, Jerry's presence, even on the first morning after his arrival, hinted at being exactly the catalyst required to bring John and Marian together. For weeks the former of the two had studiously avoided contact. Apparently to be alone with Marian, even for a short time or on the most innocent of errands, was a leap too far. If their paths crossed, and John made every effort to see they did not, it was for the briefest of encounters and with the minimum of verbal communication.

Marian felt as if she were contagious, as if she were being punished for a crime of which she was ignorant. She understood the need for caution. She fully realised the consequences of any indiscretion on her part. But to be shunned by John in the severe manner he had chosen, only served to aggravate her suffering.

Of course, politeness on John's part was one thing. It was, however, too much for Marian to hope that he and Jerry might become friends. Jonathan and John had been different in many respects, but they shared similar core values and a 'modus operandi' in their conduct which promised and delivered much. Both men were reticent over their feelings and both took pleasure in their own company.

Added to that, both were clearly attracted to the same woman, albeit for different reasons. If anything, and in spite of his arrogance, John lacked a degree of self-confidence. Marian was convinced he sought the admiration of women and took on life in the way he did simply to prove something, either to himself or, more likely, to his father.

On the other hand, Jonathan found nothing of the sort necessary. He was, until rendered a cuckold by his wife, his own man, certain of his values, self-reliant and, through a faith instilled in him from earliest childhood, satisfied to be the man God had made him.

Jerry was nothing like either them. He was famously impetuous. Of that there was no dispute. His sudden arrival at Shahjan was by no means the first evidence to that effect. And no closed book was he. He spoke his thoughts before assembling them into any sensible order and conducted his daily life as if to plan or pause for thought was to shatter some unwritten law. Marian knew there was not an ounce of malice in him. He judged no one and thought the best of everyone regardless of whether or not they had done anything to deserve it.

With only momentary consideration of the matter, Marian determined that regardless of the duration of his stay, Jerry was unlikely to impress John beyond an exchange of common courtesy.

However, one thing gave her pause. Jerry and John shared a love of horses which her late husband had not been able to equal. As far as Jonathan was concerned, horses were merely a convenient form of transport. In that at least, lay a ray of hope. In that small coincidence, Marian gambled there might in time form the foundation stone of a bond between Jerry and John.

Fortunately, the part Jerry came to play in affecting a reunion between John and Marian more than compensated for the potential complications of two opposing male egos sharing not only the same environment but each in their own way embracing the regard of a single woman.

As her house guest, Jerry enjoyed the greater portion of Marian's attention. Showering affection on Emma in an easy manner her true father found difficult to emulate, Jerry passed the majority of his time within the immediate vicinity of the bungalow. Meanwhile, as was his wont, John himself kept to his work in the leaf houses or stewarding the estate astride 'Snowden.'

It was several weeks into the picking before it occurred to Jerry he should do anything else. So bewildered was Marian by his arrival and aimless presence, she was irritated by the need to provoke him into a declaration of intent.

She was delighted to see him. Of course she was. She had not expected to do so but she could not deny the efficacy of his being close at hand. Not without being drawn to the irony of the situation, did she recall the morning he had stood beside her at All Saints Church in Karachi as she bid a silent farewell to another man whom fate had snatched away. Jerry was a comfort then and his recent reappearance made him no less so. There was something in his naïve charm and childlike paint box of emotions which eased Marian's more sombre and confused moments. To watch him playing with Emma, the two a generation apart but united by a bond of untainted honesty, brought a smile to her face and cheer to her heart; both things sadly lacking immediately prior to his arrival.

What also became apparent, and it was something which had escaped her notice in the first few days after his arrival at Shahjan, primarily to be blamed upon her own easier self-pity, was the extent to which Jerry had been ill. He ate little and rested often. He moved about the place with the fragility of a man twice his age and though he did offer to help John on the estate, noticeable relief appeared in his eyes when his offers were declined.

It occurred to Marian therefore that his coming to Assam was perhaps more than the overblown gesture of gallantry she originally supposed. He made no mention of it and his mood betrayed nothing of the sort. However, after a while she concluded that in his obvious poor state of health, the last thing he should have contemplated, let alone embarked upon, was a trek across India. In making so arduous a journey, he had surely risked a relapse or even final submission to the illness which though it had failed to affect his spirit, had clearly so ravaged his body.

One Saturday it was decided that all of them would go into Dibrugarh to polo. John, of course, would be playing. Jerry and Marian would watch with Emma from the side lines. Save for the obligatory ritual of matins each Sunday morning, this was the first time for a long time that Marian had been off the estate. It was also the first opportunity for the general populous to encounter a young man whose enigmatic status was absolutely too much to endure. Who was he, where was he from and, more importantly, why had he come to Dibrugarh? These were the three main topics of conversation frustrating would be gossips.

The last, of course, namely why he had come was still a question very much to the forefront of Marian's mind. Simple charity was not adequate as an excuse. To those residents of Dibrugarh, however, whose curiosity was stirred by the mention of his name, Jerry's health, good or bad, was the least most interesting aspect of his presence at the home of the late and much-lamented Major Jonathan Cole.

As they entered the club, there was a hush. Common courtesy dictated there should not have been and every effort was made within his immediate vicinity to convince Jerry that his presence was the least interesting event of the day. But it was to no avail. For a moment or two the level of conversational noise reduced markedly, eyes turned and the party from Shahjan was the focus of all attention.

Undoubtedly, to some, Marian herself was the main subject for scrutiny. A stranger to recent public activities, there were those keen to assess her condition. After all, she was in mourning. Much was expected of her. Those who knew her, of course, were ready to offer their support, to commiserate or to distract her from grief. By contrast, there was an equal element of bitter spinsters and forgotten widows who were looking to find fault in the way she conducted herself as the widow of a man publicly proclaimed a hero.

Jerry served as added fuel for evidence of mal practice in the administration of her responsibilities. Were they to become privy to the truth, namely that John was in fact more suitable tinder for the fire some would light, they might have rested easier in their beds.

John's impeccable behaviour, however, namely that of eliminating Marian from his life completely, gave no ground to the enemy. In that his denial of her caused consternation to Marian herself, he was sorry beyond words, but the proof of the pudding, regardless of its sour taste, was in the evidence that of all eyes turned to follow their entrance on that Saturday morning, none were towards him.

One or two unattached, young ladies averted their gaze deliberately, thereby announcing an interest in him and very probably thoughts of him which they were supposed to resist. Otherwise, he worked his way through the crowded club saloon free from sensation.

First to greet them were the Laws. Jack and Marjorie held the distinct advantage of being the only ones already acquainted with Jerry Hugo. Of course, on that previous occasion, their introduction was brief, scarcely more than a handshake before the taking of their leave, but Marjorie was not likely to concede such an advantage as a trifle.

While she had not pretended to friends that her acquaintance with the new arrival was anything other than passing, she had certainly done nothing to dispel

335

general envy at her being the only mortal beyond the confines of Shahjan to 'know' him.

Fortunately, his close association to the Dunn name was enough to guarantee Jerry for the most part safe passage through the mob. To paint Dibrugarh society as free from petty rivalries or the trite trespasses of all small colonial conclaves, would be to mislead. It was the same as all such communities, be they on the Indian subcontinent or any other sprawling land mass coloured pink on a world atlas. And, of those ready to stir mischief, in Dibrugarh at least, there was a modest but dedicated contingent. They held agendas of their own and were ever ready to disrupt the superior standing held within the community of the family named Dunn.

Trevelyan Dunn was a man whose conduct over many years rendered him more than most as a target for criticism and censure. His business ethics were highly questionable. His torrid affairs were legend. The true number of his illegitimate children was the source of permanent speculation. However, the power he wielded was such and the influence he brought to bear so effective, many thought things of him in the privacy of their own homes they would not dare nor could afford to voice in public.

Consequently, though he was unaware of it, Jerry came through his first encounter with Dibrugarh society comparatively unscathed. Many people wanted to meet him. There was much shaking of hands and many messages of welcome. That he declared himself a keen horseman and polo player met with general approval. However, at the end of the day, the one question which teased most of those gathered for the occasion, namely that of why he had come, remained unasked and unanswered.

Marian as well, returned home none the worse for wear, having circumvented the traps laid for her by those whose Christian motives were in need of keen examination.

As for the polo, it went well. Both the Dibrugarh first team of which John and Philip were primary members, and the Dibrugarh second, contrived resounding victories over their visiting rivals from Tingri. As usual on such occasions, much of the praise was heaped upon the willing shoulders of the two Dunn boys. 'Snowden' went well in the first chukka but on account of some lameness was set aside for the remainder of the match in favour of a jet-black mare with the rather unflattering name of 'Lucretia.' The change of mounts made no difference to John's performance however. He scored twice, both times taking the ball virtually the full length of the field before striking it home between the posts.

Marian was permitted a smile. Enough time had also elapsed for her to engage in the general conversation without laying herself open to raised eyebrows. And, she watched the polo with as much enthusiasm as was her custom prior to the tragedy for which she was paying so high a price. Fortunately, such enthusiasm as she expressed was and ever had been only tepid. To admire the horses was permitted, but to have become in any way excited by the performance of the players, be they a Dunn or not, would have been considered beyond the limits of propriety.

Reminiscent of the days when they had journeyed together from Bombay all the way to Landi Kotal, Jerry was ever attentive to her needs. He was less 'on his toes' than she recalled of him, probably as a side effect of his recent illness. However, he rarely left her side, preferring rather her company and the company of those who went out of their way to renew her acquaintance. The more manly ribaldry of the competing teams and their supporters, the majority of whom gathered together after the match for a lively de-briefing at one end of the club house bar where the whiskey and conversation flowed in equal abundance, was not to his taste or, Marian guessed, his stamina.

Verity Dunn, always at such events a matriarchal figure and permanently surrounded by a small throng of courtiers most of whom were women, showed little interest in cross examining the new arrival. She was introduced to Jerry, permitted him to take her hand briefly and extended him a welcome, but she was neither inquisitive nor inquisitorial. Marjorie Laws, on the other hand, and in a manner most unlike her usual self, managed to divert Jerry away to a quiet corner of the room for several minutes of concerted questions and answers.

Though Marian was too far off at the time to listen in and therefore not privy to the content of their conversation, she could well imagine the general tone of it. She only hoped for discretion. If Jerry were to confess his true feelings for her, feelings she had always known went far beyond the perimeters of their agreed platonic friendship, he might find himself the instigator of a scandal. As compassionate as she was, Marjorie and therefore, by implication, Dibrugarh society, was not ready to accept any such revelation. Enough time had elapsed for Marian to be seen again in public.

However, at this preliminary stage in the recognised mourning period, Saturday polo was perhaps not the most desirable of venues for her reintroduction. Sunday matins was the more appropriate. But this impropriety was small enough to be overlooked. What would not be tolerated however, were confessions of an amorous nature from her house guest, a stranger who had appeared from nowhere, yet was now firmly ensconced at Shahjan.

As it was, Marian's fears proved unfounded. Jerry behaved impeccably. Not only did he acquit himself well, answering all questions put to him with as little hard fact as he could engineer, but he managed to persuade the majority of those with whom he came into contact that they were safe to leave the occasion carrying a favourable impression of him to their various homes.

Two introductions did catch Marian's attention. Norman Bayden engaged Jerry conspicuously longer than any other male in or out of the club house. She noticed their conversation was earnest, the two men behaving for all the world as if they were already known to each other. While, for some twenty minutes or more, she fielded a barrage of courteous but pointed enquiries from 'ladies of the parish' as to her well-being and, more significantly, future intentions, Jerry needed no rescue.

On the contrary, he appeared pleasantly preoccupied with the now well established and generally admired Superintendent of the Jorhat-Dibrugarh Railway, a man who was soon to make his own small imprint on the history of the region with the official opening of the same. And shortly after he was set to marry his sweetheart, a 'dear, dear' girl by all accounts, due to arrive from England just in time to share his triumph.

By contrast, the next person to corner Jerry quickly provoked from him desperate glances, pleas for Marian to save him. Miss Julia Fenton, unruly, incorrigibly flirtatious and never one to stand on ceremony, cast aside formal convention by affecting her own introduction. With several carefully planned manoeuvres she extricated herself from the feminine huddle in which she had been trapped for longer than was to her liking and placed herself directly in Jerry's path as he made his way in the direction of where last he had spied Marian out of the corner of his eye.

His route blocked and with no obvious exits to hand, he had no alternative but to embrace the encounter as best he could. Since Marian had no prior knowledge of the Fenton's attending the occasion, the luckless Jerry was ill prepared. There was no warning shot across his bow and no advanced intelligence of his foe.

John was the consummate womaniser. He was as much at his ease in the company of the opposite sex as he was around horses and, like his father, tended to treat both in much the same rather cavalier fashion.

Some accused him of being incapable of deciding which of the two he preferred the more; and not without some justification. There were rare exceptions. His relationship with Marian was not undertaken lightly. Guilt in the execution of it and frustration that it was brought to an end so abruptly, haunted many of his nights. Equally, 'Snowden' was an equine friend. He favoured him above all other horses.

On the other hand, in the matter of women, Jerry was still very much an innocent and would probably remain that way. Certainly, he was no match for Miss Julia Fenton. A siren, seemingly intent upon luring every male susceptible to her rather obvious charms, Jerry stood little chance of escaping intact. She was done with John. Since he had shown himself unimpressed by her wit, charm or more obvious physical attributes, all of which, it seemed, had failed to live up to his expectations, she was hungry for a new, more susceptible victim. Like a tigress stalking her prey, she spied Jerry upon his arrival.

However, she bided her time, waiting, hidden among the crowd, gauging the perfect moment to strike. His guard was down. He was relaxed, appreciative of the welcome offered by all those whose hands he had shaken and quite unready for her ambush.

Marian saw only the pounce. So well hidden was Julia, she managed her stealthy interception before anyone had time to intervene. Jerry was alone and defenceless, his only good fortune being ignorance of the true nature of his adversary. However, by the time she was done with him the jaundiced tint to his complexion had turned pale. He fidgeted nervously, quite unable to invent any method of retreat without embarrassment or injury. Julia's claws were razor sharp, her intent nothing less than his total submission, a result achieved with such ease she appeared bored with the sport barely before it was begun, releasing him as a cat would a mouse refusing to flee from its grasp.

Jerry was saved by his own incompetence. By the time he made it back to the safe company of Marian and Jack Laws, he was shaken but relatively intact.

'Formidable what?' was Jack's succinct summary.

'Rather,' came the breathless reply.

'I'm really so sorry,' said Marian, a smile creeping to the corner of her lips. 'I should have warned you.'

'Yes, you should,' he agreed.

'Our Miss Julia can be a bit of a handful,' Jack added, a truism better offered, Jerry thought, prior to rather than post such an engagement.

'I should say,' he agreed again without protest.

'She really can be quite sweet,' Marian suggested, producing in both her male companions quizzical looks and raised eyebrows. 'She's just a little forward in her manner sometimes.'

'As in the whale was rather forward when he swallowed Jonah,' Jack quipped with an uncharacteristic attempt at humour.

'Quite,' replied Jerry.

'But did you find her to your liking?' Marian asked.

Jerry paused for a moment to consider the question. 'If I'm honest,' he mused aloud, 'Yes, I did. At first, she caught me a little off guard. She was, let's say, rather forthright in her manner and opinions, many of which she expressed in the few minutes we were together. However, she has spirit and I think spirit is a good thing in a woman.'

'Praise indeed,' Marian concluded. 'I'll obviously have to arrange a second introduction for you, somewhere a little less public.'

'Not so fast,' said Jerry. 'I think I need a few more weeks to recover my full strength before I consider another tete a tete with Miss Fenton. Pleasant enough she might be, but I've a feeling she could eat me for breakfast.'

'I should take a few years if I were you my boy,' Jack chimed in. 'A willow-the-wisp like Miss Julia Fenton needs a man with more stamina than you can muster in a few short weeks. Armies have succumbed to less.'

'Really!' Marian scolded but secretly enjoying the image of Julia Fenton reducing a whole army of men to quivering wrecks.

By the time they returned to Shahjan all discussion of Julia had ceased. John, rather the worse for drink, stabled 'Snowden' at the club overnight and travelled back with Marian and Jerry in a carriage. No doubt he would have had a thing or two to say on the subject of Miss Fenton had it been brought up. However, it was not and he did not, thereby avoiding the delicate topic of his own short-lived but highly volatile liaison with the said vixen.

Instead, he and Jerry debated the merits of the days polo, Jerry very much in awe of the triumph for the home teams, while John, emitted a casual air of complacency, indicating the inevitability of what came to be the end result.

Apparently, Tingri rarely fielded teams strong enough to challenge the talents of Dibrugarh. Some years previously they boasted a young cavalry officer by the name of Thomas Skene who combined his efforts for the Tingri first team with his role as leading goal scorer for two seasons with the Assam team. However, not as accomplished in the manufacture of tea as he was on the polo field, he had taken himself off to try his hand at rubber somewhere in southern India.

Since then, Tingri had laboured to find polo players to match the Dunn brothers. To a man, they played with gusto, but with only average talent, making a win for Dibrugarh something of a foregone conclusion, a fact John enjoyed repeating several times before the carriage arrived back at Shahjan.

It was a bold claim and easily made after the event, with the victory under their belts. Certainly, from the little Marian watched of the matches and the little she understood of the sport in general, the effort and scores on both sides appeared more evenly matched than John would have Jerry believe. Whiskey, however, is a brave lubricant to speech giving. By his rather rolling gate and occasional slurred words, Marian guessed he had downed rather more than his fair share during the after-match celebrations.

Once alone in her bedroom, with only the distant noises of the jungle for company and the occasional scurrying of a rat as it scampered through the loose thatch above her head, she considered the strange, even tragic irony of her situation.

Her husband was dead. The man she had admired and respected more than any other save her own father, was gone. His life was forfeited to no good purpose. His absence exposed a gaping wound, relentlessly slow to heal. In public, she wore black and would do so for the full two years expected of her. Day to day, she cared for her child, a child which was not his, and she played the part of widow as custom dictated.

Yet, in a room only a few yards off slept a young man whose affection for her was an open book. And away in his bungalow, in an alcoholic slumber, was the father of her daughter, a man whom she neither loved nor, it has to be said, greatly admired, but whose close proximity in the carriage during their drive home, in spite of his mild inebriation, rekindled feelings which no woman in mourning had the right to own.

Marian's life was in a spin. Change was as vital as it was unavoidable. But how and to what she had not the slightest idea. She knew much was expected of her. Public opinion was clear. Her role as dutiful wife and proud widow was as easily comprehensible as it was unsustainable. However, she had stumbled into a maze. The sides were dense and the puzzle of pathways too complex to unravel. Every determined avenue she took produced a dead end. Every corner she turned led her up another blind alley. What she needed was a guide. Marjorie Laws was a sympathetic confidante. She dressed wounds with the loving care of a most devoted nurse, but she could not heal the contagion within. She was wise and caring, honest and fair but not sage enough to show Marian the passage to open space at the centre of the maze.

Perhaps Jerry would resolve to leave when his strength returned. Perhaps John would follow in his father's footsteps and in so doing become hateful and bloated, a man to be despised. Perhaps by some trick of fate, proof would be found to secure Jonathan's right to be called father to Emma. Perhaps the world was flat. So many 'perhaps,' so little likelihood of any becoming fact.

Sleep was the only relief and the hope that when she woke in the morning her father would be at her bedside, his smiling face and unimpeachable wisdom on hand to solve the unsolvable, to fathom the unfathomable.

Chapter Twenty-Three

There was a certain predictability in John offering Jerry Hugo the position left vacant as the result of Jonathan's death, expediency being the least of it. There was equal certainty in Marian's disapproval of the idea and her praying that Jerry would have the good common sense and sensitivity to turn it down.

For as much as she was fond of him and enjoyed his company, she remained convinced his presence served more to exacerbate her problems than relieve them. Although she appreciated the selfless nature of his grand trek across India merely to be at her side, the notion of him as a permanent fixture on the estate was precisely the opposite of what she wanted. She wished him nothing but good. She wished him all the happiness and fulfilment his generosity of spirit deserved, but in truth she wished him gone from Shahjan.

She was willing to credit him with having been instrumental in restoring her relationship with John, if only by coincidence. As her chaperone, Jerry made it possible for the three of them to be assembled around the same table without fear of wagging tongues or the possibility of her becoming compromised in any way. But the price for that new liberty was too dear. Jerry's attentions towards her were too keen, too contrived to win her favour and barely a day passed she did not feel under obligation to reward the length and effort of his journey to be near her. Of course, he asked nothing of her, not at least, in word or deed. Nevertheless, she felt beholden, as if she should be indebted to him for his unswerving loyalty.

The difficulty arose in that Marian simply could not respond to his altruism in the manner she assumed he wanted. She was truly fond of him, but no more. She took comfort in his company, warmth from his affection, but there was no fire to kindle, no flame to fan. Regardless of her marriage and the suddenness of its end, a lifetime of effort would not stir in her for one minute the passion she once shared with John, the deep affection she held for Jonathan, or the unequivocal love she had felt for William.

343

Had he confronted her, she would have been helpless to provide an explanation. He was kind, faithful and courteous. His credentials were unimpeachable. He made her laugh. His unbridled enthusiasm for life was as infectious as it was uplifting and she had no doubt that were she to invite his attentions he would labour tirelessly to ensure her happiness. But still, it was not enough, nor could it be. Every day he stayed on, pretending an interest in the manufacture of tea, engineering a friendship with John which was as unlikely as it was awkward to watch, Marian felt less comfortable, precisely the opposite of what she believed he had set his sights on achieving when journeying from Lahore.

In the strangest of circumstances, however, and as if arranged for her by the fates specifically to confound, when his three months of leave were up, Jerry did not return to his regiment. Neither did he take up a career in tea planting or pursue his affection for Marian to what she feared would be its predictable and unfortunate conclusion.

The hospitality at Shahjan kept Jery there for more than six weeks, his every word and deed certain indication of an intention to remain permanently. However, almost as suddenly as he had arrived, he shocked both Marian and John alike with the announcement of his imminent departure.

Unknown to Marian, two significant introductions bore fruit which occurred on the afternoon of the polo match between Dibrugarh and Tingri.

During the course of that afternoon Jerry had been greeted by more people than he could remember. Apparently however, two people impressed him greatly. The first was Norman Bayden. During a conversation with Marian days later, Jerry admitted what he only hinted at on the day, namely an immediate rapport with the railway engineer. The carving of track through the most impenetrable jungle and across inhospitable terrain, the creation of a rail network linking one day east to west and north to south across an entire continent, was as inspiring to Jerry as it was ambitious. Not only was he invigorated by the boldness of Norman Bayden's work, he was equally impressed by the man himself, feeling at their first introduction an empathy too powerful to be ignored.

When, therefore, Jerry was approached with the offer of his becoming assistant to a man whose confidence inspired him within ten minutes of their initial introduction, there was little hesitation in accepting. Suddenly and without warning but with words of deep regret, Jerry refused John's invitation to stay on at Shahjan as temporary under manager. Instead, he determined to use his continued ill health as a means and excuse to quit the military in favour of joining the forces of those striving for a different kind of victory, namely that of constructing a communications network the scale of which had not been attempted before.

In so doing, he convinced himself and his Commander in Chief that his service to Queen and empire would be of far greater value as a builder of railways than were he to remain in uniform, an inconspicuous officer of poor constitution, stationed probably in a garrison outpost far from the nearest signs of civilisation.

Strangely, his affiliation to Norman Bayden came as no surprise to Marian. It was typical of Jerry's impetuous nature and youthful idealism. However, it did come as a considerable relief to hear of his intention to leave Shahjan of his own free will.

What she did not expect and what she found herself requiring confirmation of before she would give it the credence Jerry so earnestly asked of her, was his sudden romantic attachment to a certain young woman by the name of Miss Julia Fenton.

Anything less likely, Marian found hard to imagine. No virtuous maiden, no shy, timid country rose, Julia Fenton was so far removed from the type Marian would have predicted for Jerry that his initial declaration of an interest in her provoked a smile which nearly turned to mirth. After all, Jerry was a man who admitted with red faced humility that his lamentable accomplishments with members of the opposite sex were as legend as his grasp of international politics. His awkwardness in their company was as conspicuous as it was pitiful.

'But I thought…'

'I can imagine what you think,' Jerry interrupted, his impatience to exalt exceeding his manners. 'I know what you all think of Miss Fenton. I also know her reputation, but you're wrong. All of you. Inside, she is the sweetest, kindest girl I've ever met.'

In the mastering of her incredulity, Marian was compelled to overlook the tactless implication that Julia Fenton had so recently and quickly come to ride higher in his affections than she did. Altogether unbelievable was the concept of sweetness and kindness which Jerry claimed to have unearthed in a young woman better known to the local community as an outrageous flirt, with ideas of her beauty and elegance too bold for her own good.

That Jerry found the same young woman irresistible was extraordinary to say the least. That he imagined himself capable of capturing and calming the beast was equally as risible. Quite beyond the bounds of sanity was the notion that Miss Julia Fenton would entertain a relationship with a man like Jerry or encourage it to a happy conclusion. If indeed she had ensnared him to win his affection, it was certain to be part of some cruel game. She was surely toying with him in no lesser a way than she was in the habit of doing with any unsuspecting suitor too easily impressed by her sweet smile and deceptively inviting eyes.

'Calamity' was the word ready to spring from Marian's lips. 'Impossible, never and oh my dear sweet boy,' were others, but she kept her silence, permitting him to proceed instead with further assurances of his willing participation, Julia's reciprocal interest in him and their joint and future aspirations.

'How can this be?' Marian wanted to ask. 'How could you travel thousands of miles apparently to be with me only to fall under the spell of a temptress like Julia Fenton?'

Instead, she listened and nodded sagely, all the while restraining herself, desperate to intervene but intrigued by the confusion of his adjectives in praise of a woman with whom she was herself better but by no means well acquainted. One question after another she reserved for the pages of her diary, using them to placate her disappointment in the fickleness and mystery of the male gender.

To his face, she offered support. Rather than steer Jerry into calmer, safer waters she permitted herself the sport of advancing his cause, listing not Miss Fenton's flaws, but underlining her virtues, agreeing to the positive rather than promoting the negative.

By the time their conversation came an end, she had almost convinced herself that Julia and Jerry were the perfect couple, their few similar traits a happy coincidence, their opposites a valuable stimulus to longevity.

It was cruel. She was cruel in deceiving him in the way she did. No good would come in the furtherance of a union, however ephemeral, between the manipulative Miss Fenton and the gullible Captain Hugo, and well she knew it. But further the cause she did. And for that, she was punished by having to record the depth of guilt in her diary below exclamations of bewilderment at news of so bewildering a coupling.

More extraordinary still was the progress of said union. Jerry did not return to Marian in short measure with his tail between his legs, his heart broken and a vow of future celibacy poised on his lips. Instead, the relationship between himself and 'dear, sweet Julia, the most lovely and generous of creatures,' words employed by the love-struck boy all too often and with variable emphasis, went from strength to strength. Soon after his initial pronouncement to Marian, they were seen constantly together in public. There was nothing formal, but there was no mistaking the attachment. No amount of subtle or even unsubtle innuendo appeared to deter the odd couple from the path of true love.

So much did they become, rather quickly, the topic of general conversation that Marian noticed a welcome reduction in her own news value. The 'delightful' Jerry Hugo and 'notorious' Miss Julia Fenton were far more interesting subjects for gossip.

Marian continued on at Shahjan as before. She paid homage to public scrutiny by continuing to wear black as was expected of her. She therefore ceased to inflame the imaginations of those who would make capital from her least impropriety. Her future and the reputation of her dead husband gradually ceased to be of prime public interest. As another season progressed, there were more intriguing 'goings on' to amuse and excite.

The continuing saga of Jerry and Julia was but one of those 'goings on,' appearing as it did to be 'going on' with no end in sight save that of the obvious conclusion many drew but which few found plausible, namely marriage.

However, there were other perhaps more significant events in the schedule for Dibrugarh, guaranteed further to divert public interest away from Marian.

The penultimate section of the Assam Bengal Railway opened on 16 September 1889. Of course, it had taken longer than first planned. The weather and terrain conspired on a daily basis to delay the project. All eyes were originally on 1887 for its completion, this to coincide with the Golden Jubilee celebrations. But it was not to be. The commencement of the project was postponed several times by the snail's pace of bureaucracy and the completion by the nature of both terrain and weather.

Nevertheless, it still remained one of the most important days in the history of Dibrugarh. No expense was spared to make it an event to remember long after the name Dunn might have disappeared from the local vocabulary.

Its construction was but one in a long line of engineering feats and tests of endurance bearing witness to the greatness of empire. Though two years behind schedule, nothing could be more fitting than that its completion was achieved with only modest additional cost to the British tax payer.

No longer would Dibrugarh continue as an inhospitable backwater. Its days of being accessible only by steamer, for much of the season cut off from the civilised world by monsoons and denied so many of the conveniences of life taken for granted by those already with rail links to major cities in India, were at an end.

How better therefore to honour the Golden Jubilee of so great a monarch, albeit somewhat after the event, than by adding yet another far-flung outpost of British occupancy to Her Majesty's chest of treasures.

And what could have been more fitting than to ensure the opening ceremony was celebrated in a manner and with a carnival atmosphere to rival those of the Jubilee. And how convenient that such festivities should finally release Marian from the public gaze after nearly a year of intense scrutiny.

In the shadow of so significant an occasion, attention shifted from her and the burden of being always the faithful widow. Instead, all eyes were focussed on the coming to Dibrugarh of various invited dignitaries. A small army of them arrived as honoured guests like bees to a honey pot, their express purpose to inaugurate the latest strand of a modern, integrated railway system. For Dibrugarh it was to be a week of partying the like of which had not been seen before.

The Golden Jubilee of Her Majesty had brought merriment, national pride, bunting and a degree of pomp befitting the occasion. Time was taken away from tea production by the whole British contingent to assemble on the polo ground for unanimous rounds of three cheers and mutual patting on the back for Queen, country and empire. But the opening of a new rail link promised so much more.

It was the beginning of a new chapter for Dibrugarh and all those pioneers who had toiled so ceaselessly and against such odds to wrestle a living from the jungle. It was a pivotal moment, the significance of which was recognised by every man woman and child living and working on the numerous tea estates.

Overnight Norman Bayden was elevated. No longer was he permitted the guise of quiet, unassuming local engineer, rarely seen at social functions in respect of his being usually out in the field, trudging some newly exposed path through the jungle, inspiring his army of coolies and fellow engineers to ever greater effort.

Overnight, he became the man most people wanted to meet and shake by the hand. To him fell the privilege of welcoming the high and mighty 'up' from

Calcutta, his burden that of speech making and the chore of being the most desired guest at every dinner party.

Of course, by the date of the official opening, he had himself a new assistant. Jerry had taken up his position with the Assam Bengal Railway on 1 September, even before the application to resign his commission was decided upon by his former Commanding Officer in Delhi. His anticipation of a happy resolution was typical of his impatient nature. And, in spite of the rail link being almost complete, from the first day, as much as he was able, Jerry threw himself into his new career with the enthusiasm Marian had always noted as one of his most admirable traits.

He also moved into town, taking his leave of Shahjan with regret and near to tears, much as he had done when he and Marian parted previously in Landi Kotal. He left behind the easy comfort of Marian's bungalow for lodgings less spacious, lacking any fine views from the window and denied the ever-vigilant attentions of Booloo.

However, Marian was forced to confess, with some reluctance, that she had not seen him happier. Whether as a result of his new work or the influence of Miss Julia Fenton, whose company he seemed rarely to be without, his health returned. He became again the young man she recalled meeting a long time before at the Taj Mahal Hotel in Bombay. And for that, she could not be critical of either his decision to quit the military or the sudden reversal of his affections.

Julia Fenton was not the companion Marian would have chosen for him. They were poles apart in almost every opinion and principal. Though not proud of the fact, Marian found it impossible not to be suspicious of Julia's interest in so naïve and uncomplicated a man. Jerry lacked the dynamism of a Dunn. He had no money to speak of and no great inheritance to expect. Furthermore, his prospects were limited by the abrupt conclusion of a career which formerly promised at least a reliable income and satisfactory pension.

Of course, she blamed Julia's influence as much as anything for his decision. Why else would Jerry abandon a career he knew well and professed to love, in favour of another for which he had no proven natural aptitude. That aside, there was nothing about either of them to explain their extraordinary attachment. General perception had them down as a strange quirk of nature. More pessimistically, the same quorum of public opinion was of one accord. It was universally agreed that Julia Fenton was taking advantage of Jerry in the worst possible way and that in short time she would surely tire of the game, an all too familiar scenario and one for which she had gained her less than favourable notoriety. Quite evidently her relationship with Jerry was part of some mischievous scheme which, in the end, would leave him ruined and broken hearted.

Marjorie urged Marian to intervene. She pleaded with her to use whatever influence she had over Jerry to the better good. Even John was minded to voice his concern. He and Jerry were not close, nor were they ever likely to be, but the writing was writ so large upon the wall and he knew enough of Julia and her ways from firsthand experience that he could not ignore the danger signs.

It was all to no avail, however. When Marian attempted words of warning they were dismissed out of hand, Jerry's response being to suggest she might want to look to her own future rather than to his and that his prospects appeared rather more satisfactory than hers.

It was hurtful stuff, exchanges Jerry regretted within minutes of their occurrence and for which he apologised profusely at the first opportunity. Nevertheless, the wounds inflicted smarted enough to keep Marian from any further attempts at intervention.

In spite of her continued misgivings she permitted him free rein, watching him pursue his involvement with Julia to its ultimate conclusion, a conclusion which had Julia as the teasing predator and Jerry as the witless prey, his eyes blinded to reality.

Fortunately, his time in the limelight of Dibrugarh gossip was also comparatively short-lived. He and Julia, their courtship and its inevitable betrayal were soon to become little more than an occasional footnote to current events. During the first week in September and with each arriving steamer, new faces were to be seen around town as the population swelled for the coming celebrations; new faces, new names and new subjects to satisfy the appetite of gossip.

In 1837, the year of Princess Victorias coronation, the population of Dibrugarh represented no more than a handful of her subjects, pioneering planter families, struggling against the odds and toiling in all weathers to lay down the first tea gardens; and a military presence which could be counted almost on the fingers of one hand. There were few luxuries, few buildings in the town of any substance and although every effort was made at the time to mark the advent of a new monarch, it was a timid affair. Twenty-five years on and the Silver Jubilee fared little better. Events of the '57 mutiny stayed long in the memories of those who lived in its shadow and survived the worst of the bloodshed.

However, with the passing of a further twenty-five years or, more precisely, twenty-seven, it was a very different story. A new century was approaching fast. The British empire spanned the globe and although the voices for 'home rule' were growing ever louder, most Englishmen and women in India still slept relatively easy in their beds.

And Dibrugarh had thrived. It had grown beyond the wildest expectations of all save perhaps successive heads of the Dunn family. It was fast developing into a thriving urban community, soon to become not a backwater of Imperial endeavour but a bright light in a far corner of the empire.

For the time being, the Abors had been tamed. The Chinese seemed happy to keep their distance, suggesting no threat of any consequence. And finally, the long-awaited rail link with Jorhat was finished. No far-flung dot on the map was Dibrugarh any longer. Instead, it had become a vital and significant contributor to Her Majesty's dominions.

Noon on 16 September was the moment, an exact and planned point in time when the sacrifice and bloody-minded endeavour over half a century of families such as the Dunn's and the Laws was to be rewarded. Recent arrivals like Marian and Jerry were mere spectators. They and many others like them were new additions to the community. They swelled the ranks. They were needed and welcomed. Their families and children were nurtured and encouraged to stay. But the Dunn's, the Laws and their kind were in at the start. Jack Laws broke the first ground at Mancotta. With his bare hands, he carved a swathe through the jungle. He built a home for his family, set down roots and laid the foundation for future generations.

Trevelyan Dunn was the second to live at Kurmi. His father, a John, arrived in India at the age of sixteen as a soldier in the service of the East India Company, determined to make his fortune in a land of plenty. When he died, prematurely during an outbreak of typhoid, he left to his son no gold, silver or swollen bank account. His legacy was land stretching in every direction as far as the eye could see. It had been secured for his descendants on the back of sweat and the misery of a daily battle against hardships no Englishman in the home counties could imagine.

And Trevelyan Dunn's prize, the long-awaited reward for all those years of ruthless and uncompromising determination to succeed, of shipping season upon season of tea to English tables, was not a Golden Jubilee or the coming of a new century. Such celebrations came and went, union jacks in the streets, stirring bands and loyal toasts a plenty. But 16 September 1889 was the day he and so many of his peers had waited for and worked towards for so long. Dibrugarh was coming of age and not a soul living within its jurisdiction doubted the magnitude of the moment.

First in importance, but last to arrive, was the Governor General, the newly elevated Lord Lansdowne. Immediately prior to the great day, Norman Bayden's role as superintendent altered significantly. For several years he was chief engineer and overseer of every sleeper cut, many of which were taken under contract from jungle cleared in and around Shahjan, Medla and Bollai. But for this event he acquired the role of chief administrator, welcoming invited guests, organising their accommodation and seeing to the smooth running of planned ceremonies. And, at his side was Jerry, his duty, and one for which he appeared ideally suited, to act in the most appropriate manner as buffer, taking active control of the mundane thus leaving his immediate superior free to manage those matters most pertinent to his position.

No stone was left unturned in their joint efforts to impress, even taking into account Lord Lansdowne was fast becoming well known for the extravagance of his progresses through India. At all times he insisted upon travelling in a caravan of near regal proportions. And as he went, he consumed every ounce of hospitality reasonably afforded by the communities into which he strayed. He expected to be feted and in so doing instilled a certain trepidation into the hearts of those whose task it was to finance the privilege of his presence. But this was the first occasion he had ventured as far north from the comfort of Calcutta.

His predecessor, Lord Dufferin was a more modest man, a man who travelled little, preferring where possible to remain at his seat of government, delegating rather than taking an active part in the ambassadorial role of his office.

During the unbearable summer months, he and his numerous administrative staff relocated to Darjeeling, there to rule India from cool palaces atop cool hills, the climate akin to England, the customs and architecture as Anglo-Saxon as could be contrived. On one occasion he did engage the Brahmaputra. He steamed upstream, as far as Gauhati, riding on the mighty rivers back, one colossus upon another. The destination was that of a cricket tournament held in his honour by Prince Hetty, the Maharaja of Cooch Behar, a long-time friend and the man with whom he shared a dormitory at Eton during their formative years.

But Dibrugarh had been to him little more than a dot on the map, brought to his attention more recently only as the jumping off point for the Abor expedition. He knew nothing of the people who lived there, the scale of their contribution to the wealth of empire or the beauty of its surrounding countryside.

However, it was widely believed that with the coming of Lord Lansdowne, all this was to change. To Norman Bayden and by implication to Jerry Hugo, possibly the least eligible perhaps for such an honour, fell the responsibility of ensuring that from the moment of arrival until the hour of departure and for many months beyond, the Governor General would recall his visit to Dibrugarh as one of the highlights of his residency.

If all went to plan, he and his full entourage would arrive by train, the first passengers to set foot on the small platform at Dibrugarh station. And that is precisely what occurred. As anticipated, all day the streets were crowded. The town awarded itself a public holiday, a white man's 'Fugwa Puja.' Not a leaf was picked and the sheds fell silent as every estate owner or manager for miles around turned out to greet the Governor General up from Calcutta.

Early in the morning, predictably, it rained. By nine o'clock, the streets and surrounding roads were awash. However, no amount of water could dampen the spirits. Carriage after carriage arrived, spilling out ladies in their finest dresses and gentlemen in uniform or formal attire; feathers, top hats, canes and polished boots as far as the eye could see, mindless of mud or wet. By ten, the skies cleared. A band took to the stand on the maidan. The 'Planters Stores' opened its doors to sell paper union jacks on sticks and offered the services of a professional photographer brought up specifically from Calcutta to take souvenirs of the day.

Jack and Marjorie Laws were among the first to pose for the camera. He wore a hat which had not seen the light of day since the Jubilee. She was dressed from head to toe in a violet concoction which according to the catalogue Gerald Dickson had obtained for perusal by all his most favoured customers, was the latest thing in French 'haute couture.' It was absurdly expensive and Marjorie was kept waiting months for its arrival, but she wore it with the pride of a woman blessed with a new child.

Marian was not so fortunate. Her dress was homemade. The bolt of fabric came from the shelves of the 'Planters Stores.' It was plain Navy blue and, presumably in light of the outrageous sums of money Gerald Dickson was earning from those wealthy enough to order their dresses directly from Paris, it was reduced in price to clear. The resulting garment was simple, paid no heed to the fashion of the moment. However, it reminded John of the reason he was originally persuaded to betray his friendship with her husband.

As a gentleman, he offered to act as Marian escort. As a man, however, seeing her for the first time in so many months no longer clothed in black, he took her arm in the hope and expectation that 16 September 1889 might also prove a new starting point for the two of them.

Sadly, if he anticipated an opportunity for romantic overtures, he was to be disappointed.

Every member of 'Clan Dunn' was under orders. Trevelyan Dunn was not in Dibrugarh to waste time on celebrations or involve his family in revelry. To Norman Bayden fell the task of administration. He would meet the Governor General, guide him through the day, see to his needs and control the agenda.

But as the single most powerful land owner in the region, the largest employer and self-appointed leader of the community, to Trevelyan himself was gifted the greatest prize. He was to receive the Governor General at the grand banquet laid on in his honour. He would deliver a second, more elaborate speech of welcome than that offered by a rather tongue-tied Norman Bayden. Then, he would sit at the right-hand side of the Governor at the top table in the huge marquee which had been erected on the polo ground to accommodate all those invited to take bread in the presence of the man designated as Her Majesty's ruler in India.

It was the moment Trevelyan Dunn had worked for all his life and he expected every member of his family to play their part. Originally when planning the day, a polo match was proposed as perfect entertainment. However, with no other suitable area of open flat ground available to hold both marquee and the many carriages which would otherwise have congested the centre of town, this scheme was cancelled. Consequently, John and Philip were denied the opportunity to promote the family name through their sporting prowess. The only alternative was to ensure that all three sons stayed close to their father throughout the day, attracting attention to themselves by weight of numbers.

There were to be no excuses for absenteeism. As much as John would have liked to use the occasion as a renaissance for his relationship with Marian, a relationship he had kept on hold for a long time and in direct contradiction to his wishes, it was not to be. As a gentleman he was given licence to act as chaperone, but his duty to family was made plain and what his father failed to impress upon him by command, his mother achieved through more gentle persuasion.

Consequently, Marian found herself attached to the Dunn party throughout, tolerated she suspected, rather than accepted as a welcome addition to the family. Much to her disappointment, in accepting John as escort, she was denied the liberty to roam freely, to enjoy the carnival atmosphere.

As hot as it was by midday, the streets of the town were full. There was noise and laughter and music. There were many faces in the crowd who Marian recognised but many more she did not and all the while, keeping close to John, she obeyed not the impulse to join in but the acquired obligation to be alert, on show, a part of the community but not a part of the general mass gathered to enjoy the day.

Finally, the moment arrived which everyone had been waiting for. In the distance, some way down the newly laid track, an anonymous figure spied a thin pall of smoke rising into the warm air. A cry went up and people surged forward on to the modest platform, leaving as many still out on the streets unable to get near to where the train came to rest.

A small grand stand had been erected on a spot designed to coincide with the rear door of the Governor General's private train. It was festooned with red white and blue bunting and swathed in sashes. At each corner union jacks flew, the light breeze not sufficient to open them fully. And on said dais, in strict order of importance and rank, were seated all those singled out for special attention by the Governor General.

Jerry Hugo was denied a place, but Norman Bayden was there. So too was the commissioner, AHW Bentinck and the Reverend Thomas Powell who for this one day had forsaken his pulpit in favour of an alternative but equally elevated position. Dr Patrick Murphy also apparently merited a place among the great and good of Dibrugarh and, although too far separated from Marian for an exchange of words, was one of the few to extend her a smile of greeting. However, with no fewer than six seats reserved for the Dunn party at the front of the stand, there was no mistaking the most prominent family in Dibrugarh.

The commissioner himself was dressed entirely in white and sported a helmet embellished with much gleaming brass and an explosion of proud white plumes. His wife stood beside him. She was a wafer-thin, generally genial woman whom Marian had met but once and then only briefly at a garden party to which she and Jonathan were invited when she was well into her second pregnancy. In direct contrast, she was a monument to understatement, her dress clearly selected to prevent any chance of her outshining her husband. It was pale grey, unpretentious and, to Marian's mind, did not suit at all the bubbling, friendly personality she recalled from their previous meeting. However, a veritable regiment of Dunn's vied for position of most prominence.

At the best of times, Trevelyan Dunn had few kind words for the commissioner. 'Pompous old fart' was his favourite term for him, one for which he was reprimanded every time he voiced it in the company of ladies, something he appeared to do, presumably for effect, whenever the opportunity arose. 'Petty civil servant' and 'bumbling bureaucrat' were two other expressions used to deflate the poor man.

Unfortunately, the commissioner was not a planter. He was an appointee of the crown, a man immediately met with suspicion on account of the little practical knowledge he had of the region while being gifted with enormous influence over it and almost everything that went on within it. This was a travesty all Dunn's found intolerable, but Trevelyan Dunn in particular. Consequently, Mr Bentinck was endured on sufferance and, if absolutely necessary, pandered to, only on the grounds of what might be prised from him of later advantage.

Whether he was aware at any time of the manner in which he was played like a fish on the line by the sly elder Dunn, Marian doubted. And, as much as it went against the grain for her to find a position of accord with her favourite adversary, she was bound to agree that the commissioner was a particularly ineffectual character, a man more absorbed by the importance of his position than the benefit his good administration of the office might bring. However, the real power in India was wielded by the Governor General and it was truly awesome. A monarch in all but name alone, he held absolute sway, both in life and death over a population larger than all other countries within the empire added together.

Nominally Lord Lansdowne was answerable to Her Majesty and her government in London. In reality he was unfettered. He reigned supreme. When abroad from Calcutta he expected and was given the rites of passage reserved exclusively for Royalty. His title was never in dispute, his position incontrovertible and a mere commissioner the like of AHW Bentinck, regardless of his own self-importance, faded into insignificance beneath the shadow of single man with such monarchical powers and presence.

Somewhat pitiful therefore was the sight of a commissioner, so bent on emulation and anticipation of similar respect from the 'subjects' within his puny domain. Nevertheless, that was the measure of Mr Bentinck. Beguiled by his own ego, he was as irritating to the likes of Trevelyan Dunn as he was pitiful to witness and was, at every available opportunity, fair sport for ridicule or to be taken advantage of.

Mrs Bentinck, eventually became Lady Bentinck as reward presumably for her quiet endurance of a husband no woman truly deserved. She was aware of his foolishness and the mirth he inspired. Frequently she went the extra mile to compensate, apologising all too often for any inconvenience their presence might have caused to whichever community they descended upon, never failing to ingratiate herself with anyone generous enough to pay her heed.

As a consequence, she was generally liked. Ever grateful for hospitality freely given, she professed the memory of an elephant, particularly with regards to the names of those who had extended the hand of friendship.

For once therefore, Marian found herself favouring the tea man. Trevelyan Dunn was a ruthless ogre, a dominant, domineering and crude dictator who under normal circumstances she found it hard not to stomach. Yet she could not deny his achievements or those of his father before him. Undeterred by disease or hardship and scornful of any opposition from bureaucracy, father first and then son had established in Assam a modest kingdom of their own. For that alone, if not the means necessarily, but for the sheer courage and determination to succeed, Marian did respect Trevelyan Dunn and recognised his right to be at the head of the line for those to greet the Governor General.

As the train drew in, the crowd roared with delight. A great cheer went up and the band of the combined 1st, 2nd and 8th Gurkhas struck up; 'Land of Hope and Glory.' Then Lord Lansdowne himself stepped from the seclusion of his private carriage out into the midday sun and on to a tiny platform at the rear of the train which was surrounded on three sides with a low, gilded guard rail.

The national anthem was played. Everyone stood to attention. The singing was as rousing as it was filled with emotion, every voice raised in grand unison if not in perfect harmony.

When it was done, three cheers were raised with hats aloft. It was a moment to be remembered or savoured to varying degrees. For Norman Bayden it was the culmination of years of planning and hard work. A railway man through and through, the arrival of the Governor General's personal train along a comparatively short length of track conceived, planned and executed as a direct result of his endeavour, was the sweetest sight he could imagine. It was a personal triumph one of which and for which he was entitled to swell with pride. His reward was an introduction to the Governor General, his wife and members of his immediate staff. In time, his efforts would be recognised further afield. Though he did not know it, this his 'piece de resistance' of a career in the Indian Civil Service begun as a lowly clerk at the age of fourteen, would earn him a Knighthood.

Trevelyan Dunn would have welcomed a similar honour. However, though his ego was large enough to feast upon the idea, he was, if nothing else, a realist. He was a commercial man, a man of substantial wealth and power, but not the kind of man to merit the attention of the crown. This day, this grand celebration of Dibrugarh's and therefore his own success after a lifetime's work, was to be the sum of his reward.

When his turn came, he shook hands with the Governor General. Verity Dunn curtsied and then one at a time he introduced his sons, John, Philip and Terence in order of age and, as it happened, stature. Finally, and only she suspected because of her proximity to his eldest son, Trevelyan invited Lord and Lady Lansdowne to meet Mrs Jonathan Cole, widow of the late, Major Jonathan Cole.

Quite against her wishes, this caused a pause in the proceedings. Though the general clamour made for difficult conversation and, by necessity therefore, it was brief, Lady Lansdowne hesitated in her progress to single Marian out for particular attention. She offered her own personal condolences for the loss of her husband, assuring Marian that her late husband's valour was not only a credit to the nation but had been duly recognised by the Governor General in Calcutta and by Her Majesty in London.

This was something of a repeated assurance, one Marian had been offered previously. Nevertheless, coming as it did directly from the lips of Lady Lansdowne herself, she appreciated the gesture the more.

Of course, she was somewhat embarrassed to be singled out. Her intention had been to remain low key, enjoying the day and perhaps viewing it as a beginning to a future as yet undetermined. She had no wish to steal Dunn glory.

Therefore, as modestly as she was able, she accepted the commendations from the Governor General's bejewelled consort. With some embarrassment she hoped interest in her would switch quickly to someone more deserving, for though she would have been churlish to resent such complimentary attention, being introduced to a pairing of such eminence meant less to her than to others within her immediate vicinity.

The moment was soon gone, however. Generous were the words and gracious the sympathy. Marian was in no doubt however that both the Governor General and his wife would have preferred to be elsewhere. This was no grand Durbar. In terms of entertainment fit for a Governor General, the best Dibrugarh had to offer was modest. Yet, the significance of the day was not to be underestimated. Lord Lansdowne had been sufficiently briefed in advance of the occasion, with regard to trade and defence of the empire, that he appreciated fully the potential of a rail link so far to the north.

His presence was acknowledgement enough of the facts, even though the banners, bands and bunting were more home spun perhaps than he was used to. Rail link or not, Dibrugarh was a long way from the elegant avenues and sophisticated galas of Calcutta or Delhi and a world away from the luxury of his private residence in Darjeeling.

However, practice, patience, and perhaps even a certain acquired attitude of resignation, disguised either tedium or disappointment. Whether or not the present Governor General was an effective ruler or accomplished politician, history alone would later decide, but from what Marian saw of him during the course of his sojourn in Dibrugarh he appeared to be an accomplished manipulator of good will.

Later in the day, Trevelyan Dunn gave an emotive speech, too long possibly and with one reference too many to the achievements of his own family rather than the general efforts of a whole community. Much of it also was a competent rendition of words quite obviously composed by his more literate wife. But it was well received.

The Governor General listened or appeared to listen, nodding his head sagely from time to time. Meanwhile, those in the crowd close enough to hear applauded their approval as each milestone of achievement in the life of Dibrugarh was retold.

When he was finished, Trevelyan Dunn called for three more cheers and with a seemingly impossible feat of magic assumed a stature which had him towering over every soul turned out for the day. He exploited his moment in the sun to its fullest.

Norman Bayden, the man who had designed and built the Jorhat to Dibrugarh rail link, who had lived the laying of every sleeper and length of track, slipped into the background, his contribution overshadowed by the great planter.

In time, Norman Bayden would receive his Knighthood. His services would be recognised. Trevelyan Dunn's would not. His best hope would be to die with the assurance that his sons and their sons would carry on what he and his own father had begun. His ambition was to have the name Dunn known not only the length and breadth of Assam, but in every drawing room in England. Undoubtedly, Norman Bayden would retire quietly to Tunbridge Wells, his work ended, his knight's ribbons neatly packed away in a box, obscurity companioning his twilight years.

Not so for Trevelyan Dunn. He took to the stage that fine September afternoon already as convinced as was possible of his own immortality. No quarter was given to rank. He moved with the ease of a man who had rehearsed for just such an event all his life.

To the vast majority of those assembled at the new Dibrugarh station, sight alone of the Governor General and his famously elegant wife was enough to make it a day to remember. But Trevelyan Dunn was the equal of any Governor General. Rank or title impressed him not a jot. If he gave his respect at all, it was to a man, or woman, and very few were women, who could match him in stamina, effort and achievement. Plumed hats and any number of aids or equerries were not sufficient to have him bend low.

He knew well the reputation of Lord Lansdowne and he knew only too well the power at his fingertips. But in itself, that was not enough. He introduced himself not as a subordinate but as if the two of them shared the same pedestal; not the most diplomatic approach but the only way he knew.

Not in any sense of the word could Trevelyan Dunn be defined as a man of diplomacy; forthright yes, frank always, a man not to beat about the bush or shirk from stating his mind. It made for an odd pairing. A peer of the realm, a man appointed to the highest office by command of the Queen Empress herself, a man used to subservience, absolute obedience and, in his presence, just a little fear, found himself face to face with a rugged, ruthlessly ambitious buccaneer who scorned all authority and despised officialdom.

Marian watched in fascination. At any minute she expected if not sparks, then at the very least what might be described in diplomatic parlance as 'tension.'

She studied their coming together in the hope that her diary pages would swell with the electricity of conflict when later she sat down to write.

The day, the event, the hour, they were all worthy of record. However, setting aside the pomp, the ceremony and the general hurrah of celebration, the subtle contest of wit between a Governor General and a warrior planter absorbed her attention to the point where she scarcely noticed the constant and close proximity of her escort for the day.

At one point, mid-way through the Governor General's after-dinner response to the three official welcomes he received respectively from Norman Bayden, Trevelyan Dunn and the never brief AHW Bentinck, a man whose speeches were well known to be as featureless as the vast acreage of grouse moors he held in the Scottish Highlands, John took hold of Marian's hand.

It was achieved rather clumsily, as if to take hold of the gloved hand of a woman was for him a novelty. However, although John had fathered her child and on many occasions during their ill-timed and quite inexcusable affair made love to her, an act of physical union he performed with the natural ability of a man well practiced at the same, to hold her hand seemed an accomplishment of excruciating difficulty. Consequently, it was the performance of said task rather than the act itself which momentarily diverted Marian's attention from the more absorbing drama of Trevelyan and Lord Lansdowne coming head-to-head. Like a modern-day gladiatorial contest, both opponents were highly skilled. However, their techniques, weaponry and understanding of the rules of engagement were poles apart. It was a fascinating conflict which, in the end, produced no outright winner and was spoilt only by the distraction of John's flawed attempt at affection.

Soon after dark, with some hullabaloo, Lord and Lady Lansdowne took their leave of the town, presumably to spend the night aboard their private train, the accommodation therein and thereon considered by all concerned rather better than anything Dibrugarh had to offer. They took with them their aids and all the paraphernalia deemed so essential to a successful progress beyond Calcutta.

Fewer in number therefore, but no less celebratory in mood, the remaining throng continued their revelries long into the night. General festivities and private parties lit up the night sky and kept awake the jungle wildlife into the early hours. Few occasions in the history of Dibrugarh could have been feted with so much vigour or by so many people at the same time.

For every inhabitant of Dibrugarh and tea gardens for miles around, it was a day and night beyond anything that had gone before, even a Golden Jubilee. And for Marian, it was certainly one to place prominently in the pages of her diary, a quite extraordinary episode in a life already made remarkable by events of the previous three years.

She returned to Shahjan comparatively early. Impatient to see her daughter and nervous of the subtle but evident change in John's approach towards her, she resisted the chorus of complainants who would have had her stay.

John wanted the carriage brought so he could return with her. However, Marian was adamant he should not. Instead, she took her leave of the party at the same time as the Laws, availing herself of their kind invitation to bring her home, making for themselves in the process a considerable detour.

Jack Laws was weary. He complained several times of it, so much so Marjorie eventually bid reluctant farewells to her circle, the three of whom besides Marian were embroiled at the time with her in a rubber of bridge. Quite how or why in the middle of such general mayhem they determined on playing cards was a mystery. In the club that evening, in the huge marquee on the polo ground and around the streets of Dibrugarh there was not a single quiet alcove suitable for such an activity. Nevertheless, undeterred by noise or jostle, the ladies were seen to be dealing cards.

Consequently, poor Jack was ready and waiting for departure. Marian's desire to return home therefore served as a convenient lever for him to pry his wife from the game.

As they drove away from the lights of the town, the noise of celebration followed them. Somewhere, many miles down the newly laid track, the Governor General's train was heading back towards Calcutta. By morning Dibrugarh would have had its moment. For weeks there would be little else talked about. Eventually wagging tongues would return to gossip of relationships and rumours of relationships, of fashion, of the weather and general tittle tattle, much of which would be either brought to Marjorie's attention or instigated by her.

However, not so 16 September. That night the parties large and small went on until dawn. That night there was no gossip. There was just a general hoorah for the success of a community built upon the pluck and determination of a small colony of English men and women, thousands of miles from home. It was a night for pride and revelry and both were indulged to the full.

Wet roads and darkness meant a journey of over an hour in the carriage before reaching Shahjan, ample time for Jack to shut his eyes and fall asleep. Meanwhile Marjorie ran through a long list of all the people she had spoken to during the course of the day. She retold the gist of each conversation and speculated as to the intimacies of various new liaisons. Not the least of these was that of a young Jerry Hugo, swept into the net cast so skilfully by Miss Julia Fenton for which Marjorie insisted upon expressing her frank objections and her views as to its likely outcome.

Marian was in no mood for discussions, but she complied, avoiding firm commitment but at least admitting a certain scepticism as to the prospects for Jerry and Julia. Marjorie of course was more forthright. She was in no doubt that in short time there would be wedding bells in the air; either that or one of the two would find themselves alone on a ship bound for home shores. Quite obviously, to Marjorie anyway, it was a union headed directly for the most jagged of rocks. Disaster could not be avoided. One of them, and she suspected Jerry, was destined for a broken heart.

Miss Fenton, Marian was convinced, failed in so many areas. She was possessed of a most unforgiving ego. She was selfish, spoilt and, worse still, blind to her own failings. But of all her many faults, a whimsical interest in members of the opposite sex was the least attractive.

Much of what Marjorie expressed, Marian agreed to, either in part or full. However, her thoughts were on another relationship altogether, namely that of herself and the newly attentive John Dunn. His behaviour throughout the day was discreet, as, by definition, it needed to be. Nevertheless, his actions and attentions were enough to set alarm bells ringing for Marian and have her in a state of such confusion that speculation as to the eventual outcome of the Hugo v Fenton battle of strength and or endurance were of minor interest.

At Shahjan she said her farewells to the sleepy Jack and animated Marjorie as quickly as their kindness in bringing her so far out of their way would allow. Before going to bed, she looked in on Emma who was wide awake and restless. Cradled in her mother's arms however, she soon dosed off, returning to her cot unawares. Marian then sat out on the veranda for a while.

With fewer than usual mosquitoes pestering, but with the evening air sultry, it was pleasant enough, the quiet a welcome relief after the crash and clamour of the day. Mindful of the watershed her life had reached, she stared into the distance. It was too dark to make out the lines of planting. All she could see with any certainty was a soft sea of tea bushes to the forefront of her view. Away in the distance, right and left, the cultivation was brought up short against a black cliff face where the jungle began. From deep inside there were strange, eerie sounds, night hunters on the prowl, their prey sending out distress calls, some too late.

To Marian, Shahjan was Marian. In spite of all that had happened to her, in spite of the alien landscape, uninviting climate and the times when her heart longed to be anywhere else but Assam, for more reasons than she could number, she had never been happier.

If she had joy in her life, it was Emma, if woe it was the knowledge that the father of her child was not the man who most deserved to be so. Opening the pages of her diary, she began to write, the oil lamp on the table in front of her casting a weak light over the blank vellum.

'Great celebrations today. Lord Lansdowne came to open our new railway. All went off well. Trevelyan stole the show as we all knew he would. Certainly, a day to remember. Weather started poor but improved by mid-morning. My boots and the bottom of my dress got a bit muddy, but it was the same for everyone. John escorted me. He could not have been more attentive. I wish Jonathan were here to advise me; better still Papa. Is life so confusing or do I just make it seem so?'

Chapter Twenty-Four

Between the end of September and the first days of December, two events of significance occurred in Dibrugarh which extinguished finally what until then had been almost incessant telling and retelling of the day Lord Lansdowne came to call. For weeks after the event, all conversation revolved around that one day. Every detail was talked about, examined and dissected until the carcass was reduced to nothing but bare bone; every dress commented upon, every hand held scrutinised for clues to something more, every social 'faux pas' explored until even the jungle creatures themselves tired of the chatter.

Finally, halfway through October, came what proved to be a pivotal moment. An initial piece of news served to derail the stale cargo of gossip. Premature perhaps, but not without an accompanying chorus from those who had always suspected as much, Jerry Hugo announced that he and Miss Julia Fenton were betrothed.

Conveniently, Jerry set to one side his original motive for taking 'home leave' in Assam. He also appeared content finally to abandon for good those feelings for Marian which, at one time, though not openly admitted, were as plain as daylight. Instead, he professed a deep and irrevocable love for a young woman recognised not only for her uncanny ability to entice men into such declarations, but her rather too obvious delight in spurning the same.

That Jerry had fallen under Julia's spell was neither novel nor surprising. This was not the stuff to make tongues wag. The novelty, and it was sufficient enough to have tongues wagging considerable distances from Dibrugarh, lay in Julia's own sudden commitment. Formerly, she was rarely out of the company of some fawning suitor or other. In that, she was both conscientious and dextrous. However, her sincerity, or, more appropriately, lack of it, was where her reputation lay. All too often soft words spoken one day turned to stone the next. Like a spider she set her web to ensnare, only to cast aside whichever victim strayed too close to her sticky bonds of silk.

How and why Jerry seemed to have succeeded in securing her hand where so many others had failed was therefore the subject of intense debate. It served as a long overdue alternative to what was in danger of becoming a perpetual need to describe and re-describe the details of Lady Lansdowne's Parisian dress or her husband's inordinately large retinue.

Marian herself was more perplexed than intrigued. Jerry's sudden display of emotional fickleness caught her by surprise. News of his engagement served only to heighten her sense of disorientation, leaving her strangely hurt. She had never returned his affection when it was offered. During their time together travelling from Bombay to Landi Kotal she considered it her duty to dampen his ardour. And at their parting, three years before, Marian resisted the wounded look in his eyes, cruelly sending him on his way to the mountains of Waziristan with not an inkling of hope to warm the chill nights.

Yet, somehow and in a way she found quite curious, news of his engagement to Julia Fenton was not a happy event. Neither did it give her the sense of relief she should have found. Of course, it was not expected in the first place. She did not imagine for one moment Julia would change her ways for a man like Jerry. He was so clearly not her equal in the sport of love. In that particular skill, she towered over him like a colossus. Her knowledge of the game and her ability to circumvent the rules at will were so much more honed than his.

And yet, it came to pass. The engagement was made public and the bands were read. General opinion predicted disaster, with Jerry regretting bitterly the day he set his sights on the wayward Miss Fenton.

None of this was said to his face, of course. Instead, many congratulatory messages reverberated through the planter community, until, with what seemed suspiciously like a concerted effort to appear unanimously enthusiastic, everyone expressed their good wishes.

Of course, to a certain extent opinions may have been swayed by the fact that in Dibrugarh marriages were comparatively few and far between. Indeed, when they did occur, they usually merited something of a 'to do,' so disproportionate was the imbalance in the ratio of men to women.

The white population of Assam, indeed the whole of British India was predominantly male. Consequently, reservations or not, mostly smiling faces and hearty applause was the norm to greet news of such uncommon events. The union of Jerry Hugo and Miss Julia Fenton might have seemed incongruous on paper but after the initial shocked abated, it was welcomed. More than that and regardless of any misgivings, it was used as an excuse for a mood of good cheer.

Even Marian, forever perplexed by the sudden reversal in Jerry's affections and the rapid development of his new relationship, determined to set aside her immediate feelings of regret at such a contract. Instead, she tried to join in with his pleasure at the prospect of winning a wife and, as he put it, 'such a corker at that.' Many times, he begged Marian's confirmation that Julia was one of the most attractive of girls.

This was never in doubt. Not a soul questioned that Julia was blessed with qualities to attract beyond most of her peers. Allied to that was a definite animal magnetism and poise, both of which were wont to have heads turn in her direction the moment she entered a room.

However, such pleading on Jerry's part betrayed a lack of diplomacy in demanding of Marian repeatedly such firm assurances as to the better qualities of another woman.

Unfortunately, he was equally prone to seek confirmation of Julia's many other, finer points; her wit, her intellect, her integrity. Such conversations placed Marian on the horns of a dilemma. While she had no desire to deflate Jerry's ardour or appear spiteful, she found it difficult to exude confidence in some of the many virtues Jerry claimed for his fiancé.

Deft avoidance of anything too emphatic was her best technique. However, Jerry was nothing if not persistent. He gave the impression that without full sanction from Marian, his future happiness was in jeopardy. Time after time, he approached her on the subject, imploring clear, unqualified support for his cause, as if without it there was some doubt as to the likelihood of the wedding ever taking place.

Fortunately, but in a twist of fate she would have extolled heaven itself to be without, any question of Marian's sincerity on the topic of Julia Fenton and the forthcoming marriage between herself and Jerry was put on hold. Her obviation was rewarded, but in the worst possible way.

Suddenly, with absolutely no pre-warning, but with the most devastating impact, Jack Laws died. Returning home one Wednesday evening November, after watching polo with his friends and enjoying perhaps one whiskey too many in the club bar, he sat out on his veranda to enjoy the last rays of the sun and a cup of his own Pekoe tea. A few minutes later, Marjorie left off from the rearranging of her linen closet to join him. When she found him, his tea was untouched and he appeared asleep. But he was not. The tiredness of which he had complained for so many of the previous weeks, had claimed him, the sleep into which he sank permanent.

After that, talk of weddings seemed trite, no matter who's they were. Jack Laws was adored by his wife to the point of distraction. More than that however, he was loved and respected by the whole community. His sudden and untimely passing cast a dark shadow. Like a black cloth spread across the countryside, news of his death engulfed everyone with whom he had come into contact during his half century in Assam.

As if parched and dried by the sun, Marjorie shrivelled. Naturally she turned to Marian for support. Selflessly, Marian complied, eager to repay just a little of the kindness and understanding shown by Marjorie during her own dark hours. But though she was dedicated to the task and deeply affected by the pain of Jack's going, she was all but helpless to serve her friend.

Marjorie was beyond consolation. She was beyond kind words and deeds. Had a wild creature ripped open her chest and torn out her heart, she could not have suffered more. Husband, lover, father, companion and friend, Jack was the breath of life to her. Without him there was no oxygen, nothing to sustain her. As the final gasp left his body so her own suffocation began.

Try as she might, Marian was helpless to ease the agony of Jack's passing. She brought no relief because there was no relief to bring. Inside Marjorie died the same night as her husband. In person, she lingered on. As a physical being, the pathetic ghost of a half woman, she moved and breathed, but there was nothing left. She withered away. Like the discarded shell of a crab, she was whole but empty.

There was of course a funeral. Modestly planned, it was not destined to remain that way. No one could have guessed, not least Marjorie herself, how many people valued the memory of Jack Laws. They came into town from far and wide, determined to pay their respects.

In life, he was a quiet, self-effacing man. Marian remembered most his generosity and good humour. Happy for the most part to stand beside his wife, on the surface at least the less dominant of the two, Jack rarely involved himself in controversy, apparently content to let the likes of Trevelyan Dunn lay claim to centre stage.

Self-evidently however, he was a man of character and courage. Every 'maund' of tea produced at Mancotta, every tree felled to prepare the land, every timber laid to erect his home, bore his sweat. His ambitions were never as grandiose perhaps as others and consequently his achievements not as conspicuous. Set against estates like Kurmi, Mancotta was modest, its output not enough to merit its own label, the harvest pooled with other smaller estates to yield a hybrid tea for the general palate.

Yet, and it was a yet surely the envy of many who attended his funeral, foremost among the inventory of his wealth was the enormous respect in which he was held as a man.

It was cold on the morning of his funeral. During the night it rained heavily, rendering the roads in many places almost impassable. And yet they came, filling St Thomas' church, raising the roof in song and thanking God for Jack Laws brief spell on earth.

Marian sat with Marjorie throughout the service. AHW Bentinck read a passage from the New Testament and then, of all people, Trevelyan Dunn stood to give the eulogy, after having already been one of eight to bear the coffin.

Trevelyan was not a man of letters or reading. Therefore, his words bore little embellishment or metaphor. Nevertheless, and as surprising as it was for Marian witness a Dunn stand up to give such an address in the first place, he spoke with genuine warmth and affection of a man who, in life, he was seen to treat, if not as a rival, then as something of an irrelevance to his own unstoppable march.

In the true sense of the word, he and Jack were not friends. Trevelyan would have been the first to admit as much. They were equals, men of similar spirit, pioneers in a hostile corner of the empire. But as men, they were dissimilar in too many ways to be close. No matter. There was mutual respect and with that respect came a degree of affection.

In the end, it was a simple speech, spoken simply. Not a member of the congregation doubted the sincerity of his words or the relevance to their own feelings for the man. Trevelyan himself was both loved and despised with equal vehemence and, on balance, Marian supposed, most would have chosen the latter. On the other hand, with the exception of his wife and immediate family, Jack Laws was neither loved with any great passion nor hated with any bile. Because of his quiet almost secretive nature, few people knew him well enough to do either. For all those who came to his funeral service however, there was the unmistakable desire to express a deep sense of loss at his going. They knew they were saying goodbye to a good man.

Had Marjorie counted heads she might have taken some comfort. But she did not. For the duration of the service, she sat head bent low, tears beneath her dark veil, blurring her vision. And when finally came time for the blessing, she let out a cry so pitiful not a soul could doubt her desolation.

More useless than she had ever felt in her life, Marian took Marjorie's arm as they processed from the church to the small patch of consecrated ground prepared to receive the coffin. Marjorie did not falter. Proud to the last, she saw it through, erect but broken, accepting words of condolence but not hearing them.

And afterwards, there was no wake. The club bar stayed closed. From far and wide they came to pay their last respects. Then as quietly and unobtrusively as they arrived, they dispersed. Few lingered to catch up on old news or reacquaint themselves with old friends. So sombre the mood, so sad the occasion, there was no room for anything but reflection.

Marian was in the carriage with Marjorie, ready to draw away. Before they could, however, Trevelyan approached.

'Your husband was a fine man,' he said to Marjorie through the carriage window. 'Assam will be the poorer for his going,' he added, stating in a few words the sentiment of everyone present. Then he turned and the carriage pulled away.

Ten days later, noticing she had not risen for her usual early breakfast on the veranda, Marjorie's bearer entered the bedroom and found her lifeless body. Beside the bed was an almost empty glass of water and a small box which had once contained a quantity of laudanum sachets, none of which remained.

She left no note. None was necessary. Her love for her children and grandchildren was well known. To leave them in such a manner would have been an ordeal almost beyond endurance. But without, Jack there was nothing in life to sustain her.

Marian was shocked and distressed by the news, but not surprised. On their way home from Jack's funeral Marjorie had stayed silent, the shadow of death even then upon her shoulders There were no words Marian could say, no deeds she could perform to rid her friend of that permanent veil. Her faith was strong. Aside from Marian's own mother and the rather exaggerated piety of her younger sister, Marjorie displayed a devotion to the Christian ideal unequalled by any other woman she had met. Yet, even that was not enough. So great was her loss, so utter the devastation of Jack's withdrawal from the world, there was little alternative but that she attempt to join him.

Her funeral, all too soon after that of her husband, was a more modest affair, attended only by those more intimately connected. Jack was a planter. Over a period of fifty years the list of his acquaintances was many and spanned considerable distances. Marjorie, was merely a wife. That said, she was also a devoted mother. Sadly, her children had chosen for themselves careers and marriages in voluntary exile far from Mancotta and the intimate circle of friends to which Marjorie had laid claim was small.

However, as many as could attended her graveside, save the one or two whose moral consciences were pricked, finding it impossible to condone by their presence an act they believed to be against the will of God. Life was a precious gift. Those who thought to squander it willingly in suicide were not to be applauded.

Fortunately, Marian and sufficient others were not deterred by any such moral dilemma. They included Verity Dunn who in rendering the eulogy, took upon herself the role her husband had adopted with such surprising dignity at the service for Jack. The numbers in attendance were fewer and the weather was not much improved, but the sentiments were similar. Gone from the world in the space of what seemed like a few short days were two people whose contribution to Dibrugarh society could not be measured. So congenial had been their manner, so quietly generous their friendship, so measured the belief of their own importance, Assam itself was a poorer place for their passing.

In quieter moments, moments Marian noticed occurring and reoccurring all too often, fond memories of Jack and Marjorie lingered long. Recollections of them hung on the senses like the soft perfume of jasmine in the evening breeze, giving pleasure with every inhalation.

For many weeks afterwards, at irregular intervals, she rode to Mancotta. There she would sit on the veranda, looking down across the estate, imagining Jack and Marjorie at her side, the three of them taking tea together from porcelain cups decorated with rose petals. Possibly because her own parents were so far off, so much a memory rather than a presence, Marian missed the company and affection of two people who, in their own way, she had come to look upon as surrogate mother and father.

The bungalow was closed up, blind to the fate awaiting it. No one knew what would become of Mancotta. Surely it and the estate were willed to their eldest son. But he was in England and unlikely, it was thought, to return to Assam for his inheritance. In the interim work on the estate continued. John took upon himself the day-to-day management, unwilling to watch a lifetime's work by a man he respected, through want of care, revert to jungle. Picking for the season was drawing to a close when Jack died. With Marjorie's death the leaf sheds fell silent. All that remained for John to oversee was the packing and dispatching to the market in London, a task for which a handful of coolies only were needed. Over winter there was still much to be done and it remained to be seen what would become of the estate before the following spring.

Though she missed terribly both Jack and Marjorie and found it difficult to come to terms with their absence, from a purely selfish point of view, Marian loved the strange solitude of an almost deserted Mancotta. It was a place of great sadness where once there had been a quiet atmosphere of joy. Nevertheless, isolated from the rest of the world, she found tranquillity there. Her visits became more frequent, the time spent mostly in reflection, gazing out across the garden into the distance.

When she had first arrived in Assam everything seemed so clear, so straight forward. She and Jonathan were intent on making a life for themselves. With optimism they set about the task of laying the foundations of a future. At times she missed home. There were days when waves of longing washed over her, thoughts of her father, her family and the sights and sounds of London, colouring grey an otherwise perfect sky. Sometimes the discomfort of life in the tropics weighed heavily; dripping water inside the bungalow, rats racing through the rafters, mysterious bouts of illness which came and went with little warning but considerable vehemence. There were even periods, short though they were and inspired as they were by tragic events which had overtaken her, when she loathed the name Shahjan.

Yet, above it all, there was a sense of purpose, the like of which Marian had not felt in a long time. With Jonathan at her side there was tangible meaning to life. Dibrugarh was a long way from home. It was an alien environment with little promise of easy or graceful living. Every civilising influence was hewn as if from rock. And yet, she was at ease. Not in love, but finding love for the man she had encountered by accident on the other side of the continent, she had no regrets. She looked to their future with the same excitement and pleasure she recalled as a child when her father returned home after a business trip abroad to the midlands.

And for some time, there was little interruption to that mood, little to dampen her spirits. Home sickness, like so many other ages, came and went in short bouts, unpleasant but endured, a small price to pay for the luxury she and her husband had found together and the life they were building for themselves at Shahjan.

Steadily, as if part of some carefully devised plan to destroy what she had, to pull down brick by brick the structure of her new life, fate conspired against her. Losing her first baby was punishment perhaps for complacency. Having to face the truth of Jonathan's death was a test to vex Job himself. And now Jack and Marjorie were gone. The wheel had come full circle. Even her vanity accepted with little pain the disappointment of Jerry Hugos rapid and, to most minds, inexplicable transference of affection.

Back in the summer of 1885, when she arrived in Bombay, it was in the shadow of a deep sadness. In love then, but thwarted by death, she asked nothing of India save consolation. She found instead vibrancy, fascination and colour she had not believed possible. Nothing of her life in London or the provinces prepared her for the novelty or breathtaking allure of everything and everyone she encountered along her route. Caroline Farrer gave hints. Her extravagance mimicked in a strange way the extraordinary varieties and contrasts of life in the Raj.

By the winter of 1889, however, it was all gone. The beauty and solitude of Mancotta was all that remained and it was not enough to eliminate the dark chapters of tragedy which had pursued her so relentlessly. Like a small patch of blue in an otherwise ominous and grey sky, Emma lifted her spirits. She alone inspired her mother to seek hope where the harvest promised little.

Nevertheless, Marian had reached a point of decision. She was a nomad. She had no husband, no home, no place to call her own save an almost forgotten bedroom at 32 Princes Gate, a room she had known since infancy, a room which when the door was closed, shielded her like a warm blanket from the coldest winter blast.

More and more, as she sat alone on the veranda at Mancotta, she longed for the sanctuary of that room. More and more the pages of her diary looked back rather than forward. Less and less was her ink devoted to ambitions for the future. And inevitably, as inevitable as the tide turning, came the conclusion that her time in Assam was drawing to a close.

It was not the first time such thoughts monopolised her thinking. At each crisis, the safe haven of 32 Princes Gate, loomed large. But it was the first time she felt herself resigned, all alternatives, as few as they were, uninviting. The beauty of Mancotta would endure. Should the house crumble and the jungle reclaim what had been prised from it, paradise would remain. But it was plastic, a beauty made sterile with the departure of Jack and Marjorie. It invited lonely introspection. In the hands of an artist, it begged to be reborn on canvas with brush and paint. But only a fool would trust themselves into its hands. And Marian was no fool. Day after day she visited. Hour after hour she sat alone, sometimes with Emma playing at her feet, in awe, the stillness a reward she had done nothing to earn. She willed herself to believe the deceit that within the silence lay protection from decisions she might postpone but from which she could not escape.

'Marry me,' said John as he sat down beside her.

Knowing where she was, knowing the ritual and reason for time spent at Mancotta, he had ridden from Shahjan to be with her. Marian had not expected him. Indeed, she was unaware he knew the location of her solitary vigils. However, she was not offended by his arrival. She barely noticed him dismount from 'Snowden's' back or his broad brimmed hat as he laid it on the table to her right-hand side along with his gloves and crop.

'If you marry me,' he repeated, employing the verb 'to marry' as mundanely as he would 'to sit,' 'to go' or 'to eat,' 'I will buy Mancotta for you and you can make it your home.'

That he should propose marriage to her or any other woman in so matter of fact a manner, as if he were asking the time or commenting upon the weather, was not at all surprising or a matter for rebuke. In any other man it might have given pause for thought. In most, it would have shocked a woman of more fragile sensibilities. In Marian's case, she would have been less than honest if she professed an expectation of anything better.

John was a man like his father, a man of few words, in part because of a directness passed down through the male line and in part because, like his father, he viewed the use of adjectives, hyperbole or metaphor as the flimsy luxury of those with time to fritter.

What Marian was not prepared for, however, was John's apparent willingness to ignore the history of her location. Mancotta belonged to Jack and Marjorie. It was their home. They were gone from it but their spirit lingered on. It was not a property to be bought and sold. It was a home. If she listened hard enough and long enough, she could hear the laughter and sorrow of fifty years. She could see children playing along the foot polished wooden slats on the veranda. Through the windows she could glimpse their faces and smile at the thought of Jack sitting in the same chair John now filled so much more completely. Then she could shed a new tear for the sadness of Marjorie's final desperate act in the bedroom only a few feet behind her.

'No,' she replied. 'I could never live here. Buy it by all means. Do with it what you will. But this could never be my home.'

To the first of his suggestions, the answer was yes.

***

For the second time, as if by some quirk of nature, some whim of fate, Marian married a man with whom she was not 'in love.' On balance there was more about John of which she disapproved than aspects of his character she admired. Furthermore, as much as he was the son of his father and likely to become more so with the progress of time, there was every chance her opinion of him would deteriorate.

His ambition, his occasional ruthlessness and his complete disregard for any virtue which was not tangible or consumable, only served to heighten their obvious differences. Arm in arm they were an unlikely couple, not perhaps as curious as Jerry and Julia, but something of an oddity nevertheless.

However, try as she might, Marian could not escape the inescapable. Nor, for reasons she was at a loss to comprehend, did she want to. Marriage was the last thing on her mind and John, in truth, the least eligible candidate for such a union. Yet, even on the veranda at Mancotta, with her mind on home and her heart heavy, she could not deny the stirrings within her as she became aware of his proximity.

She cursed herself for it; of course she did. Many were the nights, when Jonathan was alive that silently she begged his forgiveness for the weakness of her sex. She knew all too well the depravity of her actions. Guilt flayed her to the bone for having succumbed so readily to carnal desires which, in spite of their consequences, she was unwilling or unable to resist.

And now, with a degree of inevitability she also preferred to deny, John claimed her as his own.

Save for Marjorie, whom Marian hoped had carried with her to the grave information given in strictest confidence, no one in Dibrugarh society knew of their earlier affair. There were those who suggested her period of mourning was

375

shorter than convention would have it, but thankfully they were few. Generally, it was agreed that if Marian was at all premature in taking a new husband, she was prudent in not wasting a moment in securing a father for her daughter. She could only guess at the public reaction were she to make known the awful yet convenient truth that Emma far from gaining by default a different father was finally in receipt of the one to which she was naturally entitled.

Of course, before she could become Mrs John Dunn, a role she looked forward to with the relief of knowing that her future security was guaranteed and some incredulity that she should have volunteered an attachment to a man with whom she had so little in common, there was the small matter of another no less likely joining of hands.

Former Captain, Jerry Hugo, recently appointed Assistant Manager to Sir Norman Bayden, Superintendent of Way and Works of the newly commissioned Dibrugarh to Sadiya Railway, took as his wife Miss Julia Fenton.

She was the elder daughter of Mr and Mrs Horatio Fenton and, it was much rumoured, better acquainted than she might have been with a significant proportion of the unmarried men in the congregation. More scandalous, but still unproven, were tales of her having seduced or been seduced by several of the husbands present at the wedding service, one of whom went by the name of Trevelyan Dunn, Marian's future father-in-law.

Naturally this was all gossip and speculation of the worst kind. Nothing was proven. Nevertheless, the general consensus appeared to be that there was an inordinate amount of smoke for no fire.

At the appropriate moment during the wedding ceremony when the rather too pious Reverend Powell invited any of those present to speak up should there be any just cause or impediment as to why the two prospective candidates placed before him could not be joined in holy matrimony, there was a relieved silence.

On 20 December 1889 therefore, Miss Julia Fenton became Mrs Jerry Hugo and only she knew that the tiny embryo stirring within her was not the result of a joyous union between herself and her husband.

The service itself went well. The reception at the club was modest but attended by a respectable gathering of friends who had taken Jerry to their hearts in the short time since becoming a part of the community.

This might have surprised Jerry, but it came as no shock to Marian. After all, he was one of the most easily likeable people she had encountered during the course of her adult life. Though she was unable to return his affection on the terms he once so often intimated, something which in many ways she regretted, not least because he was a man upon whom she could always have relied, she valued his friendship beyond measure and there were no fake tears at the parting of their ways. She only hoped that when, in the course of time, the hope and optimism of his wedding day turned to dust, as was forecast by all those in attendance, he would not blame or hate her for it.

She could not have married him herself. For convenience yes; had she agreed to marry Jerry rather than Jonathan or John, something she could have done, she would have been assured of attention and affection bearing no bounds. Jerry would have gone to hell and back to provide for her, faced dragons to protect her, sacrificed his own life if needs be to keep her from harm.

But she could not have returned that devotion. In time, and in spite of his protestations to the contrary, his love, unrequited, would have become tainted. He would have become desperate, bitter and filled with resentment. And she would have been rightly blamed for the wanton destruction of a good soul.

In rejecting his advances, in refusing to reward him as he would have wished for the sacrifice made in travelling across a continent to be with her, she realised all too well the hurt she caused. She knew also the sadness in his heart on the day he said 'I do' and 'I will' to a woman who though uniquely attractive and infinitely superior in her talent to seduce, was not the true claimant to his heart. Nevertheless, be his marriage to Julia a success or failure, Marian took comfort in the wisdom that Julia could never wound Jerry to the same degree than had she herself weakened.

Jonathan had survived her infidelity precisely as she knew he would. He coped because while there was love between himself and his wife, there was never that degree of uncontrollable, ruinous passion which, throughout history has been the destruction of so many noble but fragile hearts.

Before Christmas, Jerry left with Julia for a new home in Sadiya and Marian's affection went with him. What would become of them only time would tell. Doubt persisted, but at least Jerry went with the good wishes of all those who knew him, Marian's included. As for herself, with little ceremony, she remained behind at Shahjan to marry John.

When the day came it was overcast but stayed dry and held, as it was, quietly on the south lawn at Kurmi in the presence of a handful of witnesses and well-wishers, attracted little public comment. And, all said and done, Marian was content. It was certainly no punishment. Their love making aroused in her feelings of insatiability beyond anything she imagined as a young woman growing up in London. John was kind too, in his way. He respected her and, as so many outside observers were quick to remark, took to Emma 'as if she were his own.' And Marian wanted for nothing, save perhaps the luxury of intimate conversation. She was quickly distracted from self-pity, however, by the advent of another child in the February of 1890.

How Jerry would come to terms with the disappointment which was bound to follow the initial novelty of having claimed Julia as his wife, Marian could only wonder. He never wrote. He divided his time equally between his work and his wife, conscientious towards both but with only he knowing which of the two yielded the greater measure of satisfaction.

From time to time, news of him filtered back to Dibrugarh. John's enthusiasm for polo introduced him to players from far afield, men who either knew Jerry personally or spoke with others who were in direct contact. One or two bragged they knew his wife rather better than they should and, with more whiskeys inside them than was good for discretion, thought nothing of passing such information on.

However, John did not. He knew Mrs Jerry Hugo. He knew all too well her appetites and her easy inclination for deception. Not once did he doubt that her fidelity to the marriage vows would be as short-lived and as unlikely as a blue moon. But he saw no need to expose Marian to the truth.

To a degree he liked Jerry. John was not the kind of man to have noticed Jerry's infatuation for Marian. He was barely aware of his own emotions. Yet he took no delight in conversations which made mock of another man's pride or self-respect.

Fortune favoured therefore John's ignorance of the fact that Julia's first-born was not welcome evidence of a successful marriage, but of a bastard sister to him. Indeed, it was a secret Julia determined to conceal from her husband and the outside world until such a time as she was presented with the opportunity to exploit so devastating a revelation to its full advantage.

Chapter Twenty-Five

Her Royal Highness Queen Victoria, Empress of India and sovereign to the better part of half the worlds civilised population, breathed her last on 22 January 1901 at the age of 81. Her eyesight was failing and for many months she had suffered from insomnia. It was a little after six in the evening. Her children and grandchildren were at her side, among them the German Kaiser. Within a year of her death, Guglielmo Marconi achieved a wireless transmission in morse code across the Atlantic and in so doing gave birth to a new age of instant communication. However, that January news of the great Queen's death travelled rather more slowly to Dibrugarh.

In Calcutta, Lord Curzon, Viceroy since 1899 was notified as a matter of urgency. An era was at an end. Dangerous uncertainty was bound to follow in the aftermath of a monarch who had been on the throne, unchallenged and with a uniquely personal grasp on the reins of power for more than sixty years.

Those in Dibrugarh and the surrounding countryside were less vital to the political stability of the empire and therefore received the news rather later than in the capital of British India. However, when it reached them, 'Old' Trevelyan Dunn, a few years and months the great Queen's junior, was quick to encourage an understanding of just how momentous an event it was. Barely were the celebrations over for the new century. Indeed, it seemed but a short while since he recalled the festivities for the Diamond Jubilee.

Of course, while still claiming sovereignty over a modest empire of his own, he was an old man, much older if the rapid deterioration of his body was anything to go by. Consequently, John had all but taken control not only of the day-to-day running of Shahjan, but also of Medla, Bollai and Mancotta which he had bought from the executors of the Laws estate as much to please Marian as for its potential profitability.

In addition, to all intents and purposes, he had assumed overall management of Kurmi, something the 'old man' resisted, still choosing to think of himself as master of all he surveyed. However, while in public at least his role was unchallenged, in reality, he was simply too feeble in body and mind to wield the power he once enjoyed.

John managed the estates and made all the significant decisions concerning their future, particularly when it came to selecting the grades of tea grown for home market consumption.

At Medla and Bollai he concentrated on the production of Pekoe No 1 and Pekoe No 2, adding Orange Pekoe and Broken Pekoe, while at Shahjan production was turned over almost exclusively to Pekoe Souchong and Broken Pekoe Souchong. Only rarely did he consult with his father or seek his permission on matters relating to the immediate of future prosperity of the Dunn Tea Corporation. Just as his father had once been, John became sole arbiter of all major policy decisions and practical changes, while also attempting to prove himself a competent father.

Emma was a sparkling young girl, in 1901 fast approaching her fourteenth birthday. With a sea of dark hair and an independence of mind beyond her years, she had a smile to melt the hardest heart. Like her mother, she was intelligent and generous of spirit. She revelled in books, argument and horses, with a particular leaning towards the latter two.

'Young' John was just eleven. Also, a natural and fearless horseman, his favourite occupation was to ride alongside his father around the estates or practice polo with a specially shortened stick. More inclined to mood swings than his elder sister and in that respect very much the son of his father, he showed all the signs of carrying strong Dunn family traits, a prospect which encouraged his mother to fear for the moral welfare of the next generation of Dibrugarh maidens.

Finally, but by no means least, there was Katherine Verity Prunella, Marian's final contribution to the Dunn stable. When news arrived of the great Queen's death, she had just turned eight. Too young to have stamped her mark on the world, she had yet to prove herself. Possibly because she lived in the shadow of elder siblings, she tended towards a reticence not obviously inherited from either of her parents. She was not shy, but quiet. Neither did she brood like her father. Simply, she was self-contained, a child happy with her own company, her interest held by observation of people, places and events rather than active participation with or in them.

In many respects, though the youngest, she regularly appeared the most mature of all three, a thinker rather than a doer, a pragmatist rather than protagonist. While Emma was ready to take on the world to prove a cause, Katherine appeared content to concede a point to maintain the 'status quo.'

Marian loved equally all three of her children. Tested on the matter she would deny vehemently any bias in favour of one. However, secretly, she could not resist that certain vulnerability Katherine seemed to have about her at all times. She was neither frail in body or mind, and yet, there was something in her personality which reminded Marian of her own younger sister, after whom, rather fortuitously, she was Christened.

The younger Katherine was by no means as head strong and, fortunately, displayed a willingness to listen and learn which her namesake had not done at the same age. Nevertheless, there was something about Katherine which bore an uncanny resemblance to her aunt, be it the mischievous gleam in her eye or the knowing smile she employed to get her own way in some small dispute with her mother when logical argument failed.

Of course, there was no doubting the poignancy of losing the old Queen. In England, for many months, the nation mourned in grand unison. The dirge of death was louder and lasted longer than anyone could recall. Heads of state from across the world gathered in London to pay their respects. Vast masses packed Trafalgar Square and along The Mall to glimpse the funeral cortege.

In Dibrugarh, however, by necessity, the daily routine carried on in tandem with the nation's grief. The march of the jungle was ever constant. Let slip an hour and a day's work was needed to regain the time lost. That said, for a required and respectable period, the mood was respectful. Change bred uncertainty and, in Upper Assam, exposed and undefended, uncertainty bred anxiety.

The Queen was dead, long live the king. But gone were sixty years of empire. Gone too was the Queen who, though she never set foot on Indian soil, by name and by name alone kept subjugated hundreds of millions of native Hindus and Moslems all of whom hailed her as the great white memsahib. That subjugation and grudging acceptance of it, maintained and ordered as it was by an absurdly small population of English men and women, had been, for successive generations, a delicate balancing act.

Consequently, in the January of 1901, British rule over India teetered as if on a high wire. The slightest twitch of the wire, gust of wind or, perhaps, the death of a monarch, might just cause it to topple.

Some degree of unrest was inevitable. There was always unrest. The mutiny of 1857, nearly half a century before, was the most extreme example. Then, retribution had been swift and merciless, sending a warning to other would-be mutineers or insurgents. But swift or merciless, it was not enough to quell the most dedicated and sometimes fanatical exponents of 'home rule.'

Hindus and Moslems alike were well used to martyrdom. They courted self-sacrifice. In pursuit of their faith some, the sadhus, were prepared to submit themselves to the most extraordinary acts of self-deprivation or mutilation. Indeed, all native Indians were accustomed to suffering. The harsh reality of their existence was a breeding ground for fanaticism and provided a ready supply of volunteer martyrs.

Pockets of resistance were common place; like the rumblings of a dormant volcano. However, they were usually small, disorganised and readily silenced. Even the Indian National Congress was little more than a forum for disgruntlement. There were no men of passion to lead it, none with the integrity or dedication to bring about real change.

In truth, therefore, men like Trevelyan Dunn were generally able to sleep easy in their beds safe in the knowledge of their own permanence. They celebrated the coming of a new century, mourned the death of their Queen and, in public at least, spoke of continuity, of stability and a fresh, even brighter, age of empire to come. In the privacy of their homes and with their own thoughts, however, they speculated about the coming of the end, of a day yet to dawn when the Union Jack would be torn down, when eight hundred million native Indians would round on their masters and in one voice cry 'no more.'

Not yet though. Not in the year 1900 when flags were raised in joyful celebration or in the January of 1901, when the black of mourning coloured a nation in grief. There was a breeze, barely a zephyr's breath and on the distant horizon, for those willing or able to see, there were dark storm clouds. But in Dibrugarh, life continued on much as it had always done. The Queen was dead. The citizens of Upper Assam marked her passing as befitting to her station and with the affection which was her due.

There was no shirking. Their distance from London was no excuse for lack lustre expressions of grief. Dibrugarh mourned as London mourned, the mood in the valley, for a while, sober and circumspect.

For Marian at least, it was also a time for reflection. In the April of 1901 she was to be forty years old and she felt ready to reflect on her life, to consider its worth. She had a husband, was the mother of three healthy children and, having lived in Assam for more than fifteen years might well have imagined herself settled.

But there was a restlessness. With fresh news arriving each day, describing events in London, she found herself longing for home. She dreamed once more of 32 Princes Gate, of sitting in her bedroom, at her desk by the window, and peering out across the street as she composed the next lines for her diary.

As ever and above all, she missed her father. For years her only contact with him had been through letters. Throughout he continued the same; loving, supportive, frustrated by the antics of his two other daughters and committed, come what may, to the premise that Marian, at least, never would nor could disappoint him.

She also missed her mother, not so vehemently perhaps and not with such frequency, but miss her she did; her uncompromising love, eternal optimism and staunchly held belief that there was good to be found in everyone, even politicians and the clergy, a notion she was wont to use mischievously by way of provoking animated supper table debate on cold winters evenings.

Then there was Margaret who had finally given up her calling to become a missionary in favour of a loveless and, Marian suspected, passionless marriage to a rather successful dentist. He, a somewhat portly gentleman by the name of Cedric Holmes, boasted, it was reported in her father's correspondence with a rather large pinch of salt, that among his patients were the most refined if not necessarily the most healthy teeth in the land. Prime ministers, princes, royal courtiers and a ragtag collection of higher and lower celebrities subjected themselves willingly and regularly to the torture chamber that was his surgery.

Serving tea to acquaintances of her husband whose dental hygiene required radical reform, was a far cry for Margaret from the lifetime of converting heathens which she had once imagined for herself. However, by all accounts, apparently, she appeared happy enough with her lot.

Katie's fortunes had proven themselves less mundane. And, as had always been predicted, they were less fortunate in their conclusion. Unable or unwilling to resist her appetite for adventure, the once Bohemian and romantic promise of an elopement with Mr Kenneth, eventually turned to dust.

With two small children in tow and ever mounting debts which her father finally refused to underwrite, she and her luckless husband removed themselves back to Paris. In the early 90s, under the cover of darkness, they slipped out of Italy, leaving behind a trail of bad debts in their wake.

The excuse was a need to be nearer the new centre of modern artistic influence, an influence which appeared to shift its location in direct sympathy to their indebtedness. Mr Kenneth could not create, could not find the inspiration he required unless encircled by others of a like mind.

Paris apparently was again the place he needed to be. Italy had waned as the Mecca he once supposed. Paris offered asylum and inspiration to artists from across Europe.

For years, the restored 'moulins' of Mont Martre, had played host to painters, writers and intellectuals of every hue. There they mixed cheek by jowl, to drink, be entertained and exchange ideas. Paris was a melting pot and the melting pot was on the boil.

In fact, poor Mr Kenneth was too late, a generation too late. Moreover, he possessed neither the dedication nor talent required of him to join so select a club. His work lacked any ingredients of the novelty he sought so earnestly and others achieved with so little endeavour. His output was negligible, his success and recognition invisible to the naked eye, as invisible almost as the perspective in his few completed canvases. His aims and artistic direction were as abstract as his work, with both being unintelligible to either his trusting but naïve wife or the buying public.

Their move to Paris was a final, desperate attempt to escape a net which, in Italy, was rapidly closing in on them. Creditors were knocking at the door. All other excuses for the move were a figment, a mirage to camouflage the truth.

One truth, however, was all too evident. Mr Kenneth had ceased to care for Katie. His love for her had evaporated. She had become a millstone around his neck, stifling, he claimed in many of his more hurtful outbursts against her, the genius within, suffocating the air of invention in his lungs.

No sooner were they in Paris than he turned his back on her. Their studio, and home, was a miserable affair, discarded by other better artists for its poor light and lack of warmth in winter. It was unkempt and atop a perilous flight of stairs which threatened disaster each time Katie ascended or descended with two small children in tow.

Before long Mr Kenneth employed the services of young female models and before long what success he lacked in sustaining any worthwhile patronage he made up for with a string of mistresses.

Apparently bent on self-destruction he flaunted his infidelities, his studio serving more often as a temple to seduction than a church for the mind. In the end, about the same time as Marian was looking forward with raised hopes to the birth of her third child, the torment for Katie could go on no more. She left her husband. With her two children and a 'loan' from an older, anonymous French woman who claimed to be a patron to Mr Kenneth, willing it appeared to do anything to aid his advancement towards the public recognition he so richly deserved but was being so cruelly denied, Katie caught the boat train back to England.

Where once Margaret remained behind at 32 Princes Gate, the spinster daughter with visions of a future bringing Christ to the unchristian, Katie returned to take her place, the romantic dream she once held now a deflated balloon. There was no divorce. She remained Mrs Kenneth and when pressed declared her husband to be on the verge of great achievement, soon to be formally recognised as the innovative artist he always imagined himself becoming.

In reality, her husband's life was reduced to a sordid round of whores and 'moulins.' He scraped a living with donations of money from grateful female patrons and occasional commissions to paint exotic murals on café and restaurant walls in the less sophisticated quarters of the city. Within a year he was bankrupt, alone and singularly unappreciated in the galleries of Paris. Letters flowed into 32 Princes Gate in rapid succession, begging forgiveness and money. But he received neither. Eventually his correspondence was returned unopened, so insulting to Katie were the contents within.

Over time, news of him dwindled until it ceased completely. Katie got on with the raising of her children without a father, careful to keep them away from brush and canvas lest either show the slightest inkling to pursue an artistic career.

Instead, they were taught mathematics and science, taken to the natural history museum and praised for any interest they showed in things mechanical. They remained strangers to the Royal Academy summer exhibition and were steered away from any appraisal of the plastic arts; a revenge of sorts perhaps.

Such a blinkered education was not as liberal as Katie would have wished. Nor was it in any way a reflection of her own upbringing, but it brought her comfort, that is until news arrived from Paris which though sad, came as no surprise. In October 1896, the body of Mr Giles Kenneth was found on the floor of his studio in the Rue St Germain. A young lady who was to have sat for him made the gruesome discovery. By all accounts he had been dead for several days, the cause of his demise an overdose of narcotics. He left behind him a room full of ineffectual and mostly unfinished work, a wardrobe of well-worn clothes, numerous creditors and, strangely, a half-written letter to his wife demanding once again either her return to Paris or, by way of compensation presumably, a suitable financial donation towards his continued participation in the contemporary art scene.

At the subsequent inquest which Katie did not attend, it was determined that he died accidentally by his own hand. There was no evidence to suggest he took his own life, or that he had any intention of doing so. It was a sorry end and a tragic epitaph to a union which began with such youthful zeal.

Katie's elopement with Mr Kenneth, when she was barely old enough to think for herself, was the cause of considerable embarrassment and consternation to her family. Yet, there was a wide-eyed romanticism to it and a quiet envy from Marian who, at the time, secretly admired her sisters daring and spirit of adventure.

It began with such bold optimism and ended so pathetically. Katie became a widow too young and to a man who had chosen to throw his life away.

She mourned of course. In spite of his ill treatment towards her, she mourned him as a wife should, never letting on to her children or to public scrutiny that in her heart of hearts there was an overwhelming sense of relief. She grieved for him. She was sorry for his lack of recognition as an artist and, in a strange way, she pitied herself. But her release from pain was euphoric. His body interred; he could do her no more harm. The abuse, both emotional and physical, which she had suffered long before their arrival in Paris, was at an end.

On to her shoulders fell sole responsibility for two children, but they were no burden. They were a weight she was already well used to carrying. As a sire, Mr Kenneth was adequate. As a father, however, he was of little practical use. He rarely provided for the table. He preferred instead to survive off the good nature of his father-in-law or certain of his female patrons who were prepared to pay favourably for the time he devoted to them.

Thus, Katie resumed her life at 32 Princes Gate with genuine contrition. She was older and wiser than the day she had chosen to take off for Europe with no consideration for the commotion or hurt her actions provoked. More importantly, with the passing of time, she had learned to take nothing for granted.

Like a prodigal, she conducted herself with the piety expected of a soul in search of absolution, asking for rather than demanding and hoping for, rather than anticipating, full repatriation into the bosom of her family.

Of course, there was but a short delay. Her mother knew no meaning to the word vengeance. She never admitted it openly, but she was bemused when Katie eloped, blaming herself for failing her daughter. But she held no grudge. Having Katie back home, alive, well and with two perfect children, even after so many years of absence, was better than having ten Christmases come at once. There was no need for circumspection, or process of reconciliation. Mrs Chase behaved towards her daughter as if barely five minutes had elapsed since she last went out of the front door. She did not offer forgiveness because in her eyes, the kind, blind eyes of motherhood, there was nothing to forgive.

Katie's father was more reticent. He stalled his expressions of joy, preferring instead a certain time to elapse before he allowed himself to be pleasured by the return of a smile he had missed for so long and the impetuous spirit of a child who came into the world an afterthought, an unplanned gift, unexpected, but not for one moment regretted.

His desire was not to punish. Such feelings had subsided long before. In fact, with Marian a permanent and heart felt absentee, Katie's return to the family was the release from loneliness he thought would never come.

However, he did hesitate. Some grain of indignation, some indiscernible but niggling seed, kept him from immediate capitulation. Several months elapsed before his heart echoed to the resonance so clear in that of his wife. But he did surrender and when he did, Marian was overjoyed to read news of it in his letters.

She had no idea when, if ever, she would return to England herself. She expected to one day. The prospect of not seeing her family again was too painful to contemplate. However, by hook or by crook, she had built a life for herself in Assam. It was not her original plan. Her long sea voyage to India so many years before was not intended as an overture to a life of exile, voluntary or otherwise. Had she known in advance of leaving London that she would not see her home again in fifteen years, she would doubtless not have set foot from 32 Princes Gate.

But fate had steered her hand and though John was absent from their home for much of the time, his business ambitions in stiff competition with those on the polo field, he was a good husband to her. Marian missed her father. She missed too her mother, sisters and the home in which she had grown up, but the ache of separation had dulled with time. Although never far from her thoughts, everything in London she once held so dear, the most precious jewels in her possession, were but sweet keepsakes.

In letters to her father, letters she wrote as often as she could but each time over the years with less extravagance in their detail, she encouraged his belief in the reluctance of her absence. But it was false. Apathy, indolence, whatever it was, claims she made of wanting to return home went no further than words on the page.

Each time she rose in the morning, early usually to catch the dawn, she knew England would remain a far-off haven. Assam was a wet place. Much of the time rain hindered or made impossible the normal functions of everyday life. Mosquitoes were a constant irritant. Disease was ever present, requiring extreme vigilance at all times. Creature comforts were few, social interaction limited to a small group and cultural pursuits, so much a part of the daily life she once knew so well in London, were virtually non-existent.

She understood, however. She knew why Jack and Marjorie Laws stayed a lifetime, why they built a home for themselves, why they toiled so hard to keep what they had snatched from the heart of the jungle; beauty beyond compare and peace of mind to calm the most troubled of hearts. And Marian had found the same.

When she and Jonathan first arrived in Dibrugarh, their horizons were blurred. They were adventurers. They were looking for the building blocks of a life together but there was nothing set in stone. There was no architects drawing for the months and years ahead. They were an open book. Marian still thought then of England as her home. She was abroad, away from everything and everyone she held most dear, but her thoughts were of temporary separation.

Fifteen years on, her life had altered beyond recognition. She had altered beyond recognition. Widowed, remarried and the mother of three children there was little left to remind her of the young woman who stepped ashore in Bombay, grief stricken by the loss of a man she loved.

Rarely, however, did she pause long enough to examine the changes. The pages of her diary were a chronicle of a life and feelings. Only occasionally were they devoted to introspection. However, slowly, as slowly but as inexorably as the growth of a Nahore tree, her roots had worked their way into the soil of Assam, holding her fast to the land, making the process of upheaval more difficult with the passing of each year. She had no idea now what fate would have her do in future years or where it might lead her. Whether or not she would live out the course of her life in Assam or whether there were still more twists and turns in store she preferred not to know.

However, on the day she read news of Katie's return to 32 Princes Gate, she was both happy and relieved. She relaxed in the knowledge that, in particular, her father would have for himself a companion to see him into old age. Had Margaret remained at home, the eternal spinster, she doubted the continuance of her father's sanity. The Katie she recalled was impetuous. She was also self-centred and notoriously irresponsible. Nevertheless, she was gifted with a liveliness of spirit which, if harnessed, was capable of serving well as a foil to the wit of her father.

Marian assumed the best. For her own peace of mind, she chose to believe in the better attributes of her younger sister. Katie's term at the school of hard knocks must have done much to quench the flames of wilful defiance. A mother and more recently a widow herself, it was no more than common sense to believe Katie altered for the better with the passage of time.

Although experience was bound to have changed her beyond recognition from the head strong girl she once was, Marian doubted their father could replicate exactly with Katie the instinctive bond he shared with her. She relied solely upon supposition to imagine a Katie of wit, intellect and charm, knowing only that, from memory, there were occasional but brief glimpses of all three. Still, she rested her hopes on as much, convincing herself or at least trying to do so, that to stay on in Assam was little deprivation to her father.

One day she hoped to return. But for the immediate future she was content. Shahjan was her home. 32 Princes Gate was a distant, happy memory, a place she returned to in her thoughts only during the worst of times. And such times had been few over the recent years. In truth, the eleven years she had spent as Mrs John Dunn were spoilt by little in the way of heart break. His demands upon her as a husband were no more or less than she deserved. Their relationship was one of mutual respect.

For her part, she conceded to his ambition, adjusting early on in their marriage to the knowledge that she and her children took second place in John's determination to outshine his father. That was a conflict of mythic proportions. The obsessive need to better his father, a need magnified with the years, rather than dulled by its constancy, was to Marian a curiosity, at most a hindrance to illusions she held of a family environment for her offspring echoing that of her own childhood.

It was a disappointment also that John had proved himself unwilling to devote the energy to his wife and children which he found in abundance for the expansion of the Dunn estates, the many triumphs he and his brother Philip enjoyed on the polo field, or his apparent addiction to the sexual favours of other women. Where once the cuckolding of Jonathan was as nothing to his desire for Marian's embrace, so he had moved on, his needs sated in the arms of other men's wives or the untouched delicacies of other men's daughters.

Fortunately, there were compensations, material rewards to repay the disappointment of owning a faithless husband. Over a period of six months during the winter of 1892 and into the beginning of 1893, John built for Marian a new bungalow. It was large enough to accommodate a generous family and filled with every modern convenience. These were obtained through the good services of Messrs Evans and Dickson of the Planters Stores. With the aid of their library of up-to-date catalogues, orders were placed and goods were delivered by the now regular services of the extended Assam Bengal Railway.

At Marian's request, the veranda faced due west to catch the evening sunsets, a reminder of Mancotta and therefore of Marjorie and Jack Laws. There she would sit most days. Sometimes with her children around her, sometimes alone, she waited for her husband to return from the fields tired and hungry or from the direction of Dibrugarh and another inevitable victory on the polo field, as often as not brandishing a silver trophy and the signs on his face of one Scotch too many.

Some nights they made love. When they did, there was passion and affection, yet there was an awareness on Marian's part, forever present, that however hard she tried or however often she gave herself to him, she alone was not enough. Just like his father, John could not satisfy his sexual needs in the arms of one woman. From forbidden fruit came the greatest desire, the deepest passion.

Marian knew there were other women, many other women. From the start, even before she agreed to marry him, she knew there would be others to feel the strong grip of his hands and the weight of his body upon theirs. It was the price she paid, a compromise she accepted with open eyes, if not with an open heart.

However, she could not deny the pain of his constant infidelity. It was not without considerable dexterity that each time he came to her bed, she filled her mind, not with visions of the other women he had been with, but of that one afternoon so many years before, when, on the flooded river bank some distance through the jungle, the closeness of his body alone was enough to render her incapable of speech.

She would recall how, on that first occasion, the touch of his hand on her shoulder had made her yearn for more, how, in the weeks that followed, his lips on hers threw into turmoil the wedding vows she had exchanged with the man she then called her husband. How could she reasonably demand of John the same integrity she had denied Jonathan. How could she expect absolute fidelity from the father of her eldest child, when it was in his embrace, she had proved herself capable, so spectacularly, of betrayal.

John's affairs with other women, some more public than they might have been and others with fresh-faced virgins almost as young as his own daughter, were no easy burden to carry. They wounded. They erected a barrier to mutual affection which was unlikely to be breached.

When she married Jonathan, Marian neither loved him nor was she in love with him. Over time, however, and indeed in shorter time than she imagined, she grew to love him. His death stuck daggers into her heart. Her grief was pure and unspoilt by hypocrisy. But with John, there would never be love; fondness which grew; an understanding of his driven nature which provoked affection; and always an animal desire for him which she wanted to deny but which faded not one iota over the years or in the knowledge of his sexual duplicity; but never love.

As penance, Marian actively deprived herself of loving him and in so doing made it impossible for him to love her. In reality, she doubted he was capable of expressing love. Indeed, she doubted he had any real comprehension of the word. Somewhere in the male Dunn gene pool there was a defect. Whatever it was, it eliminated 'love' from the vocabulary. As if by some surgical procedure it had been removed several generations in the past. And, sadly, all the women who took on the Dunn name were doomed to survive without it.

In a rare moment of feminine intimacy, shortly before she and John were married, Verity Dunn warned Marian of what to expect.

'In many ways, my son is a good man,' she declared as if prompted by a question. 'He works hard and plays hard. He's a good provider and he will see to it that you and your children are protected. But you would be wise not to expect more. Like his father and brothers, he has no more to give.'

Prophetic words. Words only a mother could speak with any certainty, and only a caring mother-in-law would admit to her future daughter.

But Marian knew it already. She took no pride in John's affairs with other women. Each time he returned home, late at night and went straight to his own room, she fought to contain the hurt and anger. But all she could ask of him was discretion, a little respect. Dibrugarh knew the Dunn tradition for infidelity. Dunn ways were tolerated like the rain and mosquitoes. Trevelyan Dunn and even his father before him, set the trend. Few people expected better of the sons.

There were occasions when Marian felt shame. To show herself in public was, she believed, to risk the scorn of every wife who was able to keep her husband at home. But she had chosen to marry a Dunn. John's behaviour was no more or less than she or anyone else expected of him, even his own mother, and nothing for which his wife should be blamed. Mothers across the region laboured hard to keep their daughters from his grasp and husbands, if cuckolded, were certain to guard their secret closely.

Consequently, to a greater rather than lesser extent, Marian's reputation in the community remained untarnished by the behaviour of her husband. There were those who criticised her for choosing to re-marry having once been made a widow, those, more pious than the rest and with their original husbands intact, who disapproved of any woman occupying more than one marital bed in a single lifetime.

However, public censure was the least of her concerns. If she had sleepless nights, demons taunted her not with village gossip or behind-the-back whisperings, but with the frailty of her own self-respect. The greatest danger to Marian was that of too much introspection, too much self-recrimination. And so, over the years, she taught herself resignation. Only occasionally did she allow the behaviour of her husband to inspire a mood of deep depression.

It was no easy task. When all was said and done, however, the life she had made for herself in Assam was a good one. In her letters home she wrote not of tragedy or heart ache but of the beauty in the landscape, the joy and satisfaction she gained from her children and the achievements of a man whose virtues matched stride for stride his faults.

Chapter Twenty-Six

For a while at least, news of the old Queen's death did indeed cast something of a long shadow. The new order, and there had to be a new order, was a beast of mystery. The spirit of empire, if not the reality of it, continued on intact. No one expected otherwise. That much was held to be sacrosanct. A monarch was flesh and bones, mortal, ephemeral, a man or woman like any other, but empire was like a mighty oak. It would last a thousand years, sturdy, impregnable, resolute. Monarchs would come and go but empire would remain.

Or so went the hope and belief of every man and woman with Anglo-Saxon blood in their veins. However, like it or not, and most did not, change was coming, inexorable and unstoppable, even to the far reaches of Upper Assam.

Only the mighty Brahmaputra remained constant. Unimpressed by time or change, its coffee brown waters passed by Dibrugarh as they hand done for millennia, ever Southwards until an eventual union with Mother Ganga and their final exit into the Bay of Bengal. During the March and April of 1901, the rainfall was exceedingly heavy, heavier than it should have been for the time of the year and certainly heavier than was welcome. By those who had earned a living from the planting of tea for a generation or more, much was made of their having rarely, if ever, been as much rain for the time of the year.

Day after day, night after night, it poured from the heavens. In sheets it descended, drenching the land, destroying much of the new seasons leaf and rendering tea production of any kind virtually impossible. Worse, with a more rapid than usual spring thaw beginning in the mountains, the Brahmaputra swelled until it could contain itself no more.

A wretched and mighty flood ensued, inundating huge areas of what was normally dry land. Low-lying plantations all but disappeared beneath the swirling, muddy waters, in places rising so high, that the roof tops of bungalows and leaf sheds were all there was to be seen together with the upper canopy of jungle.

Wherever they were able, livestock were moved or escaped on their own to higher ground. Sadly, many less fortunate, the lame, the old or the sick, perished, their half-submerged carcasses floating back and forth with the currents, bloated and hideous until finally, trapped against some natural obstacle, or beached, they became a feast for grateful vultures.

Hundreds of people, if not thousands, were made homeless and where life had carried on as normal in the lee of national mourning it was brought to an abrupt halt by the forces of nature.

Shahjan was lucky. It escaped the worst. The flood waters did not reach to its boundaries. It got by with a severe drenching. The new seasons production stopped before it was begun and lakes of quickly polluted water appeared across the estate, staying wherever the ground dipped enough to contain them. Elsewhere, the slightest natural channel or undulation became a petty river, carving a way, impatient to join up with the huge mass of fast-moving water headed so furiously towards Calcutta, carrying everything before it foolish enough to be standing in its path.

Newly installed drying machines in two leaf houses were half-submerged. One was started up briefly to see if it would run. However, with a foot of muddy soup surrounding it, its heavy, fast revolving fly wheel spewed water in every direction. In the end, all efforts to carry on as normal were abandoned. At times, during the height of it, the only sensible means of transport was a small dug out which John used to negotiate his passage from one place to another.

Bollai, Kurmi and Mancotta suffered similarly. Medla, however, fared less well. Lying close to where the banks of the river normally kept back the waters sprawl, it succumbed almost completely to the flood. It was all but swept away, effectively washed from the landscape.

When, eventually, the waters did subside, nothing was left of it. Where once endless rows of tea bushes stood, the merciless flood retired leaving little more behind than a quagmire wasteland. Years of work were torn up or buried beneath the mud; buildings, machinery and trolley lines. All evidence of agriculture or human intervention were virtually gone.

Fortunately, no one lived at Medla. There were temporary coolie huts and a makeshift eat house, but no bungalows to drown in the murky currents of the flood waters. There were also two leaf houses, a drying shed, a packing room and a wash house. When the water departed, they went with it. Only hints of their existence could be found; shards of broken timbers in nearby treetops, sections of roof sticking out of the mud, but little else.

And Dibrugarh itself was not spared. Usually protected from high-water surges by the steep mooring ghats along its waterside frontage, even those were overrun. For days, the town watched and waited as the flood waters rose ever higher. Finally, they scaled the last hurdle. Water surged through the streets, sweeping away anything and everything not fixed or tied down.

Within a day, the newly appointed commissioner for the region, a man better liked than AHW Bentinck but if it were possible, even less effective, declared a state of emergency. Quite what was proposed by such an edict remained a complete mystery to a greater portion of the local population. Their sole concern was personal survival or the preservation of estates which had taken several generations to build up.

Extraordinary powers of arrest and detention, the shooting of looters on sight, the confiscation of essential assets or the occupation of vital strategic locations, seemed of little relevance to men and women gripped by so unwelcome a calamity. Personal survival was the thing on most minds, followed quickly by the need to rescue homes and livelihoods.

As best they could the Assam Valley Light Horse Volunteers turned out to lend a hand, but in spite of all efforts to the contrary, their contribution was little more than superficial. Since their numbers were made up predominantly of planters and local business men, the ranks were necessarily depleted, each volunteers' efforts being concentrated closer to home, the survival of their own families and possessions of more immediate concern than the general good.

Turn outs were necessarily poor. In the end the Gurkhas were brought in to police the unfolding disaster and to assist with the arduous programme of renewal.

Worst hit were the livestock. At the height of the flood, the rain still falling from the sky with biblical vengeance and no sign of an end in sight, thousands of drowned cattle, oxen, buffalo and even horses, unable to reach higher ground or gain secure footing, were dragged to a watery grave, their sorry remains sober evidence of the fragility of life in the region.

With her children kept close by her side and the fear that John himself might be swept away in some freak surge as he struggled somewhere on the estate to save from the flood some of what he had worked so hard and so long to gain, Marian's thoughts once more turned to home.

She imagined it raining in London. She tried to remember the worst and most prolonged period of rainfall during her childhood so that she could compare one with the other. But there was no comparison. How could there be. In thirty years and more, no one in Assam could recall a scene of such devastation.

Each year, rain was expected and, during the monsoon season, flooding, but nothing on a scale with the spring of 1901. And as if the floods themselves were not bad enough, when eventually the waters did recede, they left behind a wasteland.

Many of the smaller, low-lying estates faced total destruction and their owners' complete ruin. The seasons harvest was gone before it was begun. There would be no harvest and therefore nothing to send to the market in London. Families like the Dunn's would survive. Families like the Dunn's always did. They were survivors. They were wealthy and powerful enough to weather even the worst floods in thirty years. They had their own losses, of course and they were severe, but in the end, sustainable. In time, arrears of land laid to waste would be retrieved. In time, Medla would be replanted and its leaf houses rebuilt. Elsewhere they would pick, dry, sort and pack 'maunds' of tea at least enough to finance, new machinery, new buildings and the workforce to replant. The larger plantations had reserves enough to fight back, but many of the smaller ones did not.

It was those, and they were numerous, who needed help. Their futures depended upon assistance from the commissioner and aid from the new Viceroy in Calcutta. But when the call went out, all those who might have helped were found wanting.

For months stretches of the railway, swept into oblivion by the flood, remained untouched. Vital supplies were forced to wait downstream in Gauhati until the river became navigable again. Platitudes and messages of good intention from Calcutta were of little use to a corner of the world impoverished by a disaster not of its own making.

In the absence of any official help, John, and others like him, did what they could. So too did his father and brothers. But it was not enough. There were only so many hours in a day. They had their own land to rescue, their own buildings to repair, their own harvest to begin. What they could do for others was no more than a drop in the ocean.

Finally, and all too soon, there began from the whole region to the north and south of Dibrugarh an exodus, the sorry sight of men, women and children made refugees by the floods. With as much as they could carry and what little money they had or were given by others more fortunate, they boarded the downstream steamers on a journey which would take them first to Calcutta and thence by packet ship home to England, their tails between their legs, their heads bent low, a lifetime's work gone in a matter of days, their courage spent.

To see it all, to witness the tragedy and then look on as friends and neighbours faced the ignominy of bankruptcy was almost too much to bear. No longer was there a shadow over the land, but a shroud. The passing of Victoria Regina became of little significance, the implications of her death irrelevant. Fears for the long-term political stability of the region paled. Instead, a deep and grotesque silence descended. The 'Club' served few drinks. Polo ceased altogether. Dibrugarh itself appeared like a ghost town, commercial activity stifled, talk of growth and expansion replaced with stories of tragedy and survival. With each sailing from the ghats, more families turned their backs on a landscape laid to waste by the very rainfall which, in normal times, breathed life and hope, which helped produce the very harvest it had so mercilessly destroyed.

There were tears and there was heart break. No one escaped untouched. Those who did survive, those whose estates suffered only minor damage, those whose livelihoods were strained to breaking but did not succumb, even they struggled for consolation. Helpless to prevent such a catastrophe and with charity the only weapon in their armoury to assist the worst affected, their losses demanded extreme fortitude.

In the final analysis, so much tragedy and heart break could not be endured without some form of release. For the first few weeks, during and after the flood, furious activity by night and day was required, as Dunn's, Spekemans, Howards and every other estate owner fought to restore their lands in time for the harvest.

Patrick Murphy, by 1901 coming towards the end of his residency in Assam, relied upon the services of two younger assistant doctors. Both were bright faced bachelors newly arrived from medical school. Consequently, try as they might, they were completely overwhelmed by the scale of the problem into which they had landed themselves. Together they worked tirelessly to heal the wounded, tend the sick and prevent the spread of disease, but much of their effort was in vain.

Polluted water meant the rapid spread of cholera and typhoid. Skies filled with mosquitoes threatened incidents of the 'fever' on an unprecedented scale. An epidemic of all three or any one of them would exaggerate the catastrophic aftermath of the floods and could, if severe enough, drastically depopulate the region.

There was little the two young medics could do but patch and mend and hope for the best. Which is what they did, relying upon prayer as much as medicine to prevent the worst. At the same time, the army was fully occupied in restoring the roads and resurrecting the various lines of communication enabling Dibrugarh to keep in touch with the outside world.

Sadly and not without instilling a sense of anger which settled into the memories of the inhabitants as a need to be avenged, the outside world, in general, and central government in Calcutta, in particular, appeared uninterested in or careless of Dibrugarh's many cries for help.

Abandoned to their own devices, the plantation owners, over stretched medical officers and all those who could see no end in sight to the interminable mud and wasted landscape, recognised that their isolation was without precedent and, almost to a man, they were left with deep feelings of resentment.

In some cases, as the flood waters receded, there was relief for those whose estates had been spared. For the majority there was deep sorrow which was replaced first by disbelief and then by incredulity at the irresponsible apathy in Calcutta. In the end, salvation of a kind came from the most unlikely of sources.

For years, Marian's opinion of her father-in-law remained unflattering and unaltered. The first time they met, she disliked him. He was an overbearing, patronising chauvinist; a bully. In public at least, he treated all women as inferior. His attitude towards them as a sex and his handling of them was akin to his treatment of the natives. He took his pleasure from them, many of them, but was abusive of them.

And, in like manner, he practised a near feudal system of mastery over both his family and workforce, exploiting the loyalty and obedience of his three sons while viewing his coolies as little more than a slave workforce.

On numerous occasions, with considerable agitation, Marian recorded in her diary his offences to common decency, marvelling at the tolerance of his wife and wondering why on earth she had stayed at the side of such a man for so long. In general, she heartily disapproved of him. Many times, she was outraged by his words or deeds. And, quite as often, she found herself despising him. In life, Trevelyan Dunn was the petty tyrant she took him for when they first met. He was a man who poured scorn on and was apparently quite content to take advantage of the weakness of others, seemingly prepared to do almost anything in order to further advance his own power and wealth. At the same time, he impressed himself upon strangers only for his bulk, the ruthlessness of his business practices and his singular lack of humanity.

And first impressions of him tended not to be diluted by better acquaintance. If anything, time and familiarity endorsed the poor opinion Marian had of him. If she anticipated that age would dull the edge of his sword or soften the lash of his whip, she was to be disappointed. He continued on into grey haired antiquity as hatefully robust as he was physically unimpeded, quite beyond salvation; or so Marian supposed.

So accustomed was she to thinking badly of him, so resigned was she to the position he held as the ogre in her life, she was perhaps the last to notice but ultimately the most surprised to witness a side to him she imagined as arid as any desert.

Where, after the flood, Calcutta ignored or was ignorant of the dreadful deprivation being endured in the upper reaches of the Assam valley, from somewhere unknown, Trevelyan Dunn acquired a rare vile of altruism as pure and as concentrated as any she had seen. There were charitable organisations she had visited in London during her childhood which impressed her. Their selfless caring for those in need was as inspiring as it was admirable. She had seen with her own eyes, the poor being fed, the sick being healed and the desperate being consoled. On many occasions, she was humbled by the sacrifice of others and shamed by her own lack of commitment. Her conscience was pricked by the humanity of men and women so generous with the dispensing of charity and the dignified gratitude of those in receipt of it.

However, she was completely overcome with surprise at the actions of a man whose attributes for redemption she had many times recorded in her diary as being so buried as to be irretrievable. When it became apparent that Calcutta cared nought for the citizens of Dibrugarh and neither commissioner, nor his deputy possessed the necessary gumption or organisational skills to influence the distribution of aid where it was most needed, Trevelyan Dunn made a grab for the reins.

A long-term convert to a belief in the aimlessness of bureaucracy, he usurped the throne held so timidly by government appointees. Empowered by his own ego and encouraged by the lack of opposition, he took control. With his sons as his side, lieutenants in arms, he press ganged help from whatever quarter he chose.

With his own money he financed the setting up of committees to effect full reconstruction of the region, bringing about directly a working plan to make good the railway, restore the roads and, more immediately, to feed the hungry and treat the sick. Within weeks everyone answered to him; even the Ghurkas. Like a General at the head of his armies and in the face of mounting protest from the very bureaucratic institutions which had proved themselves so incapable of useful action, he forged ahead.

As much as Marian fought against an admission of it, without his personal intervention in what was a desperate situation, one the like of which the inhabitants of Dibrugarh and the surrounding estates had not known before, recovery would have been a pitifully slow affair. As it was, with morale improving by the day and twenty-four-hour effort from those least effected by the floods on behalf of those whose livelihoods and homes had been all but wiped off the map, within a few month's things returned to a degree of normality.

And the tyrant became the benign dictator. Trevelyan Dunn's leadership was the hub around which the wheel of recovery turned. Without his belligerence, his refusal to cede control to men whom he knew to be, in spite of their official titles, inept and incompetent, not to mention his own bloody mindedness in the face of mother nature, there would have been a greater exodus of people from the region and more land than necessary given over to the insatiable appetite of the jungle.

Quite against her best instincts and with not inconsiderable reluctance, Marian found the entries in her diary reviewing the character of a man she had known for years to be flawed in the extreme. Respect, even admiration for his tireless attention to the welfare of his fellow man compelled her to record him in a different light.

That his altruism was tainted with a degree or two of self-interest was to be expected. Nevertheless, no amount of self interest could lessen the impact of his dogged determination to rise above disaster. Whatever his agenda and however selfish, his motives, Trevelyan Moran's leadership and his personal contribution could not be ignored. Few people, if any, Anglo or native denied him the accolades he deserved.

Every 'Babu' in the region held him in high regard. Many of their villages were washed away. However, their stoicism was not entirely the gift of their faith. The hope and encouragement they gave to the villagers who respected them as the leaders of their communities, was only made possible by the practical assistance rendered by 'Dunn sahib.' The 'babus' provided solace, through faith.

'Dunn sahib,' supplied food and shelter until in turn each stricken village, where possible, could fend for itself once again.

Meanwhile, many were they who, resigned to refugee status and repatriation as their only option, owed their salvation to Trevelyan Dunn. Like Marian, in the past, they had maligned or, more often than not, feared him as a predator, as a man dangerous to cross and ruthlessly hungry for power. In a lifetime, he had acquired few friends, boasting to all who would listen, of his indifference to camaraderie. Those loyal to him, and their ranks were equally thin, were bound either by family obligation or, if not tied to him, by some degree of indebtedness.

Marian was not alone in deploring his ambition and his methods. Almost universally, he was disliked or feared in similar measure. Before the flood speeches in his favour were few, words of kindness or approval a rare commodity. Afterwards, she was among the first of swelling numbers to reverse or, at the very least, revise her opinion of him.

In a manner so predictable of him and undoubtedly a symptom of the delight he took in causing offence, he proclaimed himself frequently to be an atheist. Many were the times in the club bar he shocked a reluctant audience with his ridiculing of the need for or notion of a God, be he white and Christian or native and Hindu or Moslem.

That being the case his actions were unlikely to have been the result of a sudden conversion. Even though the transformation in his personality was something akin to that of Saul on the road to Damascus, Marian was of a mind to believe in an alternative rational for his behaviour.

Naturally enough, most of those who benefited directly from his new found generosity were too needy and too grateful to question his motives. Marian, however, could not help but include a theme of cynicism to her recording of his benevolence. She wanted to believe the propaganda. She tried to convince herself that the leopard had changed its spots. But she was held back from a completely new and more generous appraisal of him as a man.

She admired his dynamism and his refusal to permit bureaucracy to stand in his way. She respected the results of his efforts, witnessing at first hand and being impressed by their happy consequences. But there was a note of caution on the pages of her diary, a suggestion that while there was no evidence to the contrary, there might just be and indeed almost certainly was an ulterior motive to his apparently selfless catalogue of good deeds.

She was not proud of this cynicism. However, she had known the man a long time. She had seen the aftermath of his customary business practices. At first hand she had witnessed his bullying of those less durable than himself. She had watched, in even the treatment of his own sons, a heartless and incessant determination to prove them useless. And she was personally among the vast majority of those alienated by him.

Fortunately, she had taught herself to care nought for what he thought of her. As a woman she was confident enough in her own abilities and intellect to rise above his efforts to put her down. She despised his arrogance and, over the years, she was angered regularly by his patronising manner. However, it was in respect of John that her poor opinion of him was always at its most vehement.

John was a man in his own right. As his mother had so rightly once boasted, he was a good man. He provided well for his wife and children and worked ceaselessly to make a success of everything he turned his hand to. Yet he was flawed. Racked with self-guilt and a sense of inadequacy which had been instilled into him by his father from the cradle, he was incapable of shaking either off. His every word and deed were tainted by an obsessive impulse to better the man who sired him.

Their war was relentless. For years, it raged without let-up. There was no bloodshed. Indeed, to an outsider it might well have passed unnoticed. Nevertheless, it was there, an undercurrent to John's every action and thought, a cancer eating away at him day after day.

Certainly, he was a good man. Time and again he proved his worth. Save for his appetites beyond the marital bed, Marian could not have asked for better. She could not deny that her heart was empty of the emotion she once held for a young officer named William Radford and she was starved of the affection she had come to take for granted from Jonathan.

And there were times she craved such warmth and comfort. But she survived quite readily without it, persuading herself that whenever she felt the loss of either, the price of love was too dear to pay. Loving, but not being in love had been a convenient compromise in her relationship with Jonathan. Being fond of and in return being treated to at least a degree of tenderness from John was sufficient reward.

For he was an incomplete man. A life spent kicking against the pricks of his father's cruel spurs saw to that. Refusing to be broken implied a certain independence. Unbroken, a maverick, many were the times he bemoaned the submission of his younger brothers, sneering at their easy compliance to his father's every whim. Philip and Terence alike succumbed early on. Barely grown men, they caved in, seemingly content to live in the wake of their father. They offered no resistance, taking to the bit placidly, reacting to the whip with resignation and, in John's eyes therefore, existing not as individuals but as extensions of their father. His will was their will, his thoughts their thoughts and his faults their faults.

To John this was an anathema. He saw his brothers as good enough, but weak men, men whose lives were not their own, men who, because they gave in too soon, would never realise, as he had, the fulfilment of having resisted the bit and whip. So blinded was he, however, by the continual effort of his struggle, he failed to recognise the truth; he was the one in chains.

Marian lived the irony. Standing on the sidelines, watching every skirmish, living every battle, she witnessed the incarceration which her husband failed to see. Philip and Terence complied. They were the sons their father expected them to be. They did what was demanded of them, asked no questions and savoured every crumb to fall their way from his table of plenty.

And yet, in reality, it was John, not they, who was most bound to the father. His obsession to be free achieved the opposite. His constant struggle for liberty kept him a prisoner. As long as the father lived, he, not his two brothers, was destined to remain the captive.

There were periods in her life Marian became intolerant of the absurdity and tragedy of it all. She wanted to scream at John to surrender. She saw him going to waste. She longed to put an end to it. But it was no use. Even before she agreed to become his wife, she knew it was no use. John was not for turning. The pages of her diary were filled with frustration. She abhorred the futility and spectacle of two men so bent it seemed on mutual destruction.

However, she was resigned to the equal futility of expecting on her own meagre efforts to influence any resolution. John would go to the grave believing the great myth of his own independence. Until his last breath, he would deny the ropes of his queer allegiance. Of three brothers, John saw himself as and, Marian was convinced, believed himself to be, the only one to have broken free from the yoke of his father. In fact, though less visible to the naked eye, the knots binding him were the tightest of all.

And, as if to prove the point, half way through July of 1901, with the worst effects of the flood behind, life slowly returning to something resembling normal, the production of tea in full swing, the up-and-coming Dibrugarh Shield polo tournament reinstated and with Marian recording in her diary a spirit of renewed optimism, Trevelyan Dunn died.

The day it happened; he had ridden into the jungle to inspect a work gang cutting Nahore trees for sleepers. The new stretch of line to Sadiya called for more than ever. Some were needed by the railway company for the track already under construction, some for renewals to large sections washed away by the floods.

Off his horse and by all reports, determined to prove to his coolies he was still fit enough for manual labour a test for men half his age, he lent his weight to the shifting of a stubborn trunk. It was refusing to budge by elephant power alone from the deep trench into which it had settled after felling. Pulling on a rope with all his strength while cursing at the idleness of the coolies around him, he let out a faint gasp which was all but lost in the general cacophony of noise. Then he dropped stone dead to the ground, his hands still clenched around the coarse hemp rope.

'Father-in-law died today.' Began the entry in Marian's diary. 'By all accounts, his heart gave out. John went over to fetch his body back to Kurmi. He said nothing and I know he will not speak of his feelings to me. Life will not be the same here.'

It was a brief entry but prophetic. The death of Trevelyan Dunn touched the lives of every man, woman and child in the region. Most would have denied it, but it was true. In later years, few would recall him with affection. Many competing tea men indeed gained a deep sense of relief at his passing. Although on the record alone of activities immediately prior to his demise, more men than previously had cause to be grateful to him.

News of his death travelled like wild fire. At the club, the Union Jack, only recently raised to its former position, was flown again at half-mast. And the funeral was a huge affair. Mourners descended on Dibrugarh from every corner of Assam. Tea production was halted. Natives, more used to cowering in fear whenever he came near, bowed their heads in respect.

Trevelyan Dunn was younger than Queen Victoria and his empire far smaller. Nevertheless, much as it had been when the Queen Empress departed life, the impact of his death was felt by the whole community.

Marian had often imagined him dying a lonely man, attended by a tight circle of immediate family only. In her mind's eye she saw his funeral as a sorry affair, a day when more people would pass a sigh of relief at his going than tears of regret. He was so well known for his tyranny and ruthless disregard for anyone other than himself, it was hard to believe that the sight of his body contained within a coffin could or would inspire any noticeable evidence of public grief.

But it did. His most recent activities lingered fresh in the memories of the many mourners who were present at the church service in Dibrugarh and who later congregated at his grave side. Verity Dunn headed the cast list. Immediately below her, in order of seniority came his three sons and, of course, Marian as his daughter-in-law with her three children.

There followed then a small quorum of Dibrugarh's senior citizens, men like Dr Patrick Murphy, men who had seen the years through, done their time, paid their dues alongside of or in conflict with the old war horse. To a certain degree, she was reminded of the funeral of Jack Laws although, in life, as men they were poles apart.

However, besides the good and worthy of Dibrugarh itself, there was a sizeable coming together of men and women whose lives, with the assistance of one man, had been salvaged so recently from a natural disaster and which still lived vividly in their memories.

In Trevelyan Dunn's case, at the last minute and in one supreme bout of the most unaccustomed generosity towards his fellow man, as if with foresight, with some sign only known to him of his impending death, he secured for himself the post mortem reputation of benefactor. He was remembered as being a man who in a time of crisis, with the whole community floundering, stood tall, his personal support, practical assistance and considerable financial expenditure, the vital ingredients to recovery.

Was it some prior knowledge of his own closeness to the grave, Marian wondered. Was it some last-ditch attempt by him to bribe his way into heaven, to compensate for a life devoted to the proceeds of cruel ambition. Or was it perhaps just a happy coincidence which brought so many mourners to church in the rain, their unanimous display of loss a poignant epitaph for his wife.

Marian suspected the latter. Trevelyan's death was too sudden and the circumstance of it too mundane for her to suspect any advance warning from above, or below. In fact, prior to the event, she, he and most of those directly affected by his presence in the world were convinced he would never die, that he was the master of death and was determined to outlive them all. So annoyingly vigorous was he, even to the last, so demanding were his every word and deed, it was impossible to believe he could have anticipated a premature encounter with his maker.

He was old but agile. He was no athlete, but he was surprisingly athletic for his age, constantly bragging of his ability to equal the effort of any man around him, to complete any task or fulfil any work load placed before him.

He was also an obstinate opponent of illness and death. He was the sort of man who if he lost one arm in a skirmish would simply pick up his weapon in the other and carry on with the fight until his eventual triumph. When he spoke of death or dying, it was in mocking tone. He neither feared the great reaper nor respected him, pretending in public at least, to be fully prepared to flaunt the final calling.

Somewhere, it seemed, somehow, he had cobbled together a secret plan enabling him to remain on terra firma overseeing the graves of all those with whom he had engaged in conflict so lustily while they were alive. He had no fear of death because he simply had no intention of dying.

It was a boast oft-repeated in the presence of an audience, a mantra to fortify the bravado of his atheism. In her analysis therefore, Marian could not conclude any link between his more recent Samaritanism and the deadly heart failure which followed so closely on its heels. Instead, she preferred the notion, and recorded as much, that, in the end, death itself had the last word and, perhaps even, the last laugh.

If Trevelyan Moran had any final, blinding revelations, which was extremely doubtful, they were more likely to have been to spit in the eye of whoever was responsible for the shuffling off of his mortal coil, rather than to breathe a sigh of relief at having prepared so well his path to the pearly gates.

Why he laboured so steadfastly to resurrect Dibrugarh and the surrounding estates from the devastation caused by flooding, was a puzzlement. Those who knew him well which included his wife, sons and, to a certain extent Marian herself, were bound to, and did, suspect an ulterior motive.

Perhaps he looked forward to the notion of having so many helpless people in his debt. Perhaps he could not bear to see his fiefdom so ravaged. After all Dibrugarh had become a thriving community and much of its recent prosperity was a reflection of his own endeavour. Whatever it was, his efforts to affect a speedy recovery for the region were hardly likely to have been the consequence of a guilty conscience. He had no conscience, not at least one which anyone had identified.

His sudden and terminal heart attack was the direct result of Trevelyan Dunn being a man who, in taking life by the horns was unwilling to acknowledge the simple fact that he was not as young as he used to be. Had he not attempted the task of hauling a trunk which would have been more efficiently handled by elephants, he would very probably have avoided the beckoning hand of death. He died therefore as he lived; defiant to the last.

His passing was more regretted than perhaps would have been expected, in part at least evidenced by the number of mourners at his funeral. Marian only paused to wonder how much affection lay beneath the tears and the words of consolation which passed from mourner to mourner in a steady stream until fetching up in a lake of generous words at the feet of his widow and sons.

As to be expected, Verity Dunn conducted herself with extraordinary poise, not once flinching from the responsibilities inflicted upon her. Self-indulgence and self-pity were restricted to the convenience of her private grief. Her sons too carried themselves well, as indeed they did their father's coffin.

John gave the eulogy. Philip read the lesson. Terence, the only one still not to have found himself a wife and placed into a rare moment of public exposure, recited the twenty third psalm, hesitating only once to quell a distinct yet contained quiver in his voice.

The most dominated by his father, the most often derided in public for his weakness and ineffectualness, the most entitled of the three to hate the man who spawned him, Terence was in fact clearly the most affected by his father's death. So relentlessly, in life, did the father abuse and ridicule the efforts and progress of his three sons, there were times Marian marvelled at their loyalty.

She was fortunate in her upbringing. Both her parents were constant in their affection, generous with their loyalty and ostentatious in the pride they nurtured for the most trivial of her achievements. She, Margaret and Katie were spoilt with love and indulged beyond their worth. A day spent in the presence of Trevelyan Dunn and his sons was adequate proof of as much. And for that indulgence, Marian was forever grateful.

She had not been home in fifteen years. She had three children, none of whom knew their grandparents. And yet, her father's letters, far from being filled with pained recrimination at being so neglected, were constant with pride and satisfaction. Margaret had slumped into a loveless marriage with a dentist. Though settled, she remained either barren or celibate, unwilling or unable to provide her parents with accessible grandchildren.

And Katie, dear, poor Katie, who once so shamed her family, now returned from her years in disgrace both husbandless and penniless. Yet, she was loved precisely because rather than in spite of the flaws in her character, so often exploited to their extremes.

Thus, each time Marian paused to consider the dysfunctional nature of the family into which she had married, she counted her blessings. In life she held no love in her heart for her father-in-law.

Yet, in death, both wife and sons were deeply wounded by his passing. Verity proved it in the stoical manner of her public mourning. Terence and Philip, but without doubt Terence the more, could not hide the conflict between their sorrow and what Marian took to be in them an almost tangible sense of release.

In spite of everything they had endured, they did not rejoice at their father's death. Their grief was genuine. However, their relief, the relief of two souls weighed down for years by the dispute between love and hate, a dispute which had infected them throughout their lives, was real enough.

John's reaction was quite different. Perhaps because Marian knew him better than his two brothers—she sensed in him something more. There was sadness, the natural sadness of any son losing a father. There was also some degree of relief, the same relief his brothers experienced and for the same reasons. But there was another ingredient, a perverse anger.

In dying, the father denied the son a motive for being. From the first day John thought of himself as a man, he took up arms against his father. Year after year, his every waking hour was dominated by the compulsion to prove himself, to prove he was worthy of his father's respect and love.

In turn, and as if to exaggerate the torture, his father steadfastly refused to surrender. He died, the struggle unresolved, the word 'love' having never passed from his lips to those of his son.

John was frustrated by the death of his father. The war ceased but the result could not be measured. With no adversary to pursue, he was left empty, his days aimless, his future as head of the Dunn business empire strangely pointless. For weeks afterwards, he floated like a ship adrift in the doldrums, the driving wind of his own ambition having evaporated.

The sympathy Marian felt for Philip and Terence was sincere but free from concern. Her greatest fear was founded in which direction might come the wind to refill the sails of her husband's ship.

408

The passing into the afterlife of his father was for John a watershed. Sadly, and all too soon, but not entirely beyond her expectations, Marian found herself face to face with the consequences.

Chapter Twenty-Seven

Hardly was Trevelyan cold in his grave, than the sins of the father returned to haunt his sons. As quickly as Verity Dunn learned to function independently, stripped as she was of a husband whose role as master of the household had always been absolute, her comparative tranquillity was shattered.

Mrs Jerry Hugo, formerly Miss Julia Fenton returned to Dibrugarh. With her she brought several sizeable packed trunks, an adolescent daughter and ambitions for a portion of the Dunn estates. Noticeable by his absence was Jerry Hugo, a curiosity readily explained by his having little or no idea, until it was too late, that his wife had left him. Equally, once he discovered her destination, he had little inclination to pursue her.

He was distraught of course. He was deprived of a daughter he loved beyond life itself. However, so relieved was he to be finally rid of a woman who had brought him in their twelve years of marriage nothing but heart ache, shame and regret, he could not steel himself to set off after her.

The blissful novelty of being without his wife was simply too much to risk in some heroic but inevitably futile attempt at retrieval of his only child, a child, as his wife pointed out at length shortly before her departure from their home in Sadiya, was not and never had been his.

Temporarily pole-axed by the blow of an awful truth kept from him for years, but jealous of his new found freedom, Jerry procrastinated in his plans to affect a rescue, inventing each day a new excuse for not setting off in hot pursuit. While Julia went in search of Eldorado, accompanied by the physical proof of her entitlement to a share of the Dunn family fortune and therefore the hope of a new future far from the mundane life she had endured for years married to one of the most spectacularly uninteresting men possible, Jerry shored up his defences.

He was determined that, should she change her mind or fail to succeed in her quest, Julia could find no way back. Rid of her, rid of the mocking abuse of their marriage vows, rid of her brazen infidelities, her uncouth exhibitionism and her incessant lamenting of the marriage she had entered into, he made himself ready lest she attempt a return.

Uninterested in local gossip and certainly not shamed by it, Jerry embraced the renaissance of a bachelor life style, his work more than adequate compensation for any loss he had sustained. The quiet, uninterrupted nights after his wife's departure were a pleasure he had long since confined to the locker of his reminiscences.

By contrast, Julia was on a mission. She had no time to consider the more subtle nuances of her self-imposed exile. Her ambition was on fire. Her daughter had the blood of Trevelyan Dunn coursing through her veins. One night of drunken lechery had seen to that. Now she was due an inheritance, an inheritance as sure as iron, as certain as the sunrise in the morning.

Like it or not, Fanny Hugo, a charismatic, startlingly pretty and vivacious young girl, a girl gifted with similar magnetism to that which her mother exploited so relentlessly as a young woman, was being chaperoned into a drama with herself in the lead role. Naturally enough, she missed the man she had always called father. Even upon arrival in Dibrugarh, Fanny remained confused by the precipitous nature of her mother's actions, not to mention her own part in them. Nevertheless, she was wide-eyed by the distance they travelled, the various people and places they encountered and the promise of a new life described as being beyond her wildest dreams.

Understandably though and thus forgivably, she had no premonition of the devastation her presence in Dibrugarh would cause. Ignorance of her mother's well considered and long nurtured plot implied freedom from guilt. And thus, she had no cause to regret the escapade, save that of missing the warmth and affection she enjoyed so freely at home.

Initially the arrival of Julia Hugo, with daughter, was the source of measured pleasure to those who recalled her. One or two wives were sceptical, the long-held suspicions of their own husband's infidelity revived. Equally, one or two fast-ageing husbands feared for their security should the returning former temptress intend as part of her schedule a full and frank disclosure of past deeds.

For the most part, however, the new arrivals were greeted warmly. Julia was pestered for news of the world beyond Dibrugarh and to begin with she received more invitations to dine than there were days in the week. At twelve years old, Fanny Hugo was still girl enough to delight. However, at the same time, she possessed not just the smile of an angel, but the eyes of a siren. Her words invited. Her tone seduced. She was in every respect save one, the daughter of her mother, less consumed perhaps by her own vanity, but more confident. She was also, in one very marked respect, the daughter of her father, not the father she had left behind in Sadiya, the man who had loved and cared for her as his own since birth, but the father she had never known by anything other than his name.

She too was ruthless. She was a twelve-year-old girl with the head on her shoulders of a woman twice her age. She missed the man she called 'father.' Leaving him behind was not an easy task, but she shed no tears. Easily persuaded of the importance of their mission, she too deserted her home with little more than a backward glance.

By the time Fanny reached Dibrugarh with her mother, she was fully appraised of their intentions and excited by the glamour of her inheritance, if still a little in the dark as to the detail of the overall campaign.

Upon their arrival, the whole community opened its arms in welcome. Within a matter of days, however, those same arms were closed again, their welcome rescinded. In turn, first the mother, and then the daughter, became the subject of general rejection. Slowly but surely, empathy turned to antipathy and bitterness, bitterness felt most deeply by two women in particular.

Verity Dunn came to abhor Julia for the nakedness of her ambition and for shaming the Dunn name with her attempts to introduce into it a bastard child.

And for her part, Marian very soon learned to mistrust and then deplore Julia for the cold and efficient manner in which she set out to claim her husband. Eyes wide in horror and disbelief, Marian could do nothing but watch as over the course of only a few weeks, John was duped into dragging his own marriage to the edge of oblivion.

How it came about haunted Marian for years. John was disoriented. That much was true. His father's death, still recent and unexpected, had unsettled him. After the funeral he spent as little time as possible it seemed with his wife and children, preferring to be in town, at the club mostly, if not playing polo, then in the bar drinking or interesting himself in the temporary pleasures afforded by infidelity.

But Marian coped. She was used to his misdemeanours. She was hurt by them but had learned to compromise. As best she could, she tried to understand and forgive. Following the funeral, she assumed his drinking was a temporary manifestation and that his more frequent liaisons with other women, though distressing, were no threat to her own security.

Not in her worst nightmares did she foresee the dreadful consequences of Julia's influence over him. The horror of it was too much for her to comprehend. Of course, she should have been prepared. She knew Julia's reputation of old, had watched her at work, even shared the same dinner table with her. At their first exchange of pleasantries, on the morning after Julia's return, Marian should have taken heed. But the moment passed. She failed to spot the signs.

Initially, of all members of the family, John was the most vehement in the words he used to refute the claims announced all too publicly by Julia Hugo. Of course, he knew what she was like. She had been gone from Dibrugarh for more than a decade, but there was no fading to his memory. He knew she courted centre stage and he could well remember the regular pleasure she took in shocking an audience. And, though he would not admit it, he was also mildly suspicious of her sudden reappearance, convinced but not completely certain of an ulterior motive.

Consequently, he was prepared for something spectacular. What he was not prepared for were the outrageous claims he was among the first to hear and the first to ridicule. Out of hand he dismissed the preposterous notion of Fanny being the illegitimate child of Trevelyan Dunn. Privately, however, he could not deny the possibility. He was no stranger to the predilections of his father. He also recalled at first hand the moral vacuum which the former Miss Julia Fenton occupied, doubting she had undergone any substantial reformation during her years with Jerry.

What he was less willing to admit and certainly less ready to confess was the irresistible attraction he soon felt for her, one which ultimately had him turn against both Marian and his mother.

Within a month of Julia's arrival and before her much rehearsed revelations, the signs were there. He and she were seen together in company and they behaved in a manner altogether too familiar for public taste. Far from avoiding contact with her, John flirted openly, appearing intent upon seduction. Mindless of his responsibilities as a husband, he was impervious to the nodding heads and metaphorical wagging fingers of those who were witness to his unscrupulous endeavours.

And Julia was no better. Encouraging, flirtatious and clearly determined to be seduced, she paid no heed to Marian's feelings or her own reputation.

Being a Dunn, of course, John was deaf to reason and blind to the obvious. Not for a moment did he suspect Julia was playing out a scheme composed and rehearsed many times over the years as her daughter grew.

Convinced of his own sexual magnetism, it was beyond the bounds of his imagination to recognise any duplicity in the attention being paid him. He had no idea Julia was manipulating him like a skilled puppeteer. So thick was the fog in front of his face, he had no inkling of the calamity about to befall both himself and his family. Dismissing from his mind both the reasons for Julia's sudden reappearance, he slipped into her web of sticky deceit as if driven by an invisible force.

By the time he recognised the extent of Julia's betrayal, it was too late. Within weeks of her return to Dibrugarh, she was ready to strike. She had John precisely where she wanted him. Like a fish on a line, he was hooked. Utterly convinced of his own mind in the matter, he was ready to profess affection for her which far exceeded infatuation.

In a matter of only weeks, far less time in fact than she had allotted originally for her campaign, Julia scented the sweetness of victory. She held John in the palm of her hand. He was, or thought he was, 'in love' with her. He was even beguiled by the charm of her daughter and seemingly quite prepared, if Julia so required, to leave his wife and three children.

As it happened, no one was more surprised at or grateful for the speed of her own success than Julia herself. She did not assume John to be quite so malleable, or so willing to be deceived. In Sadiya, where, with years of time on her hands, she began to draft her scheme, she was denied firsthand knowledge of the ever-deepening resentment between John and his father. However, from past experience, she was aware of the extent to which a Dunn ego could be played like the sweet tune on a fiddle.

She had not begun her master stroke and yet, among her trophies was the added revenge against Marian, such revenge as she had always harboured but never imagined possible. One evening many years before, during the course of an otherwise unmemorable dinner party at Kurmi, Julia's plans to become Mrs John Dunn went awry.

Newly arrived in Assam, married but invitingly fresh and quite irresistible, Mrs Marian Cole diverted John's attention away from her. He lost interest in his dinner companion, displacing her, setting her to one side, any intentions she had then of entering the Dunn family by legitimate means dashed.

Marian was unaware of it. On that occasion, she was not acquainted well enough with John or Julia to be awake to the part she played in the dissolution of that or any other relationship. She was as ignorant of the then young Miss Fenton's intentions as John himself. Neither was she aware of the enemy she made on that night.

So completely unaware was she, it never crossed her mind that in marrying Jerry Hugo, Julia, even then, had her mind turned to spite. Naturally, at the time, Marian questioned the suitability of the coupling, and she was by no means alone. She, like so many others, commented upon the speed and incongruity of a union between Jerry and Julia. Marian was even prepared to express publicly her misgivings as to the likely longevity of such a marriage, eventually making known her surprise not that Julia had deserted Jerry but that either one of them had not left the other years earlier.

However, not once during the course of that evening so long ago did Marian consider the possibility, nor indeed was it on her mind when Julia returned to snare John, that the intention was to wreak havoc upon herself and those she loved.

Unfortunately, without exception, all Julia's plans went without a hitch. Try as she might, Marian found herself powerless to prevent them. With what might have been seen under different circumstances as admirable dexterity had her endeavours been employed in a good cause, Julia stole John. Her sleight of hand was simply too quick for the feeble awareness of her prey. And, as if to compound the felony, throughout the process, short as it was, the object of her deceit believed himself totally in command. John saw himself as the seducer. He believed he was claiming Julia as his prize; the final triumph, the last gesture of defiance in the war with his father.

While Verity Dunn recoiled at the revelation of Fanny's true parentage, a revelation proclaimed by Julia with sweet relish and with such precise detail as to the dates, times and places when she had committed adultery with her husband, John savoured every hour spent in her company. He was utterly ignorant of the concept of Greek tragedy and oblivious to the consequences of his indiscretion or the pain he was inflicting upon his family.

'Oh John!' Marian sighed in woeful resignation as he prepared himself for yet another evening at the club, another night in the company of a woman with whom he was so intoxicated that his reason was quite vanished away and his wife's feelings had ceased to be a matter of any consequence. 'Can't you see what's happening to us John? Is it so difficult for you to understand what Julia's doing?'

'Yes,' he replied coldly, his voice filled with impatience, presumably to be gone. 'Yes, it is. Do tell me. Tell me exactly what your jealousy has dreamed up for me. What dire scheme is afoot that I should beware of.'

He was in a horrible mood. He was not a violent man. He had never raised a hand against her and never would, but if he so chose, his tongue could cut deeper than the lash of the cat. Like his father, if John felt cornered or threatened in any way, he was both able and ready to strike back with words far crueller than mere blows. His temper was legend and his obstinacy like the thick walls of a medieval keep.

If Marian thought she could influence him, she was wasting her time. She knew better than to offer reason or common sense as the antidote to his lunacy. His mind was made up and when a Dunn mind was made up it was as immovable as a mountain. Words of warning were bound for deaf ears. He had no desire to hear or face the truth, particularly when it was being administered to him by his wife. He could not and would not recognise the truth. No amount of persuasion would have him believe in any other truth than the one he preferred. Julia was his prize, not he hers. She was the distraction he needed and she it was who danced to his tune.

How could HE be caught in HER spell. It was an absurd idea. He was too strong for spells. He was a Dunn, a man who controlled his own destiny, walked his own path. No man, or woman, led him by the nose. He was a leader of men. He was a man who determined the health and prosperity of hundreds, a man who had inherited and now ruled a kingdom. He would have none of Marian's pitiful protestations. She was his wife, not his master; nor was she his conscience.

So arrogant was his defiance, for Julia the game was over scarcely before it was begun. She knew John's ego, his deep commitment to the war against his father and his frailty with women. In fact, he was too easy a conquest, easy and ignorant of her clever machinations. By way of consolation however, a treat to accommodate the mild disappointment of bringing down so unchallenging a prey, one with whom she had anticipated and hoped for more sport, Julia savoured the agony of Marian's unhappiness.

That was extra bounty indeed. Her plot was to divide the forces she expected would line up against her; and divide them she did. Verity Dunn counted on and held fast to the support of Philip and Terence. Bemused but not altogether surprised by the behaviour of their elder brother, the two younger Dunns vowed loyalty to their mother. When the time came for Julia to announce her claim, together they set themselves to thwart every attempt Julia made to relieve them of any part of the Dunn fortune. Sired by their father or not, as far as they were concerned neither Fanny nor her mother were entitled to, nor would they get a penny piece or square inch of soil.

They were resolved, united, as a family, of one voice. Instinctively, they looked to John for support and leadership. They received neither. He had been lured into the enemy camp, thwarted by his own weakness. Rather than setting his battalions against Julia, as he should have done were he of sane mind, he joined forces with the enemy. Rather than contest her outrageous demands with vigorously, he rallied to her cause, more than ready to promote the legitimacy of her claim and in doing so to confront his mother and brothers head on during the ensuing conflict. It was madness personified, but it progressed with the speed of light and the contagion of a plague.

Helpless, Marian looked on, the story she told in her diary a sorry record to the awful reality of a family divided. Powerless to prevent the decay of her marriage, she could do nothing to rescue her husband from the poorly camouflaged trap into which he wandered with such casual haste.

As his mother declared to Marian many years before on the eve of their marriage, John was a 'good man.' And that much, over those years, he had proved. He was an adequate father to his children and a worthy provider. But he had an undeniable Achilles heel. He carried with him at all times an infection, a genetic disease inherited directly from his father, a disease for which there was no cure, a disease exploited with ease by the former Miss Julia Fenton.

Over the course of a few weeks, she did indeed reek the havoc she threatened, turning Dunn against Dunn, brother against brother and mother against son. In later years when Emma sat down to read the many pages of her mother's diaries, she was moved constantly by the emotions expressed within. Her mother's life was a rare documentary of an age and morality made obsolete by the all too hasty and violent advances of a new century.

However, of all the many pages, that brief period of which Marian wrote, beginning with the sudden and unannounced return of Julia Hugo to the front door of Kurmi in search of a fortune, was arguably the most tragic of all.

Marian wrote of her own sorry resignation. Her words lamented so pitifully the frightening inevitability of events as they unfolded. Julia got her fortune. But at what cost?

The Christmas of 1901 was very different from those gone before. Marian spent it alone with her children at Shahjan. Verity Dunn was also alone, at Kurmi, save for brief visits from Philip and Terence. John and Julia, along with Fanny who had become in only a few short months a pale reflection of the vibrant, pretty young thing she had been when first she arrived in Dibrugarh, celebrated together in their new home at Mancotta. By all accounts, they were an unhappy trio, much taken to violent argument and long silences.

Julia had got what she wanted. She was rid of a husband who for years had bored her and now her daughter was publicly, if reluctantly, recognised as a Dunn. In time, if Marian could be persuaded to part with the name by agreeing to a divorce, Julia might acquire that as well; but it was not essential to her needs.

Fanny's future was secure. She would never have to scrimp on the income of a railway engineers pay. She might marry, take on another man's name, go where he chose, do his bidding, lead the life he would have her lead. But she would always be a Dunn. Her children and her children's children would be Dunn's and with the name would come wealth and influence.

Inevitably, the Dunn fortunes would grow. John would see to that and, no doubt, his son after him. Quite by what magnitude even Julia could not have imagined. She had no way to predict the extraordinary rise and rise of the Dunn business empire over the course of the next twenty years.

That much aside, by the Christmas of 1901, Julia's imagination and determination were enough to have secured for herself and her daughter a new home and future. She was finally safe from the drudgery of life in Sadiya married to the mild mannered and incurably enthusiastic Jerry Hugo.

Sadly, bearing in mind the hurt they inflicted upon all those to whom they owed deeper respect, Julia and John were not happy. They lived together as man and wife and rode rough shod over the feelings of Dibrugarh society whenever they appeared together in company. John did try to salvage some good from the devastation caused by his misguided alliance. But he lived with his regret as only a man could.

To his credit, it was not long before he realised just how big a fool he had been and how so easily duped. Though he was prevented by his pride from confessing it, in time he did come to appreciate the appalling waste and tragic

418

results of his actions. Deep inside, during rare moments of reflection, he understood that he had lost a loving wife, distanced himself from his children and alienated himself from his mother and two brothers.

The only stumbling block was his refusal to make confession. He erected instead a sturdy wall of denial, a public image of his circumstances so distorted as to be a caricature.

No fences were mended because he made no serious attempt to mend any. No messages of sympathy or apology were sent out from Mancotta because in a supreme act of self-delusion, he pretended there were none due.

He continued to provide for Marian and his children, but paid them no heed. He, Philip and Terence rarely spoke, their days together as brothers in arms at an end, their sport on the polo field no longer shared. Mother and son made no contact at all. In John's eyes, his mother was the living embodiment of everything he most loathed about his father. While in hers, he was a fool to match all fools, a man so flawed she could scarcely believe he had sprung from her. Their separation was absolute, their reconciliation as unlikely as stars falling from the night skies.

But perhaps saddest blow of all was the fate of Shahjan itself. Marian stayed on in the bungalow. She and an ageing Booloo did their best to keep the place from the march of the jungle. But generally, the estate itself was let go. John rarely set foot on the land. Tea production had ceased as usual in the October of 1901. From that point onwards, little or no work was concentrated on what had for so many years been his pride and joy.

Marian was not altogether surprised at his desertion of her. Over the years, the passion of their relationship had paled to something quite commonplace. Lacking that vital spark of electricity and with only affection to sustain it, their marriage had become not much more than a mutual convenience.

John had his work and his polo. Marian had her children. When the two came together, or overlapped, their relationship was cordial. There were few complaints on either side. Marian was content with her lot. Once upon a time she craved the highs and lows of being in love. But those days were long gone. Her marriage to John was satisfactory, an arrangement as good as many and no worse than some. The mild hypocrisy of their public image was made less by their deep respect one for the other and ample evidence that their children were growing with smiles on their faces and warmth in their hearts.

That Mrs Julia Hugo therefore should have so easily seduced John was no startling revelation. She had done it before as a younger woman, if only briefly. However, she had returned to Dibrugarh fully aware of her considerable attractions and primed to use them. Once she set her sights on John, nothing followed that was not entirely predictable. In many respects, Julia was a remarkable woman. Not only was she startlingly handsome, very much aware of it and more than prepared to use such a formidable weapon to her advantage whenever it suited, but she had managed to produce and raise a daughter in her own image.

In Fanny, there was little of her true father to be recognised. She was similar in features and colouring to her mother, sported the same disarming smile and appeared on the surface at least, even at the tender age of twelve, well prepared to follow her mother's creed that with guile and charm anything in life is possible, any goal obtainable.

No, Marian did not lose too much sleep over the loss of her husband. Her own self-respect was dented and her feelings hurt by his desertion of her. However, she refused to be brought low by Julia's victory. The winning away of John from her was no great challenge. Both women knew that.

Over the years, John had sought physical pleasure and satisfaction in the arms of many other women. In competition with his father, his womanising became something of a legend. As Verity had done with her own husband, so Marian had learned to live with it in hers. She approached John's many infidelities not as infidelity at all but as a curious affliction, an ague which once understood was unlikely to threaten the core of their relationship.

Quite naturally, she was disappointed with and in John. She would have hoped for rather more resistance than he offered before finally succumbing to his adversary. More to the point, though she hid it well, she was hurt by the manner in which he turned his back on their children. After all, they were not complicit in any betrayal of their responsibilities. They had done nothing to deserve their father's indifference. If Marian despised Julia, and she did, it was not for the method she employed to trick John away, nor for the ruthlessness of her ambition, but for the cruel manner in which she appeared to encourage John to abandon his children.

However, if there were revelations, or, more precisely, if there was one overriding revelation during the whole sorry saga, a revelation which became evident in the new year of 1902, it was John's abandonment of Shahjan.

It was possible to surmise that the death of his father no longer spurred him to the personal ambition which formerly so preoccupied his every thought and deed. The emblem of his success that Shahjan was, no longer possessed the same meaning once the 'old man' was not there to have it thrust in his face. Certainly, while Marian was ready to blame Julia for most of the sins of the world, the theft of her husband being only the first item atop a long list, she was not of a mind to give her all the credit for having persuaded John to destroy, by indifference, the land, labour and love he once held for Shahjan.

To see the estate creep into decay was the saddest sight of all. For Shahjan was no ordinary tea garden. True it had been claimed from the jungle like any other. True like any other, it had taken toil and tears, and years of them, to reap a harvest. But like no other, at least in its strength of commitment, it represented the personal endeavour of one man. The land was rather poor, the lay of it unfriendly and, for some years in the beginning the leaf was good enough only for blending.

John, and John alone, believed in it. His perseverance, or down right bloody mindedness, call it what you will, was the sole reason for its success. Undoubtedly much if not most of his endeavour was inspired because his father taunted him with predictions that he had neither the talent nor drive to make it work. And Marian was aware that without so scathing an indictment of his character or will power, John might easily have turned his back on the enterprise years earlier.

Nevertheless, and regardless of the motives, beyond all predictions, Shahjan had thrived. It succeeded, cultivating eventually a high-grade leaf, easy to the wither and producing a tea with a distinct yet deservedly individual flavour. For a while, it was also a home and a happy one at that.

After Marjorie's death, if Marian needed solitude or time to reflect, she was in the habit of visiting Mancotta, drawn as if by some invisible but benign force. There, on the veranda, or walking in the cool gardens, with memories of Jack and Marjorie a pick-me-up to any mood of melancholy, she delighted as nowhere else in her surroundings.

However, in all other aspects of her life, Shahjan served as the corner stone of Marian's contentment. In the face of her husband's infidelities, discreet or otherwise, it offered solace enough to sustain her. In her letters home she claimed time after time there was nowhere else on earth she would rather be, insisting that there could be no better place to bring up three children, no finer landscape to please the eye, no sweeter music than the melody of the jungle so close at hand.

It beggared belief that so rare a place and so much sheer hard work could be let go with so little resistance. How on earth could a single woman persuade a man to a course of such wanton vandalism. What power did Julia possess over John that he was prepared to turn his back on the estate he so often professed to love, displaying for it, as he had, a depth of affection he found impossible to describe.

The answer, of course, was that she did not. All said and done, Julia was but flesh and blood. She was an accomplished temptress, of that there could be no doubt. She was gifted with some ingredient which went far beyond simple attraction. She was able to seduce and then ruin the hardest of hearts or the most resistant of men. Whatever powers she possessed which most other women did not, she had in abundance and, from all evidence, appeared to have passed them on to her daughter. But there was more to it than that. Julia was not the first woman to distract John. There were many, some prettier, some more intelligent and some in a position to offer far more in terms of a future than the bored wife of a railway engineer.

No indeed. In the harsh light of day, Marian concluded that Julia's victory was not entirely of her own making. She had an ally, a force so powerful and yet so well hidden few except a wife or a mother might have noticed its presence at all. Trevelyan Dunn was that force; John's father. From the grave, he claimed the ultimate victory over his son.

Had John stuck to Shahjan, kept it on, improved it, expanded it, made it thrive and handed it on to his own son, that would have been a victory, the prize he sought all the years his father was alive. But he was too simple a man to realise the truth. With Trevelyan in his grave John believed he had nothing more to prove, no more need to win. Shahjan was no longer of importance. It had become expendable, its purpose for being an irrelevance. Once it had been the driving force, John's 'raison d'etre.' He farmed it with passion, husbanded the soil with tender care and, aside from his love of polo, Shahjan was held higher in his affections than any living being.

For years, Marian accepted and respected the unique place it held in her husband's heart. Though his motives were flawed and the undoubted obsession he had of flying in the face of his father's derision, clear evidence of a mind less intellectually advantaged than her own, she admired not only his determination to succeed, but the quite remarkable achievement Shahjan became under his care.

To see any land spoil for no good reason would have been cause for distress. But for Marian to watch Shahjan fall into decay was a tragedy beyond compare. Nature might have done the damage. Flood waters had tried to sweep it from the surface of the earth and somehow that would have been a bearable sorrow. Nothing, however, could soothe the pain of being witness to such wilful neglect, such awful evidence that Shahjan was and always had been no more than an exhibition of one man's arrogant defiance of another.

As each day passed and still there was no sign that John intended to relent, the garden slipped further and further into decline. Like an incoming tide, the jungle crept ever nearer the bungalow, closing in around Marian, the acres laid to tea offering little resistance.

Eventually she could contain herself no longer. Unwilling to do so, but unable to resist the need, she rode one day to Mancotta. Her mission was simple and in earnest, namely to persuade John to revive his interest in Shahjan before it was too late. If she could not appeal to his humanity then she would demand that he reconcile with the estate along simple financial lines.

She was nervous. After his abandonment of her in favour of Julia, she had become something of a recluse. She rarely left Shahjan. Months passed between trips into Dibrugarh. In part this was because she was ashamed at having lost her husband to another woman but equally because there was little beyond her children and her home which was of interest.

Living alone was hard. Immediately before the arrival of the two ladies 'Hugo,' mother and daughter, Marian's relationship with John was as it had been for a few years, casual yet possessed of a mutual fondness which served as a warm blanket on cold nights and kept both from the jaws of loneliness.

On the rare occasions they slept together the passion did return. It was and always had been the corner stone of their relationship. For brief spells during the night, they came together and were joined, all emotion, all tactile intimacy exchanged in a single dynamic intercourse, the need for small and frequent gestures throughout the day unnecessary. Sadly, to her cost, Julia exploded the myth. She made a mockery of everything Marian thought of as solid ground beneath her feet.

Consequently, riding to Mancotta was a challenge she dreaded. Twice she was on the verge of turning back. She had no wish to confront her adversary, no desire to be at Mancotta with its new incumbents. She remembered it when Jack and Marjorie were alive, and, afterwards, when she was wont to go there on her own, to be alone with her thoughts. Then it was a happy place, a place which echoed to a lifetime of love poured into it. Shahjan was her home. Marian had made it so, for herself and for her children. However, Mancotta was extraordinary. There was something very special indeed about it, a cocktail of natural beauty and an atmosphere entirely its own.

On this occasion she did not expect to encounter the same again. She could not imagine the magic would endure with John and Julia living there. For a time, after Marjorie's death the bungalow had been boarded up. Under the temporary management of Thomas Gulliland who had volunteered his services as a token of respect for Marjorie and Jack alike, the estate flourished but the house was left empty. Jack and Marjorie were gone, but the beauty remained. Selfishly, Marian loved it even more then, when she could go there on her own and be alone for hours at a time in company with her thoughts, her mind at peace.

Not so as she approached the bungalow on what was a chill and dreary morning. Her mind was far from peaceful. She was agitated, even a little afraid. With no idea how she would be greeted and only an outline prepared of what she wanted to say, she shouted her 'koi hais' with little expectation of being received with any sort of a welcome.

By prior arrangement and in direct response to the note Marian had sent in advance of her visit, John was not at work but waiting to meet her. His pony was tied up outside. Its reins were hitched to a post supporting the veranda, as was his habit when returning from the fields prematurely, his intention to resume work just as soon as he could after whatever interruption had called him home.

'Snowden' had long since died. Marian remembered well just how dreadfully upset John was on the day of his death and for some time afterwards. Quite suddenly the poor animal went down with colic. Over a period of twenty-four hours he became weaker and weaker until finally he pitched over on to his side and would not budge. John knew what he had to do. He shot him where he lay and then cried like a baby, his heart break that of a father losing a child.

Since that day, he was in the habit of changing his ponies on a regular basis. The restless one, shifting constantly from one leg to another and grinding its bit like an infant chewing a rattle, impatient to be freed from its tether, was but one in a long line post-dating dear 'Snowden' who had been more man's best friend than horse, more companion than beast of burden.

'Thank you for seeing me,' was the first thing Marian said to John as they sat down together on the veranda, the view one she could have drawn from memory as accurately as any photograph could record.

'How are you?' he asked, clearly meaning it, his eyes intense and focussed upon her.

'Well. Thank you.'

'The children?'

'Well. Missing their father, but well.'

'Please!' he said, the single word enough to halt any progress Marian intended towards making her estranged husband feel guilty.

Shahjan was the purpose of her visit and it was on that basis alone John had agreed to see her. He was aware of the consequences of setting up home with his mistress. He needed no reminding of the costs or the extent to which he had deserted his responsibilities.

Perhaps he was a fool. Perhaps he was as selfish and misguided as his mistress, but he was not completely blind. He missed his children more than Marian knew or he dared admit. He was paying a high price for his final, infidelity and not a day passed he did not count the cost.

'I'm sorry,' she replied.

'You wanted to talk to me about Shahjan,' he said, 'Please let's keep the conversation to that.'

'Agreed.'

'Good.'

For the remainder of their meeting Marian was true to her word. She avoided any attempt at emotional blackmail or moral reprimands. Instead, they discussed the business in hand, the business of what was going to happen to Shahjan. Something had to be done before it was too late. The situation was becoming critical. Soon there would be no recovering what was lost. The jungle was taking back what once belonged to it at an alarming rate. Shahjan had to be saved and saved quickly. Otherwise, it would be gone forever.

Surprisingly, John agreed. He was not prepared to offer any particular excuse for his abuse of it. He confessed nothing and excused nothing. Marian was left to conclude for herself what combination of events and influences had brought about a falling out of love with the one place which had previously occupied so vital a space in his heart.

Fortunately, Julia was elsewhere in the bungalow. Not once during the visit did Marian catch sight of her, although she was aware of her influence. John's words were spoken with the guarded manner of a man who had ceased to be the master of his own destiny, his every syllable and change of tone as directed as if Julia were hovering in the wings, cue sheet open on the page.

There was no sense in appealing to John's emotions because they were no longer his own. Enhanced by practice, he spoke of Shahjan as if it were no more than an irksome patch of land, as if its past meant as little to him as its future. He feigned disinterest in the ravages of time and appeared unimpressed by Marian's graphic descriptions of decay.

'You have it,' he said in the end, by way of a convenient solution to a problem which was keeping him away from his work for longer than he liked. 'I'll make a gift of it to you. You can do with it as you wish. Keep it on and run it yourself, or sell it. I'll have the papers drawn up in the next few days. Shahjan means nothing to me anymore.'

But she knew better than that. She knew his words were not his own. Over years, she had seen with her own eyes she devotion he lavished on it.

'I don't believe you,' Marian said, a clear challenge in her voice.

'Frankly Marian, it's of little interest to me what you believe,' he replied, the sudden knife edge in his voice honed to inflict a single but deep wound, the blade stamped with Julia's own hallmark. 'For all I care, Shahjan can go back to jungle or to the devil. If you're so concerned for its welfare then best you have it. Mancotta's my home now and until Kurmi becomes mine, this is where I intend to stay.'

His words were like a venom. Before setting out to Mancotta, Marian had no idea what to expect. She hoped for an amicable, conciliatory conversation with her husband, some hope at least that Shahjan was not lost. When she arrived, she was relieved to find Julia tactfully absent. She had no wish to meet Julia or talk with her.

She wanted only to debate the future of Shahjan with her husband and, more than anything, hoped to see in his eyes some glimmer of past affection, not for herself perhaps but at least for the land he had nursed with such dedication.

His cold dismissal was not at all what she anticipated. Hence, the only conclusion she could draw was that while Julia might not have been present in any physical form, her influence was in his every word. She did not recognise John as the same man to whom she had been married for nearly twelve years. He was changed beyond recognition. There was a bitterness about him. It was clear that their meeting was convened on sufferance and that, so as not to display an ounce of weakness to the face of an enemy who in this instance happened to be his own wife, he was in no mind to give an inch of ground.

In spite of his insistence that she should have Shahjan, as far as she was concerned, Marian returned home with nothing. Her endeavour had been thwarted by a stone wall of resistance. Why John had changed, who or what had changed him, she cared not a jot. She was tired of excusing his behaviour, of forgiving him. Save for Booloo, she was alone, with three children and a tea garden going to ruin. She came away from Mancotta with little more than confirmation that her husband could not have cared less; no practical resolution and no hope of reconciliation. His fortifications were not to be breached by the inadequate forces she levelled against them. For preference, of course, she chose to lay the blame squarely at Julia's door.

Consequently, her name featured large in Marian's diary. Of the meeting with John, she wrote that self-evidently, he spoke words prepared for him by his mistress, that his coldness was inspired by her, that his dismissal of Shahjan was at her instigation and that the bitterness in his voice was a reflection of her own. It was the same bitterness and desire for revenge Julia had brought with her when she arrived back in Dibrugarh, daughter in tow, from years of involuntary exile in Sadiya with Jerry.

What the pages of her diary failed to record was anything but the most trivial of details regarding her own last days at Shahjan.

Chapter Twenty-Eight

Marian quit Shahjan, Dibrugarh and Assam with her three children on 23 April 1902, a little over sixteen years after her arrival in India. Then, the sun had shone on the Gateway to India at the entrance to Bombay. Then it had been hot and humid and an apprehensive Marian was pleased to accept Sir Archibald and Lady Caroline Farrer as her chaperones. Now, on the day of her departure, it was raining, hard enough to disguise any visible signs of her heartbreak but not hard enough to delay her going. And she was alone.

John came to see her off at Dibrugarh station. So too did Verity Dunn and Terence, though, strangely, Philip, for reasons of his own, stayed away. He preferred to excuse himself on the grounds of work rather than confront, it was believed, an older brother with whom his relationship had become so severely strained.

He did write a farewell note of some length and although Marian understood the difficulty of facing up to John in public, she deeply regretted not having a final opportunity to say farewell to him in person.

Of course, there was so much for Marian to regret, so much sorrow to hold back behind the flood gates, that Philips absence was but one disappointment to tolerate among many.

Ask me how heavy it is possible for one heart to feel and I will tell you I do not know. All I can say with any certainty is that on the morning Marian left Dibrugarh for the last time, her heart was shattered beyond repair.

She hid it well. She hid it from her children. She hid it too from all those few who came to say their farewells. She even managed to hide it from Mr and Mrs Matthew Fairhurst, majority shareholders of the Assam Frontier Tea Company and the new, proud owners of the Shahjan Tea Estate. Her home was now their home, the paradise on earth she had written of so often in her letters home, theirs to do with as they wished.

It was a day Marian had not planned for, a circumstance beyond anything she imagined possible. Shahjan was lost to her. She was homeless and stateless. Worse, apparently, she was to be denied an ounce of pity from the husband she had companioned for so many years or from the family she had assumed as her own. In the end, aside from simple vagrancy, she was presented with but one alternative.

She had no option but to return to England, to her own family, a failure. For consolation, she had her children. At least, John made no attempt to deprive her of them. After all, they needed an education. In England, they would receive one and later, when his son was of an age to determine his own future, then he would return to Assam to fulfil the responsibilities expected of him. Until that time, he and his sisters were better off with their mother, a calculation as pragmatic as it was convenient to John's circumstances.

The money from the sale of Shahjan was settled in trust. It would provide Marian with an annual income sufficient to her needs and serve to finance whatever education was deemed appropriate for all three children.

Convenient indeed was the course of action decided upon to all but Marian herself. No matter the consequences to her heart, no matter the disruption to her happiness, unanimity of approval accompanied her going. Only she, struggling like a drowning man to stay afloat, felt herself being sucked below the surface, suffocating beneath a cruel, cold sea.

She would never, could never, recover. She thought of her sister Margaret, locked into a loveless, childless marriage with a dentist. She recalled too poor Katie who returned home to England, children in her arms, dismay in her heart.

But she was not consoled by their hardships. Margaret had found happiness of a sort. She did not fulfil her dream of becoming a missionary. Her marriage was a dull, lifeless affair, but in her own way she was content. And, in spite of her hopelessness at the time, Katie recovered from being made a widow at such a young age to meet and fall in love with another man, a solid, reliable and doting barrister. He it was who first took pity on her when he was retained to disentangle the confusion of affairs after the sorry demise of Mr Kenneth in his Paris studio. His conscientious endeavours spilled over into affection, love and though it took an extraordinarily laboured period of courtship to cement the concept, marriage.

For Marian, however, there would be no such happy endings. Leaving Shahjan was too harsh a blow. She was being punished for crimes she could not identify with any clarity. Search though she did, with the intensity as if on a mission to find her very soul, she could not discover an explanation for so severe a retribution.

As a young woman, years before, she had set sail for India to find solutions, to encounter an understanding as to why and how of a young man whom she loved so dearly had been stolen from her. A lifetime later, she was returning home, not with answers but more questions. And they were questions beyond the wisdom of even the sadhus themselves, their emaciated bodies, cross legged and racked with the pain of self-sacrifice, perched like pensive crows on the ghats at Benares, Mother Ganga flowing at their feet.

Clearly, she had committed many crimes, crimes so appalling no redemption was to be accorded her. But what were these crimes. Why was she to be deprived of everything in life which made the air possible to breath and the forward motion of the years hold any reason.

Julia, the executioner, had done her job well. She had cast a spell over John, a spell which had him spurn his wife and then speak of it as 'being for the best,' a prick as painful as it was deep.

As she boarded the train, Marian cast a glance into the distance. Once upon a time, Jerry Hugo, like a knight in shining armour, crossed a continent to be at her side in her hour of need. Had he but stayed put. Had he instead but delayed his expedition for this moment.

Jonathan's death was a load she could have carried alone. Jerry came too soon. Impetuous as always, he could not hold back until her need was the greatest. He wasted the gesture on a single sorrow. He should have waited for her sorrows to double and treble. Had he done so he would have appeared on this day at the end of the platform, his armour gleaming, the sword in his hand honed to sweep away the armies rallied against her. Instead, he was a hundred miles off, the last thoughts on his mind either her timely rescue or a consideration of the contribution by his errant wife towards her downfall.

On this day, there was to be no rescue, no last-minute reprieve. The train pulled away from Dibrugarh with Marian on board, the buildings of the town she had known for so long becoming ever smaller until snatched from view by the curtain of jungle which concealed everything in its depths.

In two days, she reached Calcutta. Inside a week she was at sea, the SS Simla doing what was expected of her in transporting both cargo and passenger's home to England, the vastness of the oceans no obstacle to her progress, the coal in her holds adequate for the purpose in hand.

Marian sought solace in the wide-eyed excitement of her children. Katherine stuck close to her, but Emma and John covered every inch of the ship, introducing themselves to the other passengers, exploring all available nooks and crannies, filling their minds with novelty. Their mood was elated. Their sadness at leaving Shahjan was as nothing to the wonderment of being abroad and the prospect of standing on English soil for the first time.

Both knew Shahjan well, the estates around, a few feet of the jungle border and Dibrugarh. They had watched their father play polo, their mother tend a home and they were as familiar with the production of tea as any planter.

In Calcutta, however, they saw for the first-time grand avenues, buildings of great majesty and a vast population of people few of whose lives were not necessarily taken up with the production of tea. The stop over was all too short, barely long enough for their young eyes to focus on such a confusion of people, streets and buildings. No wonder therefore that once at sea their fondness for Shahjan was set to one side.

In such circumstances, they were not to blame for ignoring the deep anguish afflicting their mother. Their selfishness was a prerequisite of youth, their focussed enthusiasm an infection made more virulent by the narrow borders of childhood and their childhoods in particular.

Marian doubted they were aware of her despair but it mattered little. She could not resent the blindness of her children. Her pain was not their pain. She neither expected their participation nor looked to them for support. They were explorers, navigators, not victims. She was the refugee cast into exile.

Katherine tended to stay close by her mother but not in sympathy. For her this new, wider world was too new and too wide, the scale of people, places and oceans too much to comprehend without the firm grasp of a mother's hand.

In later years Emma, namely I, and John would recall the voyage to England with absolute clarity. By contrast Katherine would be able to recount little. And Marian, my mother? Well, who knows how much she chose to remember and how much she tried to forget? From the day she left Shahjan for the last time her diaries ceased. It was as if there was nothing left to say, nothing else worthy of record.

The SS Simla slipped quietly on to her berth at the Queen Victoria docks in London on a bright morning in late May 1902. There to greet the valiant ship were hundreds of smiling, happy faces, the families and loved ones of those on board who had come so far and been delivered home safe.

431

My mother had us assembled and ready to disembark long before we docked. There to welcome us ashore were a grandfather and grandmother I had never met, two aunts and two cousins, all come to bring home a woman who, in failing to continue a record of her life begun when she was younger than I, burdened me with the telling of our arrival and the days beyond.

So kind was my mother, so gentle and intelligent, I have made it my duty to retell these stories of her adult life and, where necessary, to attempt an interpretation of events and emotions. From the pages of her diaries, I have gleaned the dates and facts which have made the telling a simple task.

Sadly though, from the day we left Assam, the well dried up. Less eloquent than my mother, normally less inclined to put pen to paper, my memories of places and events are needlessly flawed by incompetence. In my continuance there is bound, I am afraid, to be both brevity and inaccuracy. In stark contrast to my mother, I do not delight in the writing down of my every action or thought. I am not the sort to compile page after page of the written word, to commit to paper the mundane or trivial of my life alongside moments of extreme joy or heartbreak.

I can recall with absolute clarity, however, the morning of our arrival in London. What child would not who had led such a sheltered upbringing. If the truth be known, I was too impressed by the symphony of sight and sound bombarding me from every direction to be absorbed in any meaningful way by the new members of my family come from Kensington to greet us. But by way of a courtesy, I will attend to them first, their collective display of familial loyalty being the only thing to raise a smile from my mother in what had begun to feel to John and I like an eternity of sorrow.

Our mother was, it can be said, overjoyed to see them. The very second she spied them from the promenade deck, even before our trusty ship was tied fast and the gang planks lowered; I stood beside her and watched, in relief I might say, as she waved and shouted and laughed with almost uncontrollable happiness to those gathered on the quayside.

Once ashore there was a procession of embraces and tears all round. However, even as a young girl, I was left in no doubt which reunion heralded the greatest joy.

My grandfather was a refined and elegant gentleman. I noticed at once he had a kind face and, something I became aware of only later, a pronounced limp hidden as best he could to conceal a fast-disintegrating hip joint. He and my mother hugged each other as if they might never let go. The final hello, his, was clearly the most coveted.

You may not be surprised therefore to read that at the moment of re-acquaintance, I remember being puzzled at my mother's mourning so deeply our leaving Shahjan. This when, quite obviously, the reality of being reunited with her family initiated such a spontaneous and overwhelming outpouring of affection.

Who suffered the most in a separation which had endured over so many years was difficult to gauge. On that morning, however, it was of no significance. After the perpetual melancholy of our long sea voyage, I was so very pleased to see my mother thus transformed. Perhaps it would be a temporary condition. Perhaps the sadness in her heart would rise again to the surface, but for a brief period at least I could see a level of joy in her eyes I had witnessed only rarely.

Eventually, my grandfather began the somewhat tricky task of dividing us all up into three carriages for the journey across town to 32 Princes Gate. We could have squeezed into two well enough but three had been brought, one, it seemed, for the sole purpose of accommodating our many pieces of luggage.

As a result, my mother rode with 'grandpapa' and 'grandmama,' taking Katherine with her because she appeared the most disoriented by the turmoil of our arrival. Meanwhile John and I shared a carriage with Aunts Margaret and Katherine and our two cousins. The latter aunt was known to us of course as Aunt Katie which, being as there were now two Katherines in the family to contend with, was the cause of some small amusement to our adolescent intellects. However, the obligatory prefix of Aunt was enough to avoid confusion of the one with our rather younger and, it must be said, less vocal sister. As nice as my Aunt Katie was and indeed still is, she has always been prone rather to monopolise the conversation.

So, what can I say of our ride through London from east to west? How can I best translate the wonderment of a girl soon to turn fifteen, whose imagination was still reeling from the sights and sounds of a brief stopover in India's first city?

I was used to Shahjan. I knew a little of the jungle, its dangers and its mystery. I was familiar with the gentile bustle of Dibrugarh. On many occasions I had experienced the excitement of polo days, of parades and of trains coming and going. I understood well and was in awe of the mighty Brahmaputra. I could name many species of tropical bird and even identify by taste or aroma a wide

433

range of different teas. But no astonishment could compare to that first carriage ride upon our arrival in England.

If my two aunts were intent upon engaging John and I in conversation, they were to be disappointed. In as much as our two cousins were expected to established the opening bars of friendship, we let them down.

I on one side and John on the other, sat with our noses glued to the windows, every novelty, and there was a novelty in every yard of our progress, a wonderment beyond compare, to be gazed upon and gasped at in unison. We were transfixed. Conversation was beyond us. The only noises to come from our mouths were unintelligible exclamations, all expressing disbelief and all shared with mutual disregard for our travelling companions.

By the time we reached 32 Princes Gate, both John and I were exhausted. We had been in the carriages for what must have been upwards of an hour, yet we knew our two aunts and cousins no better than when we first stepped ashore from the SS Simla.

Our rudeness was profound, but they appeared unruffled. Forgiving of our ill manners, their own irregular conversation was apparently unaffected by our presence, their feelings not offended by our preoccupation with matters beyond the windows of the carriage.

And for a week at least, after our arrival, John and I remained in the same generally uncommunicative state as on that first morning; so great was our continued distraction at everything we saw and heard around us.

Looking back now, to our grandparents and aunts, we must have seemed a strange pair. We must also have been, I suspect, something of an enigma to our cousins although much to our relief, they appeared to enjoy their own company almost as much as John and I relished ours. They were perfectly willing to forego the bonding process with their three relatives from India in favour of persistent games of hide and seek. These they played throughout the full four stories of a house which was in itself a considerable curiosity to us new arrivals, entirely used as we were to bungalow living.

Not to overstate the point, to John, Katherine and myself, London was a supremely magical place. Kensington Park, the palace, the serpentine lake, Knightsbridge and the sheer numbers of people on horseback, in carriages and even aboard extraordinary motorised vehicles was more than our young eyes or minds could grasp.

We were in a wonderland. All thoughts of Shahjan were obliterated by the spectacle of our every waking hour. Only Katherine showed signs of pining for what we had left behind. Mostly these were in the form of sulking or fretful bouts of tears, made worse when shortly after our installation at 32 Princes Gate, she was confined to bed with a severe fever. The doctor endeavoured to persuade my mother it was of a variety which poor Katherine must have contracted while we were still at sea. He was equally convinced that its inspiration came from direct contact with some 'darkie,' the word itself pronounced by him in a manner which left no doubt as to his distaste for those whose skin was not the same colour as his own.

Fortunately, I did not fall ill. I did not like the family physician very much. I would not have enjoyed being attended by a man of such vehement prejudices. In fact, with some determination, I stayed quite well. Mother reprimanded me for being over excited much of the time. But she was even handed. She accused John of just the same and with equal frequency.

Yet, how could we not be excited, spell bound even, by so vast and brilliant a city, two rag-a-muffin children for whom every day brought forth new enchantments. It is not difficult for me to recount those first weeks in England. I remember the exhilaration of it all only too well and I still feast upon the unbridled exuberance of my behaviour. I am bound to say too, and with a considerable degree of satisfaction, that throughout the all too brief first encounter with western life in England, I have never been closer to or felt more affection for my brother.

By the by, he returned to Assam some years ago. As predicted, he went back to be with his father and take up the responsibilities of carrying on the Dunn estates. Added to that was the need and burden of consoling a man in grief. Though she was the cause of much heart ache to my family, more particularly to my mother who was never able to forgive her for the deception and method of bringing about our exile from Shahjan, Julia's premature death after a serious fall from her horse during a violent down pour not a half mile from Kurmi, was a matter of considerable regret to us all and of the deepest possible sorrow to my father.

Although mother always stayed legally married to him, she lost the battle to keep him as a husband. Never, however, did she cease to care for him. Consequently, news of his loss was the cause of considerable sadness to her as well.

However, I am jumping ahead of myself. My brothers return to Assam and the particular tragedy of Julia's death were some ways in the future.

As much as John and I were absorbed during our first weeks in London, so too was my mother. Like a Christian reborn she was overwhelmed by the sheer pleasure of once again being among her family. She quickly returned to the habit of riding each morning in the park with my grandfather, a habit first begun when she was the same age and younger than myself. And, though my grandfather found it more difficult to mount his horse than once he had, excusing himself from too long a period in the saddle at any one time, it was as if the habit had continued unbroken. Their relationship, indeed my mother's relationship with all those dearest to her, returned to normality with remarkable speed.

There was a modest welcome home party of course, attended by friends and relatives alike. Few of these I knew or much wanted to know. Nevertheless, to all them, both John and I were introduced with monotonous frequency. The bedridden Katherine, of whom I soon became extremely jealous, was the only one spared so tedious a duty. One or two of the more stalwart guests did make the climb to her bedroom on the third floor of the house. However, most were content to postpone their introduction until she was well enough to be received into the drawing room, fit and well and prettily dressed.

Three or four 'at homes' were also held in rapid succession, for which John and I were also expected to turn out as primly as we were able. This was a chore as abhorrent as it was difficult to achieve for two young people more used to running barefoot through tea houses or plantation fields and whose only previous experiences of respectable society were the two annual polo tournaments in Dibrugarh.

By contrast, although my mother had not seen England for many years, she adapted well into London life of the twentieth century, almost as if she had not been away. Most things were familiar to her. My grandmother who was, I might say, as kind to all three of us children as could be, grieved loudly for my mother's lack of an up-to-date wardrobe, indeed any wardrobe at all. Furthermore, she could not come to terms with the shortness of my mother's hair, a shortness she had adopted long before I was born and kept to ever since.

Grand mama' also dedicated herself to the task of correcting in my mother small, but apparently bad habits which she had allowed herself to get into over the years. All in all, however, it was a relatively easy return home.

Not so for John, Katherine and myself. Because of her age, Katherine was the least affected. Of course she missed Assam. To a degree, she, like John and I, was home sick from the start. She missed all the same things we did and undoubtedly her illness lingered longer than it might have done, had she not felt quite so lost and in such a strange environment.

On the other hand, John and I were caught between two stools. We were overcome with the excitement of our new surroundings. Each dawn brought forth a feast of novel attractions; new places to visit, new things to do and, though perhaps the least inviting, new people to meet. Much of the time we were wide-eyed with the wonderment of it all.

However, there was no denying we missed home. I could say we missed our father as well, but in all honesty, I would have to confess his absence was the least of our sorrows. Even before the day he moved out of Shahjan, we saw comparatively little of him. Incidentally it was a day I shall never forget on account of the explosive exchanges between both my parents as his valises were being taken from our bungalow.

That said, we were fond of our father. Of course we were, as fond as any children could be. He was our father and we loved him, just as he loved us, in his own way. It was simply that we did not see very much of him. Occasionally we would be taken to visit him working in the leaf houses or tea sheds. As often as not, when old enough to know how to behave ourselves in public, we were taken to watch him play polo.

However, we did not know him well. Later, when he took up with Mrs Hugo, even less. I can only speak for myself and, although I am probably failing dreadfully in my duty by confessing it, of all the things I missed most in being so far from Shahjan, my father was the least of them.

I shall always love him. Should I never see him again he will always hold a place in my heart. What I know of him at first hand and from threading through the pages of my mother's diaries, convinces me that in spite of everything he is and always was essentially a good man. He was misguided and foolish perhaps in having given my mother and us up for a woman like Mrs Hugo. Certainly, he was a man who found it difficult to adopt the responsibilities of fatherhood. Nevertheless, I truly believe he always loved us. I also like to think he missed us.

Whatever the truth, for as long as my mother had anything to do with it, we were obliged to write to him on a regular basis.

No. My home sickness, such as it was, and there were times it was acute, did not gain its inspiration from any noticeable lack of fatherly affection. That was a scarce commodity even when he was in residence at Shahjan.

I missed the place. I missed our home. I missed the estate, the jungle, Booloo and all the myriad of tiny things which were as familiar to me as breathing. I missed feeling at ease and I missed the joy of being alone with my thoughts whenever I chose.

In short, I suppose, I missed most being me, the person I knew I was, not the young woman my grandmother was so intent upon me becoming. I felt uncomfortable in fashionable and restrictive clothing. I disliked the expectation that I should conduct myself as a lady at all times.

But most certainly, worst of all, I refused to accept the notion that I should be on display every waking moment, an object, to be shown off, exhibited like one of the many works of art my mother took us to see at the Royal Academy, never I might add in the company of our two cousins. Like soldiers, we were almost always on parade. Rarely after our arrival at 32 Princes Gate were we permitted to behave as ourselves, to be the children we were used to being.

In many ways, of course, it was not at all a bad thing. We were 'wayward.' We were 'high spirited.' And to a certain extent, I will admit we were in need of considerable reform. We were like mustangs in need of breaking.

However, the constrictions placed upon us, and upon me in particular, were inclined to have our hearts leap back to times before our great voyage across the seas to England. John and I were thus of two minds, frustratingly held at a fork in the road. To the left lay a broad path along which our hearts journeyed back to Assam. To the right lay the unparalleled adventure of our future in England.

Both were inviting. Both drew us towards them like a magnet. As a result, we were constantly caught betwixt and between, a most unsettling situation in which to find oneself. Needless to say, it is also one with which I have never, or not yet, come to terms.

To this day, I am still, two people. I still pine for Assam. I still have in my blood something of the girl who grew up there. I still yearn for the freedom I once had, the uncomplicated, easy, barefoot life afforded to plantation children which was as natural to me then as London was strange when we first arrived.

But unlike John, I have never been back and I doubt I will. In all but a few eccentricities I have made the cultural leap from one continent to the other. Only those who know me very well indeed catch sight of the child from Assam.

However, I digress. Thus far, this tale has been about my mother and so it should continue. I have owned up to being the narrator simply because with no further diaries to draw my stories from, you, the reader, will have to rely upon my evidence. I will try to be as fair and objective as possible, although you will have to excuse my necessarily partisan account.

Of all the people in the world I loved and treasured, my mother was by far and away most deserving of my affection. I will not claim that she is or was she the most dominant figure in my life but she certainly is and always has been the most deserving of my affection, gratitude and respect.

That said, I will continue and try as far as possible not to explore too much my own part in the tale. It is to my mother I must turn. The discovery of her diaries is what began it and, though, as I have previously stated, she ceased to write a journal at all from the day we left Shahjan, I am duty bound to continue from her perspective.

London to me, in the spring of 1902, was a strange and wonderful place, as it was for my brother and, to a lesser extent Katherine. At the same time, it was intimidating and too vast for young minds to comprehend, a fact made more potent to Katherine than myself because of our age difference. We did not, however, and I say this for the three of us because I believe it to be true, feel the pain of separation from Shahjan as deeply as my mother.

She adapted to London more quickly than we did in spite of the fact that in many respects it had changed significantly during the years she had been away. There were more people. There was more traffic and society was moving on rapidly from the strict social conventions of the latter half of the nineteenth century in which she had grown up.

Nevertheless, I was assured many times that 32 Princes Gate itself had altered little. Of course, there had been revisions in the decor and furnishings. There was also a host of new appliances cluttering the kitchens. 'Above stairs,' a telephone had been installed. But essentially, it was still the home my mother had left behind, a familiar, safe place, one she knew well and for which she held so many fond memories.

Moreover, my grandfather and grandmother were there, constant stars to guide her. Aunt Katie was unrecognisable from the selfish, whimsical young girl I was led to believe she once was. On the other hand, Margaret, save for natures cruel process of ageing, was exactly the same as she had always been. She was nervous in company and as intense on the topic of evangelism as she was silent on the subject of her dentist husband, a gentleman we did not encounter until well into the second month after our arrival.

However, and it is a 'however' I cannot emphasise sufficiently, regardless of the familiarity with her surroundings and the clear restoration of affection from those who loved her and whom, she loved in turn, my mother found the task of adapting to life in London an impossibility.

She was truly overjoyed to see her home and family again. Though young, even I was impressed by the extraordinarily close relationship she owned with my grandfather, a relationship of which I was somewhat envious when I considered the shallowness of that which I held with my own father. No brighter light shone in my mother's eyes than when they were together. The bond between them showed no scars from their years apart, a fact which could not be explained simply as a consequence of their considerable correspondence across the years. I feel certain their closeness would have remained equally as sure-footed and unfettered had there been no communication at all between them.

By the age of fifteen I was still a little gauche. I was naïve, ill-read and dangerously forthright in my opinions. Yet, I was not blind to, nor could I avoid being envious of, the unique bond between father and daughter.

Having said that, it soon became self-evident that there could be no compensation great enough to relieve the tragedy of my mother's being away from Assam. That she ceased writing in her diaries was but one symptom of a desperate and debilitating disease, a wasting sickness. Invisible to the naked eye, imperceptible to all but those closest to her, it gnawed at her, consuming her, draining the life from her like the drip, drip of water seeping from a leaking tap.

Nothing it seemed could fully compensate for the deprivation of being away from Shahjan and the life she had made for herself in Assam.

Find a human soul, wrench it from the body, cast it to the wind and there you might encounter some comparison to my mother's affliction. Otherwise, no known illness or injury can compare. It was beyond home sickness, beyond grief. It was as if a significant part of her was left behind, adrift, destined to wander the jungles and plantations alone. The greater part of her had travelled with us across the oceans. Most of her was there with us at 32 Princes Gate and most of her bathed as we did in the warmth of a home coming devoid of regret or recrimination.

But something was missing. It was a vital spark, something which I was conscious of but could neither identify nor quantify. And it was something without which my mother was lost.

Aunt Margaret, all sensitivity smothered by the monotony of her own existence, was oblivious to the problem. After the initial furore of our arrival, she came to the house infrequently and when she did, made no real effort to engage my mother intimately. Generally, she gave the impression of being singularly unimpressed by the return of yet another prodigal to the fold.

In like manner, if my grandmother was concerned for the spiritual or emotional welfare of her eldest daughter, she kept it to herself. Energy for her preoccupations was levelled at more earthly obstacles such as a regular intake of enriching meals, the latest fashions or essential manoeuvrings of the small social circle she occupied and into which she fervently wanted my mother reintroduced.

Only with Aunt Katie could I say with a degree of certainty that she recognised anything of my mother's altered state. Of course, after so many years of absence, she expected to find her much changed. My aunt knew from first hand and with bitter experience the unavoidable reversals in both character and personality which can be wrought by physical hardship or emotional trauma. She carried with her at all times the scars of one who had sustained her own wounds, who had fought her own battles.

Consequently, unlike Aunt Margaret who had clearly determined at an early age to defy any attempts at extricating herself from the bland existence she aspired to, Katie was privileged with an insight denied to her over pious sister.

She was now a fully grown woman from whom sympathy and understanding flowed readily. As best she could, therefore, Aunt Katie offered her services to my mother as both confidante and guide. Her selflessness was indicative of the degree to which she was improved by her own sorry experiences, most of which I read of either in the pages of my mother's diaries or heard directly from my aunt's own lips as years later she confessed all.

However, the wounds she tended in my mother and the remedies she offered were but a balm. She was able to soothe the pain, but she could not affect a cure. For that, my grandfather was the sole hope of salvation. He understood everything, could empathise with everything; or, if he did not, he had the wisdom to convince my mother that he did.

Of course, I do not want to create the impression that she was permanently morose, that for all the years after our arrival in England she wandered about with a cloud of melancholy hanging above her head, hovering there like some dreadful omen of doom, spoiling life for her and for all those compelled to be near her.

On the contrary. Few people were aware that it was customary for my mother to write diaries and would therefore not have noticed the writing of them had gone from her daily routine. Fewer still could sensibly imagine the uniquely different way of life we had left behind in Assam. And there can be little doubt that, with the possible exception of my grandfather, not a soul came close to appreciating the extent of my mother's inner loneliness. She was certainly not of a mind to burden others with her sorrows and regrets or wallow publicly in her own self-pity.

Those who fed on gossip, a raft of society no different be they in London or at the outer limits of the empire, were appraised of the basic facts, namely that my mother had returned to England leaving behind a husband in Assam. As time passed more trifles of information filtered out into the public domain; the husband's name was John, he was a wealthy tea planter and he had taken up with his mistress and her daughter.

Consequently, my mother received the sort of gleeful sympathy only other women can express when they believe themselves more successful in their marriages than those in need of their compassion.

And, in turn, my own father was vilified. In public he was labelled a scoundrel, while, in private I suspect, he was secretly enthused about as a man of mystery and therefore, among certain women, eminently desirable. Questions were also raised no doubt as to my mother's apparent inability to retain the warmth and affection of the man she had chosen to marry, particularly in the light of him being the second and ignoring the uninteresting fact that she had been widowed from the first.

No indeed. As best she could, and for the most part, my mother did an admirable job of it. She carried on with her life in the spirit those about her encouraged. Whether resident at 32 Princes Gate, Kensington or at 16 Adelaide Drive, Hove, a home, incidentally which John, Katherine and I enjoyed almost as much as Shahjan, she presented herself as a woman moderately content with her lot.

She made no attempt to hide the fact of being without a husband, that she was a woman alone with three children to raise or that to survive she relied entirely upon the love and support of her family, something which did not escape public notice as being less than unique among the daughters of Mr and Mrs Charles Chase.

Having said that, we were not destitute by any means. Taking up residence at 32 Princes Gate was not a matter of charity. We had funds. The money from the sale of Shahjan to Mr and Mrs Fairhurst was held in trust. From it my mother received an adequate annual income. In addition, had she selected to do so, she could have called upon it for the purchase of a modest home for us all to live in. Furthermore, the trust financed my education as well as that of John and Katherine.

No. Our long-term residence at 32 Princes Gate and sometime occupancy of 16 Adelaide Drive, Hove was a matter of choice, just as it was for Aunt Katie and her children. In spite of the moderate chaos of having so many people under a single roof, albeit one more than able to accommodate us all, my grandfather and grandmother were insistent upon our staying on permanently. They appeared ever youthful and snuffed out at its earliest opportunity any notion of our striking out alone.

And we were happy. 32 Princes Gate was not just a place of sanctuary. The atmosphere within was not that of gloom and doom. We children adapted to our new surroundings quickly. So much change combined with so much that was both new and exciting did not permit much time for melancholy. Regularly I reflected upon many things about my life in Assam which I missed. Indeed, I was conscious of them on an almost daily basis. But any misery that my deprivation inspired was quickly overwhelmed by the brilliance and bustle of London or the invigoration and freedom of weeks spent on the south coast.

Our days were simply too full and too varied in content to be brought low by pangs of home sickness. John and I and, to a lesser extent, Katherine, adapted like chameleons to fit our new surroundings. We evolved, the transition from one continent to another, from one life style to another, soon completed, the only visible signs a lingering tan to our skin which other children were without and, as my grandmother was accustomed to putting it, our habit of 'running around the place barefoot like wild animals.'

This was said of course with affection and a smile on her face. Needless to say, neither John nor I did much to correct the fault, so much so that even now, I am never more comfortable than when I can flick off my shoes and roam my own home as I used to as a child at Shahjan. The feeling is instinctive and one I am duly grateful my grandmother failed to eradicate during the long and often difficult process of converting me from a 'wild' young girl into the sophisticated and educated woman she proudly boasted by the time I reached my eighteenth birthday.

Children, of course, do adapt. Like the supple branches of a sapling, they bend easily with the wind, no matter its direction. My mother, however, was not as pliable. She tried to forget and she tried to adapt. She worked tirelessly to perfect the role into which she had been re-cast after so long an absence. There was little surface evidence of the heart break, buried as it was beneath the thin veneer of normality. On the surface, she appeared to slot back into London life perhaps more easily than any of us. For John and Katherine and I, every day brought new experiences and new hurdles. People and places, they were all very different from anything we had known before. Not so for my mother. Everything was familiar; changed a little perhaps, but familiar. Essentially, the colours were the same, only the shades had varied. Thus, within what seemed only a matter of weeks, she gave the impression of being entirely at ease with the extreme change in our surroundings.

But it was not so. As we children wrestled with the more practical problems of a new and altogether alien existence on the other side of the world from Shahjan, appearing brash and universally ignorant of even the most basic of social protocols, our mother laboured to conceal the terrible and insidious pain of separation.

I was not permitted to witness the worst of it. I can only imagine the loneliness of her nights and the sadness of a soul confined for so many afternoons to a bedroom where sorry contemplation was not given the opportunity for release as it bad been previously on the pages of her diary.

Why she stopped writing I have no idea. I have my theories, conclusions which are probably not much different from those of any observer. However, I do wish with all my heart she had continued. I cannot help but believe her misery would have been lessened had she done so. And perhaps there lies an awkward truth. Perhaps my mother was punishing herself. Perhaps she knew the solution. Perhaps she blamed herself so much for the passage of events which brought us to England, she could not bring herself to forgive. In denying herself the comfort of writing, the self-confessional which had steered her through all the problems and sorrows of her life, she was performing a penance.

If that was the case, indeed, whatever the case, I firmly believe it was a mistake. It was a mistake to blame herself for our exile or for the sequence of events which led up to it. It was also a mistake for her to believe, as I am sure she did, that she was in some way deserving of a punishment for having subjected her children to so drastic an alteration in their environment.

We tried to persuade her otherwise. With the exception of Katherine who was quite ill for several months after our arrival in England and remained a docile, inactive little thing for even longer, we adapted quickly to our new surroundings. As far as we could, neither John nor I burdened our mother with selfish demands or recriminations. We took to London and Hove and the plethora of new faces all around us as best we could, like the proverbial ducks to water.

My mother had no cause to feel guilty. But I believe she did. She was tortured with self-guilt and corroded by the constant pain of being apart from her beloved Shahjan.

I was a blossoming girl of fifteen. I was in a new century. At the time, I was too excited to notice. It is only with hindsight, with the knowledge now in my possession, I realise the corrosive sorrow which accompanied my mother from Assam as an unshakeable companion.

During the latter half of 1902 I was too busy to concern myself with intangibles. My interests lay in the company of new friends, clothes and the frustrations of being still too young to attend adult dinner parties and dances. In all but name and the occasional fond glimpse of recollection, I learned to forget Dibrugarh. On dreary days when the weather kept us at home, confined us to the house, I did engage with mild pangs of nostalgia. And I would be less than honest if I did not own certain longings to see my father, although they were less often and to a lesser extent than I expected.

All in all though, I was happy in London. So too, I believe, were John and Katherine. The former, I would say, much preferring Hove. Clearly, and very much in the mould of our father, he was a boy, and later a man, who relished time to himself. Quite at home in his own company, something by contrast which I still tend to avoid at all costs, there was nothing John liked more than to take himself off for long walks along the sea shore. For hours he was gone, come wind or shine, returning only when he was ready to do so and usually clutching some piece of fascinating but excluded from the house, piece of flotsam, which he had found washed up with the previous tide.

In so many ways, he was recognisably the son of his father; both in looks and temperament. Whether this added to my mother's torture or not is difficult to judge. She never mentioned the similarities and certainly she was as caring and

445

loving to my brother as she was to Katherine and I. Occasionally it seemed to me that he was permitted more freedom. Also, I was of the firm belief that when it came to slack rope, he was granted considerably more than I. However, I was content to account for this as a matter of our differing sexes.

When he was ready, John boarded at Harrow, an educational environment dedicated to the preparation of young minds for leadership. John was but one of many from whom much was expected if the empire was to continue through to the next century. He was taught self-belief, self-determination and self-control. His country required much of him and, while the halls of academe played a worthwhile part in his education, it was at the altar of tradition he was expected to worship. Loyalty to king and empire was paramount. Responsibility, respect and sacrifice were the virtues impressed upon him with most vigour.

It was a far cry from the attentions I received through a combination of private tutors and all too tedious yet frequent visits to bible classes, which were forced upon me regardless of my personal dislike of them.

I envied John his time away at school. I longed to be in his shoes, to think with my own mind, to walk my own path.

I dare not say I was smothered. To claim that would be unfair. I was encouraged to think for myself and to grow as an individual. My grandfather was a liberal through and through, even, dare I say it, an egalitarian, a man who encouraged his granddaughters just as he had his three daughters to think and act for themselves. Nevertheless, by comparison to John, I felt and indeed was restricted, a truth made acute by his customary long absences alone from 16 Adelaide Drive in all weathers and at all times of day when Katherine and I were rarely permitted to set foot from the house unaccompanied.

It was still an age for men. Women, or, in my case, young women, were closely constrained. I was encouraged to develop as an individual but confined to a gilded cage in which individualism had little or no productive function. My mind was liberated while my body remained imprisoned.

Thus, I yearned to be with John at Harrow. I ached to be told that my words and deeds would help shape the future of our nation. But it was not to be. I could read, but my reading was censored. I could act but my actions were futile. I could breathe, but the air I breathed was forever stale.

No wonder John became the son of his father, defying the miles separating them while I made do with becoming a woman, more alert perhaps than others of my own age, more aware and able perhaps to express that awareness, but held very firmly within the traces.

Of course, when war came in 1914, I learned quickly to become grateful for the difference. As a woman I was expected to support the heroism of the men who took part. No need for me to get my hands bloodied, no expectation that I would sacrifice my life to the glory of empire in a quagmire of mass extermination.

By then, John had already returned to the country of his birth. He went back to do precisely what his father predicted of him. True to the name 'Dunn,' in the spring of 1910, shortly after his twentieth birthday, he quit England aboard the SS Salsette bound for Calcutta, his ambition to become a tea planter. That he tried so hard in Assam to volunteer for active service on the front line in Flanders but failed was a great comfort to those of us in London who feared for his safety. Losing my brother to war as well as the husband I had taken for myself in the autumn of 1913, would have been too much of a cross to bear.

In fact, I have no doubt my grief, the grief I endured upon the death of a man who, if I am honest, I really hardly knew, was made easier in the knowledge that John was safe and far from the slaughter in Europe. Had he succeeded in his various attempts to become a soldier and had he subsequently become yet one more victim of wars insatiable appetite for corpses, I seriously doubt my resolve to endure the silent suffering expected of me.

I am even more certain that my mother would have been lost to us sooner than she was. She and John were never close in an ostentatious way. Their displays of affection one to the other were few and deliberately understated.

Yet, I know how much she loved him. I know how much his leaving to return to Assam hurt an already fragile heart. John was not just her son. She did not carry the pain of separation simply as any mother would in being parted from a child. John was more than that. He was also the reflected image of his father. Each time my mother caught sight of his face or looked into his deep and penetrating eyes, she saw a glimpse of her husband, the man she had lost, the man with whom she never claimed to be in love, but the man who had possessed her in ways no other had or would.

John was a talisman. He had responsibilities in Assam to his father and to the 'Dunn' name. His destiny was to become head of a business empire begun by his great grandfather, an empire which required the strength and commitment only a Dunn could offer. But he was more. Whether he was aware of it or not, he was the distant echo of a relationship between a man and a woman which began in lust but ended in a kind of love, at least for a while.

I was conceived in that lust. I was a coincidental penalty of deception. I came into the world with the mark of shame on my forehead. John was born because his father needed and wanted an heir. Every Dunn needed an heir. Only Katherine was blessed with the secret luxury of a motiveless birth. She was truly and innocently the consequence of passion. She had no cross to bear, no guilt for which to atone.

How strange the irony therefore that when John left for Assam and I married, a young, fresh-faced boy who betrayed me so early on by getting himself killed among the mud and blood of the trenches, the light in my mother's eyes dimmed until the flame was snuffed out for good. And when it was, poor Katherine found herself with no opportunity to enjoy the generous gift of affection John and I had taken so much for granted.

She went without. She was loved. There were smiles and tender moments, but in truth, my mother had nothing left to give. She was exhausted.

When the war ended, there was a time of relief; relief that John had failed in his attempts to join the mayhem and relief that he was still alive, still not a soldier. But it was a temporary glimmer of hope. The light soon faded and my mother returned to a darker world than before, a world which excluded my dear sister Katherine, a world where her rights had eroded to nothing.

By 1920, my mother, our mother, was lost to us completely. She had slipped into a world alone, detached, drifting, incomprehensible. Reality faded from view until finally even the comparatively simple task of recognition became a burden too great for her to bear.

Some days we talked. Some days she knew who I was, cared for my troubles and afforded me the affection I recalled as a child. On others I was a total stranger to her, the rabbit stare in her eyes a bleak reflection of the fear she felt inside.

During such times conversation was impossible. She lay in bed, the same bed she had known during all the years she lived at 32 Princes Gate, and retreated from us all. Her mind seemed unwilling or unable to cope any longer with the subtle erosion that had been with her from the day she was parted from her beloved Shahjan.

The mechanics of nature dictate that as a rule daughters and sons outlive their parents. The human psyche is not conditioned for the reverse. I positively expect to die before my own daughter Charlotte, a dear and precious child born to me four months after her father was killed in that bloodiest and foulest of battles on the Somme. And, no doubt, both my grandfather and grandmother expected the same.

However, it was not to be. No sooner had the dark curtains of dementia descended upon my mother for the final time, never to be raised again for even the merest chink of light to filter in, than her body followed the path of decay.

She was born and died at 32 Princes Gate. On the afternoon of 7 April 1921, just four days before her 60th birthday, she passed away. With the exception of Aunt Margaret's husband who was too busy removing the teeth of a cabinet minister and John, of course, who was on the other side of the world, we were all at her bedside; both my grandparents, Aunt Margaret herself, Aunt Katie, Katherine and I.

In turn, each of us said our private goodbyes and shed tears which dampened the hem of her sheets. But long before the final breath of life drifted from her lips, she was half way to Nirvana. In the last days and hours, we still knew her, loved her and mourned for her. But to her we were strangers, shadows in the room, drifting shapes.

She lies now in the churchyard at Brompton. I visit her each week and take her flowers. Though not a woman who moved mountains, not a woman whose impact on society had any specific measure, she was and remains the most powerful force in my life. She came into the world and left it in relative anonymity. Her headstone bears only the words; 'In Memory of Marian Dunn (nee Chase) 11th April 1861 to 7th April 1921, beloved daughter of Charles and Emilia. Mother to Emma, John and Katherine. You left us all too soon. God Speed.'

Yet, how imperfect is the vocabulary thus far invented to describe the love I held for my mother and still do.

There are strains of my father in me. On occasion a word, an inflection, a movement of the hand, even a thought bears his stamp. For a split second, I become him. But if there is eternity to life, it is because I am the daughter of my mother and Charlotte, my own daughter, is a reflection of me. We are not Dunn's. We are Chases. My poor, dear mother who left us too soon and should not have gone, is still with us. In my possession, rebound and carried at my side like rare jewels, are her diaries. They, the written word, are witness to a life and times, by no means extraordinary but significant nevertheless.

It is I and my own daughter who are the embodiment of the woman she was. We are the physical evidence of her temporary presence on this earth.

One day, I may have to leave 32 Princes Gate. One day, perhaps strangers will live here, sleep in the same bedroom my mother kept as her own from childhood. As long as I am here, however, I shall not mourn. For Marian Chase, who became Marian Cole and later Marian Dunn, still thrives within these walls. Rest in peace, mama.

THE END